The Darkening of

I hope you enjoy it

THE Darkening OF ALDBURY

RAYMOND HUGH

Thankyou to Hazel and Seb for their help with this project

Poole

Dorset

BH16 6FH

A CIP catalogue record for this book is available from the British Library

ISBN 978-1-8384092-0-3

Printed in Great Britain by

Biddles Books Limited, King's Lynn, Norfolk

For Loona

Who is young enough to make a difference

Chapter One

A Letter From A Friend

Legend

One explanation of the word legend in the English dictionary is "an untrue or unhistorical story" I believe this should be re defined as an historical story yet unproven. Can anyone for example say with absolute certainty that King Arthur and his knights of the round table never existed in one form of another. Indeed, there are many examples where history has had to be rewritten when new knowledge has come to light.

The story I am about to tell you is a legend of this time. It happened just a few years ago and although recent, because of the way of things cannot so far be proven. And yet it's outcome, which is still not certain, could affect not only us of this land but the whole world and worlds beyond our own. If you lived in the small rural village of Aldbury in Hertfordshire or nearby at the time of this story you may recognise some of the happenings laid out in the pages to follow but put them down to unusual but natural occurrences. The human mind sadly dictates that any other explanation can only be fantasy, to be disbelieved, to be made a mockery of. Those spouting such "rubbish" ridiculed.

Our long dead ancestors had a much deeper understanding of their natural surroundings and the hidden influences that sometimes control daily life. Sadly, today's society has a deep ignorance of our natural surroundings and an unhealthy suspicion of anything not explained by science. Such narrow mindedness in this case could mean life as we know it changing forever or worse still disappearing.

There is though hope. A child's mind as many parents are acutely aware has a deep curiosity and a desire to believe in a world that an adult wont. Thus, a child tends to be much more aware of their surroundings and open to the hidden forces that shape it, forces the average adult refuses to see or is simply blind to. The result you'll discover as you turn the pages is the burden for all our lives falls on the shoulders of a young girl. A girl who dares to see beyond the dimensions of *our world. You will also discover that the story does not end with the last page of this book. Your future, our future is still uncertain, and the little girl needs help. The reason for me telling you the story so far is to open your eyes and if you're brave enough, to try and help her. If you continue to think that this is just another "untrue or unhistorical" story, you do so not only at your peril but at the peril of time itself.*

A friend

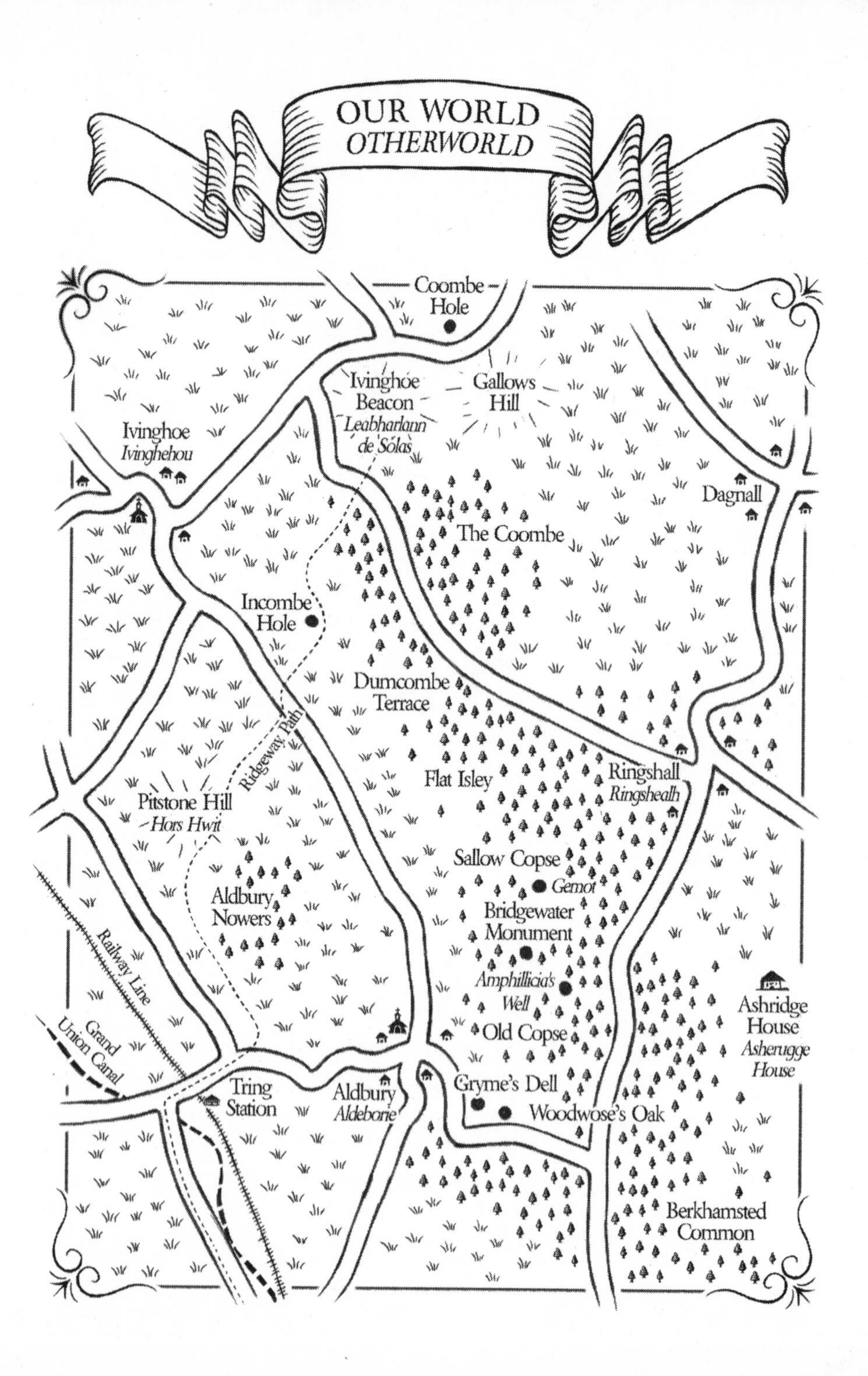
OUR WORLD
OTHERWORLD
Coombe Hole
Ivinghoe Beacon
Leabharlann de Sólas
Gallows Hill
Ivinghoe
Ivinghehou
Dagnall
The Coombe
Incombe Hole
Dumcombe Terrace
Ridgeway Path
Flat Isley
Ringshall
Ringshealh
Pitstone Hill
Hors Hwit
Sallow Copse
Gemot
Aldbury Nowers
Bridgewater Monument
Railway Line
Amphillicia's Well
Ashridge House
Asherugge House
Old Copse
Grand Union Canal
Tring Station
Aldbury
Aldeborie
Gryme's Dell
Woodwose's Oak
Berkhamsted Common

Chapter Two

The Arrival

March – Not many years ago.

Charlotte leaned forward craning her neck to view the scene through the windscreen before them. Her parents feigned calmness though in truth they were excited as she was. The view ahead was their future, hedged fields descended into a natural depression from which rose a sturdy church tower, sentinel over a scattering of rooftops, their muddled appearance due to natural development rather than an architect's plan. Rising above everything towered the wooded Chiltern Escarpment a dramatic interruption to the gentle rolling landscape before it. The three pairs of eyes staring through the windscreen were all concentrated on the church tower and the informal lay of the underlying buildings. This they knew was the village of Aldbury. Their future home. A new beginning.

From the shadows unseen forces, forces modern science refuse to accept exist watched the arrival of the three. They too were looking forward to a new beginning. The beginning of the end.

Chapter Three
Leaving London

Earlier that morning.

It was a fine spring morning. The sun was bright, the sky blue, and with the freshness in the air that only spring can bring the three combined made one feel grateful to be alive. Unless that is you were stuck in London traffic. And today unlike the weather the London traffic wasn't behaving itself. For the last half, an hour they had been stuck on the M25 without moving. They, Charlotte aged 11 and her mother and father, were only around twenty metres from joining the exit they needed and even more frustrating they could see it but to take it would mean taking the hard shoulder for a very short distance and that would mean breaking the law. Charlotte's mother was French and she possessed that Gallic spirit that liked to challenge everything and anything connected with authority. If she had been driving they would have been down the hard shoulder and off of the M25 a long time ago but it was her father driving and he was steadfastly English. Laws were there for a reason, to be obeyed and respected. Only now had the traffic started to move and it was only a matter of minutes before to everyone's relief they steered off the motorway at junction twenty for the A41. No sooner had they started moving when traffic lights brought their van to a halt at a large and equally congested roundabout.

In under a minute the traffic lights changed and her father put the van into gear edging nervously forward. I say nervously for their mode of transport was an old grey painted post office van that had been bought at auction and tended to break down when and where the roads were busiest. The A41/M25 junction was potentially prime breakdown location and Charlotte could see in the mirror that her father's lips were moving. He was talking to the van, coaxing her forward whilst giving way to anyone who wanted to push through. Their old van on appearance alone tended not to be respected by other road users and her mother swore that when they had money the first thing she would buy would be the biggest SUV available and then she wouldn't get out of anybody's way for anything. If you've ever driven in France you'll know that if her mother ever had the money this would be a promise she would most definitely keep.

Finally, after much cursing by her mother and cajoling by her father they found themselves on the A41 and the open road. They were all pleased to see they had left the sprawl of London behind and what up until that point had been rows of houses gave way to fields of green and trees still naked from winter. Charlotte observed all from the back of the van her head squeezed between the two front seats gazing out of the windscreen in front. Behind her, packed tight were her and her parent's belongings, not much for they had left most of what they owned in France but enough to fill the van to bursting. Her parents had convinced themselves that putting Charlotte in the back was both safe and legal but even so she had been well taught to duck and hide if ever a police car came into view.

The landscape was not at all what Charlotte was used to and the contrast with London made her nervous for her new life which was apparently to be in a village. For the last three years they had lived in an apartment in Bayswater. Inverness Terrace to be exact. A broad and leafy road running parallel to Queensway, lined with white painted

Georgian houses with elegant balconies. Many of the houses were now hotels, their once grand rooms divided to accommodate many more guests than was ever intended. Their apartment too had had an elegant balcony which it shared with perhaps the smartest hotel in the Terrace, The Inverness Court. Its façade is officially described by those who know about these things as Franco – Flemish something of a coincidence as Charlotte had been born and brought up in her early years in French Flanders.

Bayswater was so very different to Charlotte's early years in France. She had been born and brought up in a small country hamlet or hameau as it is called in France not a million miles from Calais. Life there was very traditional and people tended to have jobs for life seldom travelling far. Quite the opposite to Bayswater's cosmopolitan and mainly transient population. Now her parents were returning her to the country, the main difference being it was to be in an English village not a French hameau.

Those who met her father always said he looked like a writer. Physically he was tall, slim with an ease about him that tended to relax all he came in contact with. He had a kind face and a grin that he would recount often got him into trouble. He was naturally curious and was always researching, entirely for his own pleasure his surroundings. He preferred the old ways and hated the internet and social media. The World Wide Web he would often warn Charlotte was full of disinformation and that social media was responsible for a "dumbing down" of society. As a result, computers, even television were banned from their house and Charlotte could only dream of owning a smart phone. Books however were encouraged and they had so many that her father rented a lock up in which to store them. Put a bookshop next to a pub her mother would often say and your father will have found his heaven.

Her mother physically is what adults call burlesque. She had long blonde hair, not her natural colour, and a face that was determined. Her eyes were magnetic, something Charlotte had inherited and like her father, her mother too had a wide smile but not quite so mischievous. She had a vibrant infectious personality and this along with her looks attracted admiration from both men and women who often worked hard to be her friend. In France she had worked as a "coiffeuse domicile", a hairdresser that worked from home or cut clients hair in their own houses. She was very skilled at her job and had always been in demand. Charlotte was of average height. Her face rounded with a small snubbed nose, always wore a smile which went with her happy nature. She had what her mother called "Chinese" eyes though when they were wide open they had a magnetism like her mother, that was infectious. Her hair was cut in a bob and the colour of oak bark. Her naturally happy disposition had a wicked side and friends and family alike were often on the wrong end of a practical joke. When Charlotte was eight they decided to move to London, England to start a new life. Her mother's friends had thought she was mad and some even feared for her safety but her mother never ducked a challenge and so it was they ended up in Bayswater. Quite why Bayswater Charlotte never discovered. Her mother though remaining fiercely French quickly adopted all things English in particular the Royal Family whose lives she followed with great interest. To earn a living her parents had a market stall selling continental food.

Approaching the time for Charlotte to leave her primary education stress levels had risen within the family. Long whispered discussions were engaged in by her parents. Charlotte knew they were talking about her and was grown up enough she felt to be included but kept this to herself. They visited several potential schools and Charlotte passed an entry exam for the prestigious Holland Park School. Something to Charlotte's annoyance her parents appeared surprised at.

She had not long settled into Holland Park when out of the blue her parents announced they were moving. Leaving their beloved

London apartment for a village in the Chiltern Hills called Aldbury. Charlotte had never heard of the Chiltern Hills let alone Aldbury. The announcement had been a shock and not a good one as far as she was concerned. But her father had told her there was far too much temptation for a young girl in London and adolescence in a village environment with a nice local school would be much better for her.

From their ultra-modern apartment they were apparently moving to a quaint, (Charlotte had no idea what that meant) little, cottage. Though Charlotte remained suspicious, in truth the move had never been pre planned, her parents had come across the cottage quite by chance. After packing up their market stall in a commuter town called Tring they had stopped at nearby Aldbury to enjoy a sandwich beside the village pond. Whilst there they'd spotted an advert, handwritten on a dog eared and discoloured card in the cluttered window of the village shop. "Cottage to rent". The advert looked as though it had been written in haste and read as such for detail was limited and hardly enticing. However her parents quickly realised that opportunities like this rarely surfaced and had to be grabbed at. They had immediately phoned the number on the card and within minutes, for the cottage was just a couple of minutes' walk from the shop, her parents were visiting what later would turn out to be their future home. As a consequence that evening Charlotte, without consultation was told that they would at the end of the month be moving to Aldbury and that she would love it. She hoped they were right.

And so it came to be that they were now on the A41, the three of them with a van filled with sacks of clothes along with essentials and a few Knick knacks her parents had collected whilst living at Bayswater. All three, including Charlotte looking forward, with just a little apprehension perhaps, to a new dawn.

Chapter Four

A New Beginning

In no time at all it seemed her father was manoeuvring off of the A41 at the exit for Tring. After passing the local supermarket they turned right, onto a road signposted to Tring station and Aldbury. A universal cry went up as they spotted the sign and a feeling of nervous excitement started to rise in all of them. The final building before reaching more open country was Tring station, offering fast access to London and the north. After the station, visible across large open fields, nestling in something of a hollow were the cluttered rooftops and church tower of Aldbury. Acting as a backdrop to the village and an abrupt interruption to the gentle folds of the lower land rose the wooded scarp of the Chiltern Hills. This Charlotte had read was called Ashridge part of an extensive wood almost all of which was under the stewardship of the National Trust. The name, Ashridge Charlotte's father had already told her was almost certainly because the woodland along the ridge before them was made up predominantly of ash trees, hence the name ash-ridge. He had gone on to tell her that the ancients, (whoever they were), believed that the ash tree was one of the gateways to the underworld and that the squirrel had the unique ability to run down the tree following its roots to reach there. Squirrels thus were used by those with the right knowledge to carry messages back and forth between this world and its parallel. Her father had gone on to say that the handles to witches' brooms were always made out of ash as were the wands of druids and the roots were and perhaps still are used by witches to help cast spells.

It was utter nonsense of course but Charlotte like most children when told such a tale, desperately wanted to believe it was true. There's a "Peter Pan in every child," her father kept telling her. In her father too Charlotte often thought.

Her father now with the ash-ridge in site returned to the subject and Charlotte observed in the mirror, her mother's eyes glaze over as he continued with his encyclopaedic knowledge of the ash. In the Iron Age, the ash was used for building houses and throughout the centuries for fencing. Police truncheons were once apparently made from ash and ash wood was once used as a frame for a car called the Morris Traveller, Charlotte had never heard of it. Her father went on to list many further and more modern uses but his words fell on deaf ears. Charlotte and her mother were both staring through the wind-screen at the surrounding countryside, soon to be their home. Charlotte though apprehensive had to admit it was a magnificent vista and any fears she held for her new life disappeared at least for a moment. The only disappointment was that up until now they had followed a bright sun and bright blue skies. Indeed the sun and blue sky were still there but over Aldbury hung a light grey cloud that cast a shadow over the whole village.

The lane rose winding between fields before dropping to enter the village passing the village church, arriving at the village green. Even in the shadow of the cloud it was an idyllic scene. To their right sat the village shop with a central display window that was romantically bowed. The very shop where her parents had seen the card advertising their soon to be home. A post office sign hung above the door and Charlotte even from a distance could see that the contents of the windows offered much temptation to a girl of her age. To their left, on the other side of the village green and pond stood the almost obligatory village pub. Surrounding the green were a collection of houses and cottages of various shapes and sizes, each so flawless it was as though an artist had painted them in place, creating the perfect picture.

At the village green they turned right down one of four lanes that led off and after just a few metres pulled up outside a small detached, faded red brick cottage, with a thatched roof that looked as though it desperately needed replacing. The cottage beneath the thatch was plain though attractive, a cottage could never be anything else. Friendly looking sash windows, two up and one down softened the brick exterior. The window frames looked as though they'd recently been freshly painted white and specks of white on the glass portrayed a hurried or careless job. Entry was via a very plain and surprisingly modern door, this too was white but for some reason had missed out on a fresh coat of paint. Though nothing really matched, gathered together all of the features completed the frontage perfectly. Either side of the cottage were further cottages, similar in size but terraced and with slate roofs. There was a car parked in front of their cottage.

"Just like London" her father exclaimed in exasperation.

In fact every available parking place in front of the cottages was taken and they were forced to do a u turn and return to the village green for the nearest available space. Her father parked up in front of the village shop and after hauling Charlotte out over the front seat they made their way back to the cottage on foot. When they arrived a tall lanky man with a mop of black hair was waiting for them. He had the manner and air of fallen nobility with a piercing gaze and a forced smile.

"Hello" he greeted them, his voice had a cultured tone, "I saw you arrive. I couldn't mistake the van." Charlotte felt her mother wince. "And you must be Charlotte" he continued patting her on the head, "I've heard a lot about you". Why did people always say that Charlotte thought quietly to herself and why did grownups always have to pat her head, she was a child not a dog.

"Ready?" the man asked, drawing himself up. Her parents nodded. "We'll go in the back way" and gestured for all to follow him, "the lock on the front door can be temperamental" he offered by way of explanation. The man, I must call him that as he hadn't offered a name, led them around the cottage at the end of the terrace on their right following a brick path leading to the rear. They stopped before a stable door set into the side of a one story extension. The door opened easily and led into an elongated kitchen fitted with pine-wood cupboards. It was basic but could with a little kindness be described as rustic. A wooden staircase led up alongside the wall opposite and under this was a small dining table and chairs. Wooden beams lined the ceiling. The kitchen and indeed the whole cottage Charlotte was to discover had a musty smell that hinted at not only age but something else as well. It was a smell Charlotte decided that was unique to cottages. As they edged in the man opened a pine door with a latch to their right. "This is the bathroom" he said looking directly at Charlotte for her parents had already had the tour. "Before it was a bathroom, it used to be where my grandfather kept pigs" he looked to see if this information shocked Charlotte but it didn't, quite the opposite she found the information fascinating. "I've replaced the broken tiles," he said, turning his gaze to her parents. Her father nodded, her mother wasn't listening, she was too busy playing with the stable door. It was a feature that she had always dreamed of.

From the kitchen they were led into the lounge. It too had a beamed ceiling. The door with the temperamental lock was in the opposite corner and the sash window gave a view over the road to a rather grand house opposite. The only piece of furniture was a faded burgundy sofa which Charlotte recognised from catalogues was from a well-known Swedish store. Charlotte had never been in a house without a hallway before but for her the main interest was the large open fireplace. It had a cast iron grate and even without being lit generated a feeling of warmth.

"I've painted the walls white" the man told them, waving his arms, "but if you want to change it, feel free." Charlotte saw her mother squeeze her father's hand. It was obvious her mother loved it. With an abrupt turn the man led them back into the kitchen and up the stairs. They filed into the room facing them which fronted the house. The two sash windows opposite let in a great deal of light even with the gloom outside and offered a view over the grand house opposite to fields beyond. Charlotte following the hedges recognised the line of the lane via which they'd arrived. "The main bedroom" the man proclaimed again looking at Charlotte "your parents will probably want this". For a main bedroom it wasn't very big Charlotte thought and there wasn't a stick of furniture. Their old apartment had been furnished, where would her parents' sleep was her first thought. The bedroom like the rest of the house was painted white.

"I'm afraid the light doesn't work the man said flicking a yellowed switch on the wall up and down but the windows let in plenty of light and you can always get a lamp" He said this as though such a defect was perfectly normal and didn't expect a complaint. None was offered.

From the main bedroom they filed through a side door leading off from the top the stairs into what Charlotte knew was going to be her room. It was even smaller than the main bedroom if that was at all possible but to compensate had a tall sash window which reached almost from the floor to the ceiling affording fine views over the garden to the wooded scarp. Even to Charlotte at her young age it was obvious the window was not part of the original building. It was far too large and far too grand to belong to a two bedroom cottage. The window looked old though and had probably been taken from another building at some time to replace what would have been a much smaller window. The result was a room bathed in natural light with a view fit for a queen. Charlotte immediately fell in love with it. On the far side stood a simple wooden bed, the only item of furniture. The ceiling as in every other room was beamed and the walls freshly painted white. All except for a spot on the near wall where a small picture hung. The man had painted around it but only roughly, revealing in places the colour underneath, a garish yellow. The picture was set in a simple wooden frame. On reflection it might be a print rather than a painting, it was hard to tell and was of a proud looking white stag with a splendid set of antlers. It stood on what looked like a grass knoll staring into the distance. Where the picture hung the stag faced right and if the animal was actually standing in the room would be looking out of the tall sash window.

"I'm sorry" the man apologised, hands in pockets nodding at the picture. "Try as I might, I can't get the picture off the wall. Blinking pain. You may have more luck and I've left some spare paint in one of the sheds if you succeed." With his hands in his pockets he nodded towards the window." Feel free to do what you want with the picture if you manage to get it off. I don't need it".

"It's unusual," her father said looking at the picture more closely, "I quite like it, what do you think Charlotte?"

Charlotte nodded, "I like it too".

"It's been here forever" the man interjected. "I can remember it as a boy and always in the same place." With that the man made his way out of the room and back down the stairs assuming everybody would follow. Her parents obliged but Charlotte stayed behind in the room. Looking around she adored its simplicity. It had a warm feel to it as though it were an old friend and she had an odd and very strong feeling that she had been there before but of course that was impossible. She moved over to the picture. She felt drawn to it and on closer inspection it became obvious that the previous occupants had painted round the picture as well for the garish yellow hadn't completely hidden the colour before that, a misty blue. Charlotte looked closely at the stag. Certainly, it was a proud looking animal but studying its face it somehow looked sad even a little fearful and it appeared to Charlotte to be silently fighting some sort of battle. Her observation sent a cold shiver down her spine and tearing herself away she turned to the long sash window expecting to see her parents in the garden. To her surprise the window was misted up, she was sure that hadn't been the case a few moments ago. As she stared at the window trying to puzzle it out she saw that there were words scrawled in the condensation. Probably from a long time ago, where the window hadn't been cleaned, condensation she knew wouldn't settle on grease. Charlotte took a step closer in an attempt to read what was written. There were three lines and all on the top left hand pane. Some of the letters weren't all that clear as the condensation had started to run. After a few seconds she thought she had it, she mouthed the words as she read.

"You did not choose me, it is I who chose you."

As she read the condensation began to run as well as fade. Within seconds the window had cleared and Charlotte found herself looking out at the garden. Not sure what to think she studied the glass where the message had been. There was not a drop of condensation and no hint of a message left by greasy fingers. In fact the pane was so clear it looked as though it had only recently been cleaned. Outside her parents were nowhere to be seen, the garden was empty. Charlotte had a sudden urge to be with her parents. Quickly she descended the stairs to the kitchen where to her relief she found them waiting patiently with the man.

"Well?" her mother said beaming, "what do you think?". Charlotte looked at the expectant faces of both her parents and with a smile that threatened to illuminate the gloom outside she nodded.

"I love it" she replied, "I really love it." Charlotte was telling the truth. The relief of both her parents was manifest by the look on their faces. They had been worried that their daughter would robotically accept her new home just to please them but her words and facial expression had far too much feeling to be an act. It was obvious her reply was heartfelt. She really did love it, they had been so worried she wouldn't, that she may rebel.

"Want to see the garden?" the man interrupted. Both her parents murmured their agreement. It had been getting dark when they had originally visited and had only previously seen the garden from the house. They were now keen to have the complete tour. Immediately outside the stable door in a small corner sat a small wooden table with two functional looking chairs . In her excitement to see the house Charlotte hadn't noticed them when they'd entered. Both the table and chairs were of slatted wood, much of it rotting and sat on a metal frame. Once upon a time the furniture had been designed to be folded away but examining it now the joints looked to be rusted solidly together and anyone wanting to fold them would certainly have a battle on their hands. Several terracotta flower pots sat on the fragile table top with lack lustre twists of brown protruding from the soil they contained, all that remained of last year's growth. There was no sign of any new growth. A robin was perched on one of the pots and in doing so Charlotte thought was risking serious injury or even its life. Its resplendent red breast was in stark contrast to the surrounding gloom and one could see why the bird was a popular image on all sorts of cards. The robin didn't appear to be scared and cocking its head studied the gathering intently. Charlotte's father had often told her that in England the robin was considered the "gardener's friend" and that it liked the company of people. Charlotte pondered this, if the cottage had been empty a long time it was probably lonely, I'll be your first new friend she promised and hoped the little bird could read her thoughts.

As a group they walked slowly up the garden always with the robin skipping a few steps ahead. Long but narrow, the garden looked tired and unkempt, short on love. Despite this hints to its former glory were still in evidence and its potential was there for all to see. Wooden fences separated the gardens on either side, gardens that looked a lot better cared for. Our last tenant didn't really like gardening, the man told them, reading their thoughts. On the right of the garden escorted by a stone path ran a straight, narrow border. It was bare and facing north would probably remain as such pretty much throughout the year.

After approximately forty metres the garden broadened out to the right cutting into the, or what was now their neighbour's garden. Here the garden was laid to grass and in no sort of order stood a couple of plum trees and an old apple, something that would make you a millionaire in Bayswater. Here too and something of a surprise was a brick built BBQ, summer was going to be fun. On the left of the garden the border was curved and designed as a home for a colourful collection of herbaceous flowers. Just before the garden extended to the right, the border was broken by a tree that her father recognised immediately as cherry blossom. In between the curved border and the stone path the ground was laid to lawn. Pushing their way up in clumps through the grass were the unmistakable stems of daffodils and there was a profusion of daffodils scattered throughout the borders but none were close to flowering. The long finger-like leaves of crocuses were also in evidence. Their season was just coming to an end but here there was no sign of them having ever flowered or were about to. The man spread his arms.

"When they flower", Charlotte assumed he meant the daffodils, "it's quite a sight." He sounded apologetic. "This spring though has been bloody awful, hardly anything's moved. I can't remember the last time I saw the sun and with the temperature it still feels like winter. I'm amazed they," again Charlotte assumed he meant the daffodils, "even want to show their heads."

They were all surprised at this as, up until now spring had been pretty good. Lots of sun, above average temperatures and in between good spells of plant pushing rain. He was right about the temperature though, there was a definite chill in the air.

After the fruit trees there was another surprise. Stretching across the width of the garden stood a wooden pagoda. It covered a flagstone floor and unlike many pagoda's was very tastefully done. Entwined around the pagoda's wooden frame was an extensive grape vine. The pagoda completely divided the garden and an arch built on one side led via an ornate gate to several outbuildings to the rear.

"I built this myself" the man said proudly, standing under the pagoda, hands on hips. "You'll get plenty of grapes in summer, I promise you."

They all murmured their appreciation which was genuine. If he really had built it himself he had done a very professional job. The man looked reflective as he admired his work. His expression hinted to him wanting to say something further but then thought better of it. Charlotte noticed that the robin was still with them. Perched on one of the upright posts it was continuing to study them intently.

Without another word the man pushed open the ornate gate and ushered them through. They were now in the functional part of the garden. A rough grass path passed between what appeared to be two sheds after which there stood a small, rather severe looking square brick building.

"Outside toilet?" her father asked, half joking.

The man either didn't hear or purposely ignored the question. At the end of the path was a compost heap beside which a padlocked gate led, if it could be opened to an orchard. The first shed, to the left of the path, the man explained had been built as a Wendy house for his children. The other, on the right, used to be a hen house but had been used by the last tenant as a shed. Both were now empty and at their disposal the man proclaimed. No explanation was offered as to the function of the brick building. The orchard beyond the gate they were told, belonged to someone else and was private. The garden was at least eighty metres in length and without doubt the best feature of the property. If it was a good summer little time would be spent indoors.

Confirming that they were happy her parents followed the man back to the house to pay their deposit and a month's rent in advance. "All pretty standard stuff" the man had assured them referring to their contract, which he explained he'd found on the internet. Charlotte stayed in the garden gazing up at what was tonight going to be her bedroom window. The robin she noticed had not followed her parents to the back door but had stayed with her. She looked at it and it in turn stared back, showing no sign of fear.

"What's your name then" she asked the robin aloud.

As though it understood the bird replied with a typical robin tweet.

"I'm not sure I can pronounce that" and as though in reply the robin made the call again before this time flying off. You're going to be my first friend here Charlotte promised herself for the second time and headed for the house. She arrived at the back door just as the man was leaving. He made a point of solemnly shaking her hand before bidding farewell and was gone. When she entered the kitchen both parents were smiling contentedly. Her father was holding the freshly signed contract and her mother busy opening all the cupboards.

"Dad," seeing the man leave, Charlotte had a question. "What was the man's name?"

Her parents looked at each other. They realised neither of them knew, in their excitement they'd not bothered to ask and the man had never revealed it in his introduction.

"It'll be on the contract", her mother gestured to the bundle of papers in her fathers' hands. Her father flicked through them but there was no name, just a company, Sumro International, with a London address, Orme Square. The bank account into which they had to pay the rent was also in the company name. Perhaps the man's statement that he had found the contract on the internet was not quite the truth. How strange, why would he tell such an obvious lie.

"Perhaps it's on the card," her father fished out a crumpled card from his left trouser pocket. There were always crumpled papers in her father's pockets, they tended to be his filing system. The crumpled card was the card from the shop window. After a brief examination he handed the card to Charlotte's mother.

"Nothing, just a mobile number" her mother replied and added in French. "C'est bizarre." How weird.

"Never mind," her father dismissed the mystery in his usual laid back manner. Taking the card back he returned it to his pocket. "I'll ask him the next time we see him". At that moment they were all totally unaware that they would never set eyes on the man again.

Chapter Five

Settling In

It was several hours before a parking space became available close enough for them to unload the van. Her father would frequently wander, hands in pockets into the street seeing if there was a space, only to come back cursing. Her mother decided so as not to waste time they could all help cleaning the cottage before they started moving things in. Her father proclaimed it was already clean but knew he was fighting a losing battle. Charlotte's mother was extremely house proud and would clean every few hours in the day if she had the chance. As if the man who'd rented them the cottage had known this, her mother found a brand new brush and mop in one of the cupboards. Both Charlotte and her father groaned loudly when her mother appeared, smiling armed with her new find in either hand. Tired at their lack of enthusiasm her mother drew up a long list of cleaning materials she still needed and sent them on a mission to the village shop. This was a new adventure and the mission was gratefully accepted by both.

A loud bell rang as they entered the shop. Not an electric bell but a good old fashioned bell that jangled with a little too much enthusiasm each time the door was opened. Inside, the layout rather like the village could be described as rambling. The shop covered several levels with each level connected by a single and well-worn wooden step. As you passed over, much of the floor would bend and groan in protest. There were many nooks and crannies to explore and all were crammed full of merchandise. Not a centimetre was wasted. It was obvious from the layout the shop had been extended over the years to meet the growing needs of the village. As a consequence the lighting was rather informal and not always functional. In places which must have once been practical, bulbs with faded lamp shades hung from the undulating ceiling on twisted cord throwing shadows as well as light over the crammed shelves. In contrast in front of the post office counter where a wide selection of cards and stationery were displayed the merchandise was lit by a garish beam from a couple of fluorescent lights screwed tightly to the ceiling. The overall feeling of the shop was one of warmth similar to that of an old fashioned Inn. All that was missing Charlotte thought was a cat curled up in a corner somewhere.

The service counter lay to your left as you walked in and behind it stood a rather large woman with a ruddy complexion. She greeted them with a nod and a smile as they entered. She evidently recognised her father because she immediately asked.

"Did you take the cottage then?" It was obvious by her tone and expression that her question was one of genuine curiosity and not just polite chat.

"Yes" her father smiled back, "we will probably become your best customers." Charlotte doubted that. With quick thinking, she heard her father go on to ask if she knew the name of the man who'd rented them the cottage. "It's silly but he never told us. Is he local?" Without even pausing to reflect the woman shook her head.

"No, the first time I see 'im was when he came to put the advert in" and predicting her father's next question added, "and I was born and brought up 'ere and worked here" they assumed she meant the shop, "since I left school." At a rough guess, the woman was around sixty so that would mean at least forty years, probably more.

Charlotte decided to explore whilst her father and the woman continued their conversation. As she browsed she heard her father making general enquiries about the village and village life. To Charlotte the shop seemed to sell just about everything you could possibly want. For her father there was a good selection of wine and for her mother several fridges containing an impressive display of cheese and cold meats as well as vitals such as milk and butter. There was a good array of food in general including fresh fruit and veg and an equally impressive selection of cleaning materials for her mother. The selection of sweets was mind boggling, Charlotte had never seen such variety. There were even sherbet dip something her father had always bemoaned about not being able to find anymore. For those of lesser years there was also a selection of cheap colourful toys. These didn't have a display of their own but were spread randomly about the shop, finding a home wherever there was spare space. Toys were even hanging from the ceiling and these Charlotte soon discovered were reached by a brass hook screwed into the end of a broom handle, rather like those you find being used on stalls at a fun fair.

After around twenty minutes they were on their way back to the cottage arms laden with every conceivable cleaning material and for Charlotte, a sherbet dip. Her father spotted a parking space, close to their cottage on their return and dumped everything as fast as he could to grab the space before anyone else claimed it. The rest of the day was spent cleaning and unloading the van. As there were no wardrobes or drawers in the cottage clothes were folded and simply laid neatly on the floor. Some of their older clothes her mother ingeniously laid out on the floor of their bedroom to serve as a temporary mattress. Once the sheets, pillows and quilt were in place, you'd never know there wasn't a mattress underneath. Her parents also had light in their bedroom by way of an old lamp her father had picked up at Portobello Market whilst living in Bayswater.

It didn't take long for Charlotte to finish laying out her room. Most of her clothes fitted neatly under her bed frame. To keep her company, on top of her pillow she lay her favourite cuddly toy, Gromit, his eyes wide, staring intently at the ceiling. Gromit wasn't actually a cuddly toy but in fact a hot water bottle cover which Charlotte's father had bought her when she was two. The water bottle had long since perished and Gromit was well past his best but continued to go with her everywhere. On the wall adjacent to her bed, with the aid of blue tac, Charlotte attached a few pictures. They were not of pop stars, that was yet to come but scenes depicting fairies and magical creatures. On the wall opposite the window her father hung a simple wood framed mirror that despite its small size had the effect of almost doubling the amount of light in the room. The remaining wall Charlotte decided to keep bare, leaving the painting or print of the white stag to hang alone.

When they had finished her father took a calculated risk in abandoning the precious parking space to make a mysterious trip in the van. He was gone for just ten minutes and fate favoured him for when he returned the car that had been parked immediately in front of their cottage was gone and he quickly took advantage. He entered the kitchen with a flourish, brandishing a sack of logs in one hand and kindling wood in the other, purchased from the local garage. Tonight we will have fire, he said theatrically.

Thus their first evening in the cottage was spent sitting squeezed on the sofa in front of an open fire. The fire wasn't really needed as rather surprisingly the central heating worked well but no one cared. Mother created a meal from virtually nothing which they ate on their laps after which her father switched off the light so they could fully appreciate the fire's magic. Her parents shared a bottle of red wine, whilst Charlotte sipped on hot chocolate. The flames and the resulting shadows it sent prancing around the room brought out their inner fears, fears they all secretly enjoyed and imaginative tales of ghosts were soon shared. The flames, not being eternal burned at a pace, hungrily destroying their host and it wasn't long before the logs were reduced to softly glowing embers. Cold sneaked back into the room and the three of them snuggled together seeking warmth as well as comfort from each other. There came a pause in the conversation whilst all searched for an even more terrifying ghost story during which her mother said ponderously.

"I expect this cottage is haunted." She was staring into the fire as she said it and the dying embers lit her face in a fashion that accentuated her statement. It was pure if unintentional theatre and silence fell as the thought played out in their minds.

"Perhaps our landlord is a ghost," Charlotte's father said teasingly and with false bravado.

"That's not funny," replied her mother and Charlotte shivered.

There was another silence as the three reflected on the man with no name. The conversation changed to a semi serious discussion on the mystery surrounding their landlord. At first sensible reasoning ensued though this quickly, under the conditions changed to extreme and unlikely possibilities of him being a mad axe murderer or a mad doctor trapping a family, looking for body parts to sell on the black market. As the tales grew more and more bizarre Charlotte somewhat gratefully fell asleep and eventually as the last remnants of glowing ash fell through the grate her parents carried her up to bed. Tucking her daughter in her mother habitually pulled Gromit close so he lay in Charlotte's arms.

"Night ma Cherie" her mother whispered gently kissing her on the cheek. With that her parents left their daughter, retiring to their own bedroom hoping to get some sleep on their mattress of clothes. Nobody saw the robin perched on the windowsill staring through the long sash window. For a robin, it had no business being there, it was way past its bed time.

Charlotte's father was the first to wake the next morning and as he always did went downstairs to make coffee. Her mother famously always refused to get out of bed without having drunk at least one cup of coffee. Hearing her father moving about, Charlotte woke too. At first she wondered where she was and it took several unsettling seconds before her memory returned and tuned to her brain. Semi-conscious she looked around the room. Although gloomy outside the long sash window ensured the room was already well lit. Flecks of light on the walls hinted at a morning sun trying to break through the cloud. Charlotte turned her gaze to the picture of the white stag on the wall opposite. The morning light playing on the glass gave the false impression that the stag was moving. The picture was small and simple, nothing much to look at but had a presence that somehow drew attention to it. Even when she wasn't looking at it Charlotte could feel its draw, almost as though the stag in the picture was watching her. It really was very strange. Funny how the mind plays tricks for that was all it could be. Even so the sensation at times made her feel decidedly uncomfortable.

After around half an hour of lying in bed awake Charlotte stretched and decided she needed to get up. Grabbing her clothes for the day she descended the stairs to wash in the old "pig shed." She found her father in the kitchen preparing a second cup of coffee for her mother.

"Daaaaed" Charlotte said by way of a greeting.

"Yes?" her father knew, by her drawing out his title that his daughter wanted something.

"You know that old picture in my bedroom, the one with the white stag?" There was no real need to mention the deer as there was only one picture in the bedroom but Charlotte still felt it necessary.

"Mmm."

"I like it but can you move it to one of the other rooms?" She knew it was silly but the picture somehow made her feel uneasy. Her father agreed and that it wasn't a problem but first he told her he wanted her to help him in the garden. He'd see to it that afternoon.

Helping her father in the garden meant composting the dead growth from last year, turning over the soil and generally making the garden tidy in readiness for spring, when it decided to arrive that is for there was little or no sign of it even intending to arrive so far. A stark contrast to the vibrant display of spring that had greeted them at Tring. Charlotte didn't mind hard work and enjoyed the exhilaration of being outside. Growing up in France she'd often helped both her father and her grandfather, (papi), with the garden. She loved the myriad of aromas that were released into the air because of their work and in particular she loved the escaping scents of the soil as it was turned. Especially in spring when waking the earth after months of slumber, releases a freshness unique to the season. Being March, breaking the earth should have stirred all the trappings of spring but Charlotte sensed that something was wrong, the soil as it was turned still smelt of Autumn. In fact at times the freshly turned sods seemed to have no scent at all, it was as though the earth had simply ceased to live, ceased to participate with the seasons. Her father had always taught her to smell, to read the earth, to try to sense what it was feeling. He had often boasted he was so in tune with the earth that if he was driven blindfolded in a car he could tell when they were crossing a county border. His explanation, borders were originally created by people who could sense the rhythms of the earth as he. Charlotte doubted this but knew he was being sincere and understood exactly what he meant for she had inherited the same gift from her father. She was perhaps even more in tune, as he called it, with the earth than he. Her father always referred to his gift as the seventh sense. She had no idea why, what ever happened to the sixth? Her mother thought they were both mad.

Watching her father work the soil she wondered if he sensed the same as she. If he had he showed no sign of doing so and Charlotte decided not to mention it. Helping to pass the time the robin from yesterday returned to keep them company. It was almost certainly her imagination but Charlotte thought the bird actually looked pleased to see her. The robin made them both laugh as it frequently came as close as it dare in search of easy pickings. Hopping away whenever it got so close that Charlotte was tempted to reach out and touch it. At times it felt very much as though the little bird was playing a game with them. Their game, if it could be called that was interrupted suddenly by a loud and rather rough voice.

"Morning".

Such was their concentration neither had noticed the oldish man in the garden adjacent. The garden to their right if you stood with your back to the cottage. The man who was leaning with his arms resting on the fence was tall, slender, around seventy Charlotte guessed but a fit seventy. He had a narrow face supported by a pointed chin. His hair was white and combed back but not very well. He looked as though he'd shaved but again, not very well. His trousers were dull grey and by the look of them were work trousers. His shirt was of a thick material that had probably once been white, both collar and cuffs were well frayed with wear.

"Morning" Charlotte and her father duetted a greeting.

"You must be the new tenants," he said, continuing in his loud voice. "Tom told me you'd moved in".

Tom? Was that the name of their mysterious landlord? Before either of them could ask the man provided an explanation.

"I'm Tom's gardener, Tom's your neighbour. I don't believe you've had the pleasure yet."

Charlotte's father shook his head. "No" he replied, "we haven't." So Tom wasn't their landlord's name after all. Tom's gardener continued.

"I don't know why he, (Tom) wants me to come today, there's nothing to do." He waved despairingly at the garden. "The springs been so rubbish that hardly anything's moved. The crocuses haven't flowered yet and I don't think they ever will. "The daffs," he pointed at the green stems rising throughout the garden, "are normally out by now. I'm not even sure they'll flower either. And I've never seen that happen!" His voice rose to make the point. "Funny thing is". Tom's gardener was on a roll. "Just up the road at Tring and Cow Roast where

I do other gardens, everything's growing like mad. It's just Aldbury. It's been miserable here for weeks." Charlotte and her father waited to see if he had finished, he had.

"I've no idea" was her father's rather unhelpful reply shrugging his shoulders. "We've only just arrived."

"Yes well I hope it cheers up for you, by the way my name's William though everybody calls me Will". Will reached over the fence to shake hands. Charlotte's father introduced himself and then introduced Charlotte. "What a pretty name" Will observed shaking her hand. Thankfully, the fence prevented him from patting her head. If the fence hadn't have been there Charlotte was certain it would have been her head that received his greeting instead. As a child you know these things, it was a perception lost in adulthood.

"Well I must be off, there's nothing to do here" and reducing his voice to a whisper added, "I'll still charge him for several hours though, he won't notice." He nodded towards the house. "It was nice to have met you, I hope you'll like it here. Aldbury's a lovely village." Will paused and looked up at the sky. "Especially when the sun shines," he finished and with a one motion wave made his departure.

Tom, their neighbour Charlotte soon discovered, was a retired gentleman also in his seventies. Unlike his gardener his figure and reddened complexion betrayed a lifetime love of food and drink. His face was round with rapidly thinning white hair and a well-kept beard. His eyes were bright blue and full of mischief. Also in contrast to his gardener Tom was always immaculately turned out. His clothes were always classically English in style, mostly from a bygone era and there was always a touch of eccentricity such as a bright yellow handkerchief protruding from a jacket pocket or a scarlet scarf around his neck, flayed out as though he'd just been flying a bi plane. He also had a yellow checked scarf which matched a pair of yellow checked trousers and when he wore these Charlotte's father remarked always that he looked like "Rupert Bear". Charlotte had no idea what her father meant by this, she would have to Google it, that is when she could lay hands on a computer. Tom's shoes were always polished to perfection, almost to the extent that they were close to being mirrors on his feet. Tom's mode of transport was an old Renault Four and he always somehow managed to park it right outside his house. In contrast to everything else belonging to Tom his car cried out, neglect. The colour was somewhere between leaf green and aqua marine blue and resembled, Charlotte thought, water from a dirty fish tank. The car had chrome bumpers that were rusting badly and inside the burgundy seats were cracked and peeling. Tom drove the car at speed everywhere and always with the windows open no matter how cold. Over the coming weeks Charlotte and her family grew to really like Tom. He was the village eccentric and rich enough not to care. Every day at four o'clock he would sit in the one chair in his garden with a glass of brandy or sometimes whisky and a chunky cigar enjoying both whilst quietly reading a book. He was always cheerful and always greeted Charlotte and her family with great enthusiasm. Having said that they never really had a proper conversation with Tom and it was nearly always Will who would provide them with details about Tom's background and stories of life in the village.

Their other neighbours turned out to be a career couple in their thirties. Buying a cottage in Aldbury was an important rung on the social ladder for them. They both worked in London, he in insurance and her in marketing. Their garden was immaculate and punctuated with glittering modern ornaments. Charlotte's father often commented that if they'd been a couple from a generation back the garden would be full of gnomes. They had a car each and a rather flash sports car which they shared at weekends. Having three cars and inhabiting a cottage without a drive in which to park didn't make them the most popular of residents in the village though they never seemed to care. Apart from the odd "Hi" they never really got to know their young neighbours.

The two of them spent a "good morning" doing the garden. I'm using a French expression to explain time here. If Charlotte's mother was ever asked how long she'd be, she'd reply in French "a good half hour" or a "good two hours" meaning she'd be slightly longer than half an hour or slightly more than two hours. A, "petit heure" or "small hour" would mean around fifty to fifty five minutes, "a small morning," just a few hours. Her father always declared the expressions to be completely illogical, "how can you have a small hour" he would argue but his words always fell on deaf ears. Returning to the story, a "good morning" therefore meant they finished early afternoon, around one thirty to be precise. The two of them were pleased with their work. The garden had regained a level of respectability at least, though it was still a long way from looking as good as both of their neighbours. The only way that would happen quickly would be with a good covering of snow. Patience was needed.

Whilst they'd worked in the garden, Charlotte's mother had busied herself cleaning and preparing lunch and when they entered, the whole house unlike the garden smelt like spring. It really was very pleasant even if the effect did come from a bottle. After lunch Charlotte helped her mother with the washing up whilst her father went up to her room to move the picture of the white stag.

He had already decided to move it to a little spot beneath the stairs, where they ate their meals. His daughter's room he found was flooded with light, the long sash window appeared to capture the brightness then magnify it a hundred times. His daughter really was fortunate to have this room. He looked around him, everything was neatly put away and in order. Even Gromit had been neatly tucked up in bed. Their daughter was the neatest most organised person in the family and her room proved it. He turned his attention to the picture. He couldn't understand how a picture could be so difficult to move and such a small one too. He took a closer look at the picture itself. It was dull he thought and may even be an old photograph, it was hard to tell. Certainly, the picture was nothing special and normally he wouldn't have given it a second glance but for some reason and one he couldn't understand the picture held his attention. So much so that he felt a little unnerved by it. He could understand why his daughter wanted it moved. At first he looked to lift the picture of its hook. He thought the old picture wire may have become attached to the hook or nail through years of paint. The picture to his frustration simply wouldn't budge, even when he levered a good deal of force. Puzzled he peered at the picture more closely trying to see how it was attached to the wall. Being an old cottage the wall in no way could be called smooth, it had many indentations. Thus in places the picture wasn't hard against the wall. Despite this, annoyingly, he still couldn't see behind the frame well enough to find any attachment. Grabbing the picture tightly with both hands he simply tried to yank it away but again it wouldn't budge, there was not even a hint of movement. Using anymore force would risk breaking the picture and that would be a shame, it was also not theirs to damage. After several more attempts he had to admit defeat. In his frustration he thought about smashing it off with a hammer but again there was always the fact that the picture did not belong to them and smashing it wasn't their right. He was also superstitious, sometimes annoyingly so and worried that any damage he may do to the picture could possibly bring him, or worse still his family bad luck. He had never really been lucky in life and inviting further bad luck made him fearful. Silly he knew but there it was. His seventh sense told him the picture must be there for good reason and that was that. Charlotte simply shrugged her shoulders when her father told of his lack of success.

"No worries," an expression her father hated.

As a family they decided to use what was left of the afternoon to explore the village. Charlotte's father had already planned a route, as if one was needed. When he didn't have his head buried in a book he was always studying maps. "You can often learn more from a map than a book" he would often try to persuade. For the tour he'd decided they would retrace their steps in the direction via which they'd arrived the first day. This meant turning right on leaving their cottage for the short walk to the village pond, also the village centre.

An oak tree overlooked the pond under which sat a bench. The tree was a relative newcomer to the village, planted in 1976 it replaced an old elm that had previously stood there for centuries. This is where her parents, Charlotte learned, had sat to eat their sandwiches the day they discovered the card in the shop window. Just to the left of the bench stood a set of old stocks and a whipping post, a famous local landmark and one much photographed. Charlotte's father sensing his daughter's curiosity couldn't resist explaining their use and history. Her mother sensing what was coming, started to count the ducks on the pond, it was a shame there were only three. After bearing ten minutes or so of Charlotte's father in full flow and tired of repeatedly counting the same ducks she stood up and with a look that a stranger could read made ready to leave.

From the stocks they walked along the road leading to Tring, arriving shortly in front of the main entrance to the village church. A relatively modern lych gate announced the beginning of a gravel path leading to the church door. A large sign which doubled as a notice board informed strangers the church was dedicated to St John the Baptist. Charlotte with her naturally curious mind wondered who had decided which saint the church should be dedicated to. Who had made that momentous decision? The church itself was sturdy in appearance with a tall square clock tower which looked as though it had been heightened in three different stages. The tower dominated the local landscape and from a distance because of Aldbury's setting and the many trees was often the only feature of the village clearly visible. The church was attractively built of flint and stone with a brick wall enclosing the churchyard. The churchyard Charlotte thought was quite beautiful. One end raised from the road part of it had been allowed to naturalise. The graves were respectfully spaced and in a relaxed fashion, and with a good spread of trees the overall feeling was one of quiet contentment.

Between them it was decided they would leave visiting the church till another day. Instead her father, and I apologise in advance if the next few lines read rather like a guidebook, led them past the entrance to thereafter join a signposted footpath which crossed a field bordering the churchyard. An old iron fence, the type once commonly used on established country estates separated the field from the churchyard. Their way skirted the churchyard with the land on their left gently rising to in the distance meet a wood which covered the summit. A wood Charlotte's father had already told her was called Aldbury Nowers. Nowers being one of those old English words whose meaning and origin has been lost to time. Much closer and also on their left were the rather impressive outbuildings of a farm, "Church Farm," her father read loudly his nose buried in the map. The field they now found themselves tramping through was distinctly uneven with deep furrows, a good number of hollows and pronounced mounds that tumbled over a wide area. Charlotte's father enjoying playing the role of a "landscape detective" recognised the signs. At one time it was almost certain there had been a rather large building here, a farm house perhaps or a large barn.

A light, rather mysterious mist covered the field. The whole village remained under a grey cloud but here in the field the mist appeared to suck in the gloom. The scenery was beautiful, indeed it was hard to imagine a more beautiful spot yet the atmosphere was depressing, heavy weighing down on one's shoulders. It was not an atmosphere to hang around in for long, especially being next to a churchyard. Consequently the family traversed the field somewhat hastily, leaving via a style to walk through a second field behind the pretty village primary school.

The second field showed none of the disturbance of the first and the heavy atmosphere too, miraculously lifted. After leaving the primary school they passed through a gate in the hedge on their right to after walking through a small meadow come out in front of the creeper covered Greyhound pub. To celebrate their new home they had to "christen" the pub Charlotte's father persuaded. It did indeed seem a good idea and in reality no persuasion was needed. Her father ordered a local ale for himself, a large white dry white wine for her mother and Charlotte a hot chocolate. Over their drinks Charlotte learned from her father that the greyhound, as the pub sign correctly depicted, was once a popular hunting dog dating right back to the Egyptians. At one time in England they were so revered, he told her, that only Royalty or nobility were allowed to own them and if a commoner was caught with one they would probably have found themselves in the stocks. They were also well known to have been the favourite hunting dog of Henry VIII. How her father remembered all this was quite astonishing, he always seemed to have a fairly in depth knowledge on virtually every topic. Her mother taking long drawn sips of her wine remained silent, staring wistfully at the village pond. The ducks had flown, she had nothing to count. Life was so unfair.

Rising above the rooftops opposite the pub, the wooded scarp under the darkening grey sky was beginning to look a little foreboding. Several signposted paths led from the village up the heavily wooded slope and Charlotte knew it wouldn't be long before they would be exploring every single one for both her parents were keen walkers. For now though, after finishing their drinks they took the road, passing the pond back to their cottage. Before entering they decided quickly to follow the road ahead a little further to see what lay in the other direction. A short walk brought them to The Valiant Trooper, the village's second pub. Her father tried but failed badly to look surprised and despite his protestations her mother on this occasion put her foot down and it was decided, or rather her father was told that the christening of this pub could wait till another day. And so it was as the gloom grew heavier, introducing the beginning of the end to the day they returned to their cottage, pleased by what they'd seen so far of their new home.

There were enough logs left over for another fire and for a second evening they huddled together on the sofa to enjoy the fire's light. There was less drama this evening. Ghost stories had been exhausted the night before and their mysterious landlord, already forgotten. Instead the three of them sat almost in silence enjoying the hypnotic effect of the flames. Sleepy, long before the embers started to die Charlotte took herself up to bed. Outside on the windowsill the robin perched waiting for her. It waited till she was asleep and satisfied, flew off.

Chapter Six

The First Week

The next morning Charlotte's father took the van to go and collect their market stall. This was stored in a lock up they rented in Wembley. He'd estimated it would probably take him three, maybe even four trips to move everything so he would probably be gone for most of the day. Before they'd moved to Aldbury her parents had already found a lock up in nearby Berkhamsted. It was quite a bit smaller but they'd decided the "Wendy house" and the other outbuildings in the garden could be used as storage too.

After much persuasion by her parents Charlotte had been accepted at Tring School, the nearest school to them and only a short bus ride from Aldbury. The school was a large sprawling affair on Mortimer Road close to the town centre. It had, her parents been told, an excellent reputation. To attend the school Charlotte needed a school uniform and that morning whilst her father collected their livelihood Charlotte and her mother planned go into town to buy what she needed. Her father would drop them off and they were to get the bus back.

To obtain Charlotte's uniform they had been given the address, by the school, of a specialist shop in the town centre. The shop, when they arrived turned out to be a rather old fashioned affair and primarily sold sportswear. By old fashioned I mean it had a wooden floor and wooden shelves. The fittings were old but the selection of sportswear on offer was most impressive. The service too could be described as old fashioned and I mean this as a compliment. Each customer was given the utmost attention, every detail was taken care of and you were never rushed even though other customers may be waiting. Charlotte was even measured for her uniform which consisted of a blazer, trousers, a couple of white blouses and a striped tie. In addition there was also a complete PE kit. For her mother buying a school uniform was something of an adventure. School uniform was almost unheard of in France and considered there a tradition that belonged to the eccentric English. To finish the shop-keeper gave them the school badge which was to be sewn onto the blazer pocket. The badge depicted the head of a stern looking white stag on a burgundy background with the head of the animal resting on alternate waves of blue, which Charlotte assumed represented water. Ever the curious, she wondered what the badge stood for. She asked the shopkeeper and obviously embarrassed he admitted he'd no idea but assumed the head represented the Hart in Hertfordshire. Charlotte later discovered the Hart representing Hertfordshire was actually brown, not white. After purchasing the school uniform there remained a couple of hours to kill before the next bus and this the two of them spent passing quality daughter and mother time sharing cake and hot drinks and browsing the local shops along the High Street.

The bus dropped them beside the village pond and before returning to their cottage Charlotte persuaded her mother to pop into the village shop as she wanted another sherbet dip. The bell clanged loudly as they entered. The same rounded lady who'd served them before stood behind the counter busy pricing up some jars of local jam.

"Hello" she said, recognising Charlotte. There was a genuine warmth to her voice, "how are you settling in?"

"Good thanks," Charlotte replied, already warming to the smiling lady behind the counter, "this is my mum," she grabbed her mother's hand. "She's French".

"I know" the lady replied and leaning over the counter whispered dramatically, "word's got around". She smiled broadly at her mother and the two continued with small talk whilst Charlotte explored the sweet counter. They left the shop with Charlotte clutching several paper bags. Her mother protested that they contained enough sweets to last a month. In reality it would be no more than a couple of days, especially if her father discovered where she hid them.

"What did you talk to the woman about?" Charlotte asked as they walked back to their cottage. It was a genuine question though she wasn't really that interested in a reply. Her concentration was fixed on the weird sensation the sweet she'd just popped in her mouth was having. It popped and spat rather like having a sparkler in your mouth, it was the latest thing.

"Her name's Ashtynn" her mother said," unusual isn't it, I had to ask her to spell it for me. Did you know that the tenant in our cottage before us was an artist?"

Charlotte shook her head, she was busy holding her breath, something she'd been told accentuated the experience of the sweet.

"Yes apparently your bedroom used to be his studio." Charlotte half listening could understand why as the light in her room was perfect for painting. "Ashtynn says he used to be quite good, apparently some of his paintings are for sale in the village pub, the Valiant Trooper." Charlotte's mother with her French accent had trouble pronouncing the word valiant and Charlotte tried her best not to smile. "We'll have to take a look" her mother promised. Charlotte nodded, not really listening she popped a second sweet in her mouth.

Her father's last trip included bringing boxes of old books which he'd also had stored in the lock-up in Wembley. Almost all of his books were non-fiction and most of these were on history especially local history. Her father rarely read a novel. Much to her mother's dismay he unloaded all of the boxes containing his book collection into the lounge and spent the rest of the evening carefully selecting which books to display on the fitted pine shelves in the alcoves either side of the chimney breast and which to store away. On his way back he hadn't forgotten to buy another sack of logs and even her mother admitted the smell of old books complemented the scent of burning logs and combined made the lounge feel much more homely. Whilst her father was organising his reading her mother busied herself sewing the badge onto Charlotte's school blazer. After her mother had finished Charlotte tried on her uniform for her father to see and paraded around the lounge in an exaggerated fashion making them all laugh. After changing into her pyjamas she returned to the lounge carrying only her school blazer. Sitting on the sofa she thoughtfully fingered the badge.

"Look dad" she said sliding off the sofa and kneeling beside him "the school badge has the white stag just like the picture in my room".

"So it has," replied her father absently, pulling out a couple of rather large books from one of the many boxes and after a seconds' thought placing both to one side. "There's probably a local legend involving a white hart."

"What's the difference between a stag and a hart?" Charlotte asked, it was a fair question and one that most people would probably ask if they thought about it.

"I'm not sure," he admitted. "I think the word hart is more suited to mythology".

"Are white deer special then?" Charlotte looked intently at the school badge. The stag on the badge looked cross whilst the stag in the picture in her room she felt looked stressed. Neither looked happy. At this question her father stopped what he was doing and looked at her. His frame silhouetted against the fire glowed at the edges and the flickering light made his eyes look as though they were dancing. Her mother turned her gaze from the fire towards her husband. She recognised the signs, there was a story coming. She would go and prepare a pot of coffee and a hot chocolate for Charlotte.

Charlotte's father gazed at his daughter's expectant face. "The white hart or stag" he began, "is a very special animal, not just in England but world over. In the tales of King Arthur when a white hart appeared before the knights of the round table it was a sign that they were to embark on a quest. King Arthur and his knights made numerous attempts to capture the hart, probably because they wanted its knowledge but always failed if you remember." Charlotte nodded, her father was always recounting the Arthurian legends. "Indeed it's believed those who hunt it," he continued," no matter how hard they try will never capture it. The hart will always lead those in pursuit deep into the wood where it is protected by the underworld. There are tales all over the world dating back thousands of years of the white hart eluding capture. And if anyone actually did succeed in capturing it, killing it will bring great misfortune not only to them but to everybody they know. In your Tales of Narnia, The Lion, the Witch and the Wardrobe" one of Charlotte's favourite books, "the kings and queens of Narnia tried to capture a white hart but never succeeded, did they?" this time Charlotte shook her head. How she'd love to find a wardrobe like the one in Narnia. A log dislodged itself from the fire making them both jump. Her father after a brief struggle lifting it back into the grate continued. "It was also once believed in this country that the white hart had some sort of connection or could communicate with the underworld and if you ever set eyes on one it signalled a dramatic change was about to take place in your life, or the beginning of a daring adventure as with King Arthur." As if on cue the fire collapsed in on itself as a supporting log crumbled to ashes. Again the two of them jumped and her father distracted, turned his attention to rearranging the remaining logs with a stick they'd found in the garden, a substitute for a poker until they bought one. When finished her father went back to his books, the white hart or stag apparently forgotten.

After finishing her coffee Charlotte took herself up to bed. On entering her bedroom she found her room bathed in a silvery light, light generated by a full moon shining directly through the long sash window. The effect would perhaps unnerve many people but to Charlotte it was comforting, almost magical. The light brought out the richness of the robin's breast perched patiently on the window sill. On seeing the door open it skittered into the shadows, it didn't want the little girl to see it, not yet anyway. Daytime was fine but not at night. Before getting into bed Charlotte went over to the picture of the white stag, or was it a hart, what was the difference? She gazed curiously at the small picture. "I wonder because of you whether there may be a dramatic change coming?" she whispered to herself, "but then you're not real are you?" For a split second Charlotte could have sworn the hart looked at her. No that was impossible, she quickly put it down to a trick of the light. Or a full moon playing with her mind. Climbing into bed she hugged Gromit tightly. For some reason she needed his comfort more than usual that night. From the sill the robin studied the scene, careful to avoid getting caught in the moonlight. The clouds closed and the room darkened. Shivering it flew off returning to the comfort of its nest which lay, well concealed at the base of the pagoda. There was no mate to greet it and there would be no eggs or young to raise this spring. This year spring would be a very lonely affair.

The rest of the week the family spent the majority of their time exploring the local area. Much of this involved tramping the foot paths covering the Ashridge estate.

The Ashridge estate covers over 5,000 acres and includes ancient woodland as well as natural chalk downland with much of the estate falling under the protection of the National Trust. If you study a good map you will discover the woodland is divided into commons which meant in the past local people had the right to let their animals graze on the land without paying a fee. This custom only stopped a little over a hundred years ago. Lines of banks with parallel ditches run through the wood, they once formed boundaries some dating back to Saxon times or even before. There is also evidence of Roman habitation. At the estates centre is Ashridge House one of the most impressive houses in England and a grade one listed building. Today it is home to a world renowned management centre. The house is built on the site of an old monastery which was founded In 1283 by Edmund of Cornwall for the order of Bonhommes, a college of monks who wore habits of ash grey. Their origin leads back to the Cathars in Southern France who were at their height in the twelfth century. It was the building of the monastery that founded the Estate. The National Trust centre is found close to the Bridgewater monument or tower which commemorates the third duke of Bridgewater who once resided at Ashridge House. The monument is essentially a Greek column, inside which 172 steps climb to a viewing platform beneath a funerary urn affording quite incredible views over the surrounding landscape. The National Trust buildings are of wood and house a shop, an education centre and a popular café. At the Northern tip of the estate stands Ivinghoe Beacon a dramatic domed chalk hill once the site of an Iron age hill fort. The beacon too affords fabulous views over the surrounding countryside and seen from a distance is an iconic local landmark. Ivinghoe Beacon also marks the end of "The Ridgeway" a National Trail or long distance path which starts at Avebury in Wiltshire. Charlotte's father completed the route when he was just sixteen, something he reminds his family of repeatedly.

There wasn't enough time in the week to explore Ivinghoe Beacon but they quickly became acquainted with nearly all of the woodland paths in Ashridge. Every time they left Aldbury behind the weather appeared to change. It wasn't always blue skies, indeed it was often grey but never the gloom that seemed to permanently hang over the village. If you needed proof of this, outside the village spring was advancing at a pace. Bird song reverberated throughout the wood. Buds were starting to appear on the trees and blackthorn blossom shone bright even under a grey sky. The floor of the wood in places had already become a carpet of dark green. In a few weeks, the green would become a carpet of rich blue as the famous Ashridge bluebells, (Charlotte's mother insisted on calling them the French name, clochettes), reached their full splendour. For now clumps of pale yellow primroses could be enjoyed and always a pleasure to see, the delicate white flowers of wood-sorrel. Where the wood was at its dampest the small yellow flowers of the lesser celandine brightened the woodland floor and the blueish green leaves of the wild honeysuckle were already open, preparing for the summer climb.

When they weren't exploring the Ashridge Estate her parents used the van to discover their surroundings not so easily explored on foot. Nearby, Berkhamsted had some good shopping and a canal running through her that needed to be explored one day. The town also had a rather romantic ruined castle. To her mother's delight she discovered it was where William the Conqueror had received the English crown. Her mother always called him by his French title, Guillaume le Conquerant and her father in return William the Bastard a reference to his doubtful parentage. This battle would continue between them with her father declaring that William wasn't even French but Norman to which her mother would always reply in her strongest French accent, "rubbish."

Other than the vibrant town of Berkhamsted there were many delightful villages, Great and Little Gaddesden, Ivinghoe, Cheddington, (always to be associated with the great train robbery), Pitstone, Marsworth and many more. All had their own charm and their own place in history and nearly all, which was of particular interest to her father, had an enticing village pub, sometimes two!

They were, after only a few days quickly getting used to village life. Nods with other villagers were regularly exchanged, not the enthusiastic greetings experienced in Bayswater, but a discreet recognition by those more established that they had arrived and were now, almost villagers themselves. The village shop, they quickly discovered, was very much the centre of village life. Ashtynn always had a friendly greeting and regularly tried her limited French out on Charlotte's mother. She, it turned out, wasn't the owner of the shop. The owners were a young couple who had moved down from Scotland. They had a young child so the wife tended to remain at home whilst her husband spent the day running the post office counter. By keeping the shop and post office open they were providing the village with both lungs and a heart.

Midweek there was a knock at the door. The stubborn lock still wouldn't oblige and it was always a short sprint out the back door and around the side to say hello before whoever was knocking walked away. On the doorstep stood a smartly dressed woman with two young girls. She introduced herself as Emma, and that she lived in one of the newer, (posh) houses on Tom's Hill. She'd heard of their arrival and wanted to welcome them to the village. Ashtynn she said had told her that they had a daughter and thought it would help Charlotte if she introduced her own daughters, Caroline also eleven and Hanna, thirteen. The two girls smiled. It was a lovely gesture. A week later Emma invited them to dinner where they enjoyed a traditional plate of bangers and mash. Emma's husband it turned out was a music producer which of course was "really cool." When her daughters discovered Charlotte was French they immediately christened her "French Charlotte." The next morning on a trip to the village shop Ashtynn's greeting had changed from, "morning Charlotte" to "French Charlotte" and thereafter French Charlotte was to become her village title.

One evening Charlotte's father took himself to the Valiant Trooper to, "try it out." The pub had two distinct halves, the original bar dating from the 17th century and a modern extension which doubled as a restaurant. Locals tended to gather in the original bar. Charlotte had asked her father to look for the paintings by the former tenant that were supposedly for sale there. He found there to be only three and all were hung in the modern extension. All were of a view looking through a traditional sash window with ivy encroaching the panes of glass. In two of the paintings on the sill outside perched a robin and in the third a magpie wings spread back looked to be trying to land on the sill. They were well-painted but not something that he'd personally choose to buy. At £300 each he didn't consider them cheap either. On ordering his pint he asked the bar-maid about them, explaining that the artist used to live in the cottage where they lived now. "I wouldn't" know she told him, as she'd only started a couple of weeks ago and lived in Tring. She said this as though Tring was another country. What she could tell him was that the artist had simply disappeared which was a shame as they'd sold a couple of his paintings and still had the money waiting for him behind the bar.

The locals frequenting the bar greeted Charlotte's father with a healthy mix of curiosity coupled with suspicion, though all were welcoming. The main topic of conversation, perhaps predictably was the weather. Everyone had a different theory as to the grey cloud cover that had haunted the village the past eight weeks or so. All agreed that it simply "wasn't natural." "Even the blackthorn hasn't blossomed", this from a local farmer "and that's always dead on time no matter what the weather. It's just not normal." There was broad agreement. Another consensus of opinion was that the grey cloud was getting progressively heavier and that birds were no longer visiting the gardens no matter how hard one tried to tempt them. Others commented that they hadn't seen a badger for nearly two months and that the fallow deer had stopped coming into the village at night. Apparently this had been a common occurrence before. Not daring to have a third pint, Charlotte's father said his good byes. On the short walk back to the cottage he thought about the conversation in the bar especially the part about the absence of bird life. He thought about the robin that frequented their garden. It was always there, every day. They were lucky, it seemed.

On Friday, as a family they visited the local auction rooms in Tring. Charlotte had never been to an auction before and discovered it was something of an Aladdin's cave. She delighted in the fact that there were boxes of goodies that you simply had to take a chance on. Her parents put written bids on a green checked Italian sofa and a low pine coffee table. The bids weren't really serious, just a "bit of fun." The actual auction was on Saturday but her parents agreed it wasn't really sensible to attend worrying they may be tempted to bid more than they could afford. On Monday morning they received a call from the auction house informing them that their bids had won. For a grand sum of £50 they were now owners of a quality Italian sofa and a very respectable pine coffee table. Both fitted perfectly in the lounge, the cottage was fast becoming a real home.

The following weekend Charlotte and her father busied themselves in the garden planting summer bulbs in the hope that one day soon the weather would change. The robin, ever reliable perched on the fence watching everything with apparent interest. William or Will greeted them, (it turned out his was a weekly contract), this time not with a hello but by reciting a rhyme.

"And when they were dead,
The robin so red,
Brought strawberry leaves,
And over them spread,
And all the day long,
The green branches among,
They'd prettily whistle,
And this was their song –"

He was just about to continue when Charlotte's father stopped him, asking what it was he was singing. It was hardly singing, Charlotte thought to herself. Will nodded towards the robin. They both noticed he was dressed in exactly the same clothes as last week. Will that is not the robin.

"You're lucky to have him, must be the only bird left in the village" and remembering the question added, "oh that, it's from, Babes in the wood." He said this as though he were surprised they didn't know.

Charlotte immediately asked, "Dad, what's babes in the wood?"

"It's an old English tale," of course her father would know. "About two children who are found dead in the wood." Charlotte screwed her face up at this. The robin looked on as though it were listening, more than that, as if it understood.

"The robin's a good friend" Will continued, "unlike other birds they understand us. It's said that some people can talk to robins. They will warn you too if death is on the way."

"How do they do that?" Charlotte asked, a little shocked.

"By tapping on your window. I often see him" Will gestured towards the robin with his head, "sat on your kitchen sill, if he taps the window you need to be worried."

The robin with perfect timing flew to a branch in the cherry blossom. Will was deadly serious, that was clear, he believed in the old customs and meant well with his advice or warning, whichever way it was meant. Charlotte's father not wanting his daughter scared quickly changed the subject.

"What does Tom do for a living?" he asked after Will's employer.

"Nothing now" Will wiped his arm across his forward as though the weight of the conversation was causing him to sweat. "He used to be an antique dealer, a good one at that."

It made perfect sense, thought Charlotte's father. From what he'd heard and seen, for they'd not as yet been formally introduced, he could easily picture Tom as a presenter on one of the numerous television programs about antiques. The conversation passed on and inevitably came round to the dismal localised weather with Will complaining as last time that there was still nothing to do and that his employer was wasting his money by having him come every week. Not that he was complaining of course even though he was. Just as Will gestured to leave, Charlotte's father asked after their landlord and the previous tenant.

"The last tenant was an artist" Will confirmed. "Nice chap, very friendly, always had time for a chat. Elmer, his name was Elmer, unusual name." Will thought for a moment, "didn't like his paintings though. Were always of a window, and well." He paused and again gestured towards the robin who still appeared to be listening intently. "A robin, sometimes a magpie, oh and I think he painted a squirrel once but always looking at them through a damned window. It seemed to me he was obsessed with the window."

"What happened to him?" Charlotte's father asked.

"No idea" was Tom's reply. "One day he was there the next day he was gone. First time I knew he'd left was when the advert advertising your place appeared at the shop." This response brought the subject onto their landlord but this question met with less success. "No idea who owns the place" was Will's reply. Elmer was there for the past three years I think or thereabouts. Before that as far as I can remember it's always been empty. It used to be a talking point, people thought it was a waste. Such a nice cottage lying empty."

"But it's well maintained. Well reasonably well maintained," Charlotte's father added thinking twice.

"Oh yes, that's the funny thing some men used to regularly turn up and do work but they weren't from any local firm. No idea where they come from."

"And you've no idea who lived here before the artist, when it was last occupied before him?" Will shook his head.

"It was empty when I was a boy" he said, and has been for as long as I can remember, good to see people living in it now though, a building needs to be lived in. Anyway must be off, nothing to do here, wish there was." With that he waved to Charlotte and made his way down the garden disappearing along the brick path that wound around the last cottage. Charlotte and her father were left standing in silence. Charlotte, despite her age, was thinking along the same lines as her father. What about the Wendy house? It wasn't that old, it even had electricity. They both remembered the landlord stating that he'd built it for his children. Could Will be mistaken? As if reading their minds the robin flew to a new perch, the sloping roof of the Wendy house.

On Sunday it was decided to give Charlotte's mother a break and enjoy Sunday lunch at the Valiant Trooper. On arriving they found the pub was busy, mainly with families doing the same. The three pictures were still hanging on the wall, and were virtually ignored by the other diners, just the odd cry from a child, typically, "look mum, there's a robin." It was the first time Charlotte and her mother had seen the paintings by the previous tenant. Her mother's only comment was, "there's something about them." Charlotte studied them intently. Hadn't her parents noticed. That was her window in the paintings and that was their robin.

Chapter Seven

The Robin, The Squirrel And The Magpie

On Monday Charlotte started her new school. She'd argued that it was silly as in a week they'd be breaking for Easter and wouldn't it be better as she put it, "new term, new start." Her parents disagreed and Monday morning under a dark grey sky she found herself resplendent in her new uniform, standing with the other village children beside the pond waiting for the school bus. Caroline and Hannah were part of the waiting huddle and introduced her to their friends of a similar age. Everybody seemed to know each other and with the help of Caroline and her sister Charlotte didn't feel like a complete stranger. All seemed fascinated by the fact that she was French and one boy younger than her shouted out.

"I know some French. Voulez vous coucher avec moi." At this all the children laughed, even those who hadn't a clue what it meant.

Tring school Charlotte found was huge, bigger, much bigger even than the hamlet she was brought up in, in France. Surely she'd need a map to find her way around. Caroline sensing this grabbed her hand.

"Come on," she yelled. "You're in my form, I've already checked." Charlotte's form was large, around thirty plus pupils. There was a babble of excited chitchat which subsided immediately when the form teacher arrived. He was tall, around thirty Charlotte thought with tight red hair and a pale complexion. He had a kind face and casually dressed but commanded a presence that told everybody he was no push over. It was obvious that his class both liked and respected him.

"Morning" he directed at everybody.

"Morning Mr Holdsworth" his class replied in unison.

"I understand we have a stranger in our class" he said this whilst looking directly at Charlotte, "not a stranger for long though I hope. Would you care to come up and join me." It was an instruction not a question. Charlotte got up from her chair and stood beside her new form teacher. She looked across the room, what felt like hundreds of faces stared back. "Tell everybody what your name is" the teacher commanded his hand resting reassuringly on Charlotte's shoulder.

"Charlotte," it was barely a whisper.

"Could you hear that?" her new form teacher asked everybody loudly.

"Nooo" came the loud response.

"Can you tell them a little more loudly" Mr Holdsworth said smiling down at her, "no need to be shy."

Charlotte took a deep breath, "Charlotte" she shouted with an unmistakable French accent that she hadn't at all intended.

"Very good" said her teacher "and as you can probably tell by that, Charlotte is French, aren't you Charlotte?" Charlotte nodded.

"French Charlotte" Caroline shouted out and from that day on Charlotte was known throughout the school as French Charlotte. Soon she thought, the whole world will know her as French Charlotte.

At lunch time Charlotte took herself to the school library to obtain a library card and to use a computer. She search typed "robin, babes in the wood, rhyme." It wasn't long before she found the rhyme Will had recounted at their last meeting. She found the last verse and repeated it softly to herself.

"Poor babes in the wood!
Sweet babes in the wood!

Oh the sad fete of,
The babes in the wood."

Why is the robin associated with so much sadness, Charlotte thought to herself. It seems such a happy bird.

On Wednesday Charlotte's parents restarted their markets. Wednesday - Berkhamsted, Thursday – Princes Risborough, Friday – Tring and Saturday – Buckingham. This meant that her parents always left the house before she did and returned quite some time after. That is except on a Friday when it was only five minutes' walk from the school to Tring market where her mother had her stall. On Friday therefore she helped her parents close up. Every morning the robin she found waiting outside the back door, she liked to think it was there to see her off. It was also always there waiting for her on her return. Sometimes it would be sitting on the sill to the small kitchen window and remembering Wills warning she silently prayed that it wouldn't tap at its reflection in the glass. Like her father Charlotte was fiercely superstitious. She needn't have worried though, it never did and if truth be told she found the robins presence somewhat comforting.

The dark cloud covering Aldbury failed to lift during the week, if anything it grew darker. The mist hanging over the rough field between Church Farm and the Church itself also seemed to intensify and the farmer at the farm complained that if it thickened anymore he wouldn't be able to see the church from his house. Something which for him, he kept telling everybody was, a daily pleasure. An enterprising local journalist had a photograph of the phenomenon taken from the top of the Bridgewater monument. The local paper published the photograph along with a couple of pages of text, which included interviews with a number of long standing villagers. The headline – The Darkening of Aldbury.

Those who were sensitive to their animals feelings noticed subtle changes in their behaviour. Dogs in particular, started to show hints of aggression and when on a walk, often had to be put on a lead when encountering another dog. Something that had never been needed before. At the beginning of the week flyers started appearing around the village. They depicted a photograph of a cat with the headline , LOST. Beneath the photo were the words, "If found please telephone," giving a local number to contact. Midweek a second flyer appeared. It had virtualy the same wording and a photograph of a different cat. By the end of the week no less than five cats had gone missing. Their owners all told the same tale. They had let their cats out after feeding and the cats had simply never returned. A mad catnapper was suspected and for the second time that week the normally innocuous village of Aldbury found itself at the centre of a story in the local paper. "Mad catnapper at large", read the headline. The article interviewed several of the distraught owners who had lost their feline friends and advised all cat owners to keep their cats safely indoors.

Remembering the paintings in the Valiant Trooper, Charlotte would often stand in her bedroom looking out of the tall sash window towards the wooded scarp, the ash-ridge. She tried to imagine the artist in her bedroom painting the images hanging in the Valiant Trooper. She often talked out loud to the white stag on the wall.

"What do you know?" she would ask. "You were here all the time, what do you know?" How she wished the stag could talk. Staring out at the garden, at the depressing grey cloud and the brooding wooded scarp the scene she found rather unsettling almost menacing. It almost felt at times as though her seventh sense was trying to tell her something. She wouldn't particularly describe it as feeling frightened more a feeling of deep unease. There was too much mystery about their new home. There was also something about the paintings that puzzled her, she couldn't quite put her finger on it.

One morning, as she would most mornings since seeing the paintings, Charlotte stood where she thought the artist would have had his easel and tried to imagine him painting. She moved her right hand in imaginary brush strokes as she imagined the artist would have done. She thought hard about the paintings in the pub. With an exclamation she knew what it was that had been puzzling her. She had to be sure though. Opening her door she shouted down the stairs to where her father was brewing coffee in the kitchen.

"Dad, can we eat in the pub tonight?"

They had a market the next day so her father, being practical, said "no" but when she kept pleading and seeing the same pleading expression etched across her face, her father eventually agreed that they would have lunch there the first Monday of Easter half term. Charlotte groaned, that was almost a week away.

On Sunday, her father announced with the weather forecast looking promising they were to embark on a day's circular walk to Ivinghoe Beacon and back. With a superb, packed lunch prepared by Charlotte's mother, they set out before most of the village had woken. "Early morning is the best part of the day," Charlotte's father encouraged, on seeing his daughter's sleep strained face.

After the church they crossed into the field backing onto the churchyard just as they had done on their first exploration of Aldbury. The rough field was still covered by a mist and, like the cloud it had grown considerably thicker from the time when they'd first passed through it. Charlotte, looking at it half expected a headless horseman to ride out from its depths for it resembled the obligatory mist used to set the scene in old horror films. None did of course.

A steady climb took them across the greens of the local golf course, all the time heading for Aldbury Nowers. As they climbed it wasn't long before they left the mysterious cloud that cast a permanent shadow over Aldbury behind. The sun radiated on the morning dew making it glisten, creating sparkling diamond nets of the webs spun by spiders in the taller grass. The air was crisp fresh and a joy to breath in. As they neared the wood they stopped and turned to admire the view. It really was quite magnificent. The church tower of St John the Baptist stood proud, in the distance to their right the scattered hillside village of Wigginton was just visible and almost directly before them, rising above the trees the Bridgewater Monument. From their viewpoint it also became clear just how localised the strange weather affecting Aldbury was. Blue sky was everywhere except directly above the village, where hung a deep grey, and an increasingly angry looking cloud. So dense was the gloom, apart from the church tower it was hard to distinguish a single building in the village. The three stood in silence, trying to make sense of the strange phenomenon, then with a cheery, "ok let's go" from her father, they continued their walk.

Aldbury Nowers was just magical Charlotte thought, like a wood out of a fairy-tale. Further on the chalk grass ridge of Pitstone Hill was breath-taking as were the views it afforded. After crossing a narrow lane, connecting Ivinghoe with Aldbury, originally a Roman road Charlotte's father informed them they climbed, following the rim of an impressive coombe with the name Incombe Hole. For those who aren't local, describing Incombe Hole simply as a coombe does it an injustice. It is a deep, very deep and very steep sided impression in the hillside, created during the last ice age. There is a real sense of drama about Incombe Hole that is impossible to capture on film or put into words. You really have to experience it for yourself. Eventually after following a well-trodden chalk path over a series of hillocks, with effort they climbed the final steep slope to reach the summit of Ivinghoe Beacon. Standing two hundred and thirty three metres high at the entrance to the Gade Valley the views from the Beacon were more than worth the effort. From its summit one is rewarded with an extensive panorama over the Vale of Aylesbury and along the Chiltern Escarpment into

Berkshire as well as to the Dunstable Downs and the Quainton Hills. It is easy to see why in the Iron Age fort used to occupy the summit, the fort's inhabitants would have been able to see their enemies approaching miles before they got there. On the far side of the Gade valley, facing the Beacon a figure of a lion had been cut into the chalk hillside. The lion represented Whipsnade zoo and continued a tradition of cutting chalk to create an image that dates back thousands of years.

"The end of the Ridgeway" Charlotte's father declared hands on hip gazing into the distance. "And to think around 40 years ago I was standing on this spot after completing it."

"WE KNOW." Charlotte and her mother shouted in unison.

From the summit, the trio descended a spur to Gallows Hill, the northern most point of the National Trust, Ashridge Estate. On older maps the hill is named Gallows Nap, Nap or Knap being an old English name for summit or small hill. A large Bronze Age barrow or tumulus dominates the hilltop and at one time this was almost certainly a site of some religious significance. In the Middle Ages a set of gallows stood on the summit. Here people were hung for their crimes and after death often left to rot. The gallows would have been in full view of the road, the Icknield Way, now the B489 skirting the hill below and a macabre reminder to those traveling along it to stay on the right side of the law. The stocks at Aldbury seemed almost pleasurable in comparison Charlotte thought.

Her father busied himself exploring the barrow and declared that he had identified where the posts to the gallows once stood. Ignoring him, her mother proceeded to lay out their packed lunch. Rather disrespectfully Charlotte thought since so many people had died where they now planned to enjoy their picnic. Smoked salmon pate and rind washed cheese baguettes with onion confit were consumed with enthusiasm. Hardly a thought was given to the poor souls who had once suffered or to the original occupant or occupants of the barrow on which they were enjoying their meal. Only Charlotte had the sensitivity to feel a little uncomfortable between mouthfuls.

The Coombe although nice in its own way was nowhere near as dramatic as Incombe Hole. Much of The Coombe was wooded, some of which by imposing pines, planted in formal rows by the hands of man, without any sympathy to the natural surroundings. The remaining leg of the walk following the base of the Chiltern scarp was leisurely in comparison but equally pleasurable. As they approached Aldbury, dusk was slowly drawing in and, as a consequence the cloud above the village, a lot less noticeable. On returning to their cottage they all felt they'd made good use of their day. That night another fire was lit and luxuriating in the light from the flames they enjoyed tales by her father about the people who once called the surrounding hills their home. Long, long before "Jesus walked upon England's pastures green."

The next day was Easter Monday. A fact which Charlotte's father had forgotten when he'd made the promise to lunch at the Valiant Trooper. Knowing the pub would be busy, he persuaded Charlotte to allow him to move his promise to Tuesday. Begrudgingly she accepted, and the day after her father did indeed keep his promise and the following evening they dined at the Valiant Trooper. Arriving early they found themselves to be the only people in the restaurant. The pub was eerily silent with only the slightest sound of chatter coming from the old bar. To Charlotte's dismay the pictures were no longer there. In their place hung three typical local scenes of bluebells. Trying not to appear too desperate she persuaded her father to ask the waiter if the pub still had them.

"No" came the reply, "somebody came in a few days ago and bought all three, nearly a thousand pound he paid and in cash too." He turned to leave and as if he thought it was important, paused, turned and added. "No one local, I'd have known."

With that the waiter disappeared. Charlotte almost oblivious to her food strained to recall the images that not long ago had hung on the wall. The magpie she remembered came across as quite menacing. The paintings of the robin, not at all but one of the two if her memory wasn't playing tricks, wasn't true to life. In the second painting she was sure the robin had been backed by a night sky with a full moon and robins simply do not come out at night. Why paint a night sky? Perhaps it had simply been a matter of the artist's impression. Maybe, but she had an underlying feeling that this wasn't the case. The artist, she was convinced, had painted what he'd seen. Why did it even matter, she had no idea, she just knew it did and for some reason she knew she had to find out.

On returning to their cottage Charlotte told her parents that she didn't feel like sitting round the fire and wanted an early night. In her room she stared out of the tall sash window. There was no moon that night and even if there had been, its light wouldn't have been able to penetrate the dense cloud. There was also no robin. Just darkness and the odd glow coming from the windows of nearby houses. Sighing Charlotte climbed into bed. Not for the first time, she needed Gromit more than she liked to admit and held him close. Outside the robin dropped down onto the sill from the roof above. It was more skittish than usual and after just a quick glance flew back to its nest at the base of the pagoda.

The next morning Charlotte awoke still with the question of the painting of the robin nagging at her. She'd slept well enough but that morning she felt tired, completely unrefreshed. "Why does everything in this village disappear?" was her first thought, their landlord, the last tenant, village cats and now the paintings. She felt somehow that they were all connected. Don't be silly she kept telling herself with a shiver, you're just being over dramatic. She moved to the window and gazed out at the scene outside. The dark grey cloud was still there, threatening everything that lay beneath it though not with rain, despite the clouds dark ominous shades it never felt as though it was about to rain. Indeed the village was suffering something of a drought. Charlotte lowered her gaze to the garden and felt her body freeze. Sitting on a branch of the ornamental cherry sat a bird, not her robin but a magpie. It sat quite still and she thought, looked completely unafraid. What made her feel really uncomfortable was and there was absolutely no doubt, it was staring straight at her. Not at the window but straight at her, the bird had somehow caught and held her eye. She remembered the painting of the magpie in the Valiant Trooper and found herself repeating a rhyme her English grandmother had taught her.

"One for sorrow,
two for joy,
three for a girl,
four for a ......" she tailed off. Please let there be a second she whispered to herself. Somehow with a sense of certainty she didn't understand she knew there wouldn't be. She continued to stare at the magpie and the magpie continued to stare back. Why did she feel so afraid, it was just a magpie after all? It couldn't do her any harm.

That morning and for the rest of the week her parents noticed a change in their daughter. Gone was their happy go lucky little girl. Instead Charlotte appeared withdrawn as though she were worried or afraid of something. Their first thought was that perhaps she was being bullied but from her own account she had made friends quickly both in the village and at her new school. And Caroline along with girls they didn't know frequently knocked on the door asking if Charlotte could come out. That week to their delight, Charlotte did on occasion still go out but it was never for long and on returning she'd nearly always go straight to her room. Her room was where she spent most of her time. When either of her parents went into the garden they would look back at the house and see their daughter gazing out of the window. She never appeared to move, just standing there staring. At what they couldn't fathom.

There was the odd occasion when the magpie wasn't resident in the ornamental cherry and whenever her parents ventured out into the garden it would always miraculously disappear. Charlotte was always relieved when this happened but even so, when it wasn't there she could still feel it's presence. There was never a sign of a mate just the one for "sorrow" and always staring steadfastly at her, not her window but most definitely, her.

At the end of the week Will reliably turned up to work on Tom's garden. Charlotte was pleased to see him and as her father was in the garden putting up bird feeders in a vain attempt to attract a few feathered friends she ventured out. Her father beamed his pleasure at seeing his daughter outdoors. Her robin too looked delighted to see her and skipped down the fence as if to say hello. The magpie had gone but Charlotte wasn't fooled. It wasn't visible but she knew it was still there, she could feel its presence.

"Hello French Charlotte" Will leaned over the fence to shake her hand. Charlotte smiled and shook his solemnly.

"Hello" she returned, smiling.

"So what's going on French Charlotte, your dad here's worried about you." Her father looked away with embarrassment. He hadn't wanted his daughter to know he was worried in case it made her worse.

"Nothing, just this weather I'm fed up with it."

"I can understand that" Will chuckled, I think everyone is." Out of the corner of her eye Charlotte could see her father looking relieved at her answer and this made her feel somewhat better.

"Will," it was the start of a question. "What do you know about magpies?" Where did that come from Charlotte's father asked himself, listening.

"Well not much," Will admitted, "they're thieves I can tell you that much." Charlotte didn't question this, instead she asked.

"Yes but don't they have a rhyme?"

Tom chuckled again, "yes I thought everybody knew it" and without stopping launched into verse.

"One for sorrow,
two for joy,
three for a girl,
four for a boy,
five for silver,
six for gold,
seven for a secret never to be told."

"What's the secret?" Charlotte asked, almost before Will had had time to finish. Will thought about this before replying.

"As far as I know no one knows," he started slowly. "As far as I know no one's ever seen seven magpies together before. Mind you." Will changed his tone, he spoke slow and deliberately so as to invoke a sense of the dramatic. "Legend has it that whatever the secret is you don't want to find out. It's not good. You don't ever want to see seven magpies together," he stopped abruptly. Several seconds later he asked. "Why do you want to know?"

"No reason," It was a child's response and both her father and Will understood if translated meant – "I don't want to tell you."

Will didn't push further and the three of them continued talking, mainly about the weather. Hearing the chatter Charlotte's mother joined them and for nearly forty minutes talk and laughter were exchanged over the fence. Even Charlotte partook in the laughter and her parents shared a feeling of warmth, they hadn't heard their daughter laugh for days.

Over the following weekend the magpie disappeared and Charlotte began to wonder if she had simply been silly in her fear of the bird. It was after all just a bird. Even the grey cloud hanging over Aldbury appeared to thin a little though never leaving entirely. Even so, every villager felt their spirit lifted. On Sunday, Tom whilst having his brandy and cigar in the garden after his usual cheery greeting opened out to Charlotte for the first time about life in the village. His stories made her laugh. There was once the big house he couldn't possibly tell her about he teased, "oh the things that went on there," he chuckled. He went on to detail the old traditions that still survived in the village today, the May Fair, a tug of war over the village pond and an annual beer barrel race between the two pubs. Their chat lasted for only as long as Tom had brandy in his glass, so around half an hour but in that short time Charlotte thought she'd discovered more about the village than her father had with hours spent studying local books.

On Tuesday, the magpie was back and the cloud had thickened, if anything it appeared blacker and even more menacing than before. Charlotte had almost forgotten about the magpie and it was something of a shock when after getting out of bed she casually looked out of her window and saw it sitting in the ornamental cherry. It was in exactly the same place as before and sat motionless staring at her through the window. That morning too, two more cats disappeared and all the dogs in the village were strangely silent. Some, to their owner's surprise even refused to go for a walk.

The magpie sat there for three consecutive days staring at or rather through the long sash window at her. It never moved except at dusk when it flew off in the direction of the wooded scarp, the ash-ridge. Charlotte never saw it arrive, it just seemed to appear each morning out of thin air. On the fourth morning that all changed. Charlotte rose and put on her dressing gown, a ritual she performed every morning. Automatically, she then looked out of the long sash window to see if the magpie was there, which she knew it would be. That morning though as soon as her face appeared at the window the magpie launched itself into the air and after two or three thrusts of its wings left them spread wide diving directly at the long sash window. Just as she feared the magpie was going to smash through the window it pulled up as though wanting to land on the sill for which it was far too large. As though realising this, with impressive agility the bird flew almost vertical before levelling out and returning to its perch on the cherry blossom. Before Charlotte had time to catch her breath the magpie launched itself again. The manoeuvre was repeated again and again until Charlotte's screams brought her parents running into her bedroom. Flying through the door they found her lying face down on the floor with her hands over the back of her head as though protecting herself from attack.

"Que se passe t'il, que se passe t'il?" cried her mother arriving first.

Her father arriving seconds later asked virtually the same question in English, "what's the matter, what's the matter?"

"The magpie, the magpie," Charlotte gestured towards the window, "it's trying to attack me." Her parents looked out of the window.

"What magpie?" They asked, speaking in unison.

"There is no magpie," added her father. Charlotte got to her knees and nervously peered out at the ornamental cherry, the magpie was nowhere to be seen.

A few minutes later Charlotte was recovering in the kitchen sipping a large bowl of hot chocolate. Her parents were still trying to make sense of it all. Charlotte not wishing to worry them explained she must have been dreaming. Her parents, knowing their daughter, knew there was something more, much more but pretended to accept her explanation blaming her hormones, after all she would soon be a teenager. All three kept their true thoughts to themselves. Her father remembered his daughter's strange questions about magpies to Will. He was searching for a connection. Charlotte and her mother were both thinking the same thing. What Charlotte had described was exactly the image they had seen hanging in the Valiant Trooper painted by the previous tenant. Her mother wondered if the room was haunted whilst Charlotte now realised that what the previous tenant had painted, as she had always suspected, hadn't been a work driven by his imagination. The episode confirmed to her he had painted exactly what he had seen. This was the case with all of his paintings, of that Charlotte was now sure. What then had a robin been doing on the sill at night and long enough for the artist to paint it?

The rest of that day Charlotte sat in the lounge reading and, wishing they had a telly. She craved for simple distraction, a distraction that didn't require her to think. A television would have been perfect. With a book you needed to use your imagination and her imagination kept taking her to places she didn't want to be right now. She could have gone around Caroline's but she felt her parents needed her more than she needed them. Her parents, worried about her, had decided not to do their market. Charlotte wished they would have gone, as their obvious concern made her feel guilty. Attending the market, like a television for her would have been a good distraction for them.

Although she didn't dare look, Charlotte had a strong feeling the magpie had gone, that it was no longer sitting in the tree. To be sure she didn't go up to her bedroom until several hours after nightfall. Her mother had still to hang curtains in her room and without them Charlotte knew she wouldn't be able to resist looking out. It was strange how the mind encouraged temptation even when it wasn't wanted. The magpie was never there after dark and only then would she feel safe. The word safe implied she may be in some sort of danger, a rather extreme thought but that was exactly how she felt. When eventually she did go up rather than try and sleep she continued to read in bed. Sleep she knew wouldn't come easy that night and she had no desire to try, at least not yet. The book she was reading, Mystery Schooner by Terence

Roberts was engrossing and she only had three chapters to go, with a little effort she'd finish it before midnight. Despite her resolve it was only ten minutes before Charlotte's eyes closed and the book slowly slid to the floor landing with a dull thump. Giving in to her body's needs, she fell into a deep repairing sleep. Her mother recognised the thud and went up to her daughter's room. As quietly as she could, she carefully closed the book marking the open page with an old leather bookmark. After kissing her daughter gently on the head she softly closed the door to join Charlotte's father in the lounge. They were out of logs and with no fire, staying in the lounge held no attraction for either of them. Within minutes of their daughter falling asleep they had climbed the stairs and they too were soon asleep, comfy on their mattress of clothes.

Charlotte wasn't sure what had woken her. She suddenly found herself awake, not simply awake but wide awake. She had no idea what time it was and to her annoyance found her clock had stopped. From her bed she looked across to the window. Playing in the glass there appeared to be a faint glow. She couldn't explain why but she felt it not to be a natural light, it definitely wasn't a light generated by electricity. It appeared to be moving and with a life of its own. Surprisingly, she felt quite unafraid. Climbing out of bed she put on her dressing gown and stepped in front of the long sash window. The light she saw looking more closely appeared to be coming from the pagoda. It didn't appear to be threatening, indeed quite the opposite and she felt strangely as though it were calling her. After what had happened earlier she should have felt very uneasy by its presence but for some reason she felt calm. Not only calm, but incredibly relaxed. She should have felt petrified at the slightest idea of venturing out into the dark but the light had some sort of hold on her and kept calling softly. Not physically but by reaching into her mind and by the same method it was also reassuring her. Almost in slow motion Charlotte slipped her feet into her slippers and stealthily opened her bedroom door. She waited nervously for a squeak, and almost collapsed with relief when none came. The stairs were more difficult, many of the boards were loose and creaked at the slightest pressure. Charlotte however was still a child and if you can remember back to your childhood, we were all experts on where to tread on the stairs without making a noise, an essential skill for a successful night's raid on the fridge. Charlotte was no different, even so with every step she worried about waking her parents. With the utmost care she lifted the latch on the stable door and pushed both halves open, wincing as the door protested at being woken at such an hour. For several seconds she remained frozen waiting to see if her parents door sounded. Nothing, there came not a sound and neither did their door move, it remained closed. Slowly and still feeling strangely at ease Charlotte walked up the garden path towards the pagoda where the soft and gently hovering light beckoned. The night air carried cries from the wood, nocturnal creatures going about their business. Charlotte if she noticed paid them no attention, the light was quite hypnotic, nothing else mattered. On entering the pagoda she found the light to be a small sphere and to be hovering high in one corner. A gentle mist almost like the last trails of steam seconds after a kettle has boiled swirled In a whisper like fashion around it. The mist would almost disappear and then return never quite revealing its true source. The effect was mesmerising and Charlotte felt a strong urge to reach out and touch the light. Inch by inch, centimetre by centimetre she raised her arm and as she did so the light brightened before disappearing completely and the strange mist with it. For a split second she thought she saw the robin sitting on her outstretched hand and the next moment it had disappeared too. It happened so quickly she couldn't be sure if it was ever there. She was trying to come to terms with what she had just witnessed when there came a rustling from above. She looked up startled. On the roof of the pagoda, on all fours staring down at her was a squirrel, it's magnificent bushy tail stretched skywards for balance. It made no sound and for a few seconds it crouched motionless, silently staring at her. Seconds later, without warning it was gone, scurrying across a shed roof and after from tree to tree into the orchard heading for the wooded scarp.

"A robin, a magpie and now a squirrel," Charlotte whispered to herself, remembering what she knew of the last tenants paintings. "I wonder if he ever really did paint a squirrel, I wonder what's next." She no longer felt afraid but a strong determination to find out.

Chapter Eight

A World Rarely Seen

There came a gentle tap on the door.

"Charlotte, Charlotte" Charlotte recognised the voice as her mother's.

Opening her eyes she looked at her clock. It read just after nine. She was normally awake and up by seven. Why did she feel so tired? Slowly the events of the night came back to her. They felt so real but at the same she knew they must have been a dream, a realistic one maybe but all the same, just a dream. It was all too bizarre. Charlotte looked at her clock once more, it was fine. In her dream she remembered quite clearly that her clock had stopped, that confirmed it, it must have been a dream.

What's the time mum?" There was a pause whilst her mother looked at her watch.

"Just after nine," her door opened and her mother popped her head round. "Are you ok?" she asked with a smile that failed to hide her concern.

"I'm fine mum, just overslept."

"Breakfast then? I'll make you a hot chocolate."

"With milk." Her father always made it with water and it was disgusting.

"Of course," retorted her mother, as if she'd make it with anything else. Feeling rather insulted she closed the bedroom door. Charlotte listened to her mother descending the creaky staircase and when she heard her step off the last stair and into the kitchen she got out of bed.

Avoiding looking out of the window she skipped her dressing gown, preferring to get straight into her clothes. After brushing her hair she felt she was ready. In slow steady steps she drew in front of the long sash window. All this time she kept her head bowed staring at her feet. With a deep breath she slowly lifted her head at every moment telling herself not to be silly. With her head level she slowly opened her eyes. Stop being silly she continued to tell herself. The sky was a menacing grey of course and the garden appeared sad as though it were troubled. Her eyes narrowed as she forced herself to focus on the cherry blossom, to both her surprise and relief there was nothing there. Nothing, there was no magpie staring back at her. She blinked and looked again, no it definitely wasn't there, it had gone. For the umpteenth time she told herself she was just being stupid, it was just a bird. She knew magpies were attracted by shiny objects, perhaps it had been attracted to something in her room. Then she remembered the painting by the last tenant. Coincidence she tried to convince herself, failing dismally to do so. There was movement in the garden and she saw it was the robin hopping along the fence towards the house.

"Hello robin," she felt like waving to her little friend but refrained from doing so, that would just be too silly. She was just about ready to go downstairs and had her hand on the door latch when her eye caught the picture of the white stag. There was something different about it. She let go of the latch and moved over to the picture. Studying the image closely everything looked the same except it wasn't, what was it that was different. What was it that was bugging her? Then she realised what it was, it was such a huge change that she had missed the obvious. The stag was no longer looking towards the wall with the long sash window, facing what she knew to be east. Instead it was facing into her room, the opposite direction, it had changed to facing west. That was impossible. Charlotte closed her eyes and opened them again, quite sure she must be going mad. No, the stag was definitely facing in the opposite direction.

Had it always been like that? Once more she found herself questioning her sanity. No she was sane, she was sure, yesterday and every day before then the stag had always faced east, towards the wall with the long sash window. She looked more closely, there was something about the stag's expression too. Studying the picture, she saw what it was, the face of the animal was different, its expression had changed. The one it had now was definitely one of fear, she could even see it in the animal's eyes.

"Charlotte." It was her mother. Charlotte quickly decided she'd say nothing to her parents. She didn't know why for they had always been great listeners and had always been able to tell them anything without being judged. But on this occasion she had an underlying feeling that it wasn't the right thing to do. They'll probably spot the change without her help anyway. If they were meant to notice they would. Decision made, she descended the stairs for breakfast.

Her mother should have been at her market but worried about her daughter, she'd forced her father to do the stall on his own. Charlotte knew he'd hate that. The hot chocolate was great, the way only her mother could make it and she'd baked butter croissants as well, perfect just perfect. The smell was delicious and reminded Charlotte of their local village boulangerie before moving to England. For the first time since she'd arrived here she felt homesick, you could never experience the same smell in England or anywhere else in the world for that matter. The aroma radiating from a French boulangerie was unique to France. Just as the smell from a fish and chip shop was unique to the U.K.

The rest of the day was spent cleaning the cottage and preparing a meal for her father. This included baking a cake which, shamefully, wasn't intact by the time he came home. It just wasn't meant to be. For the meal they bought everything from the village shop. Ashtynn as usual gave them a cheery welcome and told them they were virtually, "villagers" now, after which the conversation typically turned to the weather.

"It's making everybody grumpy," Ashtynn complained. "Sometimes people are real rude to me. Oh but never you two," she smiled sweetly.

Charlotte's father returned around seven in the evening declaring it had been another gloriously sunny day. Not in Aldbury, they both told him. Together they ate their meal at the table in the kitchen before retiring to the lounge to enjoy the log fire. Her father after drinking too much red wine and having lots of fresh air almost immediately fell asleep, his head on her mother's shoulder who didn't seem to mind. She enjoyed the peace. Charlotte's thoughts turned to the night ahead. She didn't know why but she was feeling a little afraid. The dream from last night still seemed so real and the stag changing direction along with the change in its expression she still couldn't find an explanation for. Put together she was feeling more than a little unnerved. She simply couldn't pretend any longer. Since arriving in Aldbury nothing had been entirely normal. Facts had to be faced, something very strange was happening and not for the first time she felt that somehow she was part of it, or at least was being drawn into it. Things were happening around her that were testing her mind. Almost on a daily basis she found herself questioning, could she be dreaming, was she going insane or was she actually experiencing some of the bizarre phenomena. Charlotte looked across at her parents. Her mother had fallen asleep too. How nice it must be to be an adult, not to have to worry about anything.

Careful not to wake her parents Charlotte took herself up to bed. She half expected to find the stag in the picture facing the wall with the long sash window, just as before. To her disappointment or perhaps relief, she wasn't sure which, it wasn't. The stag was facing inwards towards the bedroom wall, the wall that divided her room from her parents. She knew deep down the stag wouldn't have changed back but then it shouldn't have changed in the first place. She had no idea why but she no longer fought against the unusual, the unexplained, instead she was readily accepting it. The impossible to explain had become the new normality. Aldbury wasn't like the rest of the country, the natural laws that governed life here were somehow different. What did concern her, perhaps more than anything was the expression in the stag's eyes. They still held their expression of fear, worse still a dread that affected her too. Charlotte hadn't an explanation for any of it, none of it made sense. All that she did know was that she was being drawn into whatever it was that was happening in Aldbury and somehow the stag or white hart was a significant part of the puzzle. Sighing, she undressed and climbed into bed. Laying on her back she automatically pulled Gromit under her arm. Instinctively she checked her clock. The second hand moved with short steady flicks round the dial, it was working. The time read ten fifteen. Pulling Gromit closer she lay staring at the ceiling. Within minutes her eyes closed and she was asleep.

Charlotte woke with a start. She had heard something tapping, something loud enough to wake her. Opening her eyes she found she was still lying as she had when she'd fallen asleep, on her back, looking up at the ceiling. She turned her head to look at her clock. The second hand wasn't moving. The clock read midnight. There came another tap followed by several more. It was coming from the window. She looked over. There was the robin, her robin and with its beak it was tapping on the window. On seeing her move it flew off. Instantly Charlotte recalled what Will had told her about a robin. A robin tapping on the window was a warning that death was on the way. She shivered but there wasn't time to contemplate further for illuminating the lower pane of the window was the unmistakable light from the night before. With an urgency she couldn't explain she got dressed, slipped her slippers on and slowly whilst treading very carefully made her way down the stairs to the kitchen. With a deep breath she lifted the latch as quietly as she was able and stepped outside closing both halves of the stable door behind her. There was the light, hypnotic as ever hovering in the same corner of the pagoda. Slowly Charlotte made her way up the garden path, why didn't she feel afraid, she should feel afraid. On reaching the pagoda Charlotte experienced the same urge from the night before, she desperately wanted to reach out and touch the sphere. Remembering what had happened last time she tried to resist, she didn't want the light to disappear but the temptation proved to be too strong and before she knew it her arm was reaching high, her fingers craving for contact. Just as she thought she might be able to scoop the luminous sphere into her hand it disappeared, vanished and the light with it. In its place, just visible in the dark that was blinding after the light sat a squirrel, almost certainly the same squirrel that she'd seen the night before. This time it made no attempt to flee, it simply remained sitting peering down through the naked twists of vine. Charlotte had the uncomfortable feeling that the animal was studying her, silently sounding her out. Without warning it scurried down a post, across the slabbed floor of the pagoda to the garden path almost running over her slippered feet as it did so. It moved so quickly that Charlotte didn't have time to feel startled. With her eyes fighting the gloom, she watched as the squirrel far from running in fear proceeded to scurry up and down the garden path almost reaching her feet before turning and running back. This it did several times, before Charlotte realised the animal, or at least she felt the squirrel was trying to encourage her to follow it. Trying not to feel stupid for surely this time she must dreaming Charlotte started down the garden path after the little creature.

The squirrel in response took off, scurrying ahead constantly pausing to look back, checking to see if she was following. By its manner Charlotte thought it appeared to be both nervous and in a hurry. From the pagoda it led her along the brick path, around the end terrace house and out onto the street. From there it darted left and right but always following the road to quickly reach the village green. Charlotte half expected a car to pass or someone to see their passage from a window and ask her what the hell she was doing but no one did. All of Aldbury it seemed were sleeping that night. From the green the squirrel bore left, past the village shop to follow the road towards Tring. Increasing in pace, it suddenly flew across the road disappearing under the lych gate and presumably up the gravel path to the church or up one of the many trees in the churchyard. It was after all a squirrel. With the animal out of sight Charlotte started to run, she had no intention of losing it. On reaching the entrance to the churchyard she hesitated. She needed to get her breath back and there was also her position to consider. Being alone the atmosphere the dark created, especially after midnight she found unnerving. She wasn't afraid to admit she felt scared. In her garden for some reason she had felt completely unafraid, it had almost felt as if something was keeping her safe but now alone in the street that feeling had deserted her. She was alone at night and just about to enter a churchyard, the realisation was unsettling to put it mildly. Gathering herself together the squirrel she saw hadn't disappeared up a tree after all but sat waiting before the dark arched wooden door to the church. Contemplating what to do next she looked around at the cool, silent stone tombstones. Tombstones never move of course but at night Charlotte thought they appeared to be even more still than they were in the day. Utter nonsense but why when daylight gave way to night did graveyards or churchyards go from having an ambience of welcoming tranquillity to one that felt threatening. They don't, she fought her mind to reason. Churchyards don't change, it's only our perception of them that does. To quote a common phrase, "it's all in the mind." She pictured her father, he loved exploring graveyards. "Imagine the history that lies beneath this earth," he would say to her. Imagine the memories stored in every graveyard. Graveyards are not something to be afraid of he had taught her, they're a celebration of people's lives, they are to be cherished, to be enjoyed. Remembering her father's words gave Charlotte the courage she needed. Her father even though he wasn't with her had managed to settle her nerves.

Concentrating once more the squirrel she saw was getting more and more impatient running back and forth up the gravel path to the church door trying to entice her to enter the churchyard. She looked up at the church itself and the church tower rising boldly towards the heavens. Her eyes were drawn to the clock, it somehow looked different. The hands were moving but not around the clock face, they were writhing, moving in a way that made them look as though they were alive. The movement made her feel a little dizzy. Attempting to understand what she was witnessing Charlotte rubbed her eyes. To her horror she saw that what should have been the solid hands of the clock had been replaced by a writhing serpent and that the serpent was being held by a hand at the centre of the clock face. Though the serpent's body was writhing both its head and tail were touching the same number. At first she thought that number was one but she was wrong. There was something else different about the clock, it had not twelve numerals but thirteen and both ends of the serpent's body, its head and tail were landed on XIII, thirteen. If at all possible it was thirteen o'clock.

Out of the corner of her eye she saw that the squirrel was becoming frantic at her hesitation. Wondering for the umpteenth time whether this was reality or just a dream she took a deep breath and started to walk determinedly up the gravel path to the church door. The squirrel continued to run back and forth just a few feet before her. She was almost within touching distance of the church door when the squirrel appeared to leap into the path itself, there's no better way to describe it, the squirrel simply vanished into the path. Charlotte stopped for a moment, wondering again if what she had just seen was reality or a trick of her mind. She took a step forward peering at the ground to see if there was some sort of hole a rabbit hole perhaps, anything that the squirrel may have dived down. All she could see was a stone slab, nothing else, certainly no hole. She took one more step forward onto the slab itself and help! The ground started to swallow her up, her body helpless started descending into the earth. There was no friction, no pain, she just slowly felt herself being pulled underground, bizarrely it was almost a pleasant feeling. Her eyes screamed silently as they came level with the ground and then blackness. She was still breathing, she could hear herself breathing the sound of each breath being magnified in the all-enveloping blackness. It didn't feel as though anything forcibly had held of her but try as she might she found she was unable to move. After what felt like an eternity that was in reality probably only a few seconds she felt herself rising. Again the force was very gentle, even so there was no way she could fight it. Whatever it was had complete control over her. Seconds more and her eyes were at ground level, gazing across the turf of the churchyard, the grass already sodden with early morning dew. Seconds more and Charlotte found herself standing once more on the stone slab just a few feet from the church door. There was no sign of the squirrel. Almost in a trance she slowly made her way back to their cottage. Aldbury looked the same, the village shop, the pond but at the same time everything felt different. The silence for one, yes it was the early hours and the village was asleep but there wasn't a sound, nothing at all, the silence was all enveloping, suffocating. As she walked Charlotte had the feeling that what she was passing through was a photograph, a three dimensional image, nothing felt real. It was something of a relief when she arrived in front of their cottage, her parents van was outside and beside it Tom's old Renault Four. She touched her parents van, reassured by the cold feel of the metal. Several chocolate wrappers were scattered on the passenger's seat evidence that it had been her father who had driven the van last.

Feeling much better Charlotte followed the brick path around the end of terrace cottage to the stable door. Smiling through a deep sense of relief she went to enter only to discover the door wouldn't budge. She pushed hard but the door simply wouldn't move, not even a fraction, it may as well be part of the wall. She took a step back trying to work out what was wrong. This was definitely her cottage, her back door, why wouldn't it open. She wondered about trying to wake her parents, but how was she to explain what she was doing outside their house in the early hours of the morning. They'd never believe the truth and she couldn't think of an alternative excuse, especially not one that would sound remotely credible. She looked up to the heavens seeking divine guidance. The cloud that was so menacing during the day appeared to be circling above her, more and more she felt as though she'd been led into a trap. As she was trying to work out what to do Charlotte saw a movement close to her feet. Glancing down, she saw it was the squirrel and as earlier she recognised the signs that it again wanted her to follow. Unlike earlier, she felt a little uneasy at doing so a second time. She wasn't sure what was happening to her, what the squirrel had led her into and was beginning to feel more than a little vulnerable. However with little other option she felt she had nothing to lose. Thus although apprehensive she found herself once more putting her faith in God's creature, a squirrel, yes a squirrel, she must be mad, maybe stupid too. Maybe, but she was ready for wherever fate took her and for whatever fate had in store.

Like some sort of re-enactment the squirrel, just as before, led her up the road, past the village shop and up the gravel path to the church door. Just as before nobody in Aldbury stirred. And just as it had done before the squirrel appeared to disappear underground, vanish into nothing or rather the path. Meekly Charlotte stepped forward onto the stone slab and immediately felt herself being pulled under, swallowed by blackness. This time she knew, whatever it was that was happening to her it wasn't death, she had survived whatever it was before and felt strangely confident she would do so again. Seconds later she felt herself being gently pushed to the surface and a few seconds more she was standing in the churchyard of St John the Baptist.

The tactile breath of a chilled breeze playing with her face brought Charlotte to her senses. She instinctively looked up at the clock on the church tower. There was no serpent, no hand and only twelve Roman numeral figures circling the clock face. The time on the clock read seven minutes past midnight. How was that possible? The clock must have stopped. In something of a trance Charlotte made her way slowly down the church path. No longer did she feel afraid, indeed the silent tombstones felt rather like old friends, one and all providing an inconspicuous welcome. A welcome to where though? This time Aldbury felt like Aldbury, that at least was reassuring. Looking about her Charlotte could see no sign of the squirrel and after waiting a minute or so in case it returned she gave up and started to retrace her steps through the village to their cottage. Nothing had changed physically but somehow it felt she was no longer walking through an image, everything felt as well as looked real. What she was experiencing now was a living breathing village. It hadn't before, she couldn't put it into words, she just felt as though in the last hour she had experienced two different Aldbury's. Saying hello to an old friend, she tapped her parent's van as she passed. After a slight hesitation during which she said a silent prayer Charlotte tried the stable door. Either her prayer had been answered or no prayer had been needed for the door opened without a struggle. Exhausted Charlotte climbed the stairs to her room, never had she been so pleased to see Gromit. The stag she noticed hadn't changed again, it was still facing the wall and her clock now working read seven minutes past midnight, just as the clock on the church tower. What had just happened, what had happened to time, there was no way she'd only been gone seven minutes, what did it all mean? They were mind bending questions and at that moment Charlotte found herself too tired to care. As her head touched the pillow she fell into a deep, a very deep sleep.

The next morning Charlotte woke to the sound of her parents busying themselves downstairs in the kitchen. She looked at her clock.

Seven thirty, she hadn't overslept. She looked across to the picture of the white stag, it was still facing towards the wall, west and still looking terrified. Sitting Gromit upright she got out of bed and walked deliberately to the window. She looked out almost not caring what she would see. The dark cloud above Aldbury was as menacing as ever, the garden in the gloom depressing but on the plus side there was still no magpie, just the sleeping cherry blossom. True to form the robin came tripping down the fence. With a flutter it was in the air and flying towards the cottage and seconds landed deftly on the sill before her. With its head cocked to one side it looked into the room and directly at Charlotte. Charlotte in return found herself smiling and instinctively gave a little wave. The robin chirped loudly and took off flying back to the fence. Next she saw Will arrive next door. He was starting early. Dressed in his usual garb in his right hand he carried a pair of shears. On seeing the robin he stopped and Charlotte could see he was taking time to talk to the little bird, shears resting on his right shoulder. Charlotte tried to lip read, to try and understand what he was saying but it was impossible. Will with a slow swagger then made towards the back of the garden where Charlotte assumed he was going to prune the small collection of fruit trees that grew there. Her eyes followed the robin as it hopped and skipped after him.

"Charlotte," her mother shouted up the stairs. "Breakfast's ready." The smells wafting into her room told her that there was competition between her parents that morning. Her mother's freshly baked croissants versus her father's, full English breakfast. She would have both she decided instantly, she was starving.

Her parents delighted in seeing their daughter wolfing down two breakfasts.

"Well you seem better" declared her mother beaming.

"I feel it," Charlotte replied, her mouth full and for some reason she did, in spite of the rigours of the night. Or had it all been a dream.

It was a question she hadn't stopped asking herself. "Why aren't you at the market?" Charlotte realised suddenly that it was Friday, market day in Tring.

"Didn't fancy it today" it was her father who replied. "And the weather forecast is rubbish. Wind and rain, there won't be anybody there. It'll just be a lot of effort for nothing." Charlotte could tell that this wasn't the whole truth, they were at home she knew in part because they were worried about her. The rubbish weather forecast had probably been a relief to them both, it had provided a convenient excuse.

"What have you got planned today?" It was her mother asking the question. Charlotte thought for a moment an expression of deep concentration spread across her face. It was an expression both her parents loved, their daughter always thought carefully before answering a question and her thought process was always a physically visible one. She was rarely flippant with an answer.

"I think I'll visit the church this morning," her reply surprised both her parents. Charlotte saw the looks on their faces and quickly added, "and go and see Caroline this afternoon." The latter she knew was an answer expected of an eleven year old girl. It worked, her parents visibly relaxed.

"I'll come with you if you like, to the church, not Caroline's" her father joked. Charlotte had wanted to go alone but couldn't refuse her father. Her parents would immediately become suspicious if she did.

It was just after ten when the two of them left for the church. The cloud overhead was almost black, that morning and Aldbury as a consequence even more depressing than usual. Charlotte couldn't help feeling a little anxious as they walked up the gravel path to the church door. The events of the night before remained clear in her mind. She kept telling herself it had all been a dream but still couldn't help half expecting to see the squirrel come scurrying up the path.

"Are you alright?" her father sensed the tension in his daughter. Charlotte desperately wanted to tell him everything that had happened that night or what she thought had happened during the night. But all the time there was something stopping her, a voice deep inside that kept warning her not to. Stranger still she felt it important that she listened, that she trusted the voice, even over her father.

The church had that unique atmosphere that only churches have. The air cool and motionless carrying and expanding the slightest of sounds with a clarity that cut through the air as would a shard of glass. Her father picked up a small guide book, paying by dropping some coins into a small wooden collection box. The sound as they landed reaching every nook and cranny. They moved slowly, her father studying every word in the book, closely inspecting each feature the guide referred to. Charlotte followed with forced patience. She wanted to examine the spot outside. The place where in her dream, if it had been a dream of course, the place she had been sucked underground. After what seemed an age they left via the heavy porch door. The light outside despite being distinctly gloomy was still bright enough to hurt after the soft luminosity inside the church and they both blinked as their sight struggled to adapt. Before Charlotte had time to examine the ground closely her father touched her arm and gestured.

"Come on let's have a look around the churchyard."

Obediently she followed him. As her father passed between the tombstones trying to read many of the epitaphs Charlotte spent her time taking in the churchyard as a whole. It was obvious the churchyard was lovingly cared for but discreetly so, always allowing nature to have the final say. Passing around the back of the church brought the two of them level with the pitted field. The field they'd passed through on their first exploration of the village. The light mist that had hung over the field on that day had become steadily thicker and looking at it now appeared almost impenetrable. As they both tried to peer in they could hear children's voices playing wolf in its depths. Although the children sounded close their presence could only be identified by little more than moving shadows, mere ghosts of their physical being.

Both were relieved, though neither would admit it, to leave the mist behind and return to the church entrance. Charlotte and her father had felt uncomfortable in its presence but neither said anything to the other. Standing in front of the church porch Charlotte discreetly examined the ground beneath them. In the place where she was pretty sure she'd been sucked underground lay a large stone slab, just as she remembered it. As far as she could see there was no inscription, it was just an ordinary looking slab. Studying the stone more closely it looked as if at one time it may have acted as a base for something.

"What are you looking at?" her father asked, interrupting her concentration. She obviously hadn't been discreet enough. As she searched for a convincing answer, footsteps, bold and forceful sounded crunching on the gravel path. Striding briskly up the path came judging by his attire the vicar. He was a stout man, with flame red hair and a beard that not one bird but several could nest in. His manner was both confident and full of purpose and Charlotte's first impression was of a Celtic warrior minus his sword. As soon as he smiled her impression collapsed, she had never seen one so broad. So bright was the vicar's smile it almost extinguished the foreboding sky. The vicar, so you know, was much loved in the village and in return he loved the village back.

"Morning French Charlotte" the vicar boomed with a voice that complemented his appearance perfectly. "What have you found there that's so interesting?"

How on earth did the vicar know who she was and how did he know her name? Those questions however would have to wait for now. Right this minute she needed to find an answer and quickly. Thinking on her feet Charlotte replied and her reply, she thought was genius.

"I was just seeing if there was an inscription." The vicar drew close, shaking her father's hand as he did so.

"Let me see. It's always a pleasure to find a young one interested in something we have here at the church." He bent over and after only a second's glance answered, "oh no you won't find anything on there."

"Why not?"

"That's not a grave," replied the vicar. "That used to be a base for a sundial."

"What happened to the sundial?" Charlotte's father asked the obvious question.

"Some basta," he started and on remembering Charlotte's presence corrected himself, hoping his slip hadn't been noticed. "Someone stole it back in the eighties. God knows where it is now." Her father made a disapproving sound with his tongue.

"People will steal anything these days," he commented with genuine sadness.

"They knew what they were doing," continued the vicar waving to a passer-by. "The sundial was almost as old as the church, one of the oldest in the country. In fact it was even featured on television once, probably the reason it was stolen." He gave a loud sigh. "Anyway, I must get on. Good to meet you French Charlotte," he said, patting her head. "He shook her father's hand again. From their manner it was obvious they'd met before, it was strange her father had never said. "I wish this bloody weather would change, people are beginning to blame me." And with that the vicar pulled open the door and disappeared inside his church.

Before returning to the cottage they stopped at the village shop. Charlotte's mother wanted some rice, she was preparing butter chicken for lunch, a rare venture into Indian cuisine. The bell as was its function announced their arrival.

"Morning French Charlotte," came the greeting from Ashtynn. "Back to school next week then." Charlotte groaned loudly at the thought then went in search of the rice whilst her father remained chatting at the counter.

"More cats have gone missing," Charlotte could hear Ashtynn telling her father. "And the police are worse than useless," was Ashtynn's considered opinion. The conversation then turned predictably to the weather. "It's just not natural, "Ashtynn kept repeating. Charlotte couldn't find any rice. "Oh I'm sorry we're out," Ashtyn apologised. "There'll be a delivery tomorrow."

After buying some sherbet dips they made their way back to the cottage, the bell sounding loudly after them. On arrival they were immediately sent on their way again this time to the supermarket, they were sure to have rice.

"You can't have butter chicken with French fries," Charlotte's mother told them, Charlotte couldn't see why not in fact she really liked the idea. In addition to rice her mother had provided them with a list for other, "essential" household items. Her father groaned when he read it and boldly wrote red wine at the bottom. As they drove, climbing slowly out of the village drops of rain started to fall on the windscreen and before they'd passed the railway station it was tipping down. The rain hadn't stopped when they left the supermarket and it was a desperate dash to the van to avoid getting soaked. As they approached Aldbury the rain petered out and by the time they'd passed Church Farm it had stopped completely. The cloud overhead in contrast was darker and more threatening than those unleashing the rain surrounding the village. Yet the village remained bone dry, not a drop of rain fell on the dusty and very thirsty soil that was a feature of Aldbury that year. Not long after passing Church farm Charlotte's father brought the van to a halt. He got out stepping into the road, gesturing for Charlotte to do the same. He took her hand and stood gazing across the fields towards the hilltop village of Wigginton. In the near distance and over the hills the rain was clearly falling, you could even smell it from where they were standing and yet from their vantage point they were in the dry. Her father looked up at the cloud, his look was one of puzzlement.

"It should be raining here too" he said simply, holding out his upward palms. "It's just not natural" he added, confirming Ashtynn's view and that of many villagers. It was the first time Charlotte had heard her father accept that what Aldbury was experiencing was not of the natural world. She'd always respected her father's view and this, his first verbal acceptance of the inexplicable frightened her more than anything that had passed before.

After what turned out to be a very good butter chicken Charlotte went in search of Caroline. She found her at home with several other girls from the village and spent an enjoyable afternoon playing games on a computer. An activity that was something of a novelty. The evening was spent in front of the fire with all three of them quietly reading. Nothing unusual happened that night. Charlotte slept soundly, there was no tapping at the window and no trip to the churchyard. The next morning the white stag was still facing west and still with fear in its eyes. The magpie didn't appear again, only her friendly robin. The weekend passed the same way and if it wasn't for the picture with the white stag Charlotte could have forgotten all about the strange events that had recently befallen her. Sunday afternoon was spent preparing for the beginning of term and that evening Charlotte was packed off to bed early in readiness for school the next day. It took a while for her to fall asleep, surprisingly she found herself quite excited at the prospect of returning to an education and as a result her head buzzed with thoughts of school.

Tap, tap, tap. Charlotte woke with a start. Tap, there it was again, tap, tap on the window, the tapping was continuous and fast. Charlotte sat up, there was the robin, tap, tap, tap, it looked desperate. There was no light this time playing in the lower panes, no light calling her from the pagoda as on the last two occasions. Charlotte felt surprisingly alert as well as focused, she didn't know why but she knew she had to act fast and question nothing. Quickly she got dressed and this time, after her last experience put on some shoes. Well-practised, she tripped silently down the stairs and out of the stable door onto the brick path where she found the robin waiting perched on a flowerpot. The squirrel to her consternation was also waiting, running in an excitable manner up and down the brick path. Charlotte after last time was still unsure whether to trust the animal. She knew it wanted her to follow it and had good reason she felt to fear where it may lead her. Completely out of character she decided to throw caution to the wind and after only a couple of seconds hesitation made to follow the rodent. The squirrel darted into the street and Charlotte this time knew exactly where it was heading. Such was its haste the squirrel almost disappeared from view and she found herself having to run simply to keep it in sight. The robin she noted stayed behind at the cottage. It was only a couple of minutes before Charlotte arrived at the church door, where as she expected the squirrel sat waiting. The animal appeared overly animated and kept glancing right as though watching for something. Charlotte looking in the same direction realised it was scanning the pitted field, the one covered by mist. The mist unlike during the day was swirling violently, angrily almost as though someone or something was stirring it. The movement like the flames of a fire she found mesmerising and if something inside, perhaps her seventh sense hadn't have warned her she could have easily spent hours and hours watching it. With some effort Charlotte tore her eyes away and remembering her last midnight visitation, fleetingly looked up at the clock on the tower. The hand held serpent writhed restlessly against the clock face, its head and tail despite its agitation remaining firmly on the figure XIII.

On seeing her approach the squirrel did its disappearing act, diving head first into the ground. Charlotte without hesitating followed, stepping boldly onto the slab. The base for a stolen sundial she now knew and immediately felt the familiar sensation of being pulled beneath the turf. Within seconds the sensation was reversed and she found herself once more standing in the churchyard, the same churchyard but just as last time, not the same. The squirrel she saw was sitting waiting for her. So to her surprise was her robin, or was it her robin, this one she thought looked a little different. She couldn't be sure. Bizarrely the robin and the squirrel appeared to be communicating with each other. As though they'd come to a decision the squirrel suddenly scurried down the only other path in the churchyard, one that led directly to the small village green and pond. Charlotte knew to follow and was just about to do so when she felt a compulsion to take another look at the mist. She glanced backwards and to her surprise found there was no mist. Instead she saw shadows. Shadows that defined the dark, shadows that were moving not swaying but moving of their own accord. They appeared to be beckoning, inviting her to join them in a dance. Charlotte liked to dance, it was fun, it would be fun to dance now. She was sorely tempted but at the back of her mind she sensed the squirrel willing her to hurry, to follow it and quickly. In her head alarm bells were also ringing, bells she knew for definite being rung by her seventh sense. She turned to follow the squirrel and to her surprise found it almost impossible to break away. The shadows were hypnotic, drawing her in willing her to dance. With an humongous effort she tore herself away, determined not to let her eyes wander in the direction of the mist again. She knew she'd come close to being under the influence of whatever it was encouraging her and that whatever it was had nothing but mal intent.

To the squirrel's obvious relief Charlotte followed it out of the churchyard to the village pond. The robin remained in the churchyard, perched on a tombstone watching them leave. From the pond the squirrel bore left running past The Greyhound pub following the road leading to Ivinghoe. All the time Aldbury felt the same as it did the last time she'd followed the squirrel. What she was walking through looked like her village but that was all, it was completely devoid of atmosphere, better put it lacked a heart, there was no soul. She was familiar with many of the people who lived in the half-timbered houses and cottages that lined the road along which she now walked though she doubted if she'd find anybody living in the true sense, behind the drawn curtains.

The squirrel continued to follow the road until it drew level with a small wood on the left separated from the road by a stone wall. Pausing, it looked back to see if Charlotte was close enough and apparently satisfied she was hopped over a low break in the wall into the wood. Charlotte followed though a little reluctantly for at night, as with a churchyard a wood takes on a completely different personality. Taking in gulps of crisp night air she stepped over the broken wall into the wood and almost immediately jumped back out onto the road. Watching her from the cover of the trees were two sets of eyes. The squirrel quick to notice ran back, trying to reassure her. The eyes followed, emerging from the moon shadows into the moonlight. Under the light of the moon the two pairs of eyes she saw belonged to two dogs and by their stature Charlotte recognised them as greyhounds. These greyhounds however were huge and curiously spotted with each wearing a gold collar that glowed platinum under the moon's silvery light. Fleetingly she remembered the pub sign back in Aldbury and her father's approval of its correct depiction of the greyhound. She wondered if there was any connection with the sign and the two hounds stood before her. Unmoving they held Charlotte's gaze and she found herself starting to fear not just for her safety but for her life. If they felt so inclined the dogs could easily tear her apart. They were strong, fearsome looking animals though their expression was in no way aggressive and by their manner if anything appeared to be offering subservience. It was only this that prevented her from turning and fleeing. As Charlotte struggled to understand the situation she found herself in she could have sworn, for a split second both the dogs bowed their heads. It had been the slightest of movement but she was sure that was what she had witnessed. It turned out there remained no further time for deliberation for the two hounds without warning turned and started to make their way through the wood with the squirrel between them, a most peculiar procession. Charlotte somehow knew they intended her to follow and meekly fell in behind. After breaking from the wood the hounds led the way uphill across open ground heading for the wooded Aldbury Nowers. Maintaining a wide flank the hounds never deviated, it was evident they knew where they were going and the only time they paused was for a second or so to sniff the air. The squirrel followed closely behind holding the centre ground and Charlotte brought up the rear all the time desperately trying to keep up. As they reached the tree line the hounds bore left keeping to the eastern slope of the hill before later turning right to follow a high bank and parallel ditch, an earthwork dug thousands of years before. It was only a matter of minutes before they left the cover of the wood once more to emerge onto the South Western slope of the hill. Before them clearly visible in the moonlight the Chiltern escarpment ran serpent like across the shires. The hounds came to a halt in front of a magnificent beech tree, it was by far the biggest tree Charlotte had ever seen. Normally the tree alone would have held her attention but hovering among the lower boughs there was a sphere of light. It was a light she recognised and it was the light that captivated her.

The light within the sphere pulsated, not a steady pulse but a pulse that matched the restless movement of the vapour. For a minute or so the sphere remained hovering above them and Charlotte couldn't help but feel she was somehow being examined. Without warning the sphere began to move, hovering it took a path leading back into the wood covered Nowers. The hounds followed and with them the squirrel, Charlotte meekly took up the rear. Where they were going she had no idea and it would be pointless asking, she had no other choice but to follow. Not long into the wood they passed between two large mounds, tombs of people who had lived and died on the hill during the Bronze Age. Here the sphere stopped and remained hovering only a metre or so above the ground whilst the hounds took up a position on the crown of each mound. They remained like this for several minutes though to Charlotte it felt like an age. Whilst struggling to keep up she hadn't had time to feel frightened but standing motionless in the dark surrounded by trees that threw witch finger moon shadows across an already darkened floor. Shadows that in her mind moved menacingly in a restless breeze, creating fear in a head already influenced by an imagination that delighted in scaring the soul. Just as Charlotte was beginning to sense she might not be able to suppress a scream, to her relief the luminous sphere started to move once more and the hounds again started following. The squirrel was next and Charlotte took up the rear, grateful to be moving and grateful that her mind could concentrate on something else other than running from shadows.

After leaving the wooded Nowers the sphere always hovering about a metre above ground led the four of them along the eastern slope of Pitstone Hill keeping just below the ridge. Their way was now open to the sky and bathed in the silvery light of the moon. The moonlit panorama was pure theatre but nobody noticed, all eyes were focused on the sphere of light leading them, a light at least to Charlotte that appeared to be getting fainter by the minute. After what felt like forever Charlotte recognised the approach to Ivinghoe Beacon. The sphere of now definitely weakening light slowed as they drew closer to the summit, keeping to the western slope and always just below the ridge. It no longer hovered a metre above ground, instead the sphere had dropped until it was almost touching. It wasn't hard to work out that they were deliberately keeping out of view, from what, Charlotte had no idea and didn't particularly care to find out.

The sphere slowed until it came to a halt around fifty metres from the summit of the Beacon, though from where they were the summit wasn't in site. On stopping the vapour that had up until now circled the light started to spread. The two hounds settled lying flat in the grass and for the first time since she'd been introduced the squirrel too sat motionless. For several minutes, agonising minutes as far as Charlotte was concerned they waited, no one moving. Reduced to a glimmer the sphere after what seemed an eternity, once again started to move edging excruciatingly slowly up the chalk grass slope. It came to a halt at the very moment the summit of Ivinghoe Beacon came into view. Charlotte drew a deep breath for there before her standing on the summit stood a white stag , without doubt the same white stag in the picture hanging in her bedroom. For the first time she realised the ground in the picture on which the stag was standing was Ivinghoe Beacon. Only now did she fully appreciate the animal's greatness. The stag's shimmering white physique reflected proud under the light of the moon, highlighting every tensed muscle. It's antlers stretching skyward were as magnificent as anything Charlotte had ever seen. Not present in the picture on the wall in her bedroom were several circles of spinning white light orbiting the stag, similar to the rings around Saturn. The animal stood rigid, facing towards distant Mentmore and Charlotte felt a tear roll down her cheek as she saw the animal's face. Just as with the image in her bedroom the stag's face held an expression of fear. A dread beyond all reasonable comprehension.

Charlotte felt the urge to run and hug the animal, a child's natural instinct to want to make things better, to offer comfort. As if sensing this the sphere began to move back down the slope. The hounds followed and after a short pause the squirrel too with Charlotte following reluctantly behind. The sphere came to a rest in something of a basin almost entirely covered by scrub. Charlotte realised unless someone was searching they were completely hidden from view. A whisper, soft and distinctly feminine made Charlotte jump. It was the first time she'd heard a human like voice in this strange world. The whisper though wasn't a whisper as we know it for it was silent. Anyone standing close by would not have heard it for it was a whisper that searched not for an ear but for a mind sensitive enough to receive it. The sphere appeared to glow a little brighter, flickering as though added strength came only with increased effort. The whispering continued and Charlotte looking up recognised the source to be the sphere itself.

"You must listen carefully child." The tone was gentle, soft as silk as perfect as one could ever hope to hear. Rather like French, her native language the words even though whispered were sung not spoken. "I am growing very weak and only have a moment in time to communicate with you." Listening Charlotte felt as though every nerve in her body was focused on receiving and understanding what the voice was telling her. At that moment nothing else mattered.

"I do not expect you to understand what is happening to you or what you have just seen little girl. All I can tell you for now is that our magnificent hart is facing west, the direction of the setting sun, the end of a cycle and thus the end of life. The extinguishing of light before the rise of dark forces. Our magnificent hart must face east as was always intended. To welcome light over darkness, a new birth from the destruction of chaos. This is not of its doing and the consequences if not reversed are….." The voice tailed off as if on reflection the consequences for now anyway maybe better left unsaid. For a moment there was silence and the light dimmed to almost nothing. The two hounds stirred uneasily. Charlotte thought the light was about to go out altogether when with another flicker it grew in strength, shining once more though with a fragility that was obvious to everyone there. The whisper came again and although the words were spoken with the same silky softness this time there was a noticeable strain. "I can no longer visit you young Charlotte, I am too weak and it is too dangerous. Next time you must visit me. Our messenger, the squirrel will be your guide, follow him, he will not lead you into danger. Alasdair and Cathasach will be your guardians." By way of acknowledgement the two hounds emitted a low growl.

"They're fleet of foot, descended from the faithful guardian of Owen once a proud prince of Gaul. Like their ancestors they will defend you with their lives." Charlotte waited for the voice to tell her more but instead the air resounded only with the sound of silence. The light within the sphere started to fade and as it did so welcomed the earth. What little light remained was just enough to see the vapour flatten out before fading into the turf. For several minutes after the last glimmer had given in to the dark nobody made a sound . Charlotte had no idea if the others had heard the sphere speak, and if they had whether they had understood a single word.

The squirrel was the first to move. It shook them all from their trance and minutes later they were retracing their steps. This time the squirrel led the way with the hounds following behind. On the return leg the hounds remained close and Charlotte in turn felt much comforted by their presence. As they entered the woodland of Aldbury Nowers it began to rain. Not hard but with a gentleness that was just enough to freshen the waking flora. The rain helped to stir everything living within the wood and Charlotte found her spirit lifted as perfumes released by the rain stimulated senses that were at this hour normally asleep. At that moment she felt an affinity with her natural surroundings as never before.

From the Nowers the squirrel led them directly down the open hillside making towards the small wood where Charlotte had first met the two hounds. Alasdair and Cathasach as she now knew them. As they did so the first light of morning appeared above the tree canopy of Ashridge. Charlotte started to panic, her parents would go mad if they discovered she'd been out during the night. Especially before the first day of a new term. On reaching the break in the stone wall the two hounds stopped. The squirrel hopped over the wall into the road and Charlotte followed but the hounds remained on the wooded side of the wall. The squirrel turned back and not for the first time that night Charlotte felt that different species were somehow communicating. After a few seconds, the squirrel turned and started running down the metalled road towards Aldbury, the hounds, slight of feet also turned and sped off back into the wood. Charlotte followed the squirrel and although at times she struggled to keep it in her sights she no longer felt worried about losing it, she knew exactly where it was heading. On entering Aldbury she was relieved to find the first fingers of light hadn't yet reached the village. Everything as before was deathly still and for the first time since she'd left her bed she started to relax. Only now did she realise just how tired she was and how cold from the spring rain. At the church, she found the squirrel waiting for her. As before on seeing her approach it dived into the path and disappeared underground. Charlotte followed, stepping onto the slab and immediately experienced the almost welcome feeling of being pulled gently underground. A robin, unseen, watched them both disappear. Before Charlotte knew it she was back in the Aldbury of now, her Aldbury. She could tell because everything felt real, she could smell the dew beginning to form and there was the odd ghostly cry from an owl. Whereas on the other side, if that was the right turn of phrase there was never a sound, the village appeared to be trapped in an unholy net with an atmosphere that was, well if she was to be honest she wasn't sure quite how to describe it. There was simply no soul that she could feel, not even using her seventh sense. What she was sure of, is that the other side mattered. Not just there but here too, the world she was standing in now and it mattered a great deal.

Automatically Charlotte looked up at the church tower. The clock's solid black hands read seven minutes past midnight. How was that even possible, she'd been gone for hours. It was then that she realised that everything was still dark, there wasn't a single sign of the first fingers of daylight in the sky above Ashridge. At the same time she realised that she was bone dry, seconds before she had been soaked. The sound of a car startled her. It's lights touched the churchyard wall before turning left at the pond onto the road towards Ivinghoe. The interruption made Charlotte realise she had to move. She looked around for the squirrel but it was gone. Quickly she made her way through the village to their cottage. Perhaps for luck she touched her parents old grey postal van. At the same time she raised her eyes to their bedroom window, on the other side of which she knew they'd be asleep, asleep on their mattress made of clothes. Looking at the four panes of glass that separated them she understood at that moment just how much she loved them. Never again would she take their love for her, for granted. Moments later Charlotte was in bed, Gromit a welcome comfort and exhausted she fell into a deep sleep. Once again she failed to see the robin perched on the windowsill. The little bird waited till it was sure the little girl had fallen asleep and satisfied she had flew to its nest at the base of the pagoda. The clock beside Charlotte's bed read seven minutes passed midnight. As her eyes closed the hands began to tick, once more recording time as it passed. That night Charlotte would dream of a world rarely seen. Hidden from sight the little robin settled down for the night. Sleep for him though didn't come so easy. He was worried that such a frail, little and inexperienced child may be their only hope. It just didn't seem possible. Somebody somewhere had got things wrong, surely.

Chapter Nine

A Quest Revealed

Charlotte woke the next morning still feeling exhausted. It took a gigantic effort simply to drag herself out of bed and into her school uniform. She was dreading the day ahead of her. Trying to keep her mind focused on school she made but a momentary glance out of her bedroom window. The magpie had completely vanished. Reliable as ever though, as if her appearance at the long sash window had summoned it, the robin hopped and skipped down the garden fence. Charlotte ate her breakfast in silence, she knew she should be concentrating on school but her head remained in another world. Her parents mistook their daughter's silent concentration as focusing on school. For Charlotte this was something of a blessing as it meant they left her in peace.

There was the usual babble of voices from the children waiting beside the pond for the school bus. That morning though far from being the usual carefree excited chatter the conversations were often niggling and at times close to being aggressive. Caroline, to Charlotte's relief greeted her with her usual friendly smile and light chatter as did two other girls she'd got to know.

School started fine and many of those whom Charlotte could already loosely call friends greeted her with a poor but warm and enthusiastic rendition of the first chords of La Marseillaise. The morning passed quickly and lunch was spent catching up with what each other had been doing over the Easter break. If only they really knew Charlotte told herself quietly, if only they really knew, how would they react?

Although she managed to get through the morning fairly comfortably by the afternoon Charlotte found herself struggling. The exertions of the night before finally caught up with her and during maths she fell into a deep sleep, her head resting on the desk. The rest of the class found this hilarious and fortunately the teacher after waking her, being experienced and having a rather caring nature decided not to make an example of her. Instead at the end of the lesson he quietly took her to one side.

"I'm not too proud to know that for many, my lessons are incredibly boring," he said with self-humour, "though I can't remember having had someone fall asleep in one. Is everything ok?" He meant the question kindly. Charlotte nodded apologising, putting it down to a "bad night's sleep."

Her maths teacher seemed to accept this and after giving his pupil a reassuring pat on the head sent her onto her next lesson where she was greeted by her classmates with exaggerated sounds of snoring. The maths teacher, more concerned than he'd let on, mentioned it to the deputy head and she in turn just to check everything was ok at home put in a call to Charlotte's parents. Her parents had sounded genuinely shocked not to mention concerned on the phone and this reassured her.

"It's probably best not to let Charlotte know I've made this call," she told them. "A new school can be a terrifying experience and I don't wish to make it harder for her by her knowing I've called you."

Her parents agreed to keep the call a secret and to keep a special eye on their daughter. The deputy head replaced the receiver. She'd been in the profession long enough to recognise bad parents and to tell when parents were being loose with the truth. Charlotte's parents were good parents of that she was certain and their concern genuine, of that she was also sure. Charlotte had also made friends quickly and was already a favourite with many of her teachers. In other words their most recent student seemed to be settling in just fine. Even so something kept nagging away at the professional mind of the experienced deputy head. Something wasn't right, she just couldn't put her finger on it. It was a feeling she wasn't used to and she made a mental note to keep a discreet eye on the little French girl who everybody called French Charlotte.

That evening Charlotte's parents made no mention of the call from the deputy head. Charlotte though wasn't stupid, she could tell that something was wrong. Her parents were being over attentive, far too nice, and hardly asked a single question about her day at school. She normally enjoyed the company of her parents but that evening she was relieved to get to bed, to get away from their smothering and badly concealed concern. Pulling Gromit towards her she wondered with a little trepidation what the night might bring. Her reflective mood made her think of the stag and she instinctively got back out of bed and crossed the room to the picture. She realised now that the picture might somehow be a living image of the animal, how else could you explain its change of direction and the change in its facial expression. The exact same expression she had seen in real life. Or had last night been real life, though it felt real she was still having difficulty in accepting it. Real or not she hadn't been able to comfort the stag when they were at the Beacon, it had been her natural instinct to want to. She still held the same feelings now, if anything, looking at the picture the urge to give some sort of comfort had grown stronger since last night. Instinctively she kissed the tip of her finger and ran it over the stags terrified face. Standing on tiptoe she then gently kissed the picture, the breath from her mouth misting the glass. Charlotte hoped that her kiss would give the stag some comfort. With a deep sigh, one far too troubled for a child, Charlotte climbed back into bed. Just before she fell asleep she thought she saw the robin at her window. It's just a dream she lied to herself. Just a dream.

Far away, yet close to home for those who know the path, in another world a message was brought to a being rarely seen. The message told of

Charlotte, the human child's innocent action in kissing the picture. The being glowed brightly, the light revealing a swirling and ever moving white vapour that encircled it. In all this darkness there was perhaps light, if only a glimmer. The innocent perception of the little human girl was quite incredible. She had no idea the strength her intuitive action would bring to their Guardian the white hart. Providing him with added strength will provide them with valuable time. Perhaps, just perhaps they may be able to overcome the dark forces they were facing after all. Overturning the years of failure that had brought them to the brink, the unthinkable, the unimaginable chaos that was now so close. They must with all their might ensure no harm came to the little human girl. Thank goodness she was unaware of the burden resting on her young shoulders for if she knew, it would surely crush her. The glow strengthened turning to light, shining so brightly that anyone witnessing the transformation was in danger of being blinded by its intensity. Emerging, but not entirely from the shining stepped a female figure, clothed from head to toe in a robe of purest white. Not a bleached white but a white with depth, a living, breathing white. Her face just distinguishable behind the veil of swirling vapour smiled with all the kindness remaining in the world. She slowly held out her delicate hand lightly touching her messenger.

"Thank you" was all she said and retreated back into the swirling luminous vapour until she was visible no longer. The light dimmed and the cloud levelled out before sinking beneath the sodden turf. The squirrel bristled with pride it's little heart pumping with renewed determination. Her touch and just those two words, "thank you", meant more than all the nuts in the wood. For a moment it sat gazing to where the entity had disappeared. All that remained was a hollow yew that had stood longer than anyone could remember. With a flick of its tail the squirrel turned to start on the long and increasingly dangerous journey to Aldbury, returning to fulfil its new raison d'etre. To guide and protect the human child. The little girl who more and more creatures living in the wood spoke of as being their last remaining hope.

Charlotte woke the next morning feeling much refreshed. She'd had, a good, uninterrupted night's sleep and her body had made the most of it by regenerating. To her surprise, she felt a little disappointed that nothing unusual had happened during the night and at the same time worried that with her deep sleep, if it had, her mind had not recorded it. She looked across the room to the picture, sad to see nothing had changed. The stag still looked terrified and still faced inwards or to the West. She now knew, facing west symbolised the ending of life or if one wanted to be blunt, death. What Charlotte did not understand was whose death. Was it death in the singular or much worse. She looked out of the window. Everything looked the same as the day before. How depressing, though thankfully the magpie still hadn't returned. Right on cue the robin came hopping down the garden fence and Charlotte found herself waving. In response, or so she thought, the robin fluttered its wings. Charlotte smiled, not everything seen from her window was depressing.

To the delight of her parents, Charlotte appeared to be her old self. Her smile had returned as had her energy. The following night Charlotte had another good night's sleep, then another and another and soon a week had passed without incident. No tapping on the window, no night time visit to the churchyard and no passage into a strange parallel world. It is quite amazing how quickly time erases one's memory and Charlotte was no different. Seven days of normal life coupled with seven nights of uninterrupted sleep and Charlotte's ventures to, well she wasn't sure where were becoming a haze. Four things prevented her from remembering everything as just another dream. The picture on her wall, the robin, the mist that had taken up residency in the field next to the church and the strange cloud hanging over the village. A cloud that appeared to be getting darker by the day. With these four things to remind her Charlotte knew that one day the squirrel would again come beckoning but for now she relished being able to enjoy the innocence of childhood.

With plenty of sleep she had no more naps at school and all of her teachers who had been asked to keep a discreet eye on her, reported a studious and hardworking child, popular with everyone. Life in Aldbury continued but one couldn't call it happy. The depressing shadow cast over the village by the cloud was unsurprisingly perhaps having an influence on the people who lived there. Arguments, often over nothing were becoming a common occurrence both within four walls and out. There was even a physical confrontation outside the village shop between two men who had been close friends for years. It had been broken up quickly by others before it had gotten out of hand. When both men were asked what the argument had been about neither could remember. There were also an increasing number of dog attacks in the village, something that before had only happened once in a blue moon, maybe even once in two blue moons. Cat owners no longer let their cats out of doors. And the vicar was becoming increasingly worried that less and less of his parishioners were bothering to attend church. He was also experiencing an increasing unease about the strange mist that was visibly thickening by the day in the field that adjoined the churchyard. He felt more and more the two were somehow linked.

The unique localised weather also brought a host of unwanted visitors. Every weekend the village was swamped with ghoulish tourists wanting to snap the enigma before it disappeared and things returned to normal. One day when Charlotte returned from school there was a television crew on the village green filming for a local news station, an emission that was to attract even more visitors. On the flip side the village shop and the two hostelries were doing a roaring trade. A local entrepreneur employed a professional photographer to take some photographers and printed them as postcards. They became a bestseller in the shop and people took photographs of each other posting the postcards in the post box outside. Charlotte's parents also took advantage of the village's new found popularity and on Sundays set up a little stall on the village green selling snacks. This led to one local resident suggesting they organise, with their unique experience, a food fair in the village hall. Not wishing to miss an opportunity a meeting was organised with the caretaker of the hall that coming Sunday, to see if the suggestion was at all viable.

Mr Clutterbuck had managed the hall for decades. He'd been born and bred in the village and was justifiably proud of everything Aldbury. Tall in stature he had a moustache that gave away his military background and if he ever shaved it off his voice would have given it away instead. He greeted Charlotte's parents with a firm handshake and bellowed.

"And how are you French charlotte? Doing well at school I hope" and gave her a firm pat on the head.

Inside, the village hall reminded Charlotte of one in a comedy Caroline's father was always watching on television, Dad's Army she thought it was called. It had a smell she considered to be uniquely English and one that revealed its past better than any description in a flyer. It reminded her mother she'd let on, of endless cups of tea and the Spitfire.

The hall was deemed suitable by all and all that remained was to find a convenient date and for her parents to sign a contract. To his annoyance Mr Clutterbuck realised he'd left both the hall diary and the contracts back at his house.

"Follow me," he bellowed "we'll do it all there." Meaning his house.

Mr Clutterbuck's house was a brick and timber affair dating from the 17th century and like many old houses in Aldbury, originally a farmstead. It was only a five minute walk from the village hall. Inside exposed beams were everywhere and antiques took up every inch of space. The walls were almost completely obscured by old paintings and prints along with photographs of his days in the RAF. A grandfather clock stood in one corner with a loud pendulum confirming with every swing the unstoppable passing of time. Charlotte's parents had told her, to avoid any embarrassing slip ups that Mr Clutterbuck's wife had passed away only last year. Charlotte demonstrating great sensitivity thought the house still had that woman's touch and that everything looked spotless. She didn't wish to imagine what a house would look like if her father lived on his own.

The hall diary and contracts were found sitting on a chair and her parents and Mr Clutterbuck settled down to confirm a date and sort out the paperwork. Charlotte passed the time examining the varied collection of pictures and photographs on the walls. On completing the paperwork her parents were offered a glass of port to celebrate which they readily accepted. Mr Clutterbuck was forced to apologise to Charlotte for not having any hot chocolate. One picture in particular had caught Charlotte's eye. It hung above the immense open fire place. Set in a dark and heavy wooden frame the picture was of a large house with trees approaching in formal lines, a variety of birds and animals created an interest in the foreground. Charlotte couldn't make out if the birds and animals were meant to be real or imaginary. The style of the painting reflected a very different age.

"You like that, do you French Charlotte?" Mr Clutterbuck had eyed her studying the picture and was pleased by her apparent interest. For him too many children today were only interested in overnight "celebrities," who as far as he could see had done nothing to deserve their adoration. French Charlotte's interest in his picture was refreshing, very refreshing, it pleased him a great deal.

Yes, what's it of?" Charlotte asked, still studying the picture.

"That," said Mr Clutterbuck standing up and walking to join Charlotte in front of the picture. "Is a painting of the original manor of

Aldbury." He paused, "well not a painting," he admitted. "A print of the original."

"What happened to the original?" Charlotte followed up quickly.

"No idea," came the reply. "No one knows what happened to the original. Probably hung on somebody's wall miles away from here and almost certainly meaningless to whoever has it, that's if it still exists at all." Mr Clutterbuck sighed his sadness and seeing her father's glass already empty moved to top it up.

"No, I meant the house." Charlotte corrected. "Not the painting."

"Oh the house. That's long gone. It used to stand behind the church in that field with all the mist. Funny business that is." Mr Clutterbuck took a moment to reflect on the bizarre. The mist unnerved him, it wasn't natural. He saw French Charlotte's expectant look and returned to the subject of the house in the painting. "House must have fallen into ruin, real pity, for as you can see," he waved an arm at the picture, "it was a magnificent building." There were murmurs of agreement from all in the room. If it was anything close to the house depicted in the picture it really must have been quite splendid, the pride of the village. "There's some weird stories," Mr Clutterbuck continued, "of how the house met its end but they're all stuff and nonsense, if you ask me."

Charlotte was just about to ask a question relating to Mr Clutterbuck's last comment when she caught her mother's eye. By her look it was obvious her mother was impatient to leave and didn't want her daughter to delay them by asking any more questions. Her father, oblivious to their silent communication raised his glass to take another sip of port, it really was rather good. Charlotte saw this and realised he had almost finished his second glass, if he started a third they could all be there for the duration. Charlotte dutifully held her silence whilst her mother proffered an apology.

"They'd love to stay but they really had to get going."

"You sure you don't want another," offered Mr Clutterbuck holding up a decanter. Her father was just about to accept when a sharp pinch on his thigh told him he'd better not.

The conversation between Charlotte's parents on the walk back to the cottage concentrated on how much money they might make from a food show in the village hall. Charlotte for once stayed silent. Her mind was focused on the manor house so beautifully captured by the artist who'd painted it. She remembered from their first village walkabout the pits and troughs along with the grass covered mounds in the field behind the church. The field now blanketed by mist and the site she now knew of the original manor of Aldbury. She didn't know why but she had a strong feeling that the old Manor and every bizarre thing that had happened to her since arriving in Aldbury were somehow linked. She just couldn't fathom how or why.

On Wednesday, the magpie was back. It sat on the same bough of the cherry blossom, as though it had never left, its penetrating stare through the long sash window touching every wall of her small bedroom. Its presence shook Charlotte to the core, she'd almost forgotten it. Worse still she was sure it was the same bird that sat in the oak tree beside the pond watching her as she waited for the school bus. That day, Charlotte found work at school hard going, try as she might she found herself unable to concentrate. Her mind constantly wandering to matters in Aldbury. Her teachers noticed too and reported back to the deputy head. If she was the same tomorrow the deputy head decided, I'll have another word with her parents. Something was seriously wrong, she just knew it, her experience told her so, she just couldn't lay her finger on what it could be and that worried her even more. Maybe she should have a quiet word with French Charlotte after all.

After getting off the school bus Charlotte deliberately avoided going straight home. Instead she asked Caroline if she could come around to her house so that they could do their homework together. Caroline agreed and from her friend's house Charlotte phoned her parents so they wouldn't worry. She planned to return after dark, by which time she knew the magpie would have gone, it was never there after dusk. Where do you fly off to? She wondered silently. The girls or rather Caroline's mother decided they could go up to her daughter's bedroom to do their work. The bedroom was airy and spacious, perhaps five times the size of Charlotte's bedroom and with built in wardrobes, felt even larger. It had a large picture window and the view from the window overlooked the whole village, it was really quite special. Charlotte though that afternoon wasn't taken by the view. On looking out of the window her eyes immediately fixed on the tree nearest to the house, a maple. Clearly visible sitting on one of the higher branches was a magpie, its intense, steady gaze fixed on the bedroom window. Refusing to be intimidated Charlotte stared back, she knew, she just knew that the bird's interest was not of the house nor the window but her.

On the short walk from her friend's back to the cottage Charlotte couldn't help continually looking over her shoulder. She had the most unsettling feeling that she was being followed and it was a feeling that made her sweat from the invisible intimidation. As a result she ran most of the way. It was a massive relief to shove open the stable door to the kitchen and find her parents sat at the table smiling. In the centre of the table sat a raclette machine and surrounding it plates brimming with all the ingredients for a good raclette. It was just what she needed, her parents had an amazing ability to read her mind. A warmth washed over her, a warmth that remained with Charlotte for the rest of the evening. She felt safe with her parents and wanted desperately to tell them about the magpie, the robin, the squirrel, the white stag and all the strange things that had been happening to her. She felt guilty for not telling them and nobody had told or indicated to her that she wasn't to. She just had a very, very strong feeling that to do so would put everybody and everything in danger. Though increasingly difficult she would continue to hold her silence. After the raclette they, all three, retired to the lounge where a log fire had already been burning for a good hour. Rather than read Charlotte's father played a cd on their ageing hifi, Enya's Shepherd Moons. When it had finished he played it again and after that twice more. Charlotte and her mother didn't complain, the music captured perfectly their mood that evening and as if the fire recognised the emotion in the room the flames swayed rather than danced, moving with a subtleness that accentuated the mystic melodies of the songs.

Tap – tap,tap,tap. Charlotte opened her eyes to find herself staring at the ceiling, she could feel Gromit by her side. Tap,tap,tap,tap, it came again. Now she was fully awake, this time she knew she was being summoned. She looked across to the window, there was the robin perched on the sill. It could see she was awake but still it didn't stop tapping, if anything on seeing her awake it tapped louder and with more frequency. Charlotte with an effort forced the feeling of sleep from her veins and after stretching hurriedly got dressed. Downstairs, remembering last time she grabbed her raincoat before lifting the catch to the stable door. Outside the squirrel was waiting as she knew it would be. As soon as it saw her it ran along the brick path not pausing to see if Charlotte was following. The robin watched them go.

Charlotte ran all the way and it felt like only seconds before she was running up the gravel path to the church door. The church loomed solid in the darkness. On the other side of the iron railings the mist in the adjacent field twisted and turned, swirling with menacing aggression. Charlotte refused to look at it, she had learned her lesson, instead she looked up at the clock on the church tower. There at the centre the clenched hand had a firm hold of the writhing snake, both the head and the tail of the serpent rested on XIII, thirteen. The squirrel she noticed had already disappeared and quickly she stepped onto the stone slab. The next second she found herself being pulled beneath the earth. Her natural reaction was to always hold her breath even though there was no need, she could breathe quite easily even when under the soil. After a pause, the invisible force was pushing her above ground and from the unnatural stillness she knew she had arrived on the other side. If that was the correct expression. The squirrel, as her feet came to rest on firm ground, was already running down the second path to the village pond and Charlotte made haste to follow it.

Just as last time they followed the Ivinghoe road. This time the two hounds, Alasdair and Cathasach, she found waiting in the road, their eyes glinting in the cloud weakened light of the moon. Unlike last time they were some way before the wood and the stone wall. Without giving Charlotte time to catch her breath, the hounds passed through a gate on the eastern side of the road and took off across open fields heading for the dark ascent of the wooded scarp. When I say pass through the gate I mean literally that. The gate was locked shut but the hounds passed through it as though it wasn't there. Charlotte touched the gate gingerly, it was solid and the wood felt almost reassuringly warm to the touch. With some effort she clambered over and started up the gradual incline towards the wooded scarp. The two hounds, to her relief, she saw had stopped running and were looking back watching her, the expression on their faces telling of their frustration at her slow progress. Well tough. Not till they arrived at the tree line did the hounds stop again allowing for a rest. Across the other side of the valley, the wooded Aldbury Nowers and the grass ridge of Pitstone Hill were but dark silhouettes against the night sky. Alasdair and Cathasach paced back and forth as Charlotte caught her breath, they looked uneasy, every muscle tensed in readiness. In readiness for what Charlotte wondered and didn't really want to know. In less than a minute the two hounds started off again tackling the steep, very steep in places, wooded scarp. The climb was always going to be hard going and wasn't helped by the soft ground underfoot made loose and greasy by the recent rain. Charlotte with her child's mind compared it to climbing up a crumbling sponge cake. At times she had to use her hands to avoid slipping, grabbing at tree roots to haul herself up. The smell of the newly disturbed earth she found strangely intoxicating. Layers of seasons past having their cover rudely pulled away, releasing sodden, musty scents of their long time slumber into the crisp receptive air of the night. Yes the strange blend was quite intoxicating and Charlotte's senses welcomed the mixture with every pained breath.

As they climbed it became fairly obvious that they were avoiding following established paths or to be more exact, paths created by the human race. Charlotte wasn't sure if this was a deliberate strategy or if they were simply taking the shortest route. If it were the shortest it definitely wasn't the easiest. On reaching the top of the ridge the hounds led them across a wide track before diving back amongst the trees and their way for the next half an hour continued through thick unforgiving woodland. A wood at night takes a completely different form to a wood during the day. The trees play tricks with your mind, teasing ingrained, but irrational fears. Charlotte was sure at times the odd tree moved, not just wave in the wind but move of its own accord. All of the time she felt she was being watched, and not just by one creature but hundreds, even by the trees themselves. Unidentifiable shapes loomed in the darkness and night shadows suggested danger lurked, ahead, behind, and on every side. A wood at night feels threatening, very threatening not at all like the cotton wool atmosphere of the day.

Fallen trees regularly blocked their passage and often the quickest way forward was simply to climb over them. The squirrel as was natural for it left the ground as they traversed the wood leaping from branch to branch overhead. Alasdair and Cathasach weaved their way through the wood as dogs do their noses constantly to the ground. Any obstacle they simply leapt or scrambled effortlessly over, the human brain maybe considered superior but the human body has some definite design deficiencies when faced with such an environment. Often the hounds ran wide on either flank and she once or twice lost sight of them. Every time this happened Charlotte felt panic rise within, her greatest fear was to be lost in a wood on her own at night. She remembered her father telling her once that everybody has one leg slightly shorter than the other and if you ever got lost in a wood you would simply walk in large circles until you died. Why did she have to remember that now.

Charlotte didn't know it but they were traversing Sallow Copse. Every now and then they crossed a human formed path some wide, some barely definable but not once did they follow one. It was a great relief, when after what seemed an eternity the little group arrived at a road. Charlotte recognised it at once and knew they were close to the hamlet of Ringshall. Almost without hesitating Alasdair and Cathasach crossed over into the wooded Witches Hollow. From there they led Charlotte along the Eastern slope of what is provocatively called Golden Valley. On reaching Pulridge Wood they stopped for a rest. They had come a long way and all three animals could see that the little girl was beginning to tire. The problem was and all three of them knew, they were running out of time. Charlotte for her part wasn't stupid, she recognised by their nervous attention that nobody had wanted to stop, she knew they had only stopped for her. Mustering up all her reserves she indicated that she was ready to move on. Hurriedly the hounds led Charlotte across another narrow lane and then across open ground before dropping into a wide valley. On reaching the valley floor the hounds swung right following a lively stream. Charlotte wasn't certain but she was pretty sure they were in the Gade Valley. She had visited the valley with her parents when they had first arrived in Aldbury and remembered that the Gade valley had been the only valley with a stream running through it. All the others except for a canal and a bourne were dry. The light gurgling of the fast running water she found helped calm her nerves and the fresh air, cooled by the stream's cold waters relieved the sweat on her brow. Alasdair and Cathasach at last began to slow and Charlotte spied in the near distance a huddle of buildings and that they were making directly for them. Even in the gloom she recognised they were approaching the tiny village of Great Gaddesden. She had been right then, they were indeed in the Gade Valley. Stopping for a few seconds the two hounds cautiously surveyed the scene before them. Like Aldbury, Great Gaddesden looked real but there was something not quite right. The two hounds started to advance once more but now taking slow, very cautious steps. The squirrel stayed where it was and Charlotte assumed she was meant to do the same. She was completely unprepared for what happened next. As Alasdair and Cathasach came close to the first houses the entire village started to disappear, not into thin air but descending into the earth just as she had done hours earlier. The process was slow and silent but within minutes the village was no more, the squat church tower being the last object to disappear. Where the church had stood, out of the blackness shone a faint light, it was a light Charlotte recognised. Alasdair and Cathasach looked round and the squirrel began to scurry forward. Charlotte followed. The four of them approached, her companions more with reverence than caution.

Where the church had stood and the surrounding churchyard was now a grass slope and where the village had been, only trees. There remained not a single building, the church and churchyard had become nothing more than a large clearing in a wood. On the grass surrounding what would have been the church was a circle of large pudding stones.

A pudding stone is the name given to boulders made up of rounded flint and pebbles compressed and held together with a mix of sand and quartz cement. They were formed around fifty million years ago and broken up during the last ice age. They are called pudding stones because their consistency is said to resemble that of the traditional plum pudding.

Close to the centre of the circle stood a particularly large pudding stone it's form quite accidently creating a natural seat or chair. Beside the stone and in the centre of the circle stood a huge yew tree, its enormous, flaked trunk a darkened hue of red. From its stature the tree looked as though it had stood there since the beginning of time. It's trunk also appeared to be hollow and the light Charlotte could see, came from within. Indeed it looked as if the light filled the whole of the tree almost as if the tree and the light were one. The spectacle gripped Charlotte like nothing had before. The light had her complete attention, it moved slivering like a snake in and around the tree, pulsating slowly as though energised by a beating heart. Unlike normal light, which Charlotte had learned at school was always a form of energy, the light before her was more of a living being. She could sense its soul, every extended glow she knew to be a heartbeat and every whispery vapour an escaping breath.

Alasdair and Cathasach edged forward entering the stone circle. Step by step they approached the old yew and when within a couple of feet lay down with their heads resting on their front legs. Charlotte saw that their eyes were fixed on the tree and the living light within. Next the squirrel entered the circle. Very un-squirrel like its movement was slow and steady, it came to rest between the two hounds. On stopping it turned its head towards Charlotte and she knew that she too was meant to enter the pudding stone circle. For a reason she couldn't understand her heart was racing and yet she felt calm, completely unafraid. As she passed into the stone circle she experienced the strangest of feelings. It may well have been her imagination but she felt sure some sort of force entered her being, a force that originated from deep beneath the ground. It reached every nerve in her body, and as it did, so she swore that she could feel the heartbeat of the Earth. As soon as both Charlotte's feet were touching the ground within the circle there was movement from outside. Silently, one by one a representative of every creature that lived in the ancient wood of Ashridge stepped out from the trees surrounding the stone circle, though not one attempted to enter the circle itself. The silent gathering humbled Charlotte, she'd never seen so many different animals gathered together in one place. They all stood motionless and in complete silence, each a proud representative of their species and their place in the natural world. Feeling the heartbeat of the Earth came a new enlightenment and Charlotte understood for the first time that she was simply one of them, different but not superior in any way. Gazing round at their faces she could sense though not understand each animal's thoughts, their feelings too. One feeling dominated all others, it was a feeling Charlotte could understand and it was the only feeling that every animal held in common. The strength of this feeling was so overwhelming that Charlotte felt like crying, the feeling was fear, absolute and unadulterated fear.

"Please sit child." It was the voice that wasn't a voice, a voice she had heard before, though last time it had been only a whisper. A voice that searched out her mind not her ears. It was soft, gentle and Charlotte would never tire of it. Obediently she sat cross legged on the grass behind the squirrel. As she did so, Alasdair and Cathasach stood up and with the squirrel left the protection of the circle to join the other animals at the edge of the wood. Charlotte was left sitting on her own.

From within the trunk the light brightened and familiar whispers of vapour trailed from the tree to fog the air around it. The light continued to grow stronger, and as it did so, the vapour thickened and gathered until it had formed a small cloud hovering over the large pudding stone that resembled a chair. Charlotte saw there was movement from within the light and small celestial bodies, shards of light started to break free and float from the broad trunk. They floated to the now lucent cloud where they joined as one. When the process was complete the cloud lifted and spread until it was no more than fading whispers of vapour. What remained was the most beautiful image Charlotte had ever seen. Sitting on the pudding stone chair was a female figure. She was made up only of different shades of light and yet her features were easily distinguishable and quite perfect. Her face radiated kindness and her eyes, though only of light expressed a gentleness that unless she'd seen it for herself Charlotte wouldn't have thought possible. She wore a gown with a hood of the purest white, woven with stiches of light that accentuated every movement.

"Thank you for coming to visit me young Charlotte." Charlotte could see her lips move but the delectable voice wasn't of their making. Her words as had been the case on the slope approaching Ivinghoe Beacon was received by her mind not her ears. "I hope your journey was not too arduous." Charlotte shook her head quite unable to speak. The lady looked down gazing into Charlotte's wide eyes, at the same time she reached out and with the slightest of touches brushed her hair. At that moment, all Charlotte's troubles left her and were replaced with nothing but joy. A joy so strong, so ecstatic, so elated that she wanted to leap up and tell the world. Another first, she now completely understood what was truly meant by the phrase, 'jump for joy.'

The luminous white lady sat with her elbows resting on her knees, her face cupped in her long delicate hands.

"My name is Leht," she said softly, "I expect you're wondering why you're here."

Charlotte just about managed a nod.

"Do not be afraid to speak in front of my friends little girl" her eyes moved to the fauna outside the circle, statuesque, every creature had their gaze fixed on the entity that Charlotte now knew as Leht. "Everything you say to me is for my ears only. Those outside the circle cannot see or hear us." Charlotte nodded again, still unable to speak. If the creatures outside the circle could not see Leht she wondered what on earth they were all staring at. "I wish I had an answer for you but I have none, for if I am honest I am not sure why you are here either." Leht's voice made the question irrelevant and her admission did not register with Charlotte for she was too intent on enjoying Leht's tones than understanding the words they formed. Leht, possibly oblivious to this continued. "The Snooks tell stories of someone transcending from the other side to help us and we have been searching for that person as the completion of the great cycle is almost upon us once more, but a young child," she smiled sympathetically at Charlotte. "I did not expect that."

This time Leht's words did register and questions quickly started to form in Charlotte's head, she wanted answers but still no matter how hard she tried, she couldn't bring herself to speak. An invisible hand was being held over her mouth. She was still searching for a way to ask a question when to her disappointment the light before her began to dim and with it the face of Leht disappeared. Her face had almost faded completely and Charlotte began to fear the lady had gone when to her relief the light brightened and the immaculate face was back but this time there shone a tiredness that hadn't been there before. Leht spoke, her silent speech was as musical as ever but like her face the tones reflected a tiredness, a weakness that hadn't been there at the beginning. Leht's next words confirmed what was clearly evident.

"I am too tired, too weak to answer your questions little girl, I know you have many, they will be answered in time but for now you must listen to what I have to say."

Charlotte once more found herself nodding.

"Good," Leht smiled appreciatively. "You will not understand much of what I have to say but it is important you remember every word, and I hope by the time the cycle completes you will understand, and you will be able to help us as the Snooks have foretold." Leht paused and the light looked as though it was about to dim once more when there was a spark and instead of dimming it glowed even more brightly than before. Leht's eyes sparkled and Charlotte began to understand that the light reflected the lady's strength and that maintaining it was a struggle for her. Leht's voice reached her mind once more.

"Since the beginning there has been a struggle between good and evil. Although we have not won every battle, overall good has remained the stronger and triumphed with every moon that has passed. With the completion of the great cycle almost upon us there is a genuine fear that may change. The dark forces have been patient, preparing well and are starting to show their hand." Leht paused once more but this time her light didn't dim and her eyes continued to sparkle. "Their ultimate goal is to learn the secret of Orme. If they achieve that they will have control both of your world and mine, the universe and everything that is beyond. Worlds that your species know nothing of. Everything will collapse into chaos even time itself and ultimately there will be nothing. Nothing at all, just a blackness so dense that not the tiniest particle will survive. It will be as things were, before the beginning of time, before what some of your species call the big bang. This time though one thing will remain. The blackness though empty will hold a feeling, a feeling that we all understand and that feeling will be fear. It will be a fear so strong that nothing will wish to disturb the blackness again. There will be no second big bang. Life, and I mean all life will be extinguished forever." Leht paused once more, though she remained smiling there was an air of sadness in her expression. "I'm sorry you have to hear this, my child. You shouldn't have to hear such things at an age that demands innocence." Charlotte remained silent, inside she wanted so much to express that she was fine, that she didn't mind but she couldn't move, a force, an invisible force was holding her still. Leht smiling leaned a little closer, her bright eyes holding Charlottes who's eyes could not possibly open any wider.

"The conclusion I have just painted need never happen young Charlotte. "What we have to concentrate on for now is where we are today, and that little girl sadly involves you and me and every living creature nearby, for the forces of darkness have decided to make their first move in our little world." Leht paused again but her light didn't dim and her image remained strong.

"In your village many moons ago one of your species dabbled with the wrong kind of magic. He succeeded in making contact with Darkness. In your world this darkness is known by many names but you my child will best know him as the Devil. In your world the Devil, as you call him, is portrayed as a physical being. He is not, he or it has no mass, it is just darkness. A blackness that devours everything. It has a mind and it uses it to create fear and with fear it controls the physical beings of all worlds to do its bidding. This man from your village tried to make a pact with the Darkness to harness power for himself. Of course he could never succeed in doing this, the Darkness took him for his own devices . Overnight he and everything he owned including his home simply vanished. The Darkness ever since has had control of the land where his house once stood and ownership of his soul. On completion of the great cycle the darkness will be able to harness his soul and through his land gain direct access to your world. The process I'm afraid has already begun." Leht took a deep breath.

"I am weakening child I must finish quickly before I fade." Her face was still clear but Leht's eyes Charlotte could see were no longer sparkling. Leht with what was now obviously taking a great deal of effort continued.

"The Darkness in our world has attacked the Sacred Library of Evinghehou, you will know it simply as Ivinghoe or Ivinghoe Beacon. You have heard the expression mountain of knowledge?" Charlotte found herself nodding again. "Well if you like, the Beacon is for us a hill of knowledge, a great library. Stored deep beneath the hill are hundreds of ancient scrolls, not scrolls as you know them but scrolls of light. Many of the scrolls are very old and some, it's said, are so old that they may have been placed in the library or under the Beacon not long after time began. They contain all kinds of knowledge. Knowledge gathered over many millennia, much of it considered sacred, and knowledge if in the wrong hands that could become world shatteringly dangerous. Some even say that in the sacred library, the most ancient scrolls hold the very keys to the universe and the oldest scrolls of all, the very first scrolls to be placed within the library are rumoured to contain some of the secrets to Orme itself. The scrolls were placed there for their protection, to stop them falling into the wrong hands. For such knowledge would, I repeat, be unimaginably dangerous if used for reasons other than good." Leht paused to take a much needed breath, her light was beginning to fade and in places her image was becoming almost transparent. Charlotte feared she would soon disappear altogether. Once more with increasingly obvious effort Leht continued with her lecture.

"To protect the scrolls, a white hart, strong in mind as well as stature was set on the summit of the Sacred Library. A white hart has the unique ability to feed off the currents of the earth and with the power of its mind can block any unwanted forces gaining access to the scrolls. To give the hart added power it was placed facing east enabling it to refresh daily, to recharge itself, to absorb strength from the new born sun. When the forces of darkness attacked the Sacred Library they failed to gain entry but they did succeed in turning our dear hart to face westwards therefore unable to regenerate naturally its strength. Without the power of the sun our dear hart would slowly lose its own power and it would only be a matter of time before the forces of darkness overcame it and possibly gain access to the scrolls. To prevent this from happening I placed rings of light around our friend. You saw them with your own eyes." Once again Charlotte found herself nodding and Leht with increasing fragility went on. "These rings have the same effect as the sun and provide renewed strength on a daily basis. However they are part of me." Leht crossed her arms before her fading figure. "Keeping them there takes a great deal out of me, I cannot sustain them for much longer." There was another pause, it was becoming obvious that Leht could fade away at any moment and Charlotte didn't know if it was a good or a bad thing but wisps of vapour were fast emerging from the great yew and gathering above Leht's fading aura. Leht spoke again but this time her words were so faint that Charlotte had to concentrate as never before to understand them.

"I must go my child for my energy is almost gone. We will meet again, have no fear of that, but not here for the journey will soon become too dangerous for you. I will send a message where to meet. Alasdair and Cathasach will ensure no harm comes to you and the squirrel will be my faithful messenger. From now on you will also have a guide to the forest. Please do not be frightened by his appearance for he is a gentle soul and I have given him the ability to speak your language, his name is Wodewose. Good luck sweet Charlotte." With that any light remaining dwindled until it was no more. The various whispers of vapour in greater haste than earlier formed a cloud over the large pudding stone before retreating and disappearing into the trunk of the yew. Within its protection Leht felt her tired being already start to regenerate. As she bathed within the yew's limbs she felt the tree's deep slow voice speak to her.

"Leht you need to be honest with the child, you need to explain to her why you are so weak, why our world is suffering. You need to be straight with her about the human connection."

"Soon," Leht answered her tree. "Soon, remember she is only a child" and with that the lady of light fell into a welcome sleep, soothed by the strong protective limbs of her yew.

Charlotte blinked as her eyes struggled to become accustomed to the darkness. Leht's light still glowed in her pupils as well as her mind. Had what happened really happened, had she really been witness to such an event? And what of the message? As she struggled to make sense of what she had just been part of with a start she realised there was someone or something standing beside her. Looking round Charlotte saw not even a metre away a figure towering above her. He had the build of a man but his body was covered in shaggy hair. In contrast he had very little hair on top of his human-like head but made up for it with a great bushy beard that appeared to grow upwards as well as downwards and outwards. He held a long roughly hewn staff in one hand with leaves that sprouted at every knobble and a small leather sack slung over one shoulder. His eyes, almost the only feature of his face visible had a rather soppy appearance. They were similar to eyes found on a dog was Charlotte's first impression, dark yet bright and expressive they spoke to you as you looked at them. Ultimately they held a kind inquisitive expression and it was this last feature that probably stopped her from turning and running in panic.

"Hello Charlotte," said the shaggy beast. His gruff voice matched his appearance but at the same time it sounded kind, definitely not threatening. "My name is Wodewose."

"Charlotte," Charlotte said realising immediately that she was being stupid, the shaggy beast , Wodewose as she now knew, already knew her name, he had just said it. "Pleased to meet you."

Wodewose shifted from foot to foot as though he felt nervous or uncomfortable. Whilst the two were making their stumbling introductions, the hounds, Alasdair and Cathasach silently re-entered the ring along with the squirrel. Woodwose looked at them, he still appeared a little nervous and perhaps a little afraid of the two hounds. Charlotte wasn't sure but there seemed to be some sort of silent communication between the hounds, Alasdair and Cathasach and Wodewose.

"We must go" Wodewose said suddenly, "and quickly." With that he grabbed Charlotte's hand pulling her to leave the ring. At the same time Charlotte realised that all the creatures that had been waiting outside the pudding stone circle earlier were no longer there, they had simply disappeared. Alasdair and Cathasach started to run but only far enough for Charlotte to realise she was to hurry. The squirrel scurried from left to right as squirrels always do.

"We must hurry," it was Wodewose again and Charlotte found herself sprinting not letting go of the shaggy beast's hand. Woodwose ran with what looked like an awkward gait and it shook Charlotte's arm to the bone but he was almost as fleet a foot as the greyhounds and at times her feet hardly touched the ground.

There was no sound, just movement and without warning the ground began to lift beneath them. Charlotte quickly realised why they were making such haste. The buildings of Great Gaddesden were rising. With an enormous leap Wodewose literally threw Charlotte into the field before them and followed, rolling several times over before coming to an ungainly halt. Alasdair and Cathasach were already in the field though poised ready to return if they thought Charlotte needed their help. The squirrel was running this way and that, its tail bristling with all the excitement.

As a group they sat or lay in the field, all trying to catch their breath and watching as the buildings of Great Gaddesden once more took their place. Everyone was gazing back at the dark outlines of the village. Where the ring of pudding stones had been with the old yew at its centre now stood the village church.

Charlotte felt Woodwose grab her hand. She hadn't noticed before but his hand was incredibly soft, almost like holding a warm towel.

"Come on, "he said, pulling her to her feet. "We need to get you home." Charlotte got to her feet, she was so thankful that she had now met two people in this strange world, who spoke her language. It made things so much easier. Now a group of five they made their way back along the valley side retracing the route by which they'd arrived when they had been just four. By the time they reached Witches Hollow dawn was firmly established, the sky already a dim greyish blue with fingers of light widening from the east. Birds were already in full song and Charlotte close to exhaustion found herself lifted by their chorus. It would take a very hardened soul not to be. Looking up at the cloudless sky and thinking of the greyness that enveloped Aldbury she had a question for Wodewose.

"Wodewose, what's the weather like in this world, is it worse than in my world?"

"Our weather mirrors yours, unless somebody wants to change it." Charlotte had no idea what he meant by this and being too tired to question, left it at that.

After crossing the road close to Ringshall they re-entered the part of the great wood known as Sallow Copse. The two hounds, Alasdair and Cathasach, as they'd done earlier led the small party deep into the wood's heart. Again they deliberately avoided following any paths created by Charlotte's fellow man and whenever one was met, it was crossed with great haste. After the challenges of the night Charlotte was beginning to tire rapidly. Traversing the wood was once more taking a lot out of her, in places it was a real scramble and the unforgiving undergrowth seemed to delight in scratching her at every opportunity. Despite the hard going and Charlotte's increasing fatigue she was still able to appreciate the wood's beauty. The leaves of the beach were starting to unfold creating a luminous green in the cover above. In places, the floor of the wood was now carpeted in bluebells stretching as far as the eye can see, and in other areas, the leaves of the unassuming dogs mercury turned the ground cover a deep green. Where the sun penetrated the nodding yellow heads of cowslips were a lovely sight as were the delicate pale purple flowers of the dog violet. Bird song continued to fill the air and the wood was bustling with their busy nest building. It was hard to believe, Charlotte thought that this was the same wood that had scared her so just a few hours earlier. The difference between daylight and the dark of night really was Jekyll and Hyde. Charlotte shivered as recalling the night passage she remembered Leht's words.

On reaching a point close to the wood's centre Alasdair and Cathasach subtly changed direction taking a more southerly route. Most people would never have noticed but Charlotte was still alert enough and familiar enough with the wood to observe the change. Between breaths she asked Wodewose where they were heading.

"They are taking you to where I live." Wodewose replied.

"Where's that?"

"You'll see, it's not far." Charlotte was amazed at the shaggy beasts seemingly effortless strides. He looked as fresh as when they had started and had an athleticism equal to an Olympian, leaping fallen trees as though he were striding hurdles. And yet his stature looked anything but athletic. If she hadn't seen it with her own eyes she'd have expected Woodrose to be the slowest of them all, plodding not running like a deer. At times she wondered at their little party, the two hounds out wide, the squirrel leaping from tree to tree above and shaggy Woodrose. Surely it must all be a dream she kept telling herself, everything was too fantastical. At any minute now I'm going to wake up and return to reality. However a voice in her head kept nagging at her, "this is reality young Charlotte, this is reality, you must believe it." And she did.

From Sallow Copse Alasdair and Cathasach led their small party across the drive to the Bridgewater monument through Aldbury Common and Old Copse eventually coming to a halt shortly before an ancient oak close to Gryme's Dell.

"This is my home." Wodewose said proudly gesturing to the tree.

Charlotte had already recognised the tree, it stood beside the road that descended from the top of the escarpment into Aldbury. She knew that on the other side of the road a little further along was a small car park.

"What do you think?" Wodewose asked. It was obvious he was very proud of his home.

Charlotte searched for a reply, she felt a simple "very nice" was too insipid but had no experience on complimenting a tree that was somebody's home. She need not have worried for Wodewose didn't wait for a reply instead he gestured for her to sit on a tree stump partly covered in moss. Woodwose himself leaned against a large fallen beech stirring the floor with one of his shaggy feet. He, as earlier looked nervous. Charlotte studied him intently, though his appearance was intimidating his manner was almost childlike as though he were only a small boy. I wonder how old you are Woodwose she questioned silently.

A few metres away Alasdair and Cathasach didn't rest but paced restlessly up and down, the squirrel came to stop, if a little precariously, on a branch a short way above them. As Charlotte was taking all of this in Wodewose spoke, his gruff voice ruffling the nearby leaves.

"I have to explain a few things," he started. "Some things that Leht didn't have time to." Charlotte wasn't sure she could take in much more though did her best not to show it. She remained politely silent waiting for Wodewose to explain.

"I am sorry," he stuttered. "I am not used to talking. Leht has temporarily given me the ability to speak and in your language but I am finding it difficult, it is very foreign to me." As he spoke Woodwose brushed his sides nervously with his hands, he needed pockets Charlotte thought lightly. Out of the corner of her eye she saw Cathasach stir and move off into the wood, Alasdair had stopped pacing and stood tense. Charlotte found herself clenching the moss in expectation that something not at all pleasant was about to happen. Wodewose appeared oblivious and without a response from Charlotte continued with his lesson.

"I am to be your guide, whilst you are here that is and especially in the woods for I am their protector and know most of what is going on within them." There was a sound that resembled indignation from the squirrel sitting on a branch above them. Woodwose chose to ignore it and carried on. Cathasach Charlotte couldn't help noticing, hadn't as yet returned. "If you have any questions," Wodewose looked kindly at her. "You must ask me. If I cannot answer I am in contact with Leht and she will help."

"Ok," Charlotte affirmed, still with one eye on where she'd last seen Cathasach.

"Take this budget," Wodewose handed Charlotte the small leather bag that had been hanging from his shoulder. She took it, holding it in both hands, mumbling her thanks.

It is unclear where the word budget originated from, in the world Charlotte finds herself now or the one we live in. It could have been either for once upon a time there was much toing and froing between the two worlds. The word was widely used for all types of leather pouches during the middle ages and before. The chancellor of the exchequer traditionally carried his papers in a budget and you can see how this developed to become the modern meaning in our world.

"Before you go back to your world you must find a safe hiding place for it." Wodewose gently touched the budget with his staff. "When you return here the first thing you must do is pick it up. You may find it will be filled with water. If you are here for any length of time you will need to drink. There are no, what you call taps in our world, only springs, streams and rivers that feed our ponds and lakes. The guardians of these waters are easily influenced and if they side with the Darkness they could easily try and poison you. The water in the budget will be pure and blessed by Leht, it will give you strength." Charlotte nodded.

"Ok" she said again. Woodwose continued.

"Whilst in our world, Alasdair and Cathasach will be your guardians." This confirmed what Leht had already told her. "The squirrel is our messenger. Only the squirrel can pass with relative ease between our two worlds, it uses the roots of the ash tree for it is the only tree which has its roots on both sides." Charlotte wanted to ask a question but Woodwose didn't give her time. He carried on with what looked to be a carefully prepared message. "If, when in your world you wish to get a message to us, you must tell the robin." Charlotte assumed he meant the robin always in their garden. "He will store the message and pass it to the squirrel who will pass it on to us. You must be our eyes in your world for we only have limited vision on what happens on the other side and the Darkness is well aware of this. Sadly, the only way we can communicate with you, is by you coming to our world. That makes it dangerous for you I know but there is no other way, we are all sorry." Charlotte wondered what all these dangers could be. She kept being told there were dangers but so far she had seen little or no evidence of any. Having said that, there was she had to admit a distinct undercurrent of danger or a threat that she had felt since first setting eyes on the magpie. A feeling she couldn't explain, it was simply there. Wodewose's gruff voice once more demanded her attention.

"One last thing young Charlotte." Wodewose was now standing upright, his staff under his arm whilst he brushed several leaves from his shaggy coat. "When we call you, you must come quickly. There have always been stories about how a human one day will be able to transcend the two worlds but we never thought it possible without the knowledge of Orme until now. However the window allowing you to pass is very short and you do not want to miss the opening or worse still get caught in between our two worlds. You must be ready at all times. Do you understand?" Wodewose had finished brushing his shaggy coat and was standing, staring at Charlotte searching for confirmation that she understood the importance of what he had just told her. Charlotte nodded again.

"Yes" she replied. "I understand." Though she wasn't at all sure that she did. Wodewose looked satisfied and for her that was all that was important for now.

"Now," he said looking pleased. "I must get some sleep, I have time for just one question. I know you must have many but for now just one please. I'm sorry." The shaggy beast was right Charlotte thought. She had hundreds of questions. Why couldn't she ask more, she was always being told there wasn't time. She was considering her one question when Woodwose spoke again.

"Quick," he urged her, "for I must go." Charlotte saw that he was looking nervously to where Cathasach had last been standing. His partner Alasdair still looked tense and remained motionless staring deep into the wood. Charlotte felt Woderose nudge her.

"Quick one question," he repeated. Charlotte thought on her feet, she was just about to re-enter her world and with this in mind asked.

"Wodewose there is a magpie that seems to be watching me, it scares me." It was a statement really but Wodewose understood the question within. He looked at her, his eyes sad.

"So I've heard," he said softly. He took her hand. "Come with me," he pulled her gently as he said this and Charlotte started to resist. "It's ok," and smiled in an attempt to reassure her. "Just to my home." Wodewose gestured towards the huge, gnarled trunk of the old oak tree. It was only around 20 metres away and she would still be in sight of Alasdair and so let Wodewose lead her. With fear threatening to rise Charlotte longed for a car to come along the narrow woodland road but knew in this world that none would.

On reaching the tree Wodewose visibly relaxed. Standing beside it Charlotte realised just how thick the tree's bark was, it's surface was literally chiselled with time. The first rays of the rising sun had started to fall on the grandiose trunk highlighting the outer bark and accentuating the grooves. Charlotte had to admit Wodewose had a magnificent home. The shaggy beast rested both his large hands on Charlotte's shoulders, his back leaning against his home.

"The magpie, is it just the one?" Charlotte nodded

"Then it can't hurt you," he said gently. "It will try and unnerve you, intimidate you, frighten you even but don't let it. It can only act as eyes for the Darkness but if the Darkness feels your fear it will use it against you and eventually control you. Just as it did last time." Charlotte saw that Wodewose instantly regretted his last remark and was quick to move on before she could ask a return question.

"We have a saying, I shall repeat it to you." Wodewose took a deep breath.

"One means anger,
two brings mirth,
three a wedding,
four a birth,
five is heaven,
six is hell,
seven is the very Devil himself." Wodewose stopped. He looked pleased with himself at remembering the entire verse.

"We have a similar saying in our world." Charlotte remembered Will repeating his version of the rhyme as if it were only a few minutes ago.

"But not the same?" Wodewose asked.

"No."

"What about the seven?" Charlotte felt the giant hands of Wodewose tighten on her shoulders. "What does it tell of the seven?"

"Just that it's a secret never to be told." Charlotte repeated the last line word for word.

"Hmm," Wodewose almost growled. "Little Charlotte," his tone sounded so low he scared her. "If ever it looks as though the magpies in your world are close to gathering as seven, you must get word to us. For if seven gather together it will be too late. There is nothing anyone can do. At least not for your world." Wodewose paused and grabbed Charlotte's shoulders so tightly that his grip started to hurt. "Do you understand?" Charlotte nodded, scared, tears started to roll down her face. Woodwose saw what he had done and quickly released his grip.

"I'm sorry, forgive me young Charlotte, I keep forgetting you're just a child."

"Almost an adult," Charlotte replied with indignation, she was angry with herself for letting Wodewose see her tears.

"You are braver than me little girl, to that I can admit without shame." For the first time Charlotte saw Woodwose grin, large white teeth exposed within his bushy beard. He took her hand once more. "I must go, If ever you lose me in the wood, make your way here and put both your hands on my home." Wodewose let go of her hand and placed both of his on the ancient oak to demonstrate. "If you do this and I am home you will awaken me and if I am distant I shall feel you and come to you with all speed. Is that clear?"

"Yes." Charlotte replied "and thank you." Still angry at herself, with her sleeve she hurriedly wiped the tears from her cheeks.

"Now, I must say goodbye until next time. Alasdair and Cathasach will see you safely back to where the squirrel can take you home." With that Wodewose stood with his right hand side leaning against the ancient oak's gnarled trunk before literally stepping sideways into the tree. In a matter of seconds he was gone.

For a moment Charlotte stood rooted to the spot marvelling again at what she had just witnessed. She felt where Wodewose had disappeared into the tree, it was solid. She had the strangest of feelings that somewhere she had seen Wodewose before but knew that this simply couldn't be. All the same the feeling kept nagging at her, it was most odd. She remembered the others and in a panic turned, fearing they may no longer be there. To her relief they were and Cathasach she saw was returning at pace. As he drew near Charlotte could see with horror that Cathasach's face was stained red with blood and blood dripped from his mouth, his expression fierce. On arriving he turned immediately and Alasdair leapt forward. The squirrel ran down from its place in the tree and scurried along the ground ahead. The two hounds started to move and Charlotte without thinking realised she was to follow and quickly. So fast did they travel that she found herself almost sliding all the way to the bottom of the deeply wooded scarp. By the time they'd reached the first houses of Aldbury she was bleeding in several places from additional scratches caused by her hurried descent. On reaching the road Alasdair and Cathasach didn't pause but raced ahead making for the familiar sight of the church. The squirrel and Charlotte followed some way behind, the squirrel constantly turning in circles making sure Charlotte was still following. When she and the squirrel reached the front door of the church they found Alasdair and Cathasach waiting for them. They were waiting, sitting bolt upright either side of the slab. The squirrel didn't hesitate, it dived head first into the ground and Charlotte leapt onto the slab only a split second after. The familiar sensation of being pulled under was immediate. Blackness soon enveloped her, though this time she saw that she was not alone. A short distance away she saw the squirrel. It was floating as she was, though its body was quite motionless and already beginning to rise. She watched as it disappeared through the ceiling above and then Charlotte too found herself starting to rise. In under a minute she was standing in what she knew was her world. It was a shock for everything was dark, it was night and yet she'd just left a place bathed in early morning sunshine. She looked up at the clock on the church tower. It read seven minutes passed midnight. She'd been gone for hours and hours and yet only minutes had passed in her world.

The squirrel, Charlotte saw, was already running down the gravel path to the lych gate. She quickly followed and continued to follow it all the way back to the cottage, never before had she felt so pleased to see her home. The squirrel escorted her all the way to the back door and only when Charlotte had closed the stable door behind her did it turn to leave. Before mounting the stairs Charlotte visited the bathroom, she must look a right mess after her adventures in the wood and was worried about what her parents might ask when they saw her scratches. She peered with heavy eyes in the mirror above the wash basin. To her surprise there wasn't a blemish on her and her clothes were just as they'd been when she'd left the cottage, shortly after midnight. Relieved and too tired to ask how, she quietly mounted the stairs. On the other side of their door she could hear both her parents breathing with the steady regularity of sleep. Even so she took great care in lifting the latch on her door. Her bedroom was just had she'd left it. Gromit she saw with guilt was unceremoniously face down half under the covers. Poor Gromit. Charlotte's eyes were drawn to the picture of the stag still with its terrified expression. Leht had called it a hart, from now on that's what she would call it. After what Leht had told her a wave of sympathy washed over her. Without thinking she went over to the picture and kissed the glass, hoping it would bring comfort in some small way. Once in bed despite her exhaustion she found sleep hard to come by, so many questions filled her head, so many. She wondered if it would be possible to reach the scrolls of light Leht had talked about simply by digging into the ground of Ivinghoe Beacon in this world. Almost certainly not. Who was the artist, the last tenant who had used her bedroom as a studio? Who had painted the magpie and those who she now considered to be her companions, the little robin and the squirrel? Was he involved somehow? Why was she able to transcend into the other world when apparently no one else could? Why the serpent on the clock tower? There were many, many more questions but one, above all others kept nagging at her, what on earth was Orme? Orme whatever it was it seemed to her to be at the centre of all this.

From questions her thoughts turned back to the moment she'd left Wodewose at his home in the ancient oak and his nervous, almost frightened demeanour. Of Cathasach, his fierce expression and the blood dripping from his mouth, what had happened? Shivering she wasn't sure she wanted to know. Charlotte's last thought before sleep finally welcomed her was more of a realisation. She remembered Woodwose giving her the leather bag, the budget as he had called it. In their haste she'd forgotten to hide it as Wodewose had requested and worse still she no longer had it with her, she'd lost it. Her last thoughts before she lost consciousness was where could it be and did it matter.

The robin waited on the sill until Charlotte's eyes were firmly shut then flew back to its nest. The squirrel scurried back to the church where it once again took the dark route back to its world. It too was exhausted. On arrival Alasdair and Cathasach were still waiting. On the step of the church lay a small leather bag, the budget. On seeing it the squirrel passed its head through the strap and proceeded to run down the path towards the pond, dragging the budget behind it. The hounds followed close behind. It took a good half an hour before the squirrel arrived home, escorted all of the way by Alasdair and Cathasach. Home was an oak of moderate age, (so a few hundred years), in a field but only a stone's throw away from the beginning of the wooded scarp. A short way above the ground a small hole pitted the oak's trunk and this led to a larger hollow within. Inside, the floor was lined with last year's leaves, they provided warmth, a soft bed and with their scent memories of last year's feasting. The squirrel with difficulty pulled the budget up the trunk and pushed it through the hole into its home. Before settling down it popped its head outside to thank Alasdair and Cathasach. Satisfied the squirrel was safe the hounds made off into the woods to their own den, though where that is I'm afraid I cannot tell you. Inside the oak, the squirrel curled into a ball and fell into a deep sleep hoping the days to come may prove to be a little easier. In his little heart he knew that almost certainly this wouldn't be the case.

Chapter Ten

The May Fair

The next morning Charlotte woke, again feeling exhausted. Why whenever she returned, she wondered, did everything return to the same state it was in before she departed? On this occasion for example, she'd been scratched to pieces not to mention covered in dirt and dead leaves, and on returning there wasn't a single sign of a scratch, and all of her clothes were spotless. Why didn't the same rule apply to how she felt emotionally, why did she not regenerate mentally? She felt terrible as though she'd not had one minutes sleep. She stored the question away along with all the others, she would ask she decided, next time she was on the other side or whatever it was called. That's another question I will ask she promised herself. The other side must have a name. Two new questions and she already had around a hundred others stored away. "This might take a while" she found herself laughing.

Seeing the time Charlotte with what she felt was an effort that should be rewarded hauled herself out of bed. She went to the window and looked out. As she knew it would be the sky was dark and the garden almost as it had been over a month ago with virtually no new growth. Only the green shoots of the most determined plants were just starting to show. The daffodils like the crocuses before them had seemingly given up. Her eyes turned to the cherry blossom. There was not the slightest sign of blossom and yet the tree by now should have been at its most splendid, radiant with colour. On its usual branch sat the magpie staring in through the window. Remembering what Wodewose had told her, Charlotte raised her hands to each ear stuck out her tongue and blew the biggest raspberry she could. The magpie didn't flinch and kept up its stare. It appeared completely unmoved by her gesture but boy did she feel better for doing it.

At breakfast, in front of her parents Charlotte tried her best to appear as her normal lively self. If it had been a public display she would have won a BAFTA for her performance. But the best acting in the world could not disguise the tired lines in her face. Her parents saw through it, though said nothing, being even better actors they played along. As a consequence Charlotte left for school tired but upbeat. She'd fooled her parents she thought and told the magpie what for. She was not a girl to be messed with. The feeling gave her an inner strength and she welcomed it. Even seeing the magpie waiting for her in the oak tree by the pond didn't intimidate her, she simply ignored it.

School was hard but not as hard as Charlotte thought it would be. The PE lesson in the morning probably helped. An hour of hockey followed by a hot shower did wonders, she felt completely revitalised and the teachers that took Charlotte that day were impressed by her performance and by her participation in class. The conversation on the bus going home was not just about the weather for a change but the upcoming May Fair. The Aldbury May Fair was the village's biggest event of the year and indeed it could be argued one of the biggest in the county. Extremely well organised, it always attracted thousands of visitors and raised valuable funds for the village school. The excited chatter on the bus was who would be doing what at the fair and most importantly who would be crowned May Queen. Charlotte already knew she would be helping her parents with their stand. The vicar had given them a site in the church yard and, as well as a selection of pre prepared French meals, her mother would be cooking Tartiflette, a dish originating from the French Alps.

After alighting from the bus Charlotte as she normally did stopped by the village shop. She opened the door, stopped, stepped back out, closing the door before re-entering. Silence announced her arrival. Ashtynn as usual was standing behind the counter. She gave Charlotte a wide grin on seeing her enter.

"Afternoon French Charlotte, how was school? Have you come for your sherbet dips?"

"School's good" and "yes," Charlotte replied. Then, "Ashtynn, what's happened to the bell?"

Ashtynn gestured for Charlotte to come closer to the counter and leaning over with one hand cupped beside her mouth Ashtynn whispered loudly.

"People started complaining it was too loud, the complaints got so bad my boss decided to take it down. In fact people here are getting so miserable, it's getting me down. I'm thinking of leaving." She emphasised the last few words with great drama, her whisper prolonged and with such gusto that her breath waved several strands of Charlotte's hair. Charlotte in turn looked shocked, Ashtynn was part of her everyday life. What the Queen was to the country Ashtynn was to her, no matter what each day brought Ashtynn would always be there with her cheery greeting. Like the Queen, Ashtynn represented stability in a turbulent world, or in her case worlds. Ashtynn saw Charlotte's shocked expression and immediately felt bad. She leant over and at full stretch patted Charlotte affectionately on the head.

"Don't worry French Charlotte," she said with a tone that was meant to reassure. "I'm only kidding, wild horses wouldn't drag me away." Charlotte looked and was visibly relieved.

"I'll miss the bell," she commented walking off to where she knew she would find the sherbet dips.

"Me too French Charlotte, me too," sighed Ashtynn. "The bell on that door has been here longer than most of the villagers, they have no right to complain."

She had a point Charlotte thought, pleased to find that the sherbet dips were well stocked. She expertly counted the coins in her pocket and picking up three dips took them to the counter. Ashtynn dropped them with exaggerated fashion into a white paper bag and handing them to Charlotte refused the coins in her outstretched hand.

"These are on me French Charlotte," she grinned. "Your smile always cheers me up, even when I'm having a bad day. Three sherbet dips is good value for that, I say."

"Your smile always cheers me up too Ashtynn," replied Charlotte wondering whether to push her luck and grab another three sherbet dips from the counter. She decided against it and opening the door left the shop to the strange sound of silence. Behind the counter Ashtynn was beaming, that was the nicest thing anybody had said to her for weeks. She wouldn't leave if only because of that little French girl.

On arriving home Charlotte's parents were relieved to see their daughter looking so much better. As they'd done quite well with the new Sunday trade, the two had planned to treat themselves to a romantic meal at The Greyhound. After this morning they were worried about leaving Charlotte on her own in the cottage but seeing her now they felt a lot better. Charlotte, her tiredness quickly catching up with her, told them she was fine with her parents going out and fancied an early night anyway. After they'd gone she realised it was the first time since they'd arrived at Aldbury that she'd been left in the cottage for any length of time on her own, certainly not on an evening. With everything that was happening she suddenly found herself feeling a little scared, even a little vulnerable especially with the dark outside. Anyone, she thought, could be outside watching her. Hurriedly she drew all the curtains and after making some hot chocolate decided to go straight to bed. Her parents hadn't yet got around to hanging curtains in her room. Because of the unusual length of the window they'd have to be made up and their finances didn't stretch to doing that for the moment at least. There were far more important things to buy first. Charlotte, as a consequence felt more comfortable without the light and got changed into her pyjamas in the dark. Climbing into bed she was comforted as always by the reassuring presence of Gromit. As Charlotte lay her head on the pillow there came a fluttering sound and outside on the sill she saw the robin. Leaning on one elbow she smiled and gave the robin a little wave. As in reply the robin hopped a couple of times chirped and flew off. That was just the medicine she needed and closing her eyes fell into a deep and much needed sleep.

Nothing happened during the night and Charlotte woke feeling very much refreshed. Once again she blew a loud raspberry at the magpie, an action she'd decided that she'd repeat every morning and laid a gentle kiss on the picture of the white hart another action she swore she'd repeat on a daily basis. At breakfast, her parents purred loudly over the dinner they'd had in the Greyhound the evening before, and seeing their daughter looking so well, all was happiness that morning.

For the next few days life played out as normal. Charlotte's parents were busy with their markets and Charlotte attended school. The dark cloud remained without the slightest sign of moving from its anchorage over the village whilst outside its borders the weather was positively balmy with spring bursting at a gallop. The organisers of the May Fair worried that the dismal village weather may put people off coming and this year's attendance they feared would be well down on previous years. A team of meteorologists from Oxford University were doing tests in the village but so far hadn't been able to find an explanation for the bizarre, localised weather. They'd also conducted tests on the thickening mist covering most of the pitted field behind the church, the site of the old manor and concluded that it was just that, nothing more than mist.

Its presence was very odd as was its denseness but it was nothing more sinister than mist. Their task now was to discover what was causing it. That may prove to be a lot harder.

Every night Charlotte expected to be woken by the robin tapping at her window but each night nothing happened. The robin still greeted her every morning in the garden and the magpie, when she was home, was always sitting in the cherry blossom. Although she didn't like it she'd become used to the bird following her around the village. She found herself worrying more with the lack of contact from the "other side" and kept wondering what was happening. Was "no news, good news" as the proverb claimed or in this case the opposite. Charlotte had a long list of questions she wanted to ask and was worried with each day that went by that one by one she was forgetting them. She didn't want to write them down in case her parents found the list and started asking questions. There was nothing she could do, she'd just have to be patient, she kept telling herself but never felt comfortable with this. With every day that passed memories of her adventures on the "other side" were fading to such an extent that they were almost becoming an irrelevance. Part of the problem was that her memories were so fantastical they were hard to take seriously, especially when the regularity of everyday life in the modern world took charge. Thank goodness for the robin, the magpie and the picture of the white hart and thank goodness for the bizarre village weather. Collectively, as they had done before they focused Charlotte's mind and prevented her from doubting that her nightly adventures had only ever been a dream.

On the bank holiday Monday, the day of the May Fair, the weather remained its dark dismal self but there was a refreshing buzz about the place. Bunting was being hung providing some much needed colour in the absence of the usual colours of spring. Stalls were being erected on the village green, in the churchyard, the school playing grounds and the field where the May Queen was to be crowned. Barbeques were being lit and a hog roast was well on the way, executed by the Greyhound pub. Excited chatter filled the air along with suppressed expectation. Any concerns about the lack of visitors were soon quashed as lines of cards started to snake towards the village, occupants eager not only to enjoy the fair but to experience the weird weather the local media had been reporting on. There might have been over the last few weeks mounting tension within the village, with villagers participating in numerous and pointless arguments but that morning everybody was looking forward to the May Fair. Everyone or nearly everyone agreed it was just what the village needed.

By mid-afternoon, the village was packed. The tea room set up in the village hall was having perhaps its most successful year ever as were many of the stalls outside. The smell of barbecued meat wetted the revellers appetite at every corner and live music helped it must be said by alcohol, prompted many to partake in an impromptu dance. Morris dancers provided a colourful and a more professional show. The atmosphere was one of fun and everybody became a friend with a stranger for the day. The normally tranquil churchyard was a hive of activity with colourful stalls lining the paths and donkey rides for the children.

"This is how it would have been most weekends, years ago." Charlotte's father kept repeating. "The village churchyard was where people came to gather to meet friends and to be with their departed. It was common for people to enjoy a picnic on a loved one's grave. Not like these days."

Nobody was listening to him and there was little time for further contemplation on the past for Charlotte's parents, like everybody else were doing a roaring trade with their French Ready Meals, hand prepared, by Charlotte's mother. The Tartiflette especially was proving to be very popular, with long queues forming. Charlotte was helping on the stand with the promise that when the Tartiflette was sold out she could go and join her friends. Her mother had promised the vicar some Tartiflette and the last portion left was scooped into a take away container for him to enjoy later. Charlotte's last task was to deliver it to the vicar who was busy helping raise money for local charities inside the church. The church, like the rest of the village, was extremely busy and it took a while before she saw him. There he was wearing a fixed smile and leaning against the fine stone screen which surrounds the Pendley Chapel for support. He was doing a superb job, shaking hands with nearly every passer-by and politely answering questions if people had one whilst dutifully thanking everyone for coming. The vicar, almost certainly from the scent of her delivery, immediately spied Charlotte.

"Hello French Charlotte," he beamed, "have you come to rescue me?" and spotting the package in her hands exclaimed. "Is that my dinner?"

"Yes," Charlotte smiled back. "My mother said to tell you that she's given you an extra-large portion and she won't accept any money."

"I take back everything I ever said against the French," The vicar joked. "Come and join me for a minute, I need a rest from talking with all these strangers." Taking his evening meal from Charlotte's outstretched hands he looked around his church and at the slowly moving line of people. Turning, he rested his arms on the stone screen to face inside the Pendley Chapel indicating for Charlotte to stand beside him. "Between you and me French Charlotte, I'll be glad when they've all gone home, but don't tell anyone I said that." He winked at her.

"I won't," promised Charlotte faithfully trying not to laugh.

"Promise?" he repeated." Charlotte nodded vigorously.

"Promise," she promised again.

They stood together, enjoying a moment's break, Charlotte resting her hands on the screen gazing casually between the stone pillars into the chapel.

"So how are you all settling into the village?" The vicar asked, his interest genuine. "And how are you finding school?"

Charlotte didn't hear him, for something else had caught her attention. Inside the chapel was Wodewose, not the shaggy, living ,breathing, slightly nervous Wodewose but a stone effigy of him. Charlotte closed and opened her eyes. It was definitely him, a smaller version of him but definitely him. He lay at the feet of a man or rather a knight dressed in armour and beside him lay a lady, presumably his wife wearing medieval dress. They both had their hands clasped in prayer. All three were lying on an intricately carved stone chest. Charlotte had seen the tomb before when visiting with her father and at the time hadn't given it much notice. She now realised why she thought she'd seen Wodewose before, it was here in the Pendley Chapel of Aldbury church. The vicar waiting for an answer to his question saw that Charlotte was distracted.

"So what's caught your eye then, French Charlotte?" he asked, unoffended by her distraction. He was always pleased when a younger person showed an interest in his church.

"What's that Vicar?" Charlotte asked pointing at the stone effigy of Wodewose.

"That," said the vicar, doubly pleased at her interest. "Is the Wild Man of the woods, although he has other names too, Woodwose or Wodewose I think." So the effigy was of her Wodewose, Charlotte struggled to contain her excitement. Wild man of the woods the vicar had said, although he looked a touch on the wild side, in the short time that she'd known him she'd hardly describe Wodewose as wild. Unkempt maybe but certainly not wild.

"And who are they?" she asked, meaning the couple laying on the stone chest. She knew her father had told her but at the time it had been just another tomb. She wished now she'd paid more attention.

"That," the vicar answered. "Is Sir Robert Whittingham. He was killed at the Battle of Tewkesbury in 1471. He'd answered the same question at least a hundred times that day and was thoroughly bored with it but now he found, not so with French Charlotte. "It was one of the battles during the War of the Roses, but of course being French you won't know anything about that." The vicar nudged her playfully.

"I do." Charlotte replied a little indignantly. "My dad told me."

"Good for him," came the vicars reply, grinning. "And beside him," he gestured at the woman lying in prayer. "Is his wife, here take a closer look." The vicar unhooked a short rope and signalled for Charlotte to enter the chapel. Charlotte thanked him and stepped respectfully round the tomb.

"What's the animal at her feet?" For at the feet of the woman lay a dog-like creature.

"I'm not sure, "admitted the vicar. "Some people say it's a deer but I think it looks more like a dog, a greyhound perhaps." Charlotte remained silent and the vicar went on. "Do you know, the whole thing," he spread his arms indicating he meant all of the Pendley Chapel. "Was moved here from Ashridge House in 1575, after the monastery was disbanded. Must have been a hell of a job and cost an absolute fortune." Charlotte was just about to ask another question. She wanted to know why the effigy of Wodewose was there when they were interrupted by a concerned looking lady dressed all in green. Charlotte knew her as a church volunteer who often did the flowers and she had to admit the church looked quite magnificent with her creations today.

"Vicar," she panted frantically touching his arm. She saw Charlotte and apologised. "Sorry to interrupt but we let an elderly lady who was desperate for the toilet use yours and now she can't get out."

"Ok." The vicar sighed, pulling a face meant only for Charlotte to see. I'm coming." The lady dressed only in green, obviously relieved scurried off. The vicar looked at Charlotte. "Bloody hell," he said, under his breath but loud enough for her to hear. “It'll be a miracle if I can get that door open, I hope the Lord's watching.” Charlotte suppressed a laugh. “We must continue our little chat another time, French Charlotte.” He patted her head. “Oh and thank your mother will you. I'm looking forward to this.” He held up his dinner and with that he disappeared in the direction of his toilet to perform a modern day miracle.

Charlotte turned back to the stone effigy of Wodewose. It was a magnificent carving she thought and apart from his size, a spitting image. Surely she found herself thinking, whoever carved the effigy must have done it from viewing a live model, it was accurate in every detail. So many questions she thought again. Where was Wodewose now and what was he doing, was he ok? She realised with a touch of sadness that she missed her shaggy friend of only a few hours. A shout interrupted her thoughts. It was Caroline.

“French Charlotte we've been looking for you everywhere, they're about to crown the May Queen. Come on.” Caroline grabbed hold of Charlotte's hand and pulled. I hope you're ok my friend, Charlotte whispered under her breath as she let Caroline lead her out of the church. Her message of course was for Wodewose.

Outside the fair was in full swing and by the smiles on people's faces, for a day at least the gloom was well and truly defeated. Rather than battle through the crowds Caroline declared they'd take a shortcut through the field behind the church, the field covered by the mysterious thick mist. The mist had become an unexpected May Fair attraction and hordes of children along with some parents were running screaming with excitement within its midst. Other parents were standing outside the mist waiting patiently for their children to come out. As part of the short-cut, Caroline led Charlotte straight through the centre of it. Deep inside the experience for both of them was surreal. The mist was so thick that others in the mist were, unless you were almost side by side, simply moving shadows. More than once a child, in their excitement would run blindly into them, on one occasion with such force that they were both sent flying. Charlotte was quietly pleased when they emerged from the other side. She had found the mist quite unnerving not to mention cold, she was shivering even though she was wearing a coat.

The first sign that something was seriously wrong was when a young mother having lost her child came to the information stand on the village green asking for an announcement to be made over the p.a. system. This was a fairly common occurrence at the fair. Almost every year children tended to get separated from their parents in the throngs of people, and announcements asking for the child or the parents to come to the information stand where the other would be waiting was standard procedure. Normally after a matter of minutes families would be reunited but on this occasion it didn't turn out that way. Several announcements were made and there was still no sign of the child, a young boy who had not long celebrated his 10th birthday . Apparently he had gone into the mist like so many other children and simply never came out. The little boy's father was still in the mist trying to find him. The mother was worried that her son with the mist being so thick may have become disoriented and come out somewhere different to where her and her husband had been waiting and wandered off. The mother, starting to become hysterical, was taken into a room in the village hall and given a cup of tea. A search party of five was quickly put together and entered the mist to work with the father in trying to find the boy. Announcements asking the lost boy to come to the information stand were broadcast with more frequency and descriptions of the lost child were broadcast also.

Around half an hour later a second mother appeared at the information stand with almost exactly the same story. She too had let her son, who was twelve play in the mist while she waited outside. The difference was this time, her son had a friend with him. They had both entered the mist together but only his friend had come out. His friend explained they had got separated whilst playing in the mist. For a while they had voice contact then they lost that too. He carried on calling, but nothing. His friend thinking he must have got out, did the same only to find his friend's mother standing alone. They kept calling for around fifteen minutes and after, like the first mother assumed her son had exited at a different point and wandered off on his own to enjoy the fair. His friend insisted that he simply wouldn't have done that. Not on his own, he would have taken him with him. The mother had to agree and so came looking for help. She apologised for the trouble she was causing and said she felt silly asking for help to find a twelve year old but didn't know what else to do. She would whack him when she found him she promised. The volunteers manning the information post thought it best not to tell the second mother that they already had a missing child in the mist. They were growing concerned and via a walkie talkie contacted the woman organising the first search to inform her that a second child was missing and under almost identical circumstances. A decision was made quickly to clear the mist covered field and check on everybody who came out. This took around 20 minutes and after the task was complete the field was taped off. There was no sign of the two missing boys.

With the fair slowly winding down and still with no sign of the missing boys, a decision was made to call the police. With surprising speed two fresh faced constables arrived in a marked police car. They listened intently to the story before talking to the two mothers and asking if they had photos. Both did, on their phones and with the help of a local resident the photos were printed off. Volunteers were then sent to the car park exits with the photos to check with each driver whether they'd seen the two boys or worse still to check that the boys hadn't been abducted and were forcibly in the back of a car or van. The situation was thought to be serious enough to warrant calling for back up and within just a few more minutes another two police officers turned up along with a PCSO to help the volunteers with the task of checking the car parks.

The original two police officers asked for more volunteers, of which there were no shortage. They quickly organised the second set of volunteers to form a line across the mist blanketed field and linking arms the line of volunteers took slow steps crossing through its midst. The thought process was that both boys may have tripped and injured themselves in the mist and were still laying on the ground unable to crawl out. It was a slow process and many volunteers felt a deep unease touching on fear as they crossed through the mist with at times almost zero visibility. Those finding themselves in the centre of the mist pulled tightly on their neighbours arms for reassurance. Reassurance not from concern that if the chain were broken they may pass the boys without noticing but from their own fear. A fear for which there was no logical reason but one that most certainly felt real. Each volunteer in the chain who experienced fear kept quiet, thinking it was only they that felt that way and not wanting to appear cowardly. If they'd asked their neighbour they would have discovered that they too experienced a similar dread. Everyone in the living chain touched by the mist felt some level of fear. For those near the centre it was much worse and for some almost unbearable. When the line had crossed the field without success the officers asked the volunteers to do the same again in reverse, just to be sure. Although many were reluctant all agreed and for a second time a human chain traversed the mist. Again nothing or rather no one was found and the officers were reasonably sure the two boys were no longer in the mist. Just to be certain, a dog handler was called in but with no more success. However the dog had shown some rather bizarre behaviour. His handler had an awful effort to persuade his dog to enter the mist. The Alsatian constantly whined and pawed the ground, refusing to move, behaviour that his handler had never experienced before. And when his dog had eventually entered the mist it howled continuously sending a chill through everybody who was near enough to hear it. The conclusion was that something dreadful had happened which the dog had picked up on but whatever it was the two boys were definitely no longer in the field.

By early evening all of the general public had left and the only people remaining were the volunteers tasked with clearing up the mess left behind. There was still no sign of the boys and by eight pm they were declared as officially missing. The mist blanketed field was cordoned off with police tape and a constable left guarding it. Both families of the missing were escorted home by specially trained personnel. The residents of the embittered village remained in shock, after what had started out as such a promising day too. Behind every door people were questioning what on earth was happening to their village, why their village. What had they done to deserve such misery. What they couldn't know was, the answer to their question went back many hundreds of years. To a time when their village was in it's infancy, when a resident had decided to hold hands with the Devil.

The talk that evening between Charlotte's parents should have been about a successful day. Instead like every other household in the village the talk was about the disappearance of the two boys and how awful it was. Everyone felt terrible for the parents and those families with young children vowed not to let them out of their sight. First the mystery of the disappearing cats, the odd missing dog and now much more serious the mysterious disappearance of two boys. Many were asking if the three were somehow linked, as were Charlotte's parents. The police although they kept it quiet were thinking along the same lines, that the three may well be linked. It was well known from cases worldwide, that many serial killers or murderers started their inhuman behaviour by killing animals. They hoped upon hope that this wasn't the case at Aldbury.

Charlotte went up to her room, she, like everybody else was in a deep state of shock. She had gone through that mist with her friend, Caroline and like many of the adults, felt the fear that they'd experienced when passing through it. Caroline kept on and on after it was commonly known the two boys were missing that the kidnapper in the mist, for that was by far the most popular theory, could have taken her and Charlotte. Charlotte for her part, was questioning the day's events and beginning to form her own theory, it was one very different to everybody else's and knew if she expressed it, she would be laughed at. She remembered what Leht had told her about the Darkness and how it manipulated people through fear. She thought about the fear she'd felt when passing through the mist. She'd experienced fear before of course, we all have, but the fear she'd experienced in the mist was unlike any she'd felt before. It hadn't produced the adrenaline that fear normally induces. The fear she'd felt in the mist was a cold fear that crept up on and tried to take over every nerve in her body. It came on slowly until it almost suffocated every other human emotion. With no adrenaline, there were no emotions, no muscles primed to fight it, she'd just felt helpless, her body yielding to the power of fear. The feeling only left her when with immense relief she'd emerged with Caroline on the other side. She dreaded to think what would have happened if she'd been on her own in the mist for any length of time, if she hadn't been holding Caroline's hand.

Remembering what Wodewose had told her, Charlotte looked out to the garden searching for the robin. After only a few seconds she spotted it sitting in the apple tree. Even though it was getting dark she noticed, as well as her robin, the magpie was still sitting in its usual spot in the cherry blossom. At first on opening the window she feared the bird might fly at her. It didn't, thank God, the magpie just sat there completely motionless, staring. It remained so still that it would have been easy to assume the bird wasn't real. After what had happened earlier in the day, Charlotte suddenly felt a deep hatred for the bird. Almost as quickly her feeling was replaced by one of guilt. The magpie may have had nothing to do with what had happened to the boys. She scolded herself, she may not like the bird, but it was wrong to feel such ill towards it without having any proof.

Charlotte had never opened her window before. As the window was taller than her and almost level with the floor, her parents were scared that she might fall out and badly injure herself or worse. Thus they had strictly forbidden her to do so. Charlotte never normally disobeyed her parents but today after what had happened she felt that her action was justified. They would think so too, she told herself if they knew the truth. Whatever the truth was. Opening the window turned out to be easier said than done. It evidently hadn't been opened since it was last painted and she was surprised just how strong paint could be. For several minutes, the window resisted all attempts to open it, the last coat of paint stubbornly holding on as though a life depended on it. Eventually after a sustained push with her right shoulder the window gave a sudden shudder before swinging open and the robin having never seen the window opened before was quick to react. It flew to the sill. The magpie to her relief remained motionless in the cherry blossom. Staring at it, ready to close the window in case it attacked, for the first time Charlotte detected something odd about the bird. It's behaviour had always been odd but now she noticed something else. If she didn't know better the bird looked to be in some sort of trance.

The sill on which the robin perched was almost level with Charlotte's feet and she had to kneel to bring her face close to the tiny bird. All the time she expected the robin to fly off but it didn't, it just sat there evidently unafraid. Despite all the strange things that had happened over the past few weeks, Charlotte found herself feeling distinctly odd talking to a robin. From kneeling she lay on the floor and stretched out of the window peering left and right ensuring nobody could see what she was doing. Satisfied no one was watching her first words were.

"I can't believe I'm talking to a robin." The robin made no sort of reply and no sort of acknowledgment if it understood her, not even by cocking its head. It simply remained statue-still though a sense, perhaps her seventh sense again, told Charlotte it was listening intently. "I want you to pass this on," and she began recounting the day's events along with the irrational fear she'd experienced in the mist. The robin never moved, though the more she passed on, the more she became convinced the robin really was listening and she wasn't simply wasting her time. When she had finished the robin remained on the sill until Charlotte closed the window after which it flew back to the pagoda. At almost the same time the magpie, with a noisy launch left the cherry blossom disappearing into the cheerless gloom that always remained, whether it be dusk, night, morning or day. Seconds after closing the window a voice called up the stairs. It was her mother.

"Charlotte, who are you talking to?" She had to think on her feet.

"Nobody, just the night sky." It was a stupid answer and so stupid it was probably the reason why her mother accepted it.

"Oh ok," came her mother's reply as though such a conversation were perfectly normal.

After what had happened that day and after her message to the robin, Charlotte was convinced that she'd be woken in the night and taken to the other side. She remembered what Wodewose had told her about how important it was to always be prepared and before she retired for the night she laid out her clothes in readiness and under her bed covers wore her trousers and socks. She was prepped for a fast departure. Exhausted from the day's events it was only minutes before Charlotte's eyes closed and sleep welcomed her. The little robin watched as sleep took hold of the little girl and satisfied, flew to its nest at the base of the pagoda. Normally it would settle down for the night but not that night. Silently it waited, alert to every sound and movement.

Just after midnight a squirrel arrived in the garden. On this occasion it passed the back door running to the pagoda where the robin was waiting. The two remained together for only a few minutes before the squirrel left, returning quickly to the church where on the clock tower a writhing serpent rested on XIII. There was no tap on the window that night and Charlotte, in a deep sleep remained completely unaware of the squirrel's visit. She awoke the next morning feeling a little disappointed that her sleep hadn't been interrupted. Climbing out of bed she, as was her ritual, looked out of the window at the garden and saw that the magpie was already there, sitting in the cherry blossom. Movement caught her eye, it was of course the robin hopping and skipping down the fence. Watching it she hoped that relaying her message hadn't been a complete waste of time. She still found it hard to believe that she had spent several minutes having a conversation with a small bird. Perhaps conversation was the wrong word for it had been strictly one sided. She watched the robin for a couple of minutes before kissing the picture of the white hart, another morning ritual. Every morning she woke hoping to find the hart smiling and facing east, looking out of the long sash window, but she was always left disappointed. It was the same again that morning. With a rather defeatist sigh she got dressed and descended the stairs to the kitchen from where there rose a smell of freshly baked croissants.

The morning bus for school was almost empty, parents preferring to drive their children instead. All the local radio stations and television were covering the story of the missing boys. More than one station was linking the mystery of the disappearing cats and dogs to the tragic disappearance of the two children. Nearly all announced that one mustn't jump to conclusions at this early stage and then went on to do exactly that. Most supposed that the boys had been kidnapped and more than likely by the same person responsible for the disappearance of so many cats. The history of many infamous serial killers who started by killing animals was rolled out by much of the media and several authors grateful for a chance to publicise their often failing publications were very willing to be interviewed. Charlotte listened to the news over breakfast, they're all wrong she kept saying to herself, they're all wrong.

The police were much in evidence in the village that day. Another search was made of the mist in the field and wider searches were started using dogs in the surrounding countryside. Within the village itself the police started making house to house enquiries. Missing posters asking for information with photos of the two boys were posted everywhere and often over the weathered remains of posters asking for information on missing cats.

The following day the story was national news. The national media had been keeping an eye on Aldbury and it's unusual micro climate for some time, waiting to run with the story on a quiet news day. So far none had but the disappearance of two boys changed all that and the village became the centre of what most residents agreed was unwanted but necessary national attention. Everybody wanted the two boys found, and quickly. More importantly everybody wanted them to be found safe and sound. If the media could help do this then it was worth the intrusion.

Sadly, there wasn't to be an early conclusion to the mystery and the media quickly, too quickly for some moved on to other, more current stories. The police although working hard behind the scenes withdrew their physical presence in the village and by the weekend everything, or at least on the surface, appeared to have returned to normal. Even the police tape around the field had been taken away by the weekend though after protests from several of the villagers the parish council erected their own protection using bright yellow tape with the footpath through the field being temporarily closed. Young children were forbidden to go anywhere near the field by their parents though with elder children and especially teenagers the field and the mist, perhaps rather predictably became something of a dare.

It wasn't until the weekend that Charlotte was awoken in the night by a sharp tapping on the long sash window.

Chapter Eleven

Sir Guy De Gravade And The Hidden Gateway

The sudden noise woke Charlotte from a deep and dream free slumber. At first she wondered where she was, disorientated she needed time and time was the one luxury Charlotte didn't have. The relentless tapping soon had the desired effect and almost robotically, she got dressed and made her way quietly down the stairs. Outside on the brick path the squirrel was waiting and Charlotte, as was becoming the norm, followed it. After passing in front of the village shop and the village hall she was just about to follow the squirrel across the road to join the gravel path in the church yard when the sound of a car engine came from the direction of Tring. Seconds later headlights lit up the road in front of her and caught in two minds, Charlotte resorted to instinct throwing herself behind a hedge bordering a private garden to her left. Quite unintentionally she found herself laying in a wide flower bed and immediately started searching for the best words to use in an apology for any damage she had done. The car passed almost at a crawl and Charlotte held her breath praying the occupants hadn't seen her. On the other side of the road she could see the squirrel going frantic, and she remembered Wodewose's warning, there was only a very short window in which she could follow the squirrel to the other side. Crucial seconds were being lost and the car, frustratingly, was driving so slowly she feared it was about to stop. Charlotte found herself counting every second and she thanked God for the cold feel of the bare earth beneath her, it was the only thing that was keeping her cool, preventing her from panicking. Never before had she needed a cool head as she did at that moment. After what felt like an age she decided she had no other option but to edge out onto the road, she simply had to take the risk, if she didn't she would run out of time. On breaking cover Charlotte immediately saw why the car was traveling so slowly, it was a police patrol car. After the disappearance of the two boys police had stepped up patrols through the village. On the gravel path opposite Charlotte could see the squirrel feverishly running up and down panic beginning to set in. Weighing up her options she decided she had to take a chance and with the police car only metres away made a dash across the road behind it praying hard that they wouldn't catch sight of her in the car mirror. Her prayer on this occasion fell on deaf ears. As she dashed across the road she heard the car start to reverse. The squirrel some way ahead dived into the ground and was quickly swallowed up. Charlotte ran as fast as she could up the gravel path all thoughts of stealth long gone. She leapt onto the stone slab just as the serpent hands on the clock tower started to fade. Slowly, much more slowly than before she felt herself being pulled underground. As her eyes reached ground level she saw the shiny tough black shoes of two police officers starting to stomp up the gravel path, a second later everything went black. Never before had she welcomed the dark as much as she did at that moment.

The two officers after running up the gravel path came to a halt in front of the church door. They had both seen a shadowy figure in their mirror running across the road behind their car. The figure looked as though it might have been a child and both officers hoped beyond hope that it was one of the missing boys. Reversing quickly they had seen whoever it was run up the gravel path to the church door. Now they were there, whoever they had seen seemed to have vanished into thin air. The younger officer tried the church door. As you would expect for the time of night it was locked. He shook it in frustration and looked at his colleague, an officer with a good 20 more years' experience. Assuming the figure had been a boy the officer gestured wildly.

"Where did he disappear to?"

The older officer shrugged his shoulders. He looked around at the hushed churchyard, whoever they'd seen could easily be hiding behind one of the many tombstones. He felt a shiver run up his spine, even with all his many years' experience and much of that not pretty, he wasn't enjoying the ghostly atmosphere of a churchyard at night. After a short discussion they decided that it would be better to search the churchyard together and by the light from their torches they started combing the ground, tomb by tomb stone by stone. As the search progressed both officers failed to suppress their inbuilt fear of the unnatural and as each minute passed their imaginations started to get the better of them. Every shadow became a possible threat and every sound no matter how innocent sounded as though it came from the grave. Their experience got worse as they moved around to the back or north of the church and within touching distance of the mysterious mist in the adjacent field. Both officers had the strangest feeling that they could see dark figures moving deep within the mist. Was it possible that what they were seeing were the two missing boys, could the two boys even with the many searches still be in the mist? What they were seeing surely was no more than creations of their imagination brought on by a self-induced fear of the unknown. What their minds suspected may be there, even if it wasn't. Neither wanted to investigate the shadows in the mist and in the end, the elder officer who was in charge, had had enough. Speaking his mind.

"It must be our imagination, there's no one here. Come on we'd best be off." He wiped his brow as he spoke, for some reason he was perspiring heavily.

The younger officer needed no more encouragement and at a pace both officers returned to their waiting car, parked just in front of the lych gate. Once both doors were closed the officers relaxed. Protected by the metal shell of their car they immediately felt safe and looking at each other simultaneously broke into laughter, both loudly mocking their childish fear. To anyone watching their laughter may come across as carefree but if both officers were honest, their laughter was not the product of true mirth but derived from a deep sense of relief. As they'd circled the church and came close to the mist they'd both experienced a fear like nothing either had experienced before. A fear so cutting, reaching so deep inside that the experience would haunt both of them for the rest of their living days, forcing one into early retirement. Both would meet an early and unexplained end.

Charlotte after welcoming the surrounding darkness was now starting to worry. In the past, straight after descending into the blackness she would start to rise again but this time she hardly moved. She seemed to be suspended in nothing. She could breathe, she could see, not that there was anything to see except blackness, but that was all. Try as hard as she might she couldn't move. An invisible force was preventing her from doing so. Her complete inability to do anything about her predicament, was understandably beginning to scare her. She was just on the verge of panic, a panic where the ability to scream had been disabled, when she felt her body slowly starting to rise although at a snail's pace. It was with an indescribable sense of relief when she found herself standing on what she knew to be the other side. The squirrel as she expected was waiting for her. Scurrying up and down along the path to the pond it looked to be on the verge of having a heart attack and if ever a squirrel could look physically relieved then this one did. Charlotte realised that whatever had just happened, judging by the squirrel's reaction she'd had a very lucky escape, from what though she wasn't sure. She just knew she'd been lucky, very, very lucky and she shivered at her near escape from the unknown. Never again would she take a risk with the passage to, to where? She still didn't know where she was, was called. If it had a name at all.

Recovering quickly the squirrel ran down the path to the village pond and Charlotte followed wishing her legs didn't feel so weak. Waiting for them at the pond were the two hounds, Alasdair and Cathasach. It might have been her imagination but Charlotte felt they too looked very relieved to see her. Without hesitation the hounds took off along the road towards Ivinghoe with Charlotte and the squirrel following behind. On the two previous occasions when the hounds had led they'd hardly stopped, even for a second and normally only because the little human child needed to take a breather but tonight the two were being much more cautious. Their gait was steady, much slower and once or twice they slowed to such a degree that they almost came to a complete stop. When this happened, the hounds appeared to be checking their surroundings, their noses raised to the night sky, sniffing for a scent that didn't belong . Much had changed since her last visit Charlotte thought, she could feel a tension in the air that hadn't been there before. Tension or was it fear? The two were so closely connected.

They left the road at the break in the wall where Charlotte had originally met Alasdair and Cathasach. It took only a couple of minutes to leave the cover of the small wood and they quickly covered open ground before entering more tree cover in the form of Howlet's Wood. From there they kept to the edge of the wood skirting Aldbury Nowers before starting to climb. As they did so Charlotte could see the dark shadow of what looked like a man standing directly ahead of them. As they approached the figure Alasdair and Cathasach separated, taking a much wider girth. Charlotte wondered if she should feel afraid of the figure they were approaching but the two hounds rather than looking tense had in the last couple of minutes visibly relaxed. The squirrel too she saw had become a lot less skittish. As they approached the figure

Charlotte recognised, partly obscured by trees, the two bronze age burial mounds. The mounds that Alasdair and Cathasach had mounted when they'd journeyed last to Ivinghoe Beacon to witness the tribulations of the white hart. Just as then the two hounds mounted the tumuli and remained on each acting sentinel. The squirrel continued ahead and Charlotte not sure what was expected of her followed. Within seconds she recognised the figure before them and could not help a broad smile working her face as the unmistakable figure of Wodewose came into view.

Standing upright, silhouetted by the moonlight with his knobbled staff in his right hand, one end resting firmly on the ground and with the two hounds resplendent in their gold collars, standing guard albeit at some distance, Charlotte thought Wodewose looked almost God-like. The next moment he scratched his shaggy belly and the image was gone, Wodewose had a lot to learn if ever he wanted to become a God.

"Hello little Charlotte," Wodewose greeted her in his gruff voice. "Is that what they call you where you come from, Little Charlotte? For you are little."

Charlotte smiled, the way he phrased his question was almost childlike, completely different to the way he'd spoken last time. Had last time been with Leht's influence, after all it was her gift that allowed Wodewose to communicate with her? Had some of her influence worn off, or on the last occasion had it been Leht using Wodewose as a mouthpiece. Here and now she considered, was the real Wodewose speaking.

"Actually they call me French Charlotte," Charlotte replied without thinking and promptly regretting it.

"Then that's what I shall call you," Wodewose reflected, scratching his leg. "French Charlotte," he repeated slowly, "French Charlotte." He stood silent for a minute looking down at Charlotte, his eyes inquisitive. "What does French mean?"

"It's where I come from," Charlotte answered. "I originally come from France." Wodewose looked even more puzzled. Scratching the back of his head he asked.

"France? Then why not France Charlotte?" Charlotte was just trying to decide how best to answer this when Wodewose came to her rescue.

"If you come from France" he said defiantly. "You should be called France Charlotte, I shall call you France Charlotte." He patted Charlotte firmly on her head, pleased at his decision.

"Ok," Charlotte rubbed her head, Wodewose may have soft hands but he was strong. "You can call me France Charlotte." She even quite liked the name, the innocence of it. Charlotte then remembered one of her many questions. "Wodewose, what do you call this place, the land where you all live. Where we are now." Wodewose looked surprised at her question.

"I thought everyone knew that. It's called Otherworld, we live in Otherworld, you're in Otherworld"

What a perfect name Charlotte thought, so very appropriate. She then remembered something else.

"Wodewose," she asked again. "In our world, in the village where I live now, there's an effigy, a statue of you, at least it looks like you, in our, in our village church."

"That is me." There was definite pride in the way Wodewose answered. Charlotte was stunned, not sure how to respond. After a little thought she followed up with another question.

"But that effigy of you is close to 700 years old, how old are you Wodewose?" Wodewose looked thoughtful, he stopped scratching.

"Don't know," he said eventually. "I was born with the wood."

Charlotte wasn't sure what he meant by this and was just about to seek an explanation when she realised the squirrel was no longer with them. All questions over Wodewose's age were immediately forgotten. She quickly checked to see if Alasdair and Cathasach were still in position on their respective mounds, they were. Both were sat bolt upright sniffing at the scents carried on the night air. Charlotte let out a short sigh of relief.

"Where's the squirrel?" she asked Wodewose, still looking around her.

"Gone to get Leht," came a characteristically simple reply from the shaggy beast.

Wodewose never gave much way, Charlotte thought and then again remembered what he had told her. Speaking her language was a temporary gift bestowed upon him by Leht. He had admitted to her that even with his new gift he found talking a little awkward. She would have to show a little more patience. Just as she was forming her next question there was a rustle of leaves and up the hill came the squirrel and dragging behind it the budget. Charlotte had forgotten all about the small leather bag or budget as Wodewose called it and immediately felt a mix of relief along with guilt for losing it in the first place.

On seeing the squirrel Woodwose dropped to his knees and reaching deep inside a rabbit hole pulled out what was a largish square shaped white stone. The square was not the stone's natural shape and it had obviously been carved at some point. Charlotte also recognised that whatever Wodewose was holding had not been carved from local stone. The hill where they were gathered was of chalk and flint as was nearly all the local geology and this particular stone was neither. Oblivious of Charlotte's silent observation Wodewose placed the stone carefully on the ground and after blowing on it proceeded to clean one of the sides with some dead leaves. When he had finished Charlotte could see that a small indentation had been chiselled into the stone on the side Wodewose had been cleaning, creating a small receptacle deep enough to hold around half a cup of water. Wodewose then proceeded to place the stone on the ground with the side with the receptacle facing up. Carefully taking the small leather bag, the budget from the squirrel's neck Wodewose motioned for Charlotte to sit beside him. This she did sitting crossed legged. Now that she was sitting closely beside Wodewose, Charlotte could see that the leather bag contained a small amount of liquid, presumably water. She remembered being told she would find water or a liquid in the budget and she was to drink only this when in Otherworld. What Charlotte wondered was about to happen, some sort of ceremony?

Wodewose glanced across to both Alasdair and Cathasach, still sitting to attention on their respective tumuli. Quite by accident or was it, shafts of light from the moon found a way through the tree cover spotlighting each hound. The effect was quite surreal and accentuated the tension that so noticeably hung in the air. It looked to Charlotte as though Wodewose was either seeking reassurance or for permission for what he was about to do next, she wasn't sure which. Which or whatever it was, Wodewose appeared to relax and gently lifting the small leather bag by one corner carefully poured the liquid within into the stone recipient. As the liquid settled it immediately started to evaporate, not as water vapour which would, billow wide and without form, but in a single narrow column twisting skywards. After reaching around waist height of an average man the vapour stopped rising and gathered to form a small cloud, almost perfectly spherical in shape. After a few seconds, from within the small cloud a light began to shine. Charlotte immediately felt a familiar and unmistakable feeling of joy.

"Leht," she whispered, eyes wide.

"Hello Charlotte," came the unmistakable whisper. "I am sorry it's been so long, we had to be sure it was safe for you to travel. As it was you almost didn't make it through to our side, please my child never take such a risk again." Charlotte suspected but wanted to be sure what Leht meant by this. She wanted to ask but as was usual, when in her presence, found herself tongue tied. She needn't have worried for Leht intended to explain.

"Little Charlotte." Leht started her explanation.

"France Charlotte." Charlotte heard Wodewose whisper to himself, softly enough so as not to interrupt.

"Regrettably," Leht continued. "As increasingly seems to be the case I have very little time to talk. What you see before you is a small piece of me. When the light goes out this piece of me will have died. I can only communicate with you as long as the light is shining and this I'm afraid will only be for a few minutes." Just a few minutes! Charlotte had so many questions.

"Firstly, the gateway to our world, or to Otherworld for I gather Wodewose has told you what we call our home, the place where you find yourself now." Charlotte confirmed her understanding with a single nod of the head. Leht's voice was still delicious to hear but it had altered slightly, there was a steely edge to it which leant Charlotte to concentrate on nothing else.

"The reason you've had to wait so long before returning to Otherworld, is that we suspect the Darkness has discovered your way here. I will explain why another time. For now if you ever see anything unusual on your way to the gateway, (Charlotte understood by gateway Leht meant the slab in front of the door to the church of St John the Baptist), no matter how insignificant do not attempt to cross. It is not worth the risk. On our side we have placed a watch bird, a robin to watch over the gateway. Robin's have the unique ability to hide their thoughts from the Darkness and all its agents, they are also excellent communicators with our messengers." Leht motioned by way of a narrow beam of light towards the squirrel and the squirrel jumped up and puffed out its chest to ensure Charlotte understood that by "messengers" Leht meant him or one of his kin. Leht smiled though no one could witness this and continued with her message.

"Whatever happens from this day on, you can always trust and talk to a robin, as you have already done so. The Darkness has no power over the little bird. If for any reason we feel the gateway has become too big a risk there are other ways to cross to Otherworld but they are not as easy and in turn have their own risks." Leht paused but only for a second. "You sent a message about an unexplained mist in your village and the sad news of two missing boys."

Frustratingly Charlotte found she still couldn't speak and once again found herself only able to nod her confirmation.

"We knew something of the mist but not that it was so advanced, the fact that it is so causes us great concern. I think you already suspect that the mist is where many years ago a house once stood, not just any house but the home of an alchemist who dared to dabble with the devil, as you call the Darkness. I touched on the story at our last acquaintance. He was a knight and his name, Sir Guy de Gravade. At first his experiments with alchemy were quite innocent but as time went on he got drawn into the dark arts and eventually managed to make contact with the Darkness itself. From there the story is unclear for it happened many moons ago. All is recorded on a light scroll placed in the Sacred Library of Evingheho or under Ivinghoe Beacon as you know it but it is far too dangerous to try and find the scroll now and even if we could the message will have been written in ancient script and almost impossible for anyone to decipher today. We would need someone who specialises in such things and there is no one near. The story as I know it, either Sir Guy crossed the Darkness and the Darkness took him or he willingly sold his soul to the Darkness on the promise he would be shown the secret of alchemy. The result either way would have been the same and was always going to be so. The Darkness took the poor man's soul and everything he physically owned in your world. Overnight Sir Guy's house and all his possessions vanished. From that moment on the Darkness owned his soul and control of the land on which his house once stood. Any house built on that land after that day, has never lasted and will never last long, it will be cursed with misfortune and soon fall into ruin, as will its owners"

Charlotte remembered the picture of the old manor hanging over the fire in the house of Mr Clutterbuck and what he had told her. She had been right then. What she had felt at the time hadn't simply been her overzealous imagination, there was a connection. She must learn to trust her perception, to follow her nose. In this strange new world the inhabitants called Otherworld she sensed she needed to learn to harness her gift, her seventh sense if indeed that was what it was. To learn to use it to her advantage. Leht reading Charlotte's thoughts smiled inwardly, the human child was a quick learner, that bode them well. She wanted to say as much but at that moment though time was the most precious commodity of all, there was no time to congratulate and Leht quickly continued with her message.

"The mist is the Darkness building a gateway into your world. When or if, for we all hope it is never so, the laying of the mist is completed the Darkness will have unlocked a door to your world and your world will be finished. The Darkness will be unstoppable. You will know when the time is near for the mist will become so dark to be almost solid and quite impossible to enter. It will then rise to reveal the vanished home of Sir Guy de Gravade, the Darkness will have its own private gateway to your world and a base in which to work its evil. We must all pray, that the Darkness does not succeed in this." Leht's voice was becoming weaker by the second but it had not lost its steely tone. "As for the two boys. Fear not for they are still alive, that much we know and the Darkness has not the ability to transcend them to Otherworld. For now it has hidden them somewhere and somewhere in your world. As to where and for what purpose, I am sorry. I am unable to tell you. We too though, like their poor families are desperate to find out."

Charlotte saw that the light within the spherical cloud was quickly beginning to diminish. Not already she cried out inside, you've only just started. Leht continued to speak and this time Charlotte had to concentrate hard to understand her last few words.

"I am going little girl and my final message is the most important. It is of the utmost significance and imperative you understand my meaning. We do not have access to armies as we did before. Victory will have to be won through pureness of thought, without fear and strength of wit. We have been studying closely the actions of the Darkness and are now convinced that it is preparing to make its ascent on your world on the day everyone will least suspect. The shortest night of the year. The celebration of Oannes or as many will know it in your village, the nativity of St John the Baptist. That your church is dedicated to this man and stands beside the Darkness's intended gateway could quite simply be a coincidence though we fear this not to be the case. There is always a reason where the Darkness is concerned no matter how obscure. I fear for your church young Charlotte, watch over those who serve it." Leht's voice was now so faint her words were hardly discernible. "I have no more strength and have to leave you now my child. I have sent for help, his name is Triskelion. He will make himself known to you"

What remained of Leht's light flickered before going out. For a moment, the small cloud remained before it too vanished, dropping to the earth and fading into the ground. An uncomfortable silence fell on the little group. Charlotte rubbed her eyes, everyone and everything was a shadow. The rasping call of a fox split the night air, Alasdair and Cathasach both emitted a low growl but didn't move from their positions on the tumuli. The two hounds were no longer illuminated by the young moon which had been snuffed out by gathering clouds. Charlotte looked fearful. The darkening of the wood complimented the atmosphere that had been left by Leht's passing. There was left a foreboding that she didn't like the feel of at all.

"It is safe here," It was Wodewose who spoke. "Relax France Charlotte, it is safe here," he said again spreading his shaggy arms to show he meant between the two mounds on which the hounds sat sentinel. "If you are in trouble you can come here, it is a safe place." He repeated again.

As he spoke he pushed the stone back down the rabbit hole from where he'd retrieved it and carefully covered the entrance with leaves. Once he'd finished he looked wistfully around the wood. He spoke again and this time there was a combination of regret and sadness in his voice.

"Long ago." Wodewose started, his expression still wistful. "Leht would travel everywhere, every night she would bring light, joy and comfort to the woods. Her light at one time was always strong. For a long time now she rarely leaves her circle. She only feels safe when she is at home. Her light has grown too weak and today she only ever sends a small part of her into the wood and this too makes her weaker. I am afraid for Leht, I am afraid it will not be long before her light will go out forever." The big shaggy beast looked so sad that Charlotte thought at any moment he may burst into tears. She reached out putting one of her small arms round him hoping her action would bring some sort of comfort.

"How long have you known Leht," Charlotte asked, feeling his sadness.

"From the beginning." Was Wodewose's simple reply. "From the beginning, we are from the same day." Again Charlotte wasn't sure what the Wodewose meant, sometimes he spoke in riddles. She then thought of something else.

"Wodewose if you are so old does it mean that you are eternal, I mean will you live forever?" Wodewose looked at her as if he thought it was a rather stupid question.

"When wood dies, I die" he replied in his simple manner.

"I see," said Charlotte, not really seeing at all.

"If wood lives forever, I live forever," Wodewose tried to help her.

This time Charlotte thought she knew what he meant though to be sure she felt she needed to ask more questions and as always seemed to be the case, now was not going to be the time. She had seen that the hounds were starting to look restless and she needed answers to more important questions before they were forced to leave this, "safe place" as Wodewose described it. From what she understood after Leht's appearance there were actually two battles. One to protect the hidden library under Ivinghoe Beacon and two, to prevent the Devil or the Darkness as it was known in Otherworld opening a gate to her world. And if Leht was correct there wasn't much time to prevent the Darkness from achieving the latter. She'd been taught at school that the nativity of St John the Baptist was held on midsummer's day and midsummer's day was only just over a month away. The situation she found herself in seemed completely surreal. For maybe the thousandth time Charlotte questioned whether she simply wasn't dreaming for nothing surely could be real. The problem was, everything felt real, none of it felt like a dream and she could always remember everything that happened down to the tiniest detail. That wouldn't be the case if she were dreaming. Her mind then turned to the two lost boys, those poor boys, their disappearance definitely wasn't a dream. That snapped her out of it, no matter how strange and whatever she was involved in, it was real and it was happening now.

She thought of her parents and how they, on a daily basis, in complete innocence of the danger that threatened them worked so hard to make a living. More than anybody she wanted to protect her parents. She thought of her mother and father asleep, oblivious to the fact that she was out of doors in a wood and in a completely different world. At that moment she felt a million miles away and completely overwhelmed by the situation in which she found herself. Why her? What had she done to be given such an impossible burden? A tear rolled down her cheek. She hadn't the faintest idea where to begin.

"Are you ok France Charlotte?" Wodewose was looking at her, his dog like eyes bathed with concern. Charlotte looked up trying to hide the tear on her cheek. She remembered Leht's words. "Pureness of thought, without fear and strength of wit." She had already failed with one, the thought made her angry. She looked back at Wodewose and the squirrel, then at Alasdair and Cathasach. God only knows what suffering they've already had to endure. For whatever reason I'm here, they've put their faith in me, maybe even put their lives at risk for me. I owe them, she told herself, and I owe my parents. If only for all of them, I will fight until there isn't a breath left in my body.

The two hounds, Alasdair and Cathasach as though sensing the change, the new determination in the little human girl tensed and raised their noses to the air. Both let out a long blood curdling howl. A new found respect shone in their eyes. Far away in an invisible pudding stone circle, a light shone within an ancient yew.

"The Snooks may just be right after all." Leht shone. "I just hope I live long enough to see the human child succeed."

With her newly found strength Charlotte thought in more analytical terms about what Leht had told her since they'd first met. She needed an answer to what for her was the most pressing question. Which was more important, the protection of the Beacon and its hidden library of light scrolls or the prevention of the Darkness completing its gateway to her world? And if they succeeded with one would it help them to find a solution in achieving the other? Charlotte's thoughts ran to Leht. She was moved, deeply moved by Wodewose's concern for her, and now she thought she understood why, for if she had understood Wodewose correctly, they had known each other since birth. How long ago that was she had no idea, definitely hundreds, probably thousands of years. Charlotte couldn't imagine having a friend for that long and now his friend, Leht appeared to be dying. Why? After so many years, why now? Charlotte knew she'd have to be sensitive in trying to find the reason, if she ever had the time. From the way Wodewose had spoken she felt pretty certain that he didn't have the answer. Only that he could see the end was near.

Charlotte's thoughts turned to the poor white stag or white hart as they called it in Otherworld. Its terrified expression and its selfless and lonely battle to protect the library of light scrolls. With Leht's help and her rings of light the Darkness was being held at bay, but by her own admission Leht was weakening and it was only a matter of time Charlotte considered before the protective rings were broken and then what? Would the Darkness easily overcome the white hart and gain instant access to the library or could the poor animal still resist? She shuddered at the thought. Charlotte turned to Wodewose who remained kneeling, patiently watching her, waiting. The kindness in his dog-like eyes that at their first meeting had swept away her fears had returned.

"Wodewose can I ask you a question?" Wodewose nodded cautiously. "What would you say is the greatest danger. The Darkness entering Aldbury or the Darkness gaining access to the sacred library?"

"The sacred library." Wodewose didn't hesitate.

"Why?"

"Because of the big secret." Wodewose looked nervous. "You are not offended?" Charlotte raised her eyebrows.

"Why should I be offended?"

"Because it is not your village."

"Of course not," Charlotte reassured him, hoping she sounded convincing. "It's so important that I understand everything and lying to be kind will simply send me down the wrong track."

"Good," Wodewose looked relieved. "What track?" Charlotte couldn't help smiling. Faced with an almost impossible adversary and Wodewose had managed to make her smile. Unintentionally perhaps but that was his magic.

"Never mind for now," she didn't fancy having to explain herself out of that one. "Wodewose when you say the big secret, do you mean

Orme?" Charlotte was hoping he would shed some light on what Orme was. Using the word though bought a reaction from Wodewose that she never could have predicted. He started trembling and fear filled his eyes.

"Please, France Charlotte," Wodewose's normally gruff voice almost a squeal. "You must not say that word and I cannot say it. Please never say it again. Promise me. Promise."

Charlotte, dismayed not to mention shocked at his reaction, quickly took hold of both Wodewose's soft hands. "I promise Wodewose, I promise. I'll never say it again."

Wodewose seemed to calm down on hearing her promise though he still looked a little nervous. Removing his hands from Charlotte's grasp, he picked up the little leather sack, the budget and handed it to her.

"You must hide this, France Charlotte, and you mustn't lose it." Charlotte felt she was being scolded and blushed at the thought of her earlier stupidity. "You cannot take it to your world. Leht said it wouldn't pass and it's dangerous to try. Leht said to tell you that this is very important."

"Ok Wodewose." Charlotte acknowledged, "I understand and I won't, I promise." Charlotte made sure her expression matched the sincerity of her answer.

"You must hide it in a special place and you must leave the budget slightly open, like this." Wodewose loosened the cord round the neck and pulled the bag apart a little so there was enough of a gap to slide a finger in.

"Why?" Charlotte asked, "why must I leave the bag, the budget I mean, open?"

"So that Leht can get in." Wodewose said this as though it was obvious why. It wasn't of course, not to Charlotte, and she was just about to ask how Leht was expected to get in such a tiny opening when the two hounds who had remained silent during their conversation simultaneously let out a low growl. The sound almost froze Charlotte's blood and Wodewose immediately stood up, grabbing Charlotte's hand he pulled her up too.

"We must go, France Charlotte, don't forget the budget." As he said this he took hold of her hand and closed it around the leather bag. Alasdair and Cathasach descended from their positions on the tumuli and started down the wooded slope. The squirrel followed with Wodewose and Charlotte taking up the rear. The two hounds despite their undisguised urgency appeared to prefer caution over haste which meant they progressed at times almost at walking pace. For this Charlotte was grateful. It meant she wasn't constantly trying to catch her breath and gave her the chance to continue talking to Wodewose, to ask more questions of him. There was one she didn't think he'd know the answer to but it was worth a try.

"Wodewose," she asked as they made their way downhill through the wood. "Do you know the man who lived where I do now, his name was Elmer. He was an artist."

"Yes." Charlotte found it hard to quell her excitement. It wasn't the answer she'd expected. Frustratingly though as was Wodewose's way he hadn't expanded on his affirmation.

"Do you know where he is now Wodewose?."

"Yes." Charlotte felt she could strangle him. Before she could the hounds brought the little party to a stop. They had reached open ground and the hounds were pacing slowly back and forth, noses to the ground. From their viewpoint the tip of the Bridgewater monument was just visible above the dark treeline opposite and to their right lights from Aldbury twinkled in the gloom. Seeing the lights made Charlotte realise just how much she wanted to reach the safety of her cottage. She so wanted to share her burden, to tell her parents the truth, to tell them all about Otherworld and the dangers that faced them. What was the feeling, the voice inside her that kept telling her that to do so would be disastrous, maybe even put her parents in peril. It wasn't even a feeling it was a definite message, a message from somewhere, someone, that had taken up residence in her mind. Not feeling able to tell her parents, she'd even thought at one time about going to the police, but an eleven year old girl with stories of the devil, a shaggy man in the woods, a secret library under Ivinghoe Beacon. She'd receive short shrift, a pat on her head and told kindly not to waste their time. No she had to accept that the burden was entirely hers and the sooner she did so the sooner she could concentrate on the enormous task ahead.

After around a minute, the hounds apparently satisfied, made off again, across open ground heading for Walk Wood. Charlotte felt Wodewose grab her hand.

"I don't like being out of the wood," he explained, apologising for his action and quickened his pace. Charlotte in turn was determined to prise a multiple syllable answer from Wodewose.

"Well Wodewose." Charlotte tried again, "where is he?"

"Who?" Another one syllable answer. Charlotte swore she could strangle him.

"The artist, the man who used to live where I do now. You said you know where he is. Where is he?" There's no way Charlotte thought Wodewose can one syllable his way out of that one. At that moment they reached Walk Wood and Wodewose let go of her hand.

"Oh." Wodewose replied nonchalantly, "he's on the other side." Charlotte gritted her teeth she wasn't about to give up, she'd come this far.

"Yes Wodewose, I know he's on my side but where on my side?"

"No Wodewose," countered. "He's here, he's in Otherworld, he's on the other side of the valley." Wodewose pointed to the top of the wooded scarp, the ash-ridge opposite. If Wodewose's answer hadn't come as such a shock she would have carried out her desire to strangle him. And Otherworld far from being an appropriate name as Charlotte first thought was a blinking stupid name, any name beginning with "other" was too easily corrupted and confused. Despite Wodewose's provocation she held back from doing him physical harm. So the artist is here. He'd crossed over just as she had done. Charlotte had constantly been told that she was the only one from her world who could do that. Could she trust anything anybody told her. Wodewose interrupted her thoughts.

"If you like, next time you come to Otherworld I can take you to him."

"That would be nice," Charlotte said softly. "That would be nice Wodewose," she repeated trying to stay calm.

Just as Charlotte had finished her sentence the little party arrived back at the break in the wall. Alasdair and Cathasach were already in the narrow lane trotting back and forth checking to see if the way was safe.

"I must say goodbye now France Charlotte," Wodewose said solemnly, shaking her hand. "I don't like roads, not safe for me, I'm going home now. The squirrel will take you back, he will show you good place to hide the budget." He touched the small leather bag, clasped tightly in her hand. "Goodbye France Charlotte." With that Wodewose virtually leapt across the road swiftly disappearing into the dark heading, at least for him anyway, to the safety of the wood. Charlotte continued watching until Wodewose had completely faded from view. She'd searched for answers but found only more questions.

The squirrel brushing her leg forced her to refocus. Alasdair and Cathasach looked as though they were in a hurry to escort her home. Obediently Charlotte fell in behind them following the road back to Aldbury. As they approached the village the hounds suddenly made a left passing through a gate into the last field before the village. The squirrel followed, passing underneath and Charlotte clumsily climbed over. When they were all gathered in the field the hounds made off heading for the wooded scarp. Where are we going now, wondered Charlotte, I don't fancy going into a wood again. Unlike Wodewose she felt safer on open ground where there were no hiding places for the mal intentioned and where there was a lighter shade of darkness. As it turned out she need not have worried for the hounds came to a halt before an oak tree, within a stone's throw of the tree line. Why stop here? Charlotte asked herself, feeling more than a little nervous. She would feel a lot easier if they weren't quite so close to the inky blackness that announced the beginning of the wooded scarp. The squirrel prevented her from dwelling on her fears. It from what she could make out had disappeared underground just as it always did before the church porch. Was this another gateway to her world? Leht said she was worried that the Darkness may know about the gateway at the church. Charlotte was in the process of contemplating whether to try and follow the squirrel when it reappeared before disappearing once more. On closer inspection Charlotte could see that it was disappearing into a hole beneath the tree, the entrance almost completely hidden by a swollen root. The squirrel popped its head out once more, then surprised her by jumping and grabbing the small leather bag by its front two paws. Almost but not quite pulling the budget out of her grasp. Charlotte to her credit, understood what it wanted at once. She was getting used to the ways of Otherworld. The squirrel was showing her where to hide the bag. Dropping to her knees she gently pushed the budget under the tree root and into the hole. The squirrel went in after it and after just a few seconds reappeared. Everyone now apparently satisfied, Alasdair and Cathasach took off across the field once more, this time heading downhill making for the dark, structured shapes of Aldbury.

The village, as Charlotte knew it would be, was deathly still. As they approached the churchyard Alasdair and Cathasach raced ahead up the path to the church door. The squirrel rather than following jumped onto a car roof parked in front of the Greyhound pub and waited. Charlotte stood holding her breath beside the pond. After what felt like an age Cathasach reappeared at the church gate. The squirrel on seeing him immediately leapt from its perch to follow the hound who had turned and disappeared back up the church path. Charlotte needing no prompting quickly followed. On arriving before the church door Charlotte spied a robin perched on the porch's castellated roof. she now knew it to be Leht's robin and this knowledge gave her comfort. Alasdair and Cathasach were as before sitting beside the stone slab. The squirrel after looking over its shoulder dived underground and Charlotte stepping onto the stone slab disappeared with it. To her relief, this time there was no stuttering, her passage underground was smooth and within seconds she felt herself rising once more. In no time at all she found herself standing in what she knew was her world and breathed a long sigh of relief.

Minutes later Charlotte was safely in her cottage. Her robin had been waiting for her at the back door. Before she climbed the stairs to bed, Charlotte stopped for a quick wash and as all young girls do on a regular basis to check herself in the mirror. Thank goodness she did, to her dismay the mirror reflected an image of a girl covered with dirt. How? She was always immaculate when returning from Otherworld. Then it dawned on her, this wasn't dirt from Otherworld this was good fresh Aldbury dirt from her world. It was from her diving into a neighbour's garden to avoid the lights of the police car. She'd picked it up from the flower bed. The event seemed so very long ago. She thought of the crushed flowers and immediately felt guilty. Worried at any moment her parents might wake up, Charlotte scrubbed herself clean before finally creeping up the ever complaining stairs and falling into bed. This time she spotted the robin perched on the sill watching her. Far from feeling upset by the intrusion, she found its presence comforting. With the slightest of smiles she hugged Gromit and curled up on one side to sleep. So many questions she reflected, so many questions' and her eyes closed. The robin took one last look and satisfied flew back to its nest at the bottom of the pagoda. Sleep brought little relief for Charlotte. In her dreams she searched for answers and found only more questions.

In Otherworld the squirrel once again was escorted by Alasdair and Cathasach back to its home in the oak tree. This time before running up the trunk to its entrance it checked on a small burrow beneath the tree's roots. There sat the budget it's neck slightly open, snug and away from prying eyes just as they had left it. Satisfied, the squirrel ran up the tree to the hole, the entrance to his home. From here the squirrel thought I can keep watch over the budget and felt justly proud at his ingenuity.

On ensuring the squirrel was safely tucked up in its nest Alasdair and Cathasach turned and almost flew up the steep wooded escarpment. Ahead of them a small black figure hurriedly dodged between the trees. As the ridge flattened out the two hounds pounced and with ruthless efficiency ensured the figure had made its last ever move. For the next few minutes they prowled the surrounding woodland. Not a single movement could they detect. Rather than reassure them this made the two hounds even more suspicious, there should be some sort of movement, the sound of a mouse or a night bird. A wood was far more active at night than during the day. As if in response the haunting call of a tawny owl reverberated around the trees. Reassured, although maybe not entirely Alasdair and Cathasach continued their search of the wood. Their inspection brought them to an ancient oak. An oak which had seen more moons than almost any other tree in Ashridge. Its chiselled bark bearing testament to its great age. The two hounds came close to the old tree, their ears primed. With their keen hearing they picked up a steady rumble from somewhere within the trunk. Wodewose was asleep. Satisfied they turned to start on their long journey back to their den.

Wodewose was overjoyed to be back at his tree. He was very fond of the little human girl, France Charlotte, but he found talking her language so very tiring, (if you've ever tried to speak a foreign language, one you rarely use for any length of time, you'll know exactly how

Wodewose feels), and she always asked so many questions, many of them very difficult to answer. As he settled down to sleep a voice came to him through the root vine.

(Scientists in our world have often claimed that plants can communicate with each other. In both worlds, trees and plants can do this via their roots. In Otherworld the network is known as the root vine. Trees communicate in complete silence, passing messages from root to root using currents that run cobweb like beneath the earth. An entire wood could be chatting away and you wouldn't know it. Bear this in mind next time you go for a walk amongst the trees.)

Wodewose recognised it was Leht talking to him from within her yew, the only tree in Ashridge older than his. Both Wodewose and Leht could communicate using the root vine and Wodewose spoke the same language as the trees which made it even easier for him. Leht's silent voice always soothed Wodewose, her tone was perfection and he never tired of hearing it. Having said that Leht rarely used the root vine and Wodewose knew for her to do so, what she had to say would be very important. Therefore though tired and needing to sleep, Wodewose concentrated hard.

"Wodewose," Leht's musical tones flowed effortlessly soothing whilst at the same time guaranteeing attention. "The little human girl. I've still no idea why she's here but with every hour that passes I feel more and more that she could be our saviour. She after all is the first human who has successfully transcended between both worlds for well over a thousand years. Many have tried since and failed with disastrous consequences as you well know." Leht paused to let what she was saying sink in. "Wodewose, you must teach France Charlotte," (Leht used Wodewose's adopted name), "the ways of the wood and everything in it. She is human, though through no fault of her own and does not understand the ways of the natural world. You must teach her what is good and what is bad in the wood. You must show her where she can find safety and where she might encounter danger. You must tell her where to find the three receiving stones. Give her the map I gave you though don't let her take it to her side or it will be destroyed and the three receiving stones rendered useless. Under a tree in Gryme's Dell, the tree where the lone Accipiter sits you will find a small frog made of the purist silver from Llywernog. You must find it Wodewose and give it to the human child for it will help protect her. It is a powerful charm and was placed there many moons ago by Sucellus. It seeks to protect whoever possesses it, however the charm will only work if the bearer remains ignorant to its purpose. You can never tell the human child its purpose Wodewose or its power will become worthless. The charm can never be taken to the other side, it will burn up perhaps causing serious injury to the bearer. The frog will not be easy to find Wodewose, the fall of the wood over many, many moons has it buried deep but find it you must." Leht fell silent and just as Wodewose thought she had gone, her voice returned.

"Wodewose, the Darkness is slowly entering our wood. I am worried that the human child can no longer travel safely at night when it is hard to know if the gnombres are hiding in the moon shadows. I am sending for her tomorrow but after tomorrow she must only travel during the the day and even then she must remain in the light for as you know shadows, even the weaker shadows of day can be dangerous. Do you understand Wodewose?" Wodewose a little overwhelmed by all that was being asked of him took a little time before grunting his confirmation.

"Please do not feel overburdened Wodewose, I have sent for help, you will not be alone." They were Leht's last words, at least for that night. Wodewose waited for more to come through the vine but his trusty tree received nothing more, at least not from Leht. Revelling in the heady seasoned scents that filled his home, Wodewose allowed himself one final scratch before falling into a deep slumber. A slumber so deep that he didn't hear Alasdair and Cathasach prowling outside. Nothing would be able to wake Wodewose that night, not even the Darkness if it tried to.

Chapter Twelve

Triskelion

"Thank goodness today is Sunday!" was Charlotte's first thought when she woke, for she was feeling exhausted. The smell of an English breakfast wafted temptingly up the stairs, confirmation it was indeed Sunday. Her father always cooked breakfast on Sunday and if her parents were feeling extravagant, they would wash it down with a bottle of bucks fizz. How can the French, her father would often tease, the country who invented champagne not come up with bucks fizz. "Trust the English to improve on it."

Charlotte took her time getting out of bed. Feeling tired she blew a kiss to the white hart rather than kissing the glass itself. Stretching she wandered over to the long sash window and standing on tiptoe stretched for a second time, extending her arms so her fingers just about touched the beamed ceiling. Like this she stared out of the window at the same time yawning widely. There was the magpie, she'd been expecting it. The robin on seeing her came hopping and skipping along the garden fence. Everything else remained grey and gloomy, Aldbury had become the ultimate definition for the latter. In other words nothing had changed since yesterday. Charlotte then saw that it had. Something caused her to look across to the trees at the bottom of Tom's garden. With the back of her hands she rubbed the sleepy dust from her eyes. There it was, in the higher boughs of one of Tom's apple trees sat another magpie. Unnervingly, like the first magpie, it sat motionless staring straight at her window, or in truth at her. Charlotte found herself whispering the second line of the verse Will had taught her.

"Two for joy." Charlotte racked her brains trying to remember the rhyme Wodewose had recounted. It finally came to her. "Two for mirth," she repeated, again whispering. Which is it and does it at all matter? The first sounded like she should be happy, the second that the Darkness maybe mocking her. She much preferred the first. Trusting in Wodewose's advice and therefore knowing that, with only two birds, she hadn't anything to fear, at least for now, Charlotte blew a large raspberry at each. Feeling much better for her atypical rudeness, she dressed and descended the stairs where she knew that a full English breakfast was waiting for her.

Her parents had excelled themselves. Breakfast was huge, her father had even made fried bread and there was black pudding. Her mother not to be defeated had made her a huge bowl of hot chocolate and Charlotte proceeded to disgust both her parents by dipping her fried bread into her beverage and leaving it there until it was just starting to go soggy. At which point she dangled the bread above her and let the soggy portion fall into her upturned mouth. "And we're led to believe the French are sophisticated," her father bemoaned, his head in his hands.

When all had finished her mother cleared the plates and placed a steaming pot of fresh coffee on the table. Whilst her parents sipped, enjoying the slow stimulation from the caffeine, Charlotte dared to ask her father a question.

"Daaaaad." The way she pronounced it Charlotte let the tone dip in the centre before rising again to level with the same note with which she started. Fathers everywhere will recognise this verbalisation. Usually, but not exclusively from daughters when asking for something, that they knew, may meet with resistance. "Dad," Charlotte repeated this time using the shortened version, have you ever heard of Sir Guy de Gravade?" Her father enjoying his coffee looked surprised at the question. He had expected his daughter to ask for a lift or something similar, not this.

"Why do you ask?" Charlotte should have been ready for such an answer or rather question but she wasn't, not at all. How stupid of her.

"Oh,." She had to think quickly. "Oh, um," pause. "It was something we touched on at school, local history. "Charlotte crossed her fingers on both hands hoping for protection from her lie. She hated lying to her parents. To her relief her father didn't really appear interested in her answer. His question had been simply, an automatic response.

"Funnily enough," he replied taking a long sip of his coffee. "I've just read a bit about him in a book I picked up from a charity shop in Berkhamsted." Her father took another sip and Charlotte waited struggling to hide her impatience. "Didn't say much though, just that he was an alchemist who messed with the devil, who in turn took his soul and everything he owned. In the book they called him the Wizard of Aldbury. Apparently that's his common title. Typical type of story from that period," her father finished obviously not impressed. If only he knew, Charlotte thought, starting the washing up before her parents asked her.

After breakfast she went to the village shop for the Sunday papers, some more coffee and of course, sherbet dip. Her mother, after the tragedy of the two boys, who still hadn't been found, was nervous about her going on her own but Charlotte insisted she'd be alright and her mother had relented. Ashtynn, she found, busy sorting the papers and complaining loudly that the delivery had been late that morning. On seeing her, Ashtynn broke off from her sorting and with her usual broad smile, called out.

"Good morning French charlotte, how are we this morning?"

"France Ch," Charlotte started correcting Ashtynn before remembering where she was and stopped herself.

"Sorry?"

"Oh nothing," Charlotte replied, angry at herself for being so careless. "Nothing, yes we're all fine thanks. Have you got the Sunday Telegraph?" She was studying the mass of papers spread all over the floor. In response Ashtynn grunted a confirmation and proceeded to tip toe among the various piles of papers, swooping up the odd copy here and there before eventually straightening up and handing a jumbled bundle to Charlotte.

"I think they're all there," she said, red faced. Charlotte had a quick flick through and confirmed she thought so too.

"There's nothing in the papers about those two poor boys. I think it's shameful how quickly they've been forgotten." Ashtynn was bending over sorting the papers again and Charlotte only just caught the last bit. Straightening once more Ashtynn slammed a sorted pile down on the counter. "And if you ask me, French Charlotte," Ashtynn nodded towards the window. "That mist out there is getting thicker by the day, it's almost darker than grey. It's not natural. It's like something out of the X Files. Do you think its aliens that's doing this, come to invade us? There's loads of stories about people being abducted by aliens, perhaps that's what's happened to those poor boys." Ashtynn plonked another completed pile of papers on the counter.

"I don't know, Ashtynn." Charlotte handed Ashtynn the money for her shopping. "Maybe, anything's possible."

"Well don't you be going near that mist, French Charlotte." Ashtynn warned, smiling again. "We don't want those aliens to get you. With you being French, we don't want an international incident do we?" Ashtynn rested her hand on Charlotte's head and rubbed her hair. At least it wasn't a pat.

"Don't worry Ashtynn I won't. I'll see you later," and with a wave Charlotte closed the shop door to the sound of silence. It felt so strange.

On closing the shop door, instead of going straight home Charlotte wandered over the road to the church gate. She stopped and gazed down the gravel path to the church door. It was open and people passed her on their way to Sunday service. The vicar was at the door greeting people as they arrived and saw Charlotte standing at the gate.

"Morning French Charlotte," he shouted, waving. "Coming to church?" In response Charlotte held up the Sunday papers.

"Got to take these to my dad." She shouted back.

"Ah another time then, tell your dad if he wants the real truth to come to church." The vicar grinned widely at his teasing.

"I will, promise." But the vicar had already disappeared inside.

Charlotte remained where she was for a few minutes before finding herself walking up to the road a few more metres to the field with the mist. She had no idea what made her to do so, only that she felt it perfectly normal. She stopped beside the gate leading into the field. Placing the papers on top of the adjacent ivy-clad wall she rested her arms and chin on the front page and stared into the mist which started only a couple of metres away. Ashtynn was right, it had thickened a lot since the May Fair. The mist was now a definite, darker-than-grey, and almost impossible to see into further than the first metre. It had even enveloped the tape barriers erected by the parish council. So much so, in places they were no longer visible. As she stared, Charlotte felt little rivulets of fear start to meander their way into her subconscious. Her skin responded with goose bumps and her toes started to tingle. The fear, like an incoming tide kept lapping at her mind, growing, second by second, minute by minute. The attack on her mind was relentless and the fear was close to taking complete control when she heard Leht's words.

"Pureness of thought, without fear and strength of wit."

Hearing these words again sparked something deep inside her. An inner strength she had no idea she possessed. With grim determination Charlotte started to fight back. With strength of mind she started to fight back. I've got no reason to be afraid, she kept telling herself, you can't harm me. A battle raged in her mind, one that could have gone either way and then slowly she felt the tide turning. The lapping subsided, the tide of fear was going out and Charlotte found herself regaining control of her subconscious. Before long, all sense of fear had vanished and she was back to a normal Sunday morning simply staring at a mist. She no longer felt afraid.

"Hey what are you doing there?" The shout startled her. She turned to see a man waving from the church gate. Charlotte didn't recognise him and assumed he was a church goer. "Get away from there little girl, it's not safe." He waved his arms again, gesturing to her to get back.

"Sorry," Charlotte called back and dutifully did as she was being told. She crossed the road and started to walk back down to the village centre. On the way she passed the garden where she'd hidden the night before. Several crushed plants were evidence of her hiding place along with an impression of her torso in the freshly dug earth. The owners would not be pleased. The man who had shouted at her, remained at the church gate watching.

"Sorry to shout," he said, as Charlotte passed him, his tone much softer. "It's just that, that field is dangerous, we don't want anything to happen to you."

"I know," Charlotte replied. "Thanks." She hadn't minded being admonished, for what she had done had been stupid. What on earth had made her do it? The one positive consequence of her action was she'd overcome her fear and that gave her a confidence she hadn't possessed before.

At the same time in Aylesbury after working through the night, a police officer was struggling to get to sleep. Every time he closed his eyes a fear crept over him, a fear so intense that he wanted constantly to scream out loud. With the fear came a blackness, not the familiar darkness that was relaxing, inducing sleep but a blackness with something lurking in its depths. Something so terrible that his fear of it made it difficult to breathe. Death he considered not for the first time would be welcome to feeling like this.

Several minutes later Charlotte was back at the cottage where her parents were still in the kitchen.

"Papers," she shouted cheerfully as she closed the door.

In a world virtually unknown, but in reality only a step away, Wodewose stretched, a loud yawn accompanying his one and only morning exercise. His limbs responded well, they felt primed. Leht's words from the night before were still playing out in his mind and bore a burden on his shoulders he wasn't sure he wanted and certainly wasn't used to. Yet summer was around the corner and his ancient oak's anticipation of rain filled balmy days was infectious. As a consequence Wodewose felt good that morning. Stepping out of his woodland home he found that the early morning sun was already bringing a shine to the emerald green canopy overhead and in places even starting to warm the woodland floor. Grass grew where the sun regularly reached the ground and early summer flowers were starting to make their presence bringing splashes of colour to the different shades of browns and green that were everywhere. Birds busied the air, flying high and low busying themselves feeding their young and constantly repairing nests. It was a joyful scene and in its midst Wodewose felt ready for anything. So good did he feel, he was ready for more exercise and stretched a second time before giving his shaggy coat a good scratch, removing the last of yesterday's woodland memorabilia.

Wodewose didn't normally plan his days. A normal day for him would be spent ambling around his wood, chatting to the trees and acknowledging the birds and the beasts that lived under their cover. Many moons ago it would have taken him several weeks to cover every corner of his wood but over recent moons his wood had become smaller and smaller and today he could pretty much cover every corner, ditch, valley and hollow within a couple of days.

"First things first," he thought to himself, but what came first? He wasn't used to planning. The little frog he thought, sounded important and shouldn't be that hard to find. He knew the exact tree, Leht was talking about. The bird in the tree was a sparrow hawk and it always rested between hunts in the only oak in Gryme's Dell. And the Dell a deep hollow was only a five minute walk from his home. It made sense to him to find the frog first and then he could give it to France Charlotte that night. His mind wandered to tonight. He liked the human child but not only was she full of questions, many of which he didn't like and found hard to answer, she always arrived at the most inconvenient hour and one of his favourite pastimes was sleeping. Since the arrival of France Charlotte, he wasn't getting a lot of that.

After a mix of roots and fresh young grass for breakfast, Wodewose set out to find the little silver frog, as Leht had asked him to. He touched his favourite trees as he passed and hummed tunes that the wind had taught him over the changing seasons. In no time at all he arrived at Gryme's Dell. The sparrow hawk he saw was already in its tree preparing to hunt for its breakfast. The morning sun hadn't as yet reached the bottom of the Dell and much was still covered in a deep, rather depressing shadow. "Never mind," he thought to himself, "the sun when upper will make my heart flutter." He had made the rhyme up himself and was quite proud of it. Pleased he casually strolled down the steep slope of the Dell, repeating the rhyme rhythmically as he went.

"The sun when upper will make my heart flutter."

The trunk of the oak rested almost at the bottom of the Dell, though not quite. Its gnarled roots started maybe half a man's height up the southern slope. "Perfect," thought Wodewose. Kneeling, he would be head height with the base of the tree. Before starting, he made a short tour of the Dell stroking the trunks of the many beeches. He could sense they felt nervous and wished to calm them. Maybe it was his early morning visit that had unsettled them, they weren't used to it. Satisfied he'd done his best, Wodewose went back to the oak. Kneeling he studied the ground around its base. "Now where would I hide a little frog?" he mused, "stupid place if you ask me." He started to brush away the earth from the oldest roots. At first it was easy, the leaf mould from recent years was soft to the touch and shifted without protest. After removing several seasons of the stuff the going became more difficult. Hardened chalk along with flint hurt his hands and roots that were solid with many moons of growth blocked nearly every attempt as he struggled to dig deeper. "Why me?" Wodewose complained on finding his way blocked by another root, "why choose me, Leht. Why not a coney?" (rabbit).

Not far away Alasdair and Cathasach were racing at near record pace across open fields closing fast on the wooded scarp. Both hounds were praying hard that they weren't going to be too late. On reaching the tree line they thrashed through the undergrowth without the slightest thought for themselves. The steep incline with its loose earth presented a considerable challenge but hardly damaged their pace. Every sinew in the hound's bodies was working at full capacity, muscles pumped like pistons, they had to get there, they had to get to Wodewose before it was too late.

Wodewose tried communicating with the tree through its roots, but the roots he was able to touch were too old, he could only sense the tree's feelings, not talk to it. He sensed the tree felt nervous even a little wary, perhaps it was due to him messing with its base. If he could dig down deeper he'd be able to touch the younger more sensitive roots and through these he'd be able to talk to the tree, reassure it and ask the old oak to help him find the little frog. For now though he'd just have to carry on digging.

Just as he sensed he was getting somewhere there was the sound of running feet and the hounds Alasdair and Cathasach appeared at the rim of the Dell. Their appearance upset Wodewose, he couldn't talk to the hounds and they always looked aggressive and Wodewose hated aggression, it was not something he understood at all. The two hounds ran, round and round the rim of the Dell circling in opposite directions, growling as they did so. At that moment, the oak talked to Wodewose, he'd finally reached a sensitive root. The tree was speaking to him with much excitement and in such a hurried fashion it was stumbling over its words. Wodewose was struggling to understand, and the hound's strange behaviour didn't help. Then he understood, the tree knew where the little frog was hidden and could help him retrieve it. The second message was relayed with a much greater sense of urgency. Wodewose had to get out of the Dell and fast, for if he didn't he may never get out at all! The tree's warning did not have the effect it intended, the message stunned Wodewose not into action but quite the opposite, he froze with fear. As he did so, many of the shadows in the Dell started to move independently. Black shapes started to rise from the dark floor, at the same time growing legs. Alasdair and Cathasach didn't hesitate, they threw themselves down the sides of the Dell snapping and charging, teeth bared at every moving shadow. The noise was hideous, and the battle played out with such speed and confusion you'd be forgiven for thinking that the Dell was one living mass. The sparrow hawk, seeing Wodewose's and the hound's plight, joined in, diving and ripping at the mass of writhing shadows.

The oak brought Wodewose to his senses.

"The frog Wodewose, find the frog or the gnombres will get it."

Wodewose wanted to run, run like the wind, to run far away from the turmoil and as quickly as possible. Only those who know Wodewose well and the true character of a "Wild man of the woods," will understand what a supreme effort it was for the gentle beast not to listen to his instincts and flee. With gritted teeth Wodewose remembered Leht, he would not fail her. Concentrating he did his best to block out the noise and to listen to what the oak was trying to tell him.

"Place your arm there Wodewose, round to the left, feel for a tunnel. I will guide you." The oak spoke with a calmness that helped to screen the rage that was all around them. Wodewose lay almost flat on the slope to achieve what the oak was asking him to do. Something sharp dug deep into his left shoulder and a pain he'd never thought he'd experience shot up his arm, the very arm under the oak searching for the little frog. Wodewose refused to cry out, instead he winced and concentrated even harder on his task.

"You're almost there Wodewose, you're almost there, feel for the tunnel it is made from the roots of the oak before me. Wodewose strained and strained then he had it. A tunnel almost perfectly smooth created by tightly entwined roots many, many moons before. He reached for the tunnel's end, the hairs on his arm pulling at his flesh in protest at the tight space. Then he had it in his grasp, it was tiny and he couldn't see it but he knew he had the frog, it felt alien to the touch. He remembered what Leht had told him, the frog offered protection to the bearer and for a split second Wodewose relaxed. It was a mistake, another stab in the same shoulder this time so painful it forced a loud cry. He remembered too late that the little frog could only protect through ignorance, his knowledge made the little frog powerless to protect him. The battle was now so intense Wodewose felt sure, without protection he was about to die and started preparing himself mentally for such a fate. The oak, witnessing this spoke to him again.

"Get out of the shadows Wodewose, get into the light, hurry."

For the second time the voice of the tree spurred Wodewose into action. He pulled his arm from the root tunnel yelping in pain as many of his hairs remained below ground. His cry caught the attention of just about every living being in the Dell and on mass and in one movement all made for his direction. By this time, the light from the rising sun had almost reached the lower depths of the Dell and although there were still a great many shadows there were also far more patches of light and

Wodewose dived for one. As he did so he saw Alasdair leap and grab something black in his jaws behind him. There was a scream and the being wriggled, before falling limp. Alasdair instantly disposed of it, tossing it effortlessly into the air.

Wodewose struggled to his feet ready to run for his life. The sunlight made the sweat clinging to his hair glisten as though he were draped in a cloak sewn with hundreds of miniature diamonds. The writhing shadows froze, and as one started to melt into to the ground, disappearing beneath the mass of trampled leaves. An eerie silence fell on the Dell, and for seconds nothing or no one moved. The wood was in shock. The commotion had been heard quite some distance away and the root vine was buzzing with horrific details of what had just occurred. Alasdair and Cathasach warily trotted up to Wodewose, panting heavily. Their bodies were covered in scars and blood dripped from their jaws. Cathasach lay to one side of the shocked Wodewose whilst Alasdair, with sensitivity that he rarely let anyone see, gently licked Wodewose's injured shoulder.

After several minutes, Cathasach rose and standing on all fours started pacing back and forth. Alasdair stopped his canine first aid and joined his colleague. Wodewose couldn't talk to the hounds but understood what they wanted, they wanted him to follow them. He slowly hauled himself up wincing with the pain in his shoulder. He leant against the trunk of the oak silently thanking it. The tree's quick thinking may well have saved his life. Below, the floor of the Dell was peaceful. Apart from the many mounds of disturbed leaves, no clue remained of the violence that had just taken place there. There was no sign of the writhing shadows, shadows with sharp teeth and even sharper claws and not one drop of blood. It was as though they'd never graced the dell with their presence. Such is the way of the gnombres.

Turning, Wodewose followed Alasdair and Cathasach up the slope and out of Gryme's Dell. Both hounds were limping, Cathasach quite badly. After leaving the Dell, Wodewose allowed Alasdair and Cathasach to escort him home. He had never been so pleased to see his old tree. He realised that as well as the oak he probably owed his life to the two hounds and feeling very guilty at his earlier mistrust turned to thank them. He was too late, on turning he found they were already running into the wood heading home. He watched until they were gone and started to slide into his tree. Once safely in the trunk he opened his left hand. There in the softness of his palm shone a tiny silver frog. It was a beautiful thing, he just hoped it had been worth all the trouble. Sobbing softly Wodewose fell into a disturbed slumber.

Charlotte spent the morning finishing homework and helping her mother prepare Sunday lunch, a traditional roast. Although that day lunch was actually going to be eaten during the evening, for her father had surprised them all by announcing they were going for another walk around Ivinghoe Beacon. Rather than walk to the Beacon as before, this time they took the van, parking in the National Trust car park straddling the road connecting Ringshall with the B489. Being a Sunday and sunny, the car park was packed and an ice cream van was doing a roaring trade. A steady stream of visitors were walking to and from the Beacon and Charlotte and her parents joined the throng.

On reaching the summit they found the view to be even more glorious than normal. The sun was strong and being spring, the air, as well as being crisp was crystal clear. Where they were standing, Charlotte realised, was exactly the spot the white hart occupied in Otherworld. Facing west as she knew the hart would be, she tried to imagine how he'd be feeling. The fight he was putting up, his immense silent struggle with the forces trying to enter the Sacred Library. His selfless struggle was for everyone in Otherworld and for every living person standing on the summit alongside her and beyond. Looking around at the array of smiling faces enjoying the spring sunshine made her angry that they were ignorant of the sacrifices being made on their behalf in another world. A large and noisy family arrived on the summit all holding ice creams. She studied their innocent merriment. Watching, even she, who knew the truth, found it hard to believe that there was a battle going on right now, on this very spot, in another world or another dimension that almost nobody believed in. Deep down she knew she had no right to be angry. People's actions would be very different if they knew the struggle taking place and the dangers ahead. Gazing across the mouth of the Gade valley Charlotte wondered about Otherworld, she was still confused as to where it was exactly. Where she was going when she transcended as Leht called it. Once more she studied the happy faces of the people on the summit, "how lucky you all are" she whispered quietly, "how lucky you are to be ignorant as to what is happening, right here, right now."

That night Charlotte was awoken by the now familiar tapping from the robin on her window. Her roast dinner still wasn't fully digested and its continued presence made her feel heavy and overly comfortable beneath her quilt. She really didn't feel like getting up, tonight she resented the tapping, tonight she wanted it to go away. It wouldn't and she knew it wouldn't. The tapping came again and this time Charlotte angrily threw off her sheets. A little less carefully than usual she ran down the stairs and out onto the brick path, grabbing her coat off of the hook on the wall as she left. The squirrel was waiting as usual and looking a little agitated. Charlotte fully awake, knew her roast dinner slumber had cost her a couple of valuable minutes and time was of the essence. Without waiting for the squirrel, she sprinted down the path and up the road towards the church, praying as she ran that her passage wouldn't be disturbed by a passing car. Unknown to her, Charlotte had no need to worry about a police patrol car that evening. The officers who were due to check the village, the same officers as the night before, deliberately avoided Aldbury that night. There was something unnatural about the place, something that terrified them both. Their silent bond made their decision easy, their superiors would never know.

In spite of her haste, the squirrel soon overtook Charlotte and was standing waiting for her as she started up the gravel path to the church porch. The writhing serpent on the clock face was still quite clear and to her relief she realised she'd got to the church on time. (It's quite disturbing how quickly the human mind adapts to the unusual, turning it into the norm. This may well be one reason why so much of the world is in crisis today. Much of what the human race today accepts as normal simply isn't. Charlotte, as proves my point didn't question what a writhing serpent was doing on the clockface, she was just relieved to see it was still there. After only a few weeks her mind was accepting the writhing serpent as normal, if it hadn't been there that night, that would not have been normal. Charlotte would have questioned why.)

On arriving in Otherworld there was an immediate change to the Aldbury she'd just left. In Otherworld it was raining and raining heavily. It was the first time, Charlotte realised, she'd seen it rain in the village for months and wondered if it had also started to rain in her world. She already knew the answer was no. But why, and why wasn't there always a cloud hanging over Aldbury in Otherworld as there was in hers? The mist was always there just as it was in her world but there wasn't always a dark cloud. She thought that everything in Otherworld mirrored her world. In Aldbury that apparently wasn't the case. She'd have to ask Wodewose. She then remembered one of her first questions to the shaggy beast. A question about the weather. Wodewose had replied that the weather in Otherworld mirrored her world unless somebody didn't want it to, or something along those lines. Charlotte couldn't remember his exact words, is this what he had meant, was the rain natural or something more sinister. She held out her arm watching the droplets fall on her pale palm. Instinctively she brought her hand up to her nose and sniffed at the wetness on her skin. Rain water always has a distinctive smell but this rain had no scent. Something primeval in her told her this water was lifeless, not of the natural world. It was as though the rain was simply a prop. As she puzzled over the latest riddle the rain began to fade and very quickly the only drops that fell were from the trees in the churchyard. I've found you out, Charlotte whispered to herself and had the uncomfortable feeling that someone or something was listening to her.

Alasdair and Cathasach were waiting to escort her and without hesitation trotted down the church path to the village pond. Charlotte immediately saw that both hounds were limping, Cathasach quite badly. What had happened? and knew it couldn't have been good. The two hounds were acting overly cautious and the resulting slow pace meant that Charlotte had no trouble in keeping up. Unlike on previous occasions they didn't follow the road. Instead, as soon as they were out of the village the hounds cut right into the field making directly for the wooded scarp. Charlotte thought they'd pass by the oak to pick up the budget but no, the two hounds were taking the shortest route to the wood. As they crossed the field the rain started again, or perhaps here it had never really stopped and if anything it was a lot heavier. With little or no wind the rain fell in vertical lines, showing no mercy. Alasdair, Cathasach and the squirrel didn't seem to notice but Charlotte being a human was not suited to it and in no time at all her rain coat had given up and wet clothes clung to her body at every opportunity. To make matters worse after no time at all her wet clothes became very cold wet clothes and not only did they make her feel extremely uncomfortable, after only ten minutes she began to shiver. The warm roast dinner was beginning to feel a million years away.

The wood offered some semblance of shelter. There was something different about rain in a wood to anywhere else. The sound was unique for one, the atmosphere as the first drops hit the tree cover and then drip by drip fall through bouncing of the lower vegetation another, and lastly there was the smell as the droplets finally came to rest on the rotted soil. Combined, all three can be quite intoxicating. Not tonight though, the tension between the two hounds was so strong that it was almost physical and all of Charlotte's attention was on them and trying to ease her discomfort. As they made their way cautiously through the trees Alasdair and Cathasach stopped frequently, occasionally emitting a low growl. Charlotte couldn't tell whether this was meant to be a warning to others or for her to take care. Either way she didn't like it and only worsened her unease at being beneath the cover of trees at night. What was reassuring, Alasdair and Cathasach kept closer to her far closer than they'd ever done in the past. The squirrel too rather than making its usual acrobatic passage through the trees kept close to the hounds. So close Charlotte observed, at times it was in danger of being trodden on.

It wasn't long although it seemed like forever before Charlotte recognised the unmistakable outline of Wodewose's tree. As they approached Alasdair and Cathasach almost crawled the last metre or so. Watching them Charlotte felt she ought to bend double though not sure why. The squirrel scurried up the trunk and proceeded to run rings around it, chattering as it did so. Within a couple of minutes a shaggy arm appeared and then a complete Wodewose holding his knobbled staff. Charlotte was immediately shocked to see Wodewose looking, not only sad but so obviously afraid. He was always nervous and perhaps always a little afraid but she'd never seen him like this, he looked utterly dejected. Her heart cried to see him looking so and it was pure instinct, a child's instinct that made Charlotte forget her fear and run to him giving him a bigger hug as she could. Her action achieved two results. His expression changed, Wodewose smiled warmly glad of her attention and he also winced with pain. Charlotte only really noticed the second.

"What?" she exclaimed stepping back, worried that she'd hurt him. "What's happened to you?"

"Somebody didn't like me," Wodewose smiled ruefully. "Nothing much though, it doesn't hurt." His last line if it was meant to reassure her was totally unconvincing. He's a totally rubbish actor Charlotte thought but kept this to herself. She squeezed his hand giving him her best smile. For a second at least all fear and all hurt left Wodewose. This human species that all of Otherworld complains about are really quite nice he considered. Though he felt it wiser to keep this thought to himself. Alasdair and Cathasach stirred, their impatience obvious. Wodewose noticed at once and squeezed Charlotte's hand.

"Come, I'll take you to see the artist as I promised to do." On hearing this Charlotte's heart leapt and the rain forgotten, at least for the moment. She couldn't wait to meet this man. Another human, and one who had not only lived in their cottage, but somehow transcended into Otherworld. Who like her had also seen the magpie and the robin. She had so many questions for him. She simply couldn't wait. With Wodewose joining them the little group made off once more through the sodden wood. Where they were heading Charlotte hadn't a clue and didn't really care. She didn't bother asking for everyone was deathly quiet. All, it was obvious, were very much keeping their thoughts to themselves and wanted it that way.

After about ten minutes the little group came upon a small muddy pool. Charlotte recognised it at once. She had passed it many times on walks with her parents. It nearly always looked as though it was about to dry up and woodland debris a permanent feature on its surface. Miraculously no matter how many days and weeks passed without rain the pool never did actually dry up. There was always a thin cover of murky water covering the mud, mud that looked as though it would suck you under if you had the misfortune to fall in. As she studied the quagmire, rain drops, some falling unchallenged, others after bouncing off of all kinds of woodland infrastructure landed with a heavy plop in the ooze. Wodewose stepping forward waved his staff at the pool's centre.

"The artist, Elmer," he said clearly. Charlotte stared at the mire before her. Had Wodewose gone completely mad? There was nothing but muddy water and more mud than water. Sensitive to his feelings, Charlotte didn't want to appear rude or offend her shaggy friend. Thus he wasn't sure how to respond and eventually ended up by simply asking.

"Where? I can't see him."

"There, in there." Wodewose lowered his staff and pointed directly to the centre of the mire. With horror Charlotte realised that what Wodewose may be trying to tell was that the artist had drowned and was lying dead somewhere beneath the filth before her. That perhaps was why he had mysteriously disappeared, he was dead. That explanation though still didn't explain how he'd travelled to Otherworld.

"In there?" she mouthed, in disbelief. "I don't fancy going in there to get him."

"No we wait," Wodewose replied as though a drowned body was an everyday occurrence. "We must wait," he said again. Charlotte as on so many occasions had no idea what Wodewose meant and as she was trying to work it out, became aware that there was some sort of communication passing between the animals. She was beginning to realise that the squirrel was not only a good and trustworthy messenger but rather like the Dutch could communicate with just about everybody. After a few more minutes, Wodewose turned to Charlotte.

"We wait, we must wait here, the dogs," Alasdair and Cathasach didn't look impressed by Wodewose calling them this, "say it's safe to do so." By Wodewose's nervous manner Charlotte could see that he wasn't at all confident in Alasdair and Cathasach's, "risk assessment" but at the same time he wasn't about to argue with them. "Come." Wodewose took Charlotte's hand. "We sit here." He led her to a rotting log on the other side of the pond. Once they had both sat down, Wodewose looked at Charlotte intently and said in the gruffest voice he could muster.

"Leht has asked me to talk to you about the wood."

Charlotte out of the corner of her eye noticed a quickness of movement and looking up saw the squirrel had joined them on the log. Alasdair and Cathasach sat a few metres away staring out into the army of trees. The rain continued to fall at a pace and Charlotte looked at her two companions beside her. Here they were, the three of them all sat side by side on a sodden log in the middle of a wood. It all felt perfectly natural now and yet a few weeks ago it would have been a scene appropriate, only for one of Grimm's fairy tales. Certainly, it would have been unbelievable. What wasn't a fairy tale was the damp from the saturated log making its presence felt beneath her, nor the steady rain that continued to find its way past her outer clothing. The damp and the cold was beginning to get to her. There was a polite cough from Wodewose and Charlotte despite her discomfort gave him her full attention.

"The wood," Wodewose started, "is a good place. It is my home and has been my home from the beginning. I can live nowhere else." Charlotte listened intently, she could tell he was speaking from the heart.

"I love the wood but it can also be dangerous, especially for someone who doesn't understand it." Charlotte knew he meant her. "And to be safe you have to know what is good and what is bad, where is safe and where not to go, where is unsafe." Wodewose took a pause. "Especially France Charlotte, if one day you find yourself in the wood on your own." Charlotte hoped with all her might that this would never happen, especially in Otherworld and at night..

"First." Woodwose continued, his dog-like eyes searching for her understanding. Try and avoid old pits or hollows, you can be trapped there by those who mean you harm." Wodewose thought back to Gryme's Dell and shivered. Hoping France Charlotte hadn't noticed he continued quickly. "In normal times they are quite safe but as you know only too well these are not normal times." Charlotte nodded in agreement, she was thankful Wodewose wasn't talking in riddles, for once he was making perfect sense. She wondered how much of Leht's influence was rubbing off with his lesson. "You must also avoid hollow paths," Wodewose paused for a moment as though searching for something and found it. "Holloways they are called in your world." He sounded pleased at finding the correct expression.

(For those who wonder what on earth Wodewose is talking about, a holloway is a sunken path. Often they can be thousands of years old, some existing thousands of years before Jesus walked this "green and pleasant land." Worn deep through constant use, in more recent times, to remain hidden, they were sometimes used by smugglers when transporting contraband.)

Charlotte loved holloways, they have a character all of their own and a strong sense of the mystique. Often and especially in woodland predominantly of beech, the banks are lined with an intricate tangle of exposed tree roots and when the trees are in full leaf, it can be like walking through a tunnel of green.

"The enemy," Wodewose's deliberately gruff voice brought Charlotte back to the here and now. "The enemy will often try to chase you into a hollow, a holloway or anything sunken, any place where shadows linger. Another pause, this time to let his warning sink in. He needn't have worried it had sunk in well enough, though just who the enemy were and how she would identify them, Charlotte wasn't sure at all. She remembered the blood dripping from Cathasach's mouth and shivered, not for once from the cold and damp. Wodewose went on to describe a number of other features to avoid, features up until that moment Charlotte had considered quite innocent.

"What I have just told you applies to both worlds."

Charlotte was shocked at Wodewose's last words. Up until now she had thought apart from the mist and of course the magpies that she was safe in her world. From what Wodewose was telling her, apparently not.

"If you know the wood," Wodewose hadn't finished. "There are safe places too. The wood can be your friend if you know where to look. Where Leht last came to us is a safe place." Charlotte remembered Wodewose telling her this at the time. "There are other similar places too and I will show them to you but not tonight." Charlotte wondered why not, after all they had plenty of time, hadn't they? Maybe not.

"If you are not near a safe place and you need one, the wood can protect you. You need to learn the ways of everything that lives here, this knowledge has been lost in your world and that is part of the problem." Charlotte had no idea what Wodewose meant by this, what problem? He was starting to speak in riddles again.

"The holly can protect you and it is difficult for the Darkness and his agents to find you if you hide in a thicket of holly. The ash and especially the rowan can help, but to be really affective you need to make a crown of woven twigs and wear it on your head." Wodewose placed his hands on his head to demonstrate. Charlotte didn't think she'd feel safe using either the ash or holly for protection and she wasn't sure whether she even knew what an ash tree looked like and had never heard of a rowan. Otherworld though she was learning fast, may look like her world but the rules here were completely different. What was fantasy in her world was reality here. She had to take what Wodewose was telling her seriously and noted his advice.

Wodewose held out his arm and opened his giant hand, in his palm shone something silver. Charlotte realised he was offering it to her and gently picked it up, it was tiny and in the dark she had trouble making it out.

"It's a frog," Wodewose helped her. Being on the subject of keeping safe he was just about to follow up by explaining its purpose when he remembered what Leht had told him.

"Whoever possesses the frog cannot know its purpose or its powers will be worthless." Wodewose just stopped himself in time. Instead he said simply.

"It's a present."

"Oh Wodewose," Charlotte was touched by his kindness. "It's beautiful." Holding it up, even without light from the moon she could make out just how intricate the little frog was, it really was perfection. She leaned over and kissed Wodewose on his hairy cheek.

"It's a present from Leht," he said quickly, embarrassed.

"It doesn't matter," Charlotte was enjoying the shaggy beast's embarrassment. "It was you who gave it to me."

"You must keep it safe," Wodewose urged her. "It's rare and worth a lot of money." He wasn't sure how else to tell Charlotte to take care of it. He had heard that in her world, her species apart from the very few valued wealth highly. In Otherworld wealth didn't really matter. It was knowledge that was most sought after, the understanding and respect of the natural way of things. These were the qualities that brought respect and with it power.

"Don't worry Wodewose, I will keep it with me always." Charlotte wore a heart shaped locket on a chain around her neck. It was very old and given to her by her English grandparents. The heart was hinged and opened so you could store something that was precious to you inside, such as a lock of hair from a loved one. She hadn't as yet decided what to keep inside the locket and the frog was so small that it fitted nicely. It was perfect. "There," she said snapping the locket shut." I'll always wear it. Wodewose looked pleased but only half. He was puzzling how to tell France Charlotte that she couldn't take the little silver frog back to her world. How was he going to do that? Charlotte for her part wasn't stupid and knew that if Leht had given it to her there had to be a very good reason, it wouldn't be just a casual trinket. There would be a purpose. I will find out in good time, she thought. Observing Wodewose's troubled expression she didn't want to burden him by probing him with awkward questions. If she was meant to know, somebody would tell her.

Up until that point Alasdair and Cathasach had remained silent, unmoving, ears pricked. So when they stirred their movement caught everybody's attention. The squirrel ran up a young beech tree. Woodwose stood up staff in hand and Charlotte, well Charlotte simply looked up. The two hounds stood rigid, their gaze fixed firmly on something deep in the woods, something coming from the direction of Aldbury Common. Charlotte, although wary, did not feel scared. She knew Alasdair and Cathasach by now, she knew their reaction to various situations and from their present reaction she knew whatever it was they'd seen they didn't consider it to be a threat. Charlotte followed their gaze into the wood, apart from the drip, drip of the rain everything was silent. In the distance she spotted a soft glow, a lone light. At first Charlotte thought it was Leht, a light was always how she started to appear. However she soon saw that this light wasn't the same, there was no vapour trail and it was slowly getting bigger. It was approaching not through the air as Leht always did but treading the earth. As the light got closer, Charlotte could see it was in fact a figure, a figure that was human in stature but definitely not human. Whatever it was, there was no doubt it was heading straight for them. Charlotte sat transfixed, even for Otherworld where nothing surprised her any more this figure looked supernatural. Surely they should be running Charlotte thought but the expression on the faces of Alasdair and Cathasach were of expectancy, neither looked tense nor displayed the slightest hint of aggression. Even the normally nervous Wodewose looked relatively relaxed. The squirrel too had come down from the beech and once more was sitting on the log beside her.

The figure came to a stop no more than two metres from them. Charlotte saw that the light was in fact a long white gown that shone with accentuated brightness in the darkness accentuated by a cloud covered night sky. As the rain fell on the cloak, the droplets bounced off becoming little shards of light before quickly fading into the night air. The closest thing Charlotte could liken the spectacle to was a sparkler in slow motion. It was quite mesmerising. The robe had a hood and it covered not a face as we know it but just a mass of characterless grey. The face was devoid of features except for two dark sockets which Charlotte assumed were eyes though they like the face were completely featureless, lacking any expression. From what Charlotte could see for the robe reached to the ground and therefore she couldn't be sure, it didn't look as though the figure possessed legs. It or he for the figure looked masculine, had from what she could tell, floated across the wood though at a walking pace.

"Hello Alasdair, hello Cathasach," the figure bowed to the two hounds who were now sitting. "Hello Wodewose and hello our master messenger," the squirrel responded by quivering its tail. The figure spoke as Leht did, by somehow talking directly to the mind, not seeking out ears. Everybody there appeared to understand what the figure was saying. The figure's featureless face turned to Charlotte.

"Nice to meet you France Charlotte, my name is Triskelion."

Chapter Thirteen

Unveiling Otherworld

Triskelion spoke with a man's voice, it was soft, calm but at the same time firm. It had strength. He addressed the group as one.

"Sorry I've taken so long but the Darkness is increasing its influence along Icknield, and on more than one occasion I had to follow the safer path of Michael." Charlotte hadn't a clue what he was talking about, he was worse than Wodewose. Triskelion then addressed only Charlotte."I understand you wish to meet Elmer? The artist and Wodewose promised you, you could." Charlotte nodded.

"Wodewose says he's there, in there." She stood and pointed to the murkiness that could loosely, very loosely, be called a pool.

"He is," Triskelion said softly. I say softly for that is exactly how he sounded but underneath there was a solidness that demonstrated authority.

"Then I'm not sure I want to see him." Charlotte replied, her voice trembling, something she was angry with herself for. She had never seen a dead body before and didn't really want to start now. Especially somebody who had lived in their cottage. There was also the question of how he had died and how did Wodewose and the others know he was there. Had they killed him and hidden his body, knowing if he was thrown into the mire the mud would suck him under? They were questions Charlotte wasn't sure she wanted to know the answers to . Especially from someone who resembled a ghost.

Triskelion either didn't hear or simply ignored Charlotte's reply.

"Watch." Triskelion spoke softly but in such a way that Charlotte knew she had little choice but to do as he commanded. She turned to look at the small circle of murky water. Since she had been concentrating on Triskelion a transformation had taken place. The pool was a perfect circle and there was no woodland debris on the surface, not even one dead leaf. The water still looked repulsive but the pool was completely free of anything alien. Charlotte glanced at Triskelion, he stood motionless, arms by his sides, his featureless eyes staring at the small circle of murky water. She saw the rest of the group were static, doing the same. Even Alasdair and Cathasach who were always alert and on guard, were, temporarily at least, off duty their attention on nothing else but the perfect circle. Who was this ghost-like creature? Charlotte asked herself who calls himself Triskelion, who demanded and received total obedience. A noise that sounded like running water made her return her attention to the mud pool. The pool was no longer static, the water had started to foam and she could see beneath the surface a glow, a glow that was growing stronger with every second. A beam of light broke the surface and remained shining unwaveringly skywards capturing all their faces in a ghostly hue. The light below the surface was now so bright it hurt to look at it but not one of them turned away. All the surface of the pool was now a mass of white foam and something could be seen rising in the midst of the agitation. At first it was simply a black shape silhouetted against the brilliance of the white thrashing water. The shape was roundish and attached to something rising beneath it. With slow and chilling horror Charlotte recognised that what at first was only distinguishable as a black round shape was in fact the head of a man. The head continued to rise, straightening as it did so until it was facing, not up nor down or to the left or right but forward, looking directly at her. The rest of the man's body followed, only stopping when he was standing erect, his feet resting flat on the surface of the water which was now so still it could have been mistaken for a mirror. The submerged light, as though somebody had thrown a switch suddenly went out. The water in the pond couldn't be blacker but the body of the man suspended above it literally glistened in the beam of light which remained. Water ran off the body in every direction. Charlotte saw, despite the draining water that the man had a mass of black curly hair and was wearing an artist's smock of dark green with plain brown trousers and brown shoes. He had a waxy complexion and deep brown eyes that were wide open and staring at her. She expected them to be expressionless but they were not, on the contrary the man's eyes were full of expression. One expression to be exact and Charlotte recognised it immediately. His eyes were almost bursting with terror, absolute and unfettered terror.

Triskelion still staring directly ahead, slowly, very slowly lowered his head. The dark water started to foam and the submerged light slowly reappeared. The body quickly started to sink and as it did so the man's face dropped until his chin was resting on his chest. Charlotte watched transfixed as the body and lastly the head vanished below the surface. The light faded and went out and the foam calmed until the water once more was so still it was like looking into a mirror. The beam of light remained for a few seconds longer before it too suddenly went out. The remaining silence was deafening, and the darkness blinding. The only sound and it was a relief from the uninvited stillness was the drip, drip ,drip of water landing on the rain soaked floor. Charlotte's head was screaming for someone to say something. Complete shock had frozen every nerve in her body and her lips refused to move, she too was an unwilling participant in the absolute quiet.

Slowly Triskelion raised his head and turned, looking directly at her.

"There," he said, the silence broken. His tone was even softer if that was at all possible. "You have met your artist." Charlotte should have felt terrified by what she had just been party to but there was something very calming in Triskelion's voice, as though he read her distress and without using words was reassuring her.

"Is he dead?" Charlotte immediately regretted the question, of course he was dead, how stupid of her.

Nothing however she should have remembered is how it first appears in Otherworld.

"No," Triskelion replied without hesitation. His tone firm, squashing any doubt but still soft enough to ask for understanding. "He is suspended until it is safe to release him."

Like so many answers she received in Otherworld Charlotte had not the faintest idea of what Triskelion was talking about and asked the only question she felt reasonable.

"When will that be?" Charlotte used a tone she hoped would convince the ghost-like newcomer that she knew exactly what he was talking about.

"That France Charlotte is, as you say in your world, the million dollar question. We simply do not know." Charlotte was more than a little shocked at this admission. The ghost, Triskelion seemed so in command of everything, it was almost reassuring to discover that he wasn't. Also, for the first time since he'd spoken she was sure she'd sensed a touch of emotion in Triskelion's voice. She was sure there'd been a touch of regret, maybe even sadness. He still hadn't explained, and Charlotte hadn't forgotten, how the artist had got there in the first place. But like on so many previous occasions she felt this wasn't the moment to ask that question.

"All will be explained in time." Triskelion spoke to her again and this time the authoritative voice was back, there was no emotion. His words were softly spoken but in a manner which said he wasn't prepared to accept any questioning. "For now, tonight, I need to show you something and it must be for your eyes only." Charlotte nodded meekly, just as it was when Leht communicated with her, she felt powerless to respond in any other way. Triskelion turned to where Wodewose and the others were grouped. Every one of them looked as though they were just emerging from a deep sleep and Charlotte wondered if Triskelion had the gift of mass hypnosis. Wodewose in particular looked very at ease and the squirrel indifferent. The two hounds in contrast looked very uncomfortable, confused, their muscles tensed. Triskelion didn't appear to notice or be bothered and addressed the group as one, once more.

"I have to show France Charlotte something and it must be for her to witness only." Charlotte sensed with his last words, Triskelion was speaking directly to Alasdair and Cathasach. "We will also be quicker if it is just the two of us. You all from what I understand, deserve a rest. Go back to your homes, get some sleep and we will all meet up again tomorrow. I will send a message as to where and at what time." Triskelion then definitely spoke directly to the hounds. "Alasdair, Cathasach, do not fret. The human child will be safe with me for the Darkness has other things on its mind, and I am aware of its movements and those of its supporters. Escort my friends back to their homes." Triskelion then turned and spoke to the squirrel directly. "As for you my little friend, I will need your services later tonight. Let Alasdair and Cathasach escort you home for now. Get some rest and we will meet later at the Great Ash, I will send a time."

Charlotte didn't at all like the thought of being left alone with Triskelion. She'd known him for under an hour and was meant to put all her trust in for want of a better word, a ghost. Wodewose must have sensed Charlotte's concern for he turned and touched her on the arm.

"It's ok he reassured her, Triskelion is a good friend of Leht, she sent for his help and trusts him completely, as do I." For a moment Wodewose had spoken as though he were a man not in his normal clumsy boyish manner.

"Please do not be concerned or alarmed France Charlotte." It was the soft voice of Triskelion. "I would not normally ask one to have faith in me so quickly but these are not normal times and time is becoming more precious with every day that passes. Worry not, I will ensure no harm comes to you." Triskelion then turned to the others and for the first time raised his robed arm, though with a slowness that was his signature. "Please be on your way, until the next moon." His voice remained soft and his words were phrased as a request but no one doubted he expected to be obeyed.

Charlotte watched as the little group, her friends disappeared into the wood. Seeing them go, Charlotte couldn't remember ever feeling so sad, so lonely. She was alone with a complete stranger in an even stranger world. Every time she crossed over or transcended into what everyone here called Otherworld she wondered if it would be the last time she'd see her world and more importantly to her, her parents. Right now she wanted to see them so badly. She couldn't begin to imagine their emotions if they woke up one morning and discovered she wasn't in her bed. That she had simply vanished, just like the two little boys. She knew it would break them. Charlotte felt like bursting into tears, never in her life had she felt as low and as vulnerable as she did now.

The stranger, Triskelion, she saw was approaching her, slow and steady as was his manner. His appearance was frightening and manner more so but Charlotte didn't run. She was past caring, after all he was Leht's friend and everyone appeared to trust him. Charlotte just prayed their trust wasn't misplaced. If his appearance wasn't so ghost like maybe it would be easier. Triskelion came to a halt directly in front of her, his robe so bright it hurt her to look at him. In the slowest of motion he raised his right hand placing it gently on her head. The softness of his touch at first surprised her and next she felt as though she were burning, not a painful burning but with all the energy of fire without the pain. The feeling was almost impossible to describe except to say that she had never felt so energised. Triskelion took his hand away. Charlotte stood rooted to the spot, her fear was gone and so was her sadness. They were replaced with equal feelings of courage and utter determination and at that moment she trusted Triskelion implicitly.

Triskelion spoke again, his soft voice demanding her full attention.

"I feel your pain little girl. I feel your distress. I have taken them both away for now. Your conduct since you have transcended into Otherworld has impressed everybody here. I have only known you for a matter of minutes human child but within that short time I have recognised something in your heart that I thought had been lost to your species forever." Charlotte not for the first time that night hadn't a clue what he was talking about but it sounded good. "You have a question?" Charlotte had hundreds, even more after tonight but at that moment, one was burning to be answered, how did Triskelion know?

"Yes, Triskelion, what am I doing here? Why me?"

Triskelion didn't answer straight away and they shared a rather uncomfortable silence accompanied by the drip, drip, drip of the rain.

"France Charlotte," Triskelion's voice when it came was slow and with thought. "I really wish I could tell you that, if I knew it would make my task here so much easier. The truth and I'm really sorry to have to tell you, is I simply don't know, nobody knows. All anybody knows is that you're here, you have been chosen and the Snooks foretold it."

Charlotte was just about to ask another question, chosen by who? when Triskelion stopped her, again he apparently had read her mind.

"I know you have many more questions France Charlotte but now I'm afraid isn't the time. Despite what I told Alasdair and Cathasach the woods are not safe and for you, especially not at night. I will answer your questions tomorrow." He paused and looked around in a manner that suggested he was wanting to drive home his warning. "I must show you something. Stay close to me, I promised I wouldn't let you come to any harm and I won't." With that he started to move off deep into the wood towards Aldbury Common and Charlotte dutifully followed. As was always the case, she had little other choice. As they moved off something made her take one last look to where she'd seen Triskelion raise the artist. The pond had returned to the state she'd always witnessed in her world, the surface lay thick with mud, and debris from the surrounding trees littered the pool's surface. What had just happened? Would she ever understand? Would anyone ever explain?

Like Alasdair and Cathasach, Triskelion avoided all human made paths, though unlike the two hounds Triskelion's pace was slow and Charlotte found it easy to keep up with him. As they progressed in silence she tried to tell whether he was floating or walking. The robe covered his feet and his movement was neither smooth nor rhythmic. It was impossible to tell. After Aldbury Common the two traversed Sallow Copse eventually coming out at Hanging Isley on the edge of the wooded scarp. The going through the wood at times had been tough. Many of the branches were body height and Charlotte often had to force her way through. In places the floor of the wood had been covered in low lying brambles which tripped and scratched at every opportunity. Though the going had been tough for her, Charlotte noticed that Triskelion although slow hadn't appeared to have found the going tough at all and asked a direct question that was straight from the child within.

"Triskelion can you walk through things?"

"No," came the equally direct answer. "I can make things move." As with many things Triskelion said Charlotte wasn't quite sure what he meant but no matter, she had another question and one that only a child could get away with.

"Are you a ghost?"

"No," came another one word reply.

From Hanging Isley the two followed the rim of the escarpment to Duncombe Terrace and then Clipper Down. After Clipper Down Triskelion appeared to be far more cautious and kept passing messages to Charlotte to be as quiet as possible. Charlotte did as she was told but if they were trying to remain hidden Triskelion's shining robe was a real giveaway. As though reading her mind, something that was beginning to make her feel a little uncomfortable, Triskelion passed another message.

"I am only visible to those I want to see me." Another riddle.

As they advanced, Charlotte realised they were approaching where her parents had parked the van on their recent outing to Ivinghoe Beacon and sure enough they crossed almost exactly where they had stopped. Shortly after this Triskelion came to a halt. They were at the top of a steep chalk grass covered slope with a scattering of scrub and the odd tree. Beneath them though not immediately visible lay the large partly wooded depression simply named The Coombe. From their vantage point they had a direct view of Ivinghoe Beacon and the Shire beyond. When Charlotte saw the Beacon she clasped her hands over her mouth. There stood the white stag or hart as they called it in Otherworld. It still faced west but everything else about the animal had changed. When she had last seen the hart with Leht, his magnificent white coat had been luminous and his antlers had shone brighter than the brightest star. Although it had been obvious he was fighting something and was scared for his life he had still demonstrated a grim determination and his strength had been clear for all to see. Around him the circles of light spun by Leht had been almost blinding. Seeing the poor hart in his current state broke Charlotte's heart. Even from a distance she could see the beast looked on the verge of defeat, dejected and so utterly alone. It's coat no longer shone and his proud set of antlers were a shadow of their former splendour. The circles of light spun by Leht to give him strength were still there but they were spinning slowly and were easy to watch without sheltering her eyes. Having said all that, Charlotte could see the hart was still not beaten, not yet anyway. Facing perhaps inevitable defeat she could see even with her being so far away, the proud animal was still refusing to give up. If only the visitors to the Beacon in my world could see this she thought. How much more they'd appreciate what was around them, maybe they'd stop taking the natural world for granted.

"Come." Triskelion instructed her and made to retrace their tracks. Not a word passed between them as they made their way back to Clipper Down. Charlotte after what she had just seen was bursting with so many questions but as always seemed to be the case, now wasn't the time. On reaching Clipper Down rather than retracing their route along the top of the escarpment, Triskelion led Charlotte to a viewpoint at the head of the down with views all the way down the valley towards Aldbury. It was a magnificent vista and one normally Charlotte would have appreciated enormously, but not tonight.

Triskelion stopped, his face staring down the valley towards her village. At that very moment the clouds parted allowing the light from the moon to shine through. Raindrops appeared to be suspended in the air as the moon's rays caught them on their way to the ground below. Aldbury for a few seconds as though the subject of a spotlight was bathed in the moon's blue tinted rays. The spectacle gave the village the appearance it was the most special place on Earth or maybe Otherworld, perhaps both.

"I am sorry you had to see that France Charlotte."

Charlotte didn't look at Triskelion, she let his words float over her, she didn't feel like talking. Instead she joined him, gazing down the valley towards Aldbury preferring to keep her thoughts to herself. Standing on a spur draped in his brightly shining cloak Triskelion shone as a beacon, a watchtower over her long suffering village. The scene reminded Charlotte of her bible lessons for what she was witnessing could almost be considered biblical. If only that really was the case. It was so beautiful, so surreal she wanted to reach out and grab it, put it in a pocket for safekeeping. Just as Oliver Twist had wanted to in the musical. Such magic could never last long of course and no sooner had the scene stirred Charlotte's deepest emotions the clouds closed and all the valley returned to darkness.

"I think you understand why I had to make you see for yourself, the predicament of our Guardian, the white hart." Triskelion's soft voice, his tone like that of a trained actor fitted the mood perfectly.

This time Charlotte responded, she nodded, she understood now.

"You can see that mere words would not have had the same impact."

Drawing a deep breath Charlotte nodded again.

"You can see how little time we have, unless something is done and done quickly our courageous hart will meet an end so horrible you cannot begin to imagine and the Beacon as you call it with its irreplaceable library will be in the hands of the Darkness. The Darkness will have access to secrets so powerful, so dangerous that it may be able not only to destroy your world and mine but the entire universe. Many of the scrolls in the Sacred Library were placed there and have remained there untouched for thousands of your years, some possibly since the beginning of time itself. Placed there by the creator or creators of everything we see around us. It is believed that one of the scrolls, maybe several, contain secrets to Orme itself and that knowledge would make the Darkness invincible. We cannot let the Sacred Library fall, France Charlotte, we simply cannot. The Sacred Library of Evinghehou must be protected at all costs."

Charlotte nodded, the magnitude of what Triskelion was telling her was beyond anything she knew. But why tell her, what can she do, why seek the ear of an eleven year human child from another world? How on earth could she play a part in what was unfolding?

"Enough for tonight," Triskelion almost sighed. He led off again descending the Down towards a farm, just visible in the valley below. On reaching the valley floor the two made their way across open fields, heading for Aldbury. The rain made no attempt to let up, if anything it was becoming heavier. The already sodden chalk soil underfoot quickly became not only sticky but greasy and twice Charlotte found herself losing her footing and ending up on her back. As they neared Aldbury Charlotte recognised the oak at the top of the field, where they'd hidden the budget. Triskelion made no attempt to stop and Charlotte thought it better to not to say anything. Perhaps he didn't know about the budget and still she didn't entirely trust Triskelion. On arriving at the church they found the squirrel waiting, looking very wet and miserable. The robin too was perched on the castellated roof of the porch. Beyond the churchyard wall Charlotte could see the mist twisting and turning more violently, more angrily than ever. Triskelion must have seen her watching, for in his soft but commanding voice he said firmly.

"Do not look at it, France Charlotte, for it will draw you in and you will be lost to us." Charlotte, shocked, looked away. Triskelion held out his hand. "Your necklace, before you go, France Charlotte I need your necklace." Charlotte was hesitant, for what possible reason could he want it? It was hers. Triskelion as seemed to be the norm answered before she could ask her question.

"The gift from Leht cannot travel to your world, it will be destroyed on the journey there. You wouldn't want that. I will keep it safe until you return. You have my word."

Charlotte, again felt she had no choice and carefully unclasped the chain and placed it complete with the little heart holding the miniature frog in Triskelion's outstretched hand.

"Thank you," his hand disappearing beneath his robe. "Fear not I will keep it safe. You must go now, till tomorrow." With that he turned and made his way down the church path. Watching him leave, Charlotte still couldn't work out if he were walking or floating. Either way with his glowing white robe and watching him pass among the tombstones, in her world he was the archetypal image of a ghost.

The squirrel Charlotte realised, was looking up at her, waiting patiently. She gave a simple nod and the squirrel dived underground with Charlotte close on its heels. Within seconds they were in her Aldbury. The real Aldbury.

"I don't need you to escort me home," Charlotte turned to the squirrel. "I'll be alright." The squirrel either ignored her or simply didn't understand for it scurried down the gravel path and past the village shop on its way to the cottage. Charlotte, tired simply followed it. At her back door, the robin was dutifully waiting. "He doesn't have to escort me home," Charlotte said irritably on seeing her feathered friend. She no longer thought twice about talking to a bird, it was a perfectly normal thing to do, especially to a robin. There appeared to be some sort of communication between the robin and the squirrel and the squirrel made off its tail bristling. "Thank you robin." Her words came out short and sharp. She didn't mean them that way, she was simply exhausted. Not bothering to bid the little bird goodnight, Charlotte pushed open the door to the kitchen. How good it was to be home. At the top of the stairs she quietly cracked the door to her parent's bedroom. Both were asleep, they looked so peaceful. Once in her own room the first thing she did was go over to the picture of the white hart. Holding the frame she planted a gentle kiss on the glass. Charlotte couldn't see it but on the summit of a hill in Otherworld the hart's coat glowed.

In bed Charlotte pulled Gromit close, so many more questions she thought, so many and fell into a deep but troubled sleep. The robin on the sill, cocked his head and rested for a few seconds watching her. If a robin could sigh, it would have done and flew back to its nest, just one more creature spending the night alone.

The next morning Charlotte awoke feeling heavy headed. The Monday morning feeling was bad enough without her feeling like this. Sitting up she yawned loudly and stretched her aching limbs. The way her limbs were complaining was a painful reminder that during the night they'd been on a trek in the rain to Ivinghoe Beacon and back. She picked up her clothes from the night before, they were where she'd left them on the floor beside her bed. She examined them closely. They were immaculate, even her shoes were spotless, not a sign of mud and everything was dry. Again she questioned, why everything returns in the same state they were when she left except the way she feels. She just could not understand the difference, it didn't make sense and it definitely wasn't fair.

Breakfast was an obligatory bowl of hot chocolate followed by toast spread with confiture de fraises and Nutella. Try it! Both the magpies were waiting in the oak for her when she arrived at the bus stop. Charlotte did her best to ignore them, turning her back to the tree. There was the usual nod from the gathering of young students when she arrived along with the odd, "morning, French Charlotte." Otherwise the babble of children waiting for the bus was strangely subdued. This was almost certainly partly due to the heavy atmosphere over Aldbury which everyone agreed was starting to become unbearable. They were well into May and everywhere outside the village, nature was displaying advanced signs of greeting summer but in Aldbury it was though winter had yet to say goodbye and spring had just simply given up. The atmosphere in the bus changed completely after it had left the confines of the village. Conversations started to flow and there were peels of excited laughter. There was no obvious reason for the sudden change in mood, The weather beyond Aldbury that morning was depressing to say the least. Indeed you could argue it was worse, for the sky was heavily overcast and rain splattered the windows as the bus wound its way between fields towards Tring. Physically though the atmosphere outside Aldbury was lighter, brighter despite the grey skies and persistent rain. On leaving Aldbury it was as though a weight had been lifted off everybody's shoulders.

Charlotte found school surprisingly easy that day. She'd expected to find it a struggle and yes she felt tired but she'd managed to stay alert without too much difficulty. In English, their teacher had asked the class to write an essay about a fantasy island. They were to imagine that they'd been shipwrecked on an island and to describe the island in detail along with their experiences on surviving there.

"Let your imaginations run riot," their teacher had told them. "Do not hold back." Charlotte knew immediately what her island would be like.

After school, on returning to Aldbury and before going home Charlotte made her habitual visit to the village shop. Caroline had told her that the shop was selling a new sweet that made your tongue go completely blue and she wanted to try them. She hated the silence as she entered, she used to love the loud greeting from the old bell as you opened the door. Inside Charlotte found the vicar, he was waiting at the till and carrying a shopping basket full of red wine.

"Good afternoon, French Charlotte," he beamed on seeing her, the heavy atmosphere hanging over the village never seemed to get to the vicar. "Unfortunately unlike Jesus I cannot turn water into wine, I have to pay for it." With some effort he lifted the heavy basket onto the counter. Charlotte expected to see Ashtynn behind the counter packing the vicar's wine but instead stood a young girl. Charlotte recognised her as a sixth former at her school.

"Where's Ashtynn?" Charlotte asked, surprised. She was disappointed too, she liked Ashtynn and her cheery welcome, she had become a little part of Charlottes life, a poor analogy perhaps but a little like homely wallpaper.

"She didn't turn up for work this morning," the sixth former said rather unkindly, as though she were Ashtynn's boss. Charlotte was just about to follow up on the sixth formers response when she saw the vicar wink at her and mouthed clearly.

"I'll fill you in outside." He gestured to the door. Charlotte nodded, enjoying the intrigue and went in search of the new sweets Caroline had been enthusing about. She soon found them and paid the sixth former, who redeemed herself by offering Charlotte a wide smile and wishing whatever it was that had stopped Ashtynn coming to work that morning wasn't something serious and that she'd be back tomorrow.

Outside the shop Charlotte found the vicar waiting.

"What have you got there, French charlotte?" the vicar asked loudly looking at her bag. Charlotte opened the little paper bag she was holding and showed him her collection of sweets. The vicar pulled a face. "Rather you than me," he smiled. "I think I'll stick to my wine."

"I'm not allowed wine." Charlotte replied pointedly.

"No, no of course not," the vicar admonished himself. "Very sensible of your parents. Talking of which," his face became serious for a moment." Does your mother bake cakes? Only I'm throwing a small party for my choir and something French," he coughed. "Would be wonderful. It might even improve their singing"

"I'll ask her," Charlotte replied, with a grin. "What about Ashtynn?"

The vicar's face changed. "Ah yes Ashtynn," he said stroking his beard. "You haven't been near that mist have you French Charlotte?" Charlotte shook her head.

"No not after the fair."

"Good, well don't." He paused and Charlotte could see that he was thinking. Whatever it was he wanted to tell her she could see it was troubling him. "I'm not sure I should say anything," he said eventually, confirming her observation. He paused again, looking at the little girl's expectant face. Without realising it he continued pulling on his beard, something he always did when deep in thought. He was questioning his decision. Seeing French Charlotte's expectant face made him feel guilty. She was only a little girl but there was something about French Charlotte that put her older than her years. He sensed she was astutely aware and had something, something inside her that no one else he'd ever met possessed. He just couldn't pinpoint what it was. Calling it spiritual was far too simple, she had spirit of a kind of that there was no doubt but her spirit he sensed belonged more to the natural world not the spiritual. He just couldn't explain it, his senses would only take him so far. Finally he relented and with a smile, "well I suppose you're old enough and you always come across as sensible."

"Thank you, that's because I am" Charlotte smiled back, her smile disguising her impatience. She desperately wanted to know what it was the vicar had to tell her.

"Glad to hear it," joked the vicar back, with an even bigger smile. "Anyway, it's a funny thing but early this morning and I mean early, for it was around five." The vicar pulled a face. "I was unlocking the church when I saw Ashtynn walking up to the shop. I thought she may have had some sorting to do and so starting early but instead of unlocking the door, she walked straight past the shop along the road and crossed over to the gate." Charlotte knew the vicar meant the gate accessing the mist covered field. The vicar had stopped talking and looked deep in thought.

"Anyway," he went on after a long pause. "I thought nothing of it until I went to buy my wine at the shop and found she wasn't there. Then you came in and asked where she was, and when the girl behind the counter said she hadn't turned up for work, it set me wondering. I know Ashtynn and you got on well, that's why I thought I'd ask what you thought." The vicar returned to stroking his beard, he was beginning to regret talking to French Charlotte about what he'd seen. She may be sensible but she was after all only eleven years old.

"Has anyone checked to see if she's at home?" Charlotte asked simply. She may only be eleven but she wasn't stupid. She could see the vicar was uncomfortable and she knew he wasn't telling her the whole story. She could tell he was holding something back, it was so obvious. Adults were nearly always rubbish actors.

"Brilliant thought, French Charlotte," the vicar replied enthusiastically looking relieved. "How stupid of me, trust a little girl and French at that," he gave her a mock punch. "To tell me, a grown man, what to do. I'll go and see her now. She's probably ill, let me dump these." He held up his bags of wine, "and I'll walk with you, it's on your way."

Charlotte waited as the vicar put the bags containing the wine on the back seat of his car. Ashtynn lived in a fairly modern house in a small estate just after the Valiant Trooper pub. It was only a further five minutes' walk after where she lived. After locking his car door the two of them proceeded to walk the first part of the route. On arriving outside Charlotte's cottage the vicar was about to bid her farewell when he hesitated and said.

"I'll tell you what French Charlotte, as I'm here, I think I'll come and ask your mother directly about baking some gateaux for the choir." He pronounced gateaux with a mock and shocking French accent.

"If you like" and Charlotte skipped down the brick path which led to the rear of the house. "Follow me she called, the front door is jammed." Her mother on hearing her daughter's voice opened the upper half of the stable door, leaning on the bottom door, ready to greet her.

"Bonjour," boomed the vicar on seeing Charlotte's mother.

"Bonjour pretre," her mother replied in the sing-song way that only the native French can manage. "What has my daughter done?"

"Oh French charlotte," smiled the vicar patting Charlotte's head. "Nothing except spending her hard earned money on too many sweets."

"Not as much as your wine," retorted Charlotte and got a mock whack on the head from her mother.

"Go and get changed," her mother held the bottom door open so Charlotte could pass. Charlotte ducked under her mother's arm and ran up the stairs to her room. Once there rather than changing she went to the sash window and lifted it open, praying her mother wouldn't hear. She needn't have worried her mother was in deep conversation with the vicar. Charlotte then lay on the floor straining to hear their conversation below, taking care all the time not to be seen.

Listening to her mother and the vicar talk wasn't difficult. Both had loud voices even when they were deliberately lowered. Her mother had invited the vicar in but he had declined politely with the excuse that if he came in he'd never leave and he had much to do. Their conversation thus was outside the back door, perfect for Charlotte to hear what was being said. At first she could hear the vicar asking her mother about baking cakes for the choir and her mother suggesting which flavours may be the most popular. The cake deliberations went on for a good five minutes, "nothing too sophisticated," the vicar kept urging. After the choice of cake along with a price had been agreed the vicar deliberately lowered his voice and as Charlotte knew, it made little or no difference. She could still hear him perfectly.

"Have you heard about Ashtynn?" the vicar started.

"Only that she wasn't at work today." Charlotte heard her mother reply. The vicar's voice came again.

"I've been the vicar here for fifteen years and I've never known Ashtynn to have a day off, not only that she didn't phone in this morning."

"Perhaps she's ill, has anyone been to her house to check?"

"That's what your daughter asked," admitted the vicar. "I'm on my way to check on her now."

"Well let me know how she is?"

"I will, I will." The vicar paused unaware that he was pulling on his beard. Charlotte's mother recognised the habit, he was either nervous or unsure what to say next. "There's something else though." The vicar lowered his tone even more but still Charlotte had no problem hearing him. Her mother waited, still leaning on the stable door. "I told your daughter." He paused again pulling even harder on his beard. "I told your daughter," he repeated. "That I saw Ashtynn this morning at five am. I thought she was going to work in the shop early."

"What at five o'clock!" Charlotte heard her mother exclaim. Her mother had never been one for early mornings and five o'clock was the Devil's hour.

"Yes but that's just it, "replied the vicar lowering his voice still further. "She didn't open the shop, she walked straight past it and." The vicar leaned forward. "I didn't tell your daughter this for I didn't want to scare her but, from the shop she walked up and crossed the road, passed through the gate and walked straight into that bloody mist. She didn't hesitate, she just walked straight into it."

"Did she come out? "Her mother sounded a little shocked.

"I've no idea," replied the vicar. "I was there early as I had lots to catch up on before visiting my needy flock." He pulled one of his faces. "I simply started doing things in the church and thought nothing more of it until I discovered just now that Ashtynn hadn't turned up for work."

"Why on earth would she want to go into that disgusting mist and at five o'clock in the morning!" Charlotte's mother made it sound as though being up at five am was far more shocking than walking into the mist.

"There's more though," continued the vicar ignoring her. "When I saw Ashtynn I was just about to unlock the church door. I called out good morning but she simply ignored me. It was early and I didn't want to wake anybody so I didn't shout too loudly, I thought maybe she hadn't heard me."

"Well that's possible," Charlotte's mother said slowly. Personally, she doubted it, even by his standards, when he spoke quietly everyone within twenty or thirty metres could hear what the vicar was saying.

Up in her bedroom Charlotte was thinking along the same lines, the vicar was simply incapable of calling out softly. If he'd called to Ashtynn she would have heard him. There was no question.

"I thought that at the time," continued the vicar "but thinking back there was something strange about Ashtynn this morning, she wasn't walking normally."

"What. You mean she was injured?"

"No, no, nothing like that. No it was as though she was in a trance as though she'd been hypnotised. She just walked, looking straight ahead, past the shop, through the gate and into that bloody mist." I don't know whether to report it or not."

"What to the police?"

Charlotte couldn't see but sensed the vicar give a nod. There was a brief silence, broken by her mother.

"Well," she said thinking. "I think you should go and see if Ashtynn's at home and if you can't get an answer, yes call the police." The vicar left a long pause before answering. He too was thinking, weighing up the options.

"I think you're right," he said eventually, once more stroking his beard. "If it wasn't for the disappearance of those two boys, I'd think nothing of it but..." his voice trailed off.

"Go on," Charlotte's mother urged, waving her hands. "Get going, you'll feel better once you've done something."

"You're right, I will." Replied the vicar. "I don't know what's happening in this bloody village. People keep asking me if it's God's work or worse still the Devil's and I haven't got an answer for them." The vicar didn't wait for Charlotte's mother to give her opinion. Instead he stepped back from the back door and shouted up to Charlotte's window. "Goodbye French Charlotte, don't eat all those sweets at once." Charlotte almost banged her head on the lower window as she was caught unawares and quickly withdrew from view.

"I won't," she shouted breathless. "And don't drink all that wine at once."

This drew an exclamation from her mother.

"I'll try my best." Shouted back the vicar. He turned to go then stopped. "Oh you've got one of those," he exclaimed.

"One of what?" Charlotte's mother hadn't a clue what he was talking about.

"A magpie." I've had one sitting in my garden for the past three or four weeks, it just sits in the same tree, staring at the house.

"I hadn't noticed it before," admitted her mother.

Up in her bedroom Charlotte was thinking furiously. So now they could see the magpie too. What did that mean?

There was no sign of life at Ashtynn's house when the vicar arrived. The garden was well attended though like everybody else's in the village, nothing was growing in it. The curtains weren't drawn but all of the windows were shut tight. The vicar rang the doorbell. He felt uncharacteristically nervous, something wasn't right, he could feel it. He could hear the bell chiming deep within the house. Listening for any other sound he waited praying silently for her to answer. But there was no reply, only the sound of silence. He waited a few seconds then pressed the bell again. Once more he could hear the chimes ringing through the house and once again the only response was silence. He tried one more time even though he knew it was futile. As he knew they would be, the chimes were followed by an unwelcome silence. From the front door the vicar moved to the front window and pressing against the glass peered in. Everything looked neat and he could see a vase of fresh flowers on a dining table, there was no sign of Ashtynn. At least she wasn't lying on the lounge floor, something he had been dreading he might find.

"Can I help you?" A rather concerned looking lady stood in the garden next door. The vicar recognised her immediately as one of his "flock." A Mrs Whittingham, he didn't know her Christian name. Mrs Whittingham recognised the vicar at the same time.

"Oh hello vicar, I didn't realise it was you."

The vicar enquired as to whether the neighbour had seen Ashtynn. "Not since yesterday," Mrs Whittingham confirmed, "and she had seemed fine then." This was in reply to the vicars second question. She then went on to say she held a key to Ashtynn's house in case of an emergency, a reciprocal arrangement between the two of them. If the vicar wanted to use it…. The vicar declined the offer politely saying there really wasn't any need. With that he bid Mrs Whittingham a good evening and walked back up the road to his car parked in front of the village shop. Not only was he looking forward to one of those bottles of wine tonight he positively needed one. On arriving home he reluctantly phoned the police.

To the vicar's surprise the police took his call extremely seriously and promised to send an officer out to Ashtynn's house that evening. In fact two officers attended her house, both experienced. They didn't need the spare key held by Mrs Whittingham to gain entry as they found the back door to be open. Inside everything appeared to be as it should be. There was fresh food in the fridge and nothing appeared to be out of place. In the kitchen they found Ashtynn's handbag and inside her bag her purse. Hanging on a hook in the hallway they found a set of keys with a plastic fob. On the card inside the fob the word shop was written in capital letters. These were later confirmed as the keys to the village shop. Reporting their findings back to the station the conclusion was quickly drawn that Ashtynn's disappearance was suspicious. Two more officers were sent to the village with instructions to meet up with the two already attending and search the field blanketed with the mysterious mist. The place where Ashtynn was last seen. As with the two missing boys this was to be sure the missing lady hadn't tripped and was lying somewhere in the field injured, perhaps unconscious. The search was made using torches and long canes with which the officers prodded the ground. The mist was so thick that the torches proved to be next to useless, the light simply reflecting back into the beam. For some reason unless they were on the very edge of the field the officers found their radios refused to work. The mist also seemed to deaden any sound and even when shouting the officers found it very difficult to communicate with each other. There was also the fear, the deep, deep, dark fear which strangled every living nerve. They found no sign of Ashtynn and the following day every one of the four officers who had been involved in searching the field reported in sick.

Later that evening police officers visited both the vicar and Charlotte's parents. They weren't really there to ask questions but to ask everyone to keep quiet about what they knew. They didn't want another disappearance reaching the ears of the media, causing panic in the village, and they didn't want the person responsible, if she'd been abducted or worse, to be aware of their investigation. They would be in touch with others, who were close to Ashtynn with the same message. And of course last but not least, if anybody hears anything to let them know immediately. Charlotte kept her thoughts to herself. Triskelion's voice rang in her head. "Don't look at the mist," he had said or "we will lose you." She hoped beyond hope Ashtynn would suddenly reappear, she really liked Ashtynn, what on earth had made her walk into the mist. As Charlotte went up to bed her mother reminded her.

"Don't you ever go near that mist Charlotte."

"I won't, I promise." Charlotte assured her mother. Never before had she been so definite about keeping her word.

Despite the best intentions of the police, word quickly spread through the village that something was up. Two patrol cars parked in the small layby outside the church, although not that unusual with all that had happened, was still not a regular occurrence and most villagers by the following morning knew something new was afoot. Two and two were soon pieced together making four. Ashtynn was as part of the village tapestry as the village church or pond and just as equally loved. Her absence was quickly noted and the correct conclusion reached. By early afternoon nearly everyone in the village was aware of what had really happened.

The team leading the investigation into the disappearance of the two boys felt the disappearance of Ashtynn could not be considered a coincidence, the similarities were obvious. The fact that Ashtynn was an adult had also upped the ante. Their theory for the moment was that somebody must be taking advantage of the mist to kidnap those who entered. What puzzled them was, so far no bodies had been found which one might expect under such circumstances and how did the perpetrator always manage to disappear with such apparent ease? To achieve this, the theory for the moment was the offender must be local. Everybody involved hoped they'd crack the case soon and find the disappeared alive. With Ashtynn's disappearance what really puzzled them and perhaps even more is why an adult would enter the mist and at five in the morning? It just didn't make sense. Yes they'd had trouble with juveniles playing dare but by all accounts the lady who worked in the shop was not of that ilk, quite the opposite. She epitomised the word sensible.

The vicar after the police had left, opened a bottle of wine, a red from the Languedoc region of France. Charlotte's mother would approve, he smiled to himself. He wasn't interested in watching television that evening, preferring instead the slow steady sound from the pendulum of his American wall clock. From a drawer in an old oak dresser he took a candle, lit it, and placed it in the window from where there were views across the fields to his church. Looking out at the night sky he prayed the light from the candle would help guide Ashtynn home. It was a deeply personal as well as spiritual gesture and he prayed harder than he'd ever prayed before that the light from the burning candle would help in some small way. Leaving the window he poured himself a second glass and retired to his favourite, cracked with age, leather chesterfield. Keeping the glass he placed the bottle on a small table beside his chair. Sipping hard he enjoyed the slow, mellowing effect the wine was beginning to have on his mind. The steady ticking of the clock also helped and after finishing a third glass he was beginning to feel at peace with the world. Feeling relaxed he began reflecting on the day's events. His thoughts turned to the mist which was now so spread it was threatening to envelope part of the churchyard. For days now he'd been feeling increasingly uneasy about the mist. Worse his feeling of uneasiness was slowly turning into something else, something much worse. He was starting to fear it. So much so he was beginning to find it hard to walk up the main path from the lych gate to the church door preferring instead to take the path from the village green. He was a man of God and had absolute faith in his maker and his religion, the bible made perfect sense to him. His personal faith though, his faith in himself was beginning to be tested on a daily basis. A feeling from deep inside him was telling him that there was something very un-Godly about the mist in the field behind his church. Worse still he was beginning to worry that his faith would not be able to protect him from it. For him to feel this way as far as he was concerned was equivalent to committing blasphemy and he hated himself for his weakness. Every day he prayed hard for guidance on how to deal with his feelings. Up until now his prayers hadn't been answered but he didn't doubt for one second that one day they would be. He just hoped it would be soon for he wasn't sure how much longer he could bear his anguish. As the clock struck midnight the vicar poured his last glass and not long after fell asleep in his chair. If he'd stayed awake and looked out of his window he would have seen a little French girl making her way up the main gravel path to the church door.

Charlotte was half asleep when she heard the tapping at the window. Triskelion had told her they'd meet again the next day. She had fallen asleep expecting to be awakened and was ready. Charlotte dressed robotically, there was no emotion, she felt completely numb. The nearest she had that night to an emotion was a grim determination not to show any fear. The squirrel was waiting, as she knew it would be. The robin on the fence. Both looked strangely subdued, the squirrel almost standoffish.

"Ok let's go," Charlotte said under her breath.

Everything she found was strangely still in the village that night, it was almost as if life had been suspended. It could almost have been Otherworld. On arriving at the church a second's glance at the clock and seeing the writhing serpent confirmed to Charlotte that the gate to Otherworld was open. She was a quick learner. The squirrel disappeared before her and one step behind she landed on the slab and felt the now familiar sensation of being pulled underground. In under half a minute she found herself standing in Otherworld.

Triskelion was standing in front of the church door. His appearance, even though she'd spent several hours with him the night before, still shocked her. Standing in front of the church door he really was the archetypal image of a ghost and in the perfect location. With her first words Charlotte told him as much.

"I assure you I am as alive as you are," he said simply. At that moment Charlotte didn't feel very alive herself but refrained from saying anything. She waited for him to move but he didn't, he remained motionless in front of the church door. The robin she noticed was in its usual place on the castellated roof of the porch. The squirrel had run up the nearest tree, the first time it had done this since she'd visited Otherworld. The two hounds Alasdair and Cathasach were conspicuous by their absence. It was more than obvious that something was wrong.

"We have only a short amount of time," Triskelion's soft voice spoke directly to her. His tone didn't change but Charlotte was sure she detected a sense of unease. "The Darkness is everywhere, it is not safe for you here in Otherworld tonight. You will have to return to your world." Charlotte should have been relieved but strangely she felt disappointed, even angry, she didn't want to return to her world, not yet. After what had happened that day she was ready for battle. She definitely didn't want to return to her world so quickly not without achieving something, no matter how small. She looked at Triskelion's featureless face. It was so hard not being able to read what someone was thinking by their expression. Her expression in reverse was easy to read, it pleaded for him to let her stay, for a little while at least.

"I have lost a friend in the mist today" she said steadily, in a manner that was far too adult for an eleven year old child. She fought to prevent her voice from breaking.

"We are aware of this," was Triskelion's unexpected reply. "We are trying to find out why." There was no sympathy in the way he said it, just the same soft, but monotone voice.

"Is she still in my world like the boys?" In contrast there was the sound of hope in the way Charlotte spoke her question.

"I'm afraid we do not know," came Triskelion's honest reply. "I am sorry. The fact that we do not know is a concern to us." Charlotte wasn't at all sure what he meant by this and was just about to ask when he cut her short.

"I know you have many, many questions France Charlotte but I have no time to answer any more questions tonight. I am sorry. One day I promise I will find the time. For now I must explain something to you and you need to listen very carefully to what I say. It could mean the difference between you surviving in our world or…" Triskelion tailed off, it was obvious what he was implying, it didn't need saying. Charlotte stared straight back at him, her expression not one of fear but resilient determination. Otherworld was slowly but surely beginning to run through her veins.

"Ok," she said, unflinching. "I'm ready." Triskelion rested his robed hand on her shoulder and she experienced the positive forces of fire without being burnt. Just as yesterday.

"I know you are, I can feel it. Now follow me." Triskelion led Charlotte down the path to the pond and stopped under the oak beside where she caught the bus to school. Standing beneath the tree, his hands clasped in front of him, he started to speak. "I am not sure I will be able to meet you here, next time you transcend." He paused letting this sink in. "My presence may bring unwanted attention to you and that is the last thing you or we want. Alasdair and Cathasach also cannot be seen in the village, it is a serious risk even for the squirrel to be seen guiding you. Strange though it may seem, it may be safer for you, at least when you first transcend to fend for yourself."

Charlotte had been ready for almost anything but not this. She realised suddenly how previously she'd always had somebody to depend on. The thought of being on her own in this strange world was not something she was at all prepared for. She didn't even know how to avoid the enemy and who the enemy was, what they looked like. She kept being told about the Darkness and it's agents but she'd never actually seen any physical proof. In her world wars were fought using bullets and bombs, you could at least recognise your enemy. Here in Otherworld it seemed to be an invisible war, there was no recognisable enemy. The only physical evidence she'd seen that people could get injured or worse was Cathasach when he'd returned with blood dripping from his mouth and from her last visit when both the hounds and Wodewose, bless him, were carrying obvious injuries.

"Your biggest friend France Charlotte when you are on your own in Otherworld is light. The Darkness and it's agents do not function well in light and if the light is bright enough, they cannot function at all. You have an expression in your world, "blinded by the light." Well the expression originated in Otherworld. If you have or are in light, the Darkness and it's agents are blinded. It has to use other senses to try to find and defeat you and those senses are not at all strong. The Darkness functions best in the dark, hence its name. The dark is when it has the advantage over us. Do you understand what I have just told you?"

Charlotte wasn't sure at all that she understood and admitted as much. What she did appreciate and couldn't understand was whenever she transcended to Otherworld it was in the middle of the night or thirteen o'clock, the furthest possible time from daylight hours.

"France Charlotte, where do you see light?" Charlotte was surprised by the question, she hadn't expected it.

"What now? Here where I'm standing, in Aldbury?" Charlotte thought Triskelion might have meant his question spiritually.

"Yes now, here where you are standing in your village. Though in Otherworld Aldbury is known by its original name, Aldeborie." He paused briefly before adding. "And physically not spiritually." Had Triskelion read her mind? Charlotte hated the idea.

She looked around her, the only lights she could see were behind drawn curtains from windows of nearby houses and being past midnight there weren't many of those. Charlotte, not believing Triskelion could mean electric light from a window, looked for some hidden light elsewhere but could see none.

"Only in windows," she finally admitted.

"Exactly, they can be your protection. Any light no matter what its source can conceal you from the Darkness. Immediately on arrival in Otherworld, you must shelter under the nearest light, do not hesitate, and stay within its beam until day break. Only when all traces of the night have gone can you step outside." Charlotte let this sink in, she could see so many obstacles to this plan with the obvious one being how she was going to get into a house if the doors were locked? And what worried her more, what would she find inside if she did manage to gain entry? She knew the houses, although they looked identical, were not the same as in her world but that didn't mean there wasn't anybody or thing behind their walls. Triskelion once again appeared to read the questions turning over in her head.

"The buildings you see aren't real, they are an image only." Charlotte remembered the first occasion she had transcended into Otherworld. She had tried to enter her cottage but the door wouldn't open. It had been solid, it most certainly hadn't been an image. She remembered too, touching her parents van. It had been cold to the touch and definitely hadn't felt like an image. Triskelion voiced an answer, precursing another predicted question.

"They feel real to you because your mind tells you they're real. You must convince your mind they are merely an image, that's all." That's all thought Charlotte, that's all. "Follow me." Triskelion didn't wait but made for a nearby house, one with a light shining from a downstairs window. Charlotte recognised the house as one belonging to a boy in the same year as her at school. Triskelion was moving surprisingly quickly and she had to run to keep up. Every now and again she glanced over her shoulder expecting a car to pass or for someone to come out of The Greyhound but nothing moved. It's all just an image she kept repeating to herself, it's all just an image. She caught up with Triskelion just as he arrived at the front door.

"Watch." His ghostly figure stood almost touching the front door. Raising his robed right hand he proceeded to knock, only he didn't knock. His hand and arm passed straight through the door. Charlotte remembered the hounds, Alasdair and Cathasach. How she thought she had seen them pass through a gate as though it didn't exist. At the time she'd thought she'd been imagining things, now she realised that is exactly what she had seen. Triskelion continued to pass his arm backwards and forwards through the door, then without notice he simply stepped through it. Like a knife through butter, not even that. More like a knife through thin air. Within seconds he reappeared. Passing through the door as though it wasn't there, which of course according to him, it wasn't.

"Now you try," he told Charlotte, stepping to one side. Charlotte stood directly in front of the door and raised her right arm, repeating over and over again, "you're not real, you're not real." With a look of grim determination she brought her clenched fist down hard on the door. There was a loud thud and an exclamation of pain as her fist was brought to an abrupt halt by solid wood. Triskelion ignored her cry of pain.

"You still believe it's real, you must remove any doubt from your mind. Now try again." To encourage her he passed his arm back and forth through the door several more times. The same door that Charlotte had just found to be solid as a rock, or rather wood.

"You're not real, you're not real," she repeated again and again and for a second time knocked on the door hoping with all her might her fist would simply pass through. Having learnt her lesson she didn't knock so hard this time, so it wouldn't hurt if her hand came up against something solid, which it did. "You're not real." This time she said it out loud and knocked for a third time, only for a third time to come up against solid wood.

"You're trying too hard," Triskelion said gently, touching her shoulder. "You mustn't try too hard, just relax and calmly tell your mind it is just an image. It's all just an image, it's not real, watch." Charlotte watched as he passed effortlessly through the door and this time rather than reappear the same way he returned by passing through the adjacent wall. Just to ram his point home he then re-entered the house by passing back through the wall and reappeared via the front door. "You see, it's like learning to ride a bike, once you've achieved it you'll wonder what all the fuss was about."

Charlotte doubted Triskelion had ever ridden a bike and was surprised he even knew what one was. She'd like to see him try. She kept these thoughts to herself and if Triskelion could read them he didn't say anything.

"Try one more time France Charlotte." Charlotte took a deep breath, trying desperately to relax and knocked. As before her fist landed against wood. Almost sobbing she leaned against the door tapping it repeatedly. The door remained as solid as ever. "Stop, stop." Charlotte did as she was told and turned to face Triskelion feeling utterly dejected. She saw that both the squirrel and the robin were at his feet. "It will come France Charlotte, fear not it will come. When you are really put to the test it will come, I promise you." Charlotte wished she had his faith. "We have to go," were his next words. "You must return to your world and be ready to return when we call you. Remember all the time that you are there, in your world, that in this world nearly everything built by your species is nothing but an image." Charlotte caught onto the word "nearly", what did he mean by the word nearly and just how was she meant to know what was an image and what wasn't?

"You will know, have no fear, you will know." Triskelion had apparently read her mind again. With that he simply disappeared, not disappeared as disappeared into the distance. He simply vanished into thin air before her eyes, one minute he was there the next minute he was gone. There remained the squirrel and the robin and both looked flustered, the squirrel running up and down the road and the robin rising and falling in the air. Charlotte realised they meant her to hurry and at the same moment she had an overwhelming sense of dread. Something inside her was telling her she had to hurry, really hurry. Not just her seventh sense but all her senses. She took off like the wind, with the squirrel before her and the robin overhead. As she leapt onto the stone in front of the church door she felt rather than saw a huge menacing shadow coming up the path behind her. As she descended into darkness she knew she'd had a very narrow escape.

On arriving in her world, Charlotte found herself shaking uncontrollably. Her legs felt as though they were about to give way and her stomach felt as if it was going to relieve itself of its contents at any moment. She was so thankful when the little squirrel ignored her previous request and led her back to the cottage. She didn't want to be left alone, not for one second. The robin was waiting to greet them both at the back door and never had she been so happy to see her feathered friend. She thanked the two of them, not caring if they didn't understand and lifting the latch almost fell into the kitchen.

For a moment she stood in silence, needing a moment to catch her breath. There was an uncomfortable feeling in her stomach and she rushed to the bathroom. Leaning over the sink her stomach finally had its wish. When her stomach had finished she turned on the cold tap and soaked the back of her neck and brow. As she did so she heard a door open and footsteps on the stairs.

"Charlotte, is that you, are you ok?" It was her mother, she must have heard her. She had to think fast. Quickly she locked the bathroom door and struggled out of her clothes. Her mother mustn't find her fully dressed. There was nowhere to hide them except in the laundry basket and she shoved everything, including her shoes in there. There came a gentle tap on the door and the door strained as her mother pushed it to see if it was locked. "Charlotte is that you?" her mother asked again, her voice strained with worry. "Charlotte, c'est toi?"

"Yes mum," Charlotte tried not to sound panicked. "Don't worry I had an awful nightmare and I've just been sick, must have been something I ate." She unlocked and opened the door.

"Probably those new sweets, "observed her mother. "Charlotte, you look awful," she added when her daughter opened the door.

"I'm ok mum, honest," Charlotte knew she didn't sound convincing but her mother appeared to accept her words at face value and after a motherly hug sent her up to bed. Despite her trauma Charlotte remembered to give the picture with the white hart a heartfelt kiss. After her experience she wondered what it must be like for the poor animal, all alone in the dark on top of the Beacon. Surrounded by enemies with no friends to turn to. The thought made her shiver, she couldn't begin to imagine what he must be going through. She saw the robin perched on the sill outside and gently touched the glass. Goodnight she whispered. Her bed that night had never felt so welcoming. Holding Gromit tight she sent herself to sleep by repeating over and over again, it's only an image it's only an image, it's-only-an-image.

Downstairs her mother made herself a coffee. She hoped her daughter was alright. There were a lot of strange goings on in the village at the moment and she was worried that the visit from the police earlier in the day may have upset their daughter without her realising. After all she was at a very vulnerable age. Climbing the stairs, coffee cup steaming she promised herself to pay much more attention to her daughter's feelings in the future. Pushing open the bedroom door with her free hand she promised herself they both would. From somewhere within the room, for there was no light, came the loud sound of a man happily asleep. Give us all strength she thought as she got into bed. Give us all strength.

Triskelion didn't like leaving the little human girl in the way he did. He simply hadn't had a choice. If he were captured by the Darkness there really wouldn't be much hope for Otherworld. Anyway he hadn't really left her, he had simply disappeared from her view. From safety he had watched the little girl make her safe way back to her world. He had seen the Scucca, one of the foulest of spirits try to catch her on the path and he'd been ready to intervene but his aid thankfully hadn't been necessary. The little girl's perception had warned her that danger lurked close by and she had been too quick. It was her next visit to Otherworld that really concerned him, he doubted very much whether anyone could risk waiting for her. Not even her guardians Alasdair and Cathasach. Their presence would simply bring unwanted attention to almost the last reliable gateway between her world and his. Certainly, the only gateway strong enough to transport a human between the two worlds with minimum risk.

On seeing France Charlotte transcend to her world Triskelion left Aldeborie for Ashridge, Assherugge as it is known in Otherworld. Before he reached the wooded scarp he stopped by the oak, home to their courageous little messenger. Kneeling he took from his robe the necklace and locket belonging to France Charlotte and reaching into a hidden hollow at the base of the tree felt for the little leather budget. He knew the neck would be left open and on finding it so dropped the necklace and locket inside. He had initially intended to keep it with him until France Charlotte returned but after everything that had happened, he now considered the charm would be safer with the budget. Standing Triskelion then rested his cloaked head against the trunk of the oak and whispered a charm handed down to him centuries ago by the holy men of Skirrid. Never had he needed to call on their magic until now. He just hoped after so many moons had passed its potency still worked and that he'd remembered the words correctly. Standing straight he knew there was little more he could do to protect the little squirrel and the hidden budget with its now precious contents and made for the nearest trees.

Triskelion knew he had to hurry. A meeting had been set up with Leht and she could no longer leave the safety of her stone circle. She simply wasn't strong enough, not anymore. He had to go to her and the gateway to her hidden circle would close a good hour before the passing of the moon. Although he could levitate, traveling this way he still wasn't able to go much faster than the jogging pace of the average human and levitation also took a lot of energy. Energy he may well need for defence. Having an invisible cloak also used a lot of energy and its power was also fallible. Those who had access to the right knowledge would still be able to see him and that could create the added risk of him traveling under a false sense of security.

After some thought he decided for the first part of the journey he would travel through the heavily wooded, Old Copse, Berkhamsted Common and Frithsden Beeches. Passing through these he would wear the cloak and travel using levitation. Invisibility worked better in a wooded environment and using levitation would also ease his way through the natural barriers a wood presents. Walking through a wood would be tough going, not to mention time consuming and with every step, just like a human he could break a twig focusing unwanted attention on his being there. From the human dwellings of Frithsden, (Frithesden in Otherworld), he would simply have to take his chances along the relatively short and open stretch to Gatesdene or Great Gaddesden as we know it.

Triskelion as it turned out needn't have worried. Either fate was looking kindly upon him that night or those seeking him were deliberately, for whatever reason allowing him uninterrupted passage. The only concern he had was traveling through Berkhamsted common. Most of the Common was made up of birch and twigs from the tree were prized by witches for their brooms. Ash was always used for the stick or handle so collectively the woods or commons of Ashridge were fertile ground for a witch wanting to make a new broom. Though he was confident he could out battle a witch he didn't need the inconvenience. Thankfully or perhaps sadly depending on your point of view the traditional witch had suffered more than most with the demise of Otherworld and today very few roamed the land. And none as far as he was aware in these troubled times travelled on All Hallows or Samhain as it is called in Otherworld to the world of French Charlotte as they had done once, in droves. As a consequence he made it to the small hamlet of Frithesden far quicker than expected and from Frithesden his passage over hills and valley to the tiny village of Gatesdene was equally uneventful. Maybe all the focus that night was on Aldeborie.

Unlike when Charlotte visited the tiny village the small cluster of buildings didn't move to allow free passage. With Triskelion there was no need. Instead he walked up the church path to the main porch just as a normal church goer would do. There he stood for several minutes enjoying the sensation generated by the earth beneath his feet. The stone circle that once stood here was placed by those who understood the energies and power of the earth. By siting their circle on this spot they had captured and concentrated the unseen currents running beneath the earth to use for their own purposes. Although the circle over the centuries had been broken and some of the stones used in the construction of the church, the influence of the old stones still remained and those sensitive enough could still benefit from their energy. Just as Triskelion could.

Feeling regenerated, Triskelion entered the porch, his right arm extended. Although locked, the church door opened before him. Once inside he took slow and steady steps up the nave to the simple altar. Facing the altar he brought his hands together as though in prayer and waited. Slowly he felt the ground beneath him opening and seconds later he was descending below the church floor. He heard the ancient floor closing above him and seconds later all was darkness. Triskelion's hands remained clasped, he could still feel the sensation of descending and knew to unclasp them before he came to a halt would be dangerous. Gradually all motion ceased and he rested suspended in space, his hands still tightly together. Directly below and rising to meet him Triskelion could see a slowly spinning circle of light. As it came closer he recognised the circle was made up of slowly spinning pudding stones held in orbit by the light in which they travelled. He knew the stones were the spiritual replica of the original circle placed on earth over 4,000 years before. At the centre of the circle though unmoving a huge yew, and before the yew on the only stone that wasn't moving, sat a female figure. As gracious and as beautiful as he remembered her.

"It is an honour to see you again, Leht," Triskelion announced his greeting with his head bowed. Leht reached out and gently touched Triskelion's face. Although he could tell Leht was so much weaker than when he'd last seen her, her touch still had the power to wipe away anxiety.

"You too Triskelion, I just wish it was under happier circumstances." Leht's voice, Triskelion noted, was as ever, full of song. Even in the darkest of times Leht was unable to sound anything but happy. He was, as he'd always been since the first time he'd set eyes on the lady of light, completely in awe of her beauty and hypnotised by the slowly spinning circle of stones that protected her. She reminded him of happier times when many such characters inhabited Otherworld. At one time it had been a magical place where light reigned and anything was possible. Slowly the lights had dimed and the spiritual world strangled as France Charlotte's species raped the adjoining world. Leht was one of the few remaining survivors from that time. Indeed she had been here, as far as he knew since the beginning and now, almost unthinkable not many moons ago, she may be forced to witness the end.

There remained a respectful silence between them. It was nearly a thousand years since they'd last seen each other and there was no need to hurry this rare occasion. It was Triskelion who spoke first.

"I too wish we were not meeting under such circumstances. There were times when we could draw upon vast resources, raise huge armies. Now apparently all our hopes rest on an eleven year old human child. It just doesn't seem possible. What can one child, and one not of this world do against the almost unlimited and growing forces not to mention power of the Darkness. How did we let our world ever come to this?" Leht remained still. Silent, she didn't want to hurry her reply.

"I disagree," she said after several minutes. "I've had time to study, to read the little girl. She has an affinity with the natural world that is close to mine. She has an awareness and sensitivity for the world around her that I did not think could be found in a human, especially not one so young. Her mind is uncorrupted, her heart is pure and she has an innocence I envy. Her parents have protected her from the vulgarities of the modern world created by her species. She is schooled in the old traditions using the written word, she has learnt to respect and understand the personality of a book. There are no moving images in her home and since she has started transcending to Otherworld rather than be overawed by it, she has accepted it. Her experiences would have crushed many including many an adult, look at our artist, but she has faced everything and championed her fear. Inside that child's fragile body lies a powerful determination and a courage I have not seen for many, many moons. Did you know the Darkness tried to influence her in her world. Rather than let it entrap her using her own fear, she faced her fears head on and came out the stronger. In these times and in both our worlds that is a very rare event."

"I did not know that" Triskelion admitted. "But that is nothing compared to what she will have to face later and she is still after all, only a child. I remain blind as to how we have any chance of achieving victory against the Darkness. It is not as though we have time to plan, we have only weeks, maybe days and as I have just admitted I am completely blind to any path we can take."

Leht raised one of her delicate hands and her light shone brighter than ever. Her voice still sang but now it sang a powerful tune. "Time is on the side of the Darkness, the more time it has the stronger it will become and the weaker we will be but time can be on our side too. The Darkness has already assumed we are defeated, it believes it's just a matter of time before it destroys both of our worlds. Its over confidence is our greatest weapon."

"I bow to your strength of will, Leht." Triskelion was just about to continue when Leht raised a finger to her mouth, signalling him to be silent. She hadn't finished.

"We've always known that the Darkness would make a concerted challenge at the end of the great cycle. At the time it was so far away, we all fell asleep and our indifference and selfish concentration on our own interests has let the Darkness almost sleepwalk to victory. We have now been rudely awoken from our lethargy and undeservedly been given a gift in the form of a human child with which to take on the evil that is the Darkness." Triskelion looked as though he wanted to say something but Leht remained holding a finger to her lips. "I admit I do not know how a little human girl can defeat the Darkness but the Snooks have repeatedly told us that the battle with the Darkness will be fought using an intelligent being that can transcend between both worlds and she is the first being that we have found who is capable of transcending successfully. Not even you or I Triskelion can do that."

"True" admitted Triskelion. "Only our messengers, the squirrels can do that and even they need the help of the ash."

"Yes that is true," Leht concurred. "We've yet to learn whether the human child can transcend on her own or use gateways other than the passage provided by the old and sacred ash. We cannot afford to make another mistake as we did with the artist. We thought he would pass and if we hadn't intervened he would no longer be with us. As it is he remains suspended in the Well of Amphillicia until we can find a way of sending him back to his world and that time may never come."

"I'm not even sure I want to find out, for we could lose the little human girl trying to do so." Triskelion was very aware of the dangers involved in trying to transcend between worlds, many beings had tried over the centuries and failed. Only with the knowledge of Orme could you safely transcend. Then with the knowledge of Orme you could transcend anywhere in the known universe and beyond and to all levels.

"We may not have a choice. If the Darkness is as we suspect aware of the gateway in Aldeborie, we will have to use another. And if our hands are forced in this way, the only way we will find out if another Gateway can be used is if the little human child, Charlotte transcends of her own accord." It was the first time either of them had used the human child's actual name and using it shook them both. It made her personal to them. "Remember also." Leht stared hard at Triskelion. "The Snooks tell us that it will be a human not just a being that will help battle the Darkness and that it will be near the time of the Great Cycle. They have to mean the human child."

"Wodewose calls her France Charlotte," Triskelion corrected Leht. "Though I'm sure you're already aware of that." Leht smiled.

"Our dear Wodewose, how is he coping with his new ability to talk?"

"The root vine informs me that everybody preferred it when he couldn't. They say it's gone to his head." Leht's smile broadened.

"He won't have his new gift forever, only as long as Charlotte, sorry France Charlotte needs his help."

"The Snooks tell us that it will be a human who helps us battle the Darkness." Triskelion's tone changed. "And yet it is the human species that has in the main brought us to where we are today, why should we put all our trust in a human?"

"Because we have no other options." Leht answered with great finality. Triskelion had to agree, he didn't want to but she was absolutely right, they had no other options and that was their failing.

"And do not forget Triskelion," Leht added. "You are in part at least, originally from human stock."

"That was when the human species respected their world and understood ours, that is not the case today and hasn't been for many a moon."

"Only right then that a human is our saviour at this time, it will be a debt repaid." Leht's smile was convincing.

"Do not forget Leht," Triskelion paused not really wanting to finish what he had started to say. "Let us not forget," he rephrased. "The Snooks have foretold that a human will help us battle the Darkness close to the Great Cycle but let us not forget also, the Snooks have constantly failed to foretell who wins the final battle."

"I know," Leht said softly. "The ending is in our hands Triskelion."

Once again there was a respectful silence between the two of them as both considered their next move. It was Leht who spoke first.

"You must confide in the human child Triskelion. You must forget her age and talk to her as though she were an adult, better still one of your trusty knights of old. You do not have to tell her everything but she has to have an understanding of how things work in Otherworld. Do not sugar coat what you tell her, she can only do battle if she is aware of the dangers and the risks involved. Do not hide them from her. I have told her something of the situation here in Otherworld and she is well aware of what will happen if the Darkness is not defeated. I have also explained to her that the battle ahead is no easy one and not one to be fought in the traditional manner. I have told her that the battle will be won with pureness of thought, without fear and with strength of wit and I sincerely believe that. We have no idea Triskelion why it is a human child that graces us with her presence at this moment in time. And Charlotte, sorry France Charlotte has even less of an idea why she has been chosen. If that indeed is the case. She has however accepted she is here and has kept the fact from everyone she knows in her world. That is a good start. Now we must help her all we can by giving her knowledge. Knowledge as you know Triskelion is strength."

Triskelion looked with affection at his old friend, the lady of light. Sat on her sacred stone in front of her yew that had been with her from the beginning, she epitomised all that was good in not just Otherworld but all worlds. He watched the slowly spinning stones and the circle of light that protected her. This hidden place of hers suspended in blackness used to be a place for her to regenerate. To retire to when she needed a rest. In recent times as she'd grown weaker it had become her permanent home and one, she very rarely left. He knew that unless a solution was found soon the fragility of Leht and what was left of her world would crumble into dust and be lost to the blackness in which they were suspended. It was an end that he did not want to contemplate. Leht read his mind. She could match him in this.

"I am not so weak, my dear Triskelion. I still have resilience and I can still be a help in our struggle. Although I rest here suspended in blackness I have eyes and ears beyond the stones. I am connected to the root vine and am probably more aware than you as to what is happening on the surface." Triskelion remained silent, he grudgingly agreed with Leht's latter statement but knew she was playing down her weakness. He knew she was using too much of what little strength she still had to help him. He was well aware that in helping him Leht was at risk of her light becoming so dim that it could no longer regenerate and extinguished forever. This would mean the end of his close friend and he would never be able to live with himself if that was to happen. Leht once again reading his mind sought to divert his fears. She spoke to him using the gentlest of melodies. Speaking only of action as opposed to fears. "Listen Triskelion, France Charlotte has the budget and the protective charm hidden by Sucellus from the land of the Gaul's. I can communicate with her through the budget by sending my light blood, by sending a piece of me to her. You must give her your map of Assherugge which shows where the stones of Avreborie are hidden for it is easier for me to communicate using those. I have asked Wodewose to give the map to her but so far he has failed to do so. I've no idea why. Without using the stones takes up too much of my energy, energy that you are well aware I no longer have. The little silver frog, it is made with silver from Llywernog and given life by Igraine one of Eire's most powerful Bandari. Sucellus must have read the future for I believe it is no accident that the charm was placed where it was. Its heart is powerful, it will offer France Charlotte protection. Not from everything that is impossible but it will be a good suit of armour. You know Triskelion that she must never know what the frog is for or its power will be lost.

"I do."

There was another silence and this time it was Triskelion who spoke next.

"Leht, you are aware that this is a battle on two fronts. We have our world to defend and we have the secret knowledge of Orme that must be protected at all costs. Part of which may and I repeat, may for nothing is written it is only spoken word. Maybe hidden in the Sacred Library of Evinghehou" founded by the forerunners."

Leht gazed at her long-time friend. She was well aware Triskelion already knew the answer she was about to give him and although he was mentally prepared for it she knew also it would still hurt. Wanting to relieve him of his pain she gently brushed his face.

"In your heart Triskelion you know that we must be prepared to sacrifice everything to defend the secret of Orme. Even our lives and all of Otherworld and the world where France Charlotte is from. I have already given a great deal of myself to help defend the Sacred Library of Evinghehou, Leabharlann de Solas" Triskelion raised his head.

"I know Leht, I just wanted to hear it from your lips. Going forward I must always prepare for such a path."

This time there was a long, long silence as both contemplated what this might mean. Leht was first to break their silence, she had witnessed the beginning and had no wish to witness the end. What remaining strength she had rose to the surface and for a moment her light shone brighter than Polaris. From where, it is rumoured she descended.

"Triskelion we must not let ourselves already feel defeated, to do so will mean we will be defeated. We must be strong of mind, and with strength of wit. Rest here for the coming day Triskelion, the stones will give you renewed strength and you will commence battle with a greater spirit. Close your eyes Triskelion, rest here with me."

Triskelion's only facial features, the shaded parts of his face where one would normally expect to see eyes faded completely and his face became void of all marks. Leht faded into her yew leaving her friend, Triskelion suspended in blackness protected from harm by the light ring of circling pudding stones. When he awoke he would experience a new strength and Leht had no doubt he would need every last drop.

The squirrel after watching Charlotte safely enter her house ran back to the church and the gateway to Otherworld. It had seen the Scucca and feared for the little human girl's safety. The speed by which the little human girl had acted had not only surprised the messenger, it had impressed him too. He was beginning to understand what all the fuss was about. On arriving back in Otherworld he was alert to whatever danger may be lying in wait. Everything appeared peaceful but he was wise to the fact that appearances meant little. The robin joined him on the church path and together, the robin half flying half hopping, they made their way to the oak in the field which the squirrel called home, at least temporarily. After discreetly checking to see if the budget was safe he ran up the trunk and in through the hole, the door to his nest. Secure in the trunk of the tree, his dry and sweet smelling bed of leaves immediately helped him relax. Within minutes the squirrel was curled in a ball and enjoying a well-earned sleep. The robin, although craving sleep as well, was reluctant to leave their messenger. Flying to one of the higher branches he decided to remain and keep watch. A little later shadows that had no business being there moved slowly uphill across the field. To the robins relief they didn't stop but slid serpent-like into the wood. As dawn broke the robin flew back to Aldeborie and to its own nest carefully tucked away in a cranny in the church wall. Before choosing to sleep it checked for any shadows that didn't belong and satisfied there weren't any settled down.

The next morning, just as any concerned parent would, Charlotte's mother popped her head around the door of her daughter's bedroom.

She found Charlotte to be fast asleep holding Gromit tightly to her chest. The room was surprisingly light despite the gloom outside. She moved to the long sash window and looked out at the garden. It was such a shame the weird weather was stopping anything from growing, she could imagine the garden would look quite beautiful under normal circumstances. Her gaze focused on the bare branches of the cherry blossom. There on the same branch sat two magpies, another she saw was sat in one of Tom's apple trees. All three unless it was her imagination seemed to be staring straight at her daughter's window. With a surge of guilt she remembered Charlotte complaining about the magpies and at the time they hadn't believed her. Studying the birds, each one motionless staring, her first thought had been incorrect. The birds she couldn't help sensing were not simply staring at the window but looking through the glass, trying to see inside. Her suspicion made her feel most uncomfortable. There must surely be a simple explanation. Knowing her daughter's love of nature she had probably been feeding the birds and made a mental note to talk to Charlotte about it when she awoke.

When Charlotte did awake it was past ten in the morning. Her mother had turned her alarm off, preferring to let her sleep. School would still be there the next day and when she'd phoned the school the receptionist had been very understanding. Charlotte did a double take when she read her clock and jumping out of bed ran down the stairs yelling.

"Mum have you seen the time?" Her mother quickly calmed her, reassuring her that the school had been fine when she'd phoned and anyway her mother told her, you obviously needed the sleep. When that was sorted Charlotte settled down to a bowl of hot chocolate, and toast spread thick with Nutella. As she ate her mother placed a pair of shoes on the kitchen table.

"Charlotte, can you explain what these were doing in the laundry basket?" Charlotte, in a panic, quickly ran several implausible excuses through her head. In the end the best she could come up with was that she must have been sleepwalking and that she'd had the strangest of dreams that night. Her mother looked intensely at her and the expression in her mother's eyes told Charlotte she wasn't convinced. To her immense relief her mother decided to leave it telling her instead that that would be the last time she ate cheese before going to bed. Charlotte hadn't had any and knew her mother knew that too. As she washed up her mother had another question.

"Charlotte, have you been feeding those magpies. They give me the creeps just sitting there staring at the house." Charlotte promised she hadn't. "Well someone must be, they're sitting there waiting for something. I'll ask your father"

Charlotte was glad in the end to escape to her room. She told her mother if she wasn't going to school then she wouldn't waste the day but spend it doing her homework. Her mother seemed pleased at this. As soon as she'd closed the door to her bedroom Charlotte went straight to the window and looked outside. There was no longer a magpie sitting in one of Tom's apple trees, that was because it was now in their garden and another must have joined it for there were now three magpies sat in the cherry blossom. All staring into her bedroom.

Charlotte was determined to ignore them, with only three, according to Wodewose they could do her no harm. She wasn't going to let them intimidate her. Going to her school bag she brought out an almost new exercise book. Today she decided she'd complete the essay they'd been set in her English class. The essay asking to invent and describe a fantasy Island. "Let your imagination's run wild," their teacher had told them. She wouldn't have to, her story would mirror what had happened to her in recent weeks, her Island would mirror Otherworld. If anything ever happened to her maybe someone clever enough would spot clues in her essay. Her story would start with an old sailing vessel, stranded on a calm, windless sea. The vessel would find itself enveloped in a strange mist, a mist that twisted and turned with anger. The ship's compass would spin madly and all time pieces would stop. When the mist lifted an Island would be revealed that didn't exist on any of the charts. Welcome to Otherworld Charlotte thought though she couldn't call it that. Neverland was no good for that was in Peter Pan. She eventually decided on Ormeland.

Charlotte worked on her essay all day even refusing to come down for lunch. It was nearly seven in the evening when she eventually closed her exercise book, satisfied. The essay had taken up almost every remaining blank page. On descending the stairs she discovered her mother had cooked a French classic. Chicken in a creamy tarragon sauce. As her parents had already eaten she was allowed to eat her dinner on her lap in the lounge. Her father had lit a fire something they hadn't enjoyed for several days and when Charlotte sat down to eat the fire had already been burning for an hour. The lounge felt positively cosy. Whilst she ate her parents chatted softly whilst enjoying a glass of genievre a strong grain based gin liquor. Charlotte's mother had brought theirs direct from a small distillery in Houlle, a small village in the Audomarois, not that far from Calais. It was sold in traditional stone bottles and Charlotte's parents kept their bottle in the freezer. They only got it out on special occasions and the celebration on this occasion Charlotte was to discover her parents had saved up enough money to buy a small car. A Volkswagen Golf and they were picking it up the next day. From tomorrow Charlotte wouldn't have to travel in the back of their old van.

After Charlotte had finished eating, her mother continued to fuss, handing her a large bowl of hot chocolate. Her father put on a CD, Beth Orton, one of his favourite singers and when that came to an end he followed with "alterum," an album by Julie Fowlis. Little was said whilst the music played. The soft melodies were wonderfully calming and Charlotte had been asleep for some time when the last embers fell through the grate and her parents called it a night. Her father half carried her up to bed and left her to tuck herself in. He didn't see the robin sitting on the sill.

He hadn't seen his daughter looking so tired for weeks. She must have had a really bad stomach, he commented getting into bed. "You're giving her too much hot chocolate," he admonished her mother.

Chapter Fourteen

Guided By The Light

The next morning Charlotte half expected to see four magpies sitting in the cherry blossom. To her disappointment almost there were only three. Only three! She was becoming complacent, that would never do. She blew them the biggest raspberry she could muster and after giving the white hart a huge kiss almost skipped down the stairs. She didn't know why but she felt full of life that morning. Breakfast was fresh pain au chocolate with, of course a bowl of hot chocolate. She was just about to leave for the bus when her father stopped her.

"I'll drive you," he said. Within a minute she discovered why. Her parents had lied, they had already picked up the car and it was sitting out front ready to take her to school. The car wasn't at all new and frayed at the edges but it was ten times better than riding in the back of a smelly van. That morning sitting in the back seat on the way to school, Charlotte felt like a queen.

"Reason for absence?" her form teacher asked.

"Too much cheese Sir." Charlotte was surprised at her own cheek, it wasn't her character to be cheeky but she felt untouchable that morning.

"Explain," her form teacher replied, not amused.

"My mother said I must have had too much cheese before I went to bed Sir, it gave me nightmares, and I was ill." Her form teacher sighed.

"I thought you being French would be able to handle a bit of cheese." He allowed himself a smile.

"It was English cheese Sir." There was an outburst of laughter from the class and the form teacher raised a hand to bring his class back to order. The trouble was he was trying not to laugh himself.

English was the first lesson after lunch.

"Have you all finished your essays?" their English teacher like the vicar had a habit of pulling or stoking his beard and he was doing it now. There came a generally unenthusiastic sounding reply of "yes." The teacher tried to ignore it. How he wished the younger generation had his enthusiasm for their language, it was so flexible, so expressive and paired with a lively imagination far better than any computer game. He wasn't about to give up. "And did you all let your imaginations run wild?" He asked, trying to inject some enthusiasm. Three maybe more of his pupils replied yes. "Ok let's hear some," and he called the names of pupils who had their heads bowed lowest. Most essays were predictable and hardly two pages long. Nina, an inoffensive and well liked pupil whose parents owned a farm near Marsworth had made a supreme effort. Her essay described a fantasy farm on an island that had cows which produced runny Nutella instead of milk. Chickens that laid chocolate eggs and sheep that when sheared their wool turned instantly into expensive designer clothes. The whole class cheered and applauded when she'd finished reading.

"Well at least someone's made an effort," the teacher tapped Nina's desk appreciatively. "Now who next?" he looked around the class. His bright blue eyes came to rest on Charlotte. "What about you French Charlotte?" Charlotte a little reluctantly opened her exercise book and flicked through the pages.

"Which part Sir?" she looked at him innocently. There sounded a ripple of suppressed laughter from the class.

"All of it of course."

Charlotte once more flicked the pages of her exercise book with her thumb. "I don't think we have time Sir." The teacher had been in the profession long enough to tell when a child was being cheeky and he saw that French Charlotte was being deadly serious.

"Let me see," he said holding out his hand. Charlotte stood up, crossed the classroom and gave him her exercise book. He flicked through it hardly believing his eyes. He whistled. "Well, you have been busy. Ok I'll read it tonight, go and sit down."

When the class had finished and the pupils were filing out the English teacher signalled for Charlotte to stay behind. He picked up her exercise book and tapped it. "I don't know if what's inside is any good French Charlotte and I'll know after I've read it but A plus for effort. It's moments like this when I remember why I became a teacher. Well done." He tapped her on the head.

"Thank you Sir." Charlotte left the classroom her chest trying its best to burst open.

Going to bed that night Charlotte couldn't help feeling a little tense. After what had happened on her last visit to Otherworld she was pretty certain she would be traveling back there soon, if not tonight and she couldn't help worrying as to what might be waiting for her when she arrived. There was also the added stress that on arrival she may well have to face Otherworld alone for the first time and would have to seek the safety of a light. She still doubted her ability to pass through a door that according to Triskelion wasn't there. It had felt very much there to her and worried it would again.

When she awoke Charlotte was surprised to see her clock read seven in the morning. She hadn't been called to Otherworld after all. The fact that she hadn't made her worry. What she wondered was happening in Otherworld and realised in some strange way she actually missed the place. Looking out of the long sash window she saw there were still only three magpies, that was a good sign at least. She blew them all a raspberry for good measure.

There was no lift for her that morning, it was back to the bus. The bus journey passed with the usual chatter about nothing in particular. After her recent adventures Charlotte found the conversation with her friends a little irrelevant and a struggle to participate in, even harder to appear enthused. After the register had been taken, Charlotte was just about to leave for her first lesson, French when her form teacher pulled her to one side.

"The Head wants to see you French Charlotte," and on seeing her shocked expression, quickly added. "Don't panic it's nothing to worry about," and gave her a wink.

Standing outside the Head's door Charlotte desperately racked her brains trying to remember what she may have done wrong, something bad enough to warrant being summoned to the Head's office. Taking a deep breath she knocked.

"Enter," Charlotte recognised the Head's powerful voice."

On entering she immediately saw her English teacher standing to one side, his hands clasped behind his back. The Head of the school was sat at her desk, on the wall behind her hung a portrait of the Queen. The rest of the walls were covered with framed diplomas and photographs capturing successful moments in the school's history. On the many bulging bookcases stood an array of highly polished silverware and more photographs. The office represented academia at its best. On the Head's desk Charlotte saw there were a number of personal photographs, mainly of her family. The Head had a book open in front of her and Charlotte recognised it instantly as her English exercise book. She immediately regretted the "I love One Direction," she'd decoratively scribbled on the back cover.

"Good morning Charlotte," the Head looked up from her exercise book. "Or should I call you French Charlotte?" she smiled.

"I don't mind Miss, either is fine" Charlotte hated the fact she was visibly shaking.

"I think I prefer French Charlotte," the Head's smile widened. "It gives you an identity."

"Yes Miss."

"I'm sorry to have dragged you away from your French lesson. In view of your nationality I don't feel we need to be too concerned if you miss a few minutes."

"No Miss." Charlotte wished she could come up with a more imaginative reply."

"Which makes this all the more remarkable." The Head held up her English exercise book. The Head looked across to her English teacher who was smiling wider than a Cheshire cat. "Mr Doorley, (the teacher's name), tells me this is an astounding piece of work." The Head placed Charlotte's exercise book back on her desk. "Not only is the volume of work, virtually a whole book most impressive. The content, Mr Doorley tells me and after flicking through parts I say I have to concur is extremely imaginative and very readable. In fact I'm really looking forward to finishing reading," the head opened her book to the title page. "Ormeland, tonight. Most impressive of all Mr Doorley praises your English, he tells me it's almost perfect and you have a natural ability to play with words. Not to let them intimidate you. That from someone in your year is praise indeed but considering English is your second language, French Charlotte." The Head paused searching for the right words. "Well I'm proud, very proud of you." She stood up and held out her hand for Charlotte to shake. Charlotte took the Head's hand, close to speechless.

"Thank you Miss," was all she could manage and that she found a struggle.

"Ok, well off you go, we don't want you to miss too much off your French class do we." The Head waved her hands

"No Miss." With that Charlotte turned and made her way out.

"Well done French Charlotte," she heard her English teacher tell her softly as she opened the door to leave.

After Charlotte had left the Head put on her reading glasses and flicked through the essay, stopping here and there to read the odd paragraph. After a few minutes she closed the book and placed it gently on her desk, stroking the cover flat. "That," she said, facing the proud English teacher. "Is one remarkable little girl. In this profession you tend to get a gut feeling about your pupils and from the first day I met French Charlotte I felt there was something inside her, something special. I believe that girl will go on to great things. So great, her name may well be written into our history, I sincerely believe this Mr Doorley. Never since I started teaching have I felt about a pupil this way, never. And thank you for bringing this body of work to my attention." She tapped Charlotte's exercise book.

"My pleasure, I'd better get back to my class." The English teacher gestured to the door.

"Yes, yes, go, go." The Head waved her arms for him to leave as she had done with French Charlotte. After the door had closed she leaned back in her chair staring at the ceiling. She'd known all along that little girl had something special and to think for a while they'd been worried about her. Don't let me down French Charlotte she whispered to herself. Don't let me down. With a deep satisfied sigh the Head stood up to leave, she had a meeting to attend in town. As she got out of her chair something outside caught her eye. Looking out of the window, there in a tree, opposite sat a magpie. Nothing unusual in that but magpies are normally always on the move and this one wasn't, it was perched motionless. Even more bizarre it appeared be staring straight at her. What do you want? Her mind questioned the bird and in a second dismissed it, her thoughts already on her meeting.

Charlotte decided not to tell her parents about her essay and her meeting with the Head. They would probably make an instant connection with the mist beside the church and her essay also contained a magpie and a robin and her mother had already accused her of feeding the magpies in the garden. She didn't want her parents asking too many questions.

For a second successive night her sleep remained undisturbed. No tapping at her window meant she should have caught up on her sleep but her mind and body were primed for action and at some point in every hour of the night she found herself awake, questioning why she hadn't been called. It was the same the following night and she was beginning to worry that in Otherworld, something may have gone terribly wrong. The only reassurance she had was the three magpies remained just that, three and the robin, in the morning was always there to greet her. This status quo she was sure would change if anything serious had happened on the other side. Just to be sure on the third morning, on her way to school she stopped to talk to the robin. She still felt very uncomfortable talking to a bird but she had nothing to lose.

"Robin, can you get a message to Wodewose or Triskelion to let me know in some way that everything's ok." The robin remained on the fence it's head cocked giving no indication it had understood. Charlotte having no time to wonder started down the brick path when she stopped and turned. "Oh and thanks," she called back.

Her request must have been answered for on the third night she was awoken by a sharp tap on her window. She had just opened her eyes when there was another sharp tap. Quickly she got out of bed and started to dress. She had to be extra quiet because she'd heard her mother get out of bed during the night on more than one occasion recently and she was worried after what had happened she may be checking on her. Just to be sure she pushed some clothes under the covers to roughly resemble her torso and left Gromit with his head just sticking out of the duvet.

Outside the squirrel was waiting for her though the robin was nowhere to be seen. Charlotte thought nothing of it or rather didn't have time to think about it as the squirrel quickly started down the brick path and she without question followed. As she ran, she made a mental note of the houses that still had lights shining in their windows. In one of these, on arriving in Otherworld she would have to seek safety. They're not real she told herself again. As they approached the village green, Charlotte started to get a strong feeling that something was wrong. She couldn't explain it but she sensed something just wasn't right. What was it Triskelion had told her? If she had the slightest doubt something was wrong, do not take the risk, do not transcend. She felt herself hesitating. Everything's fine she told herself, stop being paranoid and quickened her pace in an effort to catch up. The squirrel was already disappearing down the gravel path leading to the church door and as she too set foot on the gravel path she automatically looked up at the clock on the church tower. It read five minutes past midnight, there was no XIII and no writhing serpent. Charlotte stopped in her tracks. The squirrel she saw had reached the stone slab before the church door, it was showing no signs that it was about to dive underground. The next second a blur of grey flew across the path crashing into the waiting squirrel. The force of contact bowled it over and for the next few seconds a writhing mass of grey fur flew around the churchyard. Charlotte watched in shocked silence. It took her several moments to realise that the writhing mass was a battle between two squirrels. Never in her life had she seen a fight of such intensity and speed. She clasped her hand to her mouth when she realised one of the squirrels must be her little messenger. "Nooo," she cried silently. At that very moment one of the squirrels broke away, sprinting across the churchyard and diving into the mist in the adjacent field. Charlotte waited for it to come back but it didn't. There was no sign of it. It had disappeared.

At first she thought the mist had taken her squirrel, the messenger. Then she spotted the second squirrel. It was trotting towards her across the grass, not running but at a steady pace its tail flicking left and right in agitated fashion. Charlotte tensed before she saw hopping from gravestone to grave stone a robin, it could only be Leht's robin. Realisation slowly dawned, thankfully the squirrel approaching her was her little messenger and he had attacked. He had attacked what? Who? Charlotte wasn't sure, it had looked and behaved like her squirrel but couldn't have been. It must have been impersonating her squirrel, to lead her astray, to lead … Charlotte didn't want to think about where or what may have happened if her squirrel hadn't intervened. Would she have disappeared like Ashtynn and the two boys? She pictured the first squirrel diving into the mist. The mist wasn't taking it, it had been returning home. The thought sent a shiver up her spine. For the first time the silent, deathly still tombstones of the churchyard unnerved her. She looked up at the church tower, as she did so the steady long hand slid to III, it was fifteen minutes past midnight. The time gave her reassurance, she was still in her world, never before had reading the time given her so much comfort. The squirrel, her squirrel scuttled between her legs, she felt it's soft fir through her thin leggings. On looking down it started across the road and Charlotte knew it was taking her home, safely home. On this occasion she had no objection and knew from that night onwards, she would never object again about the squirrel accompanying her home. It was a very nervous passage back to her cottage and Charlotte couldn't help feeling that somebody or something was watching from every darkened window. Despite her discomfort nothing untoward occurred and though it felt like the longest walk in her life in no time at all. Well that's not correct for only if the Darkness has its victory would there be no time at all. In only a couple of minutes, they were back at her cottage and a stable door which she greeted as though it were a friend she hadn't seen in years.

"Thank you both," Charlotte said softly as she opened the door. She wanted to pat the squirrel on the head but knew how much she hated people doing it to her and thought better of it. Still shaking from her ordeal Charlotte climbed the stairs, sliding straight into bed. Outside on the sill the robin waited until the little girl was safely tucked in and asleep before flying back to its nest. The squirrel instead of returning to the gateway as was its habit followed the robin and after the pagoda jumped onto the shed roof. After organising the few dead leaves that were scattered on the roof into a makeshift bed, it curled into a ball hoping to get some sleep. For the first time ever it would be spending the night in this strange world, dominated by humans. He hoped it wouldn't become a regular occurrence and worried too about the hidden budget and charm at the base of the oak , in another world.

In Otherworld a robin even though it was still night left its nest, hidden in a cranny in the church wall. Flying at speed within minutes it was perched in an oak, in a field just a stone's throw from the wooded scarp, the ash-ridge. For a while it remained in the lower branches surveying the field below. Satisfied it skipped down to the trunk and in through a hole. A feeling of warmth greeted him as well as the smell of his companion. He would sleep here tonight, here he could keep watch over the budget. He was scared for his colleague trapped in the strange and from what he had heard often dangerous world the human child came from. He worried he would never see the squirrel, Leht's most trusted messenger again. The robin tried but got little sleep that night.

Charlotte woke the next morning still feeling the shock from the events in the night. Although the magpies in their garden unnerved her a little as did the ever thickening mist covering the field behind the church, she had never really felt in danger in her world. After last night that had all changed. Outside she was relieved to see there were still only three magpies. Remembering the rhyme Will had told her, she repeated the third line, "three for a girl." Was she the girl? What was the other rhyme? Charlotte racked her brains and after some searching, it came to her. "Three for a wedding." Who's wedding? She wondered, it couldn't be hers. Were either of the lines really relevant to what was happening or were they just nonsense. She had been warned in both worlds that seven magpies seen gathered together would spell catastrophe, if the lines depicting seven magpies were relevant and the warning to be taken seriously then surely the message contained in every line before must be taken so too, but what did they mean? After blowing her usual raspberry and giving the picture of the white hart a kiss, she descended the stairs to the smell of fresh croissants. As she ate Charlotte continued to puzzle over the two rhymes. There must be a key there somewhere, a clue as to what is going on. To what may happen, or what is happening. Did the long forgotten scribes who penned both rhymes foretell the future? Could they have seen all that is happening now and leave clues or warnings hidden within the verse? Charlotte had no idea but she was quite proud that she was asking such profound questions, when the rest of her world, she was pretty sure were not.

School was a daze, Charlotte's mind was elsewhere, not in this world but another where dreams were real. As the hours in the day passed she felt less and less shaken by events the night before and more and more determined to make a difference. A few days ago she had felt utterly lost, a mere pawn in a game of chess. A small insignificant dot in a world she could not make head or tail of. She simply could not see why she, an eleven year old girl, had apparently been "chosen." Whatever that meant and was at an even greater loss to understand how she could be of help. However since her early ventures into Otherworld and especially after the events the night before, an inner strength had steadily been growing inside her, a grim determination, and a belief that she may in some way make a difference. Even if it meant she died trying. Charlotte shocked herself with her last thought but she no longer felt so afraid and where the Darkness was concerned she was beginning to realise that was half the battle.

That evening she went to bed early feigning she felt tired. The opposite was true, her body tingled with expectation. Tonight she would be ready. Last night the Darkness had tricked her and by her gullibility she had put her friends from Otherworld in danger. She was determined the same thing would never happen again. Tonight she wanted to be summoned, she was ready to do battle.

Charlotte wasn't to be disappointed. At midnight there came a tap, tap, tap on her window. She was awake in under a second and fully dressed in just a few more. Outside both the squirrel and the robin were waiting. Charlotte acknowledged them with the slightest of nods and headed down the brick path to the road. Her heart was in her mouth but she was determined not to show it. As she walked up the road to the village green, like the night before she made a mental note of the houses with a light shining behind closed curtains. There were just two she counted, more on the other side of the pond. The nearest was on her road. As she stepped onto the gravel path, Charlotte glanced at the clock on the church tower. The hand held serpent writhed restlessly across the clock face its head and tail firmly on XIII. She allowed herself a wry smile. A few weeks back the writhing serpent unnerved her, scared as it would anyone seeing it for the first time. Seeing it tonight she felt relieved, calm, reassured.

After a quick look about her, Charlotte stepped onto the stone slab and immediately felt herself being pulled into the earth. In under a minute she was standing in Otherworld, in what had now been confirmed to her, to be nothing more than an image of her village. The squirrel she saw on arrival was sitting in the lower branch of a tree watching her but there was no sign of the robin. Nervously Charlotte looked around for any signs of danger, glancing only for a moment at the turbulent mist. There was nothing she could see that looked untoward and that somehow made her feel even more nervous. She had expected something to happen and was primed to deal with it or run. Snapping herself out of such wasteful thoughts she started to jog back down the gravel path, towards where she knew the nearest light would be. A house just after the village shop.

She crossed the road and was jogging past the shop when she stopped in her tracks. She froze and every hair on the back of her neck stood up. Something in the shop window had caught her eye. Not able to move she found herself staring at the bowed display window to the left of the shop door. There in the window was an upright figure, a human figure and the figure was staring straight at her. The figure was a woman and Charlotte unable to pull herself away could see she wasn't standing but floating. The figure was completely motionless, hands by her sides and without doubt floating in mid-air as if suspended by a set of invisible threads. Worse of all the woman's eyes were stretched wide open, as far as they could be and staring out of the window. Not at her Charlotte now realised but in terror at something, something behind her. In a panic, her heart pumping Charlotte spun around to see what so terrified Ashtynn, for it was Ashtynn suspended in the window, there was no doubt.

With immense relief Charlotte saw there was nothing behind her, just the empty soul stripped village. Whatever Ashtynn had seen it was not of that time. Her look of terror had been captured at a different hour and frozen by someone or something who wanted to capture her at her most terrified. And for some sick reason, someone or something had displayed her moment of terror for all to see in the shop window. Probably not for all to see, for Charlotte wasn't stupid. She knew the gruesome display was almost certainly meant for her and her alone. A warning perhaps or a promise of what was to become her if she wasn't careful. Charlotte felt physically sick at the thought. She was finding it hard to take her eyes off of the horrific display. The deliberately depraved display of Ashtynn's distress somehow held her morbidly trapped. A sharp bump against her calf caused her to scream out loud. She was preparing herself to meet a similar fate when she realised it was the squirrel. It was telling her to move. Sensing the messenger's frustration she became angry at her stupidity, maybe the suspended Ashtynn wasn't a warning at all but a trap. Without a second more hesitation Charlotte started for where she knew a light to be waiting for her. Moments later she was standing in front of a door to a low hung cottage. As it had in her world a light shone from behind a pair of dark red curtains. Charlotte walked determinedly up to the front door.

"It's not real," she mouthed. She didn't stop as she approached the door, instead she held her hand straight out in front of her as though she were going to push the door open. At the last moment she closed her eyes hoping when she opened them she would be inside the house. There was a dull thud as she came up against a solid wooden door. Charlotte cursed and took a step back. The trouble was the cottage looked real, it looked solid. When she walked through the village in Otherworld, as a whole it felt different, it almost felt like a photograph. But individually each building appeared and felt like the real thing. Taking a deep breath she took a step back and tried again, this time with her eyes open. The door remained as solid as it looked. She tried opening the door the conventional way but that was no good. She knew it wouldn't be. As a last resort she turned her back so that her gaze was of all Aldbury, the image of Aldbury, the less believable Aldbury. Surely this would work, with her eyes fixed on the buildings around the pond she started taking nervous steps backwards. Thump, Charlotte's right heel came up against a solid door. Once more she cursed. The squirrel she noticed was starting to become agitated, its tail flicking left and right. They both realised if they remained like this she was exposed and defenceless against anything or anyone that meant her harm.

"It's not real' it's not real, it's not real," Charlotte kept telling herself and with another deep breath leapt at the door but with the same result, solid wood. She felt like crying and was just about to wipe her eye to stop herself when in a flash the squirrel leapt from its position on the lawn and sailed through the door. Charlotte, shouted in frustration and threw her entire body at the door. The next moment she felt herself falling. There was no door.

She landed on a thick shag pile carpet. For a moment she was dazed and her nose hurt where she had been too slow to react to her fall. Coming round she realised she was inside the cottage, how she couldn't work out. Sitting up she looked at the front door, not quite believing what she had just achieved. The door was shut solid. Getting to her feet Charlotte looked around, her eyes exploring her new surroundings. The door had entered straight into what was a fairly large lounge. The low ceiling had several heavy exposed beams and the walls uneven, had been whitewashed. An expensive looking three piece suite faced an inglenook fireplace and in one corner sat a rather plain looking rocking chair. Nearly all of the furniture was dark oak and very solid looking. There was the odd picture, though they were far outnumbered by photographs of the family enjoying themselves. Charlotte recognised some of the faces in the photos but didn't know any of them to talk to. A staircase led straight from the lounge to the floor above. Charlotte's eyes fell on the inglenook fireplace. In the grate a log fire burned except it wasn't. The flames were strong and the logs almost white with heat but nothing moved or glowed, the fire was motionless. It's just an image, of course she told herself and for confirmation waved her hand in front of the frozen flames. The air was cold. It was then she realised the whole room was cold and tightened her coat. She inspected the room more closely. The light she'd seen through the curtains, were from three large lamps placed sympathetically around the room so as not to have any spot over lit. There was a large coffee table and on this remained a two thirds finished bottle of wine with a couple of half empty wine glasses. A small table stood beside the rocking chair and on it an almost empty brandy glass. In one corner beside the inglenook fireplace stood an upright bookcase and on it a small and rather old television set. The set was on but the image on screen was frozen. Charlotte instantly recognised the image, it was from a popular television series that always involved a murder. Her attention moved to a large wooden clock on the back wall. The time read midnight. There was another clock, one made of brass on what looked like a very old cabinet. It too read midnight.

Looking around the room it looked and felt as though it had been occupied just a few moments before. Charlotte felt very uncomfortable, at best she felt like a snoop and at worst a house breaker. "It's all just an image," she told herself again but it didn't help. She felt very much as though she were intruding and promised herself she wouldn't open any door or cupboard or read any letter of which there were several on a small table by the front door. At any moment she expected someone to come down the stairs or through a door, but no one did. For a brief moment she wondered about exploring upstairs but quickly dismissed the idea. She remembered a ghost story, on television she had once watched with a friend. A family renting a holiday cottage found after a day that they couldn't get out, they were trapped. Later one of the children had mounted the stairs to the attic and found the original family murdered in their bed. She shivered at the thought, there was no way she was going upstairs. Anyway, how did the image thing work could she mount the stairs or would she simply fall through? Charlotte walked over and put her foot on the first step. It felt solid. She then brought her second foot up and placed her whole weight on the step. It held her weight, she didn't fall through. I've got no idea how this image thing works, she mouthed to the squirrel, whom she saw had settled on the substantial window sill, looking out at the street.

Charlotte's next thought was rest. It was a good five hours before it would be daylight and it was important to get some sleep. The sumptuous sofa looked very inviting but again was it an image or was it solid, could she sleep on it? She touched one of the cushions with her hand. It felt as you would expect it to, soft, inviting, luxurious. Kicking off her shoes

Charlotte with snail pace caution lay on the sofa. It was huge, bigger than her bed and she had to admit, much more comfortable. Laying with her head resting on her hands Charlotte closed her eyes and tried to get some sleep but sleep wouldn't come. She kept thinking at any minute someone may come down the stairs and find her. Worse still if the house she was sleeping in was simply an image surely anyone or anything could walk through the wall. Then there was the light, that didn't help either but she was scared to turn off any of the lamps as they were the whole reason she was there in the first place. The light she had been told would be her protection. It was all she had. How she wished Wodewose, Triskelion or the hounds were here. Finally there was the cold, it felt like she was sleeping outside and it dawned on her if this cottage was simply an image, she was. Eventually tiredness won over all other factors, she started to feel drowsy and it wasn't that long before she drifted into sleep. Not a sound sleep. Images of Ashtynn and her look of terror haunted her. It was the same look of terror that scarred the artist and both were now in Otherworld. The thought turned over and over in her mind as her body sought desperately for a state by which it could rejuvenate. Charlotte did eventually find some release though rather like a bird which keeps one eye open she remained always aware of her surroundings and alert enough to respond quickly to any threat. It may not have been ideal and certainly not the rejuvenating sleep she needed but it was better than nothing. Just.

Daylight had started to filter through the heavy red curtains but it wasn't the light that had woken Charlotte. It was the squirrel, scurrying and jumping around the room and in no thoughtful fashion. Although her eyelids resisted, after a few seconds, Charlotte once again was taking in her foreign surroundings. Wiping her eyes she made no attempt to resist the wide yawn that followed. Ughh, she felt awful, why is it when you sleep in your clothes you feel so dirty. She needed a wash and cold water to welcome the new dawn. Stretching, she stood up. The squirrel looked pleased and stopped using the room as a race circuit. Gingerly she went through the door adjacent to the stairs, she guessed right, that it led to the kitchen. Both the digital clock on the oven and microwave she noted read, 00.00, midnight. Below the back window, through which were views across fields towards Tring, sat an old fashioned style sink with brass taps. It looked new and Charlotte guessed it was a replica. Frankly, she couldn't care less, all she wanted was to wash. She stood in front of the sink, swept back her hair and went to turn on the cold tap but found it wouldn't budge. She tried with both hands but the tap was stuck fast, it wouldn't move not even a fraction. With gritted teeth she tried one last time using every bit of strength her body could muster. This time to her utter astonishment her hands simply passed through the tap and through part of the sink as well. She jumped back in surprise, almost falling over in her haste.

Cursing, it was becoming a habit, Charlotte returned to the lounge where she found the squirrel sitting where it had rested during the night, on the window sill. Its head was squeezed through the crack in the curtains, surveying the scene outside. Charlotte spat twice on her hands and rubbed her face hard. It wasn't ideal but it did the trick. She was fully awake. The squirrel leapt down from the sill and ran to the door. Charlotte guessed intelligently that the squirrel was telling her it was time to leave. Taking one last look around the room, she went to leave. Perhaps it was over confidence, possibly the reverse but thud, she found herself walking into solid wood. This was completely unexpected, she had been sure she'd simply be able to walk straight through the door.

"It's not real, it's not real," Charlotte found herself telling herself for the umpteenth time and again she tried. This time by casually walking at the door and again thud. She looked around the room in exasperation. "None of you is real," she said out loud and once again tried the door, thud. "None of you is real," Charlotte threw at the room. No longer was she worried about being discovered. She needed to get out and shouted without caution, her voice resounding with increasing desperation. Growing inside her was the slow realisation and a rising panic if she couldn't get through the door she would be trapped inside and from what she understood if she were still trapped there at midnight she could be trapped for eternity.

The squirrel seeing her look of desperation jumped down from the windowsill, ran over to the door and leapt straight through it. Charlotte, close to tears tried once more but no, she couldn't do it, why wouldn't her mind accept that this was an image? She had accepted it. The squirrel reappeared through the door and curled itself through Charlotte's legs. It then sat as squirrels do, gazing up at her face. There was expression, feeling in the squirrel's eyes. The two remained, their eyes locked for several seconds before the squirrel in a single movement passed through the bottom of the door. Charlotte watched it go and not taking her eyes off the place where the squirrel had passed through, firmly told her mind to calm itself. Taking long steady breaths, she closed her eyes and took a long step forward. Nothing, she felt nothing. Hardly daring to breath she agonisingly brought her back foot forward and almost laughed when again she felt nothing. Standing to attention she remained too afraid to open her eyes in case when she did, nothing had changed. Her fear was she hadn't stepped far enough to pass through the door. She stretched both arms out in front of her, again there was nothing, nothing but air. Charlotte felt the gentlest of breezes caress her face, cool not yet warmed by the sun and it was this along with the motion of the squirrel rubbing against her legs that finally convinced her to open her eyes.

Her first reaction was to squint as the light from a bright morning sun confronted her eyes. She was outside. She didn't know whether to be sick, laugh or cry such was her relief, maybe all three. There was no dark grey, no depressing atmosphere. The sky was a bright blue with hardly a whisper of cloud and the sun if it weren't for the fresh morning breeze would feel positively warm. Down the road she could see her cottage with her parents car and their old van parked outside. Charlotte knew the cottage, the car and the van weren't real but she still found it hard to believe. She still half expected her mother to lean out of the bedroom window as she often did when she first got up. She felt the squirrel brush her leg again, she knew by now it was his way of telling her they had to get moving.

The squirrel, with Charlotte following ran up the road to the village green where they crossed the road together to the pond. Here Charlotte stopped to take a look back. She didn't want to but she had to be sure about what she remembered seeing the night before. She had to confirm that the grotesque image of Ashtynn hadn't been her imagination playing tricks. In her heart she knew it hadn't but she had to be sure. Suspended in the shop window, just as Charlotte had seen her during the night hung Ashtynn. Nothing had changed, her eyes remained stretched unnaturally wide in terror. Is she alive or dead, Charlotte wondered, not really wanting to know the answer. She glanced across to the church. Beyond the churchyard she could see the mist, not twisting and turning as it did after the sun had set but deathly still as though resting from a hard night. The rest of the village looked normal except of course, it wasn't. There was no movement, no sound, no birdsong welcoming the new day. No early morning deliveries to the shop, no staff walking to work at the Greyhound, no cars speeding through taking their occupants to work or to the station at Tring. In her world the village would be bustling. Her parents she thought warmly would be preparing her breakfast before going to market. Not for the first time thinking of her parents brought Charlotte close to tears. She pinched herself, in her world the time would still be just a few minutes past midnight, she would be there in the morning, ready for breakfast and no one would be any the wiser. Or at least so she hoped.

From the pond the squirrel followed the road leading to Ivinghoe or Evinghehou, as it is known in Otherworld. Shortly after passing the last house the squirrel bore right, leaving the road to traverse the now familiar field before the wooded scarp. Charlotte, quickly realised they were heading for the oak where the small leather bag, which everyone in this world called a budget lay hidden. Remembering how Alasdair and Cathasach had run through the field gate and eager to test her new found ability Charlotte attempted to do the same only to double up in pain as she ran into solidity. Not wishing to try again she clambered over the gate and started to jog across the field heading for the oak. When she got there, Charlotte found the squirrel apparently communicating with the robin, she was never sure. She also wasn't sure whether to reach for the budget or not. Deciding that was the reason she'd been brought there, she proceeded to kneel and reached into the hollow beneath the tree. Kneeling, shook the morning dew free from the grass releasing a freshness that invigorated senses, senses that would normally have been woken by a morning wash. It was just what she needed. As her hand passed beneath the tree she felt another sensation, this one quite different. This one didn't feel like a gift from nature, it felt more as though she were pushing through a force, some sort of curtain only it wasn't physical, it just felt physical. Fumbling, Charlotte recognised the leather of the budget and carefully lifted it from the hollow. Something glistened within. Looking Charlotte was delighted to see it was her necklace and charm, she still didn't wholly trust Triskelion. Opening the heart she was relieved to find the tiny silver frog safe inside.

Standing, Charlotte placed the necklace over her head and the leather strap of the budget over one shoulder. Apart from her necklace the little leather sack was empty, just as she'd left it, there was no liquid. The squirrel watched her and when she'd finished started towards the trees. The robin she noticed, took off, flying back towards the village. On reaching the fence to the field, Charlotte casually went to climb over into the wood only to this time fall straight through. The squirrel stopped to look back and Charlotte swore she could see it laughing. She really had to get the hang of how this image thing worked. Getting to her feet and with only her pride hurt, she followed the squirrel up the steep wooded incline.

On almost reaching the top the squirrel turned to follow the rim of the escarpment. It wasn't long before they were passing below the Bridgewater monument and the cluster of National Trust buildings. Everything here just as in Aldeborie was strangely silent. After the monument, the squirrel continued to follow the line of the escarpment, along the top of Moneybury Hill, always taking care to avoid following paths created by man. As they travelled Charlotte couldn't help continuously looking over her shoulder. Although it was a beautiful morning and everything looked peaceful she felt vulnerable amongst the trees, it would be easy for someone who wished her harm to hide. Her only reassurance was the squirrel, who didn't seem at all concerned.

On arriving at a large mound enclosed by a wooden fence the squirrel came to a halt. Charlotte recognised the mound as a tumulus, a burial mound similar to those on Aldbury Nowers and Gallows Hill. The squirrel scurried to the top of the tumulus where it stood on its hind legs appearing to sniff the air. At the same time, Charlotte heard what was unmistakably the sound of something running and running fast, fast through the wood making directly for them. Just as she was preparing, not for the first time in recent days to run for her life, the two hounds, Alasdair and Cathasach bounded into view. On arriving at the tumulus they didn't stop, not quite, instead they slowed and proceeded to circle the old burial site, passing back and forth through the modern day face put there to protect it from wear by twenty first century feet. Never had Charlotte felt so, relieved, so pleased to see her old guardians and happily removed her heart from her mouth. It was obvious from the hounds behaviour that they didn't wish to hang around and in no time the four of them were heading into the depths of Sallow Copse.

There is no better time to experience a wood than at dawn, the nocturnal wildlife are just settling down to sleep, whilst the rest of the wood is beginning to stir, preparing for a new day. The air invigorates and Charlotte welcomed its freshness helping with her lack of sleep. They came to rest at a small sunlit clearing or glade surrounded by tall statuesque conifers that let little light through anywhere else. Tall grass was the main feature of the glade with foxgloves pushing high around the odd tree stump. At the centre of the glade lay a fallen beech, it looked as though it had lain there for a good number of years for in places rot was causing the once proud wood to crumble and a good number of plants had made the trunk their home. The sun drenched clearing like the rest of the wood that morning, was quite magical. For Charlotte what made it all the more magical was the site of a shaggy creature curled up in the grass at the base of the fallen beech.

"Wodewose."

"Hello France Charlotte," it wasn't Wodewose who responded to her welcome. Triskelion was standing just out of the sunlight amongst the pines, his white gown glowing all the more for being in the shade. How had she not seen him? As Charlotte turned at the sound of his voice Triskelion walked into the sun, crossing to the fallen beech, gently rubbing Wodewose's head as he did so. "Our good friend Wodewose has let things get the better of him and indulged a little too heavily." Triskelion gently tapped Wodewose on the head. "Wodewose we have company," and tapped his head a little harder. It had the desired effect, Wodewose grunted, opened his eyes, blinked with the sunlight and on seeing Charlotte lifted himself onto one elbow. Almost exactly like his effigy in St John the Baptist Charlotte couldn't help thinking.

"Morning France Charlotte." Charlotte hardly recognised Wodewose's voice. It was thick as winter fog.

"Hawthorn wine," Triskelion said by way of an explanation holding up what looked like a roughly hewn wooden goblet. "Wodewose in the early hours, after a little too much of the hawthorn has been trying to teach the trees your language. The entire wood is just a little bemused." Laying on the grass, to one side of Wodewose was what looked like a leather bottle similar to the budget she had slung over her shoulder. Charlotte guessed rightly that it contained or had once contained hawthorn wine.

"I made it myself." Wodewose mumbled, starting to get up, "and very good it is too." By the time he had finished speaking Wodewose was sitting upright. Resting his back against the fallen beech, he sat hugging his knees which were tightly clenched supporting his long staff. He did look in a bit of a sorry state and Charlotte, even if his suffering was self-inflicted, couldn't feel anything else than sorry for her friend.

"It is a very good wine," Triskelion confirmed. "Wodewose has quite a talent." Charlotte wondered how Triskelion could know this for nowhere on his face could she see a mouth.

"I have some wine I've made from the primrose flower, which is even better," Wodewose boasted, his voice still heavy. "I keep it for special occasions," he added.

"Primrose wine used to be a firm favourite in Otherworld," Triskelion felt obliged to explain. "That was when the flower grew everywhere, in these sad times they are only found in clusters and are considered too precious to turn into wine. If Wodewose has some it is very rare and yes only for special occasions." Wodewose grunted in what Charlotte assumed was agreement. She wondered what those special occasions could be.

"I made it when Leht used to travel the woods. We would share it."

"That was a long time ago," added Triskelion, finding himself a seat on the fallen beech.

"How is Leht?" Charlotte changed the subject. It was Triskelion who replied.

“I went to see her after the last time we met, she is well and sends her regards. We talked a lot about you.” Charlotte wasn’t sure how she felt about this.

“Really?” Triskelion didn’t respond directly to this, instead he waved his hand across the clearing.

“Find a seat France Charlotte, we have much to talk about.” Charlotte looked about her and chose a tree stump almost covered entirely with moss. She sat down not caring that the moss was still damp from the morning dew. Several towering fox gloves, circled the rear of the stump, their flaxen like leaves almost forming a closed curtain behind her back. Sat, bathing in the sun’s rays, Charlotte felt rather like a queen residing on an elegant woodland throne.

“I love fox gloves,” she commented absently admiring their majesty.

“Fairy bells, not fox gloves,” Wodewose sounded a little irritable. Charlotte looked puzzled and Triskelion came to her assistance once more.

“In Otherworld we call them fairy bells not fox gloves,” he explained.

“What a lovely name,” Charlotte enthused. “Why are they called that?”

“Because fairies used to ring them in times of great celebration, such as a wedding or on an occasion of great importance. If you want an example,” he reflected. “When the white hart was placed on the hill, Ivinghoe Beacon as you call it to guard the Sacred Library of Evinghehou, fairy bells rang throughout Otherworld in support and celebration. Triskelion paused. “Or so I’m told, for that was before my time.” Charlotte thought about what Triskelion had just said.

“You say used to, don’t they anymore? I should like to hear them.”

“No.” It was normally Wodewose who was gifted with one syllable answers but on this occasion it was Triskelion.

“How sad, why not?” Charlotte couldn’t hide her disappointment.

"Because there are no more fairies." Wodewose spoke, sounding even more irritable. He looked as though he wanted to add to what he had just said but a look from Triskelion stopped him. Charlotte was shocked by his answer and couldn't help sensing the tension in the air caused by her question. She had always wanted to believe in fairies and wanted to know more but decided in spite of her curiosity, judging by the atmosphere it would be better not to pursue the matter. At least not on this occasion. An uneasy silence descended on the glade, during which Alasdair and Cathasach settled themselves in the long grass and the squirrel a comfortable spot on the fallen beech. Looking around, Charlotte not for the first time, considered what an odd party they looked. She didn't welcome the silence. For a moment, with the glory that was Ashridge and seeing her friends she had managed to push Ashtynn from her mind. Now with renewed tension in the air the horror that was Ashtynn came flooding back. There was also the artist, he too had had the same horrific expression on his face and from what she understood he had been in the care of Triskelion. Why had he looked so terrified? What had he, what had they both witnessed to induce such a terrified expression? And how had they both got here, to Otherworld? She kept being told that she was the only one who could transcend. Was she being fed a lie? The thought made her feel ill at ease. She glanced at Triskelion, she still didn't trust him and suspected more and more that he may have the ability to read what she was thinking. Conscious that her doubts may not please him Charlotte did her best to divert her thoughts, she needed to talk, that was the only way to stop her mind asking questions. Questions that may not be palatable to the being in the luminous white cloak, though not a ghost apparently. She quickly came up with an innocent question to ask Triskelion, one she was sure wouldn't offend or bring suspicion and was just about to ask it when the rapid tapping by a great spotted woodpecker, ratatatatatat somewhere in the wood broke the silence for her.

"You want to know how old I am," it was a statement not a question. Charlotte nodded uncomfortably wondering how much more Triskelion had read of her thoughts.

"Well now," Triskelion had slid forward and was leaning on an upright branch of the fallen beech. He was looking almost relaxed and seemed to be enjoying her obvious discomfort. "That is not an easy question to answer." Charlotte waited for him to expand on this and almost a whole minute passed during which she found herself gritting her teeth in an attempt to block any further thoughts forming. She was determined not to provide Triskelion with any more thought fodder for him to read. (If you think Charlotte is making something of a meal of this you try sitting for a minute without thinking of anything. You'll soon discover it's a lot harder than it sounds). After what seemed an eternity Triskelion spoke. "My grandfather was human just like you, he is buried near the Sacred Library of Evinghehou, on what you in your world now call Gallows Hill. Charlotte remembered the ancient burial mound on the hill, where not so long ago with her parents she'd enjoyed a picnic. She wondered if Triskelion meant there, that very tumulus. Without having to ask, the way Triskelion gripped her mind she knew she was right. Her face reddened. She'd fallen at the first hurdle in trying to hide her thoughts from him.

"Please do not feel bad France Charlotte, you weren't to know." Triskelion's dismissal didn't really help, she still felt bad, very bad. "Do you not wish to know how with a human grandfather, I am like this, how you see me today and I am not a ghost" Triskelion had read her again! Charlotte knew he was trying to move things on. She nodded, yes she really did want to know. Why couldn't she say so, where was her tongue?

"My human grandfather knew and understood how Otherworld worked. He could transcend between worlds like you. He fell in love with a banduiri from this world, her name was Aodh and was born on the hill you call Ivinghoe Beacon. They had a spiritual marriage, indeed fairy bells rang out on that day and from their original union I was later born to this world." Charlotte listened carefully, she only half understood what Triskelion was telling her. He'd made no mention of his father, only his grandfather. "As for my age," Triskelion said suddenly. "I do not know exactly but I am old enough to remember when a man you call Jesus walked on your earth, indeed at one time not too far from here. So well over two thousand years, maybe even three." Charlotte couldn't begin to imagine anyone being that old. And to think that Triskelion was around the same time as someone she'd learnt about and believed in since she was an infant. The thought was almost, no it was, it was simply mind blowing. She had so many questions though it was Wodewose who spoke next.

"I'm older," he said bluntly and with an obvious touch of pride. "Who's Jesus?" Charlotte laughed.

"I'll tell you one day," Charlotte promised him. Wodewose seemed happy with that. Still thinking, Charlotte recalled what Leht had told her just before she disappeared on Aldbury Nowers. "I've sent for help, his name is Triskelion" were Leht's last words to her that night. Charlotte thought about those words and another question formed in her mind. Triskelion answered before she could speak. He could be so annoying.

"Is that why Leht asked for my help, because I originate from here? The answer, France Charlotte is yes. Leht was right, you are very perceptive." Triskelion then said something Charlotte wasn't expecting. "You are annoyed at me for answering your questions before you have time to ask them with your own mouth. I was trying to save you the effort, would you prefer if I waited and let you speak your questions?" Charlotte found herself nodding again though this time found her tongue.

"If you wouldn't mind Triskelion," she answered, a little too meekly for her liking.

"Your wish, granted." He promised. There was another silence broken only by a series of rhythmic grunts, Wodewose had fallen asleep.

"You said we have a lot to talk about?" Charlotte asked, lowering her voice.

"Yes."

"Can you explain what you mean by that?" She wished everybody in Otherworld would stop speaking in one syllable, it would be a lot easier not to mention quicker. Triskelion read her thoughts, though felt it wise not to tell her.

"There has been talk, or rather the Snooks have foretold of a human child who can transcend between worlds, arriving to help us with what maybe the defining battle with the Darkness."

"Who or what are Snooks?" Charlotte had no idea.

"Snooks," Triskelion said patiently," are traditional storytellers from Vlaanderen. They travel anywhere and everywhere, to wherever those in Otherworld wish to hear their stories.

"And they can foretell the future?"

"Sometimes, not always. They are better known for telling tales and adventures from the distant past, stories that have long been forgotten." Charlotte thought about what Triskelion had just told her. She knew, because her mother was French that by Vlaanderen, Triskelion was referring to Flandres better known by those whose tongue is English as Flanders. Her mother had often told her of the traditional story tellers who used to travel between estaminets, the Flemish equivalent of an English Inn. Never had her mother told her that they could foretell the future. Charlotte looked intently at Triskelion.

"And how does this human child help? And how do you know they mean me?" Triskelion took his time in answering.

"That," he said finally. "The Snooks cannot tell us. That, France Charlotte is why we have to talk." Charlotte ignored his answer.

"And this human child," she repeated. "Does she help Otherworld defeat the Darkness?" Triskelion once more took his time in answering, it looked to Charlotte that this was one question he hadn't wanted her to ask.

"That." He let the word hang in the air. "That, the Snooks cannot tell us either. I have to be honest and tell you we simply do not know why you are here and how you can help. All I can tell you is that the Snooks have foretold it. You are the only child who, as far as we know can transcend and now that you are here and she has met you, Leht believes in you. The human child in the books of the Snooks can only be you, Leht believes this. It is Leht who has instructed me to talk to you, to seek your thoughts and to help you wherever I can. I have promised Leht to protect you. With my life if necessary."

Charlotte looked at Triskelion, to the sleeping Wodewose. Alasdair and Cathasach, their heads resting on their front paws. Relaxed but ever alert. Finally to the little squirrel, their messenger who at that moment was busy eating pine nuts. She thought of her world, the weapons of mass destruction that were available to the human race. The sophistication, the power, and the accuracy of them. The hundreds of millions of humans that could be called upon to fight if necessary. How on earth she thought could the five of them make any difference to a battle or war that according to Leht could mean not only the destruction of the Earth but the entire universe and everything beyond it. Triskelion held up his hand.

"France Charlotte, I apologise but I think you have a question that you may find difficult to phrase. Do you mind if I answer it before you try?" Charlotte reluctantly accepted defeat. He couldn't help himself.

"The weapons, you are thinking about. Guns, bombs, nuclear warfare, they all play into the Darkness's hands. You cannot destroy the Darkness with such weapons. Using them is exactly what the Darkness wants. It craves destruction. Their use will only strengthen him or rather it. In Otherworld too we used to have bloody battles. Huge armies pitted against each other but no more. Yes blood is still shed today," Charlotte thought back to Cathasach's bloody mouth, to Wodewose's injuries. "But the main, the most important battle of all will not be won through the spilling of blood but by, as Leht told you. Pureness of thought, without fear and strength of wit. And if I may I would like to add a fourth requirement, without anger for thoughts of anger will simply strengthen the Darkness, not defeat it" Charlotte nodded as though Triskelion had just revealed a new dawn. A dawn which she completely understood but in truth still couldn't see how any of those qualities no matter how noble could win against cold steel or a gun.

"You will come to understand in time, France Charlotte. What we do know for sure, is to win against the Darkness, the victor must have the ability or someone on their side have the ability to transcend both worlds and you," Triskelion pointed at Charlotte. "As far as we are aware, apart from the messengers, are the only being in the whole of Otherworld, both worlds capable of doing that today."

Charlotte thought about Ashtynn and the artist and quickly wiped the thought from her consciousness. Instead she sat contemplating what Triskelion had just told her. She should have felt proud by what Triskelion had just told her but she didn't, not at all. If anything she felt unworthy and a little, if not completely overwhelmed. Careful not to involve Ashtynn or the artist she considered what Triskelion had just told her about the ability to transcend and quickly got in a question before he had a chance to tell her his answer.

"Why do I always have to transcend by stepping on that stone in front of the church?" It was something that had been puzzling her for some time. Triskelion looked up to the brilliant blue sky as though searching for an appropriate answer. Wodewose continued to snore.

"A long time ago," Triskelion started by bringing his head down and looking directly at her. "A sacred tree, a great ash from the mountains grew on the spot where the stone now lies. It grew on a current that led deep into the earth. The root of the ash, after a certain age, reaches Otherworld. The ash at Aldeborie or Aldbury as you call your village with the strength of the current grew old way beyond its natural life and the roots if you like, became a superhighway or a super gateway as we prefer to call it, between your world and mine.

"Aldeborie?"

"Yes France Charlotte, in Otherworld we keep with the names christened by the forerunners."

"And what happened to the ash?"

"The ash was felled when your ancestors built the first church. Early builders of all the churches in your land were sympathetic to the original beliefs of the local population. They understood about earth currents, how they flowed and how their power could be harnessed in a building. Just as their ancestors had always known. Churches were built on sites that had always been sacred and nearly always in line with the currents of the Earth running beneath. This is why so many of your churches when compared to the layout of the streets and houses close by have such a peculiar alignment. Their dedication was also often carefully considered and where possible sympathetic to local beliefs attached to the site before. Unfortunately although the original builders of your church at Aldeborie understood the spiritual significance of the site, they didn't realise the value of the old ash and simply felled it." Triskelion stopped and looked at the sleeping Wodewose. "Part of the old tree was saved though, Wodewose's staff is cut from the sacred ash of the mountains."

Charlotte looked at the knobbled piece of wood gripped between the shaggy beasts knees. Fresh leaves sprouted at regular intervals throughout its length. If Triskelion were right and Wodewose's staff was from the sacred ash it would have to be close to fifteen hundred years old, perhaps even older, much older. And yet looking at it now, the staff appeared as if it were only cut yesterday. The leaves always fresh and as far as Charlotte could tell, survived off nothing but fresh air. Charlotte's thoughts wandered back to what Triskelion had told her about the church's origins. How many people she thought simply drove through Aldbury every day, passing the church without giving it a second thought. Did they ever really consider what the building actually stood for and why a decision had been taken to build the church there in the first place? Who had dedicated the church and why did they choose St John the Baptist, the forerunner? Why the site was so important to the original builders and its alignment? The way the church was aligned, was it simply aesthetical or had there been a greater reason, lost to the modern world? St John the Baptist is so much more than just a church. Her thoughts returned to the ash. Charlotte had another question.

"If the ash was felled all those years ago, how come the gateway between your world and mine still works?"

"The gateway was so well developed, it remained even though the tree was no longer living. There was however a problem created when your ancestors felled the ash. The living tree had a second purpose. Its boughs above ground protected the location of the gateway from unwanted eyes. What therefore concerned the druids, the custodians of the gateway in your world and their equivalent in Otherworld was that without the tree the gateway's location could be revealed to sources of mal-intent. Sources that could exploit the gateway for evil. Worse still the Darkness through its agents may become aware of it. This fear came to the fore not so many moons later when Sir Guy de Gravade whose dwelling quite by accident was almost next door to the gateway, fell in with the Darkness. When this happened it was decided the gateway had to be sealed and hidden for eternity. As the sacred ash grew in your world it was in your world the gateway had to be sealed. A sundial was commissioned to be carved from the finest stone from Ynys Mon, stone that could hold a spell for not all stone can. The stone was taken to a sacred cave hidden deep beneath Cader Idris. Here it was worked upon by scribes who specialised in binding a spell along with a key into stone. An art, which today in both our worlds is sadly no longer practiced or even remembered. The leaf decoration on the pillar, sprouting from the green man at its base, disguised a message that could only be read by those who had the knowledge. The number who had such ability could be counted on one human hand. The sundial was placed on the site of the gateway, its purpose to hide, seal and protect its existence. The gateway could only be opened using the esoteric message carved into its column. Over the centuries the gateway was forgotten until that is, some 20 of your years ago the sundial disappeared, stolen as it was reported at the time. Its disappearance created shock waves in Otherworld, especially with the nearing of the great cycle. The gateway had virtually been forgotten and the sundial's disappearance seemed too much of a coincidence. The spell worked into the stone by the stone scribes under Cader Idris should have prevented any theft. The question arose therefore, was the dial taken by someone who could read the hidden message carved into the pillar and unlock the gateway? In Otherworld the ability to interpret a message of the stone scribes beneath Cader Idris had long died out. And it seemed incredulous that there existed in your world, somebody capable of reading the hidden language of the ancients and activating the key. We always believed that if anyone were to be found with such ability, they would be found living here in Otherworld. Not in your world. I am ashamed to say, such has been the arrogance of Otherworld France Charlotte, we have walked whilst fast asleep into this crisis."

Charlotte was about to ask a question but Triskelion held up his cloaked arm to stop her.

"Let me finish, France Charlotte, please. Not long after the disappearance of the dial, rumours started that the Darkness was preparing a breach into your world. Worse still whilst we were focused on understanding what that meant and how the Darkness meant to achieve such a breach, using hidden forces the Darkness attacked the Guardian, protecting the Sacred Library of Evinghehou. I am ashamed to say we were caught completely off guard, asleep. At the same time all this was happening the Snooks started to tell tales about an impending battle with the Darkness, a battle that would involve a human who could transcend between both worlds. Later the Snooks expanded on their prediction and the human became more precisely a human child." Triskelion paused for a few seconds, he looked uncomfortable. "Sadly, the expansion of their tale came too late for Elmer, the artist who lived where you are living now. We thought him to be the human the Snooks predicted had come to help us but of course as we now know we were, very, very wrong. An attempt to bring him from your world to ours ended in disaster. He encountered something terrible as he transcended and if we hadn't put him into suspension he would have passed into his afterlife."

"What is suspension?" Charlotte risked interrupting Triskelion in mid flow. She had to fully understand what was happening. This time Triskelion offered no objection.

"Suspension, to put it bluntly, France Charlotte means suspending someone on their journey to their afterlife, or as you call afterlife in your world, death. Whilst he is in the sacred waters of Amphillicia's Well he is safe from reaching his afterlife."

Charlotte remembered the muddy pool from which Triskelion raised the artist. By the grand sounding name, Amphillicia's Well, was he referring to that?

Triskelion broke his earlier promise by not waiting for a physical question. On this subject he was too impatient, quick to answer her thoughts

"Don't be deceived by appearances, France Charlotte."

"Are you ever going to be able to get the artist out of suspension?" Charlotte politely ignored Triskelion's lack of control. If it was me, she thought, I'd prefer to reach my afterlife than lie in that mucky pool of mud forever.

"The only way we can bring Elmer out of suspension," Triskelion said slowly is by returning him to your world. Charlotte quickly realised the significance of what he had just said.

"And you have no idea, how to do that do you?"

"No." Triskelion admitted.

"So he could lie there in what's her name."

"Amphillicia's,"

"Well forever." The thought horrified Charlotte.

"Yes," Triskelion admitted again. Leht had told him to be brutally honest with the human child, he was beginning to wish he'd fought her on this.

Charlotte took a deep breath, it could be her lying there in that cesspool. She thought back to the one time she'd transcended and because of the police had taken longer than planned. How slow her passage through the blackness had been, how she had begun to panic. How Triskelion had told her afterwards not to take risks when transcending.

"Triskelion what would happen if I don't make it through the gateway. If I get stuck?" Triskelion looked around the sun drenched glade, why did life on the surface look so easy when, so often it was just the opposite.

"France Charlotte, from the time you are called."

"You mean the robin tapping on my window?"

"Yes, from that time you have exactly seven minutes to enter the gateway, the closer to the seven minutes the weaker the gateway becomes, which is what happened once with you."

"And if I try but are too late?" Triskelion looked at the little human child, known to Otherworld as France Charlotte. Determination framed her every question. Leht had been right he thought, there's more to France Charlotte than her fragile appearance lets on.

"If you're lucky the gateway will have closed by the time you reach it. If you're not, if you enter but enter so late the gateway will close before you have time to exit."

"You mean I will die," Charlotte asked bluntly.

"No something far worse." Triskelion paused to emphasize what he had just said. "You will live for eternity but you will live suspended in blackness, your eyes open but being able to see nothing but black. Your mind will continue to function and you will forever keep your memories but after a while you may wish you never had them as they will fast become too painful to bear. Every minute will be mental torture, every minute will pass so slowly it will seem like an hour, and every day a year. Every second you will pray for the torture to end, every second you will pray for your afterlife but your prayers will never be answered, your afterlife will never rescue you. Now do you understand why I told you not to take risks?"

Charlotte remained silent for a minute or so trying to imagine the nightmare scenario Triskelion had just portrayed. She had come close, too close to what he was describing. The thought made her, not for the first time, feel physically sick.

"Thank you yes." Charlotte's voice was strong but a slight waver revealed her battle with her emotions "I'm glad you've explained that to me, now I know." Charlotte continued to think hard, with every answer came many, many more questions, so many questions.

"You also need to be aware," Triskelion interrupted her thoughts. "The longer you stay in Otherworld the weaker the gateway becomes. If possible you should always try to return within 24 hours, any longer becomes a risk. The longer you stay the greater the risk. You may find the gate to your world will refuse to open and become trapped, with the outcome I have just described."

"Will I ever need to stay here longer than 24 hours?" To her credit, Charlotte's voice was now steady. Triskelion didn't answer straight away, which Charlotte thought was an answer in itself.

"France Charlotte, I am not a Snook, I cannot foretell or see the future."

Charlotte simply nodded, her eyes concentrating on the tall blades of grass waving gently in the breeze. She considered his answer a cop out and had another question. Triskelion was actually letting her ask them.

"Triskelion you let me transcend this time with nobody to meet me in Otherworld, as you told me a welcoming party may well attract unwanted attention.

"That is so." Triskelion confirmed.

"Is that because you think the Darkness is already aware of the gateway? Charlotte didn't allow Triskelion to answer straight away. She went on to explain what had happened to her, in her world. How she had almost been tricked by a squirrel that wasn't her squirrel and the frightening dark shadow that had chased her up the church path when she last transcended from Otherworld. She simply could not believe that the Darkness and his agents as Triskelion and Leht called them, couldn't know about the gateway. They must have seen her and the squirrel making their passage, especially being so close to the mist. And now, there was the missing sundial. Why hadn't she been told about this before? Surely if Triskelion or Leht didn't know who had stolen it, the conclusion must be drawn that it had been taken by someone or something acting on instructions from the Darkness. After what happened with the fake squirrel, she was also scared that the Darkness now knew where she lived and this knowledge could put her parents in danger, grave danger. Charlotte felt anger rising inside her. She was sure Triskelion wasn't telling her everything, that he was holding something back. Could she really trust Triskelion, she'd never felt completely comfortable with him. She looked across to where he was leaning against the fallen beech. Triskelion had his head bowed, his robed arms hanging loose in front of him, it looked as though his hands were clasped but Charlotte couldn't be sure. He always spoke to her through her mind and Charlotte through this connection was slowly learning to sense Triskelion's moods. They were always guarded and often complex, but at that moment she couldn't fail to sense what he was feeling. It was dejection. Charlotte knew after she had stopped talking Triskelion had read her every thought. She held back from asking anything else. Her silence as earlier would speak louder than words.

"I didn't know about your friend, Ashtynn, I'm sorry, very sorry. I hope you believe me." Triskelion's voice as always was monotone, soft, commanding and without feeling, however this time Charlotte sensed there was real sincerity in the way he spoke his words.

"How did she get here, Triskelion, through the gateway?"

"No, of that I am sure, we'd have known. Though I almost wish she had passed via the old gateway. I fear her appearance in Otherworld can only mean that hidden somewhere in the mist the Darkness is close to creating its own gateway, which means we may have even less time than we thought."

Time to do what? Charlotte still didn't have the first clue how they were meant to go about battling what appeared to be an impossible enemy let alone defeat it.

"Do not worry France Charlotte, your friend is not dead. If she is floating in the shop window as your mind portrays, then it is almost certain the Darkness has put her in suspension, just as we have done with the artist."

"But why?" There was no pause this time, Triskelion replied immediately.

"To mock us perhaps, to prove to us what it is capable of, that it is close to completing a gateway. There will be a reason why he hasn't sent your friend to her afterlife, she must still be of use. Placing her in the window is almost certainly intended to frighten you, remember the Darkness wins its battles through fear. It could also be using her for its own eyes and ears. When you return to your world later, I will come with you to see Ashtynn for myself."

Charlotte felt relieved at hearing this. She may not entirely trust Triskelion but she did feel safe with him or at least safer.

"We still do not believe the Darkness knows of the ancient gateway. It may suspect, that is all. The sundial may simply have been taken by a thief. The spell inscribed in the stone under Cader Idris may well have worn thin with time and was never really designed to protect the gateway from your species in the first place. The Darkness hasn't eyes or ears like you or me, it relies on its agents for this and they are not always dependable. We have a lookout, as you know at the gateway and we are confident the gateway is not being watched." Charlotte wasn't convinced by Triskelion's last statement. Something had almost caught her last time, she had only just made it to the gateway in time and then there was the planting of the squirrel and the magpies in their garden. If the Darkness wasn't aware of the gateway it was certainly aware of where she lived.

"Are there no other gateways I can use?" She thought it a sensible question under the circumstances.

"There are." Triskelion admitted.

"Why can't I use one of those?

"They are not safe, there is a great deal of risk involved and a high chance of you being lost forever, just as I described earlier. If we have no other option I will explain their existence when the time comes, though I sincerely hope it will never be necessary. The risk I feel personally, is simply too great." Charlotte considered Triskelion's answer, not if there were no other option she thought. Which brought her to her next question. Something in her mind from earlier that Triskelion hadn't answered.

"What if I'd followed the wrong squirrel that night, what if I hadn't been saved." Charlotte nodded towards the messenger who was sitting just behind Triskelion, still busy with its breakfast. "What if I'd been caught by that disgusting shadowy thing, last time I used the gateway. I've never been so scared,"

"I know, I know, France Charlotte," Triskelion, looked briefly up to the sky. "We failed you, you should have been made aware of what could happen. What the risks were, are. We just haven't, or rather I haven't had the time to talk them through with you. Until now."

Charlotte thought this a pathetic excuse. As far as she was concerned, he hadn't wanted to tell her, that was the truth.

"Leht admonished me for this. She told me I must tell you everything, treat you like an adult, not to hide anything." Triskelion's reply, she felt, was an admission that she had been right.

"So what would have happened?" Charlotte asked again, she needed to know. Triskelion took his time before answering.

"Always remember France Charlotte, the Darkness's most powerful weapon is installing fear into its victims. If you let the Darkness know that you're scared, it is half way there to taking over your mind and eventually your soul. No matter how frightening the situation you find yourself in try not to feel afraid. The shadow you felt following you last time you were in Otherworld is a misguided spirit from long ago. It is in the control of the Darkness and its name is Scucca. It was trying to do just that, stall you through fear. If it had reached you and you hadn't controlled your fear, it would have taken you over and you would have become a very valuable agent for the Darkness. The same with the squirrel, if our friend hadn't intervened the imposter would have led you close to the mist where fear would have got you in a stranglehold.

Once caught in its web of fear you wouldn't have been able to prevent yourself from being pulled into the mist, it would have been easy for the Darkness simply to make you walk in. Just as it did apparently with your friend Ashtynn. France Charlotte." Triskelion's voice had that ring of command that was there when she had first been introduced. "If ever you are followed or even feel you are being followed to the gateway, under no circumstances look over your shoulder, always keep your eyes firmly on our messenger. Suppress all fear, keep your eyes firmly fixed on our messenger," Triskelion repeated. "Do this and you will arrive safely. Now France Charlotte, think back carefully to the night you were summoned to follow the squirrel that we now know was an agent of the Darkness. Were you summoned in the normal manner?" Charlotte thought hard.

"You mean by the robin tapping on the window?"

"Yes, though it wasn't our robin, you know that now. This is very important France Charlotte, think carefully." Charlotte's mind went back to the night in question. She remembered distinctly being woken by a tap on the window.

"Yes," she confirmed, "I was." She was sure Triskelion was wrong in this.

"Did you see the robin?" Triskelion was persistent with his line of questioning, Charlotte just could not see what he was trying to get at, why it was so important to him. Charlotte again thought back to that night. She hadn't actually seen the robin, no.

"No, I just heard the tap." Triskelion picked up on this immediately.

"You said, tap, why did you say that France Charlotte?"

"Because that's what I." Charlotte stopped in mid flow, she suddenly realised what Triskelion was driving at, what he was trying to get out of her.

"It wasn't the robin, was it? She said flatly. The tap at her window that night had been the one heavy tap, repeated shortly after by another single heavy tap. Not at all like the robin's fast rat a tat, tat.

"No. I think it must have been one of your magpies." Charlotte shivered at the thought. "The robin is the one bird, I think I told you, that is immune from the influence, the powerful mind of the Darkness. If the Darkness had found a way to take over or control the mind of a robin, I would have lost my one, my only reliable contact in your world. And that France Charlotte would be a disaster." Charlotte should have felt relieved at hearing this but through Triskelion's questioning she had remembered something else associated with the robin.

"The robin tapping my window. Next door's gardener told me that if a robin does this, it acts as a warning for an impending death in the household. Is that true, or is it just silly superstition?"

"Yes, it's true," Triskelion began and was set to continue when Charlotte cut in.

"Even if you sent the robin to summon me, even if it wasn't the robin's choice?"

"The robin would have tapped on your window anyway." Charlotte let this new piece of information slowly sink in. If only she could read Triskelion's face, gauge what he was thinking by his expression. But there was no face to read and Triskelion had closed all doors that let her sense some or any sort of feeling.

"If that is the case, is the message meant for me, my mother or my father?" It was an unhealthy question but she had to know. Triskelion held up his right arm.

"You must understand, it is a warning, not a prediction or a message. If the bird has warned you, you can prevent it from becoming so. By being aware you can shape the future to your advantage. The warning is intended by the robin as an aid, not a threat. The warning could relate to either one of you or every one of you. Only the robin can tell you what you want to know and it is forbidden to do so by the unwritten lore of the land. Even if it wanted to tell you, it couldn't. It can't even tell me."

Charlotte believed him, Triskelion had no reason to lie. She felt hot and realised it wasn't just her emotions. The sun had risen considerably since they'd made themselves at home in the little glade and was now beginning to make its presence felt. Her mind was still busy trying to digest what Triskelion had just told her. Not wanting to look at him she gazed into the wood but after the glare of the sun found it difficult to pick out anything in the comparative gloom. Her inability to see anything in the physical sense brought a change of thought. Looking around the sunlit glade even with the hounds and Triskelion present she felt very insecure. Surely they would be sitting ducks for anyone out to get them.

"Shouldn't we be hiding?"

"We are hiding?" Triskelion replied, a little too casually. "That's why I chose this spot to meet."

"But surely sitting here we stick out like a sore thumb. Anybody could creep up on us through the wood." She just could not understand Triskelion's reasoning.

"You've forgotten what I told you, France Charlotte. The Darkness and most of its agents cannot see and many cannot survive for long in the light. They can only see well under the cover of darkness when we are at a disadvantage for we cannot. That is the very reason why I told you to find safety under a light in Aldeborie as soon as you arrive. In daylight, only shadows offer the Darkness any hope of keeping track of things and beneath a bright sun like today nearly all the shadows are too weak for the Darkness's operatives or agents. The only exception perhaps are what we call, gnombres. They live mainly in the shadows of trees and you could find hundreds living in one large shadow. They can watch your every move from a shadow providing that you're also in a shadow, so always be aware of this. If you're walking through Assherugge or any wood night or day try and keep your feet in the light whether it be moon or sunlight. And beware if a shadow is dark enough the gnombres can emerge from the shadow as physical beings and with extremely sharp teeth. If they trap you en masse when they are in a physical state, they will easily and wilfully send you to your afterlife. Even if the Darkness doesn't want them too, for they are very difficult to control. Like sharks they go into a frenzy at the smell of fresh blood. The gnombres one major weakness is that they can only travel from shadow to shadow, if they are touched by light, any sort of light, even moonlight, it will be the end for them. It was the gnombres who injured our poor Wodewose, lucky for him he was saved by the strengthening daylight. Alasdair and Cathasach may have helped a little." The two hounds as though in response, each emitted a low growl . Charlotte wondered just how much the two understood even if they couldn't talk.

"Always, always France Charlotte," Triskelion hadn't finished. "If ever you are alone and find yourself in danger, if possible seek out light. It could save your life. Remember what I told you the Darkness hasn't any sight, it needs its agents and its agents can be blinded by the light, especially bright light. Think back to your world France Charlotte. Religious paintings nearly always depict what you call a holy person under some sort of shining light. This originated from the ancient understanding that bright light is a defence from the Darkness, from evil."

Charlotte tried to make sense of what Triskelion had just told her. Their two worlds seemed to have been far more closely entwined centuries ago. What had happened to make them so far apart today? She then considered what he had told about the dangers of the dark, even dark shadows. If shadows held so much risk she thought why not simply meet in the middle of a field where there are none.

"Because there are other factors at play France Charlotte." Triskelion answering her thoughts made Charlotte jump. She hated his ability to do this and he was seemingly incapable of any restraint. "You will always be safest in the natural world France Charlotte. Sadly, your species have created an unnatural world just about everywhere they have cast their net. The way your species live and farm in particular has driven out nature and the natural way of things. Where this has happened the forces left behind are unpredictable, they answer neither to us or the Darkness. They are for a better word, mercenary. However natural, how safe a field may look, you can never tell with the forces that remain there, forces invisible to the naked eye, where their loyalties lie. In other parts of your land we do have their loyalty but sadly not here, not around the environs of Assherugge and Aldeborie. In contrast we have many friends in the wood and Wodewose has the ears and thoughts of every tree." The sound of loud steady breathing reminded everybody of Wodewose's presence. Sadly for you France Charlotte, although our two worlds are mirror images of each other, the way they operate are very different. I simply haven't time to teach you everything. You will have to on occasion trust your own instinct, your own wit.

Charlotte looked down at her feet. She sensed that Triskelion was preparing her to stand on her own two feet, to walk alone in Otherworld. She wondered if there was something else, maybe much else that he wasn't telling her or avoiding telling her to be more precise. Wodewose grunted loudly, shifted to one side and with his left cheek on the fallen beech, returned to his public slumber.

"You must have many more questions, France Charlotte. This may be the last opportunity we have to talk like this. You must take advantage." You can read my mind, Charlotte thought, you know all my questions, all of my doubts, why not answer them without asking me Triskelion. Why waste my time? Charlotte waited for him to say something but Triskelion remained silent. Charlotte looked at the sleeping Wodewose, she knew he trusted Triskelion. She remembered his effigy in the church and what he had told her. That the effigy was of him. Had he in the past visited her world? She asked Triskelion the question.

"No, never." Triskelion was definite. Charlotte waited for him to expand on his answer but Triskelion had finished. He could be so annoying at times and hoped he'd read her mind.

"There's an effigy in our church. It is the splitting image of Wodewose and when I asked him he told me it was of him. How can that be?" Charlotte was not about to give up.

"Long ago, our two worlds were much more closely aligned, we were almost close neighbours. I know you have already observed as much. Transcending between your world and Otherworld was practiced by many. King Arthur the last king of the Celts is a good example. Stories of his adventures are still told today in your world, though many of these adventures occurred in Otherworld. Wodewose was carved by a master of stone who visited our world from yours. Probably using the same gateway that you're using today."

"Why are our worlds so far apart today?"

"I was just coming to that." Whenever I've waited for you to finish, you never have, Charlotte thought, resenting being told to politely shut up.

"The old religions were closely linked to the natural world. They respected and understood nature. The people that represented these religions understood the rhythms, the currents and the natural forces that run beneath the earth. Forces that maintain the vitality of the planet. They respected them. They understood the great cycles and how they worked. They recognised the heartbeat of the planet and how important it was to keep that beat healthy. They were also aware of Otherworld and how each world benefitted one another."

Charlotte sat with her chin resting in her cupped hands, she was enthralled, Triskelion she recognised was for the first time since she'd met him speaking with passion, he was trying his best to hide it but failing dismally. Triskelion looked directly at her. If only I could read your face she thought, what would I see.

"Over your centuries new religions began to appear. For a while old and new were entwined like ivy, they complemented each other but as years passed the new religions grew stronger and the old ways were slowly forgotten, soon to be ridiculed by the new. Although the new religions were well intentioned they focused on your species only. The wellbeing of the Earth and every plant and creature that lived on it were forgotten. Without that respect and understanding the Earth and all it sustained started to suffer. As time went on power and wealth became more important than knowledge and respect. Knowledge only became important if it brought power and wealth. There were a hardcore under the umbrella of the new religions that practiced the principles of old but they were very much in the minority. Most became corrupted including leaders of the new religions. Power and wealth was everything, nothing else mattered."

"Those who understood the powers of old and their secrets grew fearful that in the hands of the new culture of greed, they could become abused and used as powerful weapons against their enemies. When the ancient thirteen commandments, the code of chivalry and I mean the original thirteen commandments not the more commonly known ten. When they were abandoned a decision was taken to hide the secrets of the invisible Earth. Your species call this period the Dark Ages and yes they were deliberately dark as the guardians of the old knowledge didn't want it to be known what they were doing. What they were hiding and where. They thought it best to cover up all evidence of Otherworld. It's existence remained only in what your species today call legends or tales of fantasy, when Otherworld is in fact part of your history. Otherworld's existence is no longer believed which is exactly what the Dark Ages were intended to achieve."

"Some knowledge of the old ways were passed down to those who could be trusted. A few of your people still transcended to Otherworld including the stone artist who created the effigy of Wodewose. He was sent by the Bonhommes, who at Assherugge had their own gateway to Otherworld. Sorry, by Assherugge I mean Ashridge, in Otherworld as I have told you we retain the old names." Triskelion stopped talking and it was apparent to Charlotte that he was reflecting on what he was going to tell her next or whether indeed he wanted to tell her.

"I will tell you something of the Bonhommes France Charlotte, for Leht and I feel their existence in Assherugge may have something to do with the Darkness attempting to rise so close to their old home and why it has targeted the Sacred Library of Evinghehou. The Bonhommes, although presenting themselves as disciples of one of the new religions, remained secretly, guardians of much of the old. Their monastery at Assherugge was founded by Edmund of Cornwall who's stronghold was at Restormel. The site he chose for the Bonhommes was completely impractical, there was no natural water supply for example. There must have been another and a much more important reason for installing the Bonhommes at Assherugge. There have been rumours in Otherworld, and they still persist today that the Bonhomme's brought with them from Montsegur in the south of France the mystical treasure of the Cathars and hid it here somewhere at Assherugge. In your world local names such as Golden Valley and Moneybury hill suggest people in the past suspected or knew something of the hidden treasure. The difference between our two worlds is In your world the treasure is said to be an unimaginable quantity of gold whereas in Otherworld the treasure is rumoured to be mystical, a great secret that would shake both your world and ours if it were ever revealed. We are not sure what the great secret is, what the mystical treasure could be though there are those who claim it could well have something to do with Orme. What we are certain of is until now the treasure has never been discovered. Such a hoard, physical or something more esoteric would simply be impossible to hide." Triskelion stopped, and Charlotte again felt he was reflecting on whether to add to what he had just told her.

"What precisely is Orme?" Charlotte asked, not allowing him time to come to a decision, if indeed that was what he was doing. "Leht told me something of it and when I asked Wodewose he flew into some sort of panic, it sounds almost Godly." Triskelion looked down at the ground before looking up and directly at Charlotte. She felt uncomfortable under his vacant stare. She could feel his mind searching hers, penetrating, delving deeper into her mind, deeper than he'd ever done before.

"That's very perceptive of you France Charlotte," he said slowly. "Godly is a very apt description though incorrect. Orme is not Godly or a God but if you know its secret you can become a God. Such is its power that many leaders have forbidden the word to be spoken or written down including in your world. In much of your world the word is indeed chanted but never written. I am embarrassed to say that here in Otherworld we thought your world was completely ignorant of Orme. After the disappearance of the sundial many investigations were started and we stumbled quite accidently on the fact that knowledge of Orme in your world has been around for many moons though how deep that knowledge is, is uncertain. Leht is doing her best to find out. Anyway I hope you now understand Wodewose's reaction to your question. I wouldn't throw the word around too lightly France Charlotte. It will undoubtedly bring unwanted attention."

Triskelion stopped abruptly. Charlotte sensed he wanted to add to what he had told her but something was preventing him from doing so. She was surprised when he started opening up some more.

"Returning to your original question, the Bonhommes wanted Wodewose recorded in case Otherworld ever came to an end or the wood at Assherugge ceased to exist. Thank goodness he hadn't partaken in any of his wine at the time." Wodewose emitted a semi-conscious grunt. Charlotte was a little surprised at Triskelion's last comment. Was this his attempt at humour? She hadn't thought him capable.

"How old is Wodewose, I'm not being rude, am I?" Charlotte was curious to know. There was something of the child in Wodewose.

"Of course not," Triskelion assured her. "To be honest I don't know. He is a lot older than me and possibly as old as Leht. He was born with the birth of the wood and will die when the wood is no more. The wood is Wodewose and Wodewose the wood."

Charlotte nodded her understanding, though of course she didn't, not entirely. It didn't really matter anyway.

There was more Triskelion wanted to tell her but had come to the decision that to do so would simply be too dangerous and may put the human child's life in greater danger than it already was. He had already told her more than he intended and wondered if with her probing mind whether she would spot the significance of some of what he'd disclosed. In particular what he had told her about the founder of the monastery at Assherugge, Edmund of Cornwall. When the time was right he would reveal to France Charlotte that Edmund of Cornwall had the Bonhommes build their monastery over the hidden entrance to a passage that led to the Sacred Library of Evinghehou.

Wodewose started to stir from his hawthorn wine induced slumber. Poor Wodewose , Charlotte thought. He hasn't volunteered for this just as I haven't. We're both victims of circumstance.

"Have you any more questions, France Charlotte, if not I have something I must show you. After that if Wodewose is capable I want him to explain to you in a little more detail how to survive in the wood, just in case you find yourself alone here."

Charlotte was beginning to feel more and more uneasy the way Triskelion kept pushing the point that there was a real possibility, that one day soon, she may have to fend for herself in the wood. As for questions, she still had so many and she knew, he knew she did.

"Yes." Was all Charlotte could say, stalling for time. Triskelion to his credit, waited patiently, he didn't push. "I have two for now." She said finally. "The first, why has the Darkness created a cloud over Aldbury?" Triskelion's answer was instant.

"I explained to you about the Darkness and light." Charlotte nodded. "The Darkness by installing the cloud is creating a situation where Aldeborie will effectively be in perpetual darkness. The cloud in time will become so dense that you will not be able to distinguish night from day. By preventing rainfall and creating a state of eternal darkness every living plant will wither and die, creating the perfect environment for the Darkness to establish its first ever physical base on Earth or your world whichever you want to call it. The Darkness has never had the ability to do this in the past and if it had we would have had the forces to stop it. Sadly, that is no longer the case." Triskelion's answer only raised further questions but they could wait, Charlotte moved to her second question.

"You told me that the Snooks foretold that it was a human child, like me."

"It is you, France Charlotte," Triskelion interrupted. Charlotte ignored him.

"A human child like me that would help do battle with the Darkness and that child would need to have the ability to transcend between both worlds. Why would that be necessary to win the fight with the Darkness?" This time Triskelion waited a few seconds before he answered.

"I believe," he started slowly. "That the Snooks, words were, would have the ability, not need the ability but I understand your question and yes I assume by that you or a human child like you would need the ability. Why though I cannot tell you, I simply do not know. I'm sorry again France Charlotte. I'm afraid there are many things I do not understand by your presence here in Otherworld. I wish I did as I have told you before, for it would be so much easier for all of us."

As Triskelion finished, Wodewose let out a loud yawn and stretched his arms. Alasdair and Cathasach in response both let out a low growl but didn't move from their position in the grass. The squirrel Charlotte couldn't decide was either finishing breakfast or starting lunch.

"Are you with us Wodewose?" Triskelion asked. In response Wodewose grunted and after rubbing his eyes looked around the sunlit glade.

"Have I missed anything?" he asked, looking a little bewildered. Charlotte smiled, glad that he had at last woken. He was so much easier to deal with than Triskelion.

"Nothing of importance Wodewose but we need you now. France Charlotte, I need you to come closer." Triskelion as he said this moved to one side so she could take up a place between him and Wodewose. When Charlotte was settled Triskelion withdrew from his robe what looked like a dog eared piece of paper. After unfolding it carefully he knelt and spread it open on the ground. Charlotte knelt beside him with Wodewose crouching to one side. On closer inspection, Charlotte realised that what Triskelion had unfolded was a map and from its appearance one of great age. She recognised that it was of the local area, though many of the names detailed were not ones she knew or recognised.

"This,"said Triskelion sliding his hand across the surface. "Is a map Leht wants you to have, it once belonged to my father and is very precious to me. Although it is of a great age it is self-updating and will help you find your way, France Charlotte." Charlotte hadn't a clue what he meant by self-updating and was frankly staggered to discover there were maps when Triskelion's father was alive. I must remember I'm in Otherworld, she told herself. "Give me your hand, France Charlotte." Charlotte did as she was told. Holding her hand gently Triskelion placed her palm flat on the ancient map and keeping it there proceeded to utter something in a language she had never heard before. After he had finished, Triskelion slowly raised her hand and waved his over the surface of the map. As he did so, Charlotte saw that features on the map started to change before her eyes. When all movement had finished, Triskelion spoke again. "This map will only be of use to you France Charlotte and to those you wish to have access. The maker of the map has read your palm. If the map passes into the hand of another, it will no longer function and become unreadable. Do you understand?"

"I think so." In truth Charlotte, as was so often the case recently wasn't sure she understood at all.

"You must not let anybody else touch it, or it will no longer be of any use," Wodewose helped out.

"Why thank you Wodewose," Charlotte smiled her thanks.

"This map is for your use alone. Wodewose can be of assistance but under no circumstances must he or anyone else touch it. Understood?" Charlotte nodded studying the map closely. All the place names she noticed were names from long ago, not of her time and there were places or points highlighted that would never be found or deemed to be important on a modern map. When she intensified her gaze on certain features, the more up to date ones became transparent, revealing a completely different layout underneath.

"I see you are already learning to read the map." Triskelion sounded pleased. "What you have in your hands France Charlotte is a map of this area as it was at the end of the Dark Ages. When the secret knowledge and ways of old had been safely hidden in the bowels of the Earth or here in Otherworld. You will see as you withdraw your gaze the features present in your world today come into being. Am I making myself clear?" Charlotte nodded her confirmation. She understood perfectly and in truth, she was surprised at how easy she found the map to read. "Good," Triskelion again sounded pleased. "You may need both the original year and the layout of today to help you find your way around and in particular find the places that can be of use to you or keep you safe. Now we are here, Triskelion placed his finger above a point roughly in the centre of the map. There was a name for where they were all gathered, it was written Gemot. "Here is Amphillicia's Well", the Well or muddy pool, (that was being kind), as Charlotte recognised it, was clearly marked. Triskelion proceeded to point out other landmarks Charlotte could identify with. Assherugge, her village Aldeborie, she recognised the village of Ivinghoe though on the map it was spelt Evinghehou. Ivinghoe Beacon was surprisingly not marked as Evinghehou but Leabharlann de Solas and along the side of Pitstone Hill were the words Hors Hwit. Several trees were highlighted as places of importance, as were the ancient burial mounds still visible today. Each burial mound carried the same symbol and this symbol was also present at Aldbury or Aldeborie church, the large house Assherugge, Amphillicia's Well and the Church at Great Gaddesden though the name Great Gaddesden did not appear on the map. Only the church was highlighted and the word Gatesdene. Triskelion pointed to each of the places highlighted by the same symbol. "These," he said waving his cloaked hand over the map are all gateways between our two worlds though none except the one you are using today have been used for close to a thousand of your years. How usable they are today," Triskelion paused. "Well there's only one way to find out." Charlotte noticed he was deliberately avoiding looking at her as he said this. "Ash trees are not marked as gateways as their accessibility is fluid and often only suitable for a messenger and many of the ash trees are too young to be of any use to them." By messenger Charlotte assumed Triskelion meant the squirrel or squirrels. Another symbol highlighted was what Triskelion called, "safe places." There were several of these and quite a number in the wood. Those in the wood were highlighted by a darker shade and Triskelion explained these were holly groves or large holly trees. "They can protect or hide you from the Darkness and its agents for a limited time only," he was not forthcoming on what he meant by a limited time. All of the old burial mounds were marked as safe places as was every church. All Triskelion warned her, can only keep you safe for a limited amount of time and it was important not to get trapped at one. Triskelion pointed to a third symbol of which Charlotte could only see three on the map. "These France Charlotte, are your contact points for Leht." Triskelion pointed one by one to each of the three places marked by the unique symbol. "They for a very good reason are not easy to find and you may need the help of Wodewose if I am not with you. At each location there is a stone brought from Ynys Mon, they are carefully hidden. Each has a shallow impression. Your budget, France Charlotte." Triskelion touched the small leather bag slung over her shoulder. "Your budget," he repeated. "If it has liquid, when you collect it, this means Leht has had the strength to send a part of her to you. The liquid is her light blood and very precious, do not spill any for it cannot be replaced. If ever you are of thirst or need strength you can drink a little of her blood, the effect will be invigorating and give you strength as well as courage. Though please never take more than a couple of sips." Don't worry thought Charlotte, I have no intention of drinking Leht's blood. The thought disgusted her. If Triskelion read her thoughts he didn't let her know, instead he continued with his instruction.

"To communicate you must pour the liquid gently into the impression in the stone from Ynys Mon. The glow of Leht will appear before you and she will speak with you."

Charlotte remembered a night, which now seemed so long ago when with Wodewose on Aldbury Nowers, (Aldbury Nowers interestingly was simply marked Nowers on the map, it was the only name as far as she could see that remained the same in both their worlds), had done exactly what Triskelion was describing and indeed Leht had spoken to her.

"I am obliged to present two words of warning when calling Leht. You must always make sure nobody is watching when you call Leht, understand?"

"Yes." Charlotte nodded.

"And Leht needs the dark so her light is strong. If you call her when daylight pleasures the wood her light will be weakened and so too her energy. I know it means added danger but if possible always try and call Leht in the dark. I am sorry." Triskelion made the apology sound as though it were his fault. "Lastly France Charlotte, the map cannot be carried into your world or it will be destroyed. You must leave it in the oak with the budget and your charm. There, that is all I have to say for now, I am glad we've had this discussion. I hope you are too."

"Me too Triskelion, though my head hurts."

"Mine too." Wodewose was rubbing his gently. Charlotte couldn't help but smile.

"And where do we go from here, Triskelion, I haven't a clue?" Charlotte shrugged her shoulders to emphasise her point. "I feel completely useless."

"If I am honest France Charlotte, I am not sure what our next move should be either or any move if the truth be told." Charlotte wished he hadn't told her that, she'd have felt so much better if he'd said nothing at all. As for Triskelion he still could not believe he was having this conversation with an eleven year old human child. How he missed the knights of old whose courage and sense of honour knew no limits. Whose minds and ways he understood. "The next time you transcend to Otherworld," he said almost kindly. "I hope we will meet with Leht, she will I'm sure give us direction. Though whatever action we take, we must take it fast." He fell silent. Wodewose decided it was a good moment to have a thorough scratch.

"I suppose," Charlotte thought aloud. "The more pressing problem and the more important task is protecting the Beacon and the library within." Triskelion gave a sort of half nod.

"Yes you are right of course but prioritising the Beacon and the Sacred Library may have severe consequences for your village and your world, ours too. You do understand that?" Charlotte thought of her world, her parents, her friends, and her family in France. A tear trickled down her left cheek. How she hoped that one day she'd wake up to find all of this was just a dream.

"I understand that perfectly," she replied with all the strength she could muster. It was a show of quite impressive defiance. A show that an adult would have been proud of let alone an eleven year girl. "She has the heart of a knight," Triskelion looked on with admiration, "I must stop doubting her."

"Anyway enough of that for now, I understand Wodewose has told you a bit about surviving in the wood?" Triskelion asked standing. Charlotte did the same whilst carefully folding the map and placing it in the budget.

"Mostly he told me how to stay safe." Charlotte confirmed trying to remember exactly what he had taught her.

"Well now, just in case you have to spend any time in our world on your own, Wodewose is going to teach you the culinary delights of the wood."

"You mean how to cook?" Charlotte asked. Wodewose apparently found this funny for he suddenly burst into a fit of laughter.

"Not quite," Triskelion corrected her. "More about what you can eat in the wood without having to cook, where to find a drink too if the budget is dry."

With that the little party spent the next three hours or so, wandering through the Commons of Asherugge with Wodewose showing Charlotte which leaves and sometimes roots she could eat and where best to find them. More importantly perhaps he also taught her which plants to avoid and she was surprised just how many poisonous plants there were growing freely. He also told her the best leaves to suck dew from and which roots may help her thirst if she was ever in desperate need of water. Charlotte for her part found the whole experience interesting but not all that pleasurable when it came to taste. She hoped that she would never be hungry enough to have to rely on the leaves and roots of the wood. If it was only a little later in the year, she'd be able to enjoy the "fruits of the forest", that would be far more pleasurable.

Although she had been given the map and they were marked, Wodewose confirmed where the most extensive spreads of holly were and demonstrated with enthusiasm how one should lie flat underneath, pulling the lower branches close to the body to achieve maximum protection. Triskelion emphasised again how the holly may provide her with vital shelter if ever she found herself in danger. Charlotte simply couldn't see how simply hiding under a holly bush may save her life and had to keep reminding herself, this is Otherworld. It's not the same world as hers, it may look the same but the rules here are very different. Charlotte also noticed with amusement that Wodewose kept his hidden cellar of homemade wine under a particularly large and obviously very old holly tree. He thought she hadn't seen him hide his leather bottle and goblet but his over acted nonchalance had given his secret away. It was mid-afternoon when Charlotte recognised they were approaching the muddy pool which in Otherworld everyone knew as Amphillicia's Well. She shivered involuntarily, remembering how Triskelion had raised the artist from its waters. Wodewose on arriving at the disgusting looking pool immediately got down on his knees and started drinking from the surface water, joined seconds later by Alasdair and Cathasach. As all three drank noisily, Charlotte looked on in disgust.

"You must try the waters, France Charlotte." Triskelion urged, Ignoring the expression on her face.

"You have got to be joking, I'm not drinking that."

"Please," Triskelion was as persistent as Charlotte was adamant. "Remember in Otherworld all is not what it seems. Please just try."

Giving in, Charlotte slowly got to her knees whilst trying to blot the image of the dripping artist from her mind. It wasn't easy, she kept thinking of horror films she'd watched at her friends, where all too often a hand would shoot out of nowhere grabbing the victim's throat. She couldn't help imagining the artist doing the same thing to her, his hand rising from the muddy waters and pulling her under.

"It is quite safe. Nothing will happen to you." Triskelion, it seemed, had read her thoughts, once again. Maybe, maybe not Charlotte thought but if I drink that I will be seriously ill. She stared at the muddy, even worse stagnant and foul smelling water, she'd prefer to drink out of a toilet bowl. As all this was going through her mind just as when Triskelion had raised the artist the water began to foam and the unevenly shaped pool became a perfect circle, somehow without ever changing. After a few seconds, the waters calmed and from deep below the surface there shone a light. Charlotte found herself no longer feeling disgusted, instead she knelt entranced, straining to see where the light was coming from. The water was no longer stained by mud but as clear as she'd ever seen. The light remained, dancing playfully with every minute movement on the surface. As she stared mesmerised, unable to move, a shape or something started to form above the light. Try as she might Charlotte could not pull her gaze away, whatever it was forming at the bottom of the well had her hooked. She was helpless. She should have felt terrified but she didn't. She felt no fear, quite the opposite she felt strangely calm. After what could have been a minute or an hour for time no longer seemed to matter the deep water in the well stopped moving. So still was it, it was hard to believe there was water there at all. What she was looking at appeared more like glass. Charlotte remained transfixed, at the bottom of the well, staring back at her, the smiling face of a woman. A truly beautiful face with an expression that radiated tranquillity. Her eyes were clear, shining like crystal resembling further pools of water. These pools had movement, just as a whirlpool, in hypnotic ever decreasing circles . Her hair was fire red with a touch of bronze and she wore a translucent white veil that like her hair waved in a rhythmic slow motion without disturbing the water.

"Drink." Charlotte wasn't sure whether it was the lady in the water or Triskelion who spoke to her. Whoever it was Charlotte couldn't resist and she drank greedily from cupped hands. The water was like no other she had ever tasted. It was cool and with a freshness that she never imagined possible. As the last drop cooled her throat she found she was desperate for more and eagerly dipped her cupped hands back into the water. Immediately she withdrew them with a cry of disgust. The beautiful face, the light and the crystal waters were gone. Her hands were covered in a muddy foul smelling slime and she was kneeling before the putrid pool she'd known from her walks with her father.

"You can only have one drink from the Well France Charlotte. It was important you made your acquaintance with Amphillicia, she will remember you." Charlotte didn't reply. Although she heard Triskelion she was too busy trying to wipe her hands clean, using leaves remaining from autumn.

"Amphillicia will offer you protection if you need it and the water will give you strength. Let the water run through your veins, France Charlotte, you will feel its strength. Agents of the Darkness fear the Well, Amphillicia's light can send them to their afterlife." Charlotte, reasonably satisfied she'd cleansed her hands of the foul smelling mud got to her feet. As she stood she started to experience a force, a force that pulsated, pumping its way around her body. The sensation faded as quickly as it had started and when it had left her altogether it was replaced by the satisfaction of feeling as though she had just woken from the best night's sleep.

"The waters of Amphillicia are very powerful, to have more than one drink would be dangerous. If Amphillicia believes her waters will do you harm, she will cease revealing them to you." Charlotte staring at the stinking pool of mud couldn't believe she had just drunk from it. Had what happened, really happened? It was a stupid question, she knew it had, the memory was too vivid and she felt amazing.

"If you don't like it, I can give you some of my wine." Wodewose offered Charlotte, wiping traces of mud from around his mouth. It was quite apparent that Amphillicia, on this occasion, had not revealed her magical waters to Wodewose.

"No thank you Wodewose, I'm too young, I am not allowed to drink wine," she refused graciously. Wodewose didn't appear particularly bothered by her reply.

"How do you feel?" Triskelion asked Charlotte.

"Great, really great. As though I've slept for a week." It was true, she did but she still couldn't believe she'd drunk from a pool of mud and one with a body in it somewhere. It suddenly occurred to her that there had been no trace of the artist, where was he, the Well wasn't so big that he could be easily hidden?

Triskelion enquired whether Wodewose had finished demonstrating the culinary delights of the wood. After confirming he had, Triskelion announced it was time to deliver France Charlotte back to her world. She needed the rest he advised everybody. First they walked Wodewose to his home in the ancient oak and it was obvious for all to see he was very pleased to see his tree. After bidding Wodewose farewell the little group headed north through Old Copse. As on all recent excursions in Otherworld, Triskelion avoided the paths trodden by homo sapiens. Charlotte was surprised how relaxed everyone appeared, the squirrel, Alasdair and Cathasach, even Triskelion behaved as though they'd simply visited the wood for a spot of exercise. None seemed bothered by the threat of attack, something she was continuously being warned to look out for. It was daylight yes, but there were still plenty of shadows, especially as the sun had started its slow decent. As they walked she questioned Triskelion on this.

"The Darkness and its agents are not operative in Asherugge today," he answered simply. Charlotte pushed him for more clarity. "The Darkness has many fronts to battle, its agents are elsewhere today. If there were any danger, Alasdair and Cathasach would smell it before it was within miles, I'm sure your next visit will be a little more exciting." Was his end remark Triskelion's idea of a joke, or was it a warning? Almost certainly the latter.

After descending the steep wooded scarp they all passed through the wooden fence, Charlotte included without mishap, and crossed part of the field to the now familiar oak. Charlotte paused, taking time to take in the view. Below, sheltered by the wooded scarp lay her village. From where she stood Aldeborie, looked nothing short of perfection, heaven on earth. She still found it hard to come to terms that what was before her was simply an image, not the real thing. It looked so real and from where she stood, so inviting. The perfect cover apparently, for the Darkness.

A tap on Charlotte's shoulder brought her back with a jump. It was Triskelion, winning her attention he instructed Charlotte to remove her necklace and put it in the budget along with the map after which she tucked everything, as bidden into the hidden hollow beneath the tree.

"Isn't it dangerous leaving everything in one place?" Charlotte thought it an awful risk to leave all that was so precious hidden in one place, and as far as she could see completely unprotected.

"No, this way we can keep a watch on everything. Anyway I do not think the agents of the Darkness will think of looking here." Triskelion hoped he sounded convincing as he too, despite his spell, was concerned about leaving everything in one place. The oak grew in a field that had been left to naturalise for years and he hoped the spirits who dwelled here had their allegiances' on the right side of the spiritual fence. It was always so difficult to judge with a field but he had no choice. There was simply no other way, no other hiding place he'd found suitable.

At the oak Triskelion disbanded Alasdair and Cathasach who disappeared at speed across fields following the lower line of the wooded escarpment. After they'd disappeared from view Triskelion gestured towards Aldeborie.

"Shall we deliver you home France Charlotte." As was often the case with Triskelion it was a statement not a question, though he always phrased it as though it may be. The two started to make their way across the field, the squirrel scurrying at their feet, heading for the heavily hedged lane visible in the valley below.

"When do you think I will be coming back to Otherworld?" Charlotte asked as they walked.

"Soon, very soon. Maybe even tomorrow. And when you arrive unless the squirrel leads you otherwise, you must find a light to make you invisible." Charlotte remembered the rather harrowing experience she'd had that morning, the difficulty in passing into a house and even worse getting out. She didn't fancy going through that experience again and told Triskelion so.

"You have no choice, France Charlotte or you risk being captured by the Darkness and the gateway being discovered."

"But I found it so difficult," moaned Charlotte.

"What did you find difficult?" Triskelion asked, without really sounding interested.

Charlotte told him how she kept failing to pass through the door, how she kept coming up against solid wood and how she almost panicked when she found she couldn't get out. How also she'd been really thirsty and couldn't get the taps to work and how she couldn't physically open the door even from the inside. Something that hadn't helped her feeling of panic. Triskelion stopped walking and turned Charlotte to face him.

"It really is very easy," he assured her. "It is literally a case of your mind or rather your subconsciousness telling your brain what is not there rather than letting your eyes tell your brain what they can see and their assumption it's real." From Charlotte's expression Triskelion could see she still wasn't convinced. "The important thing is to relax, close your eyes, pretend it's all a dream if you find it helps. Just keep telling yourself it's not there, that it's nothing more than a hologram. Put a single part of your body through first such as an arm or a leg and then let the rest of your body follow naturally."

"What if I have to hide in a house for any length of time, what if I find it's too dangerous for some reason to come out during the day, or worse still what if I can't get out. What if my mind won't let me. Am I still safe to stay the following evening, will the same light still be on to hide me from the Darkness?" Charlotte let all the questions that she had been storing up inside her to come tumbling out at once.

"Everything changes at thirteen, or in your time midnight. To put it simply the image you see when you arrive in Otherworld, is your world as it is at midnight. As though somebody took a photo. That image will remain for twenty four hours, after which it will be replaced by the new image. I hope that makes sense." Clear as mud, Charlotte thought. Triskelion persisted. "What you need to remember and this is of the utmost importance France Charlotte. You cannot remain inside an image for more than twenty four hours."

"What if I have no choice?" Charlotte responded. "What if there's danger outside?"

Triskelion held her shoulders, his blank almost featureless face holding Charlotte's gaze. "I am telling you, you do not have a choice France Charlotte. If there is danger outside you must face it, for if you remain inside the image longer than twenty four hours you will disappear with it."

"Where to?"

"I have no idea," Triskelion admitted. "You'll just disappear into nothing, you will no longer exist at least in the physical sense. You will have to judge your own situation and the important thing is to stay calm, stay relaxed." Charlotte looked doubtful. "I promised to always be honest with you, remember."

"I know, sorry, Triskelion." She hardly ever used his name and somehow using it now she felt closer to him. "If it's just an image, why isn't it night time for twenty four hours, how come the day comes and goes?" She was still struggling to understand how everything worked.

"I need hours to explain everything to you, and sadly time is one luxury we do not have. The map I gave you, France Charlotte. I explained the original was drawn up at the end of what your land calls the Dark Ages." Charlotte nodded hoping she'd understand his explanation. "Everything built or created after that time, in Otherworld at least, we consider superficial, not built respecting the rhythms of the Earth but simply for the convenience of your species without consideration for the natural world around it. Thus after midnight, your time, anything built by your species simply becomes an image in Otherworld. Not real.

Charlotte thought about what Triskelion had just told her. She didn't entirely agree with his summarisation of her world but realised she was in no position to start arguing the finer points. Instead she thought back to the map that Triskelion had given to her. She remembered that churches had been marked as a place of safety and that when she'd studied the map with more intensity their image had remained on the original map, they hadn't faded. Triskelion, concerned about time, intercepted her thinking.

"Sorry I have perhaps failed to explain some of the basics. Nearly all of your churches existed years before the Dark Ages and were built on land that was already considered sacred. Land that benefited from the invisible forces that exist below the earth. As I have already explained, the builders of these new places of worship for the Christian religion in the main understood and respected the old ways. Churches were constructed in line with the natural currents of the Earth and their natural force strengthened by connecting with other churches or sacred sites in the area and sometimes beyond, far beyond. Therefore a church in Otherworld, unless it was built without respecting the old ways, sympathetic to and respecting the rhythms of the earth, is not an image. In Otherworld it is as real as you and me. To gain entrance to a church therefore you will almost always have to enter by the normal means, you will not be able to pass through its walls as you would an image. Returning to your original question, everything outside or surrounding the image is real. Therefore the sun will rise and fall, clouds will pass overhead. What you will find, all or most living creatures in Otherworld tend to avoid going anywhere near the images. They are afraid of them and what they represent. The human world in Otherworld is little more than a wasteland, a desert, uninhabitable. And the desert is getting bigger by the day. Left unchecked Otherworld will soon become barren." Triskelion paused to allow Charlotte time to digest what he had just told her. He realised that she could easily be offended by how he'd painted her species, her world and hoped it wouldn't turn her against him or Leht. The last thing he wanted was for her to take any criticism of her ancestors personally. Whatever the risks he felt she had to know the truth and there was a lot worse to come. He would have to break the rest to her as gently as possible but there was so little time. "It's a lot to take in, I know." He ventured a little nervously. To Triskelion's relief Charlotte ignored how her world and her ancestors had been painted, concentrating instead on the challenges of dealing with an image. Thus her questions continued on the practical.

"There's something else I don't understand. When I am in a house I can pick something up and move it if I want to, just as I could if it were real but I couldn't turn on a tap or change channels on a television. If you know what a television is, Triskelion?" She hadn't a clue how much Triskelion knew about the modern world. If he knew, he didn't say, he simply Ignored Charlotte's last remark.

"Anything inside an image that has to react with the world outside, will not work," he clarified. "Moving something that is already an image, inside an image, that you can do. I'm not sure I've explained that at all well."

"You have," Charlotte assured him. "I understand perfectly," and for once she did understand.

"If you learn to have strength of will over your mind France Charlotte, you can actually have fun with images." He makes it sound like a game, Charlotte thought.

"That's exactly how you should think of it, as a game." Triskelion declared. "Once you've learned to will your mind you can switch the image off and on to your needs. For example if you need to go upstairs, will your mind to make the stairs solid. If you wish to sit in a chair, will your mind to make it solid.

"Could I do what you've just told me in my world?" she asked.

"No," was Triskelion's emphatic answer. "In your world everything is as it appears, if it's solid, it is solid. The only way you could pass through a solid, is if you have the knowledge of Orme."

There was that word again, Orme. She kept being told how powerful Orme was and how dangerous the knowledge of Orme could be but no one cared or dared to tell her exactly what Orme was. Charlotte recalled an article her father had once told her about. One that he had read in a Sunday magazine. The article informed how a modern military power had invested a small fortune in trying to train soldiers with a high IQ to will their way through solids, to literally pass through a solid wall. The experiment had been a dismal failure and disbanded. Now she, Charlotte, an eleven year old girl, knew the secret. What they had needed to succeed, was the knowledge of Orme. Triskelion and Leht had told her that they had recently discovered that there was some knowledge of Orme in her world. Behind how many featureless doors of government Charlotte wondered were agents searching for what seemed to her to be the master, the ultimate secret.

"Come we must go." Triskelion urged, interrupting her thoughts. "Time is running short and I wish to see your Ashtynn before dusk starts to settle."

With haste the two finished crossing the field and after passing through the gate, turned left to follow the road into Aldeborie. The sun was just beginning to set and in that lazy fashion that only summer allows. If it hadn't been for the squirrel scurrying right and left before them and Triskelion's ghost-like appearance they could have simply been two friends wandering home after a relaxing stroll in the countryside. Nothing regrettably was further from the truth. The squirrel, Charlotte could see was jittery and with her newly discovered sensitivity she could feel that Triskelion was tense, very tense. As for her she expected any minute for someone to lean out of a window, to open a door, to have to stand to one side to let a car pass but of course none of the three happened. They passed The Greyhound, normally at this time of day and in such fair weather there would be a crowd milling outside but that evening all was silent. There were lights on inside and Charlotte could see the bar, but no one was serving and no one was waiting to be served, the room was empty. As they skirted the pond, she strained her eyes to see if Ashtynn was still on display in the shop window. Please let her not be there, Charlotte prayed silently, over and over. After a few more paces she saw her prayers weren't to be answered, or maybe they hadn't been heard. In view, the unmistakable outline of the woman who always had such a warm welcome for her. Her position hadn't changed, she remained hanging or rather floating motionless in the shop window, still with the look of terror disfiguring her face. Triskelion stopped when they reached the village green raising his right hand to indicate he wanted Charlotte to do the same. She knew he'd said something to the squirrel for it ran off at speed towards the church, leaving the two of them to face Ashtynn.

"You must not be afraid, France Charlotte," Triskelion held her hand offering reassurance. "Your friend is held in a state of suspension and can do you no harm." Ashtynn would never harm her, Charlotte knew that. What scared her was how Ashtynn's lifeless form hung suspended in thin air, eyes open wide, staring. It was her expression, in particular her eyes that unsettled her more than anything else. What had she, Ashtynn seen to cause such a grotesquely contorted expression. Triskelion's voice freed her from her disquiet.

"I want you to walk with me until I stop," Triskelion instructed her. "You must not show any fear or you will attract the attention of the Darkness. It will be able to sense it."

"Ok." Charlotte gave one nod of the head. Her mouth felt as if it was full of sand, her tongue caressed her lips searching for the smallest drop of moisture. She found none. Triskelion took a step forward and then another and Charlotte thinking of her friends and family timed her stride with his. When they were about two metres from the window Triskelion stopped, staring directly at Ashtynn's far away eyes. He held his gaze for about a minute then turned his attention to Charlotte.

"Now, France Charlotte, I want you to walk up and down in front of the shop. I want you to walk slowly and look straight ahead at all times. No matter what happens you must never look to your left or right and neither are you to look back. Just turn around and walk back when I tell you to, at all times you must look straight ahead. Can you do that, France Charlotte?" Again Charlotte gave a single nod of her head. She so wanted to scream, to run, Triskelion just didn't know how much but then again he probably did.

"Good," he approved. "Ok turn left." Charlotte did as she was told. "Start walking and continue till I say turn. Remember to keep your eyes straight ahead at all times." Charlotte refusing to let herself tremble, even though every nerve in her body was telling her it wanted to, started to take short steady paces. As she walked she counted each step, it was something to focus on and helped to blot out everything else. After ten steps she heard Triskelion say, turn. She did as she was told. Triskelion she saw, stood where she had left him, and concentrating on nothing else but Ashtynn's face. What was he doing? What was he looking for? Did she really want to know? "Ok walk, France Charlotte, walk right past me until I say turn again, and remember keep looking ahead." Charlotte started walking back, one, two, three, she counted. Four, five, six. She was doing fine until she drew level with Triskelion. For some reason when she reached him, she paused. She had no idea why, it wasn't a deliberate action.

"Keep walking," Triskelion told her quickly, "keep walking." Charlotte did as she was told but couldn't help looking left towards Ashtynn. She didn't move her head, just her eyes but that was enough. She caught Ashtynn's gaze and Ashtynn caught hers, as Charlotte walked, eleven, twelve, thirteen Ashtynn continued to hold Charlotte's eyes with hers. Charlotte couldn't help letting out a gasp. Ashtynn's eyes were moving, they were following her, not in a human fashion more like the eyes of a ventriloquist's dummy. Being worked by a third party.

"Keep walking and look straight ahead, France Charlotte." Triskelion's voice was as soft as ever but it felt as though he were shouting at her. Charlotte focused her mind on counting her paces, forcing her eyes front. On twenty Triskelion told her to turn again. She did so, Ashtynn was now in full view, ahead to her right but she refused to look at her. She kept her gaze focused firmly on Triskelion and started to walk towards him. "Stop," he said as she drew level. Charlotte did as she was told. "Good, now walk with me to the pond." Again she did as Triskelion instructed, relieved to be putting distance between herself, the shop and Ashtynn. At the pond Triskelion stopped and turned his head towards her. Charlotte waited for an explanation but none was forthcoming. Instead Triskelion simply bade her farewell, instructing her to meet the squirrel in front of the church porch and journey back to her world without delay. We will, he assured her meet again soon, very soon. With that he was gone, returning along the road by which they'd entered the village, heading towards Ivinghoe or rather Evinghehou. For a brief second Charlotte felt very alone, terrifyingly alone. Her fear spurred her into action and moments later she was running up the path from the pond to the church door. The squirrel, she found waiting for her as was the robin and as she approached the squirrel dived into the ground. Charlotte quickly followed and within under a minute she found herself standing in her world. Two cars sped pass as she followed the squirrel down the gravel path, it felt good to be home. The shop window was full of goodies but free of Ashtynn, there were no eyes following her every move. On arriving at the back door, they were welcomed by the other robin.

"Night both of you," Charlotte whispered as she closed the top half of the stable door. Mounting the stairs her exertions in Otherworld finally caught up with her. It felt like she'd been away for days, not hours. Never, she thought as she opened her bedroom door, had her simple room with the long sash window felt so welcoming. As her head hit the pillow Charlotte was already asleep. Barely had she time to welcome Gromit into her fold before her eyes closed. Her body welcomed her state of subconscious, it needed to recharge but her mind was rewarded no such luxury, it remained in overdrive. Otherworld had unveiled some of its secrets but in doing so had opened doors to so many more questions. When would she know, would she ever know all the answers? The robin remained on the sill, even after the little girl's eyes were closed. It didn't feel like sleeping, there was too much happening at the moment. The messages it was receiving from Otherworld didn't bode well for the future. How it longed to leave the gloom of Aldbury, to feel the sun on its famous red breast. Duty however dictated it stay with the human child. The little girl he had been told repeatedly was perhaps their only hope. If he failed in his duty towards her he may never welcome the sun to his breast again. With that in mind he flew to his nest at the base of the pagoda, to try and get some much needed sleep though that night he doubted if sleep would come easily.

Minutes after Charlotte fell asleep the door to her parents room quietly opened. Her mother stepped onto the small area at the top of the stairs praying silently that the old floorboards wouldn't protest. She didn't want her daughter to know she was there. Peering through a crack in her door she saw a small bird fly from her daughter's sill. She thought it may have been a robin but couldn't be sure. She listened intently and was comforted on hearing her daughter's steady breathing which confirmed she was asleep. What had Charlotte been doing downstairs at such an hour. Should she quiz her in the morning? With this conundrum she returned to bed and a restless sleep.

In Otherworld the root vine was buzzing. Woodwose stirred in his bed, awoken by all the chatter and stiffened when message after message broke through the fuzziness of sleep. Gnombres were everywhere, not one shadow was free of them and among the shadows were new shadows that had no business being there. The wood was not safe that night. Nocturnal creatures decided to stay at home, preferring to go hungry than face the apparitions outside. Triskelion, decided that seeking shelter with Leht was a step too far, bedded down in a field. He was vulnerable, he knew, but it was better than sheltering in the wood, where shadows may rise up and attack him at any moment. Never would dawn be welcomed by so many.

Chapter Fifteen

Leht, Magpies And Gnombres

Charlotte woke to find her mother in her room. In one hand she held a mug of hot chocolate and in the other a plate of delicious smelling croissants.

"You slept through your alarm," her mother lied, on seeing her eyes open. In truth she had turned it off. "You looked so peaceful I decided to bring you breakfast in bed. Your father's gone to set up the market, I'll drive you to school, but depeche." Once again Charlotte found herself thinking what great parents she had. The hot chocolate worked wonders, so did the croissants and within fifteen minutes, she was washed, dressed and ready for school.

During registration, the headteacher entered the classroom, in her right hand she held Charlotte's exercise book. The class tensed at her presence, not from fear but respect.

"Carry on," she smiled as everybody looked in her direction and after whispering something in her form teacher's ear signalled for Charlotte to join her out front. "Let's talk in the corridor," she signalled as Charlotte joined her. "it'll be quieter." A sea of curios faces followed them as they left the classroom. In the corridor the headmistress handed Charlotte her exercise book.

"That French Charlotte, is quite an amazing piece of work."

"Thank you Miss." Charlotte desperately wanted to say something more imaginative but her mind rather frustratingly tended to freeze when faced with authority.

"I read it last night and couldn't put it down. It was quite addictive, where did you get all your ideas from?"

"Just my imagination, Miss" Charlotte replied conscious that this was only partly true.

"Well you've got a real talent, French Charlotte, you are very fortunate. I only wish I had a fraction of your imagination."

"Thank you Miss."

"By the way, why Ormeland? Where did that come from?" The Head asked, referring to the title. Charlotte shrugged her shoulders wishing she'd chosen another name.

"I just made it up," she lied, fingers crossed behind her back. The Head looked a little disappointed.

"Oh," she replied, "I hoped it had some hidden meaning that you had secreted away."

"Sorry, no Miss." Charlotte had her fingers crossed so hard, they hurt.

"Oh well, great piece of work anyway, well done, French Charlotte." The Head patted her on the head and made her leave. If ever anything happens to me, Charlotte thought watching the Head walk away, this lady will be the first to put two and two together and start investigating. She was just about to return to her classroom when the Head stopped and turned around.

"By the way," she called back. "You talk about magpies in your essay. It's most odd, I have one every day sitting in the tree outside my office. Most odd," she said again and with that continued on her way. Charlotte watched until she disappeared around a corner. She didn't know why but the news of a magpie at the school, threatening the Headteacher really shook her. Not that the Head would see the magpie as a threat, thankfully she simply saw it as something of an oddity. She would tell Triskelion, see what he made of it. With that Charlotte opened the door and returned to her classroom where, to her surprise she was greeted by a round of applause.

At the end of the school day Charlotte was relieved to step onto the school bus and even more relieved to step off it. After saying goodbye to her friends she'd taken just a few steps when she saw the vicar cross the road from the church with his usual briskness and enter the shop. Swallowing her fear, Charlotte decided to follow him. She always liked talking to the vicar and her dad had snaffled her last sherbet dip. As she approached the shop, she couldn't help but think of Ashtynn, her eyes horrifically wide, suspended in the window. It's not the same world she kept telling herself. Determined to conquer her fear she forced herself to stare in at the guilty window. Instead of Ashtynn, the window boasted a new promotion. A Union Jack, hung as a backdrop, surrounded by various bottles of wine, artfully situated between bunches of plastic grapes and strategically placed glasses. Two or three corkscrews created the finishing touch. A large sign read, The Best of British Wines. It all looked very impressive Charlotte thought and very patriotic.

"I hope you're not tempted to buy a bottle, French Charlotte," a booming voice warned, full of false mockery. It was the vicar of course. He wore his usual wide grin and his left hand gripped a carrier bag containing three bottles of wine.

"The window needs three or four sherbet dips," Charlotte replied smiling. She found it easy to smile in the vicar's presence even with so much gloom.

"Couldn't agree more French Charlotte, where would we all be without sherbet dips. Are you going in to buy some?" Charlotte nodded.

"My Dad ate my last one."

"The man's got excellent taste," boomed the vicar. "That's why you've got your mum." He patted her head. Charlotte laughed.

"Is that British wine?" she asked looking at his bag. The vicar bent over and putting his hand to his face whispered in mock exaggeration.

"No, tell your mum to relax, it's all French. Couldn't buy British, she'd put poison in the cakes I've ordered if she found out." He carefully lifted each bottle from the bag to show her. "See French Charlotte all French." Charlotte laughed again.

"Have you ever tried hawthorn wine?" she asked without really thinking.

"No," the vicar confessed. "Why does your mother make it?" Charlotte's mother had made wine in the past, her family constantly made fun of the fact but she hadn't a clue what wines they were.

"Yes," she lied, or rather she didn't know, crossing her fingers for the second time that day. "She also makes a very good primrose wine, though it's been a long time since it was a good year." Charlotte couldn't believe she was lying to a vicar, what had made her say such a thing. She had her fingers crossed so hard she was sure she'd draw blood.

"Really," the vicar replied. "I must see if your mother can see her way to donating some to the church. I can't buy any off her, she hasn't got a licence." He winked.

"I'll ask her," Charlotte said quickly trying to find a way out of the knot she'd tied herself in.

"You do that, French Charlotte," and looked on as the little French girl almost ran into the shop. Sighing loudly the vicar turned and walked to his car. We've lost a way of life in this country he thought sadly, placing his wine on the passenger seat.

Back home Charlotte found her mother busy preparing a Carbonnade Flamande, the Flemish equivalent of the British beef in beer. Her father was sitting in the lounge, his nose in a book depicting Roman life in Britain. After kissing both her parents hello on the cheek she raced up the stairs to her room wanting to finish her physics homework before dinner.

Knowing she wouldn't be going out again, Charlotte changed into her pyjamas and pulling her science books from her bag placed them on her bed in readiness for study. Minutes later her mother entered with a steaming bowl of hot chocolate. "Dinner will be in a petite heure," she told her. Taking her hot chocolate Charlotte settled on the floor in front of the long sash window to drink. As she sipped, she gazed out of the window. It was still a depressing site. All the trees were struggling to display any greenery and many were close to bare. The grass which should be a rich green for the time of year had been brown for weeks and any plants in the borders were either dead or dying. Will, who she hadn't seen for ages, was next door slowly turning the dead plants into the soil. Charlotte absently watched his easy way with the earth for before her eyes settled on the ornamental cherry. There resting in the tree's almost lifeless branches sat four magpies, all motionless and all staring back at her window, a fifth she observed rested in an apple tree next door. It too was staring in her direction. Staying calm, she ran the rhymes Will had taught her through her head.

Four for a boy,
Five for silver.

And the second, the one she'd been told in Otherworld, she thought hard. It came to her –

Four for a birth,
Five for heaven.

They had to both mean something. Charlotte simply couldn't believe they were both frivolous bits of rhyme, there had to be a meaning attached to their words, but what? Too tired to consider any meaningful understanding that evening, she tucked the question away for Triskelion when she next saw him. Blowing her best ever raspberry she went back to her hot chocolate and slightly less enjoyable, her physics homework.

It was just over an hour when her mother announced that dinner was ready. Carbonnade Flamande was served in the traditional way with home cut French fries and a green salad. Her father took tradition one step further and washed it down with a bottle of 3 Monts, a beer brewed not far from where they used to live in France. Testament to her mother's cooking, dinner was enjoyed in virtual silence and after jointly washing up they all retired to the lounge. Although it was the beginning of June there was quite a nip in the air and it didn't take much persuading for her father to light the fire. Charlottes' mother, taking up the entire sofa tuned into a French radio station and settled down to listen. Her father returned to his book on Roman life in Britain and Charlotte lay in front of the fire luxuriating in its warmth. Her mind wandered to Otherworld and her long conversation with Triskelion. To their wanderings in the wood and in particular Amphillicia's Well. She pushed all thoughts of Ashtynn to the back of her mind and closed the door firmly shut.

Apart from the odd hiss or sharp crack from the fire and a low murmur from the radio the three of them rested in silence, not needing words or moving electronic pictures to enjoy each other's company. Her father relished the silence but after a while his daughter's lack of chatter started to perturb him.

"You're quiet this evening," he observed looking over his book at his daughter spread out in front of the fire. "Everything alright?"

"Just thinking" Charlotte replied absently, not really thinking at all.

"Anything in particular?" her father went back to his book not expecting any detail from his daughter. Charlotte thought again about her conversation with Triskelion. It was worth asking her father she thought.

"Daaad," her father stopped reading and rested his book open on his knees.

"Hmmm?"

"Do you know, anything about the Bonhommes at Ashridge?"

"Hmmm." Charlotte recognised this as an affirmative.

"Did you know, there may be hidden treasure somewhere in Ashridge that they brought with them from the South of France."

"Where did you hear this?" her father was more than a little surprised at her question.

"At school, local history," Charlotte lied for the third time that day. "There's a valley near Ashridge House called Golden Valley which suggests that there could be treasure hidden somewhere."

Her father smiled, he relished her childish enthusiasm. It was a shame he'd have to bring her back down to earth.

"Firstly, the valley you're talking about isn't a natural valley but landscaped, and landscaped long after the Bonhommes left, so I doubt if there's any treasure to be found there. Secondly, the name Golden Valley is a generic term given to lots of valleys all over the country and refers to the fertility of the valley not to buried treasure." On seeing his daughters look of utter disappointment, he immediately regretted being so blunt. He could have let her down gently, given her some hope of finding treasure. Thinking on his feet, he continued to speak. "There is one true Golden Valley," he continued, pleased to see his daughter's expression change from one of disappointment to renewed interest. "It's not here though but in Herefordshire. Funnily enough people say that its name is a mistake, the name Gold coming from the Welsh, Dwr which means water. Historians say the Normans mistook the word which is pronounced Dore to mean the French for gold, or, or d'or. Now why would the Normans think the Welsh were speaking French? No I believe if ever the word Golden was meant as a clue to hidden treasure, then it's there at that valley. C.S. Lewis had a picture of the valley in his office at Oxford, as a child he described the valley as heaven, possibly in his adult life too."

Charlotte remained silent, deep in thought. She wasn't convinced by her father's dismissal of the Bonhommes and their supposed hidden treasure. Perhaps the person who named the valley Golden, knew of the

Bonhommes treasure and deliberately named the valley so, as a clue for those who came looking. More bizarrely though she had a feeling, a strong feeling and one that she couldn't understand and try as she might, she couldn't get rid of. The feeling told her that somehow the valley in Herefordshire, the true Golden Valley as her father had described it. was somehow connected to what she was experiencing, here and now in Otherworld. She thought about questioning her father further but his head was back in his book and her head was already fit to bursting with questions. She couldn't cope with answers that would inevitably lead to even more.

Bidding her parents good night Charlotte retired to her room. Her tiredness was beginning to get the better of her and the last thing she needed was to be summoned to Otherworld again that night. Gazing through the window at the blackness outside, she thought of the little robin, somewhere in their garden, of the squirrel almost certainly risking its life every time it escorted her through the gateway. Of Alasdair and Cathasach and poor Wodewose. She had no right to feel tired when others were making so many sacrifices for her. Charlotte turned to the picture of the white hart, to give it her customary kiss. What she saw shocked her. The hart instead of standing was on its knees, head bowed, so much so, it's nose was almost touching the ground. Charlotte with her newly discovered sensitivity couldn't help feeling that some invisible force was deliberately pushing his head to the ground, deliberately humiliating the proud beast. With tears rolling down her cheeks, Charlotte kissed the cold glass, willing the beast to have strength. The time for talking was over, they had wasted far too much time talking. Now was the time to stop talking and act before it was too late. After one last, lingering touch of the glass with her fingers Charlotte got into bed. She was ready, very ready to be summoned that night.

After visiting three of his parishioners the vicar arrived home just as the night was closing in. On the way he had stopped at the local

Chinese and was looking forward to his meal accompanied by a glass or two of crisp white. Going to his fridge he took out a bottle of white wine resting in the door. Not French but from a local vineyard at Frithsden. Better not tell French Charlotte he smiled to himself. After opening the wine he rinsed a glass from the night before, still sitting in the sink. After giving it a quick dry he took both the bottle and the glass into the lounge and set them on the small table by the window. Next he took a fresh candle and after lighting it placed it on the sill. This he swore he would do every night until the two boys and Ashtynn were found. He still hoped somehow the light from the candle in the window would help guide them, if not bodily, then their souls back home. The candle was also for his village, Aldbury for which he cared deeply. There was something hugely disturbing happening at the moment and he sensed that whatever it was, his church and his belief would both be needed and tested. Before returning to the kitchen he turned on his old hifi and from a cabinet selected a CD, George Winston – Winter into Spring. Most appropriate, he allowed himself a second smile as the sound of piano playing started to lift the atmosphere in the room. After heating the Chinese in the microwave he returned to the lounge and set the plate on the table. He was just about to settle down when a thought struck him. Walking over to his old oak cabinet, he took a simple pewter candle holder and candle from a drawer. After lighting the candle he let the wax drip for a while before placing it on the small spike. Happy he set the candle on the table and turned off the electric light. His meal was a little tepid but he didn't care. Listening to the steady ticking of his American wall clock, the inspirational piano playing of George Winston and burning candles the only light, rightly or wrongly he felt closer to God. Tomorrow he decided I'll get rid of my television set, it's too much of a distraction from the real world. A world I haven't been in tune with for a long time he admitted to himself.

Charlotte woke just after midnight. There had been no tapping at her window but tonight after seeing the desperate situation of her poor white hart she was raring to go. Quietly she got dressed, where are you, she thought searching for the robin, we need to go. Five minutes later, frustrated by the bird's non-appearance, she descended the stairs anyway and let herself outside. In the garden, there was still no sign of the robin, or the squirrel. Something's wrong she thought to herself, I'm needed tonight, I know I am. Throwing caution to the wind she walked determinedly up the road towards the church. It was Friday night and Aldbury was still celebrating the start of the weekend. The odd car passed as did one or two people making their way home from one of the two village pubs. Charlotte kept to the darker shadows hoping no one would notice. No one did, she reached the gravel path to the church, without incident. Automatically, she looked up at the clock on the church tower. The hands read thirty five minutes past midnight, there was no XIII and no hand held snake. Refusing to give up she walked determinedly up the path and stepped onto the stone, slab. Nothing happened. Nooooo, Charlotte cried out in silence, no, no, no. She jumped once or twice on the stone, but it wasn't to be. So desperate was her frustration it turned to anger and she hit the church door, crying out in pain as her fist connected with solid wood. Rubbing her hand a movement caught her eye. Feeling scared suddenly she swung round only to see her robin hopping up and down on the gravel path. Knowing it had her attention the robin continued to hop, moving down the path to the lych gate before flying back to her feet. It's trying to lead me home she realised, coming to her senses.

"Ok I'm coming" and together they made their way back to the cottage and the stable door. Thank you Charlotte mouthed to the little bird as she let herself in. Back in her room, she dressed once again in her pyjamas and gently touched the picture of the white hart.

"Sorry," she whispered. "Please don't give up." With that she climbed into bed, and closing her eyes, cried herself to sleep. The robin watched from the window sill, he waited until the little human child's eyes closed and turned to see the picture she had so caringly touched. There as earlier the white hart was kneeling, head bowed. In contrast though its white coat glowed, faintly maybe but the robin recognised it as a sign that their Guardian was still fighting. The little human child he realised, had by her action given their Guardian much needed strength. Maybe, just maybe the human child did have the resources to take on the evil threatening their two worlds. From that moment he swore he would if necessary lay down his life to protect the little girl's wellbeing. Beating out its red breast, the robin flew back to its nest already prepared for what tomorrow may bring.

Lying in bed, Charlotte's mother listened intently. She had heard her daughter climb the stairs to her room, where did she go, where had she been? Was she worrying unnecessarily, perhaps she'd only been raiding the fridge?

Charlotte spent the next day with her friends. None wanted to stay in the miserable environs of the village and it was unanimously decided to walk up to the Bridgewater monument and enjoy a tea and cake at the café adjoining the National Trust buildings. They chose a well-walked path leading off Tom's Hill Road, to climb the scarp to the café. In days gone by the path was known as Back Holloway for that was what it had been, a back way up the scarp. As the name suggests, the path is one of the Chiltern's famous Holloways, the type of path Wodewose had specifically told Charlotte to avoid. She'd argued vainly for them to take a different route and had been loudly shouted down, roundly being told not to be so stupid. Safety in numbers Charlotte told herself, what could really happen and after all it wasn't as though she were in Otherworld. Even so she welcomed the sense of relief on reaching the café safely. She envied her friends who managed to while away the hours talking and laughing about nothing in particular without a care in the world.

In Aldbury, life under the circumstances continued as it had always done. Villagers continued with their everyday routines and credit to man's resilience and adaptability, many were becoming used to their dismal environment though all couldn't help but notice that the cloud was becoming that little bit darker every day. The mysterious mist too was now so thick it looked almost solid. If you dared to put your hand in you simply couldn't see it. So dangerous was it considered that lines of tape now cordoned off the entire field and all footpaths passing through or close by had been temporarily closed. The infamous mist attracted hordes of ghoulish onlookers and there were several minor accidents as drivers pulled over without notice to take a photograph. Few took more than a couple of pictures, the incompressible sense of fear people experienced put paid to that. Some were lucky and their fear soon left them after leaving the village. For many unfortunate others, the fear grew like a cancer inside them. Such became its intensity that after just a few days many refused to leave their homes and increasing numbers descended into insanity. For some reason, never was there a connection made to the mist.

That Saturday morning a canal boat moored at nearby Northchurch. The owner, Robert Peddie had heard of the strange happenings at Aldbury and wanted to see for himself. He had recently retired as a solicitor and had bought the boat so he could spend the warmer months cruising the country at his leisure. His wife had left him several years before and both his children lived abroad. He had no one to answer to but himself and his maker and he embraced the freedom that brought. Moored close to the New Road bridge he unstrapped his old bike from the roof of his boat and started the bike ride along New Road towards Aldbury. It was a glorious day and the scenery was hard to beat, England had so many unsung treasures he'd discovered since retiring and the countryside surrounding Aldbury was certainly one of them. The only blot was the leaden sky ahead of him which he knew from local radio was the increasingly darkening cloud that refused to leave Aldbury. Although he had an idea what to expect nothing could have prepared him for the chill and the sheer dolorous sobriety of everything Aldbury. It was almost as if the whole village was dying on its feet, never he considered had he seen such a sorry sight, not even in a courtroom. He was surprised, no frankly he was amazed that he was offered a smile and a forced morning from more than one local resident. On arriving at the village green, he dismounted and leaned his bike against a wall beside the village shop. In the nearest window three police notices asked for help or information on persons that were missing. Photographs centred each poster. There were other missing posters, mainly with photographs of cats and there were also a couple depicting dogs. Many looked as though they'd been on display for some time. Inside he bought a sandwich, a fresh baguette, a slab of cheese and a couple of British wines that were promoted in the central window. He looked forward to lunch. Not far from the shop, on the other side of the road, there was a small and continuous line of cars. Nearly all were slowing, stopping for a second or two before moving on. He guessed this was where the infamous mist was to be found. He wanted to capture the enigma on camera and decided he'd be best off taking any pictures from the churchyard which backed onto the field with the mist. There he would be relatively undisturbed. Leaving his bike against the wall, he crossed the road and walked up the gravel path through the churchyard. The clock on the tower indicated it was almost eleven o'clock, no wonder he was feeling hungry he hadn't had breakfast, something he was beginning to regret. Carefully he uncapped the lens cover from his rather expensive looking camera, (a retirement present from colleagues in his office) and moved about the gravestones looking for a place from where best to capture the atmosphere. The mist he found at first quite mesmerising but this was quickly replaced by a dread, of what he knew not which made it worse. The fear of the unknown is the most powerful fear of all he remembered reading somewhere and now he was experiencing just that. He managed to get five good shots before he could stand it no more and left almost at a run. After strapping his shopping onto the back of the bike, he cycled at pace, returning to his boat on the Grand Union Canal. Rather than secure his bike to the roof, he left it leaning against the hedge on the towpath, something completely out of character. Orderliness was normally his bible. In the galley he opened a bottle of red, from Denbies in Surrey the label read and poured himself a large glass. He sipped hard. Enjoying the sense of escape the wine gave him, he quickly finished the glass and poured himself another. Taking the baguette from its bag he broke it open with his bare hands and doing the same with the cheese placed a broken slab between the bread and took a large bite followed by another good downing of wine. Feeling a little calmer he reached for his camera wanting to see if his efforts had been worth the way he was feeling. He opened the screen at his last shot. The image was hardly anything more than different shades of a shadow yet it was somehow hypnotic. He studied it more closely, unwittingly drawn to the centre of the image. There was something there, he was sure of it and impossibly something in the image appeared to be moving. He concentrated his vision, unconsciously being drawn deeper and deeper into the mist. Never had he examined one of his photos so closely. There was definitely something there, he could see it, the mist appeared to be clearing but that was impossible. And then he saw it. It looked like a building, a house, a house not of this time and there was something else. He let out a scream followed quickly by another and throwing his camera to the ground scrambled up the steps from the galley, desperate to get outside. He just about managed to reach the stern of the boat when he let out another scream, it was to be his last and by its sound, he'd known this to be the case. Seconds later he collapsed onto the deck. Several horrified walkers on the towpath ran to help except for one mother who was doing her best to hide the scene from her two small children. A passing cruiser, witnessing the scene also pulled over to offer assistance but it was very evident to everybody that they were too late. The man was already dead. Those who saw his face would never forget it. The poor man's eyes were stretched open wide and held an expression of terror that unless you were witness to, you wouldn't believe possible.

The official verdict was heart failure brought on by excessive and sudden shock. The police were suspicious even though witnesses, and there were plenty of them, all concurred that nobody else had left the boat. An expensive looking digital camera had been found on the table in the galley and there was a faint hope that some sort of explanation may have been captured in its memory. The memory card when examined was found to be full. Inexplicably the card contained thousands of images of exactly the same shot. The picture had quite obviously been taken from the churchyard of St John the Baptist at Aldbury and was of nothing else except the mist in the adjoining field. This information was not released to the general public and in particular the media. The vicar was questioned but was found to be of little help. Lots of people take photographs from the churchyard he told them, the mist was becoming a real nuisance. He promised not to pass on what the police had confided in him. After the police had left he lit a candle and prayed silently for several minutes for the poor man who had met such a dreadful end. At least he isn't missing he thought for a second and immediately reprimanded himself for such a careless notion. Needing air he left the serenity of his church for the comparatively chaotic scenes outside. Taking deep breaths he gazed across the churchyard to the village shop. He refused to take a second's glance at the mist which he was beginning to think may be the Devil himself or if not the Devil the breath of the Devil. Approaching the shop he saw French Charlotte and her mother, walking hand in hand. Feeling better for seeing the two, he briskly crossed the road calling out.

"Bonjour French Charlotte, bonjour Madame."

Charlotte's friends wandered aimlessly through the wood simply enjoying the beauty of their surroundings and nothing more. Why would you want more? Charlotte recognised much of the wood from her experiences in Otherworld and half expected Wodewose, Triskelion or the two hounds to appear out of the trees at any minute. At one point they passed a muddy pool which Charlotte recognised immediately as Amphillicia's Well. She couldn't help standing on its edge and staring into what was little more than a mass of mud. There was a general cry of "urghhhh" from her friends and, "French Charlotte, what are you doing?"

"Trying to see my reflection," Charlotte lied, she was getting good at it. There followed a general consensus amongst her friends that she was becoming quite mad. It was late afternoon when the little group returned to Aldbury. The gloom they all agreed, appeared so much more pronounced after the clear blue skies of Ashridge. Caroline offered to play host but Charlotte declined with the excuse she'd promised to help her mother with something. Yet another lie. In truth she wanted an early night, she wanted to be fresh for Otherworld. After exchanging a hug with everybody she wandered slowly back to the cottage. On the way she passed the house where she'd taken shelter in Otherworld. Outside a man who she recognised as living there was busy washing his car. He raised an arm in greeting on seeing her look across. Charlotte did the same, she felt dreadful. Even though she hadn't taken anything she felt like a burglar, a common thief. If it were the other way around, she'd hate the intrusion. On the spot Charlotte formulated a plan of action, next time she was summoned to Otherworld, which she was certain would be that night she knew exactly which house she'd shelter in, hers.

Back at the cottage she found her mother busy in the kitchen, preparing some salads that had been ordered for a picnic the following day. Her father, she knew would be packing up their market stall.

"I'm glad you're here," her mother smiled, delighted in seeing her enter. "You can give me a hand." That'll teach me to lie, Charlotte moaned to herself. For the next hour she helped her mother chop, slice and dress salads along with marinating various cuts of meat ready to be finished the following day. After clearing away and washing everything her mother announced she needed to go to the village shop for that evening's dinner. Just some cold meats and cheese, nothing fancy. Charlotte quickly offered to go with her and hand in hand they wandered up the street enjoying being mother and daughter together. As they neared the shop they were apprehended by the vicar. He was dressed in his work clothes, a clerical shirt and collar, black trousers and shoes and to add a touch of his own personality a bold tweed jacket. His red bush of a beard almost eclipsed the white of his collar and Charlotte's mother always said he looked more like a wrestler than a representative of the church.

"Bonjour pretre,"Charlotte's mother returned the vicars greeting. The vicar fell in step with them.

"So what delights are you two buying today, foie gras, cuisses de grenouille's?" The vicar wore his usual wide grin but Charlotte saw through it. He looked drawn, something was wrong, she knew her vicar too well, but would never dare ask.

"Do you know, I might try some of your English wine," her mother teased back, looking at the promotion in the window and purposefully putting on her strongest French accent.

The vicar followed them into the shop chatting as though his life depended on it. The shop they found was quite busy, a mix of locals and day trippers, the latter all wanting to have a taste of the "Aldbury experience." The vicar followed as Charlotte's mother shopped, paying careful though discreet attention as to her choices, particularly when it came to cheese. As they moved amongst the shelves raised voices were heard coming from another part of the shop. The voices became louder and within seconds a full scale argument erupted between a woman who looked to be in her seventies and a man probably in his early thirties. Charlotte and her mother, recognised both as being from the village. The vicar also recognised the pair and quickly moved to intervene. He arrived just as the man raised his arm and stopped what may have escalated into a physical assault. Holding both by the arm, he spoke to the two in soft but forceful terms. Rather like Triskelion, Charlotte couldn't help thinking. In under a minute both left the shop without a word of thanks to vicar and without speaking or making up with each other. Scattered across the shop floor were the remains of what had been a baguette, evidence of what had caused the argument. The young girl serving behind the counter arrived with a dustpan and brush and muttering to herself started to clear up. She didn't even acknowledge the vicar and the rest of the customers in the shop returned to their shopping as though nothing had happened. The vicar returned to Charlotte and her mother.

"They were arguing over the last baguette," he whispered loudly, incredulous. Charlotte's mother made a joke about how in France arguments like that normally erupted over the last jar of Nutella and having successfully lightened the atmosphere continued gathering for the evening meal. Finally they came to the wine. Her mother selected two from the English promotion and threatened the vicar.

"These had better be good, or you shall hear from me." Before he could reply, Charlotte interjected.

"How was your wine last night vicar?"

"Ah very good, "he replied blushing. "That reminds me," as quickly as possible he wished to divert their attention from last night's very good English wine. If asked a direct question he would not be able to lie. "That reminds me, French Charlotte tells me you may have some hawthorn or even better some homemade primrose wine." Charlotte's mother gave her daughter a strange look.

"As a matter of fact I have, though I didn't make it, Charlotte's grandmother did." She turned to her daughter. "How did you know we had some of your grandmother's wine?" Now it was Charlotte's turn to blush. Outside the vicar apologised for the commotion inside the shop.

"I don't know what's happening," he admitted pulling on his beard. "I know the couple who were arguing and they are normally both genuinely nice, but something's happening to the people in this village. I know there's the cloud, the cold and that bloody mist." He quickly apologised for his last remark. "There's something else though, it's as though the Devil himself is entering people's hearts. Parishioners who normally go out of their way to help others are becoming unreasonably selfish and fall out over the slightest thing. People used to offer me help all the time but apart from the few they now nearly always come to me because they want my help and some are desperate for my help even. It pains me to see them in this state and the most difficult pain to bear is that I fear I fail them. I do my best of course and I pray harder than I've ever done, I just wish I knew how I could be more helpful in some tangible way." There hung in the air an uncomfortable silence, both Charlotte and her mother felt a little embarrassed by what felt like a cry of help from their vicar and weren't certain how to respond. "Anyway," the vicar broke the silence, rescuing them. "At least you two always give me a smile, especially young French Charlotte here." In obligatory fashion he patted her on the head.

"I think you could do with some of Charlotte's grandmother's homemade wine," her mother touched the vicar's arm. "Come on, I'll fetch some for you."

"Really," the vicar tried to feign surprise, and failing miserably.

On arriving at the cottage the vicar waited outside the back door whilst Charlotte's mother went to fetch the vicar's wine from the brick outbuilding at the bottom of the garden. The vicar with hands in his pockets looked with sadness in his eyes at their garden.

"It's such a shame he muttered, your garden looked so nice this time last year. The whole of Aldbury's the same."

"You've seen our garden before vicar?" Charlotte was a little surprised.

"Yes I used to come to see the young man who lived here before you, I can't remember his name now," the vicar stroked his beard, a sure sign that he felt a little uncomfortable discussing their relationship. "An artist I think he was."

"Why did you come to see him?" It was a direct question that only a child could get away with. The vicar was beginning to regret his slip of the tongue, why were children so inquisitive and why were their questions so direct?

"Oh no particular reason, he just needed my help with a few things." His reply was overly dismissive and he knew it. "I can't tell you what they were, French Charlotte," the vicar tapped his nose. "Church business, confidential." Charlotte smiled sweetly, sensitive to the vicars discomfort, she wasn't fooled, she knew there was a lot more to his visits than he was letting on.

"No wonder he painted so many magpies, you've got four." The vicar had spotted the four birds in the cherry blossom." I have three in my garden now, "he added. "All they do is stare at the house all day, as though they're waiting for me to feed them. They give me the creeps." At that moment Charlotte's mother returned from the outhouse with three dust covered bottles in her hands.

"I'll just give them a wipe." The vicar stopped her.

"No, the dust tells a story. I'll take them the way they come. Thank you very much." The vicar held open a bag and Charlotte's mother handed over two of the bottles placing them carefully inside.

"There are two hawthorn and one primevere, the primevere is very special," she emphasised, holding the third bottle back. "You must only open it on a very special occasion, promise me."

"Promise," the vicar made a sign of faith and Charlotte's mother let the bottle go.

"How much do I owe you?"

"Do not insult me pretre, you know I do not want any money." The vicar knew this to be true, Charlotte's mother had never accepted money and was always bearing gifts. An idea came to him.

"I tell you what, I'm just about to get rid of my telly, would you like that? I'm sure the wine is worth a lot more but just a small token of my appreciation." He beamed, pleased with his offer. It was Charlotte who spoke next.

"My dad doesn't agree with television or computers, he won't allow them in the house." If the vicar was shocked he didn't show it.

"That's exactly why I'm getting rid of mine," he recovered quickly. "Far too much of a distraction."

"But you have a good excuse for one, you have no company at home, nobody to talk to." Everybody knew the vicar was a bachelor and Charlotte's mother was always commenting on how she felt sorry for him all alone in that big house, in the middle of nowhere.

"Ah but that's where you're wrong, I am never alone, God is always with me and we have many a conversation together." He sounded as though he meant it and Charlotte's mother smiled a show of respect. She wouldn't say anything more on the subject.

"Ok pretre, let me know what God thinks of the wine."

"I will," he promised and disappeared down the brick path. As he walked back to the church, he thought over the day's events. The visit from the police had shaken him and he wanted to share what they had told him. He had almost opened his mouth to French Charlotte's mother but had thought better of it. It was unfair to burden her. His mind turned to the squabble over the last baguette in the shop. Life in Aldbury was beginning to resemble hell and his job with the church was to protect his flock from descending into such a place. He hoped beyond hope that God would guide him in this. He thought of his church, a magnificent building. It was meant to be a sanctuary from evil, a place where one could get closer to God, yet in the last few days the vicar had noticed whispers of what looked like vapour or mist rising from somewhere beneath the church floor. He'd at first tried to dismiss it, putting it down to his imagination but the traces were becoming stronger and could no longer be ignored. He couldn't prove it but he was sure it was the same mist that had taken over the field behind the church. Worse, much worse he believed it to be a direct attack on his church by something evil, very evil, perhaps even the Devil himself. What scared him the most, more than anything, was his faith in his ability to deal with it, to defeat it.

Not long after the vicar had left Charlotte's father returned home and the three of them sat at the kitchen table enjoying raclette with all the trimmings. After dinner, Charlotte made her excuses and climbed the stairs to bed. She was sure, she'd be called that night and wanted to be prepared. Her father and mother retired to the lounge both with a book in hand. Around an hour later she heard them climb the stairs to bed and hugging Gromit forced herself to sleep.

The clock read fifteen minutes past midnight when Charlotte awoke. Not again, was her first thought when she saw the time, what's happening? Such was her state of mind not getting summoned scared her more than being summoned. Sliding out of bed she went over to her window and kneeling peered out into the darkness. There shone a scattering of lights, subdued by closed curtains and as she watched one by one they became fewer as life behind them retired to bed. Charlotte strained to see if anything was moving in their garden, or more specifically her robin. She saw a black cat walk stealthily up the lawn and went cold with the possibility that maybe the cat had caught her little friend. Worried she considered whether to get dressed and go and search. The night before came back to her and what a fool panicking had made of her. No she had to remain calm, no matter how hard it was and with supreme effort, and after ritually kissing the picture of the suffering white hart returned to her bed. Sleep was harder to come by though and it wasn't till past three in the morning before her eyes closed and she fully rested. The robin skipped along the windowsill wanting to make sure the little girl was definitely asleep. All the time she was awake he had to try and watch her. Satisfied at last, he retired to his nest at the base of the pagoda. He'd heard disturbing stories coming out of Otherworld and just like the little human child had wanted her to transcend that night. There would have been a very good reason why they didn't send for her. He just hoped it wasn't for all the wrong reasons.

The following morning breakfast was a solemn affair. There was no explanation for it except that the atmosphere grasping Aldbury was even more brooding than usual, hinting that something very bad was about to unfold. Charlotte passed several people on her way to and from the shop to collect the Sunday paper and nobody gave her even a hint of a good morning. All kept their heads down staring at the ground like ghosts searching for a home. The shop was busy as it always was on a Sunday morning but there was little conversation, instead a disturbing silence prevailed. The silence could be described as one of expectation, not an excited expectation, quite the opposite. It was one of foreboding. An acceptance of defeat, that this was the beginning of the end. If you want an analogy, I can only think it must feel similar to what birds and animals famously sense before an oncoming tsunami.

That morning the vicar welcomed around half the usual congregation to the normally popular Sunday service. He gave he thought a rousing performance and loudly led the singing, not something he normally did. In spite of his gallant efforts the atmosphere rose barely higher than flat and the ancient church walls for the first time he could remember, failed to inspire.

Charlotte's family passed an instantly forgettable day. Her father spent almost all of it reading and her mother apart from delivering the salads spent most of it cleaning and cooking. As for Charlotte she spent nearly all day in her room, for her the night couldn't come quickly enough. She kept studying the picture of the white hart and looking out of the long sash window. She finished all of her homework and knew that she'd made a sloppy effort but didn't really care. She had more important things on her mind.

The vicar was relieved in the evening to return to the sanctity of his vicarage. It had been a really hard day and his head felt heavy with a burden he couldn't explain. The life he had led, being part of the huge family that was the Church had always inspired him. He had devoted his life to his church and helping others, and although he'd never considered himself saintly, he thought up until now he'd done a pretty good job. In recent days though he had been tested as never before. Not in his belief but in his ability to keep the belief of others. Although he enjoyed cooking, he couldn't face preparing a meal and for the second night running he treated himself to a Chinese. On the kitchen table he'd placed the three bottles of Charlotte's grandmother's homemade wine. That morning he'd intended to keep all the bottles for a special occasion but exceptional circumstances warranted opening one now. He kept the dirtiest bottle, a bottle of hawthorn on the table and took the other two down to the cellar, where he hoped they'd be safe from his weakening will. Returning to the kitchen he opened a box he'd brought from the church. The box, previously unopened, was full of candles. He took out all twenty four and lit each and every one, securing them on anything that came to hand. One at a time he took them into the lounge placing them where he thought they made the greatest effect. When finished, in full clerical attire he knelt in the centre of the room and prayed as he had never prayed before. It was nearly an hour before he'd finished. He could, he considered, do no more and felt comforted by the thought. Several of the candles had burnt themselves out, those that hadn't he left alight. Returning to the kitchen he opened and poured the wine and distributed the Chinese onto a plate. He couldn't be bothered heating it and he didn't bother with his hifi either. That night, he wanted to be alone with his thoughts. He was glad he had gotten rid of his television, even though it was only to his garage. It would have been so easy to have simply turned it on and forgotten about the world and its challenges. That's not why he had joined the church. The wine he found was excellent, as he knew it would be. The taste was more like a sherry and therefore had to be sipped, a safety valve that was quite unexpected and if he was honest welcome. One by one the candles slowly burnt out. The vicar remained sat at his table until the last one flickered and died leaving him in the dark. The dark didn't frighten him, what he had told Charlotte's mother was true, he wasn't alone in his house. God was with him and that night he knew it to be true. Moving to the window he looked out across the fields and to his church. As his American wall clock beat midnight he thought, for a moment he saw a figure running up the church path. On looking twice he saw there was nobody there. He hoped it wasn't somebody playing the fool with the mist. More likely, he convinced himself, it was his imagination playing tricks. He blamed, French Charlotte's grandmother and her wine. After ensuring that every candle was definitely out he took a fresh one from the drawer in his oak cabinet and set it in the bay window. This he lit and left it to burn, after which he began mounting the bare, dark, heavily polished elm wood stairs to his bedroom. Let my light guide you all home he prayed as he fell into a troubled sleep.

In Aldbury as the last of the candles burnt out in the vicarage, there came a sharp tap, tap, tap at Charlotte's window. She was awake in a flash and already half-dressed it was no time at all before she was outside the back door. To her immense relief she found both the squirrel and the robin waiting for her.

"I thought you'd never come," she whispered to the squirrel. "I've been so worried." The squirrel flicked its tail twice in response and was just about to run down the brick path when Charlotte whispered sharply. "Wait," and disappeared back inside. Remembering her plan, she turned the light on in the lounge and re-joined the squirrel outside who immediately took off down the brick path. The squirrel she noticed, appeared to be in more haste than usual and Charlotte wondered as she ran, if anything was wrong. She'd soon find out. Luckily, there was nobody out on the streets that night and within almost record time she was transcending, with the messenger to Otherworld.

Charlotte rose through the churchyard floor, to in Otherworld, find the mist in turmoil. It was always twisting and turning but that night it was if a million whirlwinds were competing for space. For a split second she felt herself being drawn towards the vaporous fight but for a split second only. Shaking her head free from temptation she started down the gravel path to the lych gate, purposely keeping her line of sight away from the mist. At the road she started left, the squirrel in tow. She ran deliberately wide of the shop. With a glimpse she could see that Ashtynn remained suspended in the window, exactly as they'd last seen her. On arriving at the cottage she found the light for the lounge still on, and Charlotte breathed a huge sigh of relief. She'd been worried one of her parents may have wanted the toilet in the night and upon finding the light on, turned it off. Squeezing between cars Charlotte came to stand in front of the door that would never open. "If I manage to pass through, it will be the first time since living here, I've entered via the front door." She even managed a smile at the thought. Maybe it was finding humour at a tense moment that helped. In truth Charlotte would never know but somehow she managed to pass through the door at her first attempt. It was almost with astonishment she found herself standing in the lounge she knew so well. Everything was exactly as her parents had left it before they'd retired to bed. Her father's book lay open, face down on a chair and her mother's radio on the floor. A wine glass, still with a drop of red sat on the grate. It was the strangest feeling being in her lounge, knowing it wasn't her real lounge but an image. Yes it all felt most peculiar.

The squirrel jumped onto a sofa and curled into a ball. Charlotte didn't feel like resting just yet, she wanted to explore their cottage in Otherworld. From the lounge she passed into the kitchen, remembering to turn on the light as she did so. At all times, she must remain in the light, she hadn't forgotten. Her hand however simply passed through the switch. She tried again but no it was as if the switch didn't exist. She decided to take a calculated risk, she wanted to explore her home that wasn't her home. Charlotte hoped rays from the light in the lounge, trespassing into the kitchen would be enough to give her some protection, at least. In the diminished light, she could make out the raclette machine still sitting on the table and the washing up drying on tea towels, just as she'd arranged everything. She looked across to the stairs, she wanted desperately to see her room, would she notice any difference. She went to rest her hand on the banister, ready to climb the stairs and to her dismay found nothing solid to grasp hold of. Her hand simply passed straight through. She hadn't considered for a moment she may not be able to mount the stairs. With care she placed a foot on the first stair only to find there was nothing there, her foot passed straight through. Looking up the stairs she could see both hers, and her parent's doors and under her door shone a pencil of light where she had deliberately left her light on. Everything looked so real, it just didn't seem possible that she couldn't simply walk up the stairs to her room. With a determined effort she again tried to stand on the first step. This time so determined was her attempt, she almost fell flat on her face when her foot failed to find anything solid. The squirrel, she noticed had by this time joined her in the kitchen. It sat on the floor looking rather bemused at her futile attempt to climb the stairs. Charlotte tried for a third time and for the third time met with frustration. Without warning, the squirrel darted past her and ran up the stairs, coming to rest on the small square her parents euphemistically called a landing. There it sat looking down at her as if to say, "you see, it's easy." Charlotte, cursed under her breath.

"Don't be so cocky," and automatically clamped her hand over her mouth hoping her parent's hadn't heard. Of course they hadn't, they were in another world! Once more, she tried the stairs and again found only empty space. The squirrel, as if trying to enforce its message, ran back down the stairs, passing between Charlotte's legs, before running back up again to its seat on the "landing." Charlotte took a deep breath, what was it Triskelion had told her? "Treat it as a game." Getting worked up will only make it worse, she reminded herself. This time she tried the stairs almost if it didn't really matter to her, whether she connected with something solid, or simply air. Her plan worked, her foot rested on a solid stair, it even made a sound, how could it have been anything else? The concept, now she was standing on something solid seemed ridiculous. Steady, one at a time, she slowly mounted the stairs and it wasn't long before she found herself standing in her room. How on earth had she found it so difficult? Her bed covers lay over Gromit, exactly as she'd carefully positioned them before leaving. Her homework lay on the floor and her schoolbag sat on the chair. Everything was exactly as she'd left it and yet she knew what her eyes were telling her brain she could see, wasn't there, not in the true sense. Not a single thing was real. She moved over to the picture of the white hart and gently touched the glass with her fingers. The glass was solid, and cold to the touch. Leaning forward she kissed the picture with a message to keep hanging on in there. Was it her imagination or did the hart glow a little brighter? It must be her mind playing tricks she convinced herself and turned away to look out of the long sash window. The reflection from the light in her room made it difficult to see outside, and when she did manage to, all she could really make out were shadows.

Next Charlotte went to her parents room. The light never worked in their room, so she didn't bother trying to switch it on. She would simply have to risk the dark. With the help of time and what little light there was outside, Charlotte's eyes adjusted surprisingly well. It was her parent's bed that immediately drew her attention. She hadn't given it a thought and now she did, it was obvious. The covers were shaped just as they were in her world, covering her parents, though here in Otherworld, her parents of course weren't underneath. Looking at the bed covers and the depressions on their pillows, it appeared as though somebody had beamed their bodies up. Charlotte found the whole experience very unsettling, she was so close to them, yet literally worlds apart. She hated the feeling. In an instinctive move she lay on their bed, wishing to feel some sort of connection. As her head touched the pillow with horror she realised that there was nothing there. Instead she was free falling through space. In under a second she was in the lounge, looking down and in another second would land on the coffee table, except she didn't. She passed straight through, landing with a thud on the lounge floor. If the landing hadn't winded her, she would have screamed out in pain. Her right wrist felt as though it was broken and when she did eventually get her breath back, she found it painful to breathe. What had just happened? The squirrel appeared by her side, he apparently very sensibly had taken the stairs. Looking at his inquisitive face not only did she hurt physically, so did her pride.

"I'm such an idiot," she found herself telling the little animal. "How come you find it so easy?" The squirrel's response was to run in circles around her. Charlotte couldn't decide if he was circling her out of concern, or to mock. She hoped it was the former, he wouldn't be so cruel. "It's ok, I'm alright." She found it perfectly normal, talking to a squirrel even if she wasn't sure it understood. Which at that moment, was probably a good thing, as she wasn't sure if she was alright at all. Leaning on her elbows Charlotte dragged herself out from under the coffee table, even though in all probability she could have simply sat up, being able to pass through it. When she was fully removed, she stood up gingerly, not wishing to invite any further pain. Her right wrist hurt like hell but with relief she found she could move it and knew enough first aid to understand it wasn't broken. Her ribs were a different matter. She could breathe, but only by using short sharp breaths. Deep breaths hurt like hell and if she were honest, simply not possible. Charlotte knew she had either cracked or bruised a number of ribs. How could she have been so careless? This was the last thing she needed and all because she let her emotions get the better of her. She was so angry with herself. She was eleven, almost an adult and should have known better. At that moment Charlotte hated being a child. Trying to clear her head she searched for her next move. She needed to get some rest, it was still several hours till morning and she'd be no good to anybody without any sleep. The sofa looked inviting and without further thought sat down. Except of course she didn't, there was no sofa. For the second time in a matter of minutes she found herself spread-eagle on the floor and in severe pain. Cursing, and feeling utterly stupid she crawled to the floor in front of the fire, a place where she often curled up in the evenings. Her throw lay in a heap to one side. Thankfully, her mother hadn't tidied up and Charlotte with great relief found she could grip the throw and pulled it over herself hoping to find some degree of warmth and if at all possible, comfort. Placing both hands under her head she prepared herself for sleep. To add insult to injury the squirrel jumped onto the sofa and curled up against a cushion, to do the same.

"Stop showing off or you'll regret it," Charlotte murmured. She was more than a little bit jealous of the squirrel's ability to, "play games," with an image.

There was not a sound outside. That was the problem. It was too quiet to sleep. Charlotte could cope with the hard floor and to some extent the chill but not the silence. Aldbury maybe a village, set in beautiful countryside but it was also a cut through, or a rat run as they're called in London and even in her back bedroom, she was used to hearing the sound of the odd car passing, especially at night. Sleeping in the lounge there should have been lots of welcome noise, even in the early hours but there was nothing. Nothing at all, and the sound of silence, as it always did, unnerved her. Perhaps, because it wasn't a natural sound that silence unsettled her so. She was beginning to understand what was meant by a deathly silence, because that was exactly what it felt like. She kept thinking of Ashtynn, just metres up the road in the shop window. Her mind playing tricks, no longer placed her in the shop window. Ashtynn was walking down the road towards the cottage, a malevolent expression on her face. Eyes wild seeking her out. So vivid was the image in her mind, she felt Ashtynn could no longer be purely thought. She really was approaching, full of mal intent. Charlotte turned and turned, desperate for sleep, desperate to rid her mind of Ashtynn but wherever sleep was that night, it wasn't with her. She lay there, literally waiting for time to pass and as I've said many times before, if you've ever found yourself in a similar situation, you will understand when I say, time can never be hurried. Time takes its own time. It refuses to be rushed, which for Charlotte that night was little short of torture.

It wasn't a noise that stirred Charlotte, it was a light. She was sure she had seen a light pass the window. She hadn't been asleep but in that semi drowsy state that comes and goes when sleep evades. Her mind immediately focused on Ashtynn, and her blood ran cold. She looked across at the squirrel, whatever it was outside hadn't appeared to bother him. He remained curled in a ball, asleep. There it was again, a light, there was definitely someone or something outside the window, and what or whoever it was, was carrying a lamp or a torch. Charlotte forced herself to remain calm, she had to think clearly, panicking she was well aware could put her and the messenger in danger. She decided after some thought, her best plan of action would be to refrain from any action. Movement may attract unwanted attention. Better to keep still and wait, for what she had no idea, just to wait. Seconds that felt more like hours passed and there it was again, a light and it was definately hovering outside. Charlotte held her breath, waiting, still not knowing for what. Why was not knowing, always the worst feeling. Worse than the feeling of knowing even if knowing was dreadful. Charlotte sensed rather than could see that who or whatever it was, was outside the front door. She heard a sound, the first sound she had heard all night. She looked across in the direction from where it came and saw the source was the squirrel stirring awake. Whatever it was outside had finally disturbed its sleep. "Nice of you to join me at last," Charlotte thought to herself, still feeling jealous. The squirrel, ignoring her ran up and down the sofa, though by this action it didn't appear to be afraid, indeed quite the opposite. If anything it looked pleased.

Charlotte remained still, waiting for something to happen. The squirrel, jumped down from the sofa and ran to the bottom of the front door, rather like a dog will do when it can smell something on the other side. Charlotte watched nervously, wondering what the squirrel would do next and to her dismay it did the unthinkable, and in equal measure the unforgivable. The squirrel left her, abandoned her, left her all alone in the cottage by passing through the front door. Charlotte sucked in breath, shocked, she had never been alone in Otherworld before and from the first second hated the experience. She couldn't communicate easily with the messenger, and many others in Otherworld but always found their presence comforting. She felt safe, or safer in their company.

They knew far better than her how this strange world worked. Charlotte, waited, struggling to stay calm. It was becoming more and more of an effort, an immense effort simply to do nothing. She wondered whether she'd be safer retiring to the kitchen and remembered in the kitchen there was no light. "Stay in the light," Triskelion had told her over and over again. But could she trust Triskelion, she had always held a doubt about the ghostly figure, since the day or rather night she'd met him. Could instructing her to stay in the light be a trick to trap her somehow. She doubted it, that didn't make sense but still the feeling nagged at her.

"When are you going to learn to trust me, France Charlotte?" It was Triskelion speaking to her, via her mind as he always did. Charlotte, surprised looked around wildly. He was nowhere to be seen. As she searched, trying to see where his communication had come from the squirrel reappeared through the bottom of the door and the next moment the door appeared to radiate. A figure started to appear and Charlotte recognised him immediately, Triskelion. On seeing him she didn't know whether to be angry or cry with relief.

"Why couldn't you have found a way to tell me it was Triskelion?" She looked angrily at the squirrel, a tear rolling down her cheek. "That light was you outside?" She turned her hostility on Triskelion.

"Yes, sorry if I gave you cause to be afraid, I had to be sure it wasn't a trap." "Cause to be afraid," Charlotte felt like hitting him. She may have managed to control her fear on the surface but underneath she had been terrified. Calming herself down, she next had to deal with the bizarre image of seeing the ghostly figure alive and well in her lounge. Silence, once again dominated the room, Charlotte had had enough of silence, why didn't he say something?

"Why are you here Triskelion?" she was frustrated that it was her who broke the silence.

"I've come to collect you, we have to meet with Leht. We have to hurry as dawn is not too far away and her light will be too weak to communicate after dawn breaks." "Why wait to the last minute then?" Charlotte asked the silent question. She was still angry. She hadn't intended Triskelion to hear her, but of course he did.

"It would have been too dangerous to have travelled any earlier, the Darkness has his agents in Asherugge and everywhere could conceal a threat. Even traveling now is a risk."

"Ok, sorry," Charlotte felt she owed him that, the squirrel too and she turned and repeated her apology. She had no idea if the squirrel understood but whenever she spoke directly to the messenger, she noticed he would flick his tail.

"Are you ready, France Charlotte? We really haven't much time." She nodded and got to her feet, a loud gasp disclosing the pain she was in.

"You are hurt, France Charlotte? I felt it when standing outside, that's one reason why I was so cautious." Charlotte told Triskelion what had happened, how she had fallen though the non-existent floor and maybe broken one or several of her ribs.

"This is my fault," Triskelion scolded himself. "I should never have told you to treat the images as a game, they can be dangerous, very dangerous and many a creature has met their afterlife by tangling with them."

"No, your advice helped Triskelion, look I am hurt but I am still alive." Charlotte gave him her best smile. Triskelion appeared to accept this, all signs of sympathy gone in a second.

"Hurry we must go," and with that he passed back through the front door with the squirrel a close second. Charlotte went to follow but thud, came up against solid wood. She winced in pain as her ribs shouted loud their protest. Tears rolled down both cheeks. She angrily wiped them away with her good arm and drew a deep breath, at the same time taking an enormous step at the door. This time there was no protest, she passed through as though nothing was there.

"Only playing with you," she grinned, faced with what she assumed was the squirrel and Triskelion's concerned expressions. She was becoming quite proficient at lying. Triskelion said nothing, he simply turned and started up the road to the village pond. Charlotte with the squirrel followed. For the second time that night she had to force herself from looking across at the shop window. Why was it so hard not to look at something that she didn't want to see anyway? Why did the mind work in such a peculiar way that it fed her brain with such unwanted temptation? They were two questions Charlotte knew she'd never know the answer to. Anyway she had no time to consider them now, for Triskelion was almost running up the road which led to Evinghehou. After leaving the village behind, Triskelion passed through the gate on their right and started across the field. Charlotte followed, relieved that she encountered no problem with the gate. She knew exactly where he was heading, and in a few minutes they were at the oak where she always hid the budget. Though it was still dark the sky above Ashridge or Asherugge was a lighter colour and as the planet rotated would only get lighter. Triskelion was watching the sky, his featureless face, failing to disguise his concern.

"Quick France Charlotte, your budget." Charlotte bent down to retrieve the little leather bag from beneath the tree and cried out in pain. Her ribs felt as though they were piercing her lungs.

"I'm not sure I can."

"You have to, nobody else can do it, the tree won't let anybody else enter." Charlotte hadn't a clue what he meant but knew not to question, this was Otherworld and time was pressing. Holding her breath, she slowly got to her knees and felt underneath for the budget. She found it easily and pulled it from the hollow. It felt heavier than normal and on closer inspection discovered it contained water or some sort of liquid. Not "some sort" of liquid but a part of Leht, Charlotte found herself shaking on realising just what she was carrying.

"Quick." Triskelion sounded almost panicked. Trying not to reveal the pain she was in, Charlotte got to her feet. As soon as she had done so Triskelion didn't wait, he made off heading straight for the tree line. The going after the field, Charlotte knew was never going to be easy, made all the more difficult by her stupidly self-inflicted injuries. She was not wrong, only by taking short sharp breaths could she manage the climb and even doing this her chest still felt as though it were on fire. There was also the handicap of her injured wrist, normally she'd scrabble on all fours and this was no longer an option. Triskelion didn't appear to notice, he was like a man possessed, powering up the slope as though it were his last breath in Otherworld. She watched as his light became smaller and smaller with distance, not even the messenger waited. Charlotte was left alone to struggle, taking one step forward and half a step back as she fought against the grease of the chalk. Above her, she could see Triskelion had been joined by several others, who or what she couldn't make out, they were but shadows. Frankly, she was in too much pain to care, Triskelion could be meeting with the Darkness and it wouldn't matter to her at that moment. The ground beneath her gave way again and Charlotte had just about enough willpower left, to scream out in silence as she grabbed at an exposed root with the hand connected to her injured wrist. Her action stopped herself from sliding helplessly back down the incline but never had she felt so much pain. Her feet ran, helplessly, on the spot as she struggled to find a foothold and relieve her wrist. She felt so utterly helpless. Without finding a foothold the pain became simply too much to bear and Charlotte let go, prepared for the slide to come and primed to grab with her good hand at an obliging root or branch. As she started to slide, something grabbed her. Charlotte looked up in a panic and saw Wodewose staring down at her, his expression not one of concern but of curiosity.

"What are you doing France Charlotte? Triskelion says you are hurt and that we must hurry." Charlotte spluttered her frustration, if Triskelion was in a hurry, why hadn't he waited and helped her?

"I've hurt my ribs and wrist Wodewose, I can't get up the slope." Wodewose's expression changed to one of concern.

"Here, I'll pull you up." Holding her good wrist, Wodewose pulled Charlotte up the scarp as though she were a rag doll. On reaching the top, Charlotte a little more bruised from when she'd started out, saw that Triskelion was waiting along with the two hounds, Alasdair and Cathasach. Triskelion took only a seconds glance at Charlotte, concentrating on Wodewose.

"Where are we meeting?" Wodewose let go of Charlotte's wrist leaving her to get to her feet under her own power.

"At the "holey" tree."

"How far is it, from here?"

"Around twenty minutes, half an hour," Wodewose gave his estimation.

"We must make it in fifteen." Triskelion's command made it clear there was no other option. Charlotte looked pleadingly at Triskelion's blank face. She had no idea, if Triskelion had read her look but he certainly felt it. There was no way she could move quickly, which meant fifteen minutes, for her anyway, was out of the question.

"France Charlotte is hurt," he said to Wodewose. "You must help her." Wodewose looked at Charlotte with renewed concern in his dog like eyes.

He was so very different to the Wodewose of a few days ago when hawthorn wine had influenced his every move and thought. And before when he was a mouthpiece for Leht. This was a cool calm and collected Wodewose, a Wodewose prepared to obey orders, and without question, a side of him Charlotte had never seen before. It hurt her to talk and she tapped her injured wrist and waved her hand across her chest, to indicate where she hurt most. Before she had time to protest, Wodewose had put one of his strong arms under her legs and lifted her as though she weighed less than a feather. His arm acted as a chair, and with her good arm Charlotte held onto his neck.

"Please do not be afraid France Charlotte, I won't let you fall." Charlotte nodded, she didn't really have any choice. Triskelion didn't wait to see if she was secure, he was already making his way through the wood. Wodewose quickly overtook him, his strength and agility were quite incredible. All were running and the pace at times was almost frightening, though not once did Charlotte feel as though she were going to fall. Wodewose, at all times led the way and Alasdair and Cathasach although outside of the group, stayed very close, closer than Charlotte had ever seen them do before. How none of them tripped over a bramble or fallen branch in the dark, Charlotte couldn't fathom, it was almost as if the wood was allowing them a safe passage.

They came to a halt in front of what looked like a long dead tree. Virtually all that remained was the trunk with just the odd branch. Nearly all the trunk had been stripped of its bark, and what remained was riddled with holes, presumably chiselled by a woodpecker. Charlotte knew they were deep in Sallow Copse and surrounding them trees were all that were visible. The dark made every shadow appear a threat and if they were attacked, she could see little means of escape. Triskelion must know what he is doing and Charlotte prayed hard that he did.

Wodewose gently lowered Charlotte to the floor setting her among ferns that came up just above her waist. Triskelion paced up and down and the two hounds circled the tree continuously. The squirrel sat at the very top of the tree, Charlotte couldn't be sure but it looked to be acting as a look out. The atmosphere was so tense it could be cut simply with a breath, using a knife would be like taking a sledgehammer to crack a nut. Wodewose went over to the tree and put his arm into one of the holes in its trunk. The hole didn't look anywhere big enough to take his ample arm but somehow he slid it in with ease. He appeared to be feeling for something inside the trunk. After around thirty seconds a satisfied grunt told everyone he had found whatever it was, and Wodewose withdrew his arm. In his hand he held a stone, Charlotte recognised it as the same or similar to the one he had taken from a rabbit hole on Aldbury Nowers.

"Give Wodewose your budget France Charlotte." Triskelion's voice was the most commanding she had ever known it. She did as she was told and Wodewose took it without offering thanks. He sat the stone on the ground and opening the neck of the budget motioned to Charlotte to take out the ancient map and the necklace with the pendant. Charlotte, feeling very uncomfortable searched through what she knew to be Leht's blood for her necklace. It took a couple of seconds only to find it and with the map she quickly withdrew her hand. She expected the map to be ruined, soaked beyond saving but to her astonishment it was dry as a bone and her pendant felt warm to the touch, not just hand warm but as though it had been submerged in hot water. It too, somehow, was bone dry.

"Put it on, quick." It was Triskelion again, his obvious unease was beginning to frighten her. "The necklace." He pointed to her neck. Charlotte already knew what he meant and dropped the necklace over her head and let it drop onto her shoulders. On seeing the necklace settle, Triskelion visibly relaxed. Although he was still pacing it wasn't with such intensity. Her attention turned to Wodewose, he was gently pouring the liquid from the budget into the shallow hollow carved into the stone. Charlotte knew what was about to happen. She had seen the process before. Even so she watched on with her heart in her mouth and judging by their demeanour so did everybody else. From the newly poured liquid a few wisps of vapour started to rise, only a few. Charlotte didn't remember the process being this slow, before.

"Come ooooon." Triskelion hadn't intended Charlotte to hear him but she did, and she knew this moment was crucial to all of them. Slowly, very slowly the vapour began to thicken, rising and gathering above their heads. The pace agonisingly slow. Whisper by whisper the vapour condensed to form a sphere, always it looked as if it was struggling, the odd trail escaping before being pulled back in. After what seemed like an eternity, birthing inside the swirling cloud, a glimmer of light. The light grew steadily brighter until it was radiating, touching every extremity of the vaporous sphere. Then a voice said simply.

"Hello everybody." It was unmistakeably, Leht and Charlotte felt a flood of joy surge through her. Triskelion she noticed had with the slightest of movement wiped a robed arm across his face. With astonishment she realised he was wiping a tear from his featureless eyes. From that moment on, Charlotte was a little more trusting of Triskelion. All it had taken was for him to show some genuine emotion.

Silence fell upon the little group. All were waiting for Leht to speak again and it wasn't long before the sound of her melodic voice stirred an emotion in all of them. Even the normally restless squirrel sat statuesque, unmoving. For Charlotte nothing had ever managed to hold her attention like the voice and light of Leht.

"I hope it is not so, but this may be the last time I can address all of you together," a nervous stir rippled through the listeners. Leht continued as though she hadn't noticed and it quickly became apparent that she was reading a prepared speech. "It is no secret that I am weakening and I know not when the day will come, that I will no longer have the energy to leave my circle. All I know for now is, that time is not far away and I hope this moment does not turn out to be the last. In case it is, I do not have to tell you how important it is that you capture every word I have to say and keep my words with you. Only share my words with those you can trust and only then if they can be of help. Do not repeat anything from my lips to a stranger, not even a friend unless you are absolutely sure they are who you think they are." Charlotte wasn't sure what Leht meant by this and knew there wasn't time for questions, she'd have to do her best to understand.

"There was a time in Otherworld, when we could call upon great armies to defeat what we face today. Those times we have to accept are no longer with us, but before we despair we must come to terms that a grand army may not be what we need to defeat the challenge that faces us now. And let us not have any illusion that what we face now is perhaps the greatest threat to the right path, that we have ever faced in our time. So great is the threat that this may turn out to be the definitive challenge between good and evil since time started to measure the existence of Earth and Otherworld. A grand show of force on this occasion will only play into the hands of the Darkness. We must learn from the errors played out on Earth, where money, brute strength and the threat of physical attack wins over the right path. Violence and fear of violence will only strengthen the Darkness in its desire and attempt to control all. It wants us to do battle with anger in our hearts, never must we allow ourselves to be controlled by this emotion. To do so will lead to certain defeat. Anger must not be mistaken for courage, for courage is strength and strength of this type can control fear, and without fear the Darkness cannot control our minds. I come back to what I said at the beginning, a show of force is not what we need on this occasion to defeat our enemy. We do not need numbers, what we need instead is pureness of thought, a rejection of fear and strength of wit. If we hold a light to these three qualities, we do not need numbers to defeat the Darkness. Though we have our suspicions, I'm afraid I cannot tell you for sure why the Darkness has chosen our turf upon which to make its latest and perhaps biggest ever challenge. The fact that it has makes it all the more important we do not allow ourselves to bow to fear. No, we must see it as an honour that it has done so, as a challenge. Using the qualities I have just described, I have every confidence that those of you I see before me today. Though few in numbers, have the ability to defeat what is in front of us."

Charlotte looked around her, at the little mismatched group biting on every word that Leht uttered. It was laughable surely that any of them could take on such a formidable foe, such an impossible challenge. Her attention returned to Leht.

"Our weapon will be surprise. The Darkness, I suspect will be expecting and preparing for a traditional battle. It will not be looking for individuals, as its actions have already demonstrated, and that is, and will continue to be our strength. The Darkness will certainly not be expecting to face a human child and that, France Charlotte although you may not think it now, is a powerful weapon."

Charlotte was conscious that all eyes were on her and she blushed. She didn't want to be put on a pedestal, so far, as far as she could tell she had only put those she knew in Otherworld at risk. She still had no idea why she was there or how she was going to reward their faith in her. It was becoming a burden hard to bear. If Leht saw her inner struggle, she made no sign and continued with her address.

"We must recognise the Darkness has chosen to do battle on two fronts. The first is the Sacred Library of Evinghehou and the second is at Aldeborie where it is attempting as far as we know to create a gateway to the Earth. I have discussed this at some length with Triskelion and we have come to the very difficult conclusion that we may have to sacrifice the future of Otherworld and the Earth for the greater good of the Universe and the continuation of time." Charlotte expected a reaction to this, but no one stirred. Leht continued.

"Our defence of the Sacred Library started by the ancients perhaps even the originators is close to breaking point. If it had not been for your action France Charlotte my being here may even be in question." Charlotte found herself blushing for a second time, she had no idea what Leht was talking about, what it was she was supposed to have done. As far as she was concerned she had done nothing and certainly nothing which warranted praise. Leht continued.

"I no longer have the strength and therefore the ability to help our Guardian. It is with great sadness therefore that after speaking with Triskelion, I have decided we have no other option than to destroy the passageway to the Sacred Library." This announcement did cause a stir and Charlotte looking across to Triskelion saw that his head was bowed low, almost in shame. Leht continued.

"The passageway to the Sacred Library was constructed in such a way by the ancients that it could only be destroyed by a keystone beneath Leabharlann de Solas, I mean Ivinghoe Beacon." Leht smiled at Charlotte. "And the keystone to close the passageway requires the hand of one chosen for the purpose. Triskelion has long been the chosen one. The reason for his calling here." There was another stir and Triskelion's head remained bowed. Leht continued.

"For the chosen, to turn the key stone is almost certain to open the gate to their afterlife. The ancients intended this, to ensure the passageway was never closed on a whim. Only if there was no other way. And it is with a heavy heart, after searching for days without rest that I can see no other way to protect the secrets of the ancients. The passageway must be closed. Triskelion will go tomorrow. We must hope after the passageway is closed, the Darkness will lose interest and allow our courageous Guardian to leave." There was now real tension in the air. Charlotte thought she understood what Leht had just told them, though if her understanding was right she doubted Leht's judgement with regard to the Guardian. If by the Guardian, Leht was referring to the white hart, she could only see the Darkness exhorting some sort of terrible revenge on the poor creature. From Triskelion's almost buried head she could tell he did too and then came the realisation that Leht knew this all along, she was simply trying to give hope where there was none. The white hart would have to be sacrificed for the greater good.

An anger started to build in Charlotte's stomach, she simply could not stand by and let that happen. Leht continued.

"If we succeed in protecting the secrets of the ancients from the Darkness, there is hope that we can save both our worlds, Otherworld and the Earth. Every decision we make from now on must be the right one. My light is fading. Remember failure is not an option."

A heavy silence fell as Leht's light flickered and disappeared. Nobody really noticed, or to be honest cared that dawn was starting to make an appearance. As the planet turned on its axis, more and more of the sun revealed itself and slithers of light started to slice their way across the woodland floor. Charlotte for once couldn't find any beauty in the birth of a summer's day. Her mind was still on Leht's address. From what she understood in the next day or so she could lose the valiant white hart, Triskelion, just as she'd decided she could almost trust him and there was also a strong possibility she may never see Leht again. That left herself, Wodewose, the two hounds, the squirrel and the two robins to prevent the takeover and destruction of two worlds. Maybe even the Universe or as Leht put it, 'the continuation of time.' Laughter escaped her mouth at such a ridiculous prospect.

There was hardly any warning. Alasdair and Cathasach both emitted angry sounding growls. Immediately after, every shadow surrounding them burst into life, rising up, before tumbling like stormwater, wave after wave upon them. Charlotte found herself being thrown against the tree before Triskelion stepped in front of her with a brightly shining sword raised high above his head. Charlotte couldn't really recall what happened next. Alasdair and Cathasach twisted and turned faster than light itself, biting and tearing at every moving shadow. Triskelion cut and continued to cut at everything and nothing, his sword leaving intricate patterns of light hanging in the air. Not once did he take a single step away from his position in front of the human child, he'd keep his promise to Leht, he'd defend her with his life. Wodewose too, rose to defend their plight. With his staff he took huge swings into the mass of moving shadows. Shadows which Charlotte saw were full of tiny eyes, pointed claws and razor sharp teeth. As Wodewose's staff cut through their centre the forever living parts of his wood grew into long twines which curled around the invisible necks of the enemy, throwing them skywards. The noise of the battle alone was enough to kill a normal person. Agonising screams and rasps of empty air saying hello to the afterlife sought out every unturned leaf and every nook in a tree. Grunts of effort supreme became weaker as the battle progressed and were overtaken by a quite different sound. Gasps, gasps that were weak with the acceptance of death. There appeared to be no end to the tumultuous snarling shadows, as soon as one fell, another rose up behind. A storm swollen sea of shadows, when one wave died another followed, crashing in anger behind . Charlotte could see that her defence were tiring, both the hounds were bleeding profusely and the more their blood flowed the more ferocious came the attack from the shadows. Wodewose too, although uninjured looked tired and Charlotte could see that the initial determination in his eyes was slowly turning to fear. As long as they didn't show defeat. Only Triskelion still looked fresh and the shadows were becoming hesitant before throwing themselves upon his sword. As the battle raged, the planet continued to turn allowing the sun to cast its light over a wider area. Fingers of light started to touch the woodland floor and as the planet rotated a little more, light cleared an obstinate tree and flooded the ground surrounding them, illuminating the battlefield. Thousands of screams squeezed the air only to vanish into silence. Triskelion brought his sword down, not in anger but in relief, the tip of its blade splitting the ground where so much blood had just been spilt. Wodewose leant on his staff, his chest heaving. The look in his eyes told Charlotte he wouldn't have lasted much longer. The two hounds limped over to Triskelion, heads bowed. Their coats were almost shredded and soaked red with blood. On reaching Triskelion they lay at his feet. The squirrel suddenly came to life and let out a series of loud chafing sounds, its tail swirling left and right. Of their adversaries there was no sign. No blood, not even one plant looked as though it had been disturbed. Never a battle had been raged here. How appearances can deceive.

"Gnombres." Triskelion gazed deep into the wood where plenty of shadows still remained. Wodewose remained silent, with exaggerated care he scooped up the stone that had held the light blood of Leht and replaced it from where he had retrieved it, in the "holey" tree. Charlotte, found herself shaking after the event, a reaction that frustrated her as she had somehow managed to remain calm throughout.

"Where have they gone?" her question was directed at anybody who cared to answer.

"Anywhere where there's a shadow." It was Triskelion who answered her. "We cannot move from here until there is a wider cover of sunlight on the woodland floor. Are you ok, France Charlotte?"

Charlotte felt it a little late for him to ask her that. Her mind was still re-running what had just taken place, in particular she focused on Triskelion. If it hadn't been for his valiant and determined action Charlotte realised she may no longer be here. He owed him the greatest debt anybody could ever owe someone, her life. The slow realisation and acceptance of the fact as the adrenaline started to drain away brought on a completely different and unwanted reaction. Her stomach began to rise and for a moment she thought she was going to be physically sick. It took all her strength to prevent herself, after all the others had done for her, the last thing she wanted was for her to demonstrate how weak she was. At the same time she struggled to wipe her thoughts, she didn't want Triskelion to know them, more from embarrassment than anything else. Triskelion quietly read the human child's every thought and felt every emotion. He would never let her know, he would play along with her wish. He would also keep to himself just how impressed he was at France Charlotte's unrealised show of strength.

"No," Charlotte responded after she was quite sure she had control over her stomach. "I mean, there is no sign that there was ever a battle, no blood, no bodies and I saw, at least I think I saw many gnombres die." Triskelion leant heavily on his sword, his weight causing it to sink deeper into the ground.

"Gnombres do not die as your species do. When they die they simply disappear into the earth. There is no blood, no evidence they once lived. Even alive they become one, part of a shadow, you can step on them and not know. They only become physical when they mean you harm and as you have just witnessed, they are not easy to defeat. If it hadn't been for the light.......... Triskelion let his last sentence fade into the air. There was no need to finish, everyone was more than aware that a very different outcome could have materialised if it hadn't been for the rotation of the planet.

"It was such a shock." Charlotte was still struggling to stop herself shaking.

"For us too," admitted Triskelion. "That's what troubles me. Normally Alasdair and Cathasach can sense a gnombres attack from over a mile away." The two hounds looked up at Triskelion, their expressions making it clear, they felt responsible for what had just happened. Charlotte's heart went out to them. Triskelion, not moving from resting on his sword, expanded on his words. "On this occasion they only sensed the gnombres seconds before they were upon us. Gnombres may be ferocious but they are unruly and rarely organised. No this attack was not entirely their own doing, something or someone must have been controlling them. If it hadn't been for the light of Leht they could well have attacked earlier and I think that may have been their plan. To capture your budget with the light blood of Leht would have been a major victory for them and a devastating blow, maybe even a fatal blow for us. Something prevented them from doing so, I wish I knew what."

Wodewose, who up until now had been standing as Triskelion had done, gave what sounded like a grunt of satisfaction and proceeded to sit on the ground, his back resting against the "holey" tree. A hard scratch signalled he was fast recovering from his endeavours. Charlotte too, was slowly beginning to recover her composure and busy turning what Triskelion had just told her over in her mind. After some consideration she turned her thoughts into words.

"It seems stupid we can only meet Leht in the dark when it is so dangerous. Why, can we only communicate with Leht when it is night and where those stones are hidden." It was a very fair question.

"That's the way it is." That's no answer. Triskelion read Charlotte's opinion and ignored it. She was right of course, he had often asked himself the same question. "That's the way it has been since the beginning, who are we to question the decisions of our makers. Sometimes their decisions do not seem fair or practical, sometimes even cruel. Look at the rabbit who has been gifted a white tail and many others with white for a rear making it easier for those who hunt them. How can that be fair, yet we never question it? What has been bequeathed is ours to bear not to question. It is how we respond that will determine how we are judged." Judged by who, was Charlotte's immediate thought and didn't really want an answer. Triskelion pulled his sword from the ground.

"Come." Triskelion spoke to them all. "We must make haste, even with the light it is dangerous to linger for too long. Wodewose you must make your own way home, I will escort France Charlotte back to the gateway." Charlotte expected Wodewose to protest, if it had been her she would have made the strongest protest. There was no way after what had just happened that she would want to traverse the wood on her own. Wodewose to his credit appeared unmoved and almost unconcerned. Understanding and accepting of Triskelion's command. Struggling to his feet, which took some effort Wodewose turned to Charlotte.

"Remember France Charlotte, if ever you find yourself alone and need my help, come to my home." Charlotte new he meant the ancient oak. "If I am not there, my home will call me via the root vine and I will arrive faster than time itself." Wodewose's promise was an obvious impossibility born out of his desire to help and Charlotte thanked her shaggy friend with equal sincerity. With goodbyes said, Wodewose ventured into the wood. He avoided, Charlotte observed every shadow, hopping and skipping between patches of light. At times he almost appeared to be dancing or playing hopscotch and despite the seriousness of the situation, his eccentric moves brought a smile to her face. She immediately felt guilty at allowing herself a little levity and silently wished her friend safe passage and that no harm befall him. As Wodewose faded from view, she heard Triskelion reassure her.

"Don't worry France Charlotte, Wodewose will come to no harm." She only wished she could believe him. Something deep inside her, perhaps her seventh sense was speaking to her. Wodewose it was telling her was in grave, perhaps mortal danger.

"Are you ready?" Charlotte nodded. Alasdair and Cathasach struggled to their feet, both it was very apparent were in great pain. Charlotte wanted to go over and help but Triskelion stopped her. "You must not touch or help them, France Charlotte, to do so would be an insult."

"Why?" Charlotte asked, she so wanted to help.

"That's the way it is." It was the second occasion in just a few minutes that Triskelion had used the same excuse for an answer. Charlotte was close to hitting him, it was no answer at all. Just as in her world her compatriots would use the word "parce-que"(because) to answer a question they didn't want to expand on, it was so irritating. Triskelion didn't allow her time to hit him or ask another question. As soon as the two hounds were on their feet he made off, intending everyone to follow. As they left the "holey" tree with its concealed stone, Charlotte couldn't help but feel they were leaving Leht in the wood all alone and an overwhelming sense of sadness swept over her. God, how many of her emotions had been set alight since her arrival in Otherworld, she couldn't count. She needed something soon to douse the flames before she was reduced to ashes.

Rather than spend too long traversing the wood, Triskelion led the little group to the tumulus on Moneybury Hill. Here he mounted the ancient tomb and stood in silence for several minutes whilst the others waited. Without saying a word he moved off again, descending in an almost straight line, the steep wooded scarp. The going again was not easy and Charlotte slipped and fell on more than one occasion. The resulting pain from her injured ribs each time caused her to cry out loudly, attracting concerned looks from the hounds and the squirrel. Triskelion either didn't notice or ignored her plight. They came to a halt at the edge of the tree line. From their vantage point they could see across the open valley to Aldbury Nowers. The central valley was blanketed by a slowly rising morning mist which created the illusion that Aldbury Nowers was floating. The effect was both magical and surreal, befitting of where they were. Triskelion looked down at the two hounds and raised his arm. In a second they were off, racing across the field before them, soon to be swallowed by the mist that now shone white with the morning sun. Charlotte watched them go, wondering if she'd ever see them again.

"Where have you sent them?"

"Home, they need to rest."

"Where's home?"

"I do not know." It was another frustrating answer but Charlotte realised Triskelion was simply telling the truth. He really did not know, there were many things she was quickly discovering that Triskelion didn't know. There now, remained only the three of them. Triskelion turned to Charlotte and said simply.

"We must continue." He didn't wait to ask if she was ok to do so. Triskelion turned and started along the edge of the slope, careful to keep just within the tree line and therefore hidden from view to anyone or anything with mal intent on open ground. On reaching the field with the oak he paused. Charlotte could see he was scouring the immediate countryside. Apparently satisfied he broke free from the wood and headed across the field towards the now familiar tree. On arrival Charlotte went to take off her necklace intending to place it in the budget and in turn place it in its hiding place beneath the oak, when Triskelion stopped her.

"Not yet, we must wait here for a while." He then surprised Charlotte by stepping towards her. "May I?" Not waiting for an answer he took the pendant hanging from her necklace and rubbed it between his thumb and forefinger. "Thank you," he let go gently. Charlotte in a reflex action caught it, the little heart, to the touch, felt ice cold.

"Rest," Triskelion instructed. "I do not know for how long we must wait." With that he slowly lowered himself to the ground until he was sat on the dew sodden grass, his back resting against the tree. Charlotte did the same and there they waited, the two of them sitting in a field overlooking her village. What they were waiting for she had no idea. The squirrel she suddenly realised was nowhere to be seen and strained her neck to look behind. "He's asleep." Triskelion told her. "This tree is his home."

Like that, the two of them sat for several minutes before Triskelion broke the silence. "I think you have many more questions for me France Charlotte." She of course had and Triskelion she realised was inviting her to ask them. Where do I start she thought to herself, I have so many more now than I had at the beginning, whenever the beginning was.

"What beginning?" Triskelion was impossible at times!

"I can't tell you that, I don't know."

"Why not?"

"Parce-que, because." Charlotte gave Triskelion the French answer she thought he deserved. Triskelion, admonished, withdrew into silence. It was several minutes more before Charlotte was ready with her first question.

"Triskelion." Triskelion turned to look at her. "Why did Leht talk about the passage to the library and closing it could lead to you meeting your afterlife. Does it mean you will die tomorrow?" It was a horribly direct question but Charlotte as a child could get away with it and she had to be sure she had translated Leht's words correctly.

"Yes that is what Leht meant." Came Triskelion's equally direct reply, she had expected nothing else from him. "But I do not intend to meet my afterlife tomorrow France Charlotte, I will do my best to avoid such a fate."

"I wish I could be there to help you." Charlotte, meant it, she could not bear the thought of Triskelion bearing such a responsibility on his own.

"You will be." Charlotte stared at Triskelion's featureless face, desperately searching for some sort of expression. Hers was one of badly concealed shock.

"What?"

"The passage cannot be closed without a witness and Leht believes it has to be a witness from your world. There is only you. With every passing day the Snook's prediction becomes a little clearer and a step closer to reality. At first I did not believe it, how could a mere child." Triskelion stopped. "Sorry, I did not mean to insult you. Going back to what I was about to say. I can see now that the story they tell is not even a prediction for much of it has already become true. You are here and there is no doubt you are the human child their book revealed would come to help us"

"And there is no conclusion?" This Charlotte could not understand how a book could have no conclusion.

"No." Triskelion confirmed. "You can ask a Snook if you like for there is one traveling through Assherugge tomorrow. He hails from Godewaersvelde in Vlaanderen though I believe the conclusion is in our hands and our hands alone, not in the book of the Snooks. Asking will be a waste of time. And please France Charlotte, do not worry about tomorrow, I will not put you in danger, you will be there as a witness only and to be a witness, you must understand is an honour. Nobody from your world has ever seen the Sacred Library of Evinghehou. People in your world do not even know of its existence." Charlotte saw that it really was a great honour but try as she might couldn't feel overjoyed at the prospect. Preferring not to dwell on tomorrow her mind returned to Leht and her speech. She had another question.

"I understood Leht when she spoke but could the others, Alasdair and Cathasach, the squirrel?"

"When Leht speaks every living creature understands, rather like a Snook can tell a story to any living being which choses to listen." Charlotte thought for a moment.

"If that's the case then why wasn't Leht honest about me acting as a witness in the destruction of the passage to the library, I mean Sacred Library?" Triskelion didn't hesitate with his answer.

"Because you are their one hope, France Charlotte. They have listened to the Snooks and they see you as their last and only hope to prevent what could be the end of their world. We cannot be seen to put you at any greater risk than you already are. To do so could risk putting doubt in their hearts and we cannot allow that to happen. I hope you understand this France Charlotte." Charlotte had the peculiar feeling that at that moment Triskelion was trying his hardest to show her some sort of physical expression. She could almost feel his frustration and perhaps released him by asking another question.

"Triskelion, both you and Leht keep referring to the fact that at one time you could have called on huge armies to do battle. You both sound like my father talking about "the good old days." Now Leht after thousands of years is growing weak and the Darkness or the devil, to us is planning an attack on just about everything, you're describing what we call the Apocalypse. How has this situation been arrived at?" Triskelion stared across the field to the roof tops of Aldeborie. His face was still without expression but Charlotte could sense and sense strongly that he wasn't looking forward to providing her with an answer. "Triskelion?" Charlotte urged growing impatient. Triskelion remained staring over Aldeborie, without turning to look at her he started his explanation.

"I'm afraid it is your doing, not you personally," Triskelion saw immediately that he had started badly. "No not your doing in a personal sense but your species. Our worlds, yours and mine have never been perfect but at least at the beginning people recognised the natural way of things and respected nature's needs. The old religions as I have told you were connected with nature. In your world that quickly changed and in recent moons that change has accelerated. Apart from the very few your species has pursued a path of power and greed. Power, land and wealth are the new Gods and your new religions fight continuously with each other. Your species takes advantage of nature, exploits nature for the sole benefit of your way of life. In short you have waged war on the natural world, a natural world that supports us all for without her we will all meet our afterlife. There is no regard or respect for the other species that live in your world, both fauna and flora. Your species have completely lost touch with the animals and amphibians who have as much right to a fulfilling life on the planet you all share, as you do. Their chances of achieving such a right, and it is their right are diminishing with the daily expansion of your species.

Otherworld mirrors your world and for our world to survive, we require your world to be healthy. When our leaders saw the path your species were beginning to follow they hid the most powerful of the natural secrets, knowledge that could become dangerous in the wrong hands. One by one they destroyed the gateways allowing passage between our two worlds. This was perhaps our biggest mistake. Rather than, communicate, reason with those who held power in your world, we drew up the drawbridge, locked the gates and threw away the keys hoping you would simply go away. But of course you didn't. You withdrew from any kind of relation with nature and went about enthusiastically abusing the natural world and with the gates closed there was nothing we could do about it. Otherworld didn't even become a distant memory. We became a legend, a fantasy, not believed in. We no longer exist in your world, we are denied by your scholars. Your scientists follow their own path and one day their research will lead them to rediscover us and other worlds or universes like us, for there are many, but by then I fear it will be too late." Triskelion stopped for breath. Charlotte although shocked by what he had told her, recognised a distasteful truth in his words. Triskelion hadn't finished, although his tone, was now a little softer.

"We now find ourselves where we are today, or as the young in your world say, we are where we are. The actions of your species have smothered Otherworld. Our world is losing her lungs and as a result slowly suffocating. There used to be thousands of Wodewose's, now there are only a handful. Fairies are almost extinct and Leht who was born at the beginning of time may not survive another cycle of moons. Your species are on a path of self-annihilation and without realising it ours too. Those in your world who aren't responsible for such a path are sleepwalking into it. We too are guilty of this. Ironically, the Darkness has suffered too, it can no longer call on the resources it once could. The difference is the Darkness does not really care, destruction is its business and the destruction of everything its ultimate aim. Your species are, by your ways unintentionally helping the Darkness achieve its goal. Even with the help of your species the pace for the Darkness is too slow, it wants a more spectacular end, not a slow strangulation which is what is happening now. Hence its latest move, a move I'm ashamed to say it has been planning for many, many moons and it is perhaps our greatest failure that we did not see what it was plotting. We should have seen it was preparing the ground to establish a base in your world and a gateway to both, and even worse an attempt we believe to discover the secrets or at least some of the secrets of Orme. I believe Leht told you, if the Darkness obtains the knowledge of Orme it will have the power to return everything back to the state before time existed. With no hope of returning. The destruction of its own resources in its own demented mind is seen by the Darkness as a success." Triskelion touched Charlotte gently on the shoulder. "It will be the greatest irony of all if Otherworld is saved by a human child."

As the planet turned and the sun gained height the mist covering the valley thinned to a haze. Dark shapes slowly appeared as the vapour separated allowing fingers of light to explore its midst. A heaven sent sheet slowly being pulled back to welcome in the new day. How, thought Charlotte, could anything want to destroy such beauty, and immediately recognised Triskelion's words. Her species were guilty of doing just that.

Triskelion after his speech had fallen silent. He appeared to Charlotte to be deep in thought. She knew that he had been preparing to tell her the revelation for a long time and had found it very hard when the time had come.

"What are we waiting for?" Charlotte asked, not able to bear the silence any longer.

"To see if the gateway is safe, that the Darkness isn't watching it. We do not want to walk into a trap." Charlotte didn't like the sound of this at all. Especially after the attack in the wood.

"How can we be sure, is there definitely no other gateway I can use?"

"We can never be one hundred percent sure," Triskelion admitted. "We can only calculate the risk and that is what we are doing now and the reason why we are waiting. There are other gateways, as I have told you but for now this is still the safest." That was all very reassuring. At moments such as this, Charlotte regretted having made Triskelion promise to always be honest with her.

"Can I never take the gateway alone, do I always have to travel with the squirrel?" It was more out of concern for the squirrel than herself that Charlotte asked the question.

"Yes, as I told you the gateway was once the bed for an old and sacred ash tree. Only the squirrel, can transcend along the roots of the ash, and passage is via invitation of the messenger only. There is nothing, I nor anybody else can do to change that." Charlotte wasn't going to let this go, as far as she could see being reliant on only one gateway, and one so very close to where the Darkness was "rising", was not calculating risk at all. Quite the opposite, it was verging on stupidity, it was almost suicidal. She was just about to follow up with another question when Triskelion held up his hand to stop her.

"I can read what you are thinking, France Charlotte and yes it does seem stupid but at the moment it is the least stupid option we have."

"But surely the Darkness must realise we're using the gateway, if it doesn't it must be blind, that or stupid."

"You are forgetting, the Darkness is blind. It does not see like you and I do. To see, it relies on agents, on its own it has only sense and intuition. It survives and grows stronger by infiltrating the minds of others. At first influencing them and after, if it is able, completely taking them over. Yes I believes it suspects but that is all." That's enough, thought Charlotte. Triskelion as he tended to when it suited him, ignored her and continued. "That maybe why it has placed your friend in the shop window. It may be using her eyes for its own. To see where it cannot. In future it may be prudent not to pass too close to the window." Don't worry, Charlotte thought, I have no intention of passing close. Her mind pictured Ashtynn and her unnaturally moving eyes. The way they moved felt like the eyes were being operated by a third party.

An involuntary shiver ran down her spine. She took a deep breath and winced with the resulting pain. Triskelion turned to face her, once again he touched her shoulder.

"Look France Charlotte, I hope I will always be by your side, however if this cannot always be." Charlotte knew he was referring to the dangers he would have to face tomorrow and a lump formed in her throat. In just a few hours she had gone from doubting his true intentions to trusting him with her life and now in under twenty four hours more she may lose him to the afterlife, as Otherworld sanitized the word death. After tomorrow she may never see her ghostly friend again. Not only did the thought scare her more than she was willing to admit but she now realised if the worst was to happen, grief would grasp her and shake her senseless. Triskelion read her thoughts but decided not to comment. Fear and grief were two emotions that they could not afford. They invited weakness and if only to save herself what the human child needed above everything was courage.

"It's important you listen to me, France Charlotte."

"I am."

"If for any reason I cannot be by your side and you find the gateway closed, you must use the last resting place of my grandfather. There you will not need the squirrel for passage. I will send him a message, his spirit will help you." Charlotte was trying to make sense of what Triskelion was telling her. It was all coming too fast.

"By his last resting place you mean the large burial mound on Gallows Hill?"

"Yes," Triskelion confirmed, "though we have never called it Gallows Hill. Your species has." Charlotte recoiled on realising the disrespect her words had shown. To his credit and to Charlotte's relief Triskelion made no show of being offended, instead he continued with his message.

"If you have no other choice then you must use the ancient gateway of my grandfather's last resting place. He was knowledgeable in the art of transcending and also had the blood of your ancestors running through his veins. To use the gateway, stand on the summit and call his name, Drustans. His spirit has been resting for many a moon and at first he may not hear you. Do not worry if he does not answer straight away, you must keep calling, keep repeating his name until he does. When he answers, tell him I, Triskelion, have sent you and what it is you require. If he is able, he will aid you in safe passage to your world." Charlotte was immensely grateful for Triskelion's offer but as far as she could see, it had so many ifs, let alone buts and hoped she would never find the current gateway blocked. Now she realised why, despite the obvious dangers they persisted with the gateway in front of the church of St John the Baptist. They were not, as she'd first thought, making light with her life. The gateway, after taking all the negative factors into account, when compared with alternatives was still the one with the least risk. Not that, that gave her much comfort.

Once more silence settled between them. Charlotte far more in tune with her senses than a few weeks before could tell that Triskelion was becoming a little anxious. He could no longer keep all that he was feeling from her.

"Triskelion, why here, why has the Darkness chosen this area to attack our world. Why not a big city such as London or Paris, or somewhere in America or China. Why a tiny village such as Aldbury, sorry Aldeborie." Triskelion continued to look beyond the field to what you could call the unfortunate village. He remained silent.

"Triskelion?" Charlotte prompted. This time he replied.

"That, France Charlotte is the question we've been asking ourselves every minute of every day. The Darkness will have a very good reason and the fact we are still not sure is a major weakness in our armoury. The same with you France Charlotte, we are still not sure why you are here and for what purpose. It would help greatly if we did. We have been asleep, and we are paying for it."

"You must have some idea." She could not believe, with all their supposed knowledge that they had no clue at all.

"Yes we have several but on their own none of them make sense. There are far more sensitive places the Darkness could make its attack. The first reason of course is the Sacred Library of Evinghehou and the ancient scrolls deposited within. Passed down over the centuries are rumours as Leht has told you that the oldest scrolls contain some of the secrets maybe even the key to Orme. They are however only rumours and there are other libraries that carry the same rumours, several far stronger and more convincing than the rumours told of Evinghehou. And several of these libraries are far easier to gain access to than Evinghehou. They have much weaker defences if you know where to look. We fear that the Darkness may possess knowledge that we are not aware of. The ancients so we are told lay false paths as to the whereabouts of the master key to Orme. To create a labyrinth of false hope for those who make discovering the key to Orme their purpose in life. Labyrinths appear in many tales of old and in your world what are often referred to as legends. These tales in both are worlds are still popular today, though so old are they that their origin has been lost to time and some believe their true meaning too. Those whose thoughts travel along this path believe the labyrinth refers to the labyrinth created by the ancients to make the search for Orme almost impossible. Our concern as I said is that with its attack on the Sacred Library of Evinghehou the Darkness has discovered something we are unaware of and this worries us greatly." Triskelion rested allowing Charlotte time to digest what he had just told her. He wanted her to examine his words and using her still untainted mind to form her own questions, her own theories. Maybe she'd find answers they'd never considered. Having nowhere else to lay their faith, Leht had always wanted him to tell the little human child all that they knew. He however had always resisted, believing to do so would be a mistake, dangerous even. With time running out fast, if it hadn't run out already he had to accept there really was no other choice than to tell the little girl everything. And not for the first time, regretted that he hadn't trusted Leht's judgement from the beginning. He hoped he hadn't left it too late.

Charlotte, unaware of the turmoil in Triskelion's mind, thought hard about what she had just been told. Her father had often told her tales that had included labyrinths. Every time she spoke to Triskelion the story seemed to get more and more complicated, the cog bigger.

"How many libraries, like Ivinghoe are there?" She asked after a long pause, not sure where else to go.

"Many, nobody knows for sure how many."

"And where are they?"

"All over," Triskelion replied quickly. "Some are well known in Otherworld, some less so and some have been forgotten completely, with time. Near where you originate from in France, the Moulin de Pitgam stands over one, in Bavaria the monastery at Andechs hides another and in the Hoggar mountains, close to Tamanrasset is one of the remotest. Some of the better known libraries are under Mont St Michel, a forgotten tomb of one of the ancients and the Tor at Glastonbury. The latter, more famous two hold great secrets though, not it's believed, anything related to Orme."

"And these libraries, they're all in Otherworld, they do not exist in my world?"

"They're all in Otherworld." Triskelion confirmed. Charlotte thought about this and the gateway by which she transcended between the two worlds.

"There is no way to transcend from my world direct to one of the libraries?" Triskelion tensed, he didn't think it was possible but in truth they'd never considered it, and now the human child had raised the question, he realised they couldn't rule the possibility out. Was this something the Darkness had discovered, was there a hidden gateway at

Ivinghoe in France Charlotte's world? His thoughts were interrupted by another question from the human child.

"You said there may be people in my world who know about Orme?" The answer, Triskelion knew was yes, possibly, and there was evidence that humans have known for many, many moons but how much and whether any knowledge was still in circulation today, they had no idea. Unprepared for the content of her questions Triskelion wasn't sure how much he wanted to reveal and to be honest what he did know didn't amount to very much. The subject was very sensitive in Otherworld and not many moons ago you would be welcoming the afterlife simply for discussing Orme. He decided to play dumb and at the same time to pass on his dilemma. "I cannot really tell you, Leht knows far more than I do. You really must put your questions to her" If I ever see her again, Charlotte mused reflecting on Leht's last words. She changed the subject, thinking aloud.

"So you may die?" Sorry, Charlotte corrected herself. "Meet your afterlife?" She shocked herself with her bluntness but didn't let this stop her question. "By destroying the passage to the library you may have to meet your afterlife and yet it could all be in vain, as the Darkness may have found a direct gateway from my world. What exactly does the white hart do, why is it standing on the Beacon, sorry on top of the Sacred Library and why is the Darkness trying to destroy it?" Charlotte avoided using the word kill, the word was simply to personal. The adjective destroy placed the hart as an object and therefore made it easier for her to say. Triskelion breathed a silent sigh of relief, this question he could answer without hiding anything.

"The white hart was placed there on the inauguration of the Sacred Library. It's pureness and strength make it the perfect sentinel and a lock almost impossible to open." Not impossible Charlotte thought, the poor hart is almost broken and soon the Darkness could well prise open the door. The thought made her stomach, as earlier start to rise though this time in anger.

"You said earlier that there are those in Otherworld who believe the ancients left a false trail or many false trails, a labyrinth to make it almost impossible for anyone searching for the secret of Orme. Saying the word Orme made her go weak at the knees. She had no idea why.

"Yes that's true, that is the belief of some"

"And it was the ancients as you call them who placed the white hart as a lock or security on the Beacon?"

"Yes." It slowly dawned on Triskelion where the human child was going with this. Charlotte though wasn't about to let him destroy her thunder.

"If that's the case, couldn't the poor hart have been placed on the Beacon by the ancients simply as a diversionary tactic?" The thought that the ancients, as they kept being referred to, were prepared to allow and may have even set up her poor hart to be sacrificed for nothing, made Charlotte's blood boil. Her hart, who at that very moment was battling an unimaginable and terrible fate, who's living image in her room reflected with every second that passed, his terror. Yet he was still refusing to give in, staying loyal to those who had placed him there to the very end. Charlotte wanted to scream her anger. So strong was her feeling that Triskelion visibly flinched as the strength of her emotion touched him. This rare physical reaction broke Charlotte's trail of thought. Not realising she had been the cause she asked, her voice full of concern if he was ok. She worried that Triskelion may have been injured in the earlier battle and concealed the fact from her. Triskelion who had read all of her thoughts, like the human child, did not want to believe the ancients who he'd been brought up to revere, never to question. Could be guilty, if that was the word, of such cold heartlessness. France Charlotte didn't know it but he personally felt the terror. The fight their Guardian was putting up and he too, perhaps even more so than the human child did not want the animal's pain and its possible sacrifice to be for nothing. He prayed it wasn't true as much as he prayed, after reflecting on the human child's questions that his possible journey to his afterlife, wouldn't to be meaningless. He was not afraid to take the path to his afterlife but he was afraid what he would leave behind if his own sacrifice was for nothing. Seeing the human, child's concerned expression, relieved him momentarily from the painful questions his own mind were posing.

"Please do not worry France Charlotte, I am not injured, you must not allow your anger to take over though, the Darkness will only benefit." Charlotte recognised that she had let herself down. She understood now what they meant by Triskelion's warning that anger played into the hands of the Darkness. For a few seconds she had wanted to fight everybody and that she realised with shame, was exactly what the Darkness wanted.

"It's just so hard." Charlotte complained.

"That's why so many have failed in fighting the Darkness, it's main weapon is tempting your worst, your most destructive emotions. Recognising that fact is half the battle, the second half is blocking the temptation altogether."

'Lead us not into temptation.' For the first time Charlotte thought," I understand what that line really stands for." Before today, it had simply been a line to repeat, parrot fashion at school, to not perhaps be tempted to have another sherbet dip.

Once again silence fell between the pair. Charlotte knew every minute they waited meant there may be a problem in her returning to her world and her family. The possibility that she may never see her parents again frightened her far more than the thought of having to face the Darkness. Deep down she prayed the gateway was still open and that she could travel safely back to her world. Once there, the way she felt at that moment, she wasn't sure whether she would want to travel back again. She hoped her prayers and her doubt were deep enough for Triskelion not to read. Charlotte turned to look at him. He sat, still facing Aldeborie and she knew he was as concerned as she was about the gateway. She wondered if he had a family, a wife and children, she hadn't really ever thought about Triskelion in a family sense, how selfish of her. She wanted to ask now but something deep inside told her not to.

Triskelion remained deep in thought. In his mind he was replaying the human girl's questions over and over again. She could be right in so many ways and he was frustrated that a child, and a human child at that had shone a very different light on what they were facing. The last thing he wanted was to enter his afterlife without good reason. After talking with Leht, closing the ancient and secret passage to the Sacred Library had seemed the right and only option available to them, now he wasn't so sure. And now it was too late to turn back time. Leht had already started turning the key to the passage, the process couldn't be stopped. He would tomorrow have to finalise closing the passage and pray that his action wasn't to be in vain. He sensed the little girl looking at him, he knew that she wanted to ask him about his family and had blocked her, the subject was simply too painful. He was the last in a noble bloodline and if it hadn't been for the Darkness and the unwitting actions of the human child's ancestors, his line possibly, could have continued for thousands of years more. Perhaps even till the year time finally stopped of its own accord. Today he was the last survivor of his line, a line that had once been revered all over Otherworld and tomorrow the line could well disappear forever, in an inglorious whimper. The thought was almost impossible to swallow and he was finding it very hard to practice what he had just preached to France Charlotte, to control his own anger. The Darkness, he recognised was succeeding in weaving it's dark magic, even with him. He had to somehow ensure that his action tomorrow wasn't to be in vain, and like so many others before him in Otherworld, he now came to realise that his only hope in keeping his legacy alive, lay with the little human girl sitting beside him. What bothered him, was, the little girl's train of thought. Her uncomfortable questions had planted seeds of doubt in his mind where before there had been none. Perhaps, even France Charlotte was an agent of the Darkness, it was a doubt he had never contemplated before and one too late to contemplate now. If she was an agent, the Darkness had already won, if she wasn't, he, they, had to trust her one hundred percent. Sensing her genuine concern and torn human emotions, he was pretty sure the Darkness couldn't replicate those. France Charlotte, please do not let me down, he found himself pleading in silence.

"I am almost certain the Bonhommes must have brought something to Asherugge that the Darkness desires, something vital to its final plan." Triskelion, surprised Charlotte with this unexpected spoken thought.

"You mean something to do with Orme?" She still felt uncomfortable saying the word. Having felt its power she could now, sympathise with Wodewose's reaction when she'd questioned him on it.

"Possibly yes. The Bonhommes fled the Languedoc when their masters, the Cathars were persecuted. As I told you before the Cathars were believed to be guarding a great treasure. Whatever it was I am sure now the Bonhommes must have brought it with them to Asscherugge and hidden it here. I'm pretty sure this could be the reason why the Darkness has chosen this region to make its greatest ever challenge. It's simply too much of a coincidence."

"But why here at Ashridge?" Charlotte used the present name.

"The Bonhommes were invited here, they built their monastery in a place that made no sense, as I have explained. To a very few in Otherworld the location made perfect sense, they built their monastery over the passage to the Sacred Library. Coincidence or did they know and if they knew how did they know? I've always believed it to be a coincidence, that is until the question you asked me earlier, made me think again." Charlotte was just about to ask which question when

Triskelion continued, pre-empting it. "Your question about a gateway from your world direct to the Sacred Library, maybe not to the Sacred Library for our Guardian, the white hart, would prevent that but to the secret passageway which is virtually the same thing. If somehow the Bonhommes knew of the gateway they could have used it and hidden the legendary treasure of the Cathars in the Sacred Library. Which would mean, the treasure would have had to have been knowledge, not gold which many treasure hunters in your world believe it to be.

"And that knowledge?" Charlotte did not want to say the word.

"That knowledge must almost certainly have something to do with Orme." Triskelion confirmed.

"So if the hart wasn't guarding scrolls inscribed with secrets of……" Charlotte couldn't bring herself to say the word.

"Orme," Triskelion helped her. "Yes you could be right. If at the beginning, placing the honourable hart on the summit of the library was a deliberate diversion by the ancients. And if I am right about the Bonhommes, the hart is almost certainly guarding such secrets today." The thought made Charlotte feel so much better. The fact that her dear hart was fighting for something so very valuable didn't justify the actions of the ancients, but it certainly made them more palatable.

"How does the Darkness know?"

"About the Bonhommes?" Charlotte nodded. "The Darkness had many agents in the Languedoc and the South of France when the Bonhommes fled. It wouldn't have been hard for them to follow the monks here, to Asscherugge. And the arrival of the Bonhommes here at Asscherugge was never a secret, quite the contrary in fact." Charlotte thought about what Triskelion had just told her, it did all seem to make sense but nothing he had repeated explained how her village was involved in this. Why had the Darkness chosen Aldeborie to open a personal gateway to her world, why not Ashridge or a village much closer to the Beacon such as Ivinghoe, Pitstone, Ringshall or Little Gaddesden? Triskelion as she knew he would, read her thoughts.

"Before you ask France Charlotte, the answer is we do not know. We have no idea why the Darkness has chosen Aldeborie." Charlotte thought again, to the mist and stories of the Aldbury Wizard. "Could it have anything to do with the man who people say made a pact with the Devil? After all, the mist is sitting over the site of his old house."

"Almost certainly," Triskelion agreed. "But it would not have been your gentleman who made the pact with the Darkness. Quite the reverse the Darkness would have made the pact with Mr Gravade, he would have been forced, he wouldn't have had a choice. The Darkness would have groomed him, tuned him for its own purpose. This though he could have done to anyone and just about anywhere. The question remains why here at Aldeborie and how did the Darkness know it could create a gateway, here in your village. If we weren't witnessing it with our own eyes we still would not believe it possible. And why did the Darkness bother with Gravade when there was a gateway only a breath away in front of St John the Baptist. How did the Darkness not know. It does not make any sense France Charlotte. There is some secret the Darkness has discovered that we know nothing about and to be honest that is what is worrying us more than anything else."

"And why now?" Charlotte thought.

"Yes why now, France Charlotte. Though Leht feels she might know the answer to that." Triskelion was about to carry on, when he stopped and stood up. "I think we have to go, "he said with some urgency. Charlotte stood, wincing with the effort. Flying towards them she could see the robin, presumably the one from the church. "Quick your budget," Triskelion urged. Charlotte again wincing with pain lifted first the little leather sack and then her necklace over her head and placed both with the map in the hidden hollow under the tree. By the time she had finished the robin was resting on a branch above them, the squirrel too was there. Triskelion turned to her. "Listen, our friend the robin informs me that there has been a lot of unusual activity in the churchyard this morning."

"What activity?" Charlotte wanted to know

"Just activity, the important thing is our friend believes the gateway to be safe. Come on I shall escort you." With that Triskelion started down the gradual descent across the field. Charlotte followed trying to control the arrow like shots of pain in her chest whenever she slipped or tried to breathe too deeply. Had Triskelion forgotten how she hurt? Aldeborie was, as she knew it would be a village of ghosts. On reaching the pond Triskelion grabbed her arm. "I will see you tomorrow France Charlotte, find a safe light and I will search you out, now go." Triskelion pushed her towards the churchyard gateway, adjacent to the entrance to the village school. The squirrel she saw was already running up the path to the porch. Charlotte started to follow, the robin flew above their heads to its normal seat on the castellated roof of the porch. As she ran Charlotte couldn't resist a glance towards the shop window, she saw Ashtynn and quickly looked away. The squirrel had already reached the stone and disappeared from view. Charlotte followed expecting at any moment for a hand to grab her or hundreds of gnombres to launch an attack from the shadows but nothing happened. She felt herself being gently pulled underground and then rising to after only a few seconds, arrive in her own world. Aldbury was in darkness, so different from the sun soaked village she had just left. A couple of cars passed, their headlights snaking along the churchyard wall, the second with music blaring from open windows. A few weeks back their presence would have made her nervous, that night their modern world disturbance was reassuring. The squirrel made a chaffing sound, it wanted to go and Charlotte started down the gravel path. Her steps sounded loud on the gravel and that was something she realised for the first time that was also different on the other side. In Otherworld, in her village no matter how heavily she trod she moved in silence. How could that be? Why hadn't she noticed it before?

Their passage back to the cottage was without incident and her ever faithful robin was there waiting for them. As had become her habit Charlotte thanked them both and bid each good night. The atmosphere in the cottage was warm, welcoming like clean bath water and Charlotte luxuriated in it. Never, she thought, do I want to leave all this. Tired she mounted the stairs trying desperately not to make a sound, in spite of her pain. She didn't fully relax until she was safe in her room and the door shut. Even then she felt it too risky to turn on the light. Before undressing for bed she stepped to the picture of the white hart. In the gloom she could just about make out the hart's kneeling figure and bowed head. The desperate scene pained her more than the physical pain from her ribs. Charlotte understood enough now to realise that if one day she found the hart no longer in the picture, the battle with the Darkness was lost. As long as he was there, as long as he remained in her picture there was still hope. She stroked the cold glass gently with her fingers, whispering as she did so, sending a message of encouragement to the friend she had never met. Fight not anger filled her belly and flowed through every vein. She changed into her pyjamas and got into bed, I'm ready she told herself, I'm ready she repeated as she prepared herself for sleep. How often had she said that? She glanced at her clock, it read quarter passed midnight. Her eyes closed and the second hand hadn't even completed a full circle before she was asleep. The robin skipped along the windowsill. Once again the little girl had lifted his spirits. Maybe he would see in another season, maybe he would have a chance to raise another family and see his young fly into the world. Maybe, maybe, maybe, yes only maybe but maybe was better than the never he'd been preparing himself for, only a few moons ago.

Chapter Sixteen

The Bonhommes, Their Treasure And The Sacred Library Of Evinghehou

The vicar took his time descending for breakfast that morning. He was struggling to understand his emotions and worried about an undercurrent of fear that refused to leave him. Why did he feel so scared and scared of what? The fear was like an infection, a virus slowly taking over his body , the problem was he couldn't simply take a couple of aspirin to deaden the pain. The only remedy he knew, was hidden somewhere deep within his mind. That morning he had a meeting booked with a couple who wished to get married in the church. Both were from the village and had met in the churchyard during the May Fair, several springs before. He personally liked the couple and it pleased him immensely that both had an emotional tie to the church. He had been looking forward all week to the meeting but now the morning had arrived, he hated the idea. He simply couldn't face a union with them. The feeling he knew made no sense and he did his best to fight it. He really did struggle, but in the end he gave in to his irrational fear and from the phone in the hall called the couple to cancel. He couldn't even bring himself to arrange another date, he simply told the future bride that he was feeling unwell and he'd phone again to reschedule a meeting when he felt better. She had been very gracious on receiving his news and had genuinely wished him a speedy recovery, but her inbred politeness had failed to hide her obvious disappointment and the vicar felt wretched as he replaced the receiver. From the hallway he entered the lounge. All around were the stubs of waxed out candles. One by one he collected them up and took the remains through to the kitchen. The candle in the window he replaced, here he wanted a light to burn twenty four hours, a light to guide those in trouble home. After lighting the candle he placed it on the sill. Not moving he watched the little flame burn. Although the air was still, deathly still the flame flickered as if caught in a breeze and went out. The vicar tugged at his beard in frustration and lit the candle again, not picking it up this time but bending down to light the candle where it sat. The flame flickered, grew in strength and then died as though something had snuffed out its life. The vicar made a third attempt this time cupping his hands around the candle. The flame rose, creating a blushed translucent light within the space of his cupped hands. When the heat from the flame became too much the vicar removed his hands and stood back. For a moment he thought his extra effort had succeeded, the flame from the candle shone with force. It remained that way for several seconds, the flame burning vertical, a symbol of life, before waving as if caught in a breeze and once again going out. Exasperated the vicar temporarily admitted defeat and went to the kitchen pouring muesli and milk into a bowl. Grabbing a spoon from a drawer he returned to the lounge and stood in front of the bay window, holding the bowl in his left hand and eating with the other. Across the fields, Aldbury was just visible. The now almost solid mist obliterated his view of most of the church, only the tower was truly visible. Was it him or did everything seem unusually quiet that morning? He listened intently, craving for some sort of sound, unconsciously he needed proof there was life. His clock, he'd been concentrating so hard he'd failed to notice the pendulum on his wall clock wasn't swinging with the passing of time. He looked at the clock face, the hands read seven minutes past midnight, that's when the pendulum had stopped.

Placing his bowl of cereal on the table he went over to the timepiece and opened the lower door. The weight which controlled the swing was still high, he could see no reason why the pendulum sat motionless. Starting the swing with his hand he closed the door and opened the door to the clock face to readjust the time, thirty five minutes past nine according to the radio. Satisfied he returned to his cereal. He walked back out to the kitchen and after the last mouthful washed his bowl and spoon under the hot tap. Once more he returned to the lounge, determined to successfully light the candle. Before doing so he checked the room for drafts, he could find none. To be sure he collected a sheet of paper from his case in the hall and standing in the centre of the room held the paper flat, high above his head. In exaggerated fashion he let the paper go watching it float gently to the floor, by the line of its fall there were no draughts he concluded. He returned to the bay window and confidently lit the candle once more, there was no practical reason why it should not light, not only light but stay alight. For at least four seconds the candle burned strongly, then a breeze or draught, as far as he could see from nowhere blew the flame out. The lighting of the candle was fast becoming an obsession for him. This time the vicar decided he would call upon his faith. He knelt in front of the candle and clasping his hands together prayed loudly for help in giving strength to his guiding light. Before standing he once more lit the so far, stubborn candle. The flame flickered for several seconds as though having a struggle with an invisible foe, before straightening and burning with a steadiness that you would expect in a room free from the movement of air . Triumphant the vicar stood, and stepped back slowly, worried that any swift movement from himself may extinguish the flame once more. His clock, the only sound in the room, ticked with a steady beat . Everything was normal, he breathed a sigh of relief. Before leaving for his church he took one last look out of the window. His eyes were drawn to the tree on the lawn. On different branches sat, he counted out loud. One, two, three, four, five, six magpies. Gold or hell he heard himself asking, why he had no idea. For a moment he stood there staring at the birds, stroking his beard as he pondered. He had an idea, he couldn't reason why, it was just something he felt he should do. Going to a table in his hallway, he picked up an intricately carved bronze cross. A parishioner had given it to him, she had, she'd told him purchased it for a very good price at a brocante in Belgium. It was just what he needed. Returning to the lounge he placed it on the sill beside the still burning candle in the window. With an exaggerated intake of air he turned, and purposefully strode out of the lounge, determined he wasn't going to be intimidated by a few birds. After picking up his case in the hallway he left the vicarage for his car and church. Inside, the flame, the guiding light, continued to burn. As the vicar drove out of the drive and onto the road to Aldbury a draught gathered from nowhere and catching the flame unawares, easily snuffed it out, there would be no guiding light for lost souls that day. At the same time the pendulum slowed, stopped and if you wanted to know the time, the old clock would tell you, seven minutes past midnight. A tremor shook the windowsill and after a struggle the bronze cross toppled, falling to the polished wood floor. The magpies remained motionless, each one staring in through the glass of the bay window.

Charlotte awoke just before her alarm was due to go off. She eased herself up and immediately winced with pain, an immediate reminder that Otherworld did exist. She felt exhausted and the thought that she would be traveling back that night added to the feeling. Within a few moments she had made up her mind that she would skip school that day. For her it was a big decision. She had never done such a thing before and even with having not yet lied to her parents, she already felt an overwhelming sense of guilt. They'd understand if they knew the truth she comforted herself. Turning off her alarm Charlotte settled back under the covers and pretended to be asleep. She knew if she wasn't down stairs by a certain time one of her parents would be knocking at the door. Normally it was her father but there was no market today so it could be either of them. Secretly she hoped it would be her mother as her father made rubbish hot chocolate. Lady luck was smiling on Charlotte that morning for a little later she recognised her mother's light tap on her door and even better the smell of hot chocolate, properly made with full fat milk and Chantilly cream. After waiting for a few seconds her mother opened the door and peered in.

"Charlotte it's getting late," she coaxed, "you'll miss the bus." Charlotte in return made an exaggerated groan, there was not a hope that her acting talents one day would grace the professional stage. "Are you ok?" Her mother asked, setting down the steaming bowl of hot chocolate beside her bed.

"I'm not feeling well, mum," was the most imaginative arrangement of words she could think of and as a consequence probably the most realistic sounding. Her mother leant over and placed the back of her hand on Charlotte's forehead.

"Well at least you haven't got a temperature," she told her and gently patted her daughter on the chest. Charlotte managed to withhold a scream but the expression on her face told her mother instantly that something was wrong. "Do you want me to call a doctor," a mother's natural response. "Where does it hurt?"

Charlotte felt she probably did need a doctor but not right at that moment. The last thing she needed that day was a doctor poking around her ribs. In response she tried to pass it off as wind, probably something she'd eaten. Her mother didn't look convinced and Charlotte had to put on her best pleading expression, to stop her from making the call. To her satisfaction her mother relented, begrudgingly maybe, but she was off the hook and breathed a painful sigh of relief. Her mother moved over to the long sash window and looked out at the dreary scene outside.

"I'll ask your father to phone the school," her mother said absent mindlessly. It was obvious something outside had caught her mother's eye. "Do you know there are six of those black and white birds sat in our cherry tree now, what do they want? Are you sure you haven't been feeding them, Charlotte?" Charlotte winced at her mother's question.

"No mum, promise." Her mother once again looked concerned.

"Are you sure you don't want me to phone for a doctor?"

"Yes mum I'm sure." All Charlotte wanted now was for her mother to leave her in peace, she wanted to count the magpies for herself, if there were seven it may be too late to return to Otherworld.

"Hmmm," her mother made an expression that told Charlotte she wasn't convinced. "Ok but I will check on you all day and If I think you're getting worse, I will call for a doctor. Understood?"

"Yes mum, ok." Charlotte gave in, no more wincing, she told herself, no matter how much pain she was in. Her mother went back to the window and waved her arms at the offending birds.

"They don't even move," she complained waving her arms wildly. "They simply ignore me."

"Leave them, mum. They're not doing any harm." If only that were true. Her mother dropped her arms and transferred her attention to Charlotte's medley of posters on the wall. Please go down stairs mum, Charlotte urged silently. It wasn't to be, not yet at any count.

"Nice looking boys those," her mother commented, admiring her daughter's recent collection of One Direction posters.

"Yes mum," Charlotte hoped she sounded fatigued and her mother would take the hint. Remembering her hot chocolate she reached down and gingerly picked up the bowl. After carefully stirring in the cream with a spoon she took a long slow sip. As expected it was delicious, so much better than the watery slop her father always served up. Such was her concentration on the contents of the bowl Charlotte had almost forgotten her mother was still in her room. Her mother's voice therefore came as something of a surprise.

"Your poor cerf," she heard her mother say and looking up saw that she was touching the picture of the white hart. Her mother was unaware of the English word, stag. "Having to look out of the window at those stupid birds all day."

"He's not looking out of the window, he's looking at the wall," Charlotte replied without thinking.

"You must be ill, he's looking towards the window silly. Are you sure you're ok?" Charlotte, was just about to argue back, how could her mother be so stupid, when she stopped herself. She remembered that her hart, when they had first moved in had looked out of the window. According to Leht she recalled it was the Darkness who had forced him to turn around the other way, to face west. She looked across at her mother who was staring at the picture. Her mother sensed her stare.

"You see," her mother said triumphantly, turning to look at her. "He's looking towards the window." At that moment Charlotte realised for the first time that it was only her that could see the change in the white hart. For everyone else nothing had altered.

"I must be going nuts mum, sorry," she said quickly, not wanting to arouse any suspicion.

"You must be," her mother agreed. "Are you well enough to eat some croissants?" And to Charlotte's relief her mother left the room not waiting for her answer.

Charlotte waited until she could hear her mother's steps on the tiled kitchen floor before getting out of bed and stepping lightly to the long sash window. She counted, her mother had been right there were six magpies sitting in the ornamental cherry and all were sat motionless, staring back at her. She quickly looked across to the trees in Tom's garden. Not a single magpie. She re ran the two rhymes in her head, gold or hell she asked herself, gold or hell. Having doubted her desire to return to Otherworld yesterday now morning had arrived it was quite the reverse, it was going to be torture to have to wait until midnight.

She wanted to do something to stop all this and put a stop to it now. What or how? She had no idea, just something. Not bothering with a raspberry she turned to the heart breaking image of the white hart. Just as yesterday it was on its knees, head bowed and facing west towards the wall dividing her parent's bedroom from hers. So only I can see the change she thought to herself, no one else can. How could she not have realised before. Her mother was in her room everyday cleaning and tidying up, even when it wasn't needed. Her mother would have noticed any change in the picture and would have been very vocal about it. That was for certain. No, the white hart's plight was for her eyes only. The realisation made her feel even closer to the poor beast if that was at all possible and she gently kissed the glass. At the same time she heard her mother's footsteps on the stairs. As quick as she could and without making a noise Charlotte got back into bed. She had just finished settling herself when there was a tap on the door and her mother entered the room. In her hands she carried a tray with two steaming hot croissants, a small bowl of curled butter, a small bowl of raspberry confiture and a knife. She laid the tray gently on her daughter's lap. As she did so her mother made a disapproving clicking sound with her tongue.

"Your hot chocolate is going cold." Charlotte looked down at the bowl, a skin had started forming on the surface.

"Don't worry mum I'll still drink it," and Charlotte reached for the bowl, careful not to upset the plate of croissants balanced on her outstretched legs.

"Mmm," was her mother's only reply and to Charlotte's immense relief, left the room. As her mother descended the stairs she contemplated going against her daughter's wishes and phoning the doctor. Charlotte never let her hot chocolate get cold. Like all those of French descent she believed any loss of appetite was a certain sign of illness and she was worried about doing nothing in case it turned out to be serious. After several minutes arguing with herself she decided to wait until she had checked on her daughter later that morning. If she hadn't eaten her croissants she would call the doctor. Content with her decision she relayed it to Charlotte's father who had his head buried deep in that morning's newspaper. There came a disinterested grunt. Sometimes the laid back attitude of English men infuriated her. As far as she could see the only thing that collectively excited nearly every Englishman was football and beer. How she missed the Gallic temperament of French men that was so enthusiastically displayed every day on French roads. Sentimental thoughts filled her head for just a few seconds before reality replaced such rose tinted memories. The Gallic temperament more than anything else brought turbulence she remembered. If truth be told she quite liked her unexcitable, laid back Englishman. Her heart warmed, he was a good man and blew him a kiss across the kitchen.

"The cost of petrol's going up again." A familiar voice came from behind the paper. Charlotte's mother smiled, what else could she want for.

Much to the vicar's annoyance on his arrival in Aldbury he found the few parking spaces in front of the church were all taken. Probably hikers or ghoulish tourists. Instead he'd have to park in front of the village hall or shop. The vicar cursed loudly, it was only a short walk but he had a lot to carry that morning and most of it was heavy. As he stepped out of the car he heard two people arguing. Completely out of character he decided to ignore them. People in Aldbury were always arguing these days, it was almost certainly because of the heavy and dark almost claustrophobic atmosphere the villagers were living in. Here it was early summer and apart from humanity there was virtualy no other life in the village. If you were a bird lover you were wasting your time putting seeds or nuts out. All the birds had left, the dawn chorus a distant memory. Taking a box of hymn books from his boot, he locked the car and with his head down hurried up the church path. He couldn't resist having the odd glance at the unexplained mist. So dense was it now that even close up it looked almost solid. He couldn't believe how Aldbury had been dropped by the media, he'd made several phone calls to various news desks but no one was interested. Aldbury was old news, she had been abandoned by television, radio and the press, nobody wanted to talk about or print a repeat of yesterday. The government had sent a scientific team to examine the strange phenomenon that was affecting the village and their results, in layman's terms were that although it was all very unusual, the phenomenon was simply a freak of nature. Like the University they agreed it was unusual but that was all. The vicar no longer agreed with their findings. As far as he was concerned they had been looking in the wrong direction. They were searching the scientific world when they should have been examining the spiritual one. He was more convinced than ever that there was something very evil at the root of what was happening in the village and in the last couple of days he felt that whatever it was had turned its attention on him personally. With the help of his faith he was determined to fight the entity but troublingly, with the way he felt, he was worried that he may already be starting to lose the battle. Worse still he felt the presence had somehow entered his home and if he wasn't careful it, whatever it was, would take over completely. He would feel safe inside his church, of that he was convinced, well almost.

Placing the box of books on the path, he reached into his case for the large and heavy bunch of church keys. As he opened the door he was welcomed by a fresh blast of cool air. The vicar inhaled with vigour, he never grew tired of the welcome the air in his church gave him. There was nothing like the cool blessed, for that's how it came across, air in a church to make you feel calm, at peace with yourself not to mention invigorated. The feeling that morning was to be short lived. On opening the second door and stepping into the main body of the church he sensed immediately that something was wrong. The air smelt foul and there was a definite unholy feel to the place that was more than simply his imagination. Placing the box of books on a small table he reached for the light switch. On turning the lights on, what he saw shocked him to the bone. The floor, laid with tiles from the original monastery at Ashridge was covered, completely covered by a dark swirling vapour. He knew without question the mist that had taken over the adjacent field and the foul smelling vapour covering the floor of his church were one of the same. The name mist he was now convinced wasn't the correct term. This was no mist, it was the Devil's own breath and for some reason it was assaulting him, his church and his village. His natural instinct was to leave, to run, to get as far away as he could from the brazen invasion but perhaps without realising it himself, he was stronger than that. He may be scared, more scared than he'd ever been but he wasn't going to go down without a fight, he owed that at least to his lord and to his flock. He'd lived with the feeling of fear for several days now and perhaps bizarrely was becoming accustomed to it. With a cool head he returned to the porch and locked the door, he couldn't let anybody else see this, he had to protect his parishioners even if it meant sacrificing himself. Returning to the main body of the church, the vicar picked up the box of hymn books along with his case and crossed the nave to his office. Here too the dark mist covered the floor but it was nowhere near as intense as the main body of the church. He sat at his desk and opened his diary. Thank God he thought, he'd cancelled his meeting with the couple planning their wedding, he couldn't let anybody see his church like this. There were two other entries entered in his diary for that day, both ageing parishioners whom he visited regularly. I won't let them down he decided, I'll visit them as normal. For the next hour he read, sorted, rearranged and rearranged again, papers that had been sitting on his desk for weeks. If you'd asked him he wouldn't have remembered a single paper he'd read that morning, it was simply a way of passing time. On three occasions he heard a person or persons try to open the main door. On the second occasion whoever it was knocked loudly, twice before leaving. Tiring eventually of shuffling papers the vicar left his office determined to have a closer examination of the evil that was fouling his church. Returning to the body of the church he strode down the nave passing beneath the restored yellow monochrome painting of John the Baptist preaching, stopping only when he'd reached the altar. For a short moment he stood motionless his hands resting on the altar rails, staring at the cross. With courage in his heart he knelt, and with the foul smelling mist almost reaching his waste the vicar for the second time that morning put his hands together and prayed. With his eyes fixed on the cross, he prayed for guidance on how to rid his church of the evil that had so audaciously entered the home of the lord. Forgiveness for his sins so he may fight freely, without weakness, the evil that he sensed was making Aldbury its home. For the safe return of those the breath of the Devil had taken and above all for the salvation of his parish and every living creature that lived within its boundaries. As he prayed the courage in his heart grew stronger and as it did so the dark mist that covered the floor of the church started to twist and turn, swirling back and forth as though it were a thousand serpents all eager to feast upon the flesh of the man daring to defy them. The movement only calmed when the vicar had finished praying and stood once more. Walking back down the nave he stopped at the pulpit mounted a few steps and stared down at the floor of his church. He couldn't be certain but he was pretty sure the foul smelling vapour, mist, cloud whatever you wanted to call it had risen a good few centimetres since the time he'd first entered. When would it stop? How could he stop it?

Charlotte finished her hot chocolate along with her croissants and almost immediately fell back to sleep. Both her mother and father checked on her over the next few hours and were glad to find her resting. At lunch, her mother arrived with a bowl of freshly made French onion soup and a crusty baguette fresh from the village shop, spread with French, crystal salted butter. Charlotte, feeling refreshed ate quickly and even asked for a second bowl. This was the sign her mother had been hoping for, her daughter was definitely on the mend. She spent the afternoon in and out of bed, checking on the magpies outside and whispering messages of encouragement to the white hart. There was no change with either. Tea was a steaming bowl of Beef Bourguignon. Her mother really was spoiling her. Like the soup the stew was accompanied with crusty buttered baguette and as with the soup Charlotte managed seconds. Her mother took great delight in seeing her daughter eat so well.

"School for you tomorrow my fille," she told her. Charlotte only hoped, more than her mother could ever know that, that would turn out to be the case. After tea, the hours dragged by. The sun it seemed to Charlotte was simply refusing to set. Eventually the leaden sky outside did dim enough to turn into darkness and Charlotte relaxed under its shadow, even falling into a state of semi-conscious. In a few hours she hoped she'd be woken by the familiar tapping of the robin on the window. Below she could hear her parents moving around the kitchen. On hearing their mundane actions a slow and unwanted realisation touched her. I hope this isn't goodbye she whispered and several tears escaped down her cheeks. It was her last thought before sleep, real sleep waved its wand and her eyes closed. Outside on the window sill, the robin hopped nervously, he was pleased that his prodigy was getting some rest. His little heart was beating furiously, every living creature except human it seemed sensed that something which could be life changing was about to take place.

From the pulpit the vicar returned to his office. The foul smelling vapour was definitely rising. Close to his office on the north side of the church, there was a modern mainly glass extension where coffee mornings and choir practice were held. For reasons unknown the extension was still free of any of the black stuff and he moved here to organise his briefcase. Returning to the old church he noticed that the vapour appeared to be thicker outside a low door almost opposite his office. The door he'd been told secured a small storage area though the key to the door had been missing as long as anyone could remember and the cupboard being of no significance and not needed had been forgotten about. The old door had simply become a feature in the church, nothing more. Looking at his watch, the vicar pushed his discovery to the back of his mind. He had to get going or he'd be late for his first appointment. His more elderly parishioners, he was well aware, tended to set their watches by his visit. Being of the 'old school' they were always punctual and expected the same in return. Locking the door behind him he strode down the path and crossed the road to his car. Both his appointments that morning were close to Tring Station. The first a widower he only knew as Mr Barnet lived in a terraced cottage. He'd entered the army halfway through the second world war and lived to tell his experiences, not that he ever did. Unlike many of his colleagues, after the war he'd remained in the army and the army consequently became his life. He married only when he retired, to a widow almost twenty years his senior. Too late to have children he lived, devoted to his wife until old age took her from him just a few years later. Another parishioner had told him of the man's plight and he had made a surprise visit, to check on him. Expecting the door to be slammed in his face the reverse happened. Mr Barnet had welcomed him in and ever since that day the two had become formal but close friends. Mr Barnet had never attended church but enquired always as to the church's business and never let the vicar leave without giving him a cash donation, usually totalling close to £50. The only request he'd ever made in return was a burial plot that captured the sun for most of the day. This the vicar had promised faithfully he would provide, though with the current residency of the thickening cloud, this was for the time being, a promise, if called upon, he would not be able to keep.

His second visit was to a widow, Grace who lived in a grand house almost opposite Mr Barnet's humble terrace. She was close to eighty and her boundless energy often left him exhausted after a visit despite him being nearly half her age. She still kept her own house and the only luxury she allowed herself was a weekly gardener, a man named Will. Unlike Mr Barnet, Grace regularly attended church and had a superb singing voice. She once told him that in her younger years she'd been an opera singer, though she only mentioned it the once, and cleverly diverted all questions on the subject thereafter. Her husband, the vicar found out from others, had been a brilliant physician. In her house there were photographs of him and they as a couple everywhere but she never mentioned her husband and he was careful not to pry. Though he'd known both the parishioners he was visiting that day for several years he knew scarcely anything about either of their pasts. Neither were secretive, just private and it was a trait that he'd come to recognise and respect from a certain generation. A generation that had based their lives on their duty to their country, not rights. A generation, no matter how successful, lived with humility and always did what they considered was the right thing, not what would be best for them.

Both visits went as expected and between them, Mr Barnet and Grace's positive attitudes lifted his spirits, driving back to Aldbury he felt almost refreshed. His mood improved even further when he found there was parking in the layby at the entrance to his church. He was glad he'd kept the appointments in his diary, they had primed him for whatever surprises waited for him inside his church. Locking his car he strode up the gravel path, key at the ready. At the heavy front door he paused, automatically his free hand reached for his beard. Without thinking he freed his beard and moved his hand to the crucifix hanging from a chain around his neck. With thumb and forefinger he caressed the gold cross still totally unaware of his action. Clenching the key he turned it in the lock and opened the door to the porch. The air smelt fresh, untainted. He was pleased to see there was still no violation in the porch. To be sure he turned on the light, no, for some reason the porch was unaffected. Or perhaps, he hoped the foul smelling vapour had gone altogether. His heart in his mouth the vicar opened the inner door with nervous expectation. What he saw made his heart leave his mouth and plunge to the floor. The repugnant odour hit him seconds after the sight of the dark vapour. Not only, what he considered to be "the breath of the Devil" still covered the floor of his church, it had got considerably higher. Quickly he strode across the nave to his office. Sitting at his desk he made a couple of notes on the day's visits. After he'd finished he realised he was hungry. Apart from a few biscuits that Grace had offered him and a bowl of cereal for breakfast he hadn't eaten that day. There was a tin on the bookcase and he opened it. Inside he found three slices of carrot cake left over from the last coffee morning. He took out all three and a teaspoon from his briefcase. Thank goodness he'd gone to cubs, there he'd learnt to always "be prepared" and he was, for cake anyway. After finishing off all three slices in quick succession he found himself still feeling hungry. One by one he opened the drawers to his desk. In the bottom left drawer he found amongst several bunches of keys and a tin opener an unopened packet of digestive biscuits. He took the packet of biscuits and split the wrapping using a pen. Taking two out of the packet he began to eat, Digestives were good but they were dry, he needed a drink. On top of a little used filing cabinet were a kettle three mugs and a jar of coffee. There was milk in the fridge in the glass meeting room but he didn't bother. Black coffee would suffice. Stirring the dark mixture he sat back at his desk to enjoy his coffee and biscuits. He was on his third biscuit when he remembered the contents of the third drawer. Opening it he shuffled around inside and pulled out three sets of keys. After one last inspection, leaving only the tin opener, he shut the drawer. Taking out another biscuit he examined the three bunches of keys. There were around ten different keys on each bunch, all attached fairly randomly to a ring in no obvious order of size or type. None were labelled. "Why on earth does a church need thirty keys" he asked himself. Picking up his mug of coffee he walked to the low cupboard opposite his office, where the mist appeared to be at its most dense. Kneeling, making sure he kept his cup of coffee above the vapour, one by one he tried each key from the first bunch. None matched though he did recognise one of the keys as being a spare to the vicarage. Removing it from the ring he placed the key in his pocket. After finishing his coffee he started on the second bunch. Just like the first, none of the keys from the second bunch fitted the old lock. Frustrated he dropped the second bunch on the floor and took up the third. Before trying any more he shifted his position, his knees were beginning to hurt and the top of his legs cramp up. Ready, he selected the largest and oldest looking key from the third bunch, and more for elimination than anything else, inserted it in the lock. The key seemed to fit perfectly but then so had several other keys before and that was as far as it had got, none of them would turn. The vicar started to turn expecting another false dawn, a sudden jar as metal came up against metal. Holding his breath the key continued to turn. There was resistance, yes but the key carried on turning as his hand told it to, and after a few seconds a loud click announced the cupboard door was unlocked. Surprised or shocked or both the vicar knelt motionless, hardly daring to breathe. Recovering his composure he slowly withdrew the key and started to turn the iron ringed handle. Everything worked, turning the ring just a little further he would have the door open. Even so he couldn't bring himself to do it. It's only a cupboard, he kept telling himself, and yet the courage that had given him strength that morning for some unexplained reason deserted him now. In its place, a nagging ice cold fear that prevented him from opening a simple cupboard door. Annoyed at his weakness he picked up all three bunches of keys along with his mug and retreated, for that was what it was a cowardly retreat, to his office. Frustrated, for all he had to do was open a door he sat back down in his chair to gather his thoughts. On the wall in front of him hung a print of a fifteenth century painting by Giovanni Bellini, depicting the decapitated head of John the Baptist, the forerunner. On the wall above the picture hung a tapestry, embroidered by a parishioner. It was a line from the bible, John 15:16 ,"Ye have not chosen me, but I have chosen you." At that moment, the message felt rather personal. The vicar lowered his gaze. The painting did nothing to lift his mood and he considered reversing it but that would, he felt, be admitting defeat. This simple defiance of his fear he found gave him courage and rather than shy away from the painting he started to take it in, studying it as he'd never done before. It made him think of the sacrifices that people had made over the centuries in the name of his faith. Many, the ultimate sacrifice as had John the Baptist. The numerous martyrs who preferred death to denying what they believed in. He began to feel ashamed, how could he be so weak. He dug deep inside himself, searching for a new resolve to defeat his weakness only to find strength continued to desert him, he couldn't even bring himself to rise out of his chair.

The vicar had no idea how long he sat in his office fighting his own personal battle. It must have been hours not minutes for when he broke from his fight with his fear, outside he could see from his window, shadows were darkening faster than he cared for. Soon, very soon it would be nightfall. With effort he rose from his chair, he was safe in the house of God he told himself, I will not let this demon defeat me. His strongest desire was to leave his church, lock the door and drive home perhaps picking up a curry en route. Though so very tempting he was determined that that wasn't going to happen, not just yet anyway. From his office he went to each room and the main body of his church turning on every light that he knew existed. For good measure he also lit a few candles. When done, he strode to the altar and kneeling prayed for nothing more than courage. Whether it was a trick of the mind or a higher being answering his prayers, something resembling courage slowly crept through his veins. Turning he almost ran back down the nave, playfully kicking out at the offending mist. Anybody watching may have thought the vicar had gone quite mad, when the opposite was true.

"Come on then," he shouted loudly as he went. "Is this the best you can do."

He couldn't remember leaving the nave to confront the low cupboard door that only hours earlier had troubled him so. To be honest he didn't really care for those few lost minutes, all that mattered was, he was here, kneeling in front of the door. Defying the fear that he was convinced the Devil had planted within him.

"Come on then," he shouted again and turning the handle pulled the door hard towards him.

Mrs Fowler was surprised to see the lights on in the church, not only on but so many. Money was tight and the vicar was well known to be frugal. So much so that some people, rather unkindly suggested he invented the word. Mrs Fowler knew this not to be the case, a retired accountant who helped the vicar with his books, she respected the vicar's sensible attitude to money. His only excesses, it could be argued, were food and drink but his extravagance in this area meant that attendees at his regular coffee mornings had doubled and this had gone on to equate to more 'bums on seats,' at his services. As a result, the amount in the collection at each service had almost doubled, making a tidy profit. When all things were considered, and in harsh reality, this was what really mattered if the church was to fulfil its commitments. The second thing that bothered Mrs Fowler was that the vicar hadn't mentioned to her any activity that was to be held in the church that evening and he always kept her abreast of all church activities. She was sure, quite sure that he'd mentioned nothing to her about this evening and judging by the number of lights, whatever the activity was it must be big. More put out than anything else she decided to take a look for herself, she didn't like not being kept in the loop. Leaning her bike against the churchyard wall, beside the lych gate she walked purposefully up the path to the door only, to her surprise to find it locked. She shook the door to make sure it wasn't just jammed but no, it was definitely locked. Standing back she listened to see if she could hear any activity taking place inside. There wasn't a sound. Perhaps the vicar had simply forgotten to turn out the lights. With so many on it was hard to believe but at the moment it was the only rational explanation. Mrs Fowler shivered, a feeling she couldn't understand kept telling her something wasn't right. Maybe it was the cold blackness that everyone referred to as mist, she never felt comfortable when near it and although she would never admit it to anybody, the phenomenon scared her. There was something sinister about it and she didn't believe the scientists who put it down to a 'freak of nature.' A sudden urge to leave gripped Mrs Fowler, it felt almost as though something was warning her off, something with ill intent in mind. As she turned to leave she saw the vicar's car parked beside the lych gate, how had she not spotted it when she arrived? This confirmed the vicar was still in the church, he must be if his car's there. Fighting her mounting urge to get going she knocked on the stout door one more time, this time, as loudly as she could. She stepped back and waited for a reaction but none came, no sign of movement and definitely no sound. Something was wrong of that she was sure, but with some shame she decided it wasn't going to be her that found out what it was. After one last knock she hurried down the path to her bike and mounted to cycle to her cottage on the Ivinghoe road.

At first the vicar thought the cupboard door must be jammed for it still wouldn't open. As a last resort he turned the handle almost full circle and that did it, the door swung open so easily he fell sideways with the unexpected motion. A dark foul smelling vapour billowed out into the passageway and for a moment he thought Satan was about to smother him to death. He closed his eyes tight waiting for what he believed to be the inevitable, holding his breath to try and keep the foul smelling vapour from entering his lungs. He waited and waited but nothing happened, the ever increasing pain in his chest told him he was still alive. Pushing himself up he opened his eyes and unable to hold his breath any longer inhaled in one long drawn desperate gasp, welcoming the sensation of cool air, God's air as it entered his lungs. Using the open cupboard door for leverage he pulled himself back onto his feet and surveyed the scene around him. He'd found the source of the mal odorous vapour, twirls of the black stuff were rising from the floor in the long locked cupboard. He crouched in front of the opening and felt the floor nervously with the flat of his hand. The floor he found like much of the church was laid with stone slabs. Growing in confidence he ran his left hand over the surface pressing down in places where the mist was rising more densely. There were obvious cracks between the stones and as he pressed down on one there was the slightest of movement. The stone slabs he realised were tightly laid but they weren't set, they were loose. That was odd, very odd. There was something underneath and whatever it was, this was where the vapour was coming from. The vicar made up his mind there and then that he was going to find out but not right at that moment, not at night. He'd return in the morning and take a closer look. For now though after both the mental and physical exertions of the day he needed to eat, almost certainly Chinese, he also desperately needed to sleep. Heaving himself up he returned to his office to collect his case. After doing so he went to turn off the light when a voice in his head stopped him. To turn off the light would be a mistake the voice told him. The vicar paused, this wasn't his mind telling him this was the voice of a stranger, an entitas, a presence and most importantly he sensed a friend. A friend that wanted to help him, could this be the divine guidance he'd been seeking? It made sense. He remembered his teachings, 1 John 1:5, "God is light and in him is no darkness at all." This was the house of God, that night he knew no matter what the cost financially his church must have light, there must be no darkness. He left the light on, the same with the passage light and every other light in the church, not one light could he bring himself to turn off. Finally he was standing outside, exhausted, the fresh night air a sensory relief from the contamination within his church. It was never a feeling he'd expected to experience for the church was his place of work, the home to his faith, his maker. It's where you went to find peace, not confrontation. Before he'd always found relief inside his church not outside. With his mind diverted he thumbled to retrieve the keys from his left hand, the same hand that was also clutching his case. Lack of coordination caused the keys to drop to the ground in front of the door. Cursing loudly the vicar stooped to pick them up. As he did so the lights from the windows picked out a white stone slab, the slab where an old sundial had once stood. On the slab, so neatly positioned it surely must have been placed there lay a large feather. Oily black with long shades of white, the vicar recognised it instantly as coming from a magpie. They weren't his favourite birds at the moment and he brushed the feather onto the grass in disgust. The sight of the empty slab annoyed him. People stole anything these days, nothing was sacred. He wondered where it was now, whether the thief would ever benefit from a conscience. The theft of the sundial was why he locked the church at night. Locking a church went against everything he believed in. A church was a place of sanctity, of refuge, if you needed God's help he and his house should be available twenty four hours a day, not between eight in the morning until six in the evening. A church was where you could talk to God without being judged, where you could ask for help when you were desperate and if you were desperate at midnight then God's house should be at your disposal. The vicar placed the key in the lock, he couldn't turn it. The same voice that dissuaded him from turning off the lights was now doing the same with the door. Something or someone was telling him that his church was going to be needed that night, that it had to remain open. Praying he was doing the right thing the vicar withdrew the key from the lock without having turned it. That night he would leave his church open for whoever needed it. He prayed the voice in his head wasn't the Devil playing tricks. Too late if it is, he thought and strolled down the gravel path to his car, swinging the keys in his hand as he went, a theatrical but false display of confidence. Inside, his car felt like a fortress, he felt safe, secure, nothing could hurt him. Of course he was wrong and it was this very same sense of security that often caused everyday sensible people to drive so dangerously. He sat back in his seat relaxing fully for the first time that day. He turned on his radio and settled down to some good old fashioned rock playing on Absolute Radio. He put the key in the ignition but as with the door he couldn't bring himself to turn it, or better put he didn't feel the need to turn it. As the notes of Led Zeppelin's Stairway To Heaven filled his car, the vicar gazed along the path to the church door. He hoped he was doing the right thing leaving the door unlocked. He couldn't live with himself, if because of his non action something was stolen or worse still, vandals defaced anything that was sacred inside. He simply couldn't leave his church unprotected, he couldn't leave his church unlocked and not watch over it. He would spend the night in his car, in some ways he felt more comfortable here than in his vicarage. Since the magpies had started invading his garden the vicarage hadn't felt the same. Golden Earring's Radar Love was the next song to play followed by Mike Oldfield's Tubular Bells by which time the vicar was already asleep.

Charlotte was ready for the tapping on her window. She didn't feel nervous or scared, a little apprehensive, yes but overall she felt determined. Whatever the outcome she wanted the uncertainty to be finished. When the tapping came she was dressed and ready within seconds. Before going outside she turned on the light in the lounge as before. In just over a minute she was standing on the brick path where both the robin and squirrel were waiting for her. On seeing her the squirrel didn't hesitate, it started along the brick path towards the road. Charlotte followed only to stop suddenly at the sound of an approaching car. The car passed, the occupants unaware of the young girl crouching behind a wheelie bin. She waited for several more seconds before taking to the road, running as fast as she could without making a noise. She'd lost valuable seconds and throwing caution to the wind ran around the corner before the shop, without checking first to see if anybody was there. Luck that night was on her side, there was no one. She knew Ashtynn was no longer in this world and therefore she wouldn't see her suspended in the window, however she still couldn't help feeling her eyes were there following her every move. Even if she was being watched, Charlotte was past caring. She was prepared for Ashtynn but what she wasn't prepared for was seeing the lights on in the church. This was completely unexpected. Whenever she'd transcended before the church had always been in darkness. She hesitated before crossing the road, not sure what to do, the squirrel she saw had already crossed and was running back and forth, a sure sign that it was stressed. Her biggest enemy she knew, was time and time was the one thing she couldn't change, she had to work within its laws. It took just seconds for Charlotte to analyse and prioritise the risks and the next moment she was crossing the road to the lych gate. Her second shock was finding the vicar's car parked in the layby before the lych gate. What was going on? Was the vicar still in the church? If he was she'd have to take a risk in him coming out and seeing her, within minutes the gateway would close. On instinct, she crouched as she ran past the vicar's car and started up the gravel path towards the front door of the church. As she ran, as she always did she looked up at the clock on the church tower. To her relief there was the hand-held serpent writhing thirteen o'clock, normality at last after a night of surprises! With the lights on in the church, she was worried at any moment the door in front of her may open. It didn't, the door remained shut and the next moment Charlotte felt herself being pulled under on her way to Otherworld.

She arrived breathless, with no idea how much time she'd had left before the gateway had started to close, Charlotte knew it couldn't have been much. Despite the dangers she felt relaxed now she was standing in the ghostly apparition of Aldeborie. The agitated moves of the squirrel refocused her attention. Gathering her thoughts she hurried down the gravel path to the lych gate. There was the vicar's car, what was it doing there, she wondered again and what was he doing in the church past midnight? Maybe she'll never know. She tapped the car door only to see her hand pass straight through. Her subconscious had already worked out the car was an image only. Taking advantage she put her head through the car door to take a quick peep inside. She immediately felt guilty for doing so and went to withdraw when she spotted the radio, it was on or to state it correctly, had been on when the hour struck XIII. Had then the vicar been sitting in his car, had he seen her and worst of all if he had would he tell her parents? In many ways, at that moment the thought of facing her parents was more daunting than facing the Darkness. Quickly she moved on. In the bowed shop window Ashtynn hung motionless, only this time Charlotte knew what to look for and sure enough, Ashtynn's eyes she saw followed her as she passed. Although seeing her eyes move was unsettling, it no longer scared her, she was getting tough. As she drew close to her cottage her blood ran cold, there was no light, she'd turned the light on in the lounge only moments before and now it was off, there was no light. She had not been prepared for this and panic started rising from her stomach. One of her parents must have discovered the light on and turned it off. What were the chances of that happening, virtually none, she'd only been gone for a few minutes. No matter, it had happened. Quickly she needed to find another light. The light was on in the house opposite and Charlotte ran to it but just as she was ready to pass through the door the light went out. Instinctively she ran to the next light, this being in the house where she'd spent her very first light night. Again, just as she was about to prepare herself for entry the light went out. Charlotte couldn't believe her misfortune, what was happening, then a thought struck her which sent her cold. Triskelion had told her that nothing inside an image could be changed if it was connected in some way to the outside. Therefore you couldn't change channels on a television, you couldn't turn on a tap and you shouldn't be able to turn a light on and off. Then what the hell was happening, how were these lights being turned off? That didn't matter for now, with a fast growing sense of urgency she knew she had to get to safety. Something was afoot and she had the uncomfortable feeling she was being played with rather like a cat with a mouse before the kill. Lights still shone from houses on the opposite side of the pond, in fact three houses in a row all had lights shining behind closed curtains. Charlotte with the squirrel beside her took off, running without looking back. She had to get under a light and fast. Just as she drew level with the first house the light behind the curtain disappeared, it hadn't been turned off there's a subtle difference and Charlotte was sensitive enough to notice. Her heart sank and she moved to the second house where the same thing happened, with little hope she moved on to the third house and as she now expected the light inside was extinguished by someone or something. Worse still she thought she saw something, a shadow move inside. The image should be empty, nothing should be moving inside and if it was it can't have been from her world. Spinning round she saw that lights were still shining bright in The Greyhound and ran across the road ignoring the sharp stabs of pain in her chest. The pub was her last hope. Even in her current plight Charlotte worried quite illogically that she was nowhere near eighteen and may get into trouble. The issue never came to fruition, for as she approached The Greyhound, one by one the lights in the windows went out including the lights illuminating the pub sign. Charlotte stood rigid, surrounded by darkness, she looked around wildly. She was fast running out of options and there was no doubt this time, shadowy figures were moving in every darkened window and looking up the road to Ivinghoe, shadows that should be still were moving too, moving towards her.

The squirrel who had been running in circles around her feet started back towards the village green and Charlotte having run out of options followed it. Within seconds she knew where it was heading, the church. Of course the church, a "safe place" and it's lights were on. The squirrel almost skidded to a halt in front of the church door and turned back towards Charlotte who was only just inside the churchyard gate and starting to run up the path. The squirrel turned its head the other way, looking over its shoulder, checking there were to be no nasty surprises. The foul black mist twisted and turned, thrashing manically, never had he seen it looking so angry. Stones flew past his head as Charlotte came skidding to a halt beside him, crying out in pain. He looked up and saw that her face and worse still her eyes expressed a mounting fear and fear, he knew, was their biggest enemy. The little girl had to control her fear or they would both be meeting their afterlife. He rubbed against her legs and standing rested his two front paws on the church door. Looking down Charlotte knew exactly what her little friend wanted of her and verging on panic threw herself at the heavy wooden door expecting to pass through. Her ribs screamed as her side slammed against solid wood. A natural reaction to the pain, tears rolled down both her cheeks. The squirrel was scrabbling at the door, he couldn't pass through either. In a flash Charlotte tuned the handle, the door gave way and she tumbled inside, followed by the squirrel who jumped nimbly over her. As shadowy figures gathered outside she managed to close the door and drop the latch after which an uncomfortable silence settled. Laying on her back on a large doormat, Charlotte stared up at the porch ceiling. A bright light blinded her, she didn't care, it was such a lovely feeling being blinded by a light.

She lay on the mat for several more minutes, not daring to make a sound let alone move. She was worried, whatever it was outside would be listening, attempting to hear her breathing even though it was obvious to whoever had been stalking her where she was hiding. The absolute silence scared her more than noise, at least with a sound you could have a go at guessing what was happening, where your enemy were, but with silence you had not a clue and that was far worse. Eventually more because her muscles were starting to protest than courage Charlotte slowly got to her feet. She again found herself wondering what the vicar had been doing in the church at such a late hour. And why had the door been unlocked? Maybe she'd find out, for now though she was simply thankful it had been. Not wanting to spend all night in the porch she tried the inner door. That too was unlocked, the squirrel she noticed was holding back making no attempt to follow her. After what had just happened Charlotte thought she was ready for anything but she was wrong. Peering through the partially opened door the immediate assault on her sense of smell made her retch. Some deep inborn instinct told her the smell was of decomposition, to be more exact of rotting flesh, human flesh. Rather than close the door she felt strangely drawn to find the source of the offending odour. She wasn't sure what she expected to find, it was certainly not a dark heavy cloud or vapour covering the floor of the nave. She immediately worried for the safety of the vicar, was he lying under the slow swirling mass that covered the floor. Worse still was it his body that was the cause of the wretched smell. Instinctively she looked down at where she was standing. The vapour with the door slightly ajar should be pouring into the porch but it wasn't, an invisible barrier or something similar was holding it back. Charlotte stood wondering what to do next. Seeing the vapour made her question whether they'd be safe inside the church. She still believed they would be but now, on seeing the malodorous cloud, there was an element of doubt. And how was she going to get out, would outside really be safe when daylight came. If the mist, for she was sure that was what it was, could enter the house of God, surely the Darkness could find a way of getting around daylight, after all there were lights on in the church and the foul smelling cloud hadn't been repulsed. There was one big difference between the mist outside and the mist, vapour whatever you wanted to call it, inside the church. Outside the mist was restless, it swirled with an aggression that suggested it wanted to do battle, here inside the church in contrast the vapour though foul smelling was distinctly idle, hardly moving at all. Holding her nose Charlotte decided against her better judgment to take a closer look. Slowly she opened the door wide and stepped inside. The vapour came up almost to her waist and like any vapour it simply moved out of her way as she moved through it. Apart from the smell, now she was standing in it, she didn't feel uncomfortable. Slowly she walked up the nave. On drawing level with the Pendley Chapel she stopped. The effigy of Wodewose was completely submerged by the vapour. For a reason she couldn't explain she didn't feel like going any further and retraced her steps. The door to the passage leading to the vicars office she noticed was open and she was tempted to take a look. Stepping into the passage she noticed immediately that here the vapour was that much denser. She also observed that here too all the lights were on. What had the vicar been doing. She couldn't help noticing also that a door, a very old looking door to a cupboard was wide open. She hadn't even noticed a cupboard being there before and certainly had never seen the door open. She bent over cautiously trying to see inside but the vapour was too thick and almost filled the entire space within. If anything the cupboard appeared to be the source of the vapour. She thought about closing the door and decided better of it. She'd leave things as they were. She wasn't frightened but the foul smelling vapour and the strange atmosphere was starting to unsettle her. She'd done with exploring and decided to return to the porch where for some reason the sanctity of the church remained untainted.

In the porch Charlotte found the squirrel calmly sitting on a stone bench looking completely unconcerned. Perhaps it knows more than I do she hoped. Feeling tired she joined the messenger. She had no option than to simply wait until dawn. Being a porch there were no soft surfaces on which to lie or rest. She thought about going back into the church and retrieving some kneeling cushions but simply couldn't face the atmosphere a second time. Resting her elbows on her knees she cupped her hands and slowly leaned forward until her head lay comfortable in her hands. It wasn't ideal and her ribs complained at the slightest movement but it would have to do, she must try and get some sleep and closed her eyes. The squirrel watched her intently and seeing an opportunity gently eased itself onto Charlotte's lap. There was no protest from the little girl and he curled into a ball to sleep. Charlotte welcomed the warmth and she found the squirrel's presence on her lap comforting. She too drifted into an unlikely sleep.

Charlotte was sure she was dreaming. She was hearing the sound of a latch being lifted. For the last few hours she'd drifted in out of sleep, interrupting a number of vivid dreams and the sound of the latch must be yet another. The noise came again followed by the sound of hinges that could do with a touch of oil. Cold air brushed against Charlotte's face and the sudden change in temperature brought her round. This wasn't a dream, the church door was open and somebody had opened it. She jumped up and the squirrel leapt into the air, her ribs stabbed at her flesh and her heart felt as though it was trying to leave her body via her mouth. She didn't know whether to shout or scream such were the myriad of emotions along with the pain, pain that hit her like a boxer's punch.

"Sorry France Charlotte, did I scare you?" Triskelion stood, framed in the doorway. Charlotte fought with her emotions, she wanted to cry, she was so pleased, so relieved to see her ghost and yet she wanted to hit him hard, she was so angry at him for frightening her so. It was becoming a habit. In the end she did neither, she just collapsed back down onto the stone bench, limp from self-torment.

"Triskelion," was all she managed to say, followed with some effort. "How did you know I was here?" As if in answer the robin hopped onto the porch step.

"The robin," Triskelion confirmed, "are you alright?" Charlotte wondered what sort of answer Triskelion expected from her. Couldn't he see she wasn't. He apparently could read her mind after all, could he not read her emotions too. She'd been scared half to death several times, her ribs screamed fire and she'd slept, sat on a hard bench with a squirrel on her lap. In the end she decided to say nothing, she'd let Triskelion work her thoughts out for himself. Charlotte waited for words of understanding, perhaps words of sympathy too but Triskelion much to her annoyance remained silent. Unlike him, she had no idea what he was thinking, she was at such a disadvantage.

"You need to see something."Charlotte glad to flex her muscles, stood up and opened the inner door to reveal the foul smelling cloud covering the floor of the church. Triskelion stepped just inside the door, the vapour Charlotte observed unlike with her swirled wildly about his form as though it were violated by his presence.

"It has begun," Triskelion spoke slowly, his voice gravelly.

"What has?" Charlotte asked, her voice full of trepidation, she had never heard Triskelion speak in such a tone.

"The Darkness, the Darkness has decided to make its move." Charlotte wasn't sure what she'd expected for a reply, now she had heard it she realised she had been waiting for this all along.

"Is the vapour the Darkness and why has it entered the church?" Charlotte already knew the answer to her first question but sought confirmation.

"Yes although the vapour is a tool of the Darkness for the Darkness has no form, only presence. "As to why it has entered a church, I'm not sure, I wish I knew. It may simply be a demonstration of force but worryingly I feel there is more to it than that." Charlotte told him about how she came to be in the church and that the vapour seemed to be coming from an old cupboard that she'd never seen open before. She wanted Triskelion to see it but he showed no interest. No that's wrong, to put it correctly he showed no desire to go any further into the church.

"There must be some connection with the church and the house of Gravade." Triskelion made no attempt to hide his thoughts. "Normally the Darkness would not be able to enter a church. It may be another reason why it has chosen your village to establish a presence in your world." Silence fell, Triskelion appeared to be thinking. Charlotte sensed that he was very, very worried. The squirrel hopped outside. Its action spurred Triskelion into action. He grabbed Charlotte's arm. "Come France Charlotte, we must go, if the Darkness is here, it is not safe for you." You neither Charlotte sensed. Triskelion handled her gently out of the door into the churchyard. To her surprise it was raining, that gentle summer rain that refreshes so deliciously, though of course it didn't. The rain in the moonlight was pleasant on the eye but the droplets smelt of nothing, there was nothing fresh about the liquid falling to earth.

"Come," Triskelion led Charlotte down the path to the pond. Leaving the churchyard they turned left to follow the road to Evinghehou. The trials of the night were still vivid in Charlotte's mind and she searched for where she'd tried to find safety under light a few hours earlier. Her mind must have been playing tricks, for in the three houses and The Greyhound lights were blazing just as she'd first seen them. That is before somebody or something had turned them off. Triskelion was reading her thoughts and felt obliged to put the little human child out of her misery.

"You're questioning how the lights were extinguished, France Charlotte?" Charlotte looked up at Triskelion's blank face.

"Yes, you told me that anything connected to the outside couldn't be changed within an image."

"That's correct." Charlotte thought for a few seconds, was she being stupid or was she missing something.

"Then how were the lights turned off?"

"They weren't."

"They were, I saw them go out, that's how I ended up in the church. I had nowhere else to go." Didn't Triskelion believe her, did he think she was imagining things?

"The lights were not turned off, France Charlotte, they were on all the time. You let the Darkness play with your mind, it told your mind what to see." Triskelion's answer stunned her into silence, it had all seemed so real. Worse still if the Darkness could take over her mind like that, what else could it make her see or what frightened her more, do. Triskelion sought to reassure her. "Do not worry, it is not easy for the Darkness to take over your mind, normally it can only influence. It would have taken a supreme effort for it to have done so last night and a sign that it is wary of you." Charlotte was about to ask another question but Triskelion took her arm once again. "Let's leave the village first, then we can talk." Charlotte nodded and hastened her pace. The squirrel was already metres ahead, she'd learnt that night that her little friend was more than just a messenger. He'd gained her new found respect.

On reaching the oak, Triskelion appeared to relax. His manner softened and his previously tense arms swung loosely at his sides. He stood in silence, his blank eyes watching over Aldeborie whilst Charlotte, taking care, reached under the tree for the budget. As last time, she found there was a small amount of liquid in the leather bag. She'd have to take extra care, she'd be carrying a piece of Leht with her. Not only did it feel strange but the responsibility scared her a little and Charlotte had had enough of that feeling to last her a lifetime. Reaching into the bag she lifted out her necklace and pendant. Although it had been lying in liquid when she pulled it free, as before and like the map, she found it to be bone dry and also, as last time the little charm was noticeably warm to the touch. Carefully she placed the necklace over her neck and joined Triskelion who was still looking across the field to the rooftops of her village. The rain continued to fall and although it was approaching daylight, the light with the covering of clouds was still extremely weak. Charlotte hadn't a watch but even without one she could tell by the freshness it was still early. She looked across to Triskelion who remained motionless, watching over her village though his mind she sensed was elsewhere. She wanted to ask him a question, one that had been bothering her for some time. After tonight her question couldn't wait any longer.

"Triskelion, the Darkness must be watching me, it must know where I live." The thought worried her perhaps more than anything, at the back of her mind always were her parents. She'd prefer the afterlife to losing them. Triskelion didn't move, he didn't look at her and made no attempt to respond. As she waited Charlotte thought of something else. It was stupid of her but she'd never really fully connected the magpies with the mist and the Darkness. She'd grown so used to their presence, she no longer considered them dangerous, if anything they were there to be mocked. Now after what had happened during the night, re-establishing the connection made her worried for her parents. Triskelion, unmoving continued to stare across Aldeborie or to be precise to the square tower of the church. He was questioning the presence of the foul vapour, such an act wouldn't be for bravado only, there had to be a greater cause, what could it be? The question frustrated him, it also worried him deeply. He heard France Charlotte and read her fears. He didn't really want to answer for she may not respond well. He had no choice.

"The Darkness hasn't been following you, not until recently anyway." Charlotte waited for Triskelion to expand, to explain what he meant but as was his way silence followed. Obviously, Charlotte thought, Triskelion felt that was a good enough answer. Why did he never explain anything fully, how she wished she could read his mind.

"What about the magpies in my garden, how do you explain them?" There came another very long pause before Triskelion answered.

"The magpies aren't watching you," he answered finally. "They're watching the cottage, to be precise the room with the picture of our Guardian."

"My room?"

"Yes, so the robin informs us, Leht is pleased you're in that room, you're being a great help to the Guardian." Charlotte said nothing, she wanted Triskelion to continue, there were too many questions attached to what he'd just told her. She always assumed it was her the magpies were interested in, if it wasn't why did they watch her at the bus stop and what about the vicar? Charlotte once again found herself waiting for an explanation. It wasn't to be, instead Triskelion changed the subject. "France Charlotte, I think I mentioned that a Snook is visiting the wood today, they tell their stories only at dawn or dusk. Before we do what we are programmed to do today I would like you to hear one speak, for the Snooks have confirmed it is indeed you who has been chosen. If you wish to ask a question or two afterwards then please feel free." The way Triskelion spoke, Charlotte understood that she wasn't being offered an option. And what did he mean when he said she had been chosen? Chosen by whom? At the same time she was kicking herself. Today was probably the most important day of Triskelion's life, maybe even his last. She didn't want to contemplate the latter but the fact that she hadn't even had the thought to ask if he was ok was unforgivable. How could she have been so insensitive.

"It's fine France Charlotte, I feel fine about today, I am feeling strong. It is good that we are taking action. There has been far too much debate, far too much inaction. It is important to act on one's convictions. It is because we haven't had the courage to act on our convictions before, because of indecision, because of lethargy we are where we are today. My heart, far from shrinking with fear, burns strong to think that my action will thwart the Darkness and provide hope, maybe even a future for life in both our worlds. Come we must make haste, it is important you meet with a Snook." Charlotte wished she had Triskelion's conviction, his courage. She knew that fear was a weakness, a weapon of the Darkness, no matter she couldn't help the feeling, and she didn't feel ashamed.

Wodewose greeted them as they reached the treeline, he must have been watching them all the time, perhaps like her he was afraid of what was to come. She already knew he was afraid to leave his wood. There was no Alasdair or Cathasach to greet them and she hoped it wasn't because of their injuries from the battle yesterday. If Triskelion read her thoughts he didn't say anything and this only increased her concern for the two.

"Morning France Charlotte," Wodewose smiled his widest smile in greeting but Charlotte wasn't fooled, she could see her shaggy friend was nervous. Triskelion nodded his greeting to Wodewose and started up the scarp slope. Charlotte tried to hide her pain at the scramble and failed, more than once, Wodewose watching her and wearing a concerned expression offered assistance. When the land flattened out, Triskelion led them left to follow the rim of the escarpment. Their route took them across long forgotten holloways, paths that had once had a purpose, lay abandoned, silent, one or two for centuries and reclaimed by nature.

After passing below the shadowy National Trust buildings Triskelion bore right heading into the densest part of the wood, Sallow Copse. Charlotte had a feeling she knew where her ghost was leading them and she was right. It was the grass covered glade with the fallen beech and the stump backed by foxgloves which Charlotte thought resembled a woodland throne. On the map she remembered the glade as being marked as Gemot. This time the curtain of foxgloves backing the stump were in full flower and their proud and colourful stature created an even more royal scene. On the tree stump where Charlotte had rested last, sat a figure dressed in a tunic and trousers of beech leaf green complete with a poppy red trim. He resembled a human yet everything about him was crooked as though he'd been badly put together by his maker. His face was pale, long and bony with a long crooked nose and deep set dark eyes. On his head he wore a droopy coned hat also with a red trim. His shoes were not green or red but brown and curled up at the front. Sat on the "throne," his knees were raised, supporting what looked like a very old book. The book lay open and from it the Snook was reading a story to a small group of animals and birds gathered in the glade. None of his audience seemed to be paying too much attention, though none made a noise and so perhaps that particular observation was unfair. Charlotte was astonished to hear the Snook telling a story in her native language, French and with an accent and using expressions that she recognised were unique to her region.

"Do all the animals and birds understand French?" Charlotte whispered to Triskelion.

"No, when the Snook speaks, those who are listening hear his words in their own tongue and dialect." That's incredible, Charlotte thought and settled down to listen. The story the Snook told, she recognised at once. It was folklore and came from a village just outside Dunkirk. It was about a fish, a pike that lived in a lake and was so big it ate small children. What a tale to tell just before breakfast, not that anyone seemed to care as most of the audience were eating as they listened. When he had finished, the Snook carefully closed the book remaining seated whilst his audience slowly dispersed. There was no kind of applause or noise resembling appreciation, his audience simply faded away in silence. Charlotte had no idea whether anybody enjoyed the tale. When the glade was clear Triskelion and Wodewose approached beckoning for Charlotte to follow. The Snook greeted them in silence, just the faintest of smiles acknowledging their presence.

"Morning Fridolin," Triskelion greeted the Snook. So that was his name. The Snook smiled once more but didn't speak. "This is the girl I told you about, the human child." Triskelion gestured for Charlotte to come closer. Not knowing why she felt shy, she wasn't normally, Charlotte stepped forward. Standing in front of the Snook she saw that he had opened the book at a new page. The paper looked very old, yellowed in places and thick like parchment but what caught Charlotte's attention was there weren't any words printed on the pages, not a single one. The Snook, from what she could see had been reading from pages that were blank. The Snook on seeing her interest in his book, closed it slowly and rested his hands on the cover.

"So you are the little French girl, my book predicted would visit us in Otherworld." The Snook's speech was slow, careful and easy to follow, especially as he spoke with her in French. "You, I understand are from les Ch'tis like me, though different worlds of course." Charlotte simply smiled, not sure how to respond. "Triskelion here tells me that you have one or two questions for me."

"Have I?" Charlotte looked up at Triskelion.

"Yes, you asked me how the story involving you ends, what happens to the little French girl, now's your chance to ask the storyteller." Of course, Charlotte remembered, she turned back to the Snook. The Snook spoke before Charlotte had a chance to. A habit in Otherworld that she still couldn't get used to.

"Let me see," his long bony fingers parted his book and he let it fall open upon his lap. The pages, Charlotte saw, were as previously, blank, void of a single word. Charlotte thought the whole thing to be a charade, it was ridiculous, an empty page left the Snook free to make up whatever he wanted. The so-called prediction was no more than a vivid piece of the Snook's imagination.

"Wait," the Snook told her, sensing her doubt. As she watched she saw why the Snook had asked for her patience. Slowly both pages filled with the most beautiful writing she had ever seen. The words came from nowhere, or so it seemed. The first word on each page was of a decorative design, intricate and exaggerated, rich with the richest of colours. Every word sang to her as she identified it. "I shall read to you, Charlotte from les Ch'tis," and the Snook started to read. He ran his bony finger along each line as he read. The story he told, mirrored in short her visits to Otherworld so far. Charlotte waited with bated breath for the conclusion. It was rather like a Christmas present she had to unwrap before the big day arrived. She was to be disappointed, the Snook turned a page to continue reading and not a word appeared, the new page remained blank.

"What does that mean? What's happened?" Charlotte couldn't hide her frustration. The Snook looked up, taking his time.

"There is no conclusion, Charlotte from les Ch'tis, the ending depends on you, what you do, which action you take. Your story could end well, or." The Snook hesitated, "or it could end not so well." The Snook rested his hand on the empty page, holding Charlotte's eyes with his own.

"But that's ridiculous," Charlotte blurted out. "Who's heard of a story without an ending."

"It is what I told you." Triskelion was right Charlotte remembered, he had.

"There are plenty of stories without an end," the Snook added and Charlotte had to admit that he was right too.

"But how do you know the story's about me, it could be about any French girl?" Charlotte still wasn't convinced and frustration hadn't yet left her. The Snook looking completely unmoved by her outburst, turned back a page and lifted the book so she could see the page clearly. There was no written word, instead the page was filled by a picture, a masterpiece of a painting finished in minute detail. The composition was of a girl running up a path to a church. Charlotte recognised the church from the tower as St John the Baptist at Aldbury or maybe Aldeborie for she had no idea in which world the picture was painted. The clock on the church tower was faced with Roman numerals and there was no hand held serpent, the numbers ran to XII. As she ran up the path the girl in the picture was looking back as though looking at a pursuer. The face of the little girl, Charlotte recognised with shock as her own. "Oh," was all she could say. Seeing her face in the book of a complete stranger stunned her into silence. She even recognised the clothes she was wearing in the picture, in fact she was wearing them now. The only difference was, in the picture she had no coat and she appeared to be holding something though what, by the angle of her body she couldn't tell. The Snook closed the book and as before rested his hands on the cover. He smiled apologetically and as he did so started to fade. In under a minute he was gone, fading into nothing before Charlotte's disbelieving eyes.

"Snooks only appear at dawn and at dusk. They are never seen at any other time." Triskelion told her rather unhelpfully.

"I think you look really nice in your picture, France Charlotte." It was Wodewose. He said it whilst rubbing his back on the trunk of the fallen beech.

"Thank you Wodewose." Charlotte acknowledged and smiled her thanks. If only there were more Wodewose's around, Otherworld would be a much more pleasant place.

"I tried to tell you, France Charlotte, I know you doubted me. It was important you heard it straight from the lips of a Snook." Charlotte looked at Triskelion's blank face, without features it was so hard to gauge what he was really thinking.

"I never doubted you Triskelion," Charlotte replied, not sure if she had or not. "But I'm not sure that book, that picture proves anything.

Someone could have taken a photo and copied it into the book after I'd already visited Otherworld. They could have made the story up after my arrival here."

Triskelion stood facing her, "France Charlotte that story along with the picture was placed in the Snook's book a long, long time ago."

"When last week, last month, a few months ago?" Charlotte didn't see that, that mattered. Somebody still could have captured her picture when she was making her way to the gateway to transcend.

"Longer than that, France Charlotte. Much longer."

"Well how much longer?" Why couldn't Triskelion come out with everything in one go, why did she always have to follow up an answer with another question.

"Just over two thousand five hundred of your years before someone you know as Jesus walked your world. So nearly five thousand of your years in total." Wodewose continued to rub his back as though there were no surprises in Triskelion's answer. If Triskelion had wanted to shock Charlotte into a greater silence, he had almost succeeded, almost. She managed one short question.

"Including the picture?" Charlotte's voice was so quiet it was a blessing that Triskelion did not need his hearing to understand her.

"Yes."

Charlotte was finding what she had just been told, very difficult to comprehend. A story and a picture of her placed in a book nearly five thousand years ago, it simply wasn't possible. It must be fake. Triskelion saved her asking another question. He was carefully reading her thoughts.

"The book does not lie, France Charlotte, a Snook cannot change what has been written. Only a Snook can read what is within the cover of their book but they cannot change a word, nor can they add to it. The ancient who made your entry did so without leaving their name. For reasons we will never know they did not wish to be identified with the prediction. That does not change anything, you are in the book, France Charlotte, you are part of the history of Otherworld. You have never had a choice in the matter, you have not chosen to be here but somebody has chosen you. From the day you were born it has been your destiny." Charlotte tried to clear her mind, she wasn't sure she wanted Triskelion reading her thoughts at that moment. She needed to think without him interrupting. Triskelion read her torment and respected her wish, he remained silent.

The light rain continued to fall. The odd break in the clouds allowed rays from the rising sun to shine through. Somewhere there would be a rainbow. Nobody in the glade noticed the rain. Charlotte, standing stared at the ground, deep in thought. Wodewose either bored or feigning disinterest, continued to scratch whilst looking nowhere in particular. Triskelion knew it was the latter, feigning disinterest was Wodewose's way of disguising his nervousness. He tried not to pay too much attention to France Charlotte, he wanted her to have the space to sort out her thoughts. At the same time he was conscious of the time and the danger of staying in one place for too long. Trying not to make the others aware he searched the wood sounding out the interior with both his sight and his inner senses. It was daylight so they should be safe but the Darkness was getting stronger with the passing of every hour and who knew what influence it could bear on those who were normally incorruptible. Wodewose and the squirrel recognised Triskelion's concern, his fake nonchalance couldn't fool them. The concern of all three was lost on Charlotte. Her thoughts were still with the Snook and his book with no name. She needed more answers, knowledge in Otherworld was a powerful weapon, that she had learnt very early on and without fully understanding what was going on she felt handicapped. The Snook could not finish her story and she was worried that maybe it was because her appearance in Otherworld was a non-event. That she had failed before she had even started and her failure led to victory for the Darkness. The reason why the following page was blank.

"What about the artist?" Charlotte immediately won the attention of both Wodewose and Triskelion. "What about the artist?" she repeated. "He used to paint in my room, he painted pictures of both the robin and a magpie, did the Snooks tell stories about him?"

"The Snooks can only speak about Otherworld, their book, the book contains text relating to no other world. Therefore no, there is nothing in their book about the artist, the artist is of your world, not ours and therefore not in the book." Charlotte could not accept Triskelion's answer.

"But the artist IS in Otherworld, you showed him to me he's in that pond with the fancy name, (Charlotte was frustrated she couldn't recall the name) and the story the Snook told, I recognised it. It is a famous story where I come from, in my country, in my world, not yours." Triskelion continued to gaze deep into the wood. For once he agreed with Wodewose, France Charlotte had every right but even so he wished she didn't ask quite so many questions.

"The artist, France Charlotte, I told you was a mistake. When he lived in the cottage, we did not know the Snooks foretelling of a human child, you. There have always been rumours that a human living in your cottage would transcend to Otherworld to help us do battle with the Darkness. I never believed the rumours but when the artist arrived, we thought it must be true after all and brought him forcibly to Otherworld. A decision all of us deeply regret. At the time I'm afraid we were grasping at any glimmer of hope that came our way. You must understand it was at a time when there was no or very little hope. I am not proud of what we did. As for the story about the fish eating children, it is a tale from Otherworld. The story is very old and told at a time when transcending between our two worlds was not that uncommon.

There are many tales, most of which your people call legends that have their roots in Otherworld."

"The artist painted the magpie and the robin, did you know?" Charlotte asked

"We heard, where are the paintings now?" So, thought Charlotte, Triskelion doesn't know everything.

"He sold them in one of the village pubs, somebody brought the last three all in one go." Triskelion fell silent. Having the three remaining paintings all brought by the same person at such a sensitive time could not be a coincidence. What worried him more, in Otherworld they knew nothing of it. It suggested the Darkness had established contacts with humans in or close to Aldbury as the village was called in the adjoining world. Not only established contact but had humans working for it which was a very big step, much more than simply having influence.

"Who owns the cottage where we live? The question had been bugging Charlotte.

"I'm not sure," admitted Triskelion. His answer surprised Charlotte, she'd been sure he knew. "Sympathisers, an organisation of sorts. Whoever it is they appear to know something about Otherworld. They let our agents, we prefer to call them friends in your world, let the cottage but contact with them is very difficult and becoming more difficult with every moon that passes. Our friends are very knowledgeable but are unaware who it is they are working for. They're simply doing what they do for a cause." What cause? Charlotte wondered but her seventh sense was telling her not to ask.

"Was the man who rented my parents the cottage an agent working for you then?"

"Yes and his father before him and his father's father, going back many, many of your years. Their task was to find an occupant who was receptive to the picture of our Guardian. There were many failures until you arrived. You could see the picture for what it was, a living image.

Leht discovered that not only could you see our Guardian in real time you could also pass on your thoughts, your feelings. Already you have been a great help to our Guardian, more than you know." Triskelion was right about her not knowing. She had no idea how she had been of help to the white hart. "When the Snooks started telling stories of you transcending to Otherworld and our robin passed on information to say that you were receptive to the picture, we or rather Leht knew that you were the one to help us in our struggle. I say Leht for I admit I doubted how a human child could help us. I believed for a long time that it must be an error though now I see, it is I who made the error." There followed an uncomfortable silence, Triskelion's pride had been dealt a serious blow.

"So why are the magpies following me?" Triskelion still hadn't answered her question.

"They are eyes and messengers for the Darkness, just as our robin is for us."

Charlotte thought of Will and the rhyme he had told her and then Wodewose and his rendition of Otherworld's version. Both were similar but at the same time very different. Did they have any kind of meaning or were they just stuff and nonsense? Now she'd experienced the ways of Otherworld, Charlotte doubted it to be the latter. She went to ask Triskelion but he'd already read her mind.

"Many of what you call rhymes were written at a time when people understood the ways of the natural world, of the hidden power it possesses. In both our worlds, in many cases the original meaning of these rhymes has been lost to time, which is a dangerous thing, in some cases a very dangerous thing. The rhyme of the seven magpies holds a special place in both your world and ours though as to its meaning I'm afraid it has been lost to us. Leht has searched but so far found nothing, not a clue to their origin nor to the identity of the original scribe. They could well have been scribed as a warning or as a prediction. What worries us deeply is that both rhyme's feel as though their meaning is somehow relevant to what is happening now. Even more worrying the Darkness appears to be aware of their meaning and using its knowledge to its advantage."

There were six magpies in her garden Charlotte remembered and Will had told her she would not want to witness seven. She rehearsed the last line of each of the rhymes in her head. 'Seven for a secret never to be told. Seven you'll see the devil himself.' Will had been very convincing when he'd told her she would never want to witness seven magpies together. It was very obvious he believed in the rhyme and that he was genuinely afraid of witnessing such an event. Triskelion reading her thoughts cut in.

"The number seven is sacred in both our worlds, throughout the Universe, it is not a number you can bend. The symbolism of the number seven and the magpie, agents of the Darkness cannot be ignored. We must all pray the Darkness never achieves bringing seven magpies together." A loud yawn from Wodewose brought a welcome release to the tension building between Charlotte and Triskelion. Charlotte looked across to see her shaggy friend stretching his limbs awake.

"Wodewose is right," Triskelion returned his gaze to the surrounding wood. "Time is not on our side, we must make haste France Charlotte, to stay here any longer is inviting trouble." Charlotte, like Wodewose stretched to loosen her stiffness and winced as her body protested.

"I'm ready." Charlotte hoped that she was. She had no idea what was to come in the next few hours. Triskelion, she hoped could not read the battle raging inside her. Her battle to prevent expectation descending into nervousness and after descending further into fear. If Triskelion could read her uncertainty he was honourable enough not to allow her to know.

"Good, then follow me" and stepping out of the glade Triskelion made off into the wood expecting all to follow.

The vicar opened his eyes. Three things had coaxed him from his sleep. Cramped muscles, the strengthening light and the noise of car engines as early rush hour took advantage of the cut through that was Aldbury. At first, as sleep refused to leave him he wondered where he was. His eyes as consciousness won through started to focus and he recognised the tops of the trees in the churchyard. Turning his very stiff neck he saw his church. The door to the porch was shut and light shone from the high windows. Slowly everything from the day before came back to him. Rubbing his eyes and stretching he let out a loud extended yawn, a yawn so pronounced that it hurt the back of his neck. Rolling his head to relieve the pain he sat up and turned on the radio. The sound of Status Quo assaulted his fragile mind. Quickly he pressed another button to hear the news on radio five live. The wit of the two news presenters was a bit too sharp for his fuddled brain that morning but simply the sound of conversation he found relaxing. Twisting round in his seat he checked to see if the coast was clear. Seeing that it was he opened the car door and stepped outside. Standing he stretched again and took a deep breath. After the stale air of his car his lungs welcomed the crisp morning air. Almost fully awake he brushed himself down and straightened out his clothes. He couldn't let people even suspect he'd slept in his car all night. Crouching down before the side mirror he crunched his red beard into shape and ran his hand through his hair. It would have to do. Locking the car he walked down the road to the shop. He was feeling lazy, the shop had a small machine that did coffee and it was just what he needed. Whilst there he also brought a couple of readymade sandwiches, cheese and mayonnaise and beef and horseradish. Breakfast was sorted. A young lad took the money, the vicar didn't recognise him. He was both courteous and efficient and returned to his smart phone before the vicar had had a chance to open the door to leave.

That morning the car seemed a more agreeable place to enjoy breakfast than the office in his church, though in truth he knew he was simply putting off the inevitable. The radio announcers trolled through the news, laughing whenever they had the opportunity. They could have been announcing that aliens had landed for the vicar digested none of it, he simply enjoyed the electronic noise, it helped him not to feel so alone. The coffee was good and the sandwiches excellent. After roughly fifty minutes or a 'petite heure' the vicar had finished breakfast and was ready for the day or so he hoped. Once more he stepped out of the car. A horn tooted in recognition as a car passed, the vicar raised his arm in a polite greeting. He had no idea who he was waving morning to. Grabbing his briefcase he once again locked his car and strolled down the gravel path to the front door. In the porch nothing had changed, the air was cold, fresh and smelt welcoming. On opening the inner door he was disappointed to see nothing had changed there either. The malodorous vapour continued to cover the floor of the nave. The only consolation was that the vapour didn't appear to have risen since yesterday. Still he couldn't let anybody see his church like this. He returned to the porch and locked the outer door. He went to turn off the light but the same voice as yesterday told him that was wrong, he left the light on.

"God is light and in him no darkness at all." The vicar memorising the words spoke them out loud. He would leave all the lights on. Picking up his briefcase he bowed to the altr as he crossed to his office. The low door to the cupboard remained open and just as yesterday the vapour remained thick within. He placed his briefcase loudly on the desk. If anybody was hiding he wanted them to be aware of his presence. He didn't want any surprises. Grabbing a mug he made himself a coffee, his second coffee of the morning, he would probably need many, many more. Sitting down at his desk he took a long sip. It was nowhere near as good as the coffee from the shop but it was warm, wet and welcome.

He looked up at the painting of the severed head of the Forerunner, John the Baptist on the wall opposite. This morning the picture gave him nothing but strength. What's the worst that can happen to me he considered. Death of course, the *thought* no longer frightened him. As long as he kept his faith he could greet death without fear, his God would take care of him. In that he had no doubt.

Finishing his coffee he stood up and picked up an old iron cross that leaned against the wall in one corner of the room. He had no idea what it was doing there, it had been there the day he'd arrived. He assumed that it must have once stood over a grave though he had no proof. Well it would be needed today. The cross was surprisingly heavy and it took some effort to carry it across the passage to the low cupboard. There he lay it carefully on the stone floor and knelt ducking his head into the cupboard and the dense foul smelling vapour. To his surprise he found he could breathe easily enough but the smell which he thought represented rotting flesh made him wish he'd resisted the sandwiches. The cupboard was completely empty and he felt it strange that it hadn't been put to use. Space was of a premium even in a church. Feeling with his hands he tried to prise his fingers between the cracks of the stone slabs making up the floor or at least get a strong enough grip so he could lift one. Although there was movement he wasn't even close to prising one free. He'd have to resort to plan B. With his left hand he dragged the iron cross into the cupboard. Lifting the rear end he managed to prise the tip of the cross into a crack between two stone slabs enabling him to use the cross as a leaver. Pushing down on the other end of the cross the stone resisted at first before grudgingly lifting from its position. Sweating profusely with the effort he managed to prise the stone onto another and let it drop. Before going any further he slid the iron cross back out and carried it back into his office standing it upright in the corner, in exactly the same position as he had found it. Satisfied he returned to the cupboard and little by little started to pull the stone slab towards him. It was much heavier than he'd imagined and took a good few minutes to remove the stone from its home. With one gone the others were easier to manoeuvre and in just over an hour he had managed to remove all the stone slabs from the cupboard floor. They were now strewn across the passage leading to the glass meeting room. Returning to his office he lifted a torch from a hook on the wall. The lighting in the church wasn't always that reliable and Aldbury itself was prone to the odd power cut. The torch was primed and ready for such occasions.

As with fog the light from the torch reflected when meeting the vapour creating a blinding glare. Refusing to give up the vicar wafted the vapour in the cupboard with his spare hand. His effort paid off for his action granted him the odd glimpse of a wooden floor. Feeling with his hands confirmed this. Removing the torch from the cupboard the vicar left it on the floor just outside, its beam pointing in through the door. Using his hands he felt the wooden floor. The stones had been resting on wide, heavy wooden boards, he was surprised they'd been able to take their weight. Feeling around the edge of the cupboard he realised the boards were either nailed or screwed to a ledge on either side. Nailed he thought as he could feel no groove in the heads. The boards he decided would have to be prised up, there was no other option.

Otherworld

Charlotte and Wodewose followed close behind Triskelion with the squirrel leaping from tree to tree above them. The rain continued to fall though so fine was the spray when it landed the experience was refreshing rather than uncomfortable. Charlotte having traversed the commons of Ashridge on numerous occasions in both worlds had become acquainted with the various environs of the wood and was able to recognise as well as memorise their route. From Sallow Copse, Triskelion she became aware was leading them across Aldbury Common and Old Copse. He was heading for the exotically named mud pool, of that she was almost certain and felt a touch of pride when Triskelion stopped at the noxious circle of mud.

Drawing everybody to a halt Triskelion turned to address Wodewose and the squirrel. They both acted as if they knew what was coming. Charlotte had long recognised how all in the wood respected and obeyed Triskelion. Never had she heard anyone question his apparent authority or his judgement. What was coming now? She was about to find out.

"Both of you, as you are aware can no longer come with us. Wodewose you go back to your oak and my little messenger you go back to yours. Listen hard to the root vine for when France Charlotte returns to the wood she may do so alone and will need a friend. I hope to be with her but nothing is certain and we must be prepared for the possibility that I may not return." Triskelion finished as abruptly as he had started. There were no hugs, no tears. The squirrel and Wodewose simply turned and disappeared in different directions. Charlotte remained with Triskelion and though he was by her side she was overtaken by an overwhelming sense of loneliness. It was a desperate feeling. Triskelion touched her arm and bent his featureless face to face hers. He spoke, not in the soft but commanding manner that Charlotte was used to but in a deep powerful voice and in a manner that told her she must hang onto every word. That hers, their lives may depend on her understanding and if necessary acting on every detail .

"France Charlotte I told you yesterday that Leht believes she knows why the Darkness has chosen this time to act and I believe she has mentioned the great cycle to you." Charlotte nodded.

"Yes but I do not understand what the great cycle is." Triskelion's voice returned to normal, soft spoken but always commanding attention.

"The great cycle is a powerful current beneath the earth that disappears deep into Otherworld and stays there, sometimes for thousands of your years before resurfacing. Through Leht's connections we discovered that the great cycle will resurface on or close to what you call mid-summer and the point where it will resurface is beneath the Sacred Library of Evinghehou. The great cycle alone would be enough for the Darkness to make its move, for the current of the great cycle has enormous power and if you know how to harness it, can be used to one's advantage. In the wrong hands the power that the current wields can become a most dangerous tool. The Sacred library of Evinghehou also has the two strongest earth currents in this land meeting at its centre, they exist in your world too and meet beneath your Beacon just as they do in Otherworld. Their union we believe is why the sacred library was placed there by the ancients. We do not believe the earth currents are affected by the rising of the great cycle, nor do we believe they can be used by the Darkness but nothing can be ruled out." Triskelion paused, normally he would never be so free with this type of information, especially to one so young and a human at that but times had changed. He had no idea why, he just knew that he had to put his faith in the young girl. He hoped France Charlotte wouldn't follow with a question for he knew nothing else other than what he'd just told her.

Charlotte tried to digest what she had just been told. She sensed rightly that Triskelion was dreading a question. It was so difficult, nothing they talked about was idle chat. Everything had consequences, huge consequences and the subject matter mind boggling, always. She thought about Orme, the key to being a God Triskelion had told her and there was the great cycle to consider and now the Earth currents. It was simply too much to take in, she wished he hadn't have told her everything. As a result and to Triskelion's relief Charlotte's question was relatively simple, well perhaps not simple but one he could at least answer.

"You believe the Darkness knows about the rising of the great cycle?"

"We wish it were not the case but yes we think it must do and this is another concern, a grave concern. We were too concerned with what your species was doing than to keep an eye on the Darkness. Looking back we believe now that the Darkness may have started his action with its possession of Gravade, many, many moons ago. If that is the case it must have known about the rising all that time ago and has been planning without our knowledge ever since. We believed at first that the Darkness wanted to possess the Great Library of Evinghehou because of the rumours that inside were scrolls revealing the secret or some of the secrets to Orme. With Leht's recent discovery the Darkness may have a completely different or second reason to want to gain access to the Great Library. The Darkness may be looking to harness the power from the rising to search for the scrolls. With the power from one it may be able to access the second. We simply do not know. Whatever the truth, all the more reason to destroy the passage today, we cannot afford to risk the Darkness using the one physical entrance for access."

He had relayed to France Charlotte what Leht suspected in the simplest terms possible. He was aware of the enormity and complexity of the information she was expected to digest and hoped that his words didn't spell defeat simply by their burden on such small shoulders. What words could never describe are the consequences if the Darkness won the ultimate battle. He knew that Leht had told the little girl how time could end if the Darkness discovered the key to Orme. That after such an event all that would remain was blackness. Words, simple words explained the outcome but what words could never do was describe the death, the horror, the destruction as sun after sun, planet after planet, moon after moon and all forms in the universe, all existence were torn apart and replaced by a blackness. A blackness with nothing within it but the feeling of fear. No language no matter how descriptive, how sophisticated, how sensitive could even begin to explain the end of everything.

Charlotte stood deep in thought. The rain had stopped, all that remained were irregular drips as the weight of water became too much for the leaves in the canopy overhead and the resulting droplets fell, bouncing several times before they reached the ground. She breathed in the freshly moisturised air. A luxury that so many of her species saw as an inconvenience. For her the sensation was delicious, it was one of the great pleasures of life and free. She thought about what Triskelion had told her about the early inhabitant of her village, Sir Guy de Gravade and his pact or possession by the Darkness. That was well over a thousand years ago, the Darkness thus, if Leht was correct had been quietly planning this day since all that time before. If that was the case, what hope had they now? Simply destroying the passageway seemed far too simple a defence. Surely the Darkness would be prepared for such an attempt. Triskelion read everything Charlotte was thinking. She was right of course. They were banking on the Darkness not knowing about the passage. There was one other small factor in their favour, they knew that the Darkness had been completely unprepared for the arrival of a human child. One that could transcend back and forth between two different worlds, one that the Snooks recently predicted would do battle. France Charlotte was their ace card, if only he knew how to deal it.

"Is the passage we're about to close, the only entrance?" Charlotte's question, though perhaps an obvious one, still surprised Triskelion.

"There is another way in," he admitted after some thought. Charlotte sensed he didn't want to tell her and was a little surprised when he continued. "The second entrance though is not a physical entrance, it can only be used as though transcending through a gateway and even then my understanding is, a being such as you or me cannot use it. Our Guardian holds the key, that is all I know. It may not even be true. Leht may know more but if she does she has never relayed it to me. You are carrying Leht," (Charlotte knew Triskelion was referring to the liquid in the small leather bag around her neck), when you next speak to her ask her yourself." Charlotte felt uncomfortable at his last sentence, perhaps she was reading more into his words than he'd meant. It just felt to her by his last remark that he did not expect to be present when she next saw Leht.

Next and to her surprise Triskelion knelt and appeared to kiss the disgusting looking mud in the pool. Her senses told her he was talking but not in any language she recognised. As quickly as he'd knelt he rose to his feet.

"No more questions France Charlotte, we must go." Triskelion made it clear their conversation had ended. As was always his way he made off into the wood expecting her to follow, which of course she did. She wondered what he'd do if she started in the opposite direction. "Stay close to me," he instructed her and Charlotte knew instantly Triskelion had read her last thought.

It wasn't long before they arrived at a road, Charlotte recognised it as the road that ran from Dagnall to Northchurch. The road was silent, devoid of traffic as she knew it would be. The two of them, an odd couple to anyone who saw them, crossed the road to enter the deeply wooded Berkhamsted Common. On re-entering the wood something took over Triskelion. He surged ahead like a being possessed, never following a path but crossing many en route to wherever. He seemed not to notice or paid no attention to Charlotte's struggle with the underwood as she tried to keep up. He uttered not one word during their passage and neither did he once pause to look over his shoulder to see if she was close behind him. Charlotte had never seen him like this, it was though he had forgotten she existed. After what she judged to be around twenty minutes, the land started to rise and though not in view she recognised from their surroundings that they were not far from Ashridge House, as it was known in her world. On approaching the incline, Triskelion began to slow at last and shortly after came to a standstill where he abruptly commanded.

"Stop."

For Charlotte, his command couldn't have come soon enough. She was badly scratched, trying to follow in his footsteps and her deep breathing from her struggle to keep up sent stabbing pains rebounding around her chest every time her lungs expanded. She needed a rest badly. Triskelion on coming to a halt turned to face her and surely, she hoped it must be obvious to him that she was in pain. That she needed a few minutes but as earlier and to her disappointment Triskelion appeared not to notice. He was facing her yes but it felt as though Triskelion was completely unaware of her presence. His featureless eyes were fixed on her and even though she couldn't see any expression Charlotte knew Triskelion was looking far beyond at something far, far away. Looking at him now she saw that his cloak was shining brighter than she'd ever seen before. Even though it was daylight such was its exuberance it hurt her eyes to look at him. What she asked herself is going through your mind Triskelion, please let me in. She knew her plea would be in vain.

When Triskelion spoke it sounded to Charlotte as though his voice originated from a distant place. It was him talking but he sounded different, it was almost as if someone or something was using him as their mouthpiece.

"You must not be afraid France Charlotte." His slow steady tone reached deep inside her, to parts of her mind up until that moment she had been unaware existed. His voice had her transfixed, unable to move. Triskelion had her full attention, nothing else mattered.

"What you are about to see, no human in the modern era has ever set eyes on, you will be the first and there may never be another after you. The Sacred Library of Evinghehou contains secrets, solutions, answers to questions that will take your scientists thousands more years to discover if they ever will at all. For this reason France Charlotte you cannot be witness to the entrance. The hidden door to the passage must remain hidden even after the passage is destroyed. It's secret must for all time remain a secret. For this reason I am about to block your senses, if I don't, the sentries placed at the inauguration to guard the entrance will and the experience will not be a pleasant one for you. Please no questions, there is no more time. Are you ready?" Charlotte wasn't sure if she was at all but knew it was too late to have a choice. Otherworld held her captive. Triskelion in any case did not wait for an answer, Charlotte saw him raise his arm and she closed her eyes as he slowly moved to place his hand on her forehead. Whatever Triskelion intended it was instant, as if somebody had switched off the master switch to her brain. Everything went blank.

By everything going blank, it wasn't only that Charlotte couldn't see, she couldn't hear either, she couldn't feel. She knew she wasn't dead but it must be the closest thing to it. There was no way of describing how she felt because there was nothing to describe, she didn't feel anything, how can you put words to something that simply isn't there. She had no idea how much time had passed before her first sense started to return. This was her sense of smell. The inside of her nose quivered with the smell of air, not air from a wood freshened by rain but air laden with age. An atmosphere heavy with time that in contrast also had a virginal feel to it. Slowly other senses started to return. Her limbs awoke feeling stiff and the pain in her chest returned with a vengeance. Blood, if that was how to describe the feeling returned to her hands and finally to the tips of her fingers causing them to tingle. As all her senses returned Charlotte realised someone or something had hold of her left hand. Several seconds later she recognised the grip as Triskelion's. A feeling of strength surged up her arm and through the rest of her body as the last of the sensory barriers withdrew. The last sense to return was perhaps her most vital, her sight. At first there was the tiniest speck of light. The speck slowly broadened to fill her vision though the next step failed, her eyes refused to focus. There was light and central a dark singular shape but nothing was sharp, everything was fused together. A familiar feeling started to form in her stomach, that of panic. Panic that her sight from this moment on will always remain a blur. As Charlotte struggled with her emotions she felt her left hand compress as Triskelion tightened his grip. His action had the desired effect, drawing long shallow breaths Charlotte slowly regained control over her rising fear. Keeping a cool head she concentrated everything she had on her vision. Slowly, very slowly the part of her brain which controlled her sight started to function. Her focus started to sharpen, the wavering light started to fall away. Charlotte closed her eyes, she found it easier. Tears formed by her desperate attempt to focus rolled down each cheek. Instinctively she started to count to ten, slowly and deliberately she let the numbers build. All the time she could feel Triskelion feeding her reassurance. She arrived at ten and slowly opened her eyes, blinked and opened them again. For a second the blur remained but for a second only, a huge sigh of relief accompanied the complete return of her sight.

On regaining her vision Charlotte's first realisation was that they were no longer outside. They were in what looked like a tunnel, a tunnel constructed entirely of brick, both the floor and the curved ceiling. Not modern bricks but small rough bricks from another age. Their colour was a deep red and reminded Charlotte of the bricks you found everywhere in Flandres, (Flanders). The only light was from the soft glow of Triskelion's cloak who stood beside her. The bright white light that had almost blinded her before, was no longer present. The tense and intense Triskelion had gone, standing beside her he was now calmness personified. At that moment, Triskelion's light was the softest Charlotte had seen it, not dim for that would have meant sadness or depression but soft reflecting a deep calm. As a consequence with such a soft light she could only see the first metre or two ahead of them and as a consequence all she could deduce was that the tunnel stretching before them sloped downwards. Behind them the tunnel ended abruptly with a solid brick wall. Charlotte had no idea how they had arrived at where they were, there was no sign of an entrance and what worried her more, no sign of an exit.

"You are ok France Charlotte." Triskelion's voice sounded deeper in the confines of the tunnel. 'You are ok,' Charlotte recognised from his tone his words were meant as reassurance not a question. "The passage is too narrow for me to hold your hand, you must keep close behind me, do not let me out of your sight, do you understand?" Triskelion let go of her hand. Charlotte smiled and hoped it didn't come across as weak.

"Yes" she answered needlessly and added, "Triskelion how do we get out?" If Triskelion wanted to reassure her he failed completely. He ignored her question.

"Stay close to me," he instructed for the second time and stepped forward into the tunnel or 'passage' as he called it, ahead. Charlotte wondered how on earth she'd keep her footing, the soft glow from Triskelion's cloak hardly illuminated him let alone where she was expected to put her feet. As it was she needn't have worried, as Triskelion advanced flames erupted from solid iron torches on either wall, lighting their way. After that, every few steps as though there were some sort of sensor another pair of torches would miraculously flare up and the ones passed die just as quickly as they'd burst into life. Triskelion didn't hurry, his pace remained steady and at all times he kept staring straight ahead. Not once did he speak and not once did he look back to see if Charlotte was close behind him. The slope of the tunnel was gradual and with the light from the torches easy to negotiate. After only a few minutes the way flattened out and at the same time angled right. As it did so an unmoving white light could be seen shining someway in the distance. The light was like nothing Charlotte had seen before, it definitely wasn't daylight and neither was it powered by electricity. The light was also constant with no sign of movement. There was no transmatic dance played out on the walls so the light was not the product of a flame and yet the source, the luminary felt as though it had a heart, a soul may be a better way to describe it. Spiritual, Charlotte found the word she had been looking for, spiritual was how it felt for the light wasn't just physical, she could feel it's presence. As they approached the light remained constant, it didn't get any brighter but it's spirit grew stronger.

Charlotte's heart started to beat faster, not through fear the increased beat was one of expectancy. The passage without warning opened out into a small vaulted undercroft. Like the tunnel it was constructed entirely of ancient brick and Charlotte assumed that they must be beneath the old monastery built by the Bonhommes. The room was quite magnificent to behold but it wasn't the intricate brickwork that held her attention. In the centre of the room was the source of the light. A simple stone pillar rose from the brick floor. It was roughly her height and from its top shone a light that lit the whole undercroft. For the first time Charlotte understood the real meaning of the expression, "bathed in light", for that was exactly what it felt like. She felt as though she were being bathed in a translucent lather. From what she could see, the light appeared to have no source, if anything it appeared to be an entity in its own right. The light was spectacle enough but it wasn't the light that ultimately held her attention. Cupped in the light above the pillar the head of a woman stared out. Charlotte couldn't make out whether the head, she, were somehow alive or carved from stone for the appearance changed from one to the other and then back again at irregular intervals. When the head appeared alive or at least flesh and bone, it was that of a pale skinned woman with piercing blue eyes. She wore a rich red head scarf from under which escaped wisps of fine red hair that trailed over her forehead contrasting with her pale skin. The head from what she could make out appeared to be supported by the light with the neck and light becoming one where her shoulders should be. There was nothing else in the room except, carved on a stone lintel over the entrance to the passage opposite, a message.

"Alterum orbem terrarum eam appellant"

Charlotte had no idea what it meant. As she stood in silent admiration Triskelion, removing his sword from his cloak knelt on one knee before the pillar. The tip of his sword he placed in a groove worn into a brick and holding it upright he bowed his head so his forehead came to rest on the sword's simple handle. Triskelion remained in this state of reverence for several minutes, during which the light from his cloak faded completely and Charlotte feared for a moment he may have met his afterlife. Never had she witnessed Triskelion offer such devotion or for that matter any kind of devotion. Such a personal display of what was indisputably a deep adoration for the lady graced in the light, moved Charlotte almost to tears.

Keeping his head bowed, Triskelion rose to his feet, replacing his sword beneath the folds of his cloak. Bringing up his head he turned to face Charlotte. She waited for him to say something but not a word or explanation was offered. Facing forward once more he set off down the tunnel leading from the opposite side of the undercroft, the one beneath the inscribed lintel. Charlotte, after a last glance at the magic contained in the undercroft, hurried after him. What had she just witnessed, the only thought in her head.

Once again the tunnel sloped downwards, this time for several hundred metres before levelling out. Although it was hard to be certain, Charlotte had the feeling that they were all the time curving left. The absence of any distinguishing features and the repetitive ebb and flow of the flaming torches started to play tricks with her mind. It was beginning to feel like they were caught in a hamster's wheel, that the tunnel may never have an end. Arriving in a small room therefore probably saved her from imminent insanity. The room was square and at its centre a spiral staircase descended into the earth, there was no other exit apart from the tunnel by which they had entered. Again Triskelion turned to look at her and again he said nothing. After presumably checking she was still there he disappeared down the spiral staircase. Charlotte followed, she had no choice and she couldn't bear the thought of retreating back through the tunnel alone. There was no handrail in the brick stairwell and the steps narrow. The flaming torches lit the way yes but they also hinted at an unfathomable drop, deep enough that if she lost her footing she knew she wouldn't survive the fall. For this reason Charlotte couldn't bring herself to look down, just the slightest hint of what was below made her feel dizzy and close to losing her balance. The only way she could manage was to stare straight ahead at the wall. As they descended the bricks blurred before her eyes, she lost all track of time, her only salvation was hearing Triskelion below her. His sometimes irregular step and the sound of his cloak falling about him were the only relief from total and disorientating monotony.

She felt no relief when the staircase finally came to an end. As her foot left the last step her whole body and all her senses felt numb. They'd been beaten into submission by the mind numbing descent. Coupled with the constant fear of falling Charlotte felt mentally and physically exhausted. Triskelion looked as though he too had suffered from the demands of their descent. The glow from his cloak looked weary and his stance which was nearly always erect had lost some of its rigidity. Thankfully, he looked as if he was in no hurry to head down the next tunnel. This was directly opposite the last step though in which direction it headed, Charlotte had no idea, they could be beneath Australia for all she knew. Triskelion's hesitance to continue gave her a chance to take in her surroundings. The staircase she saw finished in another small room, identical to the one from which they'd descended except for one detail. In the room at the top of the staircase, there was only one tunnel providing access, it was the same in the room in which they stood now but at one time there had been two. In the wall directly behind the brickwork wasn't as uniform. Set into the wall the angle and line of a number of bricks created a perfect arch. They had once framed the entrance to a second tunnel, a tunnel for whatever reason had been bricked up. Charlotte wanted to ask why, if only to say a few words. She was beginning to detest the silence between them since they'd entered the passage. It wasn't to be, with little warning Triskelion started down the tunnel/passage that was before them and their routine continued to remain the same as did their surroundings.

From the bottom of the stairs the brick tunnel continued in a straight line. As before flames leapt from torches in the wall and died after they'd passed. Every now and again Charlotte would look back over her shoulder, everything behind them was black she couldn't even make out an outline. Triskelion's pace didn't alter. It remained not slow but steady, there was now recognisable a resolve that gained in strength with every step. I would not want to get in his way, Charlotte thought following behind. As they continued she became aware of a slow change to the tunnel ahead. The shade of darkness before them looked different. Not long after she realised why, ahead of them they were approaching a door. Nothing grand just a simple wooden door. It looked solid though and filled the entire tunnel. The door had one peculiarity, as far as Charlotte could see, it had no lock and no handle, there was no clue as to how or which way it opened. Triskelion raised his hands and rested both his palms against the door. At first Charlotte thought he was going to try and push the door open but instead he leaned forward and leant his forehead against the wood. As Charlotte watched she saw that he was whispering something, he appeared to be talking to the door. She waited in respectful silence not wanting to interrupt. As the minutes passed Triskelion's whispering became more intense, at times it was almost verging on frantic. Charlotte began to worry that maybe everything was becoming too much for him. She was close to saying or doing something to try and ease his apparent stress when Triskelion's conversation with the door came to a sudden end. Leaving his hands on the door he drew up his head and turned his face towards Charlotte. For the first time since they'd entered the tunnel, he spoke.

"France Charlotte, welcome to the great and Sacred Library of Evinghehou."

Triskelion pushed gently and the door swung open to reveal the most beautiful sight Charlotte had ever seen. Nothing, nothing at all could have prepared her for what she was about to witness. With the door open the tunnel opened out onto a curved balcony and the balcony looked out onto a huge domed cavern, so deep was it she could not see where it ended below and with no railing to protect a fall, she didn't like to lean over too far. The cavern was illuminated by thousands of shining scrolls, perhaps tens of thousands simply floating in space. Stairs led from where they were standing into the dome and weaved in labyrinth fashion between the scrolls. There was never a level, every scroll was accessed by a step. From what she could see the stairways had no support they appeared to be simply floating with the scrolls. The overall impression was of a tangled ball of magical thread. The stairways were not enclosed with railings and you would have to have a very level head to take just a few steps let alone search for a single scroll. The stairways reminded Charlotte of one she'd once seen whilst visiting Oxford with her parents. It was dusk and they had been standing in Radcliffe square admiring the mellow stone architecture. Most of the lights were on in the surrounding buildings and through one large window enticingly lit, rose the most beautiful stairway she had ever seen. At that moment more than anything else she had wanted to climb those stairs. (Here Charlotte is referring to a stairway in the Hertford College library). What she was witnessing now, made that stairway pale into insignificance. The intricacy of the stairs as they wound in no particular order between the scrolls of light was beyond comprehension. As mentioned there were no levels, if you had the courage to seek out a scroll you would be either stepping up or stepping down. Charlotte remembered that all this was below Ivinghoe Beacon. Somewhere above them on the surface the white hart was fighting to protect the miracle before their eyes from the Darkness. Now she had seen with her own eyes the miracle that was the Sacred Library of Evinghehou she was determined more than ever to defend it from the evil that threatened it.

"Some of the scrolls here are as old as the hill that protects them and some much older, a few as old as time itself." Triskelion was standing on the very edge of the balcony. The slightest loss of balance and he would be gone. "Just one scroll could contain information to advance any civilisation hundreds even thousands of your years." Charlotte couldn't understand why the people who ruled Otherworld hadn't removed a scroll to advance their own civilisation, to perhaps use the information they contained to defeat the Darkness. Why risk letting the Darkness gain access to such dangerous knowledge? "Knowledge is only dangerous in the wrong hands and that is why in our world it is forbidden to access any of the libraries, the knowledge they store could turn the head of one with the purist of thought. We are all capable of such wicked persuasion, France Charlotte, even you or I. Not one person, not one being can guarantee how they would react if offered knowledge that could make them a God. That is why we have to close the passage forever. No being can have access to this library, at least not until there is an absolute guarantee that the knowledge will only be used to benefit, not to destroy. And sadly in both our worlds at the current time the wish to destroy comes too easily to many." Charlotte couldn't argue with Triskelion's words. It still though seemed such a shame that such a beautiful sight was to be permanently hidden. If witnessed it would easily become the wonder of the world. Nothing on Earth could come close to surpassing such breath-taking beauty. She had never been more certain of anything in her life.

To Charlotte's relief, Triskelion took a step back from the edge. For a horrible moment she thought he was going to throw himself off and disappear forever into the infinite space below.

"It is time," Triskelion's face remained fixed on the wonder before them. "We must do what we came to do, any delay even the slightest puts what we witness before us at great risk. Come." Triskelion stepped back into the passageway, reluctantly Charlotte followed. The door as they left the balcony slowly closed behind them. Charlotte wondered how it could move as the door didn't appear to rest on hinges. A door of such antiquity and especially one that may not have been opened for hundreds, maybe thousands of years, you would expect to grind, to protest with a sound that pained sensitive teeth. Yet there was nothing, not a sound. The door closed with a silence that was so silent, it made you take notice.

After the door had come to a rest, Triskelion didn't hesitate. Without warning and with one swift movement he withdrew his sword from beneath his cloak. Charlotte was completely unprepared for his action and froze where she was standing. Rooted to the spot she eyed Triskelion nervously, uncertain what to do and afraid of what he might do next. He in response turned his head towards her.

"Do not fret France Charlotte, I will let no harm come to you" and turned back to face the door. Setting his legs apart, Triskelion grasped the sword's handle with both hands and held it before him, with the tip facing the floor. As he did so, all of him, not just his cloak shone bright throwing beams of light deep into the tunnel behind them. With excruciating slowness he brought the sword down to the floor. When the tip met with brick instead of stopping the blade continued into the floor. Charlotte with the strength of his light saw that Triskelion had pushed his sword into a crevice in one of the bricks. It was quickly apparent that he was meeting with resistance and taking a great deal of effort to maintain the sword's downward motion. When the sword reached waist height, Triskelion doubled over using both his strength and his weight to continue the push downward. With the base of the hilt almost touching the brick, the sword or the floor, it was hard to tell which put up its strongest resistance. Triskelion was kneeling and doubled over so low he was almost spread flat in an effort to achieve the final push. Charlotte could feel his struggle, it radiated and rebound around her head till her skull felt it was in danger of splitting. As seconds ticked by each wave she received turned from effort to one of desperation and as more seconds passed she even began to sense panic, an emotion Charlotte until now hadn't thought Triskelion capable of. As the tension rose Charlotte felt, more and more, Triskelion's desperation, maybe for the first time in his life he was staring failure in the face. His light as his desperation rose shone to such an extent Charlotte had to shield her eyes at the risk of being blinded. The light then started to fracture. For a second it was as if time was suspended, nothing moved, they were all just a negative in time. Out of spontaneity, for there was no thought process, Charlotte threw herself on Triskelion and pushed down with everything she could muster.

At first Charlotte thought her effort had been in vain. Nothing happened, then there came a jerk and the sword dropped coming to rest on its hilt. The motion sent her rolling across the floor and she heard Triskelion groan as his stomach felt the full force of the hilt coming to a sudden and violent halt. At the same moment, his fractured brilliance went out leaving them both in the dark. Struggling to get her bearings, Charlotte heard Triskelion heave himself to his feet. As she went to do the same flames erupted from the two nearest torches on the wall, throwing a restless glow that danced about the passage. From the light Charlotte saw Triskelion already standing over her. He held out his hand.

"Get up," he commanded, "we must hurry." You're always in a hurry, Charlotte bemoaned as she took his hand, and thanks for the thanks. Triskelion ignored her, hauling her to her feet. "Keep close to me," he instructed as before and started briskly back down the tunnel. His pace was such that Charlotte had to run to keep up. With every forced breath, her chest felt as if it were being sliced by shards of glass. To stop breathing would be heaven she thought as she ran and quickly wiped the thought from her mind.

It was when they arrived at the foot of the stairs that Charlotte first felt it. A faint but definite tremor. It wasn't brief, it didn't come and go, once she'd felt the motion it stayed with her. If anything it started getting stronger. As they started up the steps there came the sound, a deep low distant rumble and around the same time previously still air started to play gently with her hair. Triskelion as though wanting to avoid a bullet increased his pace, Charlotte dropped to all fours and cried with her effort to keep up. In London she had caught the tube many times before and she had experienced the phenomenon of a train pushing air out of the tunnel. She knew exactly what was happening, the tunnel was collapsing behind them, forcing the air that remained in the way and unless they hurried, she knew they'd both be buried alive.

Climbing the stairs was the hardest thing she'd ever done in her life. On several occasions she slumped to the floor only for Triskelion to pull her up, insisting she kept going. All the time the tremor was becoming more intense, the rumble more menacing and the previously playful air a brisk breeze. All signs the collapse was becoming closer. It was nothing short of a miracle, Charlotte thought when they emerged at the top of the stairs. As they did so something made her look back down the stairwell. What she saw spurred her on, Charlotte somehow discovered reserves within reserves. The bottom stairs were beginning to crumble, seconds later they collapsed completely. Then the collapse began to rise. Triskelion grabbing Charlotte's hand once more virtually dragged her along the brick floor of the tunnel, her legs splaying wildly beneath her, trying desperately and usually failing to find a grip. As they battled to fight what Charlotte was beginning to accept must be a losing battle she saw a pin prick of white light ahead of them. Though distant she recognised it as the spiritual lumiere that bathed the undercroft. On seeing it Triskelion somehow discovered new reserves and started to surge ahead, with Charlotte half dragged half running behind him. The tremor by now was more a quake and the rumble more of a roar with the force of the air almost blowing them down the tunnel. At the moment they entered the undercroft the collapse of the tunnel showed itself behind them. It was terrifying, a surging, seething mass, a suffocating cloud of rubble that would bury you in seconds if it caught you. Charlotte, shocked into action sprinted through the undercroft, oblivious of the pain that hammered at her chest. The floating head that had so captivated her on their arrival, was just a blur. Survival was all that mattered now. She was metres down the final stretch of tunnel before she realised Triskelion was no longer beside her. Frantic she stopped and turned. Triskelion she saw had stopped running. His ghostly figure stood motionless. He was standing beside the stone pillar, from which the white light appeared to spring supporting the head of the mysterious woman. His cloak Charlotte saw bore a soft glow, a sign she now realised that meant he was relaxed. Triskelion sent a silent message to his France Charlotte. He was where he wanted to be, he was ready and waiting to meet his afterlife.

"Noooo, Triskelion, NOOOOO." Charlotte's call was desperate and made worse, knowing she was wasting her time.

"Run, France Charlotte, run, if not for me for your parents, for Otherworld. RUN." Triskelion's voice virtually exploded inside her. Charlotte started to run but couldn't help stopping and looking back. The wave of rubble had entered the undercroft. Its cloud started to engulf Triskelion.

"RUN FRANCE CHARLOTTE." They were the last words Charlotte was ever to hear from Triskelion. She watched in sickened horror as he crumpled with the weight of the rubble raining down on him. Somehow he managed to keep his head up and facing her. Just before he disappeared, buried forever, Charlotte witnessed what she had wanted from the day she'd first met her "ghost." The empty featureless space that was his face was no longer there. For the first time Charlotte truly saw Triskelion. The blank that had been his face had been replaced by a real face. The face of a man, a kind face, with eyes that shone with eternal hope. His mouth tightly shut, rose each side in a silent smile. It was the smile that captivated Charlotte more than anything. It confirmed his last thought to her, he was at peace, he was happy, he was where he wanted to be. A split second later he was gone.

The white light, buried, continued to shine where it was able to through cracks in the fallen debris. Charlotte tore herself away, tears streaming down her face. Only at the end had she truly trusted Triskelion, now he was gone she had so much she wanted to say to him. Not once could she remember thanking him. Her resolve now was not to let him down. Ridiculing her pain she sprinted as fast as she was able down the tunnel. She had to outrun the collapse, she had to find the outside. The tunnel changed direction and started to rise, she knew it couldn't be far now. And there it was, the end of the tunnel, a brick wall. Triskelion had led her in, senseless, literally. She had no idea how they'd got there. She stared angrily at the wall blocking her exit ahead, she was not going to allow herself to be defeated. The roar behind her was deafening and dust started to dry her mouth, a cold rush of air threatened to blow her off her feet. She heard Triskelion's last words in her head, 'RUN', and she ran, straight at the wall.

Chapter Seventeen
No Return

Any remaining perfumes left over from winter rose freely from the recently soaked ground, grateful to the persistent rain for their release. Birds spread their feathers and let them quiver, delighting in the recent gift from the heavens. Song radiated in joyful appreciation. Flora, thirsty from seasonal growth drank greedily and the young woodland fauna frolicked in free abandon whilst their elders, wiser thanked their maker for now. Vibrant was the woodland of Asherugge that day.

Charlotte felt her foot catch on something and tumbled forward. Hitting the ground hard she screamed out in pain, cries that she repeated as she found herself tumbling down a slope. As she fell sodden earth found its way into her open mouth along with a number of rotting leaves. After coming to a halt against the trunk of a tree she spat and spluttered the offending floor of the wood into the air. Her mouth wasn't dry, in the last seconds of her fall the offending foreign material hadn't been dry, it hadn't been dust. It offended her greatly and was deeply unpleasant but it hadn't been from the tunnel. The ground no longer shook. She listened, there was no longer a thundering roar, she could hear bird song and the rustle of last year's leaves, the air smelt gloriously damp and a myriad of aromas played with her senses. She was outside, she was in Asherugge. With the back of her hand she wiped dust and dirt from her closed eyes, eyes that she had kept tightly shut not wanting to witness what she'd been sure were to be her last moments. She blinked and opened her lids, maybe she wasn't where she thought she was after all, for everything was black. She closed her eyes tight and opened them once more, as wide as she could. She didn't want to believe what she saw for all she could see was black, nothing but blackness. In rapid succession she closed and opened her eyes each time hoping for a miracle, but her wish was not to be granted. Everything remained black.

Charlotte thought quickly, adrenaline still pumping around her body. Her first thought was, was she alive, was she really in Asherugge as she'd first thought or was she somewhere completely different, was, could this be her afterlife? Pain meant an escape, at least a temporary one from her anguished questioning. Her wrist ached and from the cold she knew she'd grazed her knee and her ribs felt as though they were going to spring free at any moment. The way she had come to rest, her head was lower than her feet, always an unnatural position to be in and one that left her vulnerable, she had to right herself. Pushing her question of was this life or her afterlife to one side, Charlotte forced herself to stand up using the trunk of the tree for support. Once upright she nervously felt the ground with her feet. She was still on a slope and so hadn't reached the bottom of wherever she was and the ground was uneven. Without sight remaining standing she found a struggle and it took several minutes before she felt just a little bit confident. At that moment, Charlotte promised herself if she was ever given the chance to aid someone who was blind she'd jump at the chance. For now she felt useless, trapped inside herself, she could hear, feel her surroundings but without being able to see felt completely lost. Refusing to panic, that had always got her nowhere, she carefully considered her options. She couldn't just stand there, that was admitting defeat, she may never be found and if this wasn't her afterlife she would soon meet it. She had to move, even if it was to be in the wrong direction. Moving was better than doing nothing, she had to keep her mind and body active. Anything else would be unbearable. The question now was, if she moved, in which direction? Help me Triskelion, help me, maybe wherever he was he could still hear her. Charlotte listened hard, there was plenty of noise but it all came from the wood, from her 'ghost' there was nothing. Realising the hopelessness of her situation Charlotte began to sob.

A good five minutes passed before she regained her composure. The one good thing. In her present predicament, in the five minutes that passed nobody had taken advantage, nothing had attacked her. She was still breathing, whether she was still alive or was this her afterlife was not a question she wanted to consider. Which direction had to be her next big decision, nothing more demanding than that. It was her natural inclination to descend, to go downhill and with no persuasive competition it was the direction she took. Progress was painfully slow, with her arms stretched feeling for obstacles she shuffled forward. Each time she started to gain in confidence and take longer steps she regretted it. On more than one occasion she took a fall and when you can't see where or what you're falling on, a fall can be a terrifying experience. Her greatest obstacles were trees. Their roots to be exact, especially those of the beech who liked to spread its lower limbs along the ground rather than bury them deep. Beech roots always announced their presence before she had a chance to feel their trunks with her hands. After being the cause of several falls she learnt to slide her feet rather than step forward, this way she became aware of any opposing root before it had opportunity to cause a fall. Rabbit holes came a close second to roots, they were far fewer in number but encountering one unprepared was not a pleasant and often painful experience.

Sight Charlotte was learning fast had a number of benefits beyond being able to see that she'd never considered. Balance was one, without sight she found herself swaying and had to constantly fight to avoid a fall. The second was the measure of time. She had no idea what the time was and how long had passed since she had made the decision to move. It could be minutes or several hours, she simply had no idea. It felt like hours, many hours but that maybe because every second she found a struggle. She simply had no idea. What she was very aware of, was the growing feeling of exhaustion both mentally and physically. The worst was not knowing if she was making any progress, if all her effort was going to end in nothing but pain with no gain. The not knowing was soul destroying and ate away at her sanity, sapping her few remaining energy reserves. Her early determination was draining fast and both her mind and body was in danger of shutting down. As she fell for the umpteenth time, Charlotte cracked. She started to cry and all her pent up stress and emotion poured to the surface. Her whole body shook as she accepted the reality of her situation and tears flooded down her face. In a last valiant attempt not to give in to defeat she struggled to get up. There was a tree close by, she'd knocked against it in her latest fall. Feeling with her hands she found the trunk and pulled herself towards it, intending to use its solidity to haul herself up. She caressed the trunk with both hands, from the roughness of the bark she knew she was being supported by an oak. Her recognition reminded her of Wodewose, how she needed her shaggy friend. Charlotte gripped the tree tightly, where are you Wodewose and still holding the tree she closed her eyes. She'd had enough.

The crumpled body of a child, a little girl, lay beneath the boughs of an ancient oak. The oak had witnessed much over the centuries but nothing quite like the goings on in recent days. A summer breeze played among the trees, the old oak waved. The action caught the attention of the mischievous air and the breeze in response swung low gathering in the valley and brushing a covering of leaves over the child's delicate figure, providing a semblance of warmth. A concerned robin skirted where she lay, calling for help to all that could hear. A jay, the sentry of the wood heard the robin and as is its duty sent out a cry. On hearing the jay those who called the wood their home gathered about, some close some at a distance. Feathered or furred, they had the same objective. Collectively they were determined to prevent any harm coming to the little human child. They had all heard the Snooks, the little human girl from another world was here on their behalf. She was their one hope. So it had been predicted by the book with no name and the book never lies.

Wodewose awoke from his sleep to find the root vine buzzing. His home, the ancient oak was physically shaking in an effort to wrest him from his slumber. All the wood was talking of the little human child, France Charlotte. She was in trouble, his old friend Ackley the oak had her at its roots and was calling for him to help her. What pained him more than anything, the wise old oak in his message told that France Charlotte in her distress had called for him. For him Wodewose and he had been selfishly asleep. He would never be able to live with himself if harm came to her, the first time she really needed him and he had been asleep. He hastily stepped out of his tree, Ackley grew not far from him. He would run all of the way.

"Don't let any harm come to her," he messaged his friend, "I am making haste."

"All the wood is watching over her," the message he received back gave him some relief. Wodewose started to run.

A little later he was looking down on the pile of leaves under which lay his little fragile friend, France Charlotte. Kneeling he delicately brushed away the leaves covering her face. Her normally rosy cheeked face he was shocked to see bore not a hint of red, in its place a ghastly greyish white associated more with death than a living being. Quickly and as gently as he could Wodewose brushed the remaining leaves away. What he saw pained him even more. France Charlotte's clothes were stained with the floor of the wood, evidence that she had taken a tumble at least once. There was a split in one trouser leg and blood had dried on the exposed knee matted with leaf mould. Her hair was tangled and supported a near nest of twigs and leaves. Shocking though her appearance was Wodewose with immense relief saw that the little girl was breathing, she hadn't met her afterlife as her appearance surely suggested. Gently Wodewose did his best to disentangle her hair and remove the trappings of the wood. Laying where she had fallen, France Charlotte looked so very frail and yet Wodewose observed she looked so peaceful and seeing her so, wondered if it was wise to wake her. The old oak, Ackley, spurred Wodewose into action, sending him a sharp message via the root tangled floor.

"Wodewose you have to move her, she cannot stay here, there is not even a moon to protect her tonight."

Wodewose reacted immediately shaking her gently whilst calling her name.

"France Charlotte, France Charlotte wake up, wake up." Charlotte's fuzzled brain registered the words but only just. Something shook her, was shaking her. A surge of strength, something which every living being possesses when their survival is threatened, prepared her for a fight, in under a second she was primed, ready to defend herself. Finding she still couldn't see whatever was attacking her Charlotte lashed out as hard as she could in the direction of whatever it was that had its grasp on her shoulder. Her fist found only air and she was preparing for a second strike when the voice came again.

"France Charlotte, it's me Wodewose."

"Wodewose," she whispered, letting her arms collapse. "Wodewose," she repeated and falling back onto the woodland floor started to laugh with relief."

Wodewose wasn't sure how to deal with France Charlotte's reaction, laughter wasn't at all the response he'd expected. He would never understand the strange beings known as humans.

"France Charlotte, are you ok?"

"Yes Wodewose, I'm okay, it's just that I can't see, I'm blind." Charlotte pointed to her eyes as she spoke, she had no idea if she looked blind but surely her eyes, if she cannot see, must be absent of any feeling. If Wodewose looked into him he would see that they were lifeless.

"Take my hand France Charlotte." Charlotte felt Wodewose's enormous hand clasp hers and as if she were weightless, hauled her to her feet. "I will carry you" and before Charlotte had a chance to object, Wodewose swung her under his arm. She somehow managed to stifle any cry of pain and continued to clench her teeth as Wodewose strode through the wood swinging her gently but freely.

"We must get you back to your world for now France Charlotte, it is not safe for you here tonight, you can come back tomorrow." Charlotte was just about to reply to say how could she if she couldn't see when she experienced a stinging sensation in her eyes. The pain was excruciating, something was attempting to blind her, no that was stupid she was already blind. A natural reaction Charlotte blinked and closed her eyes quickly as cutting arrows of light stung her eyes. Light!

"Stop, Wodewose stop, please put me down." Wodewose stopped, afraid he had somehow hurt his friend. With exaggerated slowness he carefully lowered France Charlotte to the floor.

"Sorry France Charlotte, am I hurting you?" he realised a little late that he may have been a little rough in his hurry to see her safely across the wood.

"No, no," Charlotte lied, "hold my hand." Wodewose did as he was told. Feeling secure Charlotte blinked her eyes open at the same time shading them with her hands, fingers cracked. At first the brightness even with the protection of her hands brought more pain. With nervous expectation she tried to put the pain to one side and forced her eyelids to stay open. The pain along with the brightness slowly calmed, fading until they were a memory only. In their place there shone a sea of colour. Taking her hands away Charlotte gazed at the scene in front of her, never before had the woodland of Asherugge appeared so beautiful. She wanted to run and embrace every colour, every shade.

"Wodewose, I can see." Charlotte's exclamation split the air with excitement.

"That's good, France Charlotte." The matter of fact way with which he replied, Charlotte felt Wodewose wasn't at all surprised at her announcement. It was almost as though he'd expected it. She was about to question him as to why and decided against it, she would leave it for another time when Wodewose was more relaxed. Right now he was tense.

"I can walk now," she told him. "There's no need to carry me."

"You do not hurt, France Charlotte, it is no trouble for me to carry you." There was genuine concern, sketched across Wodewose's face.

"No," Charlotte lied again, she had become an expert since visiting Otherworld. "I'm fine, where are we going?"

"To Aldeborie, you must go back to your world tonight and return tomorrow. It is too dangerous for you to remain here tonight." He repeated what he had warned her earlier but offered no explanation as to why. Charlotte accepted her fate.

"Ok Wodewose."

"We go quick France Charlotte, before darkness comes." Wodewose started to stride through the wood as he said this. In her excitement Charlotte hadn't noticed that the light was just beginning to fade and already shadows were beginning to lengthen, merging slowly into one. Dusk would soon be upon them, had she really been gone that long!

It didn't take them long to reach the top of the scarp, Wodewose had stridden with a purpose Charlotte had never witnessed before and she'd had to run all the way just to keep up. With the recent persistent rain the steep incline was even more of a challenge than normal. The exposed chalk surface afforded little or no grip and twice Charlotte slid to the ground, once landing on her injured wrist. Her resultant yell caused Wodewose to swing his staff, in fear they were being attacked. His reflex swing only narrowly missed Charlotte's head and this made her determined to in future keep her suffering to herself. On arriving at the tree line, Wodewose hesitated. Before them lay the open field with the lone oak, home to the messenger. Beyond in the growing darkness a scattering of lights announced Aldeborie and her passage home. Wodewose despite the growing darkness waited beneath the tree cover. He looked more nervous than Charlotte had ever seen him before but she was impatient, she wanted to return to her world, to see her parents.

"Are we going?" she asked Wodewose passing through the fence, a feat that pleased her immensely. Wodewose continued to hesitate. "Come on," she urged but still Wodewose hesitated, his fearsome face to those who didn't know him, etched with his own fear. Fear that Charlotte saw he was desperately trying to hide from her.

"I prefer the wood," Wodewose eventually gave in and admitted his mistrust. "I don't like fields, I like trees. Fields make me nervous." It was the closest Wodewose had to come to admitting he was scared of open spaces. Charlotte with shame remembered her friend's nervousness when they had, some time ago crossed the open valley floor and the open ground on their way from Leht's, the first time they had met. How could she be so insensitive.

"It's ok Wodewose, I'll be ok, you stay here, I'll see you tomorrow." She didn't like the idea of leaving his protection but the gateway wasn't far. "I'll be ok," Charlotte hoped she sounded convincing.

"I'll watch you go," Wodewose assured her, "and wait for you tomorrow."

"Thank you Wodewose." Charlotte turned to go then stopped, she turned back to face him. "Wodewose." Charlotte paused reflecting on whether to continue. She decided she had to. "You haven't asked me where Triskelion is."

"He has met his afterlife," Wodewose replied as though it were an everyday occurrence. Charlotte, visibly shocked, asked simply.

"How do you know?"

"The Snooks foretold it." From his expression it was obvious he thought that was explanation enough. There was nothing else to say.

"You must hurry France Charlotte, you must go." Charlotte reached up and kissed the side of his face.

"I'm going," and started running across the field to the oak.

She had a sudden urge to see her parents, she was only eleven and her youth had caught up with her. She had seen enough, done enough and had enough. What she had experienced in one day, most adults would never experience in a lifetime. On reaching the oak she carefully lifted the strap of the budget over her shoulder, in all the excitement she had forgotten the leather sack still contained the 'light blood' of Leht. Looking inside she was relieved to find that none of the heavy liquid appeared to have been spilt. Next she eased off her necklace and dropped it in the bag with Leht and the map. After surveying her surroundings she carefully placed everything in the hidden hollow beneath the oak. On standing she found the squirrel waiting at her feet. It looked up at her and in that moment Charlotte recognised concern on its face. Over the past weeks she had learnt to read the facial expressions of birds and animals, no more did they all look expressionless. And now what she was witnessing with the 'messenger' was a definite concern.

On seeing that France Charlotte had spotted him the squirrel started down the slope towards the lane at the bottom of the valley. Charlotte followed her breathing laboured, she could no longer ignore the pain that hampered each intake of air. Without even thinking she passed through the field gate and followed the squirrel along the lane into Aldeborie. As usual there lay everywhere a heavy silence and that evening it felt even heavier. There was, Charlotte felt, a hint of a threat as well, something she'd never sensed before, she hoped it was nothing but her imagination. It was something of a relief when they arrived at the church gate, she was almost home, she had had enough of Otherworld for one day. The squirrel waited until Charlotte had caught up then started up the path through the churchyard to the church door. Charlotte followed, as she ran she saw the robin fluttering above them, strange she thought, it's normally perched on the porch. Ahead the squirrel arrived at the stone slab and Charlotte quickened her pace so as not to be far behind. She was preparing to leap onto the stone slab when to her surprise the squirrel instead of disappearing below ground emitted a loud shriek, leapt vertically into the air and on landing belted past her back down the path from where they'd just come. Charlotte, shocked, her first instinct was to follow but blind curiosity prevented her. The stone slab was only two more paces and she wanted to see what had caused such a startling reaction. At first she could see nothing untoward, the stone slab was where it always was, it hadn't been moved, that had been her first suspicion. Focusing on the stone she saw there was something, something laying on top. Taking a step closer she saw that it was a feather and from its near perfect position, laying between two points of the square it looked as if it had almost certainly been placed there, that its presence was no accident. With curiosity still in charge Charlotte bent down to pick it up and as her eyes drew close she recognised the feather as unmistakably having come from a magpie. The realisation caused her to hesitate and as she did so the robin landed on the path before her and hopped about in a most bizarre fashion. From the squirrel's reaction and now the robin Charlotte knew something must be wrong and in a rush it dawned on her, she was in imminent danger. Adrenaline, fast becoming a familiar friend surged through her body beating her pain into submission. In under a[1] second she could taste the hormone entering her mouth and she sprang upright, coiled, ready to fight or run. Wildly she glanced around her, was it her imagination or were the gravestones moving. The whole world about her appeared to be moving and she felt a familiar feeling forming in her stomach. Fear was taking hold and soon it would rise and let its presence be known to every nerve in her body. Charlotte heard Leht's voice.

"Do not allow fear to take over France Charlotte, the Darkness will use your fear to possess you."

Leht's voice faded as stealthily as it had arrived. Charlotte swallowed hard, her own fear was her greatest enemy, she had to bury it if she was to survive. She gulped desperate to take in air, looking about her the world had stopped moving, every gravestone stood still in respectful silence. She was winning, she no longer had the same level of fear though still the adrenaline pumped, preparing her for the unexpected and the unexpected duly arrived. Something moved and whatever it was, was only a few feet away. The robin stopped its frantic prancing and flew straight to the porch's castellated roof, sitting on the cross that welcomed worshippers into its fold. Charlotte, with her eyes followed its flight and stopped, standing in front of the arched door stood Ashtynn.

At first Charlotte was surprised rather than shocked to see the friendly shop assistant and was almost ready to greet her in some fashion when she focused on her face. Ashtynn's eyes blazed white and her normally cheerful face was so contorted with hate that it verged on the grotesque. Gone was the look of terror, every muscle was now fashioned on mal intent. Her mouth stretched artificially wide in a salacious leer, teeth bared with morbid expectation. Saliva ran freely from each corner cumulating beneath her chin before dropping to the ground. Charlotte froze like a rabbit, caught in a car's headlights. Ashtynn took a menacing step forward and that did it, Charlotte regained her free thinking consciousness and flew down the church path just as Ashtynn lunged at her. She felt her coat jerk and realised Ashtynn had hold and tore the front open struggling at the same time to free herself from the sleeves. As she fought she could hear Ashtynn snarling, it was a sound no living being on Earth possessed. It was from a place that was not of her world, nor Otherworld. It was of a place where light was absent. The sound sent shivers down Charlotte's spine, she had no wish to visit such a place and pulled hard, drawing on all the reserves she still possessed including some she didn't. Her effort sent her sprawling forward, almost tumbling down the path. Steadying herself she found her footing and ran full pelt towards the village pond. At the churchyard gate she stupidly took a second to look back. Ashtynn to her relief hadn't chased her down the path, instead she had remained by the door to the church. In her hands she held what was left of her coat. Like a being possessed Ashtynn was tearing at it with everything she had, as though her life depended on it. Soon her coat would be nothing but shredded cloth, unrecognisable. Charlotte shivered, if she hadn't managed to free herself that could be her being torn apart.

A short sharp bark brought Charlotte to her senses. The squirrel, resting on its hind legs, was at her feet desperately trying to win her attention. On seeing it had succeeded the squirrel started to scurry along the Evinghehou road, heading for the hills. Charlotte followed, exhaustion beginning to set in, adrenalin the fuel that had kept her going till now almost on empty. On leaving Aldeborie the squirrel took the now familiar route across the field to the lone oak. Surely, Charlotte thought the Darkness and its agents must know where they're heading, they'd taken this route so many times before. One day they'll walk right into a trap, maybe this was to be that moment. As she struggled to keep up Charlotte kept glancing back over her shoulder expecting to see Ashtynn or shadows in hot pursuit. Always there was nothing, the scene behind was of near perfect serenity, a perfect lie. In any case she was so tired she was almost past caring, content to place all her faith in the squirrel, the messenger and in this growing mood struggled up the grass incline. On reaching the oak to the squirrel's relief nothing or no one was lying in wait, he'd been worried gnombres may have surrounded his tree. Charlotte wasn't sure to what purpose but once more she withdrew the budget from the hidden hollow and placed the necklace and then the budget round her neck. What to do next, Charlotte had no idea, soon it would be dark and to be safe according to Triskelion she needed to find light. The only nearby light came from the valley below, in Aldeborie and despite the dangers she had no wish to return to the village where all manner of things may be lying in wait. And the thought of encountering Ashtynn in the dark made her feel physically sick. She preferred the threat of the unknown lurking in the wood to that. Anything other than encountering Ashtynn again. As it turned out the decision wasn't to be hers. Once more the squirrel took the lead and started up the slope towards the tree line. Charlotte devoid of ideas felt, like so many times before she had no other choice than to follow. This in spite, with darkness descending, the wood already beginning to take on a very different feel.

Charlotte could no longer run, the only way she could reach the tree line was with a steady walk. She knew she was close to giving up and her mind was already apologising to the rest of her for her weak mental fortitude. As they approached the first line of trees she saw movement among the shadows. Charlotte instinctively held back, the squirrel appeared not to notice and Charlotte understood why. Out of the shadows emerged a rather startling figure and one Charlotte knew well, Wodewose. He'd been waiting. Charlotte couldn't stop herself from smiling as she saw her friend striding towards her, "good old reliable Wodewose." Wodewose may not be the answer to her prayers but he was a start.

"I help you France Charlotte," and Charlotte didn't wince once as Wodewose scooped her up and swung her under his arm. Confident he had the little human girl secure he started to retrace their steps from earlier, climbing back up the wooded scarp. Even for Wodewose the climb was a struggle. Descending he'd taken advantage of the exposed chalk and loose earth for speed, when it came to the ascent the same features allowing little or no grip were a serious hindrance.

With some effort they arrived without incident at the top of the escarpment. At first Wodewose bore right following the rim, by now the cloak of darkness was covering all Otherworld and lights that falsely beckoned friendship twinkled invitingly in the valley below. Charlotte ignored them, her only thought was where Wodewose was taking her? As her mind asked the question, Wodewose changed direction bearing left into the wood, ahead a light shone through the trees. Charlotte recognised it as coming from a cottage. She'd passed it several times whilst on walks with her parents. Surely he wasn't taking her there, the thought of spending a night alone in a remote cottage, surrounded by trees didn't appeal to her at all. She'd watched far too many scary movies at her friend Caroline's involving a remote cottage in a wood and there was never a happy ending. Wodewose had no intention of stopping at the cottage, before reaching it he veered left again almost turning back on himself. Charlotte knew Wodewose wasn't far from his home, surely he couldn't be taking her there, there was nowhere there for her to hide safely. No, they were traveling deeper into the wood passing his ancient oak. He was heading for Amphillicia's Well, even in the cloak of darkness Charlotte recognised the underwood, the surrounding trees. She soon saw she'd been right. As he approached the mud pool Wodewose lessened his pace and bent low until he was almost creeping on all fours. Charlotte went to ask to be put down but Wodewose put his finger to his lips and shook his head. Something was afoot. They came to a halt and for the first time since they'd left the field Charlotte realised the squirrel was no longer with them. Wodewose hadn't moved since they'd stopped, like a pointer he was staring straight ahead, his nose raised to the air. In her compromised position, Charlotte strained her neck to see ahead. Through the trees she could just make out the debris strewn circular mire that Triskelion called Amphillicia's Well. Starlight glinted on the surface water delivered by the recent rain. Everything was still, there was no hint of a breeze, the atmosphere around and over the pond was brooding as though waiting for something to happen. Charlotte felt Wodewose tense and at the same moment she thought she saw one of the darker shadows hidden from the starlight move. With such stillness a shadow had no right to be moving. The Well Charlotte realised was being watched. Wodewose evidently having seen it too, took several steps back, not a sound did he make. On gaining what he must have considered a safe distance Wodewose quickened his pace. In a few minutes, a light told Charlotte they were approaching another woodland cottage. Light leaking from the garden illuminated an access lane. To Charlotte, after Amphillicia's Well the light looked welcoming and thought Wodewose might make for it but he must have had good reason not to, for instead he took a wide berth. On meeting the Northchurch to Dagnall road they crossed to enter the wooded Berkhamsted Common. As soon as they were once more in the company of trees Wodewose's pace quickened to a run. It was now very dark, clouds had eclipsed the few visible stars. There were no more shadows, just dark outlines, some shaded darker than others. Every shape, every darkened outline in the wood, Charlotte knew without any light could pose a threat, a mortal threat and by Wodewose's sprint she knew he was scared, not for himself but for her. Where needed Wodewose used his staff to clear the way ahead. At the beginning, when they'd first entered the wood their passage had been silent, one of stealth. The priority now it seemed was speed and haste in a wood cannot be achieved quietly. Their passage had become anything but silent and with every minute that passed, stealth it seemed to Charlotte became less and less of a factor.

As they progressed Charlotte sensed that Wodewose was beginning to tire, his pace becoming lumbered. She called for him to put her down but Wodewose didn't even acknowledge that he'd heard her. After some time Charlotte saw they were approaching what looked like a sea of black. It was, she soon realised a large open expanse of grass. Wodewose visibly slowed, not from tiredness but for the reason of caution. Soon after he stopped altogether and carefully lowered Charlotte till she was standing beside him. As he did so he put a finger to his lips signalling for her to keep silent. With his other hand he took hers and together they edged slowly forward. Before them in what little light there was loomed a huge tree, perhaps bigger and more magnificent than the beech beneath which, in Otherworld Charlotte had first been introduced to Leht's light. Wodewose she saw was making for it, step by cautious step. Charlotte remained guided by Wodewose's hand, she couldn't shake her eyes from the tree, it was a true grandmaster.

Without warning a force sent her flying. Charlotte felt leaves and branches scratch indiscriminately as she flew through the air. The odd scratch was nothing to the pain she felt as she landed, she was about to cry out when she saw the glare on Wodewose's face. His glare, not one of anger but pleading for her not to make a sound.

"Shhhhh," he confirmed in a strained whisper, "stay here till it's safe." Stay where? Lying on her back, looking up she saw she was beneath a spread of holly. A "safe place," she remembered. Rolling onto her front she strained to see through the darkness, trying to get a good view of her surroundings and more importantly her Wodewose. She could just about make out his unmistakable figure. He was she saw, steadily and very slowly stepping towards the huge tree, from its outline it looked like a beech but Charlotte couldn't be sure. Without warning there was a cry and shadows that up until that moment had simply been part of the landscape rose up from all around lunging towards her shaggy friend. With a roar that would cause the most determined foe to hesitate Wodewose burst forward diving for the great tree. Just as it looked as though hundreds of teeth bearing shadows were about to bring him down Wodewose reached the tree and after a tap with his staff stepped through the bark vanishing into the gnarled trunk. From beneath the holly Charlotte watched in horror and struggled to sustain a sigh of relief as Wodewose appeared to have made it to safety. A burning sensation against her chest, very like a bee sting diverted her attention. Forcing down a cry of pain she carefully felt beneath her jumper expecting to find some sort of insect. To her surprise there was no insect, the pain wasn't from a bite or a sting it was from the charm on her necklace. The little heart was burning hot as though it had been in a fire, so hot was it that Charlotte couldn't touch it with her bare hands. Carefully and with difficulty she pulled the charm out from beneath her jumper by the necklace and let it dangle outside her clothes. Even hanging there she could still feel it burning, but at least the pain was bearable. She felt tempted to remove the necklace altogether but a voice in her head, a voice she now trusted was telling her not to.

With her chin resting on the ground, Charlotte tried to see if the shadows, which she felt sure must be gnombres, were still there or whether after Wodewose had found the safety of the tree they had given up and left. To her dismay she saw that they remained, every one of them was statue still but she now knew what to look for and the magnificent tree she saw was surrounded. As she looked on, searching for ideas Charlotte gradually became aware of another presence, a darker far more menacing presence than the gnombres. One that expunged every morsel of good before it, turning every innocent thought to one of fear. Charlotte recognised the presence at once, it had only weeks ago got close to catching her in the churchyard. She recalled how the evil had almost overcome her through fear, terror perhaps was a more apt description of how she'd felt at the time. She remembered Triskelion had a name for the presence. He had described it as a wayward spirit and its name remained clear in her mind, Scucca. Through the branches of the holly she could just make out the dark indistinct shape of the wayward spirit. It literally loomed above her and from its presence it appeared that Scucca had grown, in strength as well as stature since their brief acquaintance in the churchyard. Even knowing fear was the spirit's greatest weapon Charlotte struggled to contain hers. Fear ebbed away at every nerve, endeavouring to unlock just one door into her mind. She had no doubt that if she were discovered, it would be the end of her, there would be no chance of escape. If Scucca found her, her only want would be for her afterlife to arrive quickly. For a brief moment, her mind moved to the plight of the white hart. What she was facing now was nothing to what he was facing on a daily basis. The thought brought renewed determination, once more she tasted adrenalin on her tongue, not fear. Beneath her, her charm was burning almost white hot. She couldn't understand why but despite the pain she felt it was a good thing that it was. She was lucky, she thought, to have two hearts.

The bed of holly on which Charlotte lay was not the most comfortable of mattresses, leaves pricked at every opportunity. Before her, the dark shape that was Scucca rose up in front of the magnificent and obviously very ancient tree in which Wodewose was hiding. The gnombres had started to move, circling the broad trunk in unruly fashion. Where she lay Charlotte could taste their ghoulish anticipation. Out of nowhere came a scream and a bolt of lightning split the sky striking the tree protecting Wodewose. There followed a sickening sound of something being torn and to Charlotte's horror a crack ran down the centre of the tree's colossal trunk. The top of the tree began to sway, not one way and then the next but in two separate directions. The tree she saw was tearing into two. At first the process was slow, then as though something had snapped the split in the trunk widened and within seconds the trunk had ruptured, separate sides crashing to the woodland floor in an ear splitting crescendo. Exposed where the trunk had once been, still holding his staff stood a terrified and unbelieving Wodewose. A cheer went up from the dark shapes surrounding the base of the stricken tree and in a bloodthirsty frenzy gnombres swarmed towards her helpless friend. As the teeth bearing shadows smothered him she saw Wodewose raise his right arm and throw his staff into the air. It was to be his final act. The staff somersaulted several times before coming to land, no more than a metre away from where Charlotte lay hidden. She felt herself tense expecting the staff to be pounced upon and her hiding place discovered. No one though appeared bothered, Wodewose's trusty staff lay where it had fallen, instantly forgotten, blending with the many other fallen boughs littering the woodland floor. His shaggy arm was the last Charlotte saw of her, "wild man" of the woods, her protector who had, like her never asked to be part of this war. In less than a minute of being exposed her dear, dear Wodewose was gone. After their success, the gnombres faded into the ground and the dark entity that was Scucca simply vanished. Charlotte closed her eyes swallowing continuously to prevent herself from crying. Despite her best effort the odd tear forced their way between her tightly closed lids. Those that got through she quickly wiped away with her fingers. She owed it to Wodewose not to show any weakness. Beneath the holly she waited and waited sure that at any moment she would be pulled into the open and meet a similar end to her friend. She waited and waited but nothing moved and she could hear nothing but silence. A silence charged with shock, for every tree in the wood was struggling to come to terms with the violent end of their father. Charlotte felt their pain, she didn't realise it but what she felt was the root vine buzzing below her. Opening her eyes through tear blurred vision she saw what remained of the once proud tree. The trunk completely split in two lay prostrate on the woodland floor, the canopy a tangled mass of broken limbs. Where she had last seen her friend there was nothing, no sign at all of his falling, just freshly torn wood and an empty space.

Charlotte had no idea how long she lay under the holly bush. It could have been minutes, it could have been hours, time no longer seemed to matter. Her body damp from lying on rain soaked leaves was cold but that didn't matter either. The fact that the charm hanging from her necklace no longer burned escaped her attention. Her mind, her body, both were incapable of feeling. A star could have landed just metres away and she wouldn't have noticed, she was that numb. She lay, vulnerable but no longer caring, at one with the woodland surrounding her. The first sound she remembered her brain registering was a rustle generated by the movement of leaves. The sound felt close but she didn't care, she chose to ignore it and her eyes remained shut. The rustle short and sharp came again and this time she sensed something before her. Common sense told her that she should open her eyes, see what was making the noise, what was causing the leaves to stir but the world outside was so horrible she preferred not to see, not to know. She kept her eyes shut, tightly shut. The sound came again and this time it was close, very close, maybe only centimetres away. Something tickled her nose and Charlotte relented, she opened her eyes, prepared for the worst.

Crouched before her, almost touching sat the squirrel, her messenger. She blinked to make sure she wasn't seeing things, she wasn't there sat her squirrel. It brushed her nose with his then backed away.

"Where did you go?" Charlotte whispered. She had no idea if he understood her question and even if he did he had no way of replying. The squirrel seeing he had her attention scurried away, ran back and scurried away again. Charlotte recognised the signs. The squirrel wanted her to follow him. With the fate of her friend vivid in her mind she was reluctant to leave the shelter of the holly, it had protected her from a similar fate. The squirrel frustrated by her reluctance to move, scurried back and forth with more urgency, kicking up leaves in the process. At one point he even had the courage to tap her on the nose.

"Alright," whispered Charlotte fiercely. "I hope you know what you're doing." Reluctantly she crawled out from under the holly. After lying in one place for so long hardly moving she found it a struggle to stand. When she managed to, she stretched hard, awakening cold cramped limbs. Pins and needles confirmed that blood had started to reach her outer limits. The squirrel watched her from the floor of the wood, twitching its impatience. Charlotte wouldn't be hurried, after everything she'd been through she deserved some time, anyway whichever way you looked at it where she was standing now was as safe as anywhere else, or as dangerous as anywhere else. Stretching by standing on her toes, Charlotte surveyed her surroundings. All was in darkness, there was no silvered moonlight and no coloured starlight penetrating the cloud. The sound of an owl electrified the air, normally its haunting cry would unnerve her, on this occasion it was a welcome sign that there was still life. The once proud tree where Wodewose had made his last stand, may have fallen but it still dominated the immediate scene. It would dominate for many more years before its body became part of the earth. Charlotte walked over to the ruptured trunk and touched where her shaggy friend had disappeared under a writhing mass of gnombres. There was not one sign that he had ever stood there. A life spanning thousands of years and nothing to commemorate it. If she ever got the chance, she would have to right that wrong. It was a promise she was determined to keep, the same for Triskelion. The squirrel brushed against her leg, she saw it was becoming desperate to make a move. Wherever it wanted to take her, Charlotte recognised it might be prudent to follow. With one last touch of the stricken tree she turned to let the squirrel lead her away. She had barely taken a step when she thought she saw something move beneath her feet. In the dark it was difficult to make out what was on the ground and with the mindset that whatever it was couldn't help them, decided to ignore it. As she went to take another step the movement came again and this time something compelled her to see what it was. Examining the ground she could see nothing out of the ordinary, nothing but the normal woodland debris. It must be a mouse she told herself and once more made to follow the squirrel. The movement came a third time and this time she had the feeling that whatever it was, was deliberately trying to win her attention.

"Wait," she hissed to the bristling squirrel, "one sec." Charlotte bent over to examine the woodland floor more closely. It was hard to see anything clearly, how she needed the light of the moon. Refusing to give up she waited for her eyes to learn to use the fraction of light that existed even under a lightless sky. What had previously been dark shapes slowly became identifiable. Still though all she could make out were last year's leaves and fallen boughs with the odd clump of something growing. She was about to give up and made to rise when the movement came again and this time she saw what she thought had made it. Lying where it had fallen lay Wodewose's staff. Surely it hadn't been his staff that had moved, that was impossible, even in Otherworld. Charlotte didn't care, she wasn't leaving it. It was all she had to remember her friend by. She gripped the staff hard as though her life depended on it and used it to heave herself up.

"Let's go," Charlotte nodded to the squirrel. The squirrel needed no further encouragement and took off, retracing the route Charlotte and Wodewose had taken only hours earlier. Under a moonless sky the wood was always an ominous place to be. You could never escape the feeling that somebody or something was watching you. Even so carrying in her hands something that had been so dear to her shaggy friend, Charlotte felt a hundred times better than she had just a few minutes ago.

Early on she realised the squirrel was leading her back via the route Wodewose had taken her, not that long ago. At every step she expected gnombres or even worse the terrifying spirit, Scucca to ambush them but nothing or no one did. Their passage through the dark wood though tense remained trouble free. The squirrel didn't let up until it reached the strangely silent Northchurch to Dagnall road. Here it stopped and resting on its hind legs sniffed the air. A previously hidden muntjac deer, ventured into the road ahead of them. At the centre it paused and with what Charlotte recognised as false nonchalance looked left and right. After a swing of its head, quite unhurried it continued to cross disappearing into the shadows on the far side. Charlotte wasn't sure what to make of what she had just witnessed. Whether the timing of the deer's crossing had been a coincidence or whether it was somehow working with the squirrel. Either way the squirrel decided it was safe to cross and after doing a spin darted across the tarmac. Charlotte sprinted close behind, beating down the resulting pain in her chest. Once more in Old Copse Charlotte now knew where the squirrel was taking her. Minutes later, as earlier she was to be proved right. Before them lay the muddy mass that in Otherworld they called, Amphillicia's Well. Unlike Wodewose earlier the squirrel did not hold back. It ran at the mass of mud, dappled with dark pools of water and headfirst dived into the mire, promptly vanishing. Charlotte hesitated, thought she saw a movement somewhere in the surrounding shadows and grasping Wodewose's staff tightly, quickly followed.

From the underwood a muntjac deer watched on. She hadn't meant to frighten the little girl but the fact she had done may be a blessing. The waters of the well will protect her, under the care of Amphillicia she will be gifted much needed strength. Pleased with the roll she'd played the deer moved off to continue her unassuming and lonesome life beneath the woodland canopy.

For a split second Charlotte saw a soft light below her and then she landed. Not in mud but in water, water clearer than crystal, water that felt warm, water that was soft and comforting, refreshing like a freshly laundered bed. There was no splash, from what she could see there was no resulting spray, just a feeling of falling gently, sinking into a mattress made from liquid. The deeper she fell the softer the glow and the more Charlotte felt at peace. Strands of red hair streaked with gold waved past her with the flow of water, shimmering like dew soaked grass responding to the morning light. Filling the pool above her appeared a face, a delicate female face that shone with kindness and a smile that bade welcome.

"Amphillicia," Charlotte smiled her recognition.

Amphillicia's smile in return was spellbinding, almost identical to Leht's, Charlotte could concentrate on nothing else. It made her feel welcome, comfortable, feelings she had almost forgotten existed. The pain that had been tormenting both her mind and body evaporated along with all her worries and suppressed fear. The glow brightened and in response Charlotte felt her eyelids drop, soon her eyes were completely closed. For a fleeting second she wondered if the squirrel was still with her and how they would leave the well, or would she be trapped forever like the artist? And her parents, her parents, when would she next see them? Her eyes remained closed and such questions became irrelevant, all her concerns floated away, she was left feeling she had not a care in the world. And what a delicious feeling that was.

Chapter Eighteen

Two Worlds

Aldbury. Our world.

The vicar returned to his office. Once again he would need the assistance of the rusting iron cross. Dragging the cross behind him he returned to the cupboard and kneeling, using his fingers felt for the boards hidden by the dark vapour. He needed to find a gap between the boards wide enough for him to insert the thin end of the cross. He quickly discovered whoever had nailed the boards in place had either been very slapdash or finished the job in a hurry for none of the boards were flush and he found more than one gap into which he felt could squeeze the tip of the cross. With a good deal of effort he managed to angle the cross into the cupboard, guiding the thin end with his left hand to one of the gaps between the boards. The task was far more difficult than he had first imagined. One, the cross was very, very heavy and kept escaping his grasp, and two the tip was wider than he first thought and slipped every time he thought he'd found a suitable position. Working in a confined space he was also hot and even when kneeling he had to bend unnaturally to work with the result that several of his limbs were beginning to complain. One or two quite loudly. The atmosphere was also most unpleasant, the dense foul smelling vapour almost filled the entire cupboard and as a consequence he was working blind. If that wasn't enough the smell made him want to vomit and he had to make himself retch on a regular basis to stop himself from being physically sick. Everything combined what he always knew was going to be a difficult job was made almost impossible. More than once he had to retreat from the cupboard to regain his composure. He had almost reached the point where he worried that what he was attempting was impossible when the tip of the cross caught and more importantly held. For a moment, the vicar didn't dare to move in case he caused the cross to slip free. For over a minute he remained motionless, trying to calm himself by taking deep steady breaths and spitting out the resulting bad taste. At last, confident that the cross wouldn't slip he brought his weight to bear on the base. He felt the wooden board start to bend under the pressure. He was determined to either prise the nails free or split the board into two. Either would be a good result, he pushed down harder on the cold iron.

A loud knocking, an unexpected distraction caused the vicar to slip. Falling head first into the cupboard, he swore loudly. The cross slipped and fell, grazing his left hand. He cursed again at the resulting pain. The banging came again, someone was knocking on the door. Nursing his injured hand he froze, he wanted to pretend he hadn't heard it but the knocking continued. "Go away," he whispered under his breath, "go away." His wish wasn't to be granted, for a fourth time came the loud repetitive banging this time with a lot more force. The vicar considered whether to answer may be his best plan of action. He remembered his car was parked out front and with all the lights on in the church it would be reasonable for anyone passing to assume he was inside. The last thing he wanted was for whoever it was at the door to become concerned and call the police. He had almost made up his mind to answer the door when the banging suddenly ceased. The vicar remained kneeling hardly daring to breathe, not sure what to do. Had whoever was knocking gone or were they standing outside listening for a noise? He continued to remain kneeling, his mind in a quandary. He was still debating when he saw a shadow pass along the wall of the passage. Whoever had been knocking on the door he realised had come around the back of the church to look in through the windows. It must be somebody who knew the church. He tried to peer out but it was too much of a risk, with the lights on he may be seen. The shadow on the wall told him whoever it was, was leaning against the glass, trying to see in. He wasn't sure how much, whoever it was could see, was he, where he was kneeling visible from the outside, he wasn't sure? The shadow moved slightly and stilled, whoever it was, was attempting to get a better look. The vicar felt he couldn't afford to take any risks, he must not let himself be seen. Slowly he slid to the floor submerging himself beneath the foul smelling vapour. For several wretched minutes he lay flat on the cold tiles trying not to retch. Twice he risked peering above the "breath of the Devil," and on the second occasion the shadow he saw was moving, whoever it was, was leaving. He risked peering around the cupboard door, just in time to recognise the figure of Mrs Fowler, the church bookkeeper disappearing around the front of the church. When he had finished he decided, he would call her, put her at ease. He would have to think of a story, he would have to lie.

He desperately needed fresh air, after lying beneath the vapour his mouth felt as though it had shrivelled, his tongue as though it were rotting. Fresh air though was a luxury he couldn't afford. Fresh water was his only other option. Going to the sink he ran the cold tap and leaning his head underneath drank as though his life depended on it, stopping only to spit out any water that had fouled by remaining in his mouth too long. After liberating his taste buds he cupped his hands and splashed water over his face and onto the back of his neck. Finally he rinsed his grazed hand. Feeling refreshed he felt ready to return to the task in hand. He was determined to discover what was under the floor. He was convinced now he had got so far that the boards and the slabs had been placed there to hide something, and whatever it was he felt, could hold the key to what was happening to the village and his church. What he may find no longer held fear for him, he was ready for anything, even if he was to meet the Devil himself.

Kneeling as before he lent into the cupboard and felt for the cross. His hands found it immediately. Sliding it back a little he felt for the crack he'd used earlier. This too he found easily, the board had splintered through his earlier exertions and the splinters guided his hand to the crevice. With both hands he guided the tip of the cross into position and when it held once again levered with all his strength. The board wasn't going to give up without a struggle and fought strongly against being dislodged. The vicar for his part was equally determined and little by little he felt his efforts being rewarded. The board began to loosen, in particular the end closest to the rear wall. Sensing victory he slid the cross further beneath the board and levered back and forth. There came a splintering sound and then a loud crack and he fell sideways as the cross no longer met with resistance. Pushing himself up the vicar felt for the freed board. Clouds of the dark vapour, the "Devil's breath," he was convinced of it billowed out of the new opening. Far from being put off by the foul smelling effluvium the vicar was all the surer he was on the right track, the result simply made him more determined. With his hands he felt for the loosened board and quickly found it. With all his strength he pulled it towards him. There was another crack and the board came away completely, throwing him backwards. In celebration he threw the board across the passage and returned to the cupboard. Feeling the floor he found the space exposed by the removal of the board and leaning further reached in with his arm. Whatever the cavity was it was large, reaching in up to his elbow, he still couldn't find anything solid, only empty space. Pushing himself back onto his knees, he found the iron cross and started on the second board. The second board too resisted strongly but proved no match for the vicars renewed vigour and within minutes it too was being thrown across the passage. The third came away a little more easily, quite a gap was starting to emerge.

Working the fourth board, the vicar, had perhaps become a little too confident and as the board prised free he lost his grip on the cross and its weight sent it tumbling into the newly exposed chasm. A loud clang echoed around the cupboard as the heavy cross landed on solid stone. The echo didn't stop there, it was followed by another and several more as the cross continued to fall. At any second the vicar expected the cross to come to a rest but the echoes never ceased, they simply became muffled as the cross fell deeper and deeper into the earth. The vicar listened intently, he knew not what he'd expected but he hadn't expected this. Whatever the cavity was the boards had been hiding it wasn't simply a hidey hole as he'd first suspected. The hole, judging by the length of the fall, and the cross was still falling, was deep, metres, possibly tens of metres deep. The cross eventually came to rest with a reverberating vibration that bounded up the shaft, filling the cupboard. There followed an eerie almost threatening silence accompanied by the smell of burning. The smell of burning lasted perhaps a couple of minutes, the stench resembling rotting flesh once more gaining the upper hand.

The vicar waited for any further noise but there was nothing more, nothing but an unnerving silence. He felt the need to freshen and again retreated to the sink, repeating his actions of a little earlier. Almost refreshed he returned to the cupboard, another couple of boards and he'd be able to get a good feel around the cavity below. However using only his bare hands the boards were always going to win. He needed something else to finish the job. Once more he returned to his office. There were drawers and cupboards everywhere, hoarding just about everything. Collections of objects built up over many decades by servants of the church. It wasn't long before he found what he was searching for. At the back of a drawer. you could always rely on the back of a drawer he mused, it was the same in his house, he found a hammer. Fully armed he returned to the cupboard. This time, after much hammering and levering the two remaining boards gave in, uncovering a large unknown.

Rather than enter head first, the vicar sat and swung both his legs over the edge into the hole or shaft. His feet immediately rested on something solid and with a little movement slipped to stop on something solid a little further below. Sliding himself further into the cupboard he allowed his legs to fall further and the aforementioned process repeated itself twice more. What his feet were discovering he realised were steps. What the floor had been hiding all these years was a spiral staircase but why, why had it been covered up? More than just covered up it had been carefully hidden. For what purpose, and who had been responsible, and when? The ultimate question of course and one the vicar feared, where did the stairwell lead? Was there a crypt, perhaps but why hide a crypt? What was down there, what was so terrible or so important that it had to be hidden from the world. There was only one way to find out.

The vicar crossed the passage to his office where he'd left his torch. As before he found it to be useless, all the light did was reflect off the vapour. He'd take it anyway he decided, without a friend to hold his hand the light if nothing else would provide companionship. Slowly he dropped himself over the edge until he was standing on a step, his head in the cupboard. He felt the walls with his hands, they were made of brick, small rough bricks. He felt for but couldn't find a handrail. Slowly, very slowly he took his first step down. Steadying himself he took another and then another. With each step he felt the wall with his hands clutching in his left hand the torch. The stairwell was thick with the foul smelling vapour, even so he found he could still breathe without difficulty and the "Devil's breath" didn't sting his eyes, it was just the smell. The odour was very, very hard to bear and the vicar began to wonder whether at the bottom he would discover it's source and hoped it wouldn't be a mass of rotting corpses. The steps he quickly discovered were narrow and being a circular stairway tapered off into nothing.

The result being he would often slip, and on one occasion came close to losing his footing completely. It was almost a relief that he couldn't see down, that would have been fatal. After what felt like an eternity he could feel no further steps and knew he'd reached the bottom of the shaft. The foul stench remained but to his immense relief there were no rotting corpses. Gingerly he felt about him. To his surprise he discovered he wasn't in a crypt but a fairly narrow tunnel that led off in two different directions. This was something he hadn't expected, though if he were honest he wasn't at all sure what he'd expected to find. A crypt, a small room perhaps but certainly not a tunnel. The thought of exploring a foul smelling tunnel without light even with his new found courage didn't really appeal to him. He'd already had enough. He turned his torch back on hoping to be able to see something but the light revealed only the "Devil's breath." The light with the vapour he found disorientating, if anything he preferred the dark and switched the torch off. This was the closest to hell one could get he surmised. Standing, not moving he listened, as before there was only silence, but a silence that was beginning to sound threatening. Fighting for courage he started down one of the tunnels, feeling all the time with his hands. He'd gone no further than roughly two metres when he came up against a brick wall, the tunnel for whatever reason had been bricked up. He felt for an opening, there was none. He was surprised to find himself feeling a little disappointed. Gingerly he made his way back to the stairwell. On arriving he once more stood still, waiting, listening. He hoped to hear something, anything but the only sound was a resounding silence. A silence that weighed heavy on his shoulders. He was beginning to hate the sound of silence, silence he was beginning to realise didn't automatically mean peace. They were two very different things. Building up courage, he didn't have much left, the vicar started to edge in the other direction, along the second tunnel. This time he found no wall blocking the passage, this tunnel was leading somewhere.

After perhaps twenty metres he came across something else blocking his way. Nothing physical, this time the obstacle was his mind, the further along the passage he travelled the greater the sensation of foreboding. In the end the sensation got the better of him, he could go no further. He stood for over a minute trying his hardest to defeat the intrusion but it was impossible. He knew it was probably only his mind playing tricks, some deep ancestral fear of the unknown but he couldn't overcome it. He would have to turn around. Slowly he edged his way back, feeling his way by sliding his hands along the brick wall. All the time the sense of foreboding was getting stronger, so much so that at times he was close to running back. It took all the self-control he could muster not to give in to such recklessness. On arriving at the stairwell he found it akin to reuniting with an old friend. He was just about to take the first step when he thought of something. The iron cross. It had fallen down the stairwell, where was it? He started to shuffle around, his feet exploring every square centimetre of floor. He shuffled up to the wall blocking the first tunnel and found nothing, he retraced his route along the other tunnel for three or four metres. There was no way it could have rebounded any further. Again nothing, it was impossible, the cross had to be somewhere, it couldn't just vanish. Not unless something or someone had moved it. Not waiting a second longer the vicar took his first step on the stairs. He had to get out of there and fast.

Amphillicia's Well. Otherworld.

Charlotte opened her eyes to find herself bathing under the softest of lights. Not just underneath, she realised for the light was everywhere, it surrounded her. Quite naturally her first thought was where was she? It felt as though she were floating, as though she were weightless and she felt wonderful. Where was she, she asked herself again, was this heaven? The surrounding light often waved and at times sparkled as though reaching her through water. As she bathed in undisturbed contentment she became aware of specks of gold rising all around her. More and more specks of gold started to rise gathering above her to form a veil of gold. As Charlotte watched in wonderment more and more gold dust drifted past her, rising to create an ever thickening, shimmering presence. As she continued to watch enthralled, the gathering of gold began to create a more structured form. A face appeared out of the cloud, a face of crystallised beauty and a smile that poured warmth into Charlotte's heart. Charlotte recognised the face before it had fully formed. Amphillicia, she remembered where she was, she was in Amphillicia's Well.

As soon as Charlotte remembered where she was, Amphillicia's face started to break up. The particles drifted apart to be absorbed by water until there remained only the wavering light in which she bathed. A few moments later the light too began to fade and in under a minute there remained not a glimmer, Charlotte found herself left floating alone in the dark. Strangely she remained feeling extremely relaxed, the surrounding darkness did not feel threatening, quite the opposite it felt soothing. Out of the darkness a thin pencil of light started to shine. At first it was hardly visible, no more than a glint, perhaps a reflection from somewhere. Slowly the light grew in strength, not once did it spread, always it remained a pencil beam and as Charlotte watched the beam started to spiral upward coated with a luminous white vapour. The spectacle looked vaguely familiar. As the specks of gold had done the luminous vapour gathered above Charlotte's head forming a tight gently swirling ball of light that pulsated to the rhythm of a beating heart. Charlotte had seen such a happening before, several times but never under water. Acting on instinct, by waving her arms she rolled herself over and looked down at the budget hanging from her neck. Her instinct had been correct, the budget was the source of the light, from its narrow neck Leht's light blood was spiralling past her.

"Leht," without realising it Charlotte was allowing her mind do her talking.

"Good morning France Charlotte," Leht's delicious voice filled the well, her melodic tones softened by the magical waters that hosted their meeting. Charlotte wasn't sure how to respond, she felt good, more relaxed than she'd ever felt and yet memories of the horrors of yesterday were, sheltered by a curtain that was only too easy to draw back. "Do not feel sad France Charlotte," Leht's voice rescued her. "Triskelion and Wodewose I have known since the day they both came into our world. That they left it fighting for its continued existence is a thing to be celebrated. We must, to honour their memory stay focused and continue the struggle. I know it is difficult France Charlotte but we must not falter." Charlotte was not about to let anybody down but at the same time she continued to feel helpless, a burden to those who pinned their hopes on her. She no longer felt afraid of the battle she knew lay ahead, she just had no idea how to fight it, how she could play her part. She was grateful for Leht's stimulating words and the healing power of the waters in Amphillicia's Well but worried once she left their protection she would feel devastated by the loss of her two friends. Would seek the comfort of her parents and abandon the fight.

"Will I ever see, Triskelion or Wodewose again?" Magic existed in Otherworld, Charlotte had witnessed magic. Phenomenon that did not exist, that were impossible in her world, actually took place here. Perhaps there existed magic that could bring her two friends back.

"I am sorry France Charlotte, I feel your pain but our friends have departed from this world, they will never return." Leht's answer could not be clearer. Charlotte wondered if in Otherworld they believed in a heaven, as they did in hers and if she ever managed to get there would she be reunited with her two friends? And what about the two hounds Alasdair and Cathasach? She had not seen them since their battle with the gnombres. Had their terrible injuries meant they too had met their afterlife and If there was a heaven, would they be there too? Leht spoke again, her voice finding joy where there should be none. Her next words revealed she understood the questions circulating in Charlotte's mind just as Triskelion had always done. "Whether we will all meet again in another place, I do not know. Luminaries in both our worlds have wondered for centuries over this enigma and a true answer has always evaded them. The truth is nobody, including me knows the answer to your hopes. The only way we will find out is when we go to our own afterlives and I'm afraid we may be disappointed France Charlotte. I too have lost two very dear friends and wish like you that I may one day unite with them in a better place. I am afraid though it may be a false hope, I am sorry."

Charlotte looked at Leht's face, all the time she'd been talking she'd remained smiling, continuing to fill her heart with joy where there should be none. She had only known Triskelion and Wodewose for a few weeks, Leht if she understood correctly had been friends with the two for thousands of years and she was still managing to smile. Charlotte felt ashamed. It should be her supporting Leht not the other way around.

"And my parents, will I ever see them again?" Charlotte felt even more embarrassed to ask Leht the question, but she had to know.

"We can only hope so France Charlotte." The way Leht spoke her words enlarged the single word hope to mean a beacon of hope but Charlotte knew if truth be told there must be very little hope. She felt she should be crying but somehow with the support of Amphillicia and Leht she felt almost euphoric. Leht's melodic voice spoke to her again, wiping all her negative thoughts from her mind.

"You did well, yesterday France Charlotte, closing the passage has frustrated the Darkness, it had not predicted your actions. You have closed a weak link."

"Triskelion closed the passage, not me." Charlotte did not want any credit. Triskelion had sacrificed himself for Otherworld perhaps even for the Universe and every universe beyond. In the process he'd even managed to protect her and nowhere in history will he be remembered for his selfless action. She remembered his face, she would never forget it. His smile, the strange head of a woman, he stood firmly beside, almost protectively Charlotte now realised as the walls crumbled taking him to where judging from his expression, he wanted to be. Charlotte wanted to ask Leht about the mysterious head of the woman but something told her not to, that this was not the time. It was never the time.

"You gave Triskelion the strength to do so France Charlotte, without you there the strength he needed may have deserted him. Now we must finish the task France Charlotte." Charlotte had no idea how she had given Triskelion strength. She even felt as though she may have been a hindrance.

"There is a second entrance, Triskelion told me." Charlotte assumed that by, 'finishing the task,' it was this entrance Leht was referring to.

"That is correct and we must ensure it is closed for eternity, with Otherworld so weak we cannot risk a malevolent discovering the other door." Charlotte tried desperately to remember Triskelion's exact words.

"I think I remember Triskelion telling me it is not a door that he or I could pass through?"

"That is correct France Charlotte, it is a virtual door that only one being has the key to. Our Guardian."

"The white hart," Charlotte mouthed the words.

"Yes the white hart, we cannot allow the Darkness to capture our friend. The Darkness could poison his mind, use him and send him in the most brutal manner to his afterlife. We have to free our Guardian from the grasp of the Darkness. If it is the last thing I ever achieve, I will be happy." Perhaps it was a blessing that Charlotte didn't read too much into Leht's last words, she was too busy contemplating how they were meant to secure the harts release. It seemed to her an impossible task. As Charlotte pondered Leht continued to speak. "France Charlotte, I have thought of a way and to succeed I need you to be with me." Before Charlotte had had time to digest what she'd just heard Leht continued, the luminous vapour surrounding her figure beginning to swirl with charged emotion. "Time is no longer with us, we must release the Guardian tonight, any delay and we may be too late. Do you understand?"

"Yes," Charlotte tried to nod but with the cushion of the well water managed only the slightest motion.

"My light is fading France Charlotte, I have not long here, follow what I am about to tell you and please no questions. Meet me this evening in The Coombe, where my light blood receptacle is hidden, whatever you do, do not forget the budget. From this moment on you must keep the budget with you always." Charlotte remained silent, no questions, she hoped Leht could read she understood. "Good," Leht sounded pleased. "You must pass a message to our Guardian, you must let him know that we are coming tonight, that he must be ready. And very important, he must raise the lights of the blue line, he must not fail in this. If he fails, he must greet his afterlife and quickly. Tell him if he has to make the greeting I will deal with the consequences. Have you got that France Charlotte?"

"Yes," but no. Charlotte had so many questions, so many and yet she wasn't allowed one. The one that rose above every other, how was she meant to pass a message to the hart, she hadn't a clue.

"The picture." They were to be Leht's last words. Leht's image quickly faded, the cloud lost its shine and then dulled to nothing. For seconds Charlotte was once more enveloped by darkness. Only for seconds, a familiar glow birthed in the depths beneath her and the waters cleared, shining crystalline once more. Charlotte felt herself rising, the waters parting to allow her free passage. A quite different light soon welcomed her, the sun was shining on Asherugge.

At first Charlotte thought Amphillicia had deposited her alone in the wood. That was until she recognised the sound of leaves being disturbed by fast moving feet. The squirrel, as though summoned bounded to her, his coat shining with rude health and his tail quivering with expectation. "So the waters of Amphillicia's well works for you too my little friend," Charlotte thought to herself. She went to brush herself down in readiness for whatever was next. She had just spent, well she wasn't sure, hours at least submerged in water yet she was bone dry. As she wondered at another example of Otherworld magic there was movement in the Well, now retuned to no more than a malodorous, muddy pool. As the two looked on, the mud started to foam and turned to foaming white water. A mist rose from its centre and Charlotte could see there was something concealed within. She watched fascinated, completely unafraid. She recalled her father telling her stories of King Arthur, she remembered tales of the knight's legendary sword, Excalibur. Momentarily she wondered if what she was witnessing was Excalibur rising from the lake or could it be Triskelion's sword? Whatever was rising from the waters, cloaked by the mist looked like it could well be a sword. Without notice the foaming stopped, the mist vanished and Charlotte heard something whistling through the air. Seconds later whatever it was landed at her feet. She cried out in alarm before bending to see what it was. She recognised it instantly as Wodewose's staff, his very own personalised sword. Charlotte could see the waters of the Well had worked magic with his staff too for fresh leaves sprouted where there hadn't been any before and clusters of red berries added further decoration. Charlotte picked it up and kissed the staff gently, never will you and I be parted she promised.

"Do you know where we're going next?" she asked the squirrel out loud not really expecting it to understand. After her conversation with Leht she had her own idea. To her surprise, in response the squirrel turned and headed into the wood. He had understood, now there's a thing. Would she never learn.

Although the squirrel was full of energy much to its frustration Charlotte wished to take her time. It was a glorious day and being June the wood was close to its greatest splendour. Charlotte had no idea why but she felt safe and needed time to think. If she needed to she knew she could run, the pain in her ribs had magically cleared, as had the pain in her wrist. She felt so good, so refreshed it was almost as though she had been reborn. Leht's final words never left her head, "the picture," the one in her bedroom, she knew exactly what Leht had meant. Charlotte wasn't surprised when the squirrel led her to the rim of the escarpment and started to descend. Yesterday the descent would have been agonising, today without feeling pain Charlotte found the descent of the almost vertical slope easy. On reaching the field she insisted on stopping. By the squirrel's reaction she could see he was frustrated but there was too much at stake to rush into things. Caution had to be king. From the cover of the trees she gazed across the field to Aldeborie. In the morning sun the village looked even more beautiful than normal, almost angelic. Rising amidst the informal gathering of cottages rose the square tower of St John the Baptist. Charlotte now knew that this was the only building in view that wasn't simply an image. St John the Baptist in Otherworld was real, as real as it was in hers. From where she stood it didn't really matter that the village was merely an image. They were too far away to take in the sterile atmosphere. The image was equally beautiful. How could, she wondered such beauty be so ruthlessly corrupted. No one could suspect that the potential end of her world will start from such an innocent setting. Perhaps that was the very key to the plan the Darkness had conceived, that no matter how obvious its presence became the world would simply ignore its progress. After all that is exactly what had happened so far.

Charlotte's mind turned to her planned meeting with Leht. Leht had said to meet in The Coombe. At the place where the receptacle for her life blood was hidden. Charlotte had no idea where The Coombe was, she knew there was more than one coombe in the local area and she also remembered the warning from Wodewose. "Coombes were a good place to hide but be careful not to become trapped in one." She remembered her map, the one Triskelion had given her. She removed it from the budget and carefully unfolding it spread the ancient parchment flat on the ground. She scanned it for The Coombe, it wasn't easy as the images created by modern man kept appearing and disappearing as she struggled to adjust to the map's sensitivities. Then she remembered, she was an idiot, the places where the receptacles were concealed were marked. She quickly found the one on Aldbury Nowers, running her finger across the surface she found the holey tree and there, she found the third. Close to the Beacon in a wooded area, the symbol for a receptacle. Hand written across the area was just one word. Coombe. Charlotte hoped she'd be able to find it, her father had always teased her about her map reading skills or lack of them and they would have to find the hiding place in the dark. She considered this for a moment. Not unless they found the place whilst it was still daylight and waited for darkness to fall. Safer that way too. Charlotte smiled, she had a plan.

Feeling pleased with herself Charlotte placed the map back in the budget and started across the field, descending towards Aldeborie. On passing the oak she stopped.

"You stay here," she told the squirrel. "There's no point in both of us going, if I'm not back in a couple of hours, come looking for me." In response the squirrel scurried back and forth at the same time running in small circles, it was obvious from his behaviour that he wasn't happy with the idea. "Please," Charlotte pleaded. At this the squirrel ran up the trunk of the oak and in through the hole that was the entrance to his nest. A few seconds later he poked his head out. "Thank you, promise I'll be back soon," Charlotte gave a short wave and continued down the slope. As she reached the Evinghehou road a small bird flew over her head. It landed on a branch of the lone oak. The robin rested there for a couple of minutes before flying back to Aldeborie, not to the church but to a small, thatched cottage.

Aldeborie was as Charlotte knew it would be, deathly silent. Nothing stirred, not only was it deathly silent the village was deathly still. Walking the road between pretty but soulless images it felt rather as though she was the only survivor after the apocalypse. Lights still burned in the Greyhound pub. Unfinished drinks sat on the bar, more on the tables, chairs pushed back every one free of their occupants. The water lay low in the pond, just enough to reflect the sun. Charlotte's mouth ran dry as she neared the village shop, the image of Ashtynn manically tearing up her coat remained fresh in her mind. She was beginning to regret leaving the squirrel behind. With her face straight ahead Charlotte glanced, using only her eyes across to the bowed window. There was no sign of Ashtynn, she could be roaming the village, unlike the gnombres she didn't require the dark or shadows. Charlotte quickened her pace to a run.

Parked out front of their cottage sat her parents newly acquired car. The light in the lounge remained on, was the light her doing or her parents, she wasn't sure. It was now nearly thirty six hours she'd remained in Otherworld. The image before her was a new one, not the one from the night she'd left. With horror she realised that having been in Otherworld so long her parents will have almost certainly risen to find her missing. The thought made her feel physically sick. Thinking what her parents must be going through if they found she was missing was worse than the thought of never seeing them again. She wasn't sure how the relation between Otherworld and her world worked, if she returned today would it be within the seven minutes of having departed or longer? She had no idea, she had never been gone longer than the twenty four hour cycle. Charlotte started to tremble, she was beginning to feel like a little girl again. If she ever returned to her world she promised herself she would remain a child as long as possible, adulthood she decided wasn't fun.

She would never return if she didn't pull herself together. Stop being stupid she told herself, the only way back was to win this. She had to stop being sentimental. With renewed purpose Charlotte walked coolly through the front door that never opened. She passed through without a problem but Wodewose's staff jammed as it came up against the door. Charlotte tugged at it but try as she might the staff would not budge, it refused to pass through the door. In exasperation she decided to leave it outside. With great care she lay the staff on the doorstep and re-entered through the door that never opened. A robin sitting in a tree opposite watched her disappear then flew off, heading for the field where a solitary oak grew sentinel. Pausing only for a minute it flew back to the thatched cottage.

Looking around the lounge it felt to Charlotte as if she had never left. Everything was as it had been when she'd switched on the light, just after midnight two nights before. Holding back tears she passed through the door to the kitchen. She found the kitchen spotless, much more so than usual. Everything had been put away except that is for a covered plate on the stove. Charlotte went to remove the lid and found her hand instead of grasping the handle passed straight through. What had Triskelion taught her? You have to convince your subconscious what you see before you is real. She tried again and again and at the fourth attempt succeeded, she lifted the lid. Underneath, carefully laid out was her favourite meal, chicken in a mushroom and cream sauce, with pureed potatoes and French fine beans. With sadness Charlotte realised the meal confirmed what she had dreaded. Her parents had woken to find her gone. The meal was meant for her, her mother would have prepared it in the hope of her safe return, it was her mother all over. It also explained the spotless kitchen, when her mother was stressed she cleaned, it was her way of dealing with things. Charlotte took one last look at the meal and replaced the lid. Covering her face with her hands she started to cry, floods of tears came streaming down her cheeks. The little human girl remained like this for at least ten minutes until there were physically no tears left to shed. Wiping her face her distressed expression turned to one of unparalleled determination. She was determined to see her parents again and the only way, it was becoming obvious this would ever happen, was to defeat the evil that was invading her village. First she had to get a message to the white hart. In this she must not fail. Determined Charlotte trod on the first step to the stairs, her foot went straight through. No, nooo, this wasn't happening. She tried again, the same. She tried a third time, the same thing again. She kicked hard and her foot swung at empty air. After returning from the solitary oak the robin looked in through the back window and immediately saw the little human girl's distress. It watched as she stamped and stamped on the first stair, her foot passing through every time. The little human child had quite understandably lost control, only a cool head would help her succeed, it was quite obvious she could not do this alone. The robin was confident now that it had done the right thing, to go against the human child's wishes and seek the messenger from his home in the lone oak.

Feeling defeated Charlotte stopped for a moment, not out of want but to get her breath back. As she stared down at the kitchen floor a most welcome and unexpected sight greeted her. The messenger sat on his hind legs looking up. "How did you know I would need you?" Charlotte even managed a laugh. The squirrel was pleased to hear her laugh but it didn't fool him, he could tell the human child was close to the edge, she needed all the support he could give her. For a few seconds he brushed between her legs, hoping to calm her. It appeared to work, France Charlotte stood straight adjusting the budget so it fell in a more comfortable fashion. Her normal senses were beginning to return. Relieved the squirrel went to the stairs and hopped onto the first step. It remained solid. France Charlotte he was pleased to see was watching his every move, that was good. Deftly, to make it look easy he hopped on and off the step a couple more times. Charlotte raised her foot slowly and brought it down, the squirrel held his breath. To his dismay her foot passed straight through.

Charlotte, in French started counting to ten, un, deux, trois…. The squirrel had made it look easy, it must therefore be easy, she just had to concentrate or perhaps that was the trouble, as before she was concentrating too hard, she had to let her subconscious relax and rule. Take over from the stressed fringes of her mind. As she made a determined effort to calm herself the squirrel hopped back onto the bottom stair, he made it look so easy. As if he'd read her thoughts the squirrel ran up the full flight of stairs, you see it is easy, just relax he seemed to be saying. Charlotte taking slow shallow breaths lifted her left leg, normally it would be her right but this way somehow it felt better. Trying not to think too hard she brought her foot down on the first stair, all the time keeping her eyes on the squirrel. She felt the stair beneath her foot, hardly daring to breathe, she brought her full weight to bear. The stair held, she started to laugh, not the crazed laughter the robin had witnessed a few moments before, this time it was quite different, this time it was from relief.

Charlotte knew the key was not to concentrate too hard, that she now realised had been her mistake, her subconscious had suspected a lie. With her eyes fixed on the squirrel she did her best to relax. Slowly she took the second stair, it held, then the third, the third stair held too. She was starting to feel more at ease, as though she really were back home. She climbed another couple of stairs, delighting in the give of the wood beneath her feet. When you missed something, it was strange how the tiniest reminiscence mattered so much. Growing in confidence by the second she reached the small "landing" without really thinking. Ahead of her, the door to her parent's bedroom was slightly ajar. The slither of light escaping through the crack tempted her to look in, she was about to push the door open when she felt the squirrel brush past her ankle. Charlotte looked down, with her new found awareness she recognised the look of concern on the squirrels face. The squirrel on seeing Charlotte look at him ran through the open door to the side, into her bedroom. "He's right I suppose, I mustn't look, it will only upset me," even so she remained sorely tempted. "Lead us not into temptation," Charlotte found it strangely calming remembering the words she'd been taught at school. She so wanted to push open the door, to see her parent's room, the temptation was so strong. With a colossal effort she managed to resist all temptation and turning away from her parents door followed the squirrel into her bedroom.

The first thing she noticed, her bed had been made. Gromit was tucked neatly under the covers staring up at the ceiling. There were no clothes lying on the floor, everything had been either hung up or put away. Her bedroom was spotless, her mother had been busy. Charlotte could visualise her, busying herself, despair mixed always with hope. Looking at her possessions, so close and yet in reality, so far away and her mother's handiwork Charlotte felt tears welling up once more. This time she managed to quell them before they saw daylight. If she was to see her parents again she had to control her emotions, she had to keep focused on why they were here and that was to send a message to the white hart. Charlotte turned to face the picture. Her heart jumped, the once proud beast was no longer standing, instead it lay on its side its head still somehow raised in defiance. Defiance maybe yes but in the hart's eyes Charlotte saw that his resistance was beginning to fail, she could see the first signs of acceptance that he was beaten. Tonight cannot come soon enough, she wished she was there now at the hart's side. Leht had been right, any further delay and the hart would be vanquished, property of the Darkness, meeting a fate… Charlotte refused to reflect on it. The message, she had to convey Leht's message, how to do that, she had no idea. In truth Charlotte did know, she was simply unaware that she knew, she may have suspected yet still she wasn't convinced of her gift. Instinctively she placed her head against the glass of the picture and concentrated hard. Through her subconscious she conveyed everything Leht had told her in Amphillicia's Well. When she had finished she kissed the picture gently and ran her fingers over the glass. Tonight we will meet, she promised. Before leaving she took a look out of the long sash window. It felt an age since she last looked out. Unlike in her world the sun shone and everything was growing as it should be for the time of year. There was not one magpie to be seen. A movement at her feet told her she must linger no longer. With one last look around her room Charlotte followed the squirrel back down the stairs to the kitchen. This time the squirrel exited via the back door. Charlotte went to follow and walked straight into solid wood. Ouch, she rubbed her nose more in shock than hurt. Unlike previous occasions she did not panic, she knew how to do this now. As though she was flicking a switch she flipped her subconscious and took a step at the door. Within seconds she was standing outside on the brick path.

"Yeees," she punched the air triumphantly. The squirrel shook his head, he would never understand the human species and continuing to shake his head started down the brick path. Charlotte followed, feeling at that moment she could take on all the world and win.

Deep beneath the church dedicated to St John the Baptist at Great Gaddesden or rather Gatesdene as we're in Otherworld, the pudding stone circle slowly orbited the ancient yew. Inside Leht prepared herself for what she knew may be her last day shining her light in Otherworld. She was sad beyond comprehension, she had lost two of her dearest friends and wasn't sure if her sacrifice tonight would save her beloved land. Her light would be extinguished and she would not be witness to the little human child's victory or failure. Since the beginning of time her light had burned in this place, she had never really considered the possibility that one day it may be extinguished. Especially under such circumstances. A tremor resonated from the roots of her trusty yew rising up the red trunk. A message had just been received via the root vine. The white hart was ready. The little human child, France Charlotte, had succeeded, she hardly dared to believe it.

"Yeees." Leht allowed herself a rare cry of celebration.

After collecting Wodewose's staff, Charlotte with the squirrel at her side in a display of bravado marched purposefully up the road to the village pond and green. Aldeborie remained deathly silent, a ghost village without ghosts. They were the only two living, breathing creatures in the village and at that moment it felt as though they were the only two left in the world. Charlotte still had a disturbing feeling that she was being watched that every window was an eye for the Darkness. If that was the case she was determined not to show any fear, she had become someone to be reckoned with. On arriving at the green she was just about to cross to the pond and continue along the road to Evinghehou when something stopped her. Not physically but a question that kept nagging away at her conscious. She desperately wanted to get out of the fake village but simply couldn't leave Aldeborie without first seeing if the gateway was still blocked. Instead of crossing the road to the pond she turned left to pass in front of the shop. Ashtynn was nowhere to be seen, the shop window had only a display of English wine. On seeing the human child change direction the squirrel scurried this way and that, circling as though his tail was on fire. It was obvious once more that he wasn't at all happy at her decision. Charlotte decided to ignore his display of anxiety, she couldn't rest until she had checked the gateway. After crossing the road, she passed through the lych gate and started up the gravel path, everything appeared to be normal. Even the mist didn't appear to be all that angry, indeed it was hardly moving. After taking a couple of steps along the gravel path Charlotte, perhaps stupidly began to relax. Only a moment later she regretted her stupidity. She sensed, not imagined, sensed that something was following her. Without hesitating she started to run at the same time taking a fleeting look over her shoulder. In a camera flash she realised that what she had just done was mirror the image in the Snook's book with no name. She started to run faster, the squirrel she saw had already raced ahead darting down the other path towards the village pond. She looked behind her again, there was nothing there but she knew there was something, her seventh sense was telling her so. No not telling, it was screaming at her. As she reached the stone slab, the gateway, a body emerged from the slowly swirling mist, Ashtynn! Charlotte squealed and leapt over the stone making to follow the squirrel. The magpie's feather she saw remained, laid neatly, blocking all access to her world. Ashtynn started to run, lunging at her and Charlotte squealed again as she felt Ashtynn's hand brush her arm. With all the force she could muster Charlotte took several hurdle-like strides before putting her head down and fleeing for all she was worth. At the church gate she allowed herself a brief look back. Ashtynn, she saw, was no longer pursuing her, instead, as last time she remained in front of the church door fighting the air with her arms in a disturbingly manic fashion. Charlotte couldn't understand why she had stopped, why Ashtynn hadn't continued to pursue her? She was much bigger and much taller, surely if she'd tried she could have caught her. Charlotte hadn't the strength to question why she was just very, very grateful she'd given up the chase so easily. The squirrel she saw was already a long way along the road towards Evinghehou and Charlotte ran after it, cursing herself for having been so stupid. The feeling of being followed had gone, why? Why was she no longer being pursued? She would never understand the ways of the Darkness.

After leaving Aldeborie Charlotte and the squirrel took what was now their regular route across the field to the lone oak. A very human trait, Charlotte touched the trunk of the oak hoping her act would bring good fortune, after all they would definitely need it.

Charlotte on touching wood was following a belief that is worldwide, the one superstition that transcends all cultures. The custom may well have originated from Otherworld where one would touch a tree to ask it's magical inhabitants such as fairies for good fortune. Sadly today many trees remain empty and so requests often go unanswered.

On reaching the tree line Charlotte half expected to be greeted by Wodewose and a new reality set in when they were greeted only by the wood itself. Where were Alasdair and Cathasach, she wondered again. After a brief pause the two of them started on their climb of the steep wooded scarp. Just as with the descent earlier, Charlotte was pleasantly surprised how easily she managed. Using Wodewose's staff for support, her chest free of pain and able to use both hands the climb was so much easier. She thanked Amphillicia and her shaggy friend at every step. Nearing the top the two of them bore left following the rim of the escarpment. Whenever they met a path or holloway they crossed in haste, even Charlotte who had been brought up on exploring footpaths no longer felt comfortable in their presence. After passing below the Bridgewater monument they left the rim and headed into Sallow Copse. At this point Charlotte felt the need to check the map, she knew roughly where they were headed but couldn't afford to make a mistake. At a small glade with a moss covered tree stump she stopped. Sitting on the stump she pulled the map from the budget and lay it open on the massed grass. Every now and again she raised her head to take a quick glance around her, seeing as far as she could into the trees. Looking for danger before danger found her. She still found it hard to understand why they had not continued being pursued when in Aldeborie, there had to be a reason and that worried her.

The wood that day was glorious, it was shouting it's splendour from the tree tops to anyone who would listen. Every shade of green imaginable were woven together in a sun dappled tapestry that had no beginning and no end. Bird song delighted in the soft summer air. It was hard to imagine anything but good could take place in this cathedral of woods. It would be easy to fall under the wood's magical spell and drop her guard but Charlotte had experienced enough in the last few weeks to expect the unexpected, that beauty didn't necessarily mean safety. In summer especially, in a wood there were so many places for an enemy to hide yet Triskelion had always told her that the wood was her friend, that it was the safest place for her to be. She thought of Wodewose, the wood hadn't been much help to him but then again would he have fared any better in open ground, almost certainly not. Charlotte, continued to be unaware that she was steadily falling deeper and deeper into understanding the ways of Otherworld, she was learning to trust her deeper senses more than those on the outside. An enemy can hide out of sight but not always out of mind. She couldn't spot any signs of danger but more importantly she couldn't sense any either and the latter reassured her more than anything. Using Wodewose's staff for support she bent low to study the map.

After several minutes of examining the ancient cartography Charlotte felt she knew roughly where they were though roughly, she knew wasn't good enough. To find the location where the stone that would receive Leht's life blood was hidden would require pin point accuracy and in this she doubted her ability. The wood had no real distinguishing features, there were trends but nothing specific, no distinguishing landmarks, at least not that she could find her way by. The wood was also a labyrinth of paths and tracks, some ancient some relatively recent, she wasn't at all sure if the old map accounted for every path that was there today. It was too easy to get lost. How she needed Wodewose, he'd be able to tell where he was just by looking at a tree. She tried turning the map so it faced roughly in the direction she needed to take. This helped but only a little, she was still not sure of the best route. The squirrel she hoped may know the way and guide her but after Aldeborie it had shown little sign of wanting to lead and no interest at all in the ancient map. She suspected his knowledge of the area was very much localised. Why couldn't she simply go to Amphillicia's Well, Leht hadn't needed a receiving stone there. As if something was directing her, Charlotte brushed the budget hanging from her neck with the back of her hand. It swayed gently at her slight touch. The budget weighed empty, to be sure she opened the neck and peered inside. What she saw confirmed her touch, there was no liquid, no light-blood that was Leht. Bending closer, she went back to studying the map.

In Aldeborie Charlotte had always suspected she was being watched and her suspicion had proved correct. Here in the wood despite what had gone before she felt safe, she couldn't understand why, she just did. What she could not realise was that in the wood too she was being closely watched. Not from windows of soulless buildings or figures lurking in shadows but by the wood itself. The root vine just like the World Wide Web when there's headline news was virtually setting the woodland floor alight. The wood had already lost its greatest friend it wasn't prepared to see the little human child go the same way. Decision making though wasn't the woods strongest point, there were limitations on what they could do and with so many plants, shrubs and trees involved in the discussion, finding a collective plan of action was not proving easy. After much disagreement, the wood came together and concurred that the only real way it could help was to try and help guide the little human child to the place where the receiving stone lay hidden. To do this the majority agreed somewhat reluctantly, they would have to enlist the help of the Moosleute.

After bending over for a good half an hour and with the sun on the back of her neck Charlotte began to feel disorientated. Sitting up she leant back and rolled her head slowly, trying to regain her senses. Even with her eyelids shut the bright sun created a kaleidoscope of colours beneath her lids. Her disorientation must have been worse than she'd imagined for she kept hearing voices, tiny shrill voices. Rather than fading as she expected them to, the voices became louder. Somewhat alarmed, she blinked her eyes open and quickly glanced around the wood. She could see or sense nothing and that made her feel uneasy. The squirrel looked totally relaxed, his tail looped over backwards, always a sign that he wasn't concerned. She listened intently, the voices definitely were not of her imagination, they were real and now concentrating harder she realised they were coming from somewhere below. Her gaze descended to the woodland floor. The foot of Wodewose's staff she saw was resting in a sea of luxuriant green moss. Charlotte stared harder, the moss appeared to be moving, not gently or with any kind of rhythm but in a quite chaotic pattern as though it were trying to relieve itself from an itch. Charlotte rubbed her eyes and bent closer to get a better look. What she saw, made her want to rub her eyes again. Otherworld was never short on surprises but the scene at her feet was completely unexpected and so bizarre that she wondered if she was either dreaming or hallucinating. From the moss, hundreds of tiny beings appeared to be popping up and down. They were on closer inspection, part of the moss, attached by stalks rather like tiny mushrooms. None were more than two or three centimetres high and as far as she could see consisted only of a face with a moss cap. All appeared unable to stay still for long and seconds after popping up disappeared into the moss once more. As she studied the tiny creatures Charlotte realised that they were the source of the tiny voices she thought she'd been imagining. Listening she tried to get a grasp of what they were saying but they were all talking at once and no one seemed to be saying the same thing. The second problem was each little being only popped up long enough to say a few words before disappearing back into the moss. She sensed the little folk were friendly and that they were trying to tell her something but their way of communicating was simply chaotic. Their massed speech did nothing but create a soup of incoherence. Nevertheless, she refused to give up, after quickly taking another glance around the wood Charlotte knelt to try and fathom what they were trying to tell her. For trying to tell her something she was sure was their intention. With one ear almost touching the ground she listened hard, if she could make out just one word it may help. After a minute or so the only two things that she could deduce with any certainty were, she was pretty sure they were speaking in English and they kept mentioning Wodewose. Anything else was completely unintelligible.

"I give up, I can't understand a word they're saying." Charlotte directed her frustration at the squirrel still not entirely sure if he understood her. The squirrel for his part gave no hint as to whether he understood or not.

Careful not to put her hands on any of the little creatures, Charlotte rested on all fours in an attempt to restudy the map. She was becoming more and more worried about being able to find the receiving stone and the little creatures, fascinating though they were, were an unwanted distraction. Balancing on her elbows with her chin resting in cupped hands Charlotte once more tried to make sense of the ancient cartography. As she did so, the trees above her began to sway and she felt the faintest of tremors running through the ground. Alarmed, Charlotte quickly knelt up, what had just happened was not a natural occurrence of that she was certain. Could it mean danger? What else was this strange world going to throw at her? She waited, tensed to see what would happen next but nothing did. There was only silence, how she hated silence, silence was unnatural, suspenseful it played with her nerves and in Otherworld there was too much of it. She was about to get to her feet, ready to run if necessary when the little moss voices started up again. This time their voices were different, they were she realised speaking in unison.

"We're the Moosleute." Charlotte didn't understand what they'd just said but she recognised it had been a sentence of some sort not just a mish mash of words. Charlotte looked back at the ground. Where the little creatures had been there was now only moss, perhaps she had been imagining things.

"We're the Moosleute," from out of the moss the little creatures all rose in unison and in unison spoke their message before sinking into their carpet of green once more.

"You're the what?"

"Moosleute," Charlotte had barely finished her question before the little creatures, once again in unison popped up to answer. "Moosleute," they popped up again to confirm.

"Moos..." Charlotte started to repeat what she thought she'd just heard.

"We're here to help."

"Help?"

"Yes, we're here to help." Charlotte quickly deduced that any communication with the Moos – something, would have to be short and to the point. They never stayed above ground long enough to get out more than a very short sentence.

"How?"

"To find your meeting place with Leht" Charlotte was astonished, A) they could speak her language, B) they knew Leht and C) they were offering to help.

"You know where I have to meet with Leht?"

"No." Charlotte gritted her teeth in frustration at their reply, the Moos whatever were worse than Wodewose.

"We don't but Woderose knows."

"Wodewose has met, has gone to his afterlife," Charlotte tried to say the words as softly as possible, the Moos whatever had obviously not heard.

"We know."

"Well –" Charlotte was cut off before she'd barely started by another cry in unison.

"Not, Wodewose, Woderose."

"Wood –"

"His wife."

"His wife!" This was a shock, Wodewose had never mentioned he was married.

"Yes his wife, her name is Woderose, she knows."

"Wodewose never told me he was married."

"They never talked." Charlotte wondered how to respond to this.

"Woderose can take you there."

"To –"

"To the place to meet Leht." Charlotte waited for the Moos-something to add to their latest revelation but for once annoyingly, they remained silent.

"How do I find Wodewose?"

"Not Wodewose, Woderose."

"Wode r o s e." Charlotte repeated slowly.

"Yes," came the cry in unison.

"How do I find her?"

"We can take you."

Charlotte couldn't remotely see how this was possible, as far as she could tell the Moos whatever were part of or attached to the moss by long stems. Without legs surely it would be impossible for them to take her to Woderose.

"Can't you simply tell me where to find her?" Charlotte thought this to be a very sensible solution.

"No," came the reply in unison.

"Then how –".

"Follow us," The Moosleute cut in before Charlotte had a chance to finish her question.

"But how?"

"This way." Again the cry was in unison but this time not from the little characters beneath her feet, it came instead from the edge of the clearing. Charlotte looked over from where the call had come from, as she did so a fresh set of little moss characters, popped up.

"This way," the Moosleute at the edge of the glade repeated. Charlotte got to her feet and went over to the patch of moss from where they had appeared. As she drew close another set of figures popped up from a patch of moss further into the wood.

"This way," they called to her. Charlotte proceeded to where the most recent call had come from followed by the squirrel. As she approached, just as before a fresh group of Moosleute popped up ahead of her.

"This way," she mimed before the latest group called her.

And so it went on. In this manner the Moosleute proceeded to lead Charlotte and the messenger across the rough centre of Sallow Copse. It was all going so well when all new cries of "this way" came to an abrupt halt. They just suddenly stopped. Confused Charlotte scouted ahead looking for the next patch of moss, perhaps the little Moss whatever they called themselves were asleep. As she searched she encountered what may be the problem, she could find no further patches of moss. She had no idea why but the next part of the wood was moss free. Charlotte walked back to the last group of moss from where the moss folk had popped up to direct her. The moss carpeted the exposed roots of an old oak in quite beautiful fashion. She waited but there was no sign of any further help. Charlotte bent low hoping they could hear her.

"Where do I go now?"

Silence. Charlotte stood up running both hands through her hair in frustration. It was obvious she was not going to get any further help from the little moss folk. Once more she retrieved the map from the budget. She was concerned that the little leather bag was still empty, there was not a drop of Leht's light blood. How was it to get there. Before, the light blood had always been inside when she had retrieved the budget from the base of the lone oak. On this occasion, since the last appearance of Leht in Amphillicia's Well, the budget had always been at her side.

Charlotte reminded herself that it had been Leht who had told her to keep the budget with her, Leht above everyone will know what is best. Feeling a little reassured Charlotte unfolded the map. Before studying it she glanced over to the patch of moss hoping to see some movement, still nothing she would have to rely on the map after all. It didn't take long for her to discover she was now worse off than before. She knew roughly she was somewhere in Sallow Copse but exactly where she had no idea and the map when she paid it close attention was covered in trees with names. Not generic names like oak or beech but personal names. Every tree had a name, that may have made sense to Wodewose but to her it only confused. Her father or a good map reader would have deciphered the map within the blink of an eye but she was not a natural map reader, quite the opposite. The more she studied the map the more confused she became. So intense was Charlotte's concentration she did not see or sense the lone muntjac deer stroll quietly into view before her. Choosing its spot carefully it stopped to face her, the squirrel ran to its feet and started to curl around the deer's nimble legs. Charlotte jumped when she sensed she was being watched and jumped even more so when she saw the lone deer, unmoving, staring at her. It was not much bigger than an average size dog though much stockier. Unlike the famous fallow deer of the Ashridge Estate who tend to travel in herds Charlotte knew from her father that muntjac deer tended to be very much lonesome animals, occasionally traveling in pairs but almost never in groups. They were also much bolder than fallow deer and not easily scared. Charlotte had often come across them when walking with her parents and just as the deer before her was doing now they would often simply stand and stare. She remembered the muntjac deer a couple of nights before that appeared to be acting as a look out on the Berkhamsted to Dagnall road. Could it be the same animal she wondered and more importantly could it be trusted? Her eyes dropped to the squirrel who looked quite comfortable sitting between the deer's four cloven hooves.

Charlotte's gaze returned to the deer who remained motionless, its eyes matching her stare. For around half a minute their eyes remained locked, neither of them moving. Charlotte spent the time trying to access her deepest senses, she wanted to trust the animal. From nowhere a gentle breeze weaved its way between the two, stirring the canopy overhead and causing the tall, feathered bracken of the underwood to bow and rise in seeming frustration. The deer raised, its head its nostrils reading the breeze, there was a message in every twist and turn. Just as the breeze had arrived from nowhere it disappeared to nowhere. In its place the air remained still, breathless and a silence loaded with anticipation descended on the surrounding woodland of Asherugge.

The deer was the first to move, with a snort and shake of its head the little muntjac scraped the ground with its right forefoot. It then turned and after a glance over its shoulder started in the same direction Charlotte had been traveling before the moss folk had ceased to be. The squirrel turned a couple of circles and followed, Charlotte guessing she had no other choice stepped into line behind. Messages of success coupled with relief passed around the root vine.

The muntjac led the two through the heart of Sallow Copse. The small deer used to the terrain surely found the going easy but for Charlotte the route it chose presented something of a challenge. She found herself constantly fighting nettles, some so tall that they managed to sting her face. If it wasn't nettles she found herself battling through brambles and sprawling raspberry bushes or parting bracken that at times towered above her. When this happened, often the only way of telling that she was still following the deer was by the giveaway movement of the foliage before her. After a hard going fifteen minutes the muntjac came to a halt in front of a huge oak on the northern fringes of Sallow Copse. Like Wodewose's oak it had a chiselled appearance with small clusters of leaves growing in haphazard fashion both from the trunk and the few remaining branches. The deer stood rigid whilst the squirrel ran up and began circling the trunk. Charlotte watched on rubbing her face, scratched and bubbling white from nettle stings. Intermittently the squirrel stopped as though listening for something before continuing to circle the trunk once more. After several minutes whatever it was they were looking for either wasn't there or didn't want them to know it was there. Could this be Woderose's home. Before Charlotte had time to find out they were on the move again, leaving Sallow Copse to enter Ivinghoe Common and Dockley Wood though unless you knew the wood well you'd not notice any difference. At one point they passed through a grove of mature hawthorn. Here the appearance of the wood can most definitely be described as witch-like. It may have been Charlotte's imagination but the little deer appeared to gather pace under the cover of the hawthorn, only slowing when once more the canopy above them was mainly beech.

In both worlds ancient lore forbids the felling or damaging of the hawthorn without good reason. To do so would bring certain bad luck, possibly even death. The hawthorn is a sacred tree and guarded jealously by woodland spirits who are quick to wreak revenge if the tree isn't respected. This applies not only to us but to all creatures habiting the wood and for some creatures respect can escalate into fear, perhaps this explains the muntjac's reaction. In our world ancient lore also forbids bringing any part of the tree into the house, again to do so would be to invite illness or even death. When cut, the flowers of the woodland hawthorn quickly give off a smell resembling rotting flesh. The chemical, trimethylamine, responsible for the smell in decaying flesh is also present in the flower of the woodland hawthorn and like rotting flesh the chemical is released into the air when dying. The most famous hawthorn in Britain is at Glastonbury and is said to have originated from a staff belonging to Joseph of Arimathea.

Not long after leaving the hawthorn grove the muntjac came to a halt in front of an immense pollarded beech. As with the old oak the squirrel ran up the trunk circling several times, stopping on occasion to, Charlotte assumed, listen. Once more whatever or whoever it was they were hoping to find wasn't in and the muntjac after the squirrel had run to the ground did virtually an about turn leading the two back into the wood heading this time for an area known as Flat Isley. Thankfully for Charlotte the undergrowth now, was much sparser and the going relatively easy. Often the floor far from being a deciduous jungle was almost bare. On occasion a pungent smell of garlic hung in the air, left over from the ramsons that not long before had carpeted the ground. After around twelve to fifteen minutes the muntjac led them through an area of woodland dominated by sweet chestnuts, their bark distinguished by long fissures spiralling the trunk. Not long after, the muntjac came to a halt for the third time. On this occasion before a sweet chestnut with a trunk that stood out, its bark being tightly twisted as though a giant hand had grabbed it and wrung the trunk as you would a flannel. As with the two previous trees the squirrel ran up the trunk and started circling with the muntjac looking on. Charlotte waited patiently, prepared for another disappointment. The stings on her face and hands were beginning to itch as well as hurt. When she scratched the action sometimes caught a thorn embedded in her skin, the resulting pain causing her to flinch and suck in breath. Thorns were also caught in her clothing and whilst she waited for the squirrel to do whatever it had to do Charlotte busied herself removing as many as she could before they buried through to her skin. On close examination not only were her clothes stained with mud but also ravaged with numerous tears, thread hanging loose at virtually every fold and crease.

A sharp bark from the muntjac broke Charlotte from her studious self-examination. She looked up to see the head of the deer raised and the squirrel scurrying down the trunk, its tail bristling with either success or excitement, possibly both. At first Charlotte couldn't see what all the excitement was about then she saw, at least she thought she saw the trunk of the tree move. She felt herself tense. For a few seconds more nothing happened then it came again, movement, definite movement. Slowly a shaggy arm appeared from the trunk. Next an equally shaggy leg and out from the trunk stepped a female image of Wodewose. She was slightly smaller and slighter than Wodewose though covered in the same shaggy hair and her face sculptured with features of femininity. Her dog like eyes reflected a complex mix of expressions though clearly evident were fear and suspicion. Charlotte immediately felt sorry for the poor creature and quickly tried to put Woderose, for that was whom she assumed she was, at ease. Stepping forward she slowly held out her hand.

"Hello Woderose, my name's Charlotte, sorry France Charlotte. I used to know your husband, Wodewose." Charlotte paused. She immediately felt very uncomfortable by what she had just said, perhaps Woderose wasn't aware of her husband meeting his afterlife. How insensitive of her to already mention his name. Why hadn't she thought before opening her mouth. Woderose rather than take Charlotte's hand shrunk back placing one hand on the trunk of her tree. For a moment Charlotte was scared she may turn and run but touching her tree appeared to calm her and after a short wait stepped forward and took Charlotte's hand before releasing it almost at once. Again she stepped back though Charlotte was relieved to see she no longer looked frightened just nervous. She decided not to mention Wodewose again, she had no wish to upset the obviously timid creature. Judging by first appearances Woderose was very similar to her husband, perhaps that was the reason they'd lived so far apart from each other. Anyway she was only eleven, what did she know about relationships. She was just surprised that Wodewose had never mentioned her, nor for that matter had Triskelion or Leht. Why ever not?

Charlotte couldn't have known but she needn't have worried about mentioning her knowing Wodewose and of his fate. Woderose already knew, she had been listening to the root vine. In fact she had been following her husband's progress ever since Leht had chosen him to help the little human girl. She hadn't physically seen or spoken to her husband for many, many moons, thousands of the human child's world years, the wood had literally become too small for them both and she had hated the old oak in which they had lived. She'd wanted a much younger home but Wodewose loved his oak and had refused to move. As a result they'd bickered continuously driving all the wood mad. It was the wood in the end that had advised them to separate and it was the wood that had found her several younger trees in which to live her life plus an old oak should she ever become home sick. Unlike her husband who had liked to roam all over the wood talking to any plant, tree or creature who cared to listen she preferred to keep herself to herself never traveling far from one of her trees. She had greeted the news of her husband's calling to his afterlife with a mix of pride, more sadness than she'd expected and a tinge of regret. The root vine had called her after Wodewose's passing, informing her the little human girl would need her help. Since receiving the message she had remained hidden in her tree terrified when this day would arrive, constantly hoping that she wouldn't be needed after all. Her hopes were now shattered, before her stood the little human girl, the human child all the wood was talking about. Seeing the little girl for the first time she was surprised how small and fragile she looked, so very vulnerable. Her little round face covered in scratches and blotched white by nettle stings, played on her female instinct to protect. The little girl's equally round eyes, wide, silently pleading. There was no way Woderose told herself she could refuse the little human child's cry for help. She also wanted to do it for Wodewose. After his passing he had become something of a hero in the wood and if she could she wanted to try and help, even if only in a very small way to finish the quest he and others had started. With her new found resolve she managed a nervous smile.

Charlotte on seeing Woderose smile couldn't help but respond with a wide grin, how a smile changed a face.

"Can you help me?

Woderose's faint smile changed to an expression of puzzlement.

"I need to find a place in the woods, can you help me? The…." Charlotte paused wondering how to describe the minute mushroom like figures who had told her to search out the nervous figure now standing before her. "The little people who live in the moss, told me you could help." It was the best she could come up with.

Woodrose remained still, one hand remaining resting on her tree, she no longer looked scared or nervous, just puzzled as though she didn't understand. Of course, it came to her. Woderose had never spoken her language, the fact that Wodewose could communicate in clumsy English had been a temporary gift from Leht. Woderose had never been granted that gift, it was obvious from her expression she couldn't understand a word she was saying. Just as Charlotte realised their communication problem Woderose received a message through her tree from the root vine. The message told her how the little human child needed her help. The expression on Woderose's face changed from one of puzzlement to a broad smile of understanding. To Charlotte's surprise Woderose stepped forward pointing to the ancient map she still held in her hand. To be sure she understood Charlotte held the map up. With a wide smile Woodrose nodded. Quickly, worried that there still may be a misunderstanding, Charlotte unfolded the map and lay it carefully on the woodland floor, kneeling before it. Woderose no longer showing any nerves knelt beside her. At first Charlotte thought it best to find out where they were now. She pointed to Woderose's sweet chestnut tree then opened her palms to the map. Woderose understood and after only a few seconds hovered a finger over a point on the map. As she did so an image of her sweet chestnut grew large on the ancient parchment. A name in freehand was inscribed beneath, Twizel. Charlotte was ecstatic, she'd understood. Woderose gazed at Charlotte, her expressive, dog-like eyes searching for confirmation that that was what the little human girl had wanted. Charlotte nodded grinning, she then pointed to the place on the map where she was meant to meet Leht. Woderose placed her finger just above Charlotte's and once more an image appeared, this time it was a small sarsen stone. Charlotte had no idea if the stone was relevant, she hoped it was. Not wishing to lose Woderose's concentration Charlotte responded quickly, nodding once more before drawing an imaginary line between the two places, Woderose's tree and the stone. She hoped beyond hope that Woderose understood. That she needed her to lead her to the stone, where she hoped she'd meet with Leht. Woderose gave another wide smile, she really looked very pretty when she smiled. It was such a shame that she and Wodewose hadn't got on. Still smiling Woderose stood up, she pointed first to herself, then to Charlotte and then to the sarsen stone on the map. She then waved an arm in the direction from where they'd just come. Charlotte getting to her feet nodded enthusiastically, she was sure Woderose had understood what she wanted and was agreeing to help. A new confident Woderose took charge indicating for Charlotte to fold the map and return it to the budget. After she had done so, Woderose took Charlotte's hand in hers and started to lead her through the wood roughly in the same direction by which they had arrived. The squirrel perhaps tired, ran up Woderose's back and took up a position, parrotlike on one shoulder. Woderose appeared not to care or perhaps more accurately appeared not to even notice. What nobody noticed was the little muntjac deer, rather than follow the trio, she turned in the opposite direction and casually walked off, welcoming the thicker foliage of Sallow Copse.

Woderose not letting go of Charlotte's hand led her to the edge of the Chiltern escarpment passing through Duncombe Terrace and across Clipper Down. Like her husband Woderose did her best to keep to the wooded areas even when it would have been quicker to cross a field.

After roughly an hour they came to the narrow Ringshealh (Ringshall), to Evinghehou road and an area in our world where people parked if walking to Ivinghoe Beacon. It was only at this point that Charlotte noticed that the muntjac was no longer with them. She looked back over her shoulder to see if it was somewhere following behind but a sharp tug from Woderose made her concentrate on the way before them. For a moment there was a magnificent view to the Beacon itself though they were too far away to make out the white hart. The view, one of the most famous in the Chilterns was quite stupendous and on a normal occasion Charlotte would have enjoyed resting a while to take it in. But in no way could this be described as a normal occasion and Woderose not hesitating ran across the open area pulling Charlotte with her, not slowing until she had reached the cover of more trees. The way forward was now steep, even so Woderose led them downhill at a pace heading for a large, semi wooded hollow known simply as The Coombe. Charlotte recognised it instantly from walks with her parents, so this was The Coombe, she should have known. By the lay of the land she also recognised that they were nearing their target and a taste of nervous expectation stimulated the tip of her tongue. As they neared the bottom Woderose led them through more open ground. The terrain was still wooded, just with far fewer trees and what trees there were, were spread apart with many showing signs of advanced decay. Fallen limbs lay everywhere, just visible in the many tufts of tall grass. A profusion of nettles grew with the grass and Charlotte simply accepted each sting as an occupational hazard. For the first time the lack of tree cover didn't appear to bother Woderose, her strides were bold, not hesitant and unrushed. Unlike when they'd first met, the Woderose holding her hand oozed confidence, every step had a purpose. As they progressed Charlotte saw Woderose was leading her to a largish circle of tall bracken. Rather than skirt round the bracken Woderose entered their cover. All of the bracken were taller than Charlotte and their feather-like leaves were everywhere, indeed they were all she could see at times not even the sky was visible. With their Jurassic like appearance the child in her half expected a dinosaur to emerge at any moment. Woderose she noticed was careful not to damage any of the tall ferns, parting each carefully with her hands and stepping between them. Still being led by the hand, Charlotte followed in Woderose's parted trail. The going was slow and sapped her already limited energy, the cover of the ferns also acted as an insulator and she was beginning to feel uncomfortably hot, goodness knows how Woderose was feeling beneath that thick coat of hair.

Thankfully, it wasn't all that long before Woderose came to a stop, at their feet lay a small sarsen stone. Charlotte recognised it instantly from the map. Kneeling carefully so as not to disturb the bracken, Woderose placed her hands on one side of the stone and gently rolled it to one side. Underneath lay strands of brown and very dry bracken. With a gentleness of touch that her husband never possessed, Woderose delicately brushed the brittle leaves to one side to reveal a small cavity. Smiling broadly Woderose reached in and lifted out a stone that had no business being in a chalk hill side. Charlotte recognised it with a sense of relief as being a receiving stone. Woderose had understood after all. At times she had been worried she was being led on a wild goose chase but no, Woderose had led her without doubt to the place pre-arranged to meet Leht. In a spontaneous reaction Charlotte slung her arms around the timid beast before her and hugged her hard. When she let go Woderose was beaming so wide her face was in danger of splitting. Placing the receiving stone on the floor Woderose stood up and lightly brushed the squirrel from her shoulder. She had noticed after all. She then placed both hands on Charlotte's shoulder, pushing gently, motioning for her to sit or kneel on the floor. Charlotte obediently did as indicated feeling even more dwarfed by the towering bracken. Woderose then held out her palms an indication Charlotte interpreted as Woderose wanting her to remain where she was. With her arms still outstretched and her palms exposed Woderose proceeded to slowly back out of the circle. Charlotte a little alarmed and not wanting to be left alone at first tried to grab Woderose's hand but with her new found confidence, Woderose pushed her back. Not roughly, gently but with commanding force whilst at the same time making soothing noises.

Woderose hoped the little human child understood. She was not abandoning her, simply leaving her for a short while. Where she was she was safe, safer than coming with her. The little girl due to the tension throughout her body was unaware of her hunger, the tension needed for drive and determination had successfully subdued it. The little girl's hunger though could not be hidden from her, her female instinct had recognised it immediately. She had to go foraging. The little girl would need to eat if she was to survive the challenge that lay ahead.

Charlotte sat cross legged, completely hidden by the cover of the bracken with only the squirrel and her thoughts for company. The squirrel, tired from the day's exertions, curled up tightly, making a bed in the dry bracken that covered the floor and promptly fell asleep. Charlotte looked on, a little jealous at the ease by which the squirrel was able to do this. She too suddenly felt tired as well as hungry, though neither was she possible to satisfy given her situation. Her hand brushed the receiving stone that lay beside her. Such had been her concentration during their passage she'd forgotten about the budget around her neck. It felt empty, something must be wrong, if she was to meet Leht the budget should contain her light blood, the receiving stone was meaningless without it. Pulling open the neck Charlotte looked inside to confirm what she already knew, the budget was empty. She tried not to worry, there was still plenty of time. Even so she couldn't help herself from starting to count the minutes in her head and as the minutes dragged by the monotony of waiting and doing nothing started to take its toll, Charlotte's eyes began to close. At first a shake of her head kept her awake but after three or four shakes, monotony coupled with tiredness won over and her head dropped, her eyes closed and she fell into a light sleep.

Woderose busied herself foraging for what she hoped the little human child would eat. She was very pleased to find some wild strawberries, though not very many. There were still some beech leaves, young enough to digest, their gathering brought back memories of her husband who used to make a rather potent beech leaf gin. Other leaves she managed to find she hoped the child would like included, salad burnet, common winter cress, dandelion, cow parsnip and the beautiful yellow archangel. For a little more sustenance, she dug up the roots of silverweed and restharrow, the latter being a good root to chew and to clear the palate. Pleased with her efforts, Woderose started to make her way back to the sarsen stone, she hoped she hadn't been gone too long.

Charlotte woke with a start, her head shooting up with a jerk that brought an instant protest from her neck. Glancing around wildly, it took seconds to remember where she was. At first the mass of green made it difficult to focus, when her eyes had settled the first thing she saw was the squirrel still soundly asleep. On her other side lay the sarsen stone and beside that Leht's receiving stone, nothing looked as though it had been disturbed. She started to relax and as she did so questions started to enter her head. What time was it, how long had she been asleep, where was Woderose, was she coming back, had anything happened to her? There was something else, she felt a weight around her neck, it was the budget, she looked down, the little leather sack was literally bulging at the seams. Gingerly she opened the neck, it was full to the brim, so much so she was in danger of spilling some of the liquid. Charlotte smiled to herself, so Leht had arrived, thank God. Carefully she pulled the neck tightly shut, as she did so there came a noise, a rustling and at the same time some of the ferns waved back and forth disturbed by something more physical than air. Realising that it was this noise and movement that had awakened her she stood ready to flee. There was no way she could fight. The squirrel woken by Charlotte's movement sat up, its ears raised in alert. Almost immediately it relaxed and bounded off in the direction of the disturbance leaving Charlotte alone. Charlotte waited not sure what to do, she felt like running but something told her there was no need. Her deeper senses were active, telling her she wasn't in any immediate danger and as usual her senses were proven right. The ferns parted and there crouched Woderose with the squirrel once more crouched on her shoulder. Woderose knelt, smiling she carefully laying out her efforts from the past few hours on the scented bracken floor. Charlotte looked puzzled and Woderose demonstrating patience showed her how to eat each of the delicacies that laid before them. Charlotte wanted to show her appreciation for Woderose's efforts but felt very uncomfortable about trying anything except for the strawberries. She knew many plants in the wild were poisonous, some extremely poisonous and what may be ok for Woderose may not be digestible for her. More importantly they probably all tasted disgusting. Woderose however, looked so hurt at her reluctance to try anything that Charlotte eventually decided to throw caution to the wind and followed her example. Surprisingly, nothing tasted as bad as she thought and one or two of the leaves were to her surprise quite enjoyable. They also helped ease the hunger that had started to let its presence be known.

On finishing their meal, Woderose stretched her shaggy arms, yawned and lay down to sleep, the squirrel followed once more curling into a ball resting against her warm thick hair. Charlotte, still tired and aware that there may be a very long night ahead allowed her head to drop between her knees, leaving the weighty budget to rest on the floor. She tried hard to follow the other two, hoping to doze off however for Charlotte sleep refused to come easily. Instead she found herself drifting in and out of consciousness only ever achieving a brief encounter with solid sleep. The enormity of the task that lay before her had started to weave its way into her mind pushing sleep away. At times, the thought of what lay ahead made her feel sick. She wanted to blame Woderose's meal but the feeling of nausea wasn't in her stomach, it had made its home in her chest and accompanied a bitter taste wetting her mouth. Time once more passed slowly and Charlotte tried to wish it faster. Time however listens to no one, no matter what world or universe you are in, it is the one constant that bonds everything and its destruction the ultimate aim of the Darkness.

After what seemed an eternity the sky started to lose its brightness. The slow turn of the planet meant Asherugge was saying farewell to the sun. Shadows started to grow longer and bond with each other. Woderose stirred and sat up. Parting the bracken she looked up at the sky and smiled weakly at the little human child.

Woderose hated the night, it frightened her. The urge to leave the little human child with dusk approaching grew unchallenged in her head. She wanted to help but there were limits to her courage, she had never wanted to be a heroine and certainly not a martyr. She knew the little human child's mission was dangerous and an almost impossible one and with darkness approaching she hoped the wood would understand that she'd done her bit. Standing she smiled again and with the slightest of waves retreated from the cover of the bracken. From there she started to run and did not stop until she'd reached the old oak given to her by the wood. The oak was the strongest tree there was and she prayed that if the little girl failed it would offer some sort of protection from the anger of the Darkness. Her weakness though made her feel guilty. She had done her best, she really had but now safe in her oak the thought of the little human child all alone. Alone with the added danger of nightfall made her feel terrible, sick with remorse. A tear rolled down her cheek, she would not sleep that night of that she was certain. For what she had just done she considered it a very minor punishment.

Chapter Nineteen

Orme

Charlotte watched Woderose leave, she made no attempt to stop her, the poor creature had looked absolutely terrified. She would never forget the look on Woderose's face as she disappeared into the fading light. It had been one of fear coupled with an obvious feeling of guilt. Charlotte was sensitive enough to recognise that Woderose had been fighting an internal battle and in her case fear had won, the need to retreat to safety had been stronger than the will to stay and help her fight. If fight was the right word that is, she still wasn't entirely sure how she would be needed. The thought of any sort of battle made her stomach churn, or this time was it the meal provided by Woderose, in all probability both. Certainly, her memory of Woderose would be living inside her for several hours more, her stomach was beginning to make that quite clear.

Waiting continued to be Charlotte's hardest chore, she needed dusk to turn into night before she could call on Leht. She could not risk wasting any of Leht's light blood by pouring it into the receiving stone too soon. The squirrel was no longer sleeping, it was sitting on its hind legs, ears pricked. At the slightest sound, and there were many as the cloak of darkness descended, the squirrel would tense, its nose searching for the slightest hint of danger. Charlotte sat still, watching and listening to dusk turn into night. She had never realised that the change had a change in sound as well as light. The sound of darkness, of night was quite different to the sound of day and daylight. Noise at night was far crisper, far more pronounced and travelled further. She remembered her father joking once that sound travelled further at night because it's cheaper. The thought brought a smile to her face, then she pushed it away, she didn't want to think about her parents, their memory made it far too painful. She needed to concentrate on the here and now, she knew it was the only way she had any hope of seeing her parents again. Charlotte crunched up her face, she refused to cry, now was not the time for weakness. For a distraction she looked up at the sky. Through the fine slits in the fronds of bracken she could just about see the brightest stars were beginning to appear in the darkening sky. Stars meant dusk was turning to night. It was time, physically shaking with nerves she placed the receiving stone between her legs and opening the neck of the budget began very, very carefully to pour. No sooner had she started when the budget jerked up and its neck closed unaided. Before she had time to wonder what was happening the now familiar vapour began to rise from the receiving stone. Though Charlotte had seen the process before, she stared in wonderment as the vapour gathered into a ball of ever changing, ever moving light. On this occasion the light instead of rising high remained close, hovering below the cover of bracken and easily within touching distance. So close was it Charlotte could feel its energy along with a much welcome unbridled utopia. She sat transfixed as the ball of light gathered tighter, slowly it began to change, to take a shape until hovering directly in front of her shone the unmistakable face of Leht.

"Hello France Charlotte," Leht smiled, her mouth unmoving her words like notes delivered on an invisible staff. Charlotte strained for a reply but remained speechless, to her frustration a weak smile was all she could manage. "Thank you for meeting me here, France Charlotte and thank you for everything you have done since Amphillicia's Well, we are all indebted to you. To you too," Leht smiled at the squirrel, the messenger, who like Charlotte sat motionless. "I can tell you that our

Guardian, received your message and is prepared for tonight, I trust the power of good will help us succeed."

"What are we to do?" Charlotte managed to find her first words, the question had been burning inside her all day. Leht continued to smile as though she had not a care in the world, as though they were simply discussing what to eat for dinner, though of course they weren't.

"We have to help move the Guardian, he cannot last another night." Leht made it sound so simple. "We must move him to somewhere where he will be safe and be able to continue his duties as a Guardian for it is in his blood. It is as you say in your native tongue France Charlotte, his raison d'etre."

"Where will we move him to?" It was the obvious question and one Charlotte felt Leht had left her to ask. Why, she didn't know. She also wanted to ask how but she'd learned that in Otherworld it was always best to ask one question at a time. If you didn't play by this rule you'd only ever get half an answer. One question, one answer that was the key to opening doors.

"Not we France Charlotte, I'm afraid it will be you alone who will help our Guardian move, I cannot help you in this. As to where, the tomb of a king from your world, the tomb of Cunobelinus or as he is also known, Cymbeline. His tomb guards the entrance to another sacred library, a library honoured with his name. The sacred library of Cymbeline. The library is also guarded by the spirits of his two sons who lie buried there. In both our world's great battles once took place on the slopes of the library. In Otherworld it was a battle between good and evil, an early attempt by the Darkness to raid a sacred library. The battle became a precursor to many similar battles with the greatest battle still to come, one which may well be imminent. We will never know which is to be the final battle until each battle is over. Both sons were killed in the battle I speak of and lie buried beneath the hill which thereafter was named in their honour, Cymbeline's Mount, though in your world it is also called Beacon Hill. Their spirits along with that of their father now help guard the library which they defended so valiantly whilst in the physical world. The tomb of their father is known in your world as Chequer's Knap. In Otherworld it is simply known as the tomb. His tomb is a mound that has a perfectly flat top. In the past, in both our worlds, the mound was used by druids and bandrui during religious ceremonies. It stands on a current that reaches deep into the earth and long ago acted as a signalling point between Cymbeline's Mount, or Beacon Hill and the original stronghold of Cunobelinus which once stood on a hill that in your world is known today as Pulpit Hill. The tomb is the smallest flat topped mound on a current which is aligned with two more flat topped hills, the hill of the dragon and the hill of Silbury at a place in your world known as Avebury. All were built at a time when those who knew how, passed regularly between our two worlds. The hill at Silbury contains perhaps the greatest library in Otherworld and is still a stronghold of ours. It must be our mission to eventually lead the Guardian to it, to help defend it if needed, but this is for another day. For now we must obtain the Guardians' release and help him safely to the tomb of Cunobelinus, where he can take on a new role. The land surrounding Cymbeline's Mount and the tomb is hallowed earth, France Charlotte, even the Darkness fears to tread there. Our Guardian and you too will be safe there, providing you keep within its boundaries."

Chequer's Knap which Leht is referring to is just off of the Ridgeway path. It is clearly visible from Beacon and Pulpit Hill. Cymbeline's Castle, marked on Ordnance Survey maps, is actually a Norman fortification that once guarded an important thoroughfare. Cymbeline's Castle is also often mistakenly called Cymbeline's Mount. It is quite clear from Leht's speech that Cymbeline's Mount is Beacon Hill. The Iron age fort on Pulpit Hill had a main entrance and a second much smaller gateway that led to a view point directly overlooking Chequer's Knap.

Leht stopped to let France Charlotte digest what she had just told her. It was a lot to take in but this was probably the last time she would be able to talk to the human child and thus she had little choice. There was also much more to tell, much, much more. The thought worried her greatly. Would the young mind of the little girl be able to absorb all that she had to pass on. She hoped so for the sake of Otherworld.

Charlotte's gaze remained fixed on Leht's ever smiling face hovering just beneath the cover of the tallest ferns. She knew many of the places Leht had just referred to, they lay between the towns of Wendover and Princes Risborough and close to Chequers, the country residence for Britain's incumbent Prime Minister. However she wasn't at all sure if she would be able to find her way there on her own. There was also the question of leading the white hart, the Guardian as Leht always called him. Surely if they managed his escape the Darkness would be frantic to find him, how was she expected to hide let alone guide such a large and distinct animal across country without being spotted. And if she did manage to find her way there, what was she to do then. She couldn't stay protected on hallowed ground forever, she wanted to get home. Leht was reading her thoughts and with a little more tact than Triskelion, gracefully interrupted.

"Fear not, France Charlotte, you will not need to guide the Guardian, he will guide you. You must stay with him until he completes his journey. After his escape you will hide in Incombe Hole, there you will remain protected until day break. At dawn you will start your journey to the tomb of Cunobelinus. The Guardian will take either the lines of Michael or Mary, he will know best the safest to follow."

The Mary and Michael lines Leht refers to are two lines of energy or earth currents that entwine, rather like the snakes on Asclepius's rod, Britain's most famous Ley line, the line of St Michael. The existence of Ley lines in our world are hotly disputed. They are invisible, pre Christian, lines that connect ancient monuments and extraordinary natural features such as Ivinghoe Beacon and Glastonbury Tor. Though modern scientists may dismiss such theories as nothing but fantasy what cannot be denied is the extraordinary accuracy with which ancient man managed to align their monuments along with extraordinary natural features. The St Michael line if you wish to research further starts at Carn Les Boel in Cornwall and finishes at St Margaret's Church at Hopton on the Norfolk coast. Along the way the line passes through hundreds of significant landmarks including St Michaels Mount, Cheesewring, Glastonbury Tor, Avebury Circle and of course Ivinghoe Beacon where the Mary and Michael currents or lines also meet. Dowsers have long claimed to be able to discover Ley lines or earth currents especially when using copper rods which as you will read later may be significant.

"Whichever line our Guardian choses it will give you strength and also help protect you. Whatever happens you must reach the tomb by nightfall, failure to do so," Leht paused before continuing. "Well you do not need me to tell you." Charlotte did not, her stomach was churning, both from the meal that Woderose had given her and the thought of what was to come. She tried to concentrate on what Leht had just told her, she still couldn't see why she was needed. Leht read her thoughts but on this occasion remained silent, preferring to let the little human child form her own opinions.

"What am I to do once, (if, Charlotte thought not once but didn't wish to appear negative), we arrive at the tomb? Leht had dreaded this question and with all her given wisdom still hadn't formed an answer she was happy with. There was no option but to be honest. The little human child deserved that at least.

"You must find your own way, France Charlotte, if I can help you I will, but where I have to go I am not at all sure that I will be able to. I am afraid that your destiny, (and perhaps that of Otherworld, Leht kept this to herself), will almost certainly be in your hands. You will have to trust your own mind, your own instincts. I am so sorry France Charlotte."

"Why, where do you have to go?" Leht could not bring herself to tell the little human child the truth.

"I'm afraid I cannot reveal that, France Charlotte." It was an imperfect answer, one that she felt deeply ashamed of. The little human child deserved better. Silence fell as Charlotte pondered this. For the first time since Leht's smiling face had formed amongst the leafy bracken Charlotte broke her gaze and looked up at the stars. Is all this really happening she asked herself, please let it be a dream. Her gaze returned to Leht, the image of tranquillity, a disguise she wore so well. She had asked herself the same question many times before but this was no dream, she already knew.

"How do I defeat the Darkness?" Charlotte's question although she was personally unaware was her acceptance finally of her role, a role that somebody or something had chosen for her without asking her consent. Leht did not reply immediately and for a moment, just a second Charlotte could have sworn she saw Leht's serene smile slip.

"I cannot help you with that either, France Charlotte, I am afraid the questions you now ask are beyond my understanding, you will have to find your own path, you have been chosen by powers unknown to all of us. Powers that are no longer with us to explain their decision. All I can tell you is that to defeat the Darkness you must do it in your world not Otherworld. You cannot defeat the Darkness here."

"How do I get back to my world?" This question too had been simmering ever since her scare at the church of St John the Baptist in Aldeborie. How was she ever going to return to her world. She didn't really care how she'd do battle with the Darkness, as long as she could return to her world and see her parents. Everything though was beginning to look more and more hopeless. Leht at one time had appeared to have the answer to everything, now she appeared not to own a single answer. And Leht was about to disappoint again.

"I'm afraid I cannot tell you that either, France Charlotte, as with everything else, after tonight you will have to find your own answers to your questions, I am truly sorry, France Charlotte." Charlotte thought hard, Leht may suddenly appear not to have an answer to a single question but she must continue trying. From Leht's account this was probably her last chance. She thought back to the gateway through which she'd transcended, so many times before, to the magpie's feather on the stone slab that was preventing her from doing so again. It all seemed too simple, a mere feather blocking her passage. Leht a little alarmed at the direction the little human child's thoughts were taking, cut in.

"You cannot unlock the feather, France Charlotte, only the Darkness can do that. If you remove the feather, the gateway will cave in on itself rather like a black hole and simply cease to exist. To try and pass after you have forcibly removed the feather or key will mean that the physical part of you will be crushed into dust though your soul and your mind will survive, slave to the calling of the Darkness. Do not let such temptation enter your mind, France Charlotte, the Darkness will only encourage it." Silence fell on the little gathering once more. Whoever named silence as golden, was an idiot, Charlotte hated silence. As earlier she thought back to her scare before the porch of St John the Baptist. If the Darkness was so keen to defeat her, to kill her, why hadn't it done so then. She had been at its mercy and yet it felt to her as though it had simply let her go. This time rather than let Leht read her thoughts she threw them at Leht with questions attached. Maybe this way she'd get a full answer. Why had Ashtynn stopped chasing her was her main one. She would have surely caught her and ...., Charlotte shivered to think. This time Leht offered an answer and was quick with her reply.

"The Darkness is spread thinly, France Charlotte. To create a new passage between our two worlds is an immense task even with the help of your Gravade. And it has a tight schedule, we know now that the Darkness needs to complete the new gateway before the coming of the great cycle. Failure to do so will maybe mean it has to wait thousands of years more before the same opportunity arises again. As we have already told you, like us the Darkness does not have the same resources as it once did. Many of the spirits it once relied upon now have their own agenda and there is a lot of infighting. Scucca is still loyal but he has to be controlled as do the gnombres who by nature are rebellious and disorganised. The Darkness does not have the power to direct all its agents all of the time. To let Ashtynn or Scucca pursue you further may have meant they'd escaped its ring of influence, it would risk no longer having control over them. It simply could not risk that happening so let you escape." There could well be another reason and Leht hoped it wasn't the case. She also had no wish to relay it to the little human child. It was one that her and Triskelion had discussed at length and that was that the Darkness may know more of what was contained in the books of the Snooks than they did. It may be that the Snooks books were simply recording the human child's transcendence into Otherworld, simply recording her presence here, nothing more. She may well have no influence in the final battle and the Darkness perhaps was aware of that. In fact by the way things were progressing it appeared more and more likely this may be the case. Leht could see no way at all how the little human child was going to do battle with the Darkness, let alone defeat it. She saw little hope for the world from where France Charlotte came. The Darkness would surely destroy it and with its destruction Otherworld would lose its anchor. What would become of her world if this happened was impossible to predict. The main goal now was to stop the secrets of Orme falling into the hands of the Darkness and tonight was to be part of that plan. If she could help start a journey that gathered all of the light scrolls that may hold the key to Orme, together in one secure place, they may when the day came, be used by good in the final battle with evil. If she could start this journey then she would have completed her own raison d'etre. The little human child had now become part of this new plan. Perhaps this was her role after all, not to do battle with the Darkness. For the first time since her birth Leht felt the feeling of guilt and it was not a feeling that sat well with her. When the little human child met her afterlife which she will surely do soon, Leht hoped she would never have to face her in a new world. She'd prefer to meet her afterlife again rather than do that.

"Do you have any further questions, France Charlotte, I cannot appear before you forever, to do so is to consume energy that I may well need later." The question was designed to move things on, Leht was beginning to feel very uncomfortable in the little girl's gaze and she still had information to relay. Information that in case beyond all her doubts and fears the little human child did succeed, she would be able to use in the search for a successful and maybe final outcome.

Charlotte thought hard, so much was going around her head and it didn't help that her stomach was raging. She had so many, so many, many questions but they were in no logical order and many were surely irrelevant. Many were simply to satisfy her curiosity. She eventually decided on one only, another question that had been tormenting her, one that she desperately wanted an answer to. The expression on Triskelion's face when he had met his afterlife, it had haunted her ever since and the head of the woman in the room that had surely become his tomb. Who was she? Leht sighed as she read France Charlotte's thoughts, she could not give the little human child the answer she so craved for. To do so would simply be too dangerous.

"France Charlotte," Leht started. "Please do not ask me this, Triskelion's reason for parting as he did is for him and personal to him. If he did not convey his reasons to you it is not for me to guess or pass on his personal wishes. As for the scarlet lady, her identity I am forbidden to reveal. Even if I wanted to, I cannot. I am very sorry France Charlotte." So many secrets Charlotte thought to herself why so many secrets, if so much was to be asked of her why were so many things kept from her? Leht reading her feelings cut in once more.

"Some things you are simply not ready for France Charlotte, please trust me in this." Charlotte though was not about to give up. She felt she deserved the right to know more.

"Would it have anything to do with the Bonhommes? Triskelion told me a lot about them."

"Why do you say that, France Charlotte?" Charlotte thought back to what Triskelion had told her about the possibility of the treasure they'd brought from the South of France and hidden somewhere at Ashridge or Assherugge. Had they as part of their haul brought the head that Triskelion had met his afterlife beside. It was a reasonable assumption. Charlotte relayed what Triskelion had told her, keeping it as short as possible. Leht's light was beginning to fade and Charlotte knew there was little time left in which to seek answers.

"Triskelion wouldn't say or wasn't sure what their treasure was, he said it may have something to do with Orme. I thought it may be gold as there is a valley called Golden Valley close by. I told my father this but he said many valleys bore the same name and that the name had nothing to do with precious metal." She paused then added. "My father said the only Golden Valley where there may really be a valuable hidden treasure is one in a county in our world called Herefordshire." Charlotte could not explain why she'd felt the need to add this. A voice, the voice deep inside her, the one she could not explain but had learned to trust urged her to reveal what her father had told her. Leht gazed down at the little human child, France Charlotte as Wodewose had christened her. What she had just told her had taken her completely by surprise. It took her nicely onto what she was about to convey but she had to choose her words carefully. They had been investigating the valley the little girl spoke of. From what France Charlotte had just conveyed to her perhaps her father knew something of what was happening. They'd never considered this in Otherworld, only that a little human child, a young girl would transcend and live amongst them.

"Your father may well be right, France Charlotte, what makes him say this?" Charlotte simply shrugged and shook her head, she hadn't been prepared for such a response and honestly hadn't any idea. Leht dearly wanted to question the little girl further but time was running out as was her energy.

"France Charlotte, you cannot ask me any further questions, time and my energy does not allow it. I am about to tell you a little about Orme, you must listen and listen only. There is little time left until my power fades and when it does our talking is finished, do you understand?" Charlotte nodded, her eyes wide with expectation. Her long queue of questions wiped from her mind, at least for now.

"Since visiting Otherworld we have made you aware of the power of Orme, it is the secret to everything around us. As Triskelion and I have told you, to know Orme enables one to become a God." Charlotte nodded furiously. "Good." Leht looked pleased and Charlotte felt herself glowing with pleasure. "I need to stress that such is its power, to know its secret may corrupt the purest soul, the temptation to use it for your own ends would simply be too great. In the case of Orme knowledge corrupts, knowledge is dangerous. That is why the ancients spread the secret to Orme throughout the world, not only in Otherworld but your world too. The secret to Orme can never be destroyed but the ancients did their best to hide it, to make it almost impossible to put together, to make it impossible to complete the jigsaw if you like. Do you follow me?" Once again Charlotte nodded vigorously. Leht continuing to smile went on.

"There are many parts to Orme. You can know some of its secrets and use them accordingly but finding all of the pieces and joining them together will enable whoever succeeds in this to have access to unchallengeable power. At first we thought the ancients only distributed the secrets throughout Otherworld but has recently became apparent that many of the pieces had also been hidden in your world. To find a place to start is difficult, what is important to you for now is what we know about your world and so I will concentrate there. There was once in your world a civilisation you call Egyptians, we do not know how much but we are aware they knew something of Orme. Thankfully, they guarded and used their knowledge carefully. We believe they were aware of the dangers if such knowledge fell into the wrong hands. That danger sadly in time became real and to avoid what surely would have been a catastrophe the Egyptian priesthood dispatched a princess with all their knowledge of Orme. Her mission to hide the secret not in one place but just as the ancients did, in many places. How these secrets were stored we do not know, they may have been written on a type of parchment, scribed in stone, or somehow stored in light as they are in Otherworld, we simply do not know." Leht paused worried that for a child the subject matter may be too much to digest. Reading the little girl's mind she was relieved to find that so far like a sponge her mind had absorbed every word. "We know that she, the princess, sailed to what you today call Spain then travelled up through the Languedoc in your native country, where we believed she may have hidden some of the secrets. This is where there may be a connection to the Cathars and the Bonhommes for this region and especially the Languedoc was their home." Charlotte nodded again, she was struggling to suppress a feeling of excitement. She knew the Languedoc Leht spoke of, she had holidayed there with her parents. Leht continued, her strength was fading fast. "We believe, though do not know for certain, that after the Languedoc the princess travelled northwards through France depositing further secrets along the way. It is my belief she travelled to Rochelle from where she sailed to Rochester in the land of the Aengles or what you now call England. The land in which you live today. From Rochester we are told she may have sailed to the land of Alba or what you today call Scotland and from there to the ancient kingdom of Inis Ealga, which today, in your world is known as Ireland. She eventually ended her journey we believe at the sacred hill of Tara. Throughout her journey the princess may have deposited, hidden is a better word some of the secrets to Orme. I return to her final destination, Tara. One of the properties of Orme is that in a certain form it burns with a cold flame. From the outside the flame emits heat but will not burn you, put your hand in the flame and the flame is cold. The main property of the flame we understand is that it generates youth, it is what you call in your world the elixir of life. To bathe in its flame can not only make you younger, the process can make you immortal. Legends told in your world of the elixir is perhaps the strongest evidence we have that some of your species knew at least this property of Orme. Further research has left me in no doubt that a number of people in your world have experimented with the use of this property and succeeded. There are too many examples over history to its use. Too many to tell you now France Charlotte. What I will tell you is that there are many stories or legends as you call them in your world relating to fires burning on the hill of Tarah, and I now believe these fires are almost certainly related to the burning of Orme. What I have told you gives you a broad understanding of how the secrets of Orme were distributed in your world. Now more specifically to the Bonhommes. Certainly, they brought with them to Assherugge a great treasure, of that there is no doubt and in all probability it was something to do with one of the secrets to Orme, possibly several secrets. There is a clue that cannot be ignored, the founder of the college of Bonhommes at Ashridge was Edmund the 2nd Earl of Cornwall. His base was Restormel Castle near a town called Lostwithiel. You cannot fail to see the word orme in the name, Restormel. Edmund rebuilt the castle and there are many features within its walls that are unique and remain unexplained."

"Do you think the Bonhommes hid the treasure inside the sacred library? Triskelion thought they may have done."

"In the sacred library, I think it is unlikely though possible. It is far more likely they hid it somewhere else but where, I personally have no idea, they were very clever for they have left no clue."

"Then it may still be hidden at Ashridge, sorry Asherugge?" Charlotte remembered the bricked up passage and quickly wiped it from her thoughts. She did not know why but she felt uncomfortable revealing its existence to Leht. She questioned her reasoning but the voice deep inside her kept telling her to do so was unwise. Leht ever weakening appeared this time not to read Charlotte's thoughts, it was very apparent she was keen to move on and thus failed to register Charlotte's quandary.

"Please, France Charlotte, no more interruptions, I have to finish what I need to say and my energy is failing fast." Charlotte could see Leht's words were true, her face had lost its shine and her features were fading fast. She promised not to interrupt again and Leht quickly moved on.

"If you succeed in returning to your world, France Charlotte the whereabouts of the treasure of the Bonhommes is one of the things we'd like you to try and find. If it exists it will be well hidden and as I have just told you, we in Otherworld know of no clue as to where. I must warn you there will be dangers involved in your search for I am sure you will not be the only one seeking the treasure and those who are also searching will not take kindly to your intrusion. It is a lot to ask of you but we cannot risk the treasure, if it is to do with Orme falling into the wrong hands." For a moment Charlotte thought Leht had finished, her light was fading fast, almost to the point of extinction but with an obvious effort some of her light rematerialized and Leht continued with her message.

I must now take you back, France Charlotte, to the beginning, to the arrival of Orme in both of our worlds. You in your world just as we do in Otherworld have an expression. It refers to blue or royal blood the latter being an expression for blue blood." Charlotte nodded she knew of the expression, they had the same expression in her country of birth, sang bleu and it also referred to the blood of a royal or nobleman. "The first ancients did not roam the land but lived in water. They ingested not air but copper from the water and as a result their blood was blue. This is where the expression originates from. We have discovered that some in your land believe that the term sang real refers to the ancestral blood of the Christian son of God, Jesus. It is much older than that. There are many tales all over your world, in many cultures of men emerging from the sea and the original symbol for Jesus who I know you follow, is a fish. Sang bleu or sang real are one and the same. There are molluscs in your world living today who intake copper and their blood being copper rich is blue when exposed to air. It is worth noting that one such mollusc in your world has been named Ormer or Ormeau which suggests that whoever named it was aware of the connection between copper, blue blood and Orme. For the blue blooded ancients there was not enough copper to be found naturally in water and they had to go in search of copper on land. Many mines therefore were dug to provide enough copper for the original ancients to survive. Evidence of these ancient mines have survived world over and the largest of these was even named after what we now believe to have been the mine's original purpose. The mine I am talking about is still known in your world by its original name, The Great Orme. I need to explain for you to understand why I say this. We have long known in Otherworld that copper is almost certainly a key ingredient in creating Orme, alchemists always worked with copper. And it would appear whoever was responsible for naming this mine, "The Great Orme," was not afraid to make public its true purpose.

Leht's light was beginning to fade again. Charlotte felt as though her head was ready to burst but then Leht, she knew would be aware of this. She was growing concerned, if Leht's light was to disappear altogether, how was she to know what to do next, she hadn't a clue, Leht hadn't told her. So far it had all been about Orme. Just as she was starting to panic, Leht's voice sounded again but it was now so weak that Charlotte had to strain to understand. Leht still hadn't finished with Orme.

"Orme and evidence of some of your species being aware of Orme is to be found everywhere in your world. Our concern is, how much is actual knowledge and how much is pure guesswork based on rumours or small discoveries . If you do manage to return to your world we would like you to make finding out your "raison d'etre". Alchemists like Gravade we now believe, were searching for Orme not gold as is commonly thought and we have suspicions that the Philosophers Stone is in fact Orme. We are worried that Gravade may have made an important discovery with regard to Orme and this is the real reason the Darkness courted him. I must now return to the Golden Valley, in the valley your father described to you is a church with connections to another in London. Inscriptions on the gravestones of both churches are in some cases almost identical and relay a rather unique message. The church in London our contacts in your world have led us to believe was once infiltrated by a group who knew something or were searching for the secret of Orme. Our informers have not told us which churches. Find out France Charlotte, find out if you can. In the past your people left messages and clues of Orme in stone with the hope that one day someone with the right knowledge will understand. If you want an example of this we are aware there is an ancient stone set in a wall of a building somewhere in the centre of a city called Truro not far from Restormel. You see the connection. I have not seen the stone, though I'm told it is mirrored in Otherworld and I'm also told it has an inscription you must read and interpret. There is much more to tell France Charlotte but I must conserve my energy. We have little contact with your world now. With what little contact we do have we have made those who we are in touch with aware of your existence, your role here in Otherworld and your possible help in such matters if ever you return to your world. In return they will do their best to aid and protect you, you have my word on this." Leht paused, it was taking all of her remaining strength to stop herself from fading altogether. She hoped everything she had just told the little human child wasn't to be in vain, though in all likelihood she knew it would be. The thought depressed her. If only they hadn't been so arrogant, they may have sought the help of the little girl's world earlier and avoided the crisis presented today. France Charlotte's species might be by their way of life slowly strangling their world and with it Otherworld but with education this could still be reversed. In contrast the secret of Orme falling into the wrong hands would almost certainly be irreversible. Leht's last reserves concentrated on their immediate mission. If they failed in this, everything she had just revealed to France Charlotte would definitely have been for nothing. She had very little light left, she had to get her final message across before it was too late.

The wealth of information that Leht had just conveyed upon her had completely muddled Charlotte's brain. She had only just accepted that there was another world, Otherworld and now Leht was filling her mind with something even more alien, even more fantastical. Where would it end? Life had once in comparison been so simple, how she longed for its return. What she couldn't understand was why did evil exist at all, where and when was its foundation. Who was its founder, who invented it? God, Orme? Why, why, why? Charlotte's wrangled contemplation was interrupted by Leht's now almost unintelligible voice

"Pay attention, France Charlotte, when I disappear you must pick up my receiving stone and carry it to two yew trees that grow side by side. Do not worry although you will not be able to see me, I will guide you there. On arriving you must touch each tree with the palm of your hand. The trees are connected directly with my ancient yew and its power will give you courage as well as strength. From the two yews you must walk and wait under a holly tree, again I will guide you. The holly tree you will identify immediately, it is shaped rather like a fir, or a Christmas tree may be a better description. When you are called, still carrying my receiving stone you must walk through an expanse of mature firs. The firs were planted by your species in rows, rather like soldiers. The manner in which they were planted, they have no place being in The Coombe. They are not connected to the root vine and recently have become agents of the Darkness. When they spy you, they will try and intimidate you but you must not be afraid. Being planted in a Coombe they cannot move, they are literally rooted to the spot." (Another expression that looks as though it has its roots in Otherworld). Although they are under the influence of the Darkness they are not in communication with it, the passage through the firs will be quite safe and they will provide cover for our advance on what you call Ivinghoe Beacon. After the firs continue until my receiving stone will go no further. There is a circumference outside of which the stone will not travel. When you reach this point place my stone on the ground and pour the remainder of my light blood bar a small drop into my stone. As you know I will appear. The remaining drop in the budget you must drink, it will help me communicate with you and help me to observe your progress."

Charlotte didn't like the thought of drinking Leht's light blood in the slightest but meekly accepted her request. She would do as bid. With that Leht's face faded into nothing and once more Charlotte found herself alone with the squirrel. With the absence of Leht's light the tall bracken surrounding them turned from a rather comforting cover to something that felt quite intimidating. Charlotte carefully parting a few fronds looked up at the sky. The heavens were clear and a weak but visible waxing crescent moon accompanied the festoon of brightly coloured stars. Was she looking at the same sky that appeared in her world. She wasn't sure if she wanted to know the answer .Life in Otherworld was becoming far too complicated, she needed no further distractions. With the help of Wodewose's staff she stood up. Her legs had fallen asleep and she had to rub them awake. Looking down at the little squirrel she noticed he appeared to have no such trouble. Bending once more she picked up Leht's receiving stone, it was really heavy. She hadn't realised just how heavy and now she was expected to carry it. Placing her left hand under the stone and using Wodewose's staff for support Charlotte advanced carefully through the bracken. What few trees there were reported her progress via the root vine to the rest of Asherugge. The whole of the wood waited with bated breath. Each and every tree knew that the outcome of the next few hours may determine their future, if there was to be one at all. Woderose in her sturdy oak put her hands over her ears and tried to blot out the commentary. She couldn't bear to listen, undeserved guilt lay heavy on her bowed head.

Chapter Twenty

A Light Extinguished

It took only minutes for Charlotte and the squirrel to leave the cover of the bracken. For what in the past few hours had been a deeply small and personal world they were thrown into a wide and open expanse, a landscape full of grandeur with nowhere to hide. Before them rose a dark seemingly impenetrable wall which Charlotte knew to be the wood of tall firs that Leht had told her they would have to pass through. Charlotte shivered at the thought and as she did so she was sure that every one of the firs moved slightly. A voice sounded in her head, the soothing melodic voice that was Leht's. This time there were no words, instead her notes span an invisible thread laying a route for her to follow. Though Charlotte found the route laid by Leht easy to follow the local flora wasn't quite so obliging. Nettles, nettles that reached taller than her were the main obstacle and though Wodewose's staff helped beat them back the weight of Leht's receiving stone meant that with each swing she almost lost her balance. In the end Charlotte for the sake of progress accepted she would simply have to get stung. She swore one day she would take her revenge on nettles by making a soup from their objectionable leaves. After skirting the wall of firs Charlotte viewed the two yews. Her first thought was that they didn't look very old, she had assumed they would be ancient. As bid she went to each yew and placed her hand on their reddish trunks. After touching the second trunk she felt a rush of blood that reached the extremities of all her senses. The feeling was indescribable, Leht had called it both courage and strength but the feeling was much more than that, it was one of invincibility. The feeling she realised sensibly had to be controlled she must not let its strength overwhelm her, to do so could be dangerous. Her increasingly strong bond with her deeper senses warned her if she didn't respect the gift from Leht's yew she may become reckless.

Once more Leht's invisible thread was ready to guide her and within minutes of leaving the two yews Charlotte recognised the holly tree that Leht had told her to wait under. It really did resemble a Christmas tree. She wondered how Leht knew what a Christmas tree looked like. Otherworld from what she'd experienced didn't appear to be particularly Christian and by her own admission Leht had never visited her world. Anyhow at that moment the question wasn't really important, it could wait for another day. Obediently she stood beneath the tree as directed and waited for further instructions. She hoped they wouldn't be long in coming, the receiving stone was becoming very uncomfortable to carry. She could, you may suggest rest the stone on the ground but the now familiar voice in her head told her this would be unwise. The budget too being almost full with Leht's light blood weighed heavy around her neck. Once again Charlotte found herself making the same mistake earlier, that of trying to count the passing of time. Time as it always does responds by dragging its feet. Only a few paces away the man planted wood of firs loomed dark, daring her to enter their fold. Charlotte looked the other way. Raising her nose to the sky she took in the night air, air that carried scents not present during the hours of daylight. She relished the stories they carried. In her mind she was no longer afraid, tense, nervous perhaps yes but not afraid. The force given to her by Leht's yew still raged but she had its influence under control. Maybe she would need its power in the near future and if she did she would free it and allow it to do its will. For now it was comforting to know she had it in reserve.

The command came as though a light had been switched on in her head. She had to move, the instruction buzzed urgency. Adrenalin wet her mouth, the enormity of what was about to happen hitting her like a train traveling at one hundred miles per hour. Leht's invisible thread led her directly to the wood of firs and the cavernous dark within. She wanted to close her eyes but knew that would be bowing to fear and whatever was to happen she knew, knew above anything else she must not let fear take over. As she passed through the lines of firs she had an overwhelming feeling of being watched and an even stronger one of hate, intense hatred. She concentrated on holding her head high, guided by Leht's invisible trail just like the thread of Ariadne. All the time determined she was not going to be intimidated by a bunch of trees, no matter how scary. At that very moment as though the firs had read her mind, every tree started to move. They began to march, was how it felt. Charlotte began to run, struggling not to let the receiving stone fall from her grasp. The budget swung wildly about her neck and Wodewose's staff rather than help was cumbersome. Her way wasn't helped by the squirrel who scared out of his wits ran up her back and onto her left shoulder. Charlotte soon gave up, running was out of the question. She slowed to a brisk walk. All around her the towering firs were moving, marching in unison, the sound they made resembled thousands of heavily booted feet. It was deafening. Charlotte continued, doing her utmost to ignore them, one bold step at a time, concentrating on following Leht's invisible thread. She heard Leht's melodic voice, she remembered her, telling her, the firs could do her no harm. Surely, surely though soon the firs would block her way, crush her into oblivion. She would have no hope against their combined strength. This must surely be the end. All the time she could hear Leht's voice trying to calm her, assuring her the firs cannot do her harm and a slow realisation descended on her. The firs were all show, all needles and no trunk. The firs were marching but they weren't going anywhere, they were marching on the spot. Their frustration, their anger was obvious, their trunks shook violently as they strained to break free. She remembered Leht's words, the firs were, "rooted to the spot," trapped by The Coombe and by the way in which they'd been planted. A renewed confidence spurred her on and Charlotte after understanding the firs could do her no harm marched through the wood wearing a broad smile. A smile in truth that hid a multitude of emotions and one that infuriated the firs, they shook furiously with rage. Though she knew the firs could cause her no harm it was a relief when they eventually left their cover, to be an object of such hate was not a good feeling. Not a good feeling at all.

Standing on open ground, before them lay the expansive chalk grassland that announced the approach to Ivinghoe Beacon. At any other time Charlotte would have gazed upon the scene with awe, but that night the view presented nothing but a challenge and worse still danger. Moving with caution she stepped forward taking small slow steps, was it her imagination or was Leht's compass starting to waiver. She was having to concentrate more and more if she was to avoid losing her thread. As though being filmed in slow motion the Beacon itself came into view. It's immediate slopes were one large shadow and at its summit the faintest of glows which Charlotte knew was the Guardian, the white hart that had kept her company since her first day in Aldbury. With one careful step after another Charlotte edged forward, her gaze fixed on the summit of the Beacon. An eerie silence surrounded her and she had a strange feeling the whole world was watching. Surely the Darkness would be too.

When the time came it was quite unexpected. Though she had been forewarned, Charlotte was still caught off guard. It was as though she suddenly came up against an invisible wall. With an abrupt jar her advance was halted. Holding the receiving stone with one hand she used the other to feel ahead of her. There was nothing, just air her hand moved freely in the space before her. Once more she tried to take a step forward but came up an invisible wall, it was the receiving stone, not her that could advance no further. Just as Wodewose's staff had refused to enter her cottage, the receiving stone was refusing to travel any further. As Leht had warned her, she'd reached the circumference beyond which the receiving stone was unable to travel. Taking a deep breath Charlotte placed the stone on the ground and kneeling on one knee slowly poured the liquid that was Leht's light blood into the receptacle. The budget as it had done before stopped pouring when the required amount of blood had been released though on this occasion that meant almost everything, only a few drops remained. Charlotte knew she was meant to drink what was left but couldn't help feeling repulsed at the idea. As she hesitated Leht's melodic voice floated about her.

"Drink me."

It was the most forceful Charlotte had known Leht to sound. Her words were not a plea but an order. Lifting the small leather bag to her lips Charlotte let the last remaining drops fall onto her tongue. The taste was unpleasant, very, very bitter and she did her best not to retch. Memories of Alice in Wonderland filled her head and she half expected to shrink or grow tall as Alice had done. Nothing happened at least not physically, she remained the same height. What the liquid did do was to clear her mind, it was though a door had been opened to Leht's soul. She could feel her as never before, so strong was the connection that she almost felt as though she and Leht were one. As Charlotte struggled with her feelings, before her glowing spirals of vapour from Leht's light blood rose skywards. Such was the mass the vapour formed not a sphere but a curtain. Slowly the luminous curtain condensed to form a shape and when the process was finished appearing in front of Charlotte stood the figure of Leht. Not since their first meeting in the puddingstone stone circle had Charlotte seen Leht as a whole. Every time she had appeared after their meeting in Leht's circle only her face had become visible, until now. Charlotte couldn't help taking a spontaneous intake of breath. She had forgotten the depth of Leht's beauty, the figure stood before her epitomised the word grace, Leht was utter perfection.

"Hello again France Charlotte and to you my little messenger" Leht's smile held both Charlotte and the messenger transfixed. "Are you ready?" Charlotte remained motionless, her new connection with Leht meant that the luminous figure standing before her already knew she was. "Reach into your budget France Charlotte." Charlotte did as she was told feeling for the map. There was something else, something that hadn't been there a few moments ago of that she was sure for the whatever it was, was large, she would have felt its presence. Her hand closed around the foreign body, it was solid and cold to the touch, it was also heavy. Carefully she withdrew the object though the neck of the small leather bag. In her hand she was shocked to see she held a knife or to be more accurate a dagger. It's blade glinted beneath the light from the stars and the waxing crescent moon. The handle felt as though it were wrapped in leather though she could not be sure. Charlotte gazed in horror at Leht's smiling face, no questions was Leht's response, you must only do as I command. Charlotte had never felt so helpless, she knew she hadn't a choice. Leht waved an arm towards Ivinghoe Beacon, her voice travelled effortlessly, melodic as always but now with an edge that Charlotte had never thought possible.

"The shadow you see covering Leabharlann de Solas, the hill covering the sacred library, to you of course Ivinghoe Beacon are gnombres. Thousands are massed waiting for the last breath of our Guardian. I am going to distract them, France Charlotte. The Darkness is convinced it has already won a battle here and has reduced its influence over the gnombres that surround our Guardian. This will work in our favour. The Guardian thanks to your message will subdue what remains of his glow and at the same I will take on his form and my image will shine brighter than the brightest star. From the place where Triskelion's ancestor rests, I will flee the northern slope. If fortune is with us, for gnombres act on instinct and the desire to devour, not with wisdom or reflection and hopefully because of these failures they will follow fearing our Guardian is escaping. I will lead the rabble into Coombe Hole where they will become trapped. The spirit of Triskelion's grandfather will help hide my approach to the ridge where I will become visible to the gnombres ." Leht stopped to allow the France Charlotte time to absorb and understand her plan. She had total control over the little human child but only wanted to use her control if it became necessary to do so. She hoped it would never come to that. Their chances of succeeding were stronger if France Charlotte acted of her own desire, using her own instincts. The strength of both of them would be depleted if she had to force the little girl. Satisfied France Charlotte was indeed following, Leht continued.

"When you see the gnombres leave the slopes of the Beacon France Charlotte you must climb to the summit with the greatest haste. The Guardian will be waiting. On his crown he will be carrying an orb of light. (When Leht says crown, she means antlers. In Otherworld, the antlers of a white hart are always referred to as a crown). Do not be alarmed, the orb may scare you by its appearance but it will do you no harm. The orb is to carry five light scrolls which our Guardian has raised from the Sacred Library. These are scrolls which I believe may contain secrets to Orme. After the closing of the entrance by yourself and Triskelion I have discovered there is another way into the Sacred Library. There is an entrance hidden in the woodland of Ashridge, an entrance until the passing of the last moon I wasn't aware existed. It is not an easy one to find or enter but I cannot take the risk of the Darkness using it. The Guardian will carry the scrolls to the library of Cymbeline where they will be deposited temporarily until we find a good time to move them to somewhere safer." Leht paused once more allowing the little human child to take in what she had just told her.

"You are holding a dagger France Charlotte, I hope you will not have to use it but you must be prepared to, if necessary. If there is the slightest danger that the Guardian may be captured by the Darkness or its agents you must strike the Guardian through the heart with the knife in your hand. You must not fail in this France Charlotte, there will be no blood. The Guardian will simply disappear and the light scrolls destroyed. The Guardian will be ready for your strike and even willing you to do so. To be captured by the Darkness will be a fate far worse. His capture and that of the scrolls simply cannot happen. Is that clear?" Leht immediately knew it was. She could feel the little human child's abhorrence at the thought but also read her understanding and her willingness to act if it became necessary.

"On reaching the Guardian you must climb on his back, he will carry you and our messenger to the tomb and the Library of Cymbeline. It is imperative you reach your destination within the hours of daylight following this moon. As I told you earlier failure to do so will almost certainly mean all of you meeting your afterlife. The Darkness is growing in strength by the hour, after the passing of the next moon you may not find shelter even during the hours of daylight. The power of the Darkness will be such that it will be able to draw a cloak over the heavens, to darken the skies to such an extent the gnombres and its other agents will be able to move freely. After the passing of the next moon you may find nowhere to hide." Leht was relieved to have finished, she was tired of talking and like Triskelion starting to tire of living. Within the hour she knew unless there was a miracle she would meet her afterlife, her light would shine no more in Otherworld. All of her was now in the open, there was no going back. So much still rested on the little human child. What both her and Triskelion had first considered to be France Charlotte's destiny in Otherworld sadly wasn't to be. She now realised they'd been mistaken. For a human child to do battle with the Darkness, she now recognised with shame had been a fantasy of theirs, a hope without reason. France Charlotte's destiny it was now clear had always been to help their Guardian carry the light scrolls, scrolls possibly carrying secrets to Orme, for it wasn't certain at all, to safety. And if that became impossible to ensure they were destroyed forever. It was a very sad destiny for such a bold child especially after a beginning that had looked to be so promising. Leht had no wish to linger any longer, what must be, must be, she had done her best, now it was time for others to take over. May the power of good protect all Otherworld and the world of the little girl.

"You are ready, France Charlotte?" Charlotte found the freedom to nod. She felt rather than read Leht's mood and did not want to believe it.

"Good, we will meet again, France Charlotte. I wish you luck. Goodbye." They were to be Leht's last words.

Charlotte watched Leht's light climb the hill to the barrow under which Triskelion's grandfather rested. The shadow smothering the Beacon made no move, so Charlotte assumed Leht must somehow appear invisible. After touching the receiving stone for luck or comfort, in truth she didn't really know, Charlotte started to creep slowly towards the lower slope. She held the dagger in her left hand, Wodewose's staff in her right. She no longer had the budget or the map, she had left them with the receiving stone, they belonged together had been her thought and were no use to her now. Charlotte did not want to be far from the summit when Leht sprang her diversion, at the same time she dare not risk being spotted by the Gnombres. Her breathing remained steady throughout her approach and she was surprised to find how calm she felt. At a point where she felt it too risky to advance any further, Charlotte dropped and lay flat among the chalkland flowers the squirrel at her side. She hardly dared to breathe, once more she silently counted time and obligingly time dragged its feet.

It took just minutes for Leht to reach the ridge that ran to Ivinghoe Beacon. She looked back to the darkened southern slope beneath which she knew the little human child lay waiting for her to lay a diversion. She hoped it was only gnombres guarding the slope. She had no way of knowing whether Scucca was among them. If he was France Charlotte was finished as would be their Guardian. So much was at stake and so much could go wrong. With a deep sigh Leht turned away, it was time, there was nothing more she could do.

A flash of light exploded above the hill which in our world is known as Gallows Hill. Such was its brilliance that even shielding her eyes Charlotte was temporarily blinded. When the light had settled a white hart its face held high, its coat so bright it looked to be ablaze stood proud on the tumulus created for Triskelion's grandfather. A cry went up around the slopes of the Beacon and the shadow that smothered it moved as one at speed towards the beast that Charlotte knew to be Leht. Leht's plan appeared to be working. With a deep breath Charlotte ran towards the lower slope and on reaching it started to climb.

Leht waited till the shadow was within twenty metres then started to run, descending the scrub covered northern slope at speed. A cry rose behind her as the excitement of a kill pumped the blood of the gnombres. The chase was on. Leht prayed her energy would last, already she could feel her light fading. She must not lose the image of a hart. She could not let the gnombres see they had been fooled, that she wasn't the hart they'd been guarding the past few months.

As Charlotte climbed she felt at any minute as though her heart may burst. With grim determination she managed to keep her pace at a run. A slow run admittedly but a running pace it was. The dagger swung back and forth in one hand, Wodewose's staff in the other, her arms acting as pistons driving her onwards and upwards. Out of the corner of her eye she saw Leht disappear over the edge of the hill followed closely by an ever changing shadow. She could hear the excited cries of the gnombres and the sound chilled her to the bone. "Good luck" she whispered between clenched teeth. "Good luck Leht."

The last few strides to the summit were the worst. She wanted to shout, to spur on her effort but worried about drawing attention, pushed on in silence, gasping and blowing as she drew in the night air and expelled what she no longer needed. At last Charlotte reached the summit, where at the centre lay the Guardian, her white hart, the animal that she had been communicating with for weeks without realising it. His head was bowed and his face looked drawn and tired through weeks of unimaginable suffering. The hart must have heard Charlotte's approach but it made no acknowledgment. Instead he bowed his head lower until his antlers, his "crown" touched the earth. Charlotte immediately saw why, through the turf rose a giant ball of light. The ball or orb as Leht called it was spinning as a planet does. Its progress was painfully slow and Charlotte kept pacing the ground ready to fight off any threat. Kind gentle, playful Charlotte who was at that moment Charlotte the warrior. There came another flash of light, this time far below the northern slope. Charlotte ran to the edge of the summit and peered over to where she thought the flash had come from. She could see nothing but outlines of the terrain and nothing appeared to be moving, not a sound reached her through the night air. Where are you Leht she whispered searching for any sign of a light, where are you and as she asked the question a second time Charlotte realised her connection with Leht had been abruptly severed. Now she really was on her own. A deep anger seethed inside her and she turned away from what she knew was Leht's last resting place.

As she descended the slope Leht saw with alarm that gnombres were coming along the lower slope of the hill and she was in danger of being cut off by their action and unable to reach the coombe. With extra effort she managed to increase her pace. Even so a number of the gnombres managed to sink their teeth into what they thought was the hart's hind leg only to find themselves falling helplessly through a beam of light. For seconds confusion gripped them before the excitement of the chase took hold once more and they flew forward with the masses homing in for the kill. It took all of Leht's remaining energy to avoid being overrun by the gnombres, her light dimmed and she knew it wouldn't be long now before her light would diminish and extinguish forever. After crossing the human built road she finally reached Coombe Hole and headed for its lowest point. Waves of gnombres followed her, high pitched cries splitting the air as they sensed the end was nigh. On reaching the bottom Leht turned to face her foe, almost immediately she was overwhelmed by wave after wave of gnombres. She made no attempt to fight them off, she knew this was her last moment. For one final time her face graced Otherworld, her smile as serene as ever. Her last vision before her light was extinguished was of the little human child on the summit of what she called Ivinghoe Beacon. She had made it after all, good luck France Charlotte. Her thought had no time to leave her before her light was extinguished forever. Instead of a message to the little human child, good luck became her last thought.

Deep below the church of St John the Baptist in Gatesdene or as we know it in our world, Great Gaddesden, a rotating circle of light flickered and went out. The stones that had orbited within the light on losing their host started to float aimlessly in the darkness. For as long as Otherworld continued to exist darkness would be their home from now on. The needles of a once proud yew dropped as one and minutes later the ancient tree collapsed to dust. A home created at the beginning of time would no longer see the passing of time.

The trees of Ashridge learnt of Leht's passing with a mix of shock and deep sadness. Many bowed their boughs in respect and some even shed their leaves in sorrow. The little human child now remained their only hope.

In Coombe Hole the gnombres a little deflated that the kill had been so easy turned to leave. On mass they started to climb the steep incline only to be dragged down time and again by an invisible force. As effort after effort failed mass hysteria started to set in and in fighting broke out. Like a shark in a frenzy they set upon each other until not one survived. From that night on Coombe Hole became the darkest coombe in all Otherworld.

Charlotte turned to see the white hart looking at her. Spinning on his crown as Leht called it was a huge ball of light. The light gave off an energy which Charlotte could feel even though she was standing several metres away. Within the sphere it was hard to believe may be secrets that in the wrong hands could destroy her world, even the universe. The hart's expression was one of pleading and Charlotte realised it was desperate to leave. She quickly ran over and climbed on its back, the squirrel doing the same, resting beneath her chin. Trying to hide the dagger she swung her arms around the hart's sturdy neck, Wodewose's staff tucked under one arm. Immediately the hart got to his feet. To do so was an obvious effort and it was very apparent that the hart had few reserves left.

From the summit of Ivinghoe Beacon the hart followed the route of the Ridgeway across the Ivinghoe Hills. I say the Ridgeway though this name meant nothing to the hart, he was following the Mary Line which ran through Ivinghoe Beacon to Incombe Hole and then onto Ivinghoe or Evinghehou. It had been a struggle to decide which line to follow Michael or Mary but Mary ran closest to their intended destination and thus he felt this line would be their safest route. If he could feed into the current it would provide him with much needed energy for as he was, he had not the strength to make it to the tomb of Cunobelinus.

Charlotte held on as though her life depended on it. It felt as though they were always either climbing or descending and with every step she feared she would fall. She was amazed, how on all fours the squirrel managed to keep his balance, constantly moving his feet to compensate for every movement of muscle. Nothing though prepared her for Incombe Hole. On reaching the edge of the impressive coombe the hart halted. Charlotte could not believe what lay before them, a gaping yawn of a hole with an almost vertical slope which descended, or so it seemed into the bowls of the Earth. Surely the hart wasn't contemplating on going down there? It was impossible. The very next second her worst fears were realised, the hart started down what appeared to be an impossible incline. The animal slid and slipped and sometimes floundered but never tumbled. Even though at times Charlotte's feet touched the ground she never let go of the harts neck and never fell off. With every second with every jarring movement she thought she may die and it was something of a surprise, a miracle even when they finally reached the bottom with her heart still beating. Bruised and battered maybe but still very much alive. The hart on reaching the bottom of the coombe literally collapsed with exhaustion and Charlotte became worried that it might drop the orb or even worse die from his exertion. Exhausted he may be but the hart was not about to give up so easily, he had a duty to fill and he fully intended to complete the task he had been given. Lying on the dew sodden grass he kept his head upright with no danger of the sphere falling from its axis. With his mind he searched for a direct connection with the Mary Line. After several minutes he found it and settled down to feed off its energy. The squirrel jumped off of the harts back and curled up against the beast's side. Charlotte took the hint, it didn't look as though they'd be moving for a while. She followed the squirrel, sliding off the harts back and kneeling, nuzzled her head against the head of the proud animal. The hart in return blew gently through its nostrils. Like that Charlotte and the hart rested for several minutes comfortable in each other's company. Eventually she decided the animal needed some rest and for that matter so she did she. Laying on her back she joined the squirrel resting her head on the hart's still sweat covered flank. She looked up at the stars, perhaps counting them would help her sleep and started what she knew was an impossible task. As she counted an uncomfortable feeling that they were being watched started to stir her deeper senses. Charlotte knew by now that her deeper senses were senses to be listened to and not wishing to alarm the other two as quietly and as casually as she was able looked all about her. The coombe was so enclosed that even with a star lit sky, where they lay they were surrounded by an almost inky darkness and from within the darkness stared two pairs of eyes. As Charlotte focused hardly daring to breathe both sets of eyes started to advance, making straight for her. Charlotte's left hand gripped the dagger in readiness only to seconds later, relax. Her senses had changed direction, they were telling her the eyes posed no threat, that there was no danger. Charlotte saw why. Standing before her were the two hounds, Alasdair and Cathasach.

Chapter Twenty-One

Cymbeline And The Mary Line

Charlotte stared in disbelief, the two hounds looked as fit and well as they'd ever been.

"Where did you two get to?" Charlotte could not stop herself from smiling and immediately felt guilty after the possibility of Leht's recent passing. The two hounds, as was their way, did not greet her as a pet dog would. They simply took up positions on either side of the little group, sitting upright, eyes, ears and noses alert. They behaved as though they'd never been missing. The hart immediately accepted their presence and Charlotte feeling much safer than she had a few minutes earlier settled down to sleep. For the first time that night she became aware of just how cold the air had become and like the squirrel snuggled up against the hart to keep warm. In no time at all, all three of the original party were asleep though the Guardian, the white hart never let his head bow once. The orb continued to spin safe in the cradle of his crown.

As the three slept a shadow, like a ray hugging the sand floated slowly across the land. Unlike the Gnombres the shadow was threatening because of its stealth. Unhurried, it patiently searched for its prey, confident that in time it would find them and when it did revenge will be used as an example to others who crossed its master. Alasdair and Cathasach tensed as the shadow skirted the coombe in which they were resting. They knew they were safe within the coombe's boundaries but in the morning they would have to leave its protection and who knew what may be lying in wait.

The planet continued to turn, almost as steady as time itself and as the hour of four approached so did the first signs of daylight. Alasdair and Cathasach began to pace up and down, when the last traces of the last moon had left the sky they must be ready to leave. Any delay may not just be dangerous, it could well be cataclysmic. The white hart snorted its greeting and shook its body urging the squirrel and Charlotte to rise from their slumber. Charlotte shivered as she regained consciousness, the cool morning air rudely awaking her. Standing, she yawned whilst stretching her arms to the heavens urging her muscles to respond. Looking around her none of her companions appeared bothered by the freshness of the morning air, neither did any of them seem to be having trouble in waking their limbs, quite the opposite in fact. Somewhere over the passage of time, Charlotte considered not for the first time since her forays into Otherworld, the physical design of the human body had taken a wrong turn.

Fully awake she climbed once more onto the harts back, the squirrel as yesterday took up a position below her chin. She still held the dagger tightly and prayed with all her might she would never have need to use it. With some effort the hart got to its feet. He looked a little better than yesterday but it was obvious to everybody in the party that the once proud beast was on its last legs. The two hounds advanced slowly following the line of the ice flow that thousands of years before had carved a way out of the coombe. The hart followed, its pace painfully slow. Charlotte could see that the sphere of light it was carrying was sapping its energy. To relieve its burden she wanted to dismount and walk alongside but the recurring voice told her this would be unwise.

Charlotte had no way of knowing that the hart was steadily following the line of Mary. Sometimes the current ran deep below ground and when this happened the signal was faint and easy to lose. At times it took all of the harts concentration not to lose the current completely, to do so he was only too aware could spell disaster. Just as the sun started to warm the morning air the first houses of Evinghehou came into view. Directly ahead of them lay the proud church of St Mary and Charlotte saw that the hart was heading straight for it.

It was no accident that the original builders of the church had placed its foundations directly over the Mary current. The full force of the current could be experienced from within the church and the hart knew this. Like a camel sensing water the hart hastened its pace coming to a halt only when they reached the main door. Charlotte knew exactly what it wanted her to do. Sliding off the harts back she went to the door, praying it wouldn't be locked. It wasn't the door swung open and without hesitating the hart stepped inside. Alasdair and Cathasach remained seated outside, Charlotte assumed rightly to guard the entrance. Looking at them she couldn't help thinking they resembled the dogs that once guarded Egyptian temples. Her thought took her to Leht and her tales of Egyptians and the princess that carried secrets of Orme to safety. Had she come here to Ashridge?

Inside the church the hart walked steadily up the nave towards the Christian altar. Carvings of witches and knights, the green man and even a mermaid followed its progress as did winged angels overhead and heads of folk that once roamed Otherworld. Charlotte watched fascinated, the carved figures though unmoving appeared to be breathing to be completely aware of the hart's presence. It was a feeling that was impossible to explain, a realisation brought about by her deepest senses. The church of St Mary was not just a building, it was a living, breathing entity that was fully in tune with the Earth. At some point the hart stopped. Facing the altar it stood erect the sphere spinning brighter than ever. Its whole body started to tremble and fingers of light emerging from the floor started to climb the animal's now shaking legs. Charlotte alarmed instinctively moved forward in case she was needed but a sharp message which she knew came from the hart told her to stay away. The light from the floor started to circle the entire body of the hart, spinning faster and faster until all that could be seen was light. She sensed that every carving in the church was participating in some way but how she had no idea. Without warning the light simply disappeared, it was as though it had never existed except the coat of the hart was now a pure white and a soft glow radiated from its frame. The hart turned to look at Charlotte and she could have sworn it was smiling. There was no sign of its former exhaustion, standing before her was a proud strong beast full of majesty, just as the animal was always depicted in tales of knights of old. Turning it strode back up the nave and outside, where Alasdair and Cathasach were patiently waiting. Charlotte closed the door quietly on a building, no a living, breathing body still surging with energy. On the path the hart stooped to allow her and the squirrel to climb onto its back. No longer did the animal feel weak, indeed she could now feel its energy. With renewed vigour the little party led by the hart continued on their way.

To Charlotte who although it had been explained to her, remained unaware exactly what the Mary line meant and as a result the route the hart took, to her was nonsensical. At times they passed straight through the centre of modern houses, through rooms with frozen televisions and half eaten meals, all captured on the passing of midnight. Although she knew they were simply images she couldn't help feeling that they were intruding. To the east Charlotte was sure lay the familiar outline of Pitstone Hill, except carved into the slope of this hill was the chalk figure of a running horse. What did it mean? An answer would have to wait, for now all of her concentration was needed to stay on the harts back. Not to fall off. It wasn't long before she recognised the approaching village of Marsworth. As at Ivinghoe or Evinghehou the hart headed straight for the church and as at Evinghehou Charlotte opened the door to allow the hart in. Once more the hart stood in the nave facing the Christian alter and as at Ivinghoe streams of light shot up and around its body. On exiting the hart looked even stronger and the glow emitting from its frame even brighter. And so they continued, Alasdair and Cathasach running on either flank with the hart heading the way. Not one road did they follow, the Mary line which flowed as would a stream dictated by a current. Fields, gardens and houses were entered and exited as though they didn't exist. Their only stops were churches where their early builders had recognised where the force of the current, the Mary line broke ground. In every case the current ran the length of the nave. After Marsworth, they stopped at All saints in the small hamlet of Buckland, not long after, after traversing the eerily silent A41 St Michael and All Saints at Aston Clinton. Next after passing through the silent rooms of many more houses, St Mary the Virgin at nearby Weston Turville. Each time the hart appeared to regenerate and by the time they reached what Charlotte considered must be the final church en route, St Peter and Paul at Ellesborough his coat was so bright it almost hurt her eyes to look at.

To her surprise the hart did not stop at the church Ellesborough, even though it appeared to stand directly on their route. Instead he skirted the building to commence a climb along the side of the uniquely shaped Beacon Hill or as Charlotte now knew it to be called in Otherworld, Cymbeline's Mount, home to another sacred library.

> *In Otherworld, those who lived in the area were wary of the church at Ellesborough. The dedication should, so the book of the Snooks read, have been given to St Michael but something had happened in the far and distant past and the saints of St Peter and St Paul had been presented with the honour. The church perhaps as a result is bypassed by both the Mary and Michael line.*

The party according to Leht were now on hallowed ground and Charlotte could sense the change. She also saw what it meant to the others. The normally regimental Alasdair and Cathasach were quite different. It was though they had been set free from an invisible leash. Instead of marching they pranced, almost playfully at times leaping into the air as though a great weight had been lifted from their shoulders. The splendid white hart despite the incline quickened his pace snorting loudly, so different to the dejected animal that had lain on the summit of Ivinghoe Beacon only hours earlier.

As they climbed the tapestry of the Vale stretched far into the distance below them. On the other side of the hill, Charlotte knew lay Chequers, the country residence of the incumbent prime minister. The near landscape bears marks, scars and is much shaped by ancient man. Clues to the importance and reverence in which the landscape was once held are scattered everywhere. Local superstitions and legends derived from long forgotten historical events still circulate though, with each generation, sadly another is lost to time. Blood once poured down the surrounding slopes into the tightly folded Warrens below and souls of the men that died here still touch those who are sensitive enough to receive them. It was and is a magical landscape and you have to have a cold heart not to be moved by it. From the Beacon or Cymbeline's Mount the hart led them above the two Warrens , Ellesborough and Great Kimble, two razor edged valleys with almost jungle-like vegetation. Finally the hart joined and followed a path, an ancient route with an ancient name, The Cradle. A path that hugs the head of Great Kimble Warren. Not long after the hart stopped and after shaking its head knelt allowing Charlotte to descend from its back. The squirrel followed. Effortlessly the hart got back to his feet and what happened next, for Charlotte anyway, was entirely unexpected. Stooping the hart tenderly nuzzled her face, a message of thanks passing between them. Fully restored the proud animal, unrecognisable from a few hours ago turned to mount The Tomb, or Chequer's Knapp as it is known in our world. Standing on its flat summit the hart bowed his head and all stood in wonderment as the spinning orb of light descended slowly into the ground. The hart, after the last of the spinning orb had disappeared beneath the earth, did not move. Instead he remained for several minutes more with his head bowed, the tip of his crown at all times resting on the ground. When he did eventually lift his head he raised it to the sky and let out a loud roar that rebounded around the tree capped hills. With a bow to his colleagues of the last few hours, the proud beast then pulled himself up and standing statuesque moved not another muscle. Charlotte knew her friend had found east and facing the beginning of everything was once more taking on his role as Guardian, a sentinel for the sacred library of Cymbeline. Her magnificent white hart, her best friend was once more fulfilling its 'raison d'etre' and she was proud, so proud.

Chapter Twenty-Two

The Return

Silence fell upon the little party. An important chapter had just been completed in the history of Otherworld and they were all aware of its significance. Alasdair, Cathasach and the squirrel all now stood looking at France Charlotte, they were seeking direction. She was now the decision maker Charlotte realised, an eleven year old child. She had not asked for and did not want the burden. Even so she immediately began to consider her, their next move. Leht had told her that she would be safe within the environs of Cymbeline but she couldn't stay here forever and a longing to be reunited with her parents was burning deep inside her. Though she was here, she did not belong in Otherworld, she missed her world, even if it was responsible for so much ruin. She had to find a way home. With the gateway before the church of St John the Baptist denied to her she had to find another. Everyone had warned her of the dangers, of trying any other way except that is, Triskelion. Triskelion she recalled had offered her one last hope. The burial place of his grandfather, the tumulus on the disrespectfully named Gallows Hill. His grandfather he had told her, would do his best to help her. She looked up at the sky, the sun was nowhere near its highest. It was, Charlotte judged only mid-morning, there was still time. Without the legs of the hart it would be a long and tiring trek but with effort she could make Triskelion's grandfather's tomb before nightfall when she would be at the mercy of the Darkness. As she saw it she had little other choice. For what she knew would almost certainly be the last time she turned to say goodbye to her friend, kissing him on the neck. The white hart standing proud, head held high did not respond. Though disappointed Charlotte understood, his new role prevented any interaction. With a determined about turn she started back along The Cradle path retracing their steps to Ellesborough. She had considered following the route of The Ridgeway path but had decided it was simply too long. The route the white hart had taken although it had served a purpose was also meandering and she felt of little use to her. Even with her newly discovered senses there was no way she'd be able to follow the thread of the Mary or Michael lines. No, although she had been warned to avoid routes laid by her fellow beings, Charlotte felt she had little choice. She would have to follow a route formed by her ancestors thousands of years before her, The Icknield Way. A route still hailed as the oldest road in England. It meant they would be following a metalled road, it was by far the quickest route and speed now outweighed every other factor. She hoped the spirits that had travelled the road over the past centuries and still oversaw the route may help her find safe passage.

The hard surface of the road soon told on Charlotte's feet and after only a few miles she was beginning to question her decision. Her colleagues too looked uncomfortable with her chosen route and when it was able the squirrel swung from branch to branch overhead rather than tread the human road. Passing through the centre of the market town of Wendover was extremely hard going. The quaint normally vibrant small town with a beating heart lay eerily silent. The High Street with its cosy marketplace, empty, soulless, devoid of any feeling. Its character created from centuries of toil resulting in both success and failure wiped clean. Not even a ghost would dare to tread the road they were now following. Looking out for the slightest hint of danger, it felt to Charlotte that the human race had been completely wiped out. What they now bore witness to, she realised was a reflection of what was in store for every town if the Darkness succeeded. A mirror image of what the future may hold if it wasn't defeated. The realisation chilled Charlotte's heart and forged a renewed determination to try and thwart the evil that was rising. How, she still had no idea, the only solid plan she'd formed was to return to her world.

Shortly after Wendover the little party passed the military base of Halton. A base that, when, if the time came would be completely ineffective against the methods of the Darkness. Indeed it may even become an instrument for evil. A military defence would quite unintentionally become a powerful weapon for the Darkness, even if it was used in the belief of doing good. Was there really any hope?

It was mid-afternoon she estimated by the time they were approaching the wooded Aldbury Nowers and Pitstone Hill. The squirrel, exhausted, was now sitting on her shoulder and the hounds normally espousing boundless energy had their tongues hanging loose and their heads bowed. So far their way had been without incident but following the road any further Charlotte felt was only inviting trouble. Although it was a climb, the soft ground of the Nowers after miles of unforgiving tarmac made the extra effort almost pleasurable. Charlotte was now relying on her senses for guidance rather than reason, decisions were no longer being decided using any form of thought process but purely on instinct. Her senses were telling her to avoid taking the shortest or easiest route, instead they trod a virtual path that took them over the Nowers descending into the valley below Assherugge where they crossed the Aldeborie to Evinghehou road. Thereafter still following her instincts Charlotte led her little party along the base of the wooded Chiltern escarpment, traveling in a roundabout fashion towards Ivinghoe Beacon. It was strange that they hadn't met any resistance, Charlotte knew that beneath the light of day she was protected but even so, she had expected something to stand in their way. So far it had simply been too easy and the thought began to worry her, was she leading her colleagues into a trap? If she were it was too late to do anything about it now, she had run out of options.

Around an hour later Charlotte found herself gazing upon Ivinghoe Beacon and the ridge that led down to the tumulus which she hoped would be her gateway home. As far as she could see there was no threat, no danger, the landscape was a canvas of tranquillity. It was difficult to believe what had taken place here under the cover of darkness only hours earlier. Rather than descend into The Coombe to where the firs would be waiting and noisily announce her presence, she decided to take a more direct route descending the chalk grassland slope and heading directly for the hill with the tumulus where Triskelion's grandfather lay in rest. If it hadn't been already his rest was about to be rudely disturbed. The final approach would be a steep but relatively short climb. Her senses seemed to be making no objections to her plan and so in her mind all was set.

The hill, she could not forget, was not long ago the place where Leht had started her diversion. Charlotte shivered at the memory and what may have taken place soon after. Anger started to rage inside her, a rage that her senses were quick to tell her to quell. Anger if it raised its ugly head would be a valuable tool for the Darkness. She did her best but controlling such a basic emotion wasn't easy. Charlotte began to understand how powerful the weapons used by the Darkness were. Tapping into and using such powerful emotions to destroy thereby causing more and more anger and stirring the desire for revenge. The act of revenge resulting in further destruction, further misery, further anger and so the cycle would continue. If the Darkness could continue stirring the anger there could only be one outcome. With the arsenal of weaponry at the disposal of her species she understood how by using such powerful emotions the Darkness could influence man to instigate his own destruction and the destruction of the planet on which lived millions of other innocent species. A planet that was not theirs to destroy. Standing, staring across to Gallows Hill she finally understood what Triskelion had been trying to tell her.

From their outlook over Ivinghoe Beacon Charlotte decided, success or failure they could wait no longer. Bold as brass she descended the chalk grass slope heading for what she intended to be her final destination in Otherworld. The hounds and the little messenger without a care for themselves dutifully followed behind. Charlotte's chosen route took them past the place where she had left Leht's receiving stone, the budget and with them Triskelion's map. None were now to be found. Something or someone had taken them. As Charlotte questioned the significance of this she sensed Alasdair and Cathasach tense, both confirmed their new state of alert with a low growl. Charlotte looked over to where the two stood, both had their heads raised to a sky, a sky that was darkening fast with clouds rolling in from the west. This was no ordinary phenomenon, Charlotte realised that at once, this was the work of the Darkness it was the cover it needed for its agents to run freely. Leht had warned her the Darkness would blacken the skies but not today, Leht had predicted after the passing of the next moon, tomorrow. She had been wrong, the Darkness was evidently stronger than Leht had been aware. What Leht had predicted would happen tomorrow was happening today, here and now, at that very moment .

Instinctively Charlotte started to run, she had to reach the tumulus before the Darkness provided enough cover to release its agents. Alasdair and Cathasach ran beside her, both beginning to bark. The poor little messenger, petrified ran between her feet, in danger of tripping her with every panicked step. As the sky blackened a wind started to howl and lightning bolt after lightning bolt ripped open the heavens. Arrow after arrow threatened to strike the earth and if one succeeded it would surely send all of them into oblivion. Still they climbed, refusing to bow to a seemingly formidable foe just as David had done when faced with Goliath. The wind tore along the side of the hill daring the four to go any further and all accepted the dare. Metre by metre despite the Darkness's best efforts they were closing on the tumulus. The sky was now so dark it was beginning to feel like night and what Charlotte had been dreading since they'd started their climb appeared in the near distance. Shadows were racing towards them and one shadow stood out from the rest, she recognised it immediately, Scucca. Adrenaline more than she had ever known pumped through Charlotte's veins, she could not be defeated now, not when she was so close. But the wind was too strong, it was slowing their progress, to such an extent that the gnombres would reach them before they could reach the tumulus. Just as she was beginning to despair Charlotte felt a new feeling rising inside of her. At first she couldn't understand what it was, perhaps it was her mind preparing her for her afterlife, perhaps it was the Darkness taking control. No it didn't feel like either of those, she was sure she recognised the feeling, she had experienced it before. Her sense's took over, they immediately recognised it as the near reckless courage given to her by Leht's ancient yew. The emotion that she had earlier suppressed, now her senses commanded her to let run riot, she had nothing to lose.

The first result was a loud cry from Charlotte's pursed lips, a cry so loud, so fierce sounding that every shadow paused momentarily in their pursuit. It was the break they needed, with a new leader to follow the squirrel and the hounds pushed forward cutting through the wind as though it were merely a breeze. With a cry that resonated victory Charlotte scrambled to the centre of the mound, the tumulus beneath which Triskelion's grandfather slept. She hoped it was a slumber he could be woken from. The squirrel quickly joined her though the hounds refused to mount. Instead they turned to face the advancing gnombres. Charlotte didn't try to persuade them, she knew it would be futile to try. Standing erect she willed their safe passage to her world, she waited to be pulled underground but nothing happened, they remained rooted in Otherworld. Alasdair and Cathasach couldn't hide their concern, the shadows were almost upon them and both turned to do battle, their teeth bared.

"Come onnnn," Charlotte screamed, "come onnnn." Dark clouds massed above them and lightning struck the ground close by throwing sparks into the air, the wind was now so strong it threatened to tear them from their footing. Charlotte only managed to hold on because of the strength given to her by Leht's ancient yew and Wodewose's staff. The squirrel lay flat cowering in a shallow depression on top of the mound the wind trying but not quite able to prise him free. Charlotte searched deep within herself, she must be doing something wrong and in a moment it came to her, she had to call the name of Triskelion's grandfather. He could only help on her calling. Raising both the dagger and Wodewose's staff to the sky she called out his name.

"Drustans." Pleading for his help, her cries as they left her carried away on the wind. The two hounds she saw were now doing battle with the gnombres, the noise quite sickening. With both arms reaching high above her Charlotte once more, shouted the name Triskelion had given her.

"Drustans, Drustans," Charlotte pleaded for Triskelion's grandfather to hear her cries, to wake from his slumber. As she cried for help she continued to raise the dagger and Wodewose's staff high above her head. Lightening raged all around her, the wind roared, dark clouds boiled above her. Win or lose this was the image she wanted in the books carried by the Snooks. A picture of a little girl fighting for Otherworld, this was the story she wanted told. Not the frightened image of a girl running from an enemy, along a church path. Again and again she shouted the name of Triskelion's grandfather thrusting both the dagger and Wodewose's staff to the sky. In response the storm grew stronger, its rage verging on the apocalyptic. It was not the reaction Charlotte sought, her feet remained firmly on Otherworld soil. In sheer frustration Charlotte pounded the ground with Wodewose's staff and almost immediately she felt herself descending into the earth, through a gateway that had been closed for over two thousand years.

As she started to descend Charlotte saw for the first time the full horror of the battle around her. Alasdair and Cathasach were both on their backs making a desperate last stand. She then saw the squirrel, why wasn't it descending with her, it looked terrified and it was the last look she saw before the gnombres with a blood curdling cry fell upon the little messenger. As her head started to draw level with the ground she felt a burning sensation against her chest. Her necklace as though it had a life of its own started to rise above her head, the heart pendant sprang open and the little silver frog she had been carrying for so long flew into the air. In response the gnombres drew back and she wished they hadn't for her last view of Otherworld were of the lifeless bodies of Alasdair and Cathasach, faithful to the end along with the squirrel, the messenger. Behind them glowered Scucca. Although she couldn't see his face she could sense his satisfaction.

Rage seethed through Charlotte, uncontrollable rage. She could not believe she had lost so much, so many friends in so short a time. She was too angry to feel sad and no longer cared what happened to her. If she reached her world she knew now exactly what she was going to do. Her thought brought her to her current predicament, she wasn't rising as she was supposed to, instead she was floating helplessly in blackness. Orbiting her were a series of objects, a sword, a shield and many smaller items, all looking as though they were made from gold. There was something else, something above her. She struggled to look up and instantly recoiled. A skeleton blocked what would have been her exit. At first she thought it was deliberately blocking her way and fear she may be suspended there forever threw her into a near panic. Something brushed against her hand and the sensation brought her to her senses, it was the hand of the skeleton. Far from blocking her she saw it was trying to help. After all the skeleton had a name, Drustans, grandfather to

Triskelion. The skeleton was family. Doing her best not to feel nauseous Charlotte reached for the skeleton's hand. As she touched it she felt bony fingers close around her wrist in a tight grip and the next thing she knew she was starting to rise. With a push the skeletal fingers released their grip and she was traveling freely upwards and upwards. On her way Charlotte passed the skeleton's grinning face and as she did so she found the fortitude to mouth her thanks. The next moment her head broke the Earth's surface and seconds later she found herself laying on the grass surface of the tumulus. The difference was she was in her world. A world that only moments ago she'd thought she'd never see again.

It was several minutes before Charlotte felt strong enough to stand. When she did she realised she wasn't alone. There were people on the summit, many with dogs. She looked down at her torn and soiled clothes. Unlike passing through the gateway in front of the church, St John the Baptist they hadn't renewed. I must look a sight she thought, tough. In her right hand she still held Wodewose's staff but in her left there was nothing, the dagger had gone. Like her little frog it obviously belonged in Otherworld. With her left hand Charlotte gently closed the heart which had held the little silver charm. She wondered where it was now and quickly pushed the thought from her mind. The question reminded her of seeing the savage and cruel end of her friends. Anger once more stirred within her and Charlotte started to walk.

People recoiled as the wild child passed them. Several asked if she was alright but Charlotte gave them no answer, she had only one thing in mind. One or two thought they ought to call the police but decided not to, not wanting to get involved. Charlotte followed the route of the Ridgeway Path. As she walked along the summit of Pitstone Hill the route taken by the hart and her fallen friends was easy to trace below but Charlotte didn't notice, she didn't care. Through the wooded Aldbury Nowers she passed a pair of tumuli where in Otherworld, in a rabbit hole between the two probably still lay one of Leht's receiving stones.

A lot of use it would be now. Soon after passing the second tumulus she bore left. Not long after she broke free of the tree cover and there before her in the valley below lay Aldbury. The village because of the low cloud and mist was barely visible, only the square tower of St John the Baptist really stood out, a beacon calling for her to come home. How many days till the great cycle rises beneath Ivinghoe Beacon she wondered, was she too late? She hadn't a clue she didn't even know which day it was. As she gazed upon her village, out of the blue a bolt of lightning struck a lone tree in a field the other side of the valley. The tree was an oak, a tree she knew well. Further bolts of lightning repeatedly struck its trunk and in no time the tree was ablaze. Still the lightening reigned down, time after time striking the home of the messenger. It was only a matter of minutes before the tree was no more, not a trace was left. As though satisfied the lightening ceased. Charlotte felt even more rage build inside her. Not only had the Darkness killed her little messenger it had destroyed his home, the one thing that preserved his memory.

"Right," Charlotte yelled out loud, "here I come" and started down the valley side towards the darkness that concealed Aldbury.

As the vicar climbed, the foul smelling vapour started to thicken, clouds of the stuff bellowing up the stairwell. He choked as trails of the black stuff, the "Devil's breath" entered his lungs. Dropping to all fours he scrambled as best he could, determined not to succumb to the cloud of evil that he was sure was trying to finish him. After an immense effort he reached the floor of the passageway and literally threw himself out of the cupboard. He hoped that on leaving the cupboard he would find some relief but the black stuff was everywhere. With his hand over his mouth and trying not to breathe too heavily through his nose he stumbled into the body of the church. The stench was terrible, the malodorous cloud covered almost everything. With a cry of desperation the vicar staggered to the door, it was locked, he remembered he had locked it, where had he put the key? He hadn't time to look, he just had to escape the evil foul smelling, suffocating vapour. Without doubt he now knew the black stuff had nothing but mal intent. For the first time he feared for his life. Holding his breath the vicar ran to the stairs that mounted the tower and started to climb, taking two steps at a time. On reaching open air he gulped greedily. His relief was short-lived. Hovering over the village the cloud that had been building over the past months had gotten steadily lower as it had grown thicker and would soon envelope the tower on top of which he sought relief. Relief from what, he still wasn't sure. As he looked up at the menace in the skies, trails from the cloud started to descend towards where he was standing, targeting him, he was sure. There was no mistaking it, black crooked finger trails of the cloud were descending on him, him alone. In the adjacent field the mist was now so thick it looked almost solid and to make things worse a familiar stench was starting to rise from its depths. A thought started to play out in the vicar's mind. Normally it would be a thought that would horrify him but something was taking over his mind. Something alien had somehow found a door to his thought process. The vicar looked down to the ground far below. The ground looked so very inviting, it would be so easy to end his misery, his torment, right now. All he had to do was fall from the tower and his suffering would be over. Surely his maker would understand, he had done his best, he simply wasn't strong enough. A calm washed over him and without any feeling of fear he stepped to the edge of the tower. He looked down, the ground wasn't even that far below. It would be over before he knew it. Something made him hesitate to look up, descending the hillside was a figure he was certain he recognised. A little girl and she was heading straight for the mist. Squinting the vicar looked harder, she looked familiar. It was French Charlotte. What had happened to her, her clothes he saw as she got closer were ripped to shreds, her face covered in scratches and everywhere she was caked in mud. And in her hand, she was holding something very odd. It looked like some sort of pole, a staff perhaps except it had leaves and berries.

"French Charlotte, NOOOO. French Charlotte turn around, don't do it, don't go in there, don't enter the mist." French Charlotte either hadn't heard him or she may be in some sort of trance for she wore the same look as Ashtynn when he had seen her enter the mist. He could not let French Charlotte make the same mistake. The vicar suddenly felt deeply ashamed at what he had almost done. How easily he had succumbed to the evil claiming his church. The evil may claim his church but he wouldn't allow it to claim him. It would have to fight a lot harder if it wanted to achieve that. The Devil if that who it was had almost taken him, well he would show him, he was a servant of God, he would not make it that easy. In his haste the vicar almost fell down the narrow stairs, blood ran freely from a graze on his forehead and the knuckles on his right hand were almost raw to the bone as he'd desperately scrabbled to avoid more serious injury. The church keys he realised had been in his pocket all the time. On reaching the door he thrust the key into the lock and after a single turn launched himself onto the gravel path outside. Pushing himself to his feet he ran down the path repeatedly crying, NO, NO, NOOO. He reached the field just as French Charlotte reached the edge of the mist.

"NOOOOOOOOO French Charlotte noooooo." His cry echoed with desperation. He saw French Charlotte turn and look at him, her face wore a very strange expression and the next minute she was gone. "Noooo," the vicar dropped to the ground sobbing the word over and over again. "No, noo, nooooooo."

As Charlotte stepped into the mist several unexplained phenomena took place in and around the village. Phenomena that were quite spectacular yet not one inhabitant of Aldbury can remember witnessing anything out of the ordinary. Lightning storms continued to rage around the village. On the ridge overlooking Aldbury bolt after bolt of lightning hit an oak growing in a wooded hollow known as Gryme's Dell. On the opposite side of the valley a house built during the reign of Victoria became the victim of another lightning storm, strike after strike demolished the gothic structure in a matter of minutes. When both storms had finished there remained no clue that the oak or the vicarage had ever existed.

In the churchyard an oily feather that once belonged to a magpie started to burn. Slowly at first before combusting with fury. Within seconds it was nothing but dust. The stone on which it had lain started to descend beneath the earth. Seconds later grass grew where it had sat, no one would ever know it had been there. Inside the church another fire started, an ancient cupboard door burned, slowly at first before flames ignited skyward. Within seconds there was no door and where it had stood a wall had taken its place. Though new if the stonework was ever tested it would match the age of much of the church.

Wodewose's staff as Charlotte entered the mist flew from her hand. Spinning furiously it flew high across the sky, over Aldbury coming to land on the wooded scarp. Within seconds far from disappearing the staff sent down roots and a new tree was born. A tree if given the chance would help protect Aldbury and her environs. Those with knowledge of such things will be aware the red berried rowan is an ancient defence against evil. To help it in its task, it just needs to be believed in.

Charlotte's silver necklace still hung loose around her neck the tiny heart locket remaining wide open. As she stepped into the mist the little heart started to burn hot and the necklace rose above her head. Within seconds it had left Charlotte completely falling to the ground behind her. I assume it must still lay there somewhere for to my knowledge it has never been found.

Charlotte had no idea what to expect, pain, shock, nausea, breathlessness. It was none of the above. As she stepped into the almost solid mist her feet were taken from under her and she found herself floating.

Not floating freely but being sucked towards a black hole, rather like water in a sink. Surprisingly, she didn't feel scared, her strongest feeling apart from anger was one of frustration. There was so much she still didn't understand, questions she wanted answers to. Otherworld held so many secrets, secrets she wanted to uncover. The world she thought she knew was not that world at all. Above all Leht had asked for her assistance, it must be your mission was how she had described it. A mission to try and discover what those in her world knew of Orme. From her experiences in Otherworld Orme was the greatest secret of all. Now it would require a miracle if she was to be able to deliver.

Black, all-encompassing blackness that's all Charlotte could see. She sensed somewhere there were walls to a house, a very ancient building and people staring at her through the windows but she couldn't see them, all she could see was blackness only blackness, just blackness. She was sure she could hear people whispering but no she was wrong, there was blackness only blackness, silent, suffocating blackness. She felt herself being dragged deeper into more blackness, deeper blackness, denser blackness, blackness all around her. Soon she sensed it would be too late, forever and ever she would be encased in blackness. Blackness would be her only friend, blackness was what she would see every day, blackness only blackness. She wasn't afraid but she was angry, so very angry. She hated the Darkness and wanted revenge. When she'd entered the mist she'd felt sure she'd be able to put up a fight but she found she was helpless, the Darkness was in complete control. More anger rose within her, she did not want to go like this, she wanted to face the Darkness, tell it what she thought, to try and shame it, she wanted revenge, above everything else she wanted revenge. Deeper and deeper she sank, there were no more whispers, only blackness, silence, suffocating silence and blackness, more and more blackness. She wanted to close her eyes to shut out the blackness. Try as she might, she found it was impossible, the Darkness wanted her to see its strength, its strength was in nothingness, with nothing at all the human soul was lost, it needed something to attach itself to. With nothing the human soul simply surrendered to its will and how it wanted the soul of the little girl he now had trapped in nothing but blackness. She was still fighting, that was good, he wanted, needed her to hate, to be angry it was her anger that would give it victory, anger would make her surrender her soul. It would not be long now before she succumbed to her fate and for all the trouble she had caused it would ensure her frustration, her anger tortured her for eternity. Even when it had succeeded in stopping time it would ensure that she would live on, the only being left, existing in nothing, nothing but blackness. Her loneliness would torture her for eternity. Yes it would have one more feeling to add to her frustration and anger, utter loneliness that would eat away at her forever and ever, crying pathetic tears for the need to see her parents. She would be made to count time except time won't just have slowed it will have stopped, she will be counting the same second, over and over and over again. Her fate will be far, far worse than death, her mind, her emotions will live on, eternal in their struggle. Every recurring second she will wish she could close her eyes, to let her emotions find a final resting place but it will never let that happen. The human child had given it far too much trouble.

Blackness, blackness, blackness, that was all Charlotte could see, could feel, she wanted something to fight, she couldn't fight blackness. Deeper and deeper she felt herself sinking, deeper and deeper, she still wasn't afraid that feeling had left her a long time ago she was just angry so very angry. Life, and death too if this was death was so unfair, so very unfair. There came a voice, it sounded like Leht, it could only be a trick, it must be a trick for there was only blackness, Leht was not here. She wouldn't listen, she wouldn't let the Darkness trick her, she would shut the voice of Leht out. A liquid entered her mouth, it wasn't adrenalin, she knew adrenalin, this liquid was bitter, very, very, bitter.

What tricks were the Darkness playing now. She looked around, there was only blackness and she was sinking, still sinking. She was sure she could hear Leht but Leht had passed, the thought made her angrier and she started sinking deeper, faster. Sinking into more blackness, more and more blackness. The bitter liquid continued to stain her mouth, she could still hear Leht, this time she could hear her words, "anger will only give the Darkness strength." The words brought back memories, she struggled to remember but the blackness was beginning to numb all and every thought. As she weakened her anger started to leave her, instead of revenge she started to feel sorry for the Darkness, something that got enjoyment from other people's misery could not be happy. From feeling sorry she moved to wanting to help it, to help bring happiness to the Darkness, she was sure if given the opportunity she could do it. To be a good friend to the Darkness. She so wanted to be its friend. She no longer felt angry.

Chapter Twenty-Three

A New Dawn

Light shone through the long sash window, the rays of the morning sun falling across Charlotte's face and she turned to avoid their brightness. Beside her she felt the familiar softness that was Gromit and she sighed with contentment. The smell of freshly baked croissants wafted up the stairs and soon she would hear her mother's voice calling her down for breakfast. Sure enough, just seconds later her mother did just that. Stretching she eased herself out of bed and walked over to the long sash window. The garden looked a picture, it had reached its peak and Charlotte considered she may simply spend the day reading, surrounded by flowers. Before she left her room she spotted something alien lying on the floor. It was a picture that had been hanging on the wall since the day they'd arrived. It must have fallen off during the night. The picture wasn't much, just a grass mound, why would anyone want to paint a simple grass mound. Where the picture had hung a number of colours revealed themselves. To Charlotte, they all looked disgusting, she would ask her father to paint over them. As she descended the stairs she could hear music, it must be the weekend, her father only played music in the morning on weekends. She recognised the album, her father often played it, it was called cuilidh by Julie Fowlis. In the kitchen her parents were already sat at the table. A plate heaped with butter croissants, steam rising unchallenged lay at the centre. An array of jars which Charlotte knew contained various confitures were laid to one side and beside them a butter dish with local farm butter. Life could hardly get better. After helping her mother wash up, her father asked if she minded going to the village shop for the Sunday paper. Charlotte didn't mind at all, her father always gave her more money than was needed and she could buy some sherbet dips. As she stepped out of the door onto the brick path she saw a robin perched on the fence. It was always there, sitting on the fence and should be used to her by now but try as she might to be friendly, the little bird remained too timid to accept titbits from her hand. She had tried almost on a daily basis and had never come close to enticing the little bird to her hand. She passed several people on the way to the shop, all greeted her with a smile and a "morning French Charlotte", or with the occasional "bonjour." As she rounded the corner to the shop she found the vicar leaving, on his way to conduct the Sunday service. In his right hand he held a carrier bag containing several bottles of wine. He beamed a wide smile.

"Morning French Charlotte."

"Morning vicar." Charlotte looked at the bag he was carrying. She saw the wine.

"Shame I can't turn water into wine, I'd be a lot richer." Charlotte laughed, he'd told the same joke many times before but she still found it funny and underneath she believed he meant it. "Tell your mother I'll be round tomorrow for the cakes I've ordered, I hope she hasn't forgotten."

"She won't have," Charlotte promised.

"Great, I'll catch you later, French Charlotte," with that the vicar gave her a wave and crossed the road heading for the church. Charlotte watched him enter the church yard then turned to enter the shop.

Chapter Twenty-Four

The Last Words

The bell rattled loudly, you could hardly call it a chime, announcing her entrance. The shop was busy with people buying Sunday papers. A smiling Ashtynn stood behind the service counter. Her smile broadened on seeing Charlotte.

"Good morning France Charlotte."

A stone, somewhere in Truro

Chapter Twenty-Five

From Your Friend

A closing letter

Dear friends

I hope you do not mind me calling you a friend. I feel if you have taken the trouble to read my story you are already involved and therefore very much a friend.

You will understand, I am sure that what is contained within the pages of this book is not the full story. Rather like French Charlotte or France Charlotte if you are reading this in Otherworld, you will no doubt have many questions, questions that need answering I know. You will, I hope understand that a battle has been won but the war has not gone away, it is still raging. Many more, even greater battles lie ahead and every one will involve you personally. I have additional information to pass on but now is not the time. When I feel it is safe to do so I will reveal more, for now I ask that you play your part. If you don't our planet may no longer exist for our children's children even our children.

If you understand the message contained within these pages, please do your very best to help the little girl. If you are of advancing years like me we owe it to future generations to try and make a difference, no matter how small. If you are young, you can make a big difference. It is your actions that will finally determine the outcome of my story.

There are those of you who will doubt my story, the modern legend laid bare in the pages before . If you are one of those people, please I beg you visit Ivinghoe Beacon. Not on a bright sunny day when you will be joined by many others but on a day beset with a storm, when rain and wind are doing battle. When you may well have the Beacon to yourself. Stand on the summit, gaze out at the view and let the weather do its worst. Let your mind fly free and feel the force beneath your feet. Do this and I am sure my friend you will become a believer.

Remember in another world a proud animal once stood where one day I hope you will stand. A white hart, a magical being prepared to enter its afterlife for our future. A white hart, the proud symbol of Otherworld. An animal it is written and spoken by the Snooks, when no longer walking this Earth, Otherworld will cease to be. Let us all do our best to ensure this never happens.

Finally I suggest in future you take a special interest in the wildlife that enters your garden. Our ancestors, even our close ancestors understood the ways of the Earth. It is time for all of us to make that connection again. To understand why things happen in the natural world. If you spy a robin it may not be there simply to gather food. If you spy a magpie..........................

Until the next time.

A friend

The war rages on

The next instalment

SYMBOLS OF ORME

Some Three Years Later...

Chapter One

Not An Average Morning

It was Saturday. Charlotte rose, crossed to the long sash window and gazed out at the tapestry of gold that draped the wooded scarp. Autumn was advancing at a pace and the leaves that remained on the trees were changing colour almost by the day. The morning sun shone uninterrupted. There was not a cloud in the sky and without the haze that came with summer the light was vibrant. Every tone, every colour caught in the sun's spotlight picked out to create a breath-taking panoramic spectacular that only nature is capable of staging.

Charlotte drew up the lower window and leaned out eager to take in the crisp autumn air. Below in the garden a robin came hopping down the garden fence. The robin was as much part of the landscape as the lawn or the cherry blossom. It always miraculously hopped down the fence just as she looked out of her window first thing every morning. Something she never failed to do.

Her parents were waiting for her in the kitchen, fresh baguette, farm butter and confiture waited with them. There was also a plate of cheese along with thick slices of black ham. Charlotte knew the ham would be her father's contribution to breakfast. On the table in front of the nearest chair sat a bowl of steaming hot chocolate, definitely her mother's doing.

After a breakfast which lasted almost an hour Charlotte dutifully dressed for a trip to the village shop. Saturday papers for her father and a good list of provisions for her mother. She loved weekends, villagers walked the road to and from the little shop with an ease and a joy in their step that only a weekend allows. Nearly all would throw a smile and many would stop and chat to her. Those that didn't usually waved a cheery, "good morning French Charlotte" or a loud "bonjour."

In the shop Ashtynn was busy serving several customers, many at the same time something she'd learnt to do through years of practice. Ashtynn knew nearly every customer by name and always made time to ask after their wellbeing. You'd think this sort of personal service on a busy day would create a queue but somehow Ashtynn always managed to clear each customer with the utmost efficiency. After gathering everything on her mother's list Charlotte quickly found herself at the counter being served.

"Morning France Charlotte," Ashtynn grinned as Charlotte placed her shopping on the counter. Ashtynn was the only person in the village who called her that. Everybody else called her French Charlotte. She had no idea why Ashtynn was different and frankly she didn't care. There was the usual small talk or better put, banter between them and Charlotte was quickly on her way. As she went to close the door Charlotte turned to give Ashtynn a final wave. Looking back Ashtynn she saw was studying her intently, ignoring her other customers. This was a surprise in itself but there was something else, something that could also be described as surprising but really requires an adjective a lot stronger. Shocked is a more apt expression for Charlotte was shocked when she saw the look on Ashtynn's face. Gone was her cheery smile and in its place a leer, a leer that wasn't only unpleasant but etched with malevolence. But what really sent a chill through Charlotte's veins was the expression in Ashtynn's eyes. Her eyes were burning, burning with a hatred that until that moment she wouldn't have deemed possible. Quickly Charlotte shut the door.

Outside she allowed herself a few moments to gather together some sort of sensible reasoning or explanation. Had she read Ashtynn's expression wrongly or and much more likely had it simply been a moment of hormonal adolescent imagination. She wanted to put it down to the latter but found herself struggling to quash the image captured by and stored in her mind. Several people passed her entering the shop, two grinned a cheerful, "morning French Charlotte." As the fifth person entered Charlotte took the opportunity to glance back through the open door. She saw Ashtynn packing a bag, laughing and joking as she did so. It had to have been her imagination. Feeling a little reassured she turned to walk home when she spied a little group huddled around something beside the pond.

Ever the curious Charlotte crossed the road to see what the attraction was. When she got there she found an artist sitting at an easel. Almost certainly he was taking advantage of the unique autumn light. His subject matter appeared to be the village pond. At sporadic intervals, the odd word of appreciation could be heard coming from the small group of admirers. Charlotte squeezed her head between the coats of some of those gathered. She was still young enough, just, to get away with such a move without causing complaint. The painting she saw was indeed of the village pond but the pond wasn't the main subject, the artist had used the pond purely as background. Background for a fantastical image. At the centre of the painting rising magically from the pond he had painted a lady. A lady unnervingly captivating by her beauty. She wore bright crystal blue eyes that stood out from a snow white complexion accentuated by long flowing reddish golden locks which tumbled into the water and beyond. She was dressed in robes of a translucent almost colourless material that blended with the surface and became the water where they touched. Staring at her face Charlotte had a very odd and also a very strong feeling that she knew the subject. That surely was impossible, the lady was a creation only of someone else's imagination. Perhaps the artist had used somebody local as a model but try as she might Charlotte couldn't put a name to the face, only that she felt strangely certain she knew the subject. As she looked on Charlotte found herself drawn to the lady's crystal blue eyes. Such was the artistry it appeared that the eyes were pleading and that her pleading was not meant for everybody but directed only at her. Charlotte was sure every other onlooker must be feeling the same way but for the second time that morning she found herself feeling very uncomfortable. As she continued to try and understand her sensitivity towards the image the artist perhaps because he sensed Charlotte's questioning broke from his work and turned to look at her. Charlotte wished he hadn't for he wore the exact same expression as Ashtynn just a few moments before. She felt her hands go clammy under his gaze and with only a moments more hesitation started walking briskly back to the cottage. As she walked she allowed herself a seconds long glance over her shoulder. The artist was still looking her way but now he wore a smile that would melt the stubbornest winter frost. Had it been her imagination, possibly but try as she might she couldn't force his original expression from her mind. And there was something else, just as with the lady in the painting she had a very strong feeling that she had seen him before, that she knew the artist. So strong was the feeling it made her feel quite uncomfortable. Her excitation was so pronounced she felt she must have met him somewhere, sometime. But where? Frustratingly she just couldn't place him.

As Charlotte approached the back door she heard a voice coming from the kitchen that didn't belong to either of her parents. Pushing the artist and his painting from her mind she listened intently. The day had started with such a beautiful morning and now the morning was turning into a most peculiar one and not one she much cared for. The upper half of the stable door was hooked open and as a consequence the voices within carried easily . She could hear her mother and by her tone she sounded upset. A man's voice, one she didn't recognise sounded as though he were trying to calm her. What now, she wasn't in the mood for any further surprises.

Taking a deep breath she pushed the lower half of the door open and boldly stepped inside. Her mother was sitting at the kitchen table and on seeing her daughter quickly wiped a tear from her cheek. She was too late, Charlotte spotted it. Her father was leaning against the door frame to the lounge, his arms folded, he smiled as she entered. The stranger's voice belonged to a tall smartly dressed man. He even had a folded handkerchief tucked into the breast pocket of what looked to Charlotte like a hand tailored suit. The man looked to be around fifty and stood tall, taller than her father, his build told he didn't have to work out to stay slim. The hair on his head was neatly cut and he wore a moustache which belonged to another age. He smiled at Charlotte as she entered. Stooping he held out his hand, which immediately won him points in Charlotte's eyes.

"You must be French Charlotte". He smiled broadly, revealing a set of badly stained teeth.

Charlotte, not quite sure how to react accepted his hand with a polite hello.

"We have to leave here," her mother stared angrily at the man who in return looked distinctly uncomfortable.

"I'm from the agency, Sumro, who rents you the cottage. I'm afraid they now require the property." This was shattering news to Charlotte, she liked living in Aldbury, most of her friends were from the village and she was happy in her school. "Don't worry" the man continued quickly, we have another property similar in character and size which you can move into."

"Is it in Aldbury?" Charlotte asked without leaving the man time to explain further.

"I'm afraid not but it's not that far from here and I can assure you it's very nice."

"It's in the back of beyond." Her mother cried a little too dramatically. Charlotte knew her mother would hate it if their home wasn't part of a framework of nearby houses, she adored social contact and the gossip that went with it.

"Anyway I must be off," the man perhaps understandably looked in a hurry to leave. "As I told you there's no hurry, we don't need this cottage back for another three months. If you wish to continue renting through us please get in touch and I'll arrange for you to visit the other property we have available. I do highly recommend it." He took out a card, offering it to Charlotte's mother. Her mother made no attempt to take it so he turned and offered it to Charlotte who was next closest. Charlotte took it politely. The man then did something rather surprising. He handed Charlotte a book that he had been carrying in his left hand. "My colleague who first rented you this cottage remembers you" he said smiling at her. I believe he has a daughter of a similar age, perhaps a year or two older. Anyway she has just finished with this at school and knowing I was coming here thought you might like it. Oh and take this too." The man handed her what looked like a brochure. "We were planning to go away for a weekend but with work I can't. You may find it useful. Right I must be off and please," the man gestured to the card Charlotte held in her hand. "Please if ever I can be of assistance I'm only a phone call away." With that the man made for the door and Charlotte's parents followed him outside.

Charlotte still reeling drew up a seat at the kitchen table. Brushing away crumbs left over from breakfast she placed the brochure flat on the table top. It was a holiday brochure for Rome. On the cover was a large photo of the Colosseum with insets of smiling people visiting other famous sights, always with a bright blue sky. Next she looked at the card he'd given her. It was headed Sumro, just that not even a sub title explaining they're letting agents. Underneath in sharp type the man's name Edward that was all. Finally the agency's address, Orme Square, London, W2 4RS and telephone number. There was no mobile. She carefully placed the card on the brochure and turned to the book. How odd, she'd only met the man who'd rented them the cottage for a few minutes. She was amazed he'd even remembered her let alone well enough to pass on a book. Charlotte still holding the book in her hands studied the cover. It looked like a very old copy and well used. The title unusually didn't shout at you. Instead it was laid almost discreetly along the bottom. It read Evelyn Waugh, she assumed the author and then the title, Brideshead Revisited. Charlotte had never heard of the author nor the title. Curious she flicked through the first few pages until she came to Chapter One. At the same time her parents returned, before she closed the book she quickly read the title. ET IN ARCADIA EGO.

Help

One way you can help in the ongoing battle is to become a member of one of the following. They all help and protect a variety of natural environments where the battle is taking place.

The National Trust

The stewardship of much of the wood at Ashridge is under the National Trust. They help to preserve and protect this unique wood, along with many other places of natural beauty all over the country.

To join the National Trust please either visit the shop by the Bridgewater monument or visit their website – www.nationaltrust.org.uk/join-us

The Chiltern Society

The Chiltern Society protect, care for and promote the Chiltern Hills. They work closely with the Chilterns Conversation board to conserve the fragile natural environment and beauty of the Chilterns.

To find out more or to become a member visit - www.chilternsociety.org.uk

Berks, Bucks and Oxen Wildlife Trust

The trust protect a wide variety of special landscapes in Berkshire, Buckinghamshire and Oxfordshire. In their own words their mission is to create a region rich in wildlife valued by all.

To find out more or to join please visit - www.bbowt.org.uk

Herts and Middlesex Wildlife Trust

To find out more please visit – www.hertswildlifetrust.org.uk

The Woodland Trust

The Woodland Trust are concerned with creating, protecting and restoring our native woodland heritage.

To find out more or to become a member please visit – www.woodlandtrust.org.uk

St John the Baptist – A special mention.

St John the Baptist is a beautiful church and one well run with benefit to the community. In recent years it has been the victim of mindless vandalism. If you ever visit the church, please give what you can to help preserve its beauty and it's daily work.

Raymond Hugh

Author's Note

Much of my story is based on real places though all the characters are an invention. Where necessary I have used artistic licence to fit in with the thread of the story.

The thatched cottage for obvious reasons is an invention. There is an excellent village shop in Aldbury though it is a little different to the one in my story. Both pubs in Aldbury featured in the book exist and both are excellent. Everything that takes place within their walls in my story is fiction. St John the Baptist features strongly though the low cupboard is also an invention.

There was once a sundial outside the St John the Baptist and it was, stolen. The tree in which Wodewose met his end, fans of a certain boy magician might recognise.

Tring school features and has an excellent reputation. Everything that happens within its walls in my story is pure invention.

Finally if after reading of French Charlotte and her battle you wish to visit the area, please respect the lives of the people who live there.

A guide to the places featured is planned.

A Personal Note

Thirty years ago I visited southern Spain with my parents. Whilst out walking in the countryside I commented on the abundance of insects, butterflies and wild flowers. My mother responded by telling me that when she was a child, it used be like this in England.

I've never forgotten her words and as I continue to enjoy the English countryside I cannot help but notice the annual decimation of our countryside heritage and the ever increasing pressures on our wildlife.

In the long term I wish to help to reverse this by forming a charity which will concentrate on reinstating our hedgerows, re-sowing flower meadows, sympathetic with the local flora. Re- creating safe ponds for amphibians to enjoy and safely breed and finally planting new and restoring orchards with traditional trees that have, in recent years become rare.

Anybody interested in helping me with this project please contact me by emailing the publisher – morningmistpublications@gmail.com.

Until then I hope the pages within this book will help to spread my message.

Raymond Hugh